AF361381

NEW BOUNDARIES IN POLITICAL SCIENCE FICTION

NEW BOUNDARIES IN POLITICAL SCIENCE FICTION

**Edited by
Donald M. Hassler and Clyde Wilcox**

The University of South Carolina Press

Published by the University of South Carolina Press
Columbia, South Carolina 29208

www.sc.edu/uscpress

Manufactured in the United States of America

17 16 15 14 13 12 11 10 09 08   10 9 8 7 6 5 4 3 2 1

Library of Congress Cataloging-in-Publication Data

New boundaries in political science fiction / edited by Donald M. Hassler and Clyde Wilcox.
    p. cm.
  Includes bibliographical references and index.
  ISBN 978-1-57003-736-8 (cloth : alk. paper)
  1. Science fiction—History and criticism. 2. Politics in literature. 3. Utopias in literature.
  I. Hassler, Donald M. II. Wilcox, Clyde, 1953–
  PN3433.6.N49 2008
  809.3'8762093581—dc22   2008006199

This book was printed on Glatfelter Natures, a recycled paper with 30 percent postconsumer
waste content.

Contents

Preface

Inside and Outside

We are lucky to be able to make a return journey to the location of our 1997 collaboration that produced the book *Political Science Fiction,* because like all return trips the journey itself and the destination will have changed in ways that are interesting and in ways that teach. We still both do the same work—Wilcox in the government department at Georgetown, Hassler in the English department at Kent State. The politics of the real world on our planet continues with event, with struggle, with individual and collective success and failure. The fictional world of science fiction continues to be reinterpreted, newly invented, and widely attended to in our culture. Yet very little is still the same in the political realities of the new twenty-first century, in the thinking about these realities, in the new and newly interpreted fictional literature of extrapolation and the future, nor in this new collection of essays that we want to identify with a version of our end-of-century title *Political Science Fiction.*

Both of us travel a lot, Wilcox much more than Hassler. Even that small fact is important in the introduction of this collection of essays. The political scientist strives to work much of the time with the real world of geographic locations and people. The literary critic works much of the time in the imagined locations of stories. Nevertheless, we both find ourselves in airports often, and now, in the preparation for this book, the airports have seemed both more full of people and more blocked off to people at the same time. When Hassler and his wife took their daughter to the Cleveland Hopkins International Airport as this introduction was being written, they were a little late and wanted to have dinner together. But since the restaurants and sports bars were all beyond the security checkpoints, they had to eat sandwiches standing up from vending machines in order to eat together. Similarly we have found that the stories, the realities, the situations that we collect in what follows about politics and science fiction in the early twenty-first century are a strange mix of much more individuality and personalness that is sharply contrasted to massive blocks in structures and systems that seem to forbid entry. We may at the same time be both safer in our constraints and more individually separated, and hence more conscious of our individual identities.

Also, this is a longer book than the 1997 *Political Science Fiction* because more people have more to say on the topic. We have given the opportunity to more people to speak here and spoken less ourselves. Also, unlike in the earlier collection, here we have arranged the essays into three separate groupings, because the basic opposition mentioned above in the way we see the overall topic of politics and this literature now seems to us so vital and instructive. In fact, the anecdotal illustration of individual family members at the massively locked-down Cleveland Airport seems to us simply a mundane image for the volumes of philosophical and theoretical thinking about the individual and society from Kant's idealized and personal worldview onward to our own most current Orwellian totalized systems. The ideas of Kant may have been the last quantum leap in how humans view themselves morally and politically; the work of cognitive neuroscience, as our opening essay by Peter R. Bergethon suggests, may be the next step. A further irony is that Kant worked more or less individually, whereas our neuroscientists work in groups—though Bergethon's essay is a fine personal statement from a scientist who is a science fiction lover too.

In any case, we were pleased to discover within the essays of this new collection an embedded conformity to a theoretical pattern that is both familiar and troubling, that we can broadly introduce here, and that does finally suggest an interrogation that continues to haunt our thinking. The question is whether identity and meaning in human affairs stem from the results of changing linear, even digital, developments that resemble evolution and "progress" or from the "eternal return" of realities such as war, death, and competitive survival. The following pointed and eloquent quotation, from Marta Petreu's *An Infamous Past: E. M. Cioran and the Rise of Fascism in Romania*, resonates with haunting echoes of how vital fascism was at key moments in recent history far beyond that small country:

> Theirs [the Legion of the Archangel Michael] was the mystique of the
> new man, of national redemption, of death, of an ancestral past that had
> become myth. Their writings . . . were designed to serve a direct political
> purpose: control public life, reshape the nation according to the Legion's
> ideology, replace the democratic state with a national totalitarian one.
> (Petreu, 61)

Surprisingly the same data about the power of images, of digital bits, of language in literature seem to yield opposing general conclusions, so we have allowed this puzzling opposition to govern our management of what follows.

On the one hand, we have received essays (some solicited) that describe a possible "new mankind." From neuroscience to blog technologies to the polemic on gender and race the message seems to be about democratization of political elements leading to genuine new identities. These seven essays are thus grouped to form our first section. Our second section includes strong essays that evoke the old power centers of competitive empires and nation-states and larger-than-life heroic systems where the rational and galaxy-spanning environment of *Star Trek,* for example, seems to represent a nostalgic symbol for human triumph. In these essays, indeed, popular culture celebrates the ancient truths of competition and aggression where, as Robert A. Heinlein said to the applause of most science fiction fans, "there ain't no such thing as a free lunch." His TANSTAAFL dictum comes from his novel *The Moon Is a Harsh Mistress* but is repeated all over the science fiction terrain. Finally our third section collects idiosyncratic essays on individual writers and, lastly, an essay on an immediate situation in international politics. In each of these last essays, a clear opposition remains between the personal and the efficient organization of a systems approach to human affairs.

Clearly one of the saddest realities from twentieth-century experience is the recurring fascist urge to link the "new man" with national power and to couple it all with a nostalgia for primitive immediacy and xenophobic savageness. Our organizational structure here bravely separates ideas about the "new humanness" from the mystical sense of old and permanent unity that, in many cases, condones and encourages savage emotion. Savage emotion, of course, makes for good reading as well as good nostalgic politics such as revenge or conquest. And, in fact, many of the essays near the end of the book about strong and individual writers hint at the underlying dramatic threats for a fanatic unity in human groups. We may be most sensible and rational if we embrace the nearly limitless possibilities for linear and digital expansion, but the finality of our past work and familial, even tribal, identities always pulls us back to admire dead images that are so recognizable. Paradoxically, even the liberalness of keeping as much knowledge and perception as we can (the making of books and the making of return books) draws us back to the shapes and mistakes of our human past. And finally, it seems to be in negotiating the minefields (and mind fields) of just those oppositions and dilemmas that storytelling and, in this case, science fiction storytelling comes in most handy. It remains such a big field that we hardly have room for all the essays that might help in these negotiations and advances and retreats.

Moving back now to our title for this collection to conclude these opening introductory remarks, *New Boundaries in Political Science Fiction* covers the full ten years of politics and of science fiction since we worked on our 1997 book. Key fiction writers such as Philip K. Dick; China Miéville, with two essays in our third section on him; Iain Banks; Walter Mosley; and the many women writers who gravitate around the leadership of Judith Merril and Ursula K. Le Guin seem to thrive on the notions of new identities and vaster political systems. And even from the time of Aristotle, the most interesting political thought is what goes "beyond," stretching the limits of practical and historical politics in what can be thought about or speculated about in fictions. Thus our last editorial move in the face of speculative vastness and complexity is to conclude this collection with an essay that makes use of a rather "comic" tone that emphasizes vividly the dynamic relationship of past and future thought and politics at a given moment in our time.

Acknowledgments

We continue to believe in some collective order possible in the world and hence need to thank the many who have helped us in this project. First of all we thank the editors at the University of South Carolina Press, who did a beautiful job of book production for us ten years ago. We have found it useful ever since, and we are glad they have invited us again to this fertile field. Several essays here have appeared earlier. We were awarded a small grant by the Research and Graduate Studies Division of Kent State University to complete the manuscript, and we thank Dean Peter Tandy for this support. Judy Smith of Kent State prepared the final text for us. Linda Merola of Georgetown University also helped with the formatting. Patrick Carr, Jason Klocek, and Rentaro Iida of Georgetown University helped with further editorial work. We thank them. Individually the Wilcox-Cook family members and the Hassler family members have generously tolerated our absorption in this work; and we thank, in particular, our wives, Elizabeth Cook and Sue Hassler.

We would also like to thank the following individuals and publishers:

Javier Martinez, publisher of *Extrapolation,* for permission to republish Fred Erisman's "*Stagecoach* in Space: The Legacy of *Firefly*" (*Extrapolation* 47 [Summer 2006]: 249–58); Carl Freedman's "To the Perdido Street Station: The Representation of Revolution in China Miéville's *Iron Council*" (*Extrapolation* 46 [Summer 2005]: 235–48); and Carter Kaplan's "Fractal Fantasies of Transformation: William Blake, Michael Moorcock, and the Utilities of Mythographic Shamanism" (*Extrapolation* 45 [Winter 2004]: 419–36);

Mabel Moreña, managing editor of *Revista Iberoamericana,* for permission to publish an English translation of M. Elizabeth Ginway's "Do implante ao ciborgue: Cyberpunk brasileiro e o corpo social" (*Revista Iberoamericana* 73 [October–December 2007]: 787–99) as "The Body Politic in Brazilian Science Fiction: Implants and Cyborgs";

Darko Suvin for permission to republish a portion of his "Of Starship Troopers and Refuseniks: War and Militarism in U.S. Science Fiction," first published in *Extrapolation* (Spring 2007);

I. B. Tauris & Co. for permission to republish chapter 8 of Lincoln Geraghty's *Living with* Star Trek: *American Culture and the* Star Trek *Universe* (2007) as "A Truly American Enterprise: *Star Trek*'s Post-9/11 Politics."

PART 1: ON THE PERSONAL "NEW MAN"

Landscapes of Change

Science, Science Fiction, and Advances in Biology

Peter R. Bergethon

In concluding his 1953 essay "Social Science Fiction" Isaac Asimov summarized:

> 1. For the first time in history mankind is faced with a rapidly changing society, due to the advent of modern technology.
> 2. Science fiction is a form of literature that has grown out of this fact.
> 3. The contribution science fiction can make to society is that of accustoming its readers to the thought of the inevitability of continuing change and the necessity of directing and shaping that change rather than opposing it blindly or blindly permitting it to overwhelm us.

Each morning I enter my office at the Laboratory of Intelligence Modeling and Neurophysics and am greeted by the wheezing and whirring of a large cluster supercomputer. The sounds are a reflection of its own thermal homeostasis as the machine controls the fans regulating its temperature, which fluctuates according to its internal activity and the external ambient laboratory temperature. Over the course of a day, I can hear the constant adjustment of fan number and speed as the computer goes about its homeostatic rounds. We share sensation of the state of the external environment (and I often have knowledge of its internal tasks, having sent them to the machine). I sense that the computer and I are in a social coordination in fashion similar to the way one becomes comfortable with the breathing and footsteps of children at home. Of course, this is a one-way socialization since the computer is not aware of me in any similar fashion (even when working on the tasks that I have sent it!).

I have resisted the geek scientist impulse to pseudo-HALify this cluster to behave like the HAL computer in Arthur Clarke's *2001: A Space Odyssey*. Pseudo-HALification would be trivially easy: I could write a few simple lines of code to have the machine greet me: "Good Morning Dr. Bergethon. Did you have a nice evening?" That output could be triggered by a sensor linked to a physical interaction with me: an audible pattern of footstep, or the information that the door has been opened with the swipe-card that only I possess. But

Pseudo-HALification gives the appearance of interaction when there really is none. I admit to the temptation because to me, having cut my imaginative teeth on a string of science fiction sentient robots and computers starting with the first book I really read (and reread five times), *Tom Swift Jr. and His Giant Robot,* complex social interactions between man and machine have always seemed natural. It is perhaps no surprise that in real life, every day we engage the question: of what would such machines be built and how would they work? Thus I resist (or have resisted) the adolescent satisfaction of reducing this quest to the level of gadget science fiction. The actual endpoint will be striking and arrives when a biologically inspired and bio-industrial crafted (probably) protoplasmic "machine" opens its own "eyes" and recognizes first itself and then my walking into the laboratory. When it chooses to say "Good Morning Dr. Bergethon. How was your commute? Will you have a moment to discuss a few issues that I have?" in its effort to engage conversation of its own interest and direction, then a new era of social and political interactions will be initiated.

This is not a science fiction scenario but a real story from a Boston medical school laboratory. It is an example of the type of rapid change to which we as a modern scientific society have become accustomed and anticipate. The value of science fiction as an essential method to understand and prepare for the implications of social and political change was proposed by Isaac Asimov in his essay "Social Science Fiction." Asimov argued that the appearance of rapid rates of change that result in entire societies becoming altered in a fraction of a generation was a completely new and unprecedented phenomenon that could be attached to the time of the French Revolution. Asimov argued that this phenomenon was a direct result of scientific and technological pressures that had been building for centuries.

> Actually, the French Revolution was not primary. Underlying it lay centuries of slow changes in the fabric of society—changes of which most men were unaware. But from the nadir of western society—the tenth century—and through the Renaissance the rate of change had been steadily and continuously increasing. . . . the French Revolution is therefore a handy way of pegging the date. The fundamental consideration is that about 1800, the tide of hastening change due to the scientific and industrial development of western society had become a colossal current that swept all other competing factors into discard.
>
> . . . Even today it is not entirely plain to many people that scientific-economic change is the master and political change the servant. . . . You may wonder how one can balance the Emancipation Proclamation against the electric light and the Bill of Rights against the X-ray tube. . . . Consider the changes in our own generation. The rise and fall of Nazi Germany, with its World War II enclosure, took place in a round dozen years. Forty years ago the word "Fascism" did not exist. In less than forty years, Communism grew from a splinter group of the Socialist left to the

predominant code of thinking of one third of the world. . . . Yet consider!
Imagine a world in which Communism suddenly ceased to be. It would
be a different world . . . your life would be changed, perhaps drastically.
Now imagine a world in which the automobile ceased to be.

. . . Technological changes lie at the root of political change. It was
the developing Industrial Revolution that placed Western Europe so far
ahead of the rest of the world. . . . the railroads of the United States were
built as the result of investments of European capitalists. And it is the
Industrial Revolution spreading outward to America first, then to Russia
and now to China and India, that has shaken and is destroying European
hegemony. (Asimov 1953, 34–35)

Since this passage was written in 1953, Lenin-Stalinist Communism reached its
apex and has fallen, China has embraced capitalism, and Europe is well under
way with its experiment to restore its hegemony, the European Union. The great
battle of our time is shaping up to be between a twenty-first-century Western
social-political culture that encourages and embraces change especially through
individual growth and a largely seventh-century vision of the world that abhors
and defies such change.

Kabul, Afghanistan—The Taliban gunmen who murdered two teachers
in eastern Afghanistan early today were only following their rules:
Teachers receive a warning, then a beating, and if they continue to teach
must be killed. The new list of 30 rules decided on during a high Taliban
meeting in September or October [2006] and since circulated over the
internet . . . Rule No. 24 forbids anyone to work as a teacher "under the
current puppet regime, because it strengthens the system of the infidels."
Rule No. 25 says teachers who ignore Taliban warnings will be killed. . . .
"If a school fails a warning to close, it must be burned. But all religious
books must be secured beforehand," rule No. 26 says. (Straziuso 2006)

Asimov asserts that it is the process of science and its success at discovery that is
the forcing function in the changing landscape of history. His argument for the
primacy of scientific and technological advances within social and political systems has a strongly positivist viewpoint. However, the turbulence in social and
political systems driven by the changing knowledge landscapes that result from
scientific inquiry suggests a cultural vector that interacts with these powerful
forces for change. This cultural influence may either oppose or potentiate the
force of science and technology. Examples of authoritarian resistance include
the resistance of "Aryan Physics" against the relativity theories of Albert Einstein
labeled as "Jewish science" by the Nazis, the Soviet preference for Lysenkoism
over genetic science, and the Taliban's pronouncements. Thus while there is no
doubt that the advance of scientific knowledge through the modern scientific
method is a major driving force for change, neither the scientific method nor
the scientific products derived from its application can be easily (or usefully)

divorced from the social and political movements that either spawned and nurtured scientific investigation or those that opposed such scientific inquiry.

Because it is the nature of successful scientific investigation to ask impertinent questions of dogmatic authority, certain political traditions enhance science and its progress and other traditions oppose scientific efforts and generate more turbulence. It is of historical and also of important scientific analytical interest that political and social empowerment of individuals and the weakening of dogmatic institutions including churches and kings fed the requisite human skeptical empiricism required for the successful practice of science by humans. It is particularly interesting that the National Socialist and Communist experiments of the twentieth century, both of which endeavored to limit scientific skepticism, have already ended in short order.

It is plausible (especially to scientists) to argue that the positivism of science is inevitable. However, science is a disciplinary approach to knowledge acquisition that is a human enterprise and endeavor. The scientific enterprise always takes place in a social and political context. Therefore it is of interest and value to inquire: how do scientists who discover new knowledge such as quantum mechanics and relativity perform the acts of impertinent questioning that might overthrow an entire edifice of classical understanding if they are not enabled and to some large degree sustained by political and social structures that allow the most risky of human endeavors and the most liberal of human actions, overturning strongly held belief systems?

Let us consider what science is and its connection to human biology. Then we may consider how knowledge gained recently in biology might impact political and social science fiction.

Science

Science is defined as a human endeavor that explores the natural world. The human brain, with its strengths and weaknesses, does the exploring. The formulation that the brain constructs an internal model of the world is a well-developed and useful theory with applications in neurology, cognitive neuroscience, education, and the social sciences (Bergethon 1999; Szentágothai and Arbib 1974; Woodcock and Dockery 1993). There is substantial experimental evidence that the nervous system employs a computational strategy in which sensory data is processed from the level of stimulation to the level of cognition by the process of feature abstraction (Hartline 1940; Dowling 1979; Hubel 1988; Mountcastle and Darian-Smith 1968). The role of the generated internal models is central to the normal function of the brain and serves as the integral context for all of the actions of the nervous system. These actions include the planning and execution of motor strategies, memory, reflexive learning, declarative (propositional) learning, and abstractions in language, graphical, and temporal concepts. Neurological syndromes that demonstrate the abnormalities of the failure to produce or to interact correctly with these internal models have been well described (Victor and Ropper 2001).

The importance of models in science (Giere 1988) and in scientific discovery (Nersessian 1992) is well established; models are also at the core of Kuhn's "normal science" and can be viewed as embodying his paradigms (Kuhn 1962). A model embodies general principles and central concepts but also iconic objects that anchor the model to reality; it relates different components of an understood system to each other, and it can be manipulated dynamically, giving causal meaning to observed relationships. This is true of both internal mental models and external models that are available to be learned or experienced.

Learning and knowledge acquisition at least at the cognitive levels above simple adaptive behavior may be usefully regarded as the process leading to alteration (revision, reconstruction, or embellishment) of internal models. Learning is a function of both the biological substrate and the environment. A variety of neural models of perception and learning have been proposed. Our lab has developed dynamic-systems models that relate how behaviors such as cognition and learning can result from using systems analysis of data to integrate a multiplicity of hierarchies in a self-organizing fashion to achieve a stable equilibrium: a state of knowledge or belief. The neural models that we have developed in our research have shown how a neural feature-extraction system such as the human brain

1. Can make a model, which is regarded as complete (i.e., real), even when it comes from the imagination or from a hallucination! The brain does not have an innate tendency to be skeptical.

2. Tries to resolve ambiguity when constructing a model. The brain circuitry is driven to complete a model created from a pattern even when adequate information is not present. Then, after creating a pattern from inadequate information, the brain will discard the original data and indiscriminately attribute "reality" to the incorrectly built model. The brain avoids ambiguity whenever possible, often sacrificing truth to do so. As a result of the drive to avoid and resolve ambiguity, the circuits in the brain are predisposed to error, bias, and misconceptions. There is a natural tendency to get stuck in a rut or trapped in a bias or prejudice. This provides a neurological accounting of two human tendencies: (A) to leap to conclusions that are often unsupported by objective evidence and then (B) to cling to those conclusions as "creatures of habit" who resist change when necessary.

It is precisely because it can compensate for these innate tendencies toward bias, prejudice, and leaping to conclusions (especially in the face of inadequate information) that scientific process has evolved successfully over the history of civilization.

All science starts with observations of the patterns of the natural world. Archeological evidence from cave paintings and the notching of bone and reindeer horns suggests that prehistoric humans were extremely careful in their recording of seasonal and temporal patterns. This kind of knowledge is acquired by simple observation. A hunter-gatherer society depends on this science to know where and when animals gather, feed, obtain water, or sleep; to know where berries, shrubs, and flowers are located and when they will bear fruit; and to know the patterns of weather, drought, and flood so that migration ensures the survival of the society. An agricultural society also depends on this basic science to know when to plant, when to reap, and when to gather and store food.

However, observation alone is not "modern" science; simple observation leads to "proto-science." Proto-science accepts observations without question or verification. The human brain always tries to organize observations of its world into unambiguous models of cause and effect or at least correlation. Models of cause and effect are built on a mode of explanation or a context. A mode of explanation establishes the way that cause-and-effect relationships explain the natural world. Historically humans and their cultures have used several modes of explanation in their attempt to formulate the cause-and-effect models that give meaning to their observations of the natural world. Three common modes of explanation seen in the history of humans are received knowledge, ways of knowing, and modern skeptical empiricism.

Received Knowledge

This mode of explanation attributes the cause for events to gods, magic, and mystical powers and leads to mythological and theological explanations for the events discovered in the natural world. Mystical attribution is usually based on "received knowledge." The observed evidence, which may be quite accurate and detailed, is interpreted in a god-demon-magic context. For much of human history, patterns of importance to hunter-gatherer and agricultural civilizations have been used to ensure survival of the society. For most of human experience, the causality relations were attributed to supernatural gods and magical occurrences. Thus a proto-science based on observation with theological attribution has existed for most of humankind's history.

Ways of Knowing

The ancient Greeks made extremely careful observations about their natural world. They developed models that explained the observations according to strictly rational, logical deductions. The starting point for these deduced models was derived from "self-evident" truths. These models of thought assumed that the actions of the universe were rational, according to a human-rationalized order. In the Greek (Aristotelian) view, the philosophical mind saw truth and perfection in the mind and imposed it onto the universe. For example, the Greek view on motion would be as follows: The gods who made the world are perfect. Circles and straight lines are perfect. Gods make motion; motion must be perfect because the gods made it. Therefore motion in the natural world is circles and straight lines. Likewise, planets move in circles and cannonballs move in straight lines.

The problem with "ways of knowing" models of explanation is that all observations are forced to fit the model. The underlying model cannot be changed by evidence. This mode of explanation is resistant to any change in the worldview, because new observations cannot alter the underlying models of cause and effect. For example, the idea that motion occurred in straight lines led medieval military engineers to calculate that a cannonball would rise to a certain height and then fall straight down over a castle wall. However, cannonballs did not land according to the medieval engineers' expectations. The Aristotelian "way of knowing" was not able to provide a means to correct the error between what was expected and what happened.

Both of the "received knowledge" and "ways of knowing" modes of explanation satisfy the brain's goals of completing patterns of cause and effect and of avoiding ambiguity. However, the particular viewpoint of these modes of explanation enhances the preset bias of the behavior of the brain. Neither the "received knowledge" nor the "ways of knowing" modes of explanation have the capacity to alter the underlying worldview. These modes of explanation are therefore limited in their flexibility and capacity to expand their field of knowledge beyond a relatively restricted plane of observation. Both are like looking at the world through a fixed-focus lens or, in the narrowest case, closing the lens completely and considering only what is already known and accepted as the extent of relevant knowledge. Neither of these modes would be expected to develop a recognizable science fiction.

Modern Skeptical Empirical Science

During the Italian Renaissance, Leonardo da Vinci, who was a very good military engineer, tried to solve the problem of the mortar shells that kept missing. Da Vinci's approach was radical for his time. He observed that when a mortar was fired, the shell followed a path that was not the one predicted by "perfect" motion. There was no straight-line motion at all! Instead the shell followed the path of a parabola. He changed his world's view based on his experiments and measurements. Da Vinci's mortars began to hit their targets, and the seeds of experimental modern science were planted.

In the scientific mode of explanation, the fundamental rules are discovered not from assumption or philosophical musing, but rather from careful consideration, measurement, experiment, and analysis of specific, relatively simple cases. Observation is the first step in constructing a model. The validity of the model is tested by making a prediction, performing experiments to test the model, making experimental measurements, recognizing that the observer may influence the experiment, and measuring that influence and changing the model when the experimental evidence requires a different worldview.

Thus, instead of using a strictly deductive logic that dictated reality from a series of self-evident propositions, modern science began by breaking from this tradition and using inductive logic. In deductive logic, the general proposition exists first, and then the specific case is logically concluded by starting at the general and working toward the specific. In inductive logic, the principles of rational order still stand, but the first step is the consideration of specific cases that are carefully studied, and then the specific case is generalized backward to fundamental principles. In a system of inductive logic, the fundamental rules are discovered not from assumption or philosophical musing, but rather through careful consideration, measurement, experiment, and analysis.

Today, we live in an era of "modern inductive" science that derives its rules from a detailed experimental system. That system is designed to balance the errors caused by the intuitive leaps made by the brain with the inspired strokes of genius that occur when the brain makes such leaps. In modern science, the role of the brain as both an indifferent observer and an inevitable participant in the observed experiment is explicitly recognized—attempts are carefully made to define and control for both roles. Modern science and its traditions have evolved the ability to counter the error-prone mechanisms in the otherwise enormously successful human brain. In this way science is intrinsically social and therefore potentially susceptible to political forces even while constrained by the reality of good models (gravity and thermodynamics, though axiomatic, are not really open to postmodern falsification).

Science Fiction

Definitions for science fiction vary and have been a subject of dispute and discussion for decades. Asimov, Heinlein, Knight, and Pohl provide useful and complementary boundaries for the definition.

Asimov's definition of science fiction was first proposed in a 1951 article for *Science Fiction Writers of America Bulletin:* "[Social] Science fiction is that branch of literature which is concerned with the impact of scientific advance on human beings." It was in 1953 that he limited his interest to the only branch of science fiction that was sociologically "significant." He recognized that other stories might be properly classified as science fiction but felt they were not significant, "however amusing they might be or however as excellent as pieces of fiction."

Robert Heinlein (1959) argued that the question of what exactly is science fiction has been best defined and inspired by Reginald Bretnor's placement of application of the scientific method in the prime position. "A handy short definition of almost all science fiction might read: realistic speculation about possible future events, based solidly on adequate knowledge of the real world, past and present, and on a *thorough understanding of the scientific method.* To make this definition cover all science fiction (instead of 'almost all') it is necessary only to strike out the word future" (63, emphasis added).

Frederik Pohl (1997) argued that science fiction is operationally identifiable because of its universal production by the "science fiction method" (just as real science is universally produced by the application of the scientific method and not just protoscientific observation and curiosity). Pohl's method is as follows: "First they [science fiction writers] look at the world around them in all its parts. Then they take some of those parts out and throw them away and replace them with new parts of their own imagining. Then they reassemble this changed world and start it going to see how it works; and that is the background to every science fiction story I know" (7–8). Pohl describes science fiction as a modeling problem, with the fictional story as the output of a new simulated internal model.

An experimental attempt to define science fiction was put forth by Damon Knight (1977), who wrote a list of promising definitions and then used them to rate a series of works published as science fiction. (This is a method quite reminiscent of the scientific technique of using a training set of proteins with known crystallographic structure as a method to predict protein structure from primary sequence data.) Knight's list is that stories contain reference to or use of

1. Science (after Gernsback)
2. Technology and invention (after Heinlein, Miller)
3. The future and the remote past, including all time-travel stories
(after Bailey)
4. Extrapolation (after Davenport)
5. Scientific method (after Bretnor)
6. Other places—planets and dimensions, for example, including visitors
from the above (after Bailey)
7. Catastrophes, natural or manmade (after Bailey)

Knight found that a story could be classified by counting up the appearance of any of these elements as follows:

science fiction ≥ 3,
borderline $= 2$
not science fiction ≤ 1

Given the nature of science, all of these definitions define a view that science fiction is a modeling exercise in which a model of scientific knowledge is internalized and used to simulate change in a society of human interest. This allows an exploration of what is possible and speculative analysis of how those possibilities might play out in a human context. Otto Von Bismarck noted that "politics is the art of the possible," and Aristotle remarked that "man is by nature a political animal." Science fiction is then a logical context in which to explore various possibilities and see how they might impact the human enterprise. Recall that the forcing function of the shape and character of the space-of-the-possible is driven largely by new knowledge and perspectives derived from the scientific realm. What could have greater effect on this field of speculation than new knowledge about biology and biological organization given the potential effect such new knowledge has on both sides of our equation: exploration of the way the universe works and the biology of the humans that perceive and interact with it?

Conclusion

Finally, I would like to present just several areas of new knowledge in the biological and biomedical sciences that will lead to new questions or reframe old questions in areas of social and political concern. From these new perspectives we can expect the generation of a corpus of political science fiction that will speculate on the implications for human society. In this discussion I will apply as a constraint obedience to Arthur Clarke's third law of prediction (Clarke 1973), which states that any sufficiently advanced technology is indistinguishable from magic. Application of the law allows postulates of advanced technology that do not require explanation, thus relieving the science fiction writer of the risks of using flawed engineering or scientific concepts. Using the Clarke restriction thus prevents me from proposing predominantly technical advances in the biological sciences (of which there are many). Such advances, while gloriously appealing to the gadgeteer, are subsumed under the genre of "gadget science fiction," and furthermore they could be easily be rolled into "space-opera" type stories. It is inevitable that these areas I will discuss can (and will) generate both gadget and space-opera stories, but that should not distract us from the interesting and significant social-science-fiction impact that such new paradigms will allow us to explore. Just as Isaac Asimov considered the atomic age of science fiction to have begun because the atomic bomb changed the general view of the seriousness of science fiction, the deep implications of biology on life, liberty, destruction, and survival and the philosophical questions of epistemology and purpose make it likely that we will soon need to have a new era of science fiction, perhaps named "the post-genomic era."

1. Bigger is not correlated with better: Human complexity is not a result of a larger number of genes but rather is an emergent property of the biological system. Biological science has always been deeply bound to philosophical, religious, and social notions. It has also been in varying degrees somewhat narcissistic. The notion that the scientific study of life requires special natural forces and special scientific treatment was expressed for centuries as vitalism. Vitalism was effectively disproved when Friedrich Wöhler synthesized the supposedly uniquely "organic compound" urea in 1828. Furthermore, Louis Pasteur experimentally laid to rest the two-thousand-year-old vitalist concept of spontaneous generation in 1859.

Still, vitalism is a stubborn idea that is tightly held. If all biological systems are to be governed by a universal set of physicochemical principles at least humans should have a special place in nature; our genetic code would be significantly larger, accounting for our special place. This assumption had remained a matter of some pride in the collective mind of humanity until recently. In the year 2000, the fruit fly was the first living creature to have its genetic code deciphered. It was found to have nearly 13,600 genes. It seemed only natural to expect that when the human genome was solved, there would be a factor of countable complexity consistent with the obvious fact that people are substantially more complicated than fruit flies. Therefore initial estimates were of at least 100,000 genes in the human genome (7.35 times the number in the fly).

The Human Genome Project completed the sequencing of human DNA in 2001. It quickly became clear that no matter how much more complicated people may be compared to flies, the number of human genes was not going to be much greater than 40,000. What a disappointment! Yet some solace could be found in the calculation in that we were at least three times more complicated than a fruit fly. Alas, recent counts suggest that the number of genes in the human genome will be on the order of 20,000 to 25,000 genes. So for comparison:

Fruit flies:	13,600 genes
Roundworms:	19,500 genes
Humans:	20,000–25,000 genes
Rice:	45,000 genes
Maize:	50,000 genes

Outside of the blow to our collective egos for not having as many genes as we thought we ought, the important lesson is that we have not understood the nature of our complexity to this point. The process of complexity is not associated so much with bigger or different counts of what building blocks make us up but rather with the process determining how those blocks are assembled.

Biological complexity is an emergent property of the biological system. The nature of these interactions is properly studied in general systems theory, a field of study formalized by Ludwig von Bertalanffy (1975). Complexity of this type is a natural vote against command-control organization such as is found in central planning. At the level of DNA biological systems, like those of physics, are constructed from a framework of rules of prohibition rather than rules of permission. Rules of prohibition (energy may neither be created nor destroyed, only changed; charge and baryon number are preserved) lead to systems of conservation as opposed to systems of permission. A conservative system has maximum choice within boundaries that are unyielding. Permissive systems approach an infinity of permitted and regulated events, thus generating an infinity of controls. In nature, permissive systems become extinct, collapsing under their own weight. Conservative systems survive and flourish. This fundamental view of the natural order of biological life will inevitably find its way into social and political science fiction in the coming years.

2. An important aspect of recent biological knowledge is a growing appreciation of the dynamic, delocalized control of living systems.

This is a logical extension of our discovery of the lack of primacy in DNA number. Until recently, the "central dogma" in biology was a one-gene ⧧ one-protein mapping. Thus a gene coded in DNA is transcribed into a messenger RNA (mRNA) template followed by translation into the proteins making up the cellular machinery. Achieving the required complexity and diversity of the human organism with the lower gene number implies that the genes are mixed and matched in variable fashion to achieve far greater diversity of form and function than gene number alone can account for. Thus diversity is a result of maximal "local" choice and not an expanded assignment by a command-control top-down source. The checks and balances used to ensure such diversity in biological systems include switches that "veto" or silence gene product formation either at the level of the gene transcription or later on at the level of interfering with the effectiveness of the mRNA translation into protein. This later RNA interference mechanism is an example of a control mechanism that is well downstream of the DNA control systems; the 2006 Nobel Prize in medicine was awarded for research on this subject by Andrew Z. Fire and Craig C. Mello.

3. Biology, evolution, and nanotechnology are probably linked.

The fact that the complicated machinery of biological cells and organisms apparently undergoes a "just-in-time" and "point-of-action" style of control has important implications when self-organizing biological systems are considered. The exciting new technology at the turn of the millennium is nanotechnology. Nanotechnology focuses on manufacturing processes that will arrange atoms in precise and detailed positions in order to gain function. In its current conception, these manufacturing processes will lead to revolutions in small, molecular-sized devices for material manufacture (food, building materials, pollution control), manipulation (nano-devices to repair diseased tissues and cure disease), and computation (nano-computers). To the biologist, nanotechnology and nanomachines sound like cellular systems. It seems likely that the control mechanisms of successful nanotechnological machines will be organized in the same fashion as the decentralized, biological, self-organizing systems described above. This implies a remarkable degree of autonomy and self-organizing systems that will *evolve* on their own. Evolution in this context is likely an emergent property of a complex, decentralized, self-organizing system. Once started such machines will evolve steadily toward evermore lifelike action.

Now we are ready to close the loop that started with the early morning entrance to the Laboratory for Intelligence Modeling and Neurophysics. Whether we engineer nanomachines derived directly from biological or noncarbon manufactured materials, it seems likely that the decentralized self-organizing processes will evolve on a variable trajectory set out by the initial conditions. Our "machine" will develop first physically and then psychologically to become an adaptive, intelligent system that will one day greet its "trajectory creator." The social and political questions that this scenario generates are quite fundamental.

Who is the creator, the human or the process wielded by the human?

When it evolves to achieve sentient awareness, does it become alive?

Is the process of becoming alive an example of "spontaneous generation"?

What are the property rights of this system?

Can it participate in self-deterministic actions?

What is our relationship as human beings to this device?

When it appreciates its changing world, will it compose its own science fiction?

What role will we humans play in that foreign fiction of these evolved entities?

There certainly will be many other questions of social and political nature as well. These questions I must leave to the science fiction writers and political philosophers who will appropriately consider whether these new perspectives support a dismal Hobbesian state of nature or a far more optimistic Lockean natural state. Certainly we will explore these issues in science fiction writings for at least several decades before we actually encounter the reality.

Bibliography

Appleton, Victor, II. 1954. *Tom Swift Jr. and His Giant Robot.* New York: Grosset and Dunlap.

Asimov, Isaac. 1951. "Other Worlds to Conquer." *Science Fiction Writers of America Bulletin* (May). Referenced in "Social Science Fiction," in Damon Knight, *Turning Points: Essays on the Art of Science Fiction,* 29. New York: Harper & Row, 1977.

———. 1953. "Social Science Fiction." In *Modern Science Fiction, Its Meaning and Its Future,* ed. Reginald Bretnor. New York: Coward-McCann.

Bergethon, Peter R. 1999. *Learning the Language of Patterns: A Teacher's Guided Tour.* Holliston, Mass.: Symmetry Learning Systems.

Clarke, Arthur C. 1968. *2001: A Space Odyssey.* New York: New American Library.

———. 1973. *Profiles of the Future: An Inquiry into the Limits of the Possible.* Rev. ed. New York: Harper and Row.

Dowling, J. E. 1979. "Information Processing by Local Circuits: The Vertebrate Retina a Model System." In *The Neurosciences: Fourth Study Program,* ed. Francis O. Schmitt and Frederic G. Worden. Cambridge, Mass.: MIT Press.

Giere, Ronald N. 1988. *Explaining Science: A Cognitive Approach.* Chicago: University of Chicago Press.

Hartline, H. K. 1940. "The Receptive Fields of Optic Nerve Fibers." *American Journal of Physiology* 130: 690.

Heinlein, Robert A. 1969. "Science Fiction: Its Nature, Faults, and Virtues." In *The Science Fiction Novel: Imagination and Social Criticism.* 3rd ed. Chicago: Advent.

Hubel, David H. 1988. *Eye, Brain, and Vision.* New York: Scientific American Library.

Knight, Damon. 1977. "What Is Science Fiction?" In *Turning Points: Essays on the Art of Science Fiction,* ed. Damon Knight, 62–69. New York: Harper and Row.

Kuhn, Thomas S. 1962. *The Structure of Scientific Revolutions.* Chicago: University of Chicago Press.

Mountcastle, Vernon B., and J. Darian-Smith. 1968. "Neural Mechanisms in Somesthesia." In *Medical Physiology,* ed. Vernon B. Mountcastle, 2:1372–1423. 12th ed. St. Louis: Mosby.

Nersessian, Nancy J. 1992. "How Do Scientists Think? Capturing the Dynamics of Conceptual Change in Science." In *Cognitive Models of Science,* ed. Ronald N. Giere, 3–45. Minneapolis: University of Minnesota Press.

Pohl, Frederik. 1997. "The Politics of Prophecy." In *Political Science Fiction,* ed. Donald M. Hassler and Clyde Wilcox, 7–17. Columbia: University of South Carolina Press.

Straziuso, Jason. 2006. "30 Rules of the Taliban Proclaimed," *Boston Sunday Globe,* December 10.

Szentágothai, János, and Michael A. Arbib. 1974. *Conceptual Models of Neural Organization, Neurosciences Research Program Bulletin* 12, no. 3.

Victor, Maurice, and Allan H. Ropper. 2001. *Principles of Neurology.* 7th ed. New York: Medical Publishing Division, McGraw-Hill.

Bertalanffy, Ludwig von. 1975. *General System Theory: Theory, Foundations, Development.* New York: Braziller.

Woodcock, A. E. R., and John T. Dockery. 1993. "Catastrophe Theory and the Lanchester Equations." In *The Military Landscape: Mathematical Models of Combat,* ed. A. E. R. Woodcock and John T. Dockery, 7–93. Cambridge: Woodhead.

Looking Within

Science Fiction Explores the Future of "Being Human"

Bruce L. Rockwood

Science Fiction writers sometimes appear to run in packs, circling an idea, borrowing from each other as they explore a new theme or sort out the implications of a new technology. Cyberpunk's exploration of the Internet is one example, and stories on the implications of nanotechnology are another. One of the major current narrative tropes of science fiction is the exploration of the role of gender and body in understanding the self and the other, often linked to the concept of the mutant as a foil for understanding ourselves (Hollinger and Gordon 2002).

There are several tributaries that feed into this narrative river. First, reflecting the golden age tradition of linking "hard" science fiction to real science (DeForest 2004) is the desire of science fiction writers to make use of the latest in cutting-edge science from a wide variety of fields. That is the whole point of science fiction from this perspective—it is popular fiction that is about, builds on, and may even explicitly seek to teach about science (Pratchett, Stewart, and Cohen 2005). It may build on a preexisting interest in science in the reader, but in any event must cultivate such an interest if it is to attract a repeat audience.

Second, since the 1960s there has been an increasing exploration of science fiction narratives by feminist, minority, and other alternative voices who see the corporate-dominated narratives in the mass media as at best unimaginative and at worst oppressive (Le Guin and Atteberry 1993). A similar trend emerged in the 1970s in both critical race theory and narrative pedagogy in legal scholarship, with the two merging in Derrick Bell's now-classic story, "The Space Traders" (Bell 1999).

Third, science fiction writers are influenced by, and seek to criticize and influence, the political and social controversies of the day. This has been true for a long time, in, for example, the dystopias of Aldous Huxley's *Brave New World* (1932), George Orwell's *Nineteen Eighty-four* (1949), and Margaret Atwood's *The Handmaid's Tale* (1985); the satire of Frederik Pohl and C. M. Kornbluth's *The Space Merchants* (1953); and Pohl's more optimistic 1984 novel of a future

New York, *The Years of the City* (Rockwood 1998). Today such writers react to a planet transformed by corporate globalization (Stiglitz 2002), the Internet, and biotechnology, where the potential of science for great good—and great evil—is compounded by a fundamentalist resurgence built upon the twin supports of ignorance and fear. David Brin's *Kiln People* (2002) and K. W. Jeter's *Noir* (1998) are two recent examples. Some social scientists see this as an ethnic, religious, and cultural "clash of civilizations" (Huntington 1996). Arguably it is really a clash between the Enlightenment ideals of modern, secular, scientific civilization, with its belief in progress, tolerance, and a natural human tendency toward cooperation (Ury 2000), and social groups within many societies that see the metaphors of the past they prefer to live by as incompatible with acceptance of the realities of the present (Lawrence; Friedman 1999; Chua 2003).[1]

These three tributaries—a commitment to narratives based on real science, an openness and sensitivity to minority and alternative voices, and a strong political, satirical, or polemical edge—are all present in the recent novels of Greg Bear, Greg Egan, Robert J. Sawyer, and Stephen Baxter. All of them take advantage of what Terry Pratchett and his coauthors of *The Science of Discworld* series call "quantum" and "narrativium" as devices for serving up compelling alternatives, either through the scientific and philosophical implications of quantum mechanics in physics as explored in Robert J. Sawyer's *Neanderthal Parallax* trilogy, or the quantum leap of punctuated equilibrium in evolution at times of great stress, as explored in Greg Bear's *Darwin* novels. Together they produce a mighty narrative river that carries the reader along in thoughtful, plausible, and highly readable visions of Earth's near future. If they are not describing Earth as it is right now, it is only a matter of luck and, perhaps, of time. They are so compelling because they speak to our present condition. Their stories reach out to a wide readership by using a setting just different enough initially to permit readers to distance themselves from criticisms of their own practices implicit in the narratives.[2] Within the page limits of the current volume, this paper will explore some of these visions and their implications for our understanding of what it means to speak of "being human" in the twenty-first century.

Greg Egan's *Distress*

The title *Distress* chosen by Greg Egan reflects both an unexplained plague facing Earth and the personal situation of his carefully conceived major character, Andrew Worth, an investigative reporter whose body is filled with the latest in recording technology and a built-in pharm unit. Worth's literal personalty and lack of ability to read body language or understand metaphors mark his as an Asperger or autistic spectrum (AS) personality, not unlike many computer programmers today. Asperger syndrome has only emerged as a distinct diagnosis in the past twenty years (Rockwood and Rockwood 2005), and Egan's novel is one of the first to fully incorporate it in to the heart of a full-length fictional work.

A well-known subsequent portrayal of Asperger syndrome is Christopher John Francis Boone, the fifteen-year-old protagonist in Mark Haddon's novel *The Curious Incident of the Dog in the Night-Time* (2003). And it appears to play a role in the portrait of the scientist Marconi in Erik Larson's novel *Thunderstruck,* as a person whose "social obtuseness . . . made him oblivious to how his actions affected others" (Larson, as quoted in Baker 2006).

Egan introduces Andrew's challenges in the context of planning his next assignment after completing *Junk DNA,* his current documentary series for the net. Andrew is offered the chance to investigate a strange new mental illness, "acute clinical anxiety syndrome," also called "distress," which has begun to spread like wildfire with no apparent cause. "We're broadcasting on May 24th— that's ten weeks from Monday. You'll need to start pre-production the minute *Junk DNA* is finished," his boss tells him (37). He is periodically using drugs to keep awake and adjust his body clock as needed, so the project would be a stretch for him: "I hit the icon for the pharm unit, and said 'Recompute my melatonin doses. Give me two more hours of peak alertness a day, starting immediately.' . . . The Pharm said, 'You'll be sorry.'" With the new melatonin levels, he has some free time, so he calls his girlfriend, Gina, to go dancing, thinking, "Rule number six. Be unpredictable. But not too often" (42). There is an alternative project Andrew finds more attractive: doing a profile of a Nobel Prize–winning physicist Violet Mosala, twenty-seven years old, who is planning to announce her solution to the Theory of Everything (TOE) at a conference in three weeks. He has not prepared for the project and would have to take it away from someone else who wants to do it, but it would be over more quickly and he could then afford some time off with Gina. He thinks to himself, "Rule number four: Discuss everything with Gina first. Whether or not she'd ever admit to being offended if you didn't" (37).

These "rules" are the sorts of internal self-policing lists that Asperger adults develop to help them navigate a world where they cannot really empathize with others or read how others take what they say and do, and yet wish to function with a modicum of social success. When Andrew poses the two alternatives to Gina, she seems "baffled" that he wants her opinion: "If you don't want to make *Distress* . . . then don't. It's really none of my business." He explains, "It affects you too. It would be a lot more money," and they could afford a holiday, but "Gina was affronted. . . . We ate in silence. . . . Had I broken some taboo about money? . . . What should I have done? . . . My head spun. The truth was, I had no idea what she was thinking. *It was all too hard, too slippery*" (52–53). Andrew's extra melatonin expires, and he crashes before their night together can be consummated; shortly thereafter she breaks up with him. He is completely surprised and does not understand why.

Andrew's lack of insight into his own AS symptoms, even as he goes on to interview an advocate of the "Voluntary Autists" shortly thereafter, is intriguing. Perhaps Egan is suggesting that missing something that is in front of your nose on a personal level, even while you are an investigative journalist exploring the implications of the same issue socially, is a characteristic of "human" nature.

Andrew Worth's home is in a mid-twenty-first-century Australia, where core cities have been all but abandoned with the final adoption of uniform standards for universal broadband: "the use of the networks for entertainment and tele-commuting" had been "transmuted from a form of psychological torture into a natural and convenient alternative to ninety percent of physical travel" (44). Advances in surgery, pharmacology, and biotechnology have intersected with assertions of the fundamental right of persons to choose from a wide range of psychosexual identities, leading to concomitant linguistic developments: "Asex was really nothing but an umbrella term for a broad group of philosophies, styles of dress, cosmetic-surgical changes, and deep-biological alterations. The only thing that one asex person necessarily had in common with another was the view that vis gender parameters (neutral, endocrine, chromosomal and gen-ital) were the business of no one but verself, usually (but not always) vis lovers, probably vis doctor, and sometimes a few close friends" (45). Discussing the issue over dinner with Gina, Andrew argues that "gender migration is ninety percent politics. Some coverage still treats it as a kind of decadent, gratuitous, fashionable mimicry of gender reassignment for transsexuals—but most gender migrants go no further than superficial asex. . . . It's a protest action, like resign-ing from a political party, or renouncing your citizenship . . . or deserting a bat-tlefield" (48).

With a civilization liberated by, yet dependent upon, advances in technology, it is no wonder that intellectual property rights—particularly the protection of patents—are at the core of contemporary international politics. Global corpo-rations have pressured states to impose a boycott on Stateless, a quasi-floating artificial coral island community in the South Pacific, whose very existence is the result of the illegal exploitation of stolen intellectual property.

In completing his *Junk DNA* documentary series, Andrew goes to Manches-ter, England, to interview James Rourke, media liaison officer for the Voluntary Autists Association. Worth takes a filmmaker's perspective on Rourke, initially seeing him as "painfully awkward, with poor eye contact and muted body lan-guage. Verbally articulate, but far from telegenic" (57). He has no sense of the irony in his observation, which might well apply to Andrew himself. And after watching the video replay of his interview, he realized he has made a mistake in thinking Rourk would not be effective in the documentary. Rourke stands in con-trast to a slick earlier interviewee whose "performance . . . left no room for any question of what was going on beneath. Andrew realizes that Rourke put on no performance at all—and the effect was both riveting and deeply unsettling" (57).

Worth challenges Rourke's reasoning in defense of the demands of the VA movement to be permitted to complete surgically their transition to fully autis-tic status. The debate becomes an exploration of what it means to function in society, and, further, what it means to be human (59–67).

Rourke argues that people with the brain damage that makes them "partially autistic" can "survive in ordinary society" up to a point—the point where they may even "convince ourselves that nothing's wrong. For a while" (59). But they eventually realize that they cannot succeed at interpersonal relations, and not merely in terms of sexual relations. Most people "instinctively" try to "understand other human beings. To guess what they're thinking. To anticipate their actions. To . . . 'know them'" (59–60). But autistic people lack this ability to model what other people are thinking, and Rourke asserts that it is mostly due to congenital or later brain injury.[3] He refers to studies of a "small region in the left frontal lobe" called Lamont's area, after the neuroscientist who discovered it in 2014 (60–61). Damage to this area means that fully autistic people cannot lie or tell when someone else is lying, while partially autistic people may lack the ability to feel consistently empathy or the intimacy necessary to believe they understand someone they love. Rourke posits that "evolution invented intimacy," and Worth guesses that "even partial autism makes [love] impossible. . . . Because you can't model anyone well enough to *really know them at all?*" (62). While Egan's novel posits a good success record for some surgical procedures to help partially autistic people regain the ability to feel empathy and the sense of intimacy necessary to maintain personal relationships, VA advocates want the option to become fully autistic: "We know that non-autistic people are capable of believing that they've achieved intimacy. But in VA, we've decided we'd be better off without that talent," Rourke argues, calling it "a talent for self-deception" (65).

Worth struggles to understand Rourke, because he thinks that surgically healing the brain lesion would help recover "that lost understanding," so Rourke makes himself crystal clear: "But how much is understanding, and how much is a *delusion of understanding?* Is intimacy a form of knowledge, or is it just a comforting false belief?" (65). There is a parallel here to Robert Sawyer's character Ponter Boddit's implied longing for the potential to believe in God, or in life after death, which has been linked by neuroscience to a tiny part of the brain found in humans (Gliksins) but not in Neanderthals (Barasts) in the *Neanderthal Parallax* trilogy. The roles of genetics and neurosurgery in brain function in both Sawyer's and Egan's novels call into question what constitutes (or should constitute) "normal consciousness" in "humanity." Joe Haldeman's novels *The Forever War* (1974) and *Forever Peace* (1997) also both explore the question of how we can truly "know" each other in a manner worth contrasting to the approach taken in *Distress.*

Worth finally accuses Voluntary Autists of wanting to get rid of something "fundamental to humanity," and Rourke, amazingly, agrees. He points out that partial autists through their personal experience have "lived for decades with a *fundamental* truth about human relationships," which they do not wish to give up. They want to "stop being punished for our refusal to be deceived" (67).

The rest of the novel builds on this theme of what it means to be human— or even to talk about being human—to be conscious, and not to be deceived.

Egan deploys plot elements of an international thriller, with corrupt corporations, interventionist governments hiring mercenaries, and the global media panicking about the spreading disease distress, all tied up with an elaborate underground of biotechnology experts, quasi-religious ignorance cults, and a life-or-death struggle over which physicist will announce the TOE and what its consequences will be. Not since Greg Bear's *Moving Mars* have I read a novel in which the mere articulation of novel ideas of physics has resulted in such sudden and profound consequences, as are portrayed here: "I was the Keystone. I'd explained the universe into being, wrapped it around the seed of this moment, layer after layer of beautiful convoluted necessity. This blazing wasteland of galaxies, twenty billion years of cosmic evolution, ten billion human cousins, forty billion species of life—the whole elaborate ancestry of consciousness flowed out of this singularity. I had no need to reach out and imagine every molecule, every planet, every face. This moment encoded them all. . . . Nothing could have been created without the full knowledge of how it was done: without the unified TOE, physical and informational" (448). Andrew almost accepts that the universe will "now unravel into empty tautology" until he sees a "way through" by recognizing that no one person, no one mind alone can explain another into being. He has to rely on his own personal experience and memories to "tear myself out of the center of the universe" and give up "one last illusion" (448–49).

From the epilogue, set fifty years in the future, fifty years since the end of the "Age of Ignorance," it appears that the last illusion was the notion of intimacy, and with it the idea that any one person can speak for another. Instead there is a universal perception of the TOE, which does not prevent a wide variety of individual responses to this single truth. "What's become impossible is maintaining the pretense that every culture could ever have created its own separate reality—while we all breathed the same air and walked the same ground" (450). Egan's insight is one of cognitive dissonance: there is no foundation, but we can all build our reality on the TOE, which is the foundation. Speaking to a group of kindergarten children, trying to explain how it was before, Andrew thinks: "Ancient history always sounds quaint, old victories preordained, but I try to convey some sense of how long and hard their ancestors struggled to learn everything they now take for granted: that law and morality, physics and metaphysics, space and time, pleasure, love, meaning . . . are all the burden of the participants. There are no immovable centers, dispensing absolutes like manna: no God, no Gaia, no beneficent rulers. No reality but the universe explained into being. No purpose to life unless we create it, together or alone" (452).

At the end of the novel, society and humanity are irreversibly changed, and the change appears to be for the better from the standpoint of the people who live within the transformed world. Andrew notes that "Love in the face of truth has turned out to be stronger than ever. Happiness never really depended on the old lies. . . . Violet Mosala once said, 'Reaching the foundations doesn't mean hitting the ceiling." The "future is unbounded" for these children, but they "already knew that, of course" (454).

Darwin's Radio and *Darwin's Children*

The two novels in Greg Bear's Darwin sequence, *Darwin's Radio* (1999) and *Darwin's Children* (2003), postulate the parallel discoveries of an anthropologist, Mitch Rafelson, and a molecular biologist, Kay Lang, and her associates, and trace their consequences in biological and political thrillers that show that even writing prior to 9/11 Bear had a strong sense of the fear verging on paranoia that already informed much of the American public's response to trends such as the AIDS epidemic, fear of the "other," terrorism, and the new science of biotechnology.

Kay Lang is working within the government health bureaucracy intending to find out the source of the newly recognized "SHEVA virus," which apparently threatens the health of mothers and newborns, causing gross birth defects and miscarriages (Bear 1999, 133). She wants to identify a cure before it spreads too widely. She is not initially aware of the intentions of her opportunistic superiors to use the possibility of a pandemic to build their personal influence under the guise of responding to a national security threat posed by the virus. Bear notes: "SHEVA would soon become an official crisis. In the politics of health, a crisis tended to he resolved using familiar science and bureaucratically tried and true routines. Until the situation showed its true strangeness, Dicken did not think anyone would believe his conclusions" (Bear 1999, 134).

As events rapidly unfold, Bear's two novels portray a grim view of any hope for the survival of democracy and civil liberties in the face of this threat as it unfolds throughout the twenty-first century. There is a clear parallel between the government's response to the "war on biological terror" in these novels and the current threats to civil liberties in response to the "war on terror" since 9/11—in both cases, the claim is that the end justifies the means, but the means can be seen as undermining the end: preservation of our freedoms and way of life (Zimbardo 2007). For example, during the hearings over the nomination of former Judge Michael B. Mukasey for attorney general in the fall of 2007, the issue of whether the president could authorize torture was front and center. In a letter that threatened to undermine his acceptability to the Senate Judiciary Committee, Mukasey indicated that "he could not say whether waterboarding, which simulates drowning, was illegal torture" (Shane 2007).

Bear's novels show some optimism at the end, as Mitch and Kay, their "new child" daughter, and her peers all begin to find ways to prove that America can accept the reality of the new children and that all kinds of humans can live together in harmony. Even then, civil liberties and democratic institutions have taken a terrible beating in the interval. Many of Bear's characters suffer an early death as a consequence of their roles as intermediaries in the creation of these "new children," who are shown to be the result of the next phase of a process of punctuated equilibrium brought about by the stress of modern society (Bear 1999, 34). Over the course of both novels the argument plays out that at various times in human evolution, circumstances (possibly periods of great stress, in the past perhaps due to climate change and today perhaps due to the impact of war, social conflict, and overpopulation) have interfaced with a retrovirus and caused a great leap in human physical evolution along the lines of Stephen Jay Gould's concept of punctuated equilibrium (Gould 2002). Apparently such a leap is occurring in the present of the novel, having first emerged in the Caucasus Mountains of Georgia in the Soviet Union during Stalin's Reign of Terror and now seemingly appearing everywhere.

Bear does a good job, both in the text and in bibliographical and explanatory materials appended at the end of each novel and updated at his Web site, in explaining the scientific underpinnings of his story and identifying where it relies on controversial or speculative research. The mechanism of reproduction leading to the new children includes an apparent miscarriage that is really the production of an intermediate form solely to produce a subsequent "new child" free of susceptibility to contemporary viral threats (Bear 1999, 239, 275, 312). The second pregnancies give rise to the popular impression of asexual or even immaculate conception taking place, a religious interpretation reinforced because they only occur among committed couples. This plays a role in the public debate over the appropriate response to take.

The theme of children with physical differences that make them readily distinct from the general population and powers that give them great potential for building a more cooperative society—but also are perceived as a threat to the survival of "humanity"—can be read on several levels. The new children could be seen as a metaphor for widespread fears of "illegal immigrants" taking American jobs or seeking such "outrageous" benefits as in-state tuition at state universities (as the Fox News Channel or Lou Dobbs might put it). They can also be seen as a surrogate for the fears of religious fundamentalists and their conservative political backers, who fear the implications of genetic engineering for their inflexible worldviews.[4] With federal government support for stem cell research held back by President Bush's policies,[5] it is not too implausible to foresee an American future when distrust and fear of science undermines our ability to compete and survive in the emerging global society. Bear even hints at this possibility in *Darwin's Children* when he mentions various incidents where new children and their families appear to be better accepted and accommodated in other countries than in the United States.

In the second novel, the United States has isolated many new children in what amount to state-run concentration camps called schools (often located in former prisons or mental hospitals), where steps are taken to deny them use of their physical and mental powers—particularly associated with their sense of smell and their ability to communicate in a group mind to achieve consensus and to build elaborate social networks, a striking parallel to the situation portrayed for all people at the end of Egan's *Distress.* At some schools, research is performed on deceased children to develop biological weapons that could be used to wipe out the emerging new species (if that is what it is). At one point an accidental, or possibly intentional, release of a new virus wipes out many of the children before the protagonists discover the cause and manage to stop it in time.

Meanwhile, governmental steps are taken to censor Internet support groups used by the families and friends of new children, which reminds one of the cooperation of Microsoft, Google, and Yahoo! with Chinese censorship of words such as *human rights* and *democracy* on blogs that make use of their portals in China. Denial of fair trials in the name of security is common: Mitch is shot and then jailed on trumped-up charges for several years when his "new child" daughter with Kay is seized and sent off to the state school in Ohio. Other emergency powers used by the government mirror the abuses of power embodied in the USA PATRIOT Act, Guantánamo Bay and Abu Ghraib, and the legislation denying habeas corpus to those held in Cuba.

Underlying much of the health and national-security state apparatus deployed against the new children is the fear that they reflect a potential pool of contagion that might somehow harm or destroy humanity. Yet there is no evidence of any violence by the new children or any deliberate harm of others by them. They are the victims of individual violence, bounty hunters, and in one incident, being burned alive in a riot by locals who surround a state school in California. This is in contrast to the more threatening portrayal of an emerging "advanced" species in the short-lived cult science fiction series *Prey,* shown on ABC for thirteen episodes in 1998.

It is only after many years, when it becomes apparent that the threat, if any, only runs one way (mutations of human viruses that might kill new children), that Bear shows the national political consensus, and lap-dog mass media that follows it, start to turn toward a winding down of the confrontation and a search for healing. The length of time it takes is reflected in several long breaks in the narrative of *Darwin's Children,* which allow the characters to grow up and assume new roles but which also suggest a parallel to the current "war on terror": a conflict without apparent end, justifying ever-increasing restrictions that seem to serve no useful purpose other than consolidate state power and reduce civil liberty.

The eventual opportunity for movement toward reconciliation between humans and new humans is an archaeological discovery that is made possible only because of an illegal dig conducted in violation of the Native American Graves Protection Act (Bear 2004, 314) by Mitch and his former college mentor Eileen Ripper. They discover near Mount Hood in Oregon indisputable fossil evidence of *Homo sapiens* and *Homo erectus*—two different species—living together in harmony (329–31). The discovery is made public in a successful public relations stunt that makes the political and social case for viewers and officials alike that if prehistoric men and women from different species had lived and worked together, supporting each other, then there is no reason we cannot do so today (450–59).

One odd note in the second book is a series of religious experiences, epiphanies, that Kay Lang and others experience, that help move the plot along on one level while providing a metaphysical context for the tremendous upheavals humanity and society have been put through by SHEVA. The entity that appears to be behind these epiphanies communicates with Kay at the end of the novel, as she slips away, unable to talk to Mitch or their daughter Stella, now with a baby of her own: "She seemed to be listening. *She felt the love rolling over her, in waves, the yearning that was at once so powerful and frightening, the sweetness that lay behind the power. Her death would not come yet but she was no longer much of this world. And so she could be embraced and told all.*" Stella recognizes the scent of "smoke from a wood fire, and flowers" coming from Kay: "Mother, you could teach me so much." Kay's "tiny freckles darken" as her she is portrayed as hearing a final internal monologue—or perhaps as communicating it to Stella through scent? *The memories fall away. We are shaped, but in ways we do not understand. Know that thinking and memory are biology and history is what we leave behind The caller speaks to all of our minds and they all pray; to all of our minds from the lowest to the highest, in nature, the caller assures us that there is more, that is all the caller can do . . . ultimately all must be chipped away, having made their contributions*" (472–73). Shades of transcendentalism and Buddhism, perhaps, but somehow out of keeping with the scientific foundation of the novels. These passages may be nods to the perceived religious revival in America and encouragement to readers in the red states who might be put off by science fiction about evolution, or they may be a reflection of the tendency of Americans to see religious implications where others might not. This contrasts with the more skeptical view of religion in Egan's *Distress,* and in the novels of Sawyer and Baxter.

Sawyer's *Neanderthal Parallax*

Robert J. Sawyer's *Neanderthal Parallax* trilogy is composed of *Hominids, Humans,* and *Hybrids.* Sawyer is a Canadian writer described as a "self-proclaimed rationalist" in a biographical sketch at *Contemporary Authors Online.* The protagonists of the trilogy are two Neanderthal "quantum physicists" and a human Canadian paleo-geneticist, who are thrown together when an experiment in quantum computing on the Neanderthal version of Earth transports one of the Neanderthals, Ponter Boddit, to the Sudbury Neutrino Observatory located at the bottom of a mine in northern Ontario.

One of the premises of the novels, which is worked out over the course of the three narratives, is that about forty thousand years ago, perhaps during a realignment of Earth's electromagnetic fields, a significant quantum event occurred: consciousness emerged in one version of Earth in the larger-brained Neanderthals and in Homo sapiens in the other version. This was such a significant quantum event that the two versions did not merge, as usually happens with minor quantum discrepancies, so proceeded to markedly different evolutionary results while their respective geologies remained essentially the same. This circumstance allows for some interesting comparisons as the two species, or races, of humanity, broadly defined, get to know each other for better and for worse as the stories unfold.

The Barasts (as the Neanderthals call themselves) have evolved along lines that reflect an environmentalist creed of treading lightly on the world. They practice population control by only procreating once every ten years, so that each cohort (or "generation," as the Barasts call them) is numbered and separated by a decade. Accustomed to northern or colder climes, they have largely left the tropical portions of their planet unpopulated, so their total population is only about 335 million at the time they meet twenty-first-century Earth. They use solar power to fuel lightweight, stackable communal travel cubes, so they do not pave over nature to put up roads or parking lots, and they grow houses organically integrated into tended, communally owned trees; these are passed on to a new resident as the older ones die. Thus the population is stable, and everyone makes "their contribution."

Lest this idealistic Eden be seen as too perfect, it has some flaws, not only from our more individualistic perspective but surely by the Neanderthals' more communitarian standards as well, particularly since they seem clearly to value objective reality and a rough-and-ready pragmatism. Many of the Neanderthals we come to know seem remarkably unreflective and deferential to authority, reflecting in part a system of governance that does not allow you to vote until you are old and wise (perhaps over fifty by our mode of counting), so the elected rulers are referred to as the Gray Council. But there is one scientist who has had her research in genetic engineering banned, in part because it would undermine the rather draconian criminal justice system the Neanderthals have evolved, in which offenders (and their near family members) are castrated so that they cannot pass on their suspect genes. Angered, she rips out the surgically implanted companion that monitors all Neanderthals nearly from birth and goes to live off the land as her ancestors did: thanks to their environmentally careful lifestyles, there are still plenty of woolly mammoths and passenger pigeons to eat.

To reduce the risk of violent crime and enhance the mean intelligence and potential of all Neanderthals, they practice selective restrictions on reproduction. In addition to castrating violent criminals and their near relatives, the Neanderthals required that for ten generations, the lowest 5 percent in intelligence were not permitted to produce children "when Two become One." Sawyer's Barasts appear to be following the logic of a well-known U.S. Supreme Court case that affirmed Virginia's enforced sterilization of institutionalized mental patients, *Buck v. Bell*, 2784 US 200 (1927), where Justice Oliver Wendell Holmes ruled that "three generations of imbeciles is enough." The portrayal of Neanderthal practices is nonjudgmental, showing the strengths and limitations of his well-realized alternative to what we conceive of as "human" society. One can feel that their laws are draconian by our standards; yet consider that U.S. voters tend to approve of isolating "convicted sex offenders" for life, putting their names on Internet registries, and prohibiting them from living (for all practical purposes) almost anywhere, lest they be within some arbitrary distance from a school, playground, or other protected location.

"When Two become One" refers to the Neanderthal practice of men living in the periphery and women in the center of Neanderthal communities, with the men and women coming together for only four days of each month. As part of the social commitment to birth control, the four days usually fall when the women are not fertile, but every ten years, when a new generation is due to be conceived, "Two become One" during the fertile period. During the balance of the year, men live with men and women with women. Every Neanderthal has a man-mate and a woman-mate. Children live with their mothers until, at ten, the boys go to the fathers, while the girls remain with their mothers until, at age eighteen, they take their own mates and after a few years produce their first child in a new generation.

Data derived from studies undertaken by human and Neanderthal scientists once they were in contact suggests that as a result of these practices, and apart from their larger brains, the average Barast is significantly more intelligent than the majority of Gliksins (as the Neanderthals refer to the extinct Homo sapiens on their world). But because of the uncompromising severity of their criminal justice penalties, there is a problem. Spousal abuse often goes unreported, because if it is punished, the children and siblings of the accused receive the same punishment, castration. It would seem this one-size-fits-all penalty would inevitably entail such unreported crime, and it is surprising that such highly intelligent people do not recognize that. Perhaps it will lead to legal reform, if Mary Vaughan, the human paleo-geneticist who marries Ponter Boddit, has anything to say about it in a future book in the series, thus far a trilogy. Another volume would answer questions still open at this point. One of the advantages of Barasts coming into contact with Gliksins is thus not only a sharing of technology, and perhaps the reintroduction of extinct species into our version of Earth, but the opportunity for comparative study of legal and political institutions.

Perhaps the most surprising to humans of the Barast innovations is the relatively recent adoption of companion implants, which record on an unerasable crystal everything each Barast sees, says, and does, in a three-dimensional image with sound, throughout his or her entire life. Individuals can use this to go back and look at themselves and find where they left their glasses. And society through the use of adjudicators can examine the crystal when a Barast is accused of a crime or one's man-mate or woman-mate goes missing. Thus there is practically no crime, and it is safe for women and children to walk outside at night and look at the stars (which are easy to see, since there is none of our light pollution to worry about).

I recall Margaret Mead speaking at my college in my senior year, describing in light of the Kitty Genovese case how in the future people would give up their right to privacy in exchange for constant video and audio surveillance to ensure their safety. We now have most public places surveilled in England and in much of America, particularly after 9/11, so it is not far-fetched to assume that if something like the Barasts' companion could be built and was tamperproof, we might well try it. Automobiles and cell phones already are commonly sold with technology that makes them easy to trace; chips are implanted in dogs to help in their recovery if they run away and could easily be implanted in children, or ex-felons, for the same reason. Passports and credit cards that can be read electronically at a distance are a step in this direction (as well as a new opportunity for identity theft). So while the stark version of this abandonment of all privacy as presented by Sawyer initially strikes the reader as too much, contemporary events suggest that such a world is not so far removed from our present reality.

In the first of the three novels, the plot revolves around a murder trial of Ponter Boddit's man-mate, Adikor Huld, who is accused of killing Ponter and hiding the body when he disappears as a result of the quantum experiment. The accuser has a personal ax to grind, and because the mine shaft into which Ponter disappears is so deep that signals recording their interaction cannot be received or stored, there is no companion recording in Adikor's crystal to document that he is in fact innocent. Because Adikor is a physicist, the adjudicators assume he could have tampered with his own companion implant to alter its recording. He is cleared only when he manages to find a way to evade detection and reopen the portal between the two Earths and Ponter returns. Thereafter, the subplots revolve around a dispute over whether to keep the portal between the two worlds open—the Gray Council has its doubts after someone shoots Ponter outside the UN Headquarters after a diplomatic visit—and around Mary Vaughan's rape, which occurs at York University in Toronto where teaches and conducts research. Sawyer uses the rape, which takes place just prior to Ponter's arrival in Mary's world, to explore whether sometimes a little castration could go a long way to solving social problems.

One cannot tell if Sawyer is advocating surgical castration as an alternative to chemical castration or the indefinite confinement for sex offenders in the United States or Canada, but given the horrific recent examples of child murders in Florida, one can see how proposals of this sort might too easily be adopted. Is it wise to promote them on the grounds of efficiency or utilitarianism, then, given problems we have had over the years with the accuracy of eyewitness identification in rape cases, the reluctance of authorities to fund DNA testing for current prisoners who claim they are innocent, the frequency of mistakes in the FBI and state crime labs, and the problem of mobs seeking vengeance—not to speak of the association of genetic engineering and procedures of this sort with Social Darwinism and Nazi practice? Sawyer's own narrative of Adikor Huld's near miss with the shears, based on a mistaken inference from circumstantial evidence as presented by a biased, emotionally driven prosecutor, is probably sufficient balance here, but it is a close call.

Another highly charged theme is why Neanderthals have no religion and no belief in God or in the concept of an afterlife, which they find inconsistent with objective reality. Mary wants a divorce from her Canadian husband, but he wants an annulment to stay in the good graces of the Roman Catholic Church, and she is reluctant to give it to him. The rapist (who proves later to be a fellow academic) complains that his career has been unjustly interfered with by the York University's affirmative action hiring practices; without justifying his actions, his grievance adds complexity to the narrative. Jock Krieger, a sometime Rand Corporation researcher with a possible CIA background, has hired Mary away from her university to work at the Synergy Corporation in New York state, to compare human and Neanderthal DNA. He is clearly looking for a way to claim the new Earth for "real humans," which leads to the crisis at the end of the third novel. The solution assumes that Neanderthals can trust human women more than human men, which is a fairly sweeping assumption, so there is plenty of room for future conflict, but at the end of the trilogy Sawyer has pretty much made his main points.

Through the perspective of Mary Vaughan, a smart but conflicted woman exploring her own faith while trying to explain it to Ponter, we come to see much of what is good, and bad, about human society, and what parts of human behavior we might wish to do without. Sawyer comes down against the God gene: if there is one, he'd like to have it out. In light of religiously driven suicide bombers blowing themselves up daily in various parts of the world, while in the United States religious fanatics try to drive evolution out of science class and demagogues trash the rights of gays and lesbians based on tortured interpretations of ancient texts often mistranslated and not literally followed in all respects by anyone, it is hard to disagree. Through the lens of Ponter's investigation of the genetic basis for religious belief in Gliksins, Sawyer makes it clear that if there is a "God gene" in humans, he would like to have it removed.

Some unanswered questions remain. The third novel is *Hybrids,* but the only physical hybrid is Ponter and Mary's anticipated girl child, and we do not know yet if she will be fertile, and if she will be fully accepted among Barasts: we can already guess she'll have the same sort of problems among Gliksins that Worf would have as a Klingon on *Star Trek: The Next Generation.* The matter of the impact of the gradual reversal of the Gliksin version of Earth's electromagnetic field on human consciousness could be further explored. Humans are portrayed as talking of visiting Mars in both versions: but just because there are Barast and Gliksin versions of Earth, does that extend to Mars, or even the whole universe? This is the same claim Egan makes at the end of *Distress,* and it strikes me as almost Ptolemaic in its retention of the sense that, in the end, Earth remains the center of the universe, and what happens to (or because of) humans has ripple effects everywhere else.[6]

The Themes

All three sets of novels discussed here, as well as Stephen Baxter's *Manifold: Origin,*[7] take advantage of human difference to explore human nature and values. Apart from Bear's nod to the implications of some religious sensitivities or epiphanies (which Sawyer's Ponter Boddit would see as probably a product of that mutant God gene and not anything to take seriously), all of these authors have thoroughly grounded their narratives in state-of-the-art scientific research and endeavored to make their stories appear both scientifically plausible and reflective of actual cultural trends.

In Egan's portrayal of an Earth integrated by an updated, more fully realized Internet, where travel is swift and a fully realized global culture exists, we see a positive portrayal of how humanity might evolve in a direction that would undermine the fear of the other that often fixates on immigrants. In contrast, Bear's stories of the fate of the new children suggest that we do have something to fear, particularly from those whose religion argues that "humans" are in God's image and thus might have trouble figuring out where new, better humans fit in, particularly if their existence appears to validate evolution. A negative reaction to the new children seems more likely in a society that devalues science education, so one lesson Bear leaves us with is that it is all the more important to fight instances such as the Kansas School Board's periodic efforts to remove evolution from the teaching curriculum.

Both Egan, in his discussion of the asex movement, and Sawyer, in his exploration of Neanderthal marital relations, take a sympathetic approach to varied gender roles and acceptance of homosexual relationships that remain controversial with far too many voters for the health of the U.S. body politic. The U.S. Supreme Court ruled in *Rumsfeld v. F.A.I.R.* (2006) that the First Amendment rights of universities *not* to invite employers to recruit on campus if they fail to follow university nondiscrimination policies can be legally trumped by the Solomon Amendment, which cuts off all federal funding to the entire university if any element excludes military recruiters.[8] If the justices would read some of these novels, they might come to do the right thing and respect the rights of all humans of whatever sort. If Greg Bear is right, we have a long road ahead before we see the dawn on some of these issues.

Conclusion: Human Nature?

These stories tell us that humans are diverse, complicated, and resilient. We can imagine the impossible, and having done so, derive lessons from it as if it were so. The Greeks and Romans did this with their gods, and the religious folk who dominate world discourse today continue to do so but generally deny they are just telling stories. (Jesus gave us oral parables, but like Homer he had no control over his transcriptions or his interpreters, and his copyright has long expired). Science fiction stories are written for people who choose to read and understand complexity, and who may see in science fiction narratives that will enable us to assemble an acceptable future. As the slogan of Yoyodyne Propulsion puts it, "The Future Begins Tomorrow." Let's go there.

Notes

1. UN Secretary General Kofi Annan received a report from a cross-cultural "Alliance of Civilizations" recently that included Anglican Archbishop Desmond Tutu and former Iranian President Mohammed Khatami. The report calls for efforts to build bridges between Muslim and Western societies, noting, "As long as the Palestinians live under occupation, exposed to daily frustration and humiliation, and as long as Israelis are blown up in buses and in dance halls, so long will passions everywhere be inflamed." The report notes that many communities see globalization as an "assault" and that "the prospect for greater well-being has come at a high price, which includes cultural homogenisation, family dislocation, challenges to traditional lifestyles, and environmental degradation." "Call to Bridge West-Muslim Divide," BBC News, November 13, 2006, http://news.bbc.co.uk/go/pr/fr/-/2/hi/europe/6142308.stm.

2. Compare Sinclair Lewis's *It Can't Happen Here,* reprinted in 2005, with Philip Roth's *The Plot against America.* Both explore fears of fascism and religious fundamentalism in the 1930s and 1940s in uncanny alternate Americas, with implications for our current president's "faith-based initiatives"—from charitable choice to Terry Schiavo's case and stem-cell research, which the controversy over Michael J. Fox's political commercial in Missouri brought to attention again in the November 2006 elections. See also "An Evangelical Identity Crisis," *Newsweek,* November 13, 2006, 30–43.

3. As of 2005 there is no agreed clear, single cause of AS. One author notes: "I had already noted that the diagnostic criteria for Asperger's were so complicated and so contradictory and so blurred at the borders as to sometimes stretch credulity. There seemed to be endless lists of ifs and buts. Was it possible, then, that around a core biological illness a large superstructure of behaviors and moods had been created by society itself? This did not mean that Asperger's was imaginary. . . . But the purely biological explanation was too simple. Many hold out hope of a cure for autism in the conventional sense, but so far such a panacea has proved . . . elusive. We might ask whether a personality disorder should be cured at all—for what would it mean to *cure* a personality?" (Osborne 2002, 185). Many young people today call themselves autistic and are demanding to be granted their civil rights as such. See the Autism Network International Web site, at http://ani.autistics.org/. *Scientific American* recently reported new clues as to the diagnosis and treatment of autism, which these young people might not readily desire. Vilayanur S. Ramachandran and Lindsay M. Oberman, "Special Section: Neuroscience: Broken Mirrors, a Theory of Autism," *Scientific American* 295 (November 2006): 63–69.

4. See Christine Corcos, Isabel Corcos, and Brian Stockhoff, "Double-Take: A Second Look at Cloning, Science Fiction, and Law," *Louisiana Law Review,* 59 (1999): 1041–1099, which suggests that images of cloning and the "mad scientist" in science fiction may have contributed to badly drawn legislation that underestimates the potential of genetic research for curing disease; and Leon R. Kass, "Triumph or Tragedy? The Moral Meaning of Genetic Technology," *American Journal of Jurisprudence* 45 (2000): 1–16, in which President Bush's former adviser on bioethics lays out some of his worries about stem cell research. See also Alexander M. Capron, "Ethical Aspects of Major Increases in Life Span and Life Expectancy," in *Coping with Methuselah: The Impact of Molecular Biology on Medicine and Society,* ed. Henry J. Aaron and William B. Schwartz (Washington, D.C.: Brookings Institution Press,

2004), 198–234, which discusses the ethical issues associated with using biotechnology to prolong human life and responds to some of Kass's criticisms of research to that end.

5. See "Stem Cells: How Far Will We Go?" *National Geographic* 208 (July 2005): 2–27.

6. It is also reminiscent of the role of robots making the universe safe, and thus empty, for humans, in the interconnected novels of Isaac Asimov.

7. Baxter's *Manifold* trilogy also takes advantages of quantum mechanics to create the context for these mammoth space operas, which transcend the whole fate of the universe without, alas, explaining it all once and for all.

8. For all of the documentation on this point, see the Georgetown University School of Law's Web site: http://www.law.georgetown.edu/solomon/.

Bibliography

Baker, Kevin. 2006. "Ship to Shore." *New York Times Book Review,* November 5.

Bashe, Patricia R., Barbara L. Kirby, Simon Baron-Cohen, and Tony Atwood. 2005. *The Oasis Guide to Asperger Syndrome, Completely Revised and Updated: Advise, Support, Insight, and Inspiration.* New York: Crown Publishers.

Baxter, Stephen. 2002. *Manifold: Origin.* New York: Ballantine.

Bear, Greg. 1999. *Darwin's Radio.* New York: Del Rey.

———. 2003. *Darwin's Children.* New York: Ballantine.

Bell, Derrick. 1999. "The Power of Narrative." *Legal Studies Forum* 23, no. 3: 315.

Brin, David. 2002. *Kiln People.* New York: Tor.

Chua, Amy. 2003. *World on Fire: How Exporting Free Market Democracy Breeds Ethnic Hatred and Global Instability.* New York: Doubleday.

DeForest, Tim. 2004. *Storytelling in the Pulps, Comics and Radio, How Technology Changed Popular Fiction in America.* Jefferson, N.C.: McFarland.

Egan, Greg. 1998. *Distress.* New York: HarperPrism.

Friedman, Thomas. 1999. *The Lexus and the Olive Tree.* New York: Farrar, Straus, Giroux.

Gould, Stephen Jay. 2002. *The Structure of Evolutionary Theory.* Cambridge, Mass.: Belknap Press.

Haddon, Mark. 2003. *The Curious Incident of the Dog in the Night-Time.* New York: Doubleday.

Hollinger, Veronica, and Joan Gordon. 2002. *Edging into the Future: Science Fiction and Contemporary Cultural Transformation.* Philadelphia: University of Pennsylvania Press.

Huntington, Samuel P. 1996. *The Clash of Civilizations and the Remaking of World Order.* New York: Simon and Schuster.

Jeter, K. W. 1998. *Noir.* New York: Bantam.

Larson, Erik. 2006. *Thunderstruck.* New York: Crown.

Lawrence, Bruce B. 1998. *Shattering the Myth: Islam beyond Violence.* Princeton: Princeton University Press.

Le Guin, Ursula K., and Brian Atteberry. 1993. *The Norton Book of Science Fiction: North American Science Fiction, 1960–1990.* New York: Norton.

Osborne, Lawrence. 2002. *American Normal: The Hidden World of Asperger Syndrome.* New York: Copernicus.

Pohl, Frederik. 1984. *The Years of the City.* New York: Simon and Schuster.

Pratchett, Terry, Ian Stewart, and Jack S. Cohen. 2005. *Darwin's Watch: The Science of Discworld III.* London: Ebury.

Rockwood, Bruce L. 1998. "Communication and Self-Governance: Is Democracy Possible?" In *Revolutions, Institutions, Law,* ed. Joel Levin and Roberta Kevelson, 189–229. New York: Peter Lang.

Rockwood, Bruce L., and Susan M. Rockwood. 2005. "Normal or Neurotypical? Mark Haddon's *The Curious Incident of the Dog in the Night-Time* and the Emerging Asperger's Community." Paper presented April 16, 2005, to the International Roundtable for the Semiotics of Law, McGill University, Montreal.

Sawyer, Robert J. 2002. *Hominids.* New York: Tor.

———. 2003a. *Humans.* New York: Tor.

———. 2003b. *Hybrids.* New York: Tor.

Shane, Scott. 2007. "Mukasey Calls Harsh Interrogation 'Repugnant.'" *New York Times,* October 31.

Stiglitz, Joseph E. 2002. *Globalization and Its Discontents.* New York: Norton.

Ury, William. 2000. *The Third Side: Why We Fight and How We Can Stop.* New York: Penguin.

Zimbardo, Philip. 2007. *The Lucifer Effect: Understanding How Good People Turn Evil.* New York: Random House.

Fractal Fantasies of Transformation

William Blake, Michael Moorcock, and the Utilities
of Mythographic Shamanism

Carter Kaplan

In a posting to the Q & A page at the Web site of British fantasy writer Michael
Moorcock, I asked about the operation of personal and group mythographies.

> My question has to do . . . with the nature of human thought processes,
> and my feeling—which I was led to by reading your Second Ether
> [trilogy]—that the source of much of our woe . . . has to do with our
> thinking in terms of archetypes and Platonic ideals. We create for our-
> selves (or they are thrust upon us) whole pantheons (or pandemoniums,
> as Milton would say) of expectations about ourselves, and we seek to
> live our lives according to the dictates and strictures voiced by the gods
> dwelling in these pantheons, and in the end we come up feeling very sad
> and very sorry, because our lives do not live up to these ideals. We are in
> a real fix, moreover, when these pantheons are controlled by corpora-
> tions who use "our" gods against us. . . .
>
> My general question is: My goodness, what's to be done! My specific
> question is: Can you reflect upon your reading in Milton and Blake?
> Thanks, Carter

Michael Moorcock answered as follows:

> In a way Jerry Cornelius and all the multiverse books are about shifting
> identities to suit one's context. Since you're going to find yourself in
> a good many more contexts than you might have a hundred years ago
> (unless a character in a Victorian long-running adventure serial!) you
> have to learn to move easily and fluidly between them while maintaining
> a core identity which provides what you might call public sector virtues
> —morality, commonality. A mixed psychic economy—the public sector
> doing what it does best, the private sector doing what it does best.

Paradoxically, of course, the "public" involves the most private, the most enduring self. To survive and thrive we don't necessarily confront our natural enemies—the lumbering dinosaur orthodoxies of big business and big government—we go around and behind them. To live to the full in the modern world, in other words, you have to learn to weave and dodge and drift and take advantage of what the moment offers. This isn't a particularly new problem for metropolitan working classes. The trick is to choose your masks. To choose your roles. And play them consciously as roles. The old notion of the person of integrity—strike them where you will they ring true—has to be revamped, perhaps. The existential moral being must learn whole sets of roles—Pierrot, Harlequin, Columbine. On we go. Blake and Milton provide us with models of Law and Chaos, rather than Good and Evil, and that can't be bad. What a lot of theological abstract fun you can have with that idea. . . .
       Best, M

I am not so much interested in the way William Blake has influenced Michael Moorcock as I am in the way that Michael Moorcock has influenced my reading of William Blake and John Milton. While I have reservations concerning what I understand to be Moorcock's emphasis regarding Milton and Blake, I am moved by his work—particularly his most Blakean production, the Second Ether trilogy—to identify my own understanding of Blake and Milton and to discover in their epics a practice of mythographic shamanism that is at least as sophisticated, as supple, and as clever as the more broadly understood shamanistic practices and rituals of archaic and preliterate peoples. Indeed, the movement of shamanism from preliterate to literate stages has enriched shamanistic practice and liberated it from the essentially conservative tendencies of the preliterate mind. At the same time, however, the advent of written language has created new forms and processes of orthodoxy. It is the task of the literary mythographer to expose such orthodoxies and to release the poetic imagination from the tyrannies of custom and institution. Suggesting the program if not the techniques of Ludwig Wittgenstein, Blake and Moorcock are engaged in a mythographic house cleaning. Through identifying, exposing, and clearing away conceptual confusion, their works pattern analytic processes that expose and clarify the complex operation of the mythologies that define our self-concepts, our social personae, and our worldviews.

A comparative examination of Blake and Moorcock spotlights the analytic utilities of Western mythographic shamanism. Moorcock and Blake are both men of working-class London neighborhoods. Blake's love for London together with the distress he felt in beholding the poverty and destitution of the lower classes are amply described and explored in his work. When removed from London during his tenure in the village of Felpham, he was a salient neighborhood fixture. The well-known account of Blake's arrest in Felpham after ejecting a soldier from his garden and the enthusiastic support he received from his neighbors in court and during his return home are indicative of how the poet was favored by the people who lived around him. In the 1960s, Moorcock's home in London's Ladbroke Grove was a center for raconteurs, musicians, visionaries, travelers, and other flamboyant personalities. Many of Moorcock's realistic fantasies—the Cornelius tetralogy and novels such as *King of the City* (2000) and *Mother London* (1988)—are built around the descriptions of life in lower-middle-class and working-class London neighborhoods. It is certainly very possible that the variability, the variety, the fecundity, the decay, the pace, the rapid rates of change, and the phantasmagoria of such neighborhood fabrics drive the complexity and the dynamics of Blake's and Moorcock's mythographies.

The activity of giving voice to the sensibility of these neighborhoods and the role played by the local prophetic heroes represent a cultural pattern with identifiable historical beginnings in Civil War London. The weakening of upper-class control in the 1640s coincided with the rise of a radical publishing underground. In the wake of the Long Parliament, during the 1640s there was a breakdown of censorship, the collapse of church courts, and the eclipse of upper-class leadership in English culture. A fierce hostility to the gentry, the aristocracy, and the monarch was revealed through an explosion of publications advancing the ideas of antinomians, Arminians, Socinians, Arians, Ranters, libertines, Independents, Anabaptists, Quakers, Levelers, and other radicals. By 1646 the theological scene in London was dominated by the lower and middle classes, who freely spoke and wrote of new liberty, universal grace, the abrogation of church law, and the sinfulness of repentance and who denounced the priestly orders and ministry of the Church of England as anti-Christian (Hill 1977, 94). The scene is eulogized by Milton in *Areopagitica,* where he describes a city in which "all the Lord's people are become prophets . . . trying all things, assenting to the force of reason and convincement. . . . A nation not slow and dull, but of a quick, ingenious and piercing spirit, acute to invent, subtle and sinewy to discourse, not beneath the reach of any point the highest that human capacity can soar to." In triumph Milton declares: "Behold now this vast City, a city of refuge, the mansion house of liberty . . ." (1930, 749). In the linked celebration of antinomianism, independent theology, professed radicalism, and a DIY approach to self-editing and self-publishing, Blake and Moorcock are heirs to the cultural revolutions of London in the 1640s.

Both Blake and Moorcock pursued careers as artisans to support their more sophisticated artistic projects, and in this respect both authors made their commercial work into subjects and themes that are explored in their more ambitious efforts. Blake, of course, worked as an illustrator. Moorcock has been an editor, a comic book writer, a paperback fantasy writer, and a rock musician and composer. Blake and Moorcock have made their careers a source of material for mythmaking, and their mythography in this respect focuses not so much on the subject of their commercial work, but rather on the activity represented by this work: the activity of the creative process itself. Stories about artisans and artistic creation are central to their mythographies. Indeed, in every sense of the phrase, Blake and Moorcock are "poets of artifice."

This interest in artifice begins with their approach to language. Following after epic usage, Blake and Moorcock select language to allegorize, aggrandize, illuminate, theorize, personify, visualize, valorize, and validate their idiosyncratic mythological systems. Such words as *ad hoc, parodic,* and *satiric* characterize Blake and Moorcock's usage. Blake draws upon the Bible, Homer, Milton, and Swedenborg for his mythological vernacular, while Moorcock parodies Conan the Barbarian, tabloid newspapers, detective magazines, George Meredith, Victorian serial fiction, Sherlock Holmes, Madison Avenue, H. G. Wells, the Beatles, and James Bond. At one end, such language is wonderfully humorous and brings a sense of proportion to the authors' metaphysical gymnastics, which, if left unbalanced, would grow cloying and burdensome. At the same time, such language accomplishes the analytic purposes of satire, adding to the farrago of perspectives and voices that cannot go too far in providing a full anatomy of the subject at hand. The complexity of their language builds into the sophistication of their composition, creating a work that is nearly unintelligible. But rather than obscurity, the effect of this complexity is itself a source of meaning.

Both Blake and Moorcock combine their ontological and metaphysical concepts so closely that their philosophies teeter dangerously at the edge of idealism. For Blake the notion of such a metaphysic is itself both the result and the cause of a fallen state. For Moorcock the scientific unification of ontology and metaphysics provides the superstructure for an elaborate joke. Moorcock repeatedly portrays characters that use science as a means to hide from the human condition. An enthusiasm for theoretical science figures among the many self-deceptions of his heroes, who, possessing incomplete knowledge of themselves, struggle unsuccessfully against the contours of a hostile and deforming landscape. It is ironic that Moorcock himself so readily promotes a scientific theory of his own. In his metaphysical scheme the world exists in a flux between law and chaos, between order and entropy. There is no good and evil, but only the interplay of these polarized states of being. Such a polarization is descried occasionally by Blake, who provides us with images of a universe laid out between poles of energy and passivity, between poetic inspiration and acquiescence to the empire of social mediocrity and the cosmo-mechanical-vegetable mundane. For Moorcock and Blake, good and evil are not to be found as tending to one or the other of these poles, but rather in the particular experiences of particular individuals who variously perceive themselves, or fail to perceive themselves, between the fluctuations of them. While Moorcock claims this is a mathematical and physical phenomenon, Blake expresses the dichotomy as a matter of perception. Moorcock's proposition that Milton "provide[s] us with models of Law and Chaos, rather than Good and Evil," is interesting and attractive, and there is much in Milton that argues for such a model. Moorcock's proposition easily dovetails with the contemporary pseudoscientific critical habits of identifying dichotomies and reading them as physical forces that drive a dialectical universe, as if our way of seeing, our way of understanding, our scientific method itself were all simply dialectical.

Milton's project transcends simple dichotomies. As I read Milton, the moral drama that unfolds in the universe is driven not by underlying dialectical energies but by the ability of human beings to choose to use reason as a tool, and this tool itself is an effect (or an artifact) of choice; very often that choice is a decision to test strongly held belief systems, or even to overturn the prevailing worldview. Milton equates morality with reason, analysis, inspiration, and communication. If reason is good, then the lack of reason or the denial of reason is evil. Evil is an absence of good; evil is not itself an active principle. The wild variables of inspiration, apostasy, and intuition are thus not evil—nor are they attributes of law or chaos—but rather they work as the arbiters between the senses and reason. They safeguard human freedom as guarantors of human judgment. In the development and education of the full person, these principles are to be cultivated, and poetry is the chief instrument of this cultivation. For Milton the transformational nature of mythography simply represents a quality of the tool in its uncultivated state. Cultivation sharpens mythography into an analytic tool that—in the familiar terms of the scientific method—allows us to investigate the influences of the observer upon the experiment; a vital and living mythographic process allows us to peer into the human brain's tendency to rationalize ambiguity and establish patterns—often credulous and fictitious patterns—of cause and effect and of correlation. As Francis Bacon says, "human understanding is of its own nature prone to suppose the existence of more order and regularity in the world than it finds. And though there be many things in nature which are singular and unmatched, yet it devises for them parallels and conjugates and relatives which do not exist" (1620, 50). A fully competent and reflexive mythographic system is keen to highlight and analyze these illusionary specters of understanding. Although cognizant of such spectral manifestations and willing to document them in grotesque and sensational detail, in his larger figure Blake embraces the process of inspiration, apostasy, and intuition in toto, offering as his Parnassus-scaling model a kind of hallucinating noble-savage-with-a-pen. From this heroic perch he casually reduces and rejects even the most sensible cultivation, characterizing it as merely the prevailing neoclassic cant of his rivals in the art world of late-eighteenth-century London. In this consideration Blake is a reactionary antimodernist who uses poetry in a scientific attempt to "return" people to a unified state with the cosmos. He sees the transformational nature of myth as the message itself, an esoteric, pseudoscientific "proof" of epistemic relativism that leaves the world in a shattered and fractured state— a bright, blistering, and gaudy "ultra-modern" universe of exotic sensation and psychological distraction—and thus he has been variously championed, embellished, and imitated by the inhabitants of such spheres. There is, and make no mistake, a price to be paid for achieving unity with the cosmos. Ultimately Blake's follower is left stranded in a Hobbesian universe whose laws are mechanical, fixed, and inviolable—where the poetical facility, once so full of promise, is reduced to a simple tool for food-gathering, conflict, or escape. Milton, on the other hand, is content to remain alienated and slug it out with existence, so long as observation, reason, and inspiration accompany him for consolation, for in that universe—let's call it a Lockean universe—the human being is liberated from the mechanism of the cosmos, and rather than being joined with the cosmos is instead separate and free to discover the secrets of the mechanism in order to transcend it. It is this Lockean universe to which Moorcock's elaborate mythography is tending. It is very possible that Moorcock's extensive mythic production, when taken collectively, portrays the transformation from the Hobbesian worldview to the Lockean.

Chaos theory and complexity science have many applications in describing the compositional process and the mythological systems that Blake and Moorcock have conceived. Three notions from chaos theory are particularly applicable in an examination of their mythologies.

First is the central notion of chaos theory itself, which is that complex interdependent systems pushed into chaos will undergo a phase transition resulting in new order. Moorcock uses this principle to drive his plots, where law and chaos become poles in an epic struggle between supernatural aristocracies of angels and demons, where the unbridled energies of chaos bring about a transformation of cosmic and political order that is shaped by the conceptual designs of law. At a more subtle level, Moorcock explains this dichotomy in terms of form and consciousness. Form and consciousness, like order and chaos, are not so much involved in a struggle as a reconciliation, for it is through form that consciousness survives, and it is through consciousness that form survives.

A second application of chaos theory that can be applied to Blake and Moorcock involves the way complexity itself can be used as a tool to create compositional interest. Blake and Moorcock use complexity in their compositions to make them more interesting, intriguing, and satisfying. The measure of this complexity is called "organizational depth." Architecture critic Charles Jencks describes organizational depth as a sort of ornamentation or elaboration that creates the "resonance," "deep character," and "integrity" we perceive in art (Jencks 1995). A complex narrative can force the reader into an act of co-creation with the author, where the reader, faced with compounding confusion, is led to create a parallel personal narrative in order to superimpose narrative cohesion upon the text. In this way consciousness can be said to enter and pervade a narrative.

A third aspect of chaos theory that has its applications in describing our authors is the notion of self-similarity and fractal scaling. Self-similarity is a concept from chaos theory that identifies an underlying pattern of order in complex phenomenon. Best illustrated by the graphic patterns created by the Mandelbrot set formula, self-similar fractal patterns can be seen in turbulence, clouds, waterfalls, coastlines, mountain ranges, and in simple organic forms, where one part of the pattern resembles the whole. Take, for example, a fern plant, in which the sprays or fronds of the fern are representative of a repeated pattern or image seen at other scales. The pointy shape of the frond is replicated in the shape of the leaves on the frond. In turn, the leaves are made up of tapering leaflets that resemble the leaves; and in turn these leaflets are edged with thin, pointed serrations that copy the pointed thematic pattern that is recapitulated throughout the plant at different scale levels: serration, leaflet, leaf, frond, and so on. According to the aesthetic of self-similarity and scaling, parts resemble not only each other but the whole as well. Self-similarity represents a transforming pattern of similarity and not exact replication. Mathematically self-similar patterns are defined by "strange attractors," reference points that establish recurring patterns of form and movement in a complex system.

In the essay "About My Multiverse," Moorcock explains that the concept of self-similarity is central to his cosmology: "Since the advent of Mandelbrot's extraordinary observations, the creation of Chaos Theory and Chaos Mathematics, I have been able to give further coherence to my notion [of cosmology], by suggesting we perceive each fresh 'plane' of the multiverse as a 'scale'—that scale alone differentiates them when so close together. The greater the variance of scales, the greater the variance of history and personal lives. Mass also changes with scale. We can also see the multiverse in terms of constantly renewing shoots and branches, growing more and more complex, each shoot a near-clone of the mother-branch, that branch in turn belonging to another and that to another until, a near-infinity of branches away, the trunk is joined. This fits best with observed reality but is much harder to visualize in linear terms" (1997, 49–50). This "multiversal" metaphysic not only provides an appropriate approach to understanding and mapping the self-similar features of Moorcock's work, but it also suggests new strategies for reading Blake. Indeed, it provides a template for identifying thematic similarities within the scope of any author's work, or within any period, or within a particular genre, and so on.

The grand mythological systems of Blake and Moorcock, driven as they are by the compositional techniques employed to create and portray these systems, are particularly well suited to an analysis that reviews the phenomenon of complexity as both an operator and a subject within an artistic work. Concepts that can be described by the vocabulary of complexity include:

1. *Organizational Depth:* The "building-in" of complexity through obscurity, vagueness, superposition (overlaying), and cluttering.

2. *Multivalent Signifiers:* Characters, themes, and plots that serve as exponents for a multiplicity of concepts, all of which are intermittently transforming and intermittently reflexive.

3. *Feedback/Reflexive Technique:* Characters, plots, and themes that serve as exponents for the processes of artistic creation, reading, and interpretation.

4. *Catastrophe/Folding/Landslides/Phase-Transition:* Sudden and disruptive changes in plot, scene, and character.

5. *Scaling:* self-similarity and fractal geometry.

The most significant similarities Blake and Moorcock share are their mythographic perspectives and procedures, and the useful (and pleasurable) shamanistic insights that such procedure affords.

What follows are some of the details of this procedure:

Blake's and Moorcock's works exhibit narratological self-similarity. Utilizing the same characters, Blake tells the same stories repeatedly in different ways, altering the story either slightly or profoundly at each retelling. He offers cosmogonies and cosmological systems; he offers psychological schemes that resemble metaphysics and metaphysical schemes that resemble psychology; he tells tales of love, birth, jealousy, hatred, misunderstanding, changing perceptions, and forgiveness. Following pagan and classical notions of sympathetic magic and the mythographic patterning of archetypical heroes, gods, and ideas, Blake outlines simultaneous and parallel actions in the world of people, in the world of myth, and in the world of the gods.

Moorcock follows the same practices and patterns, utilizing variations on the same characters and placing these characters in relations to one another that are repeated frequently in his novels so that in each successive retelling the fortunes of the characters may result in different outcomes, but the essential relationships, emotions, challenges, victories, and failures remain the same. In his Eternal Champion stories, of which his albino prince Elric of Melniboné is the best-known example, Moorcock presents a comic-book Armageddon involving the opposed "supernatural" forces of law and chaos. At the center of each of these tales is the eternal champion, a Byronic hero—a "Byronsattva," so to speak—who is reincarnated in each volume to play a decisive role in the cosmic conflict between law and chaos. Depending upon the strength and depth of the champion's character, the cosmic balance swings to a state of either more or less entropy. The key to the success of the champion depends upon his or her ability to reveal the weaknesses of the gods and transcend their influence so that the Byronsattva can emerge and exercise his or her real power to control the universe. In other sagas and cycles Moorcock variously portrays the commedia dell'arte, or harlequinade. In these stories he achieves resolution by unmasking the players. He redeems his characters by exposing them to the artificiality of the roles they play.

The practice of telling the same stories over and over again is enhanced by the bibliographic complexities that are characteristic of Blake's and Moorcock's output. Both Blake and Moorcock are notorious for their variorum. Blake altered the order of the pages in his handmade epics; he altered the position of illustrations and sometimes omitted them entirely; and he colored his illustrations and his texts differently at each production. Not only are his stories retold in different ways, but his physical texts are characterized by alteration. Moreover, the illustrations themselves add still another dimension to this textual variability. When reading Blake's illuminated manuscripts the reader is confronted with the problem of resolving the illustrations to the text. Formulating the narrative is made complicated because there are many ways to combine the illustrated and written narratives. Inconsistencies can be read into a comparison of the illustrations and the text. In formulating the narrative does the reader privilege the illustrations over the text, or the text over the illustrations? By providing illustrations to his stories, Blake has compounded the problem of interpreting his texts; but he has also opened up the possibilities for multiple readings. By leading his reader to confront these multiple readings (and viewings), he highlights the dynamics and the mechanics of mythographic practice.

Moorcock has also altered his texts. During a career that now spans more than fifty years, Moorcock has continued to revise, alter, and retitle his texts. He has reshuffled the order in which they appear in collected editions. While these textual alterations and reorderings represent a daunting challenge to the bibliographer, such practices confirm and enrich the practices of the mythographer. In effect Blake and Moorcock draw their readers into an act of co-creation that is absolved and shielded from the orthodox dictates of the textual Brahmins. The personal revelations of the reader supersede the text, thus disenfranchising the Urizenic lawgivers and deauthorizing the ecclesiastical courts of their hermeneutic bishoprics.

Once again, Blake and Moorcock are "poets of artifice." As I earlier hinted, in the Western liberal tradition of the Netherlands, Britain, and America— specifically the Lockean nexus of theological and political thought that joins Grotius, Cromwell, Milton, the "Good Old Cause," the Glorious Revolution, the English Bill of Rights, Jefferson, the Declaration of Independence, the Virginia Act of Religious Freedom, the American Bill of Rights—the archetype of this politicized intellectual tradition was patterned in London in the 1640s. The power to create artifice is not limited to the upper classes but lies within the reach of all the people.

In the Second Ether trilogy, his most Blakean production, Moorcock tells a group of related stories branching off from the central human story of love, underscoring his observations with a circumspect commentary on the role of love in the continuation of culture and the human species. Turning the facets of his jeweled lens to reveal a succession of incomplete perspectives, Moorcock explores how culture and nature use love to control individuals. His main theme in this respect is loss: boy meets girl; boy falls in love with girl; boy loses girl; boy goes crazy trying to get girl back. The madness and frustration as well as the hope and inventiveness that are driven by this loss lead to an examination of the psychological dynamics of suffering prompted by longing and the problem of being displaced in both time and space from somewhere you have been and wish to be again—and from someone you have been with and wish to be with again. In *Blood,* the first volume of the trilogy, these questions are considered in the case of Jack Karaquazian, who must come to terms with his own loss of love by confronting the mythological beliefs and philosophical assumptions that are created by his loss and are the cause of his loss. If he can identify the gods that make up his pantheon of woe and demythologize them, he has a chance of altering their influences. By understanding the mythographic dynamics of his suffering, he can redeem himself from his fallen state. But the process is spiritual as well as mythographic; it is a process of ontological growth as well as conceptual clarification. The primary tools for affecting Jack's transformation are humility, faith, forgiveness, and love.

In the introduction to *Blood,* Moorcock claims to be the editor of the work, which he has put together from fragments of typescript and handmade magazines written by one "Edwin Begg, the famous Clapham antichrist." Moorcock explains that he did not know what to make of the confused collection of material: "It looked like remains of a psychedelic undergraduate project which very properly had been abandoned. . . . However, as I worked on the manuscript I began to perceive its coherence. A complex and intriguing story emerged as all the disparate elements came together to form an unfamiliar whole" (1994, 1).

Blood opens along the Gulf Coast and Mississippi River, where Jack Karaquazian and his friend Sam Oakenhurst are riverboat gamblers. Pools of color have recently been discovered in the Gulf. Suggesting at once the computer revolution and the crude oil that drives our plastic civilization, the color is an apparently limitless source of electronic energy. At a more fundamental level, the pools of color represent the human brain's capacity for credulous rationalization, conceptual confusion, orthodox scientism, and intellectual myth, Greedy prospectors drill into the color and create an ecological disaster—a metaphysical fault in space-time that engulfs the region in webs of conceptual distortion. Rivers change course in midstream, zombie policeman bubble like burning plastic, guns shoot carcinogenic projectiles, and meat boats steam through phantom dimensions. Against the backdrop of this distortion, the gambling games Jack and Sam play take on a multidimensional significance. Do they play with cards? Video games? Complex fantasy role-playing games such as Dungeons and Dragons? Moorcock describes Jack and Sam dealing each other subsets of intellectual history and the trajectories of hypothetical civilizations. According to Moorcock, "whole universes, species and nations were created, sometimes down to the most ordinary individual, and then manipulated in a game which sometimes took decades of subjective time, yet only a few minutes of real time" (1994, 30).

All this is very well, and Sam and Jack adapt easily to their distorted universe. But then two women come into their lives: Colinda Dovero and "The Rose." Colinda offers Jack an unconditional love that he is not ready to understand or accept, until he loses her. The Rose brings both men into contact with the Second Ether, the ulterior mythological cosmos that Sam follows in his collection of handmade illustrated magazines. These magazines contain the tales of *The Corsairs of the Second Ether.*

Chapters from *The Corsairs of the Second Ether* are presented in *Blood* in staggered chronological order. The beings that inhabit the Second Ether are divided between two competing groups, the "Singularity" and the "Chaos Engineers." Captain Billy-Bob Begg, Fearless Frank Force, Little Rupoldo, Pearl Peru, Professor Pop, Kapitan Kaos, Manley Mark Male, Little Fanny Fun, Corporal Pork, Karl Kapital, and others crew the various spaceships that, at different fractal levels, they variously blend and transform into. These ships go by such names as *I Don't Want to Go to Chelsea, The Right Choice for Recovery, The Smollettsphere,* and *Now the Clouds Have Meaning.* Traveling through space and time and scaling up and down through fractal levels, the ships and their crews resemble mental states, moods, motivations, passions, and archetypes in a grand confused myth about self-fulfillment, self-understanding, and the end of the universe.

Jack and Sam "scale up" to the Second Ether (the Rose flies them there in a Dornier flying boat), where they assume a central role as both subjects and observers in the so-called Game of Time, an eternal conflict between the Chaos Engineers and the Singularity. Jack and Sam are absorbed into the personae of the corsairs—now psychic archetypes—who arrange themselves into an epic last judgment, an apocalypse of contraries, syntheses, and metamorphoses that is highly suggestive of Blake's mythographic patterns of reconciliation and redemption. Blake's epics, of course, were printed and colored by the poet himself. In this light, the "handmade" magazines devoted to *The Corsairs of the Second Ether* gain especial significance. After the corsairs have absorbed Sam and Jack, the corsairs themselves begin to combine and absorb into each other, until Fearless Frank Force, representing the Singularity, and Captain Billy-Bob Begg, representing the Chaos Engineers, are fully sexualized and ready to copulate. Through their union an enormous cuttlefish named *The Spammer Gain*—representing after a fashion St. John the Divine's vision of the Virgin of the Apocalypse—is saved from Old Reg, the Original Insect, or Satan. Through their copulation Force and Begg make it possible for *The Spammer Gain* to recover her lost fishlings, and thus the cycle of life continues. In order to achieve the union it had been necessary for Sam to sacrifice himself in the preliminary moves of this play of archetypes, or what Blake would call a "mental war." Sam's annihilation is at once an act of love and an act of self-deceit. As he lies dying he judges himself, confessing that his initial explorations in the Second Ether and his pursuit of the archetypes he sought to emulate were actually an escape act. He has been destroyed thus by his own code of conduct, and as he expires his mythic self reverts, as Moorcock says, "to the services of entropy; to roam the quasi-infinite, a demigod blessed by death's eternal simplicities" (1994, 241). At the scale of human existence, Sam's sacrifice has made it possible for Jack to recover his lost love, Colinda. Not surprisingly, and again deeply in the vein of Blake, Jack learns to forgive, trust in himself, and love.

Such patterns of sacrifice are reflected by Blake in his portrayal of judgment scenes, where eternals, emanations, and more human characters struggle to come to terms with the psychic fallout of accusation, guilt, possessiveness, jealousy, and pity. Early in the poem *Milton,* an Eternal suddenly appears in the midst of the proceedings and declares, "One must die for another throughout all eternity" (11:18). Blake revisits and further develops this concept in *Milton* and again in *Jerusalem,* explaining that the struggle between ideas and perspectives is a struggle to arrive at truth, and that the personified ideas locked in this struggle "fight and contend for life & not for eternal death" (43:41). "Such are the Laws of Eternity, that each shall mutually Annihilate himself for others' good" (*Milton,* 38:35). In respect to Sam Oakenhurst, the sacrifice is not the sacrifice of a person, but the rejection of an idea as perceived in a mental vision. Ideas are personified in order to animate them and render them as dynamic and as supple as the poet's altering visions and attributions. In the apocalypse portrayed at the end of *Blood,* the events that unfold are subject to Jack's point of view. The problem is, of course, that Jack—like comparable observers in Blake's epics—is not a reliable observer of the events he experiences.

In *Blood* Jack does succeed in redeeming himself, but, as Moorcock intimates, Jack is the fictitious product of an imagination that itself dwells in a fictitious world. *Fabulous Harbours,* the second volume in the trilogy, dilates upon this theme of artifice versus reality. Moorcock anatomizes the interaction of real life and the Second Ether by recounting a series of related stories—ranging from a commonplace discussion over lunch with the Clapham antichrist, a scatty and somewhat destitute priest still trumpeting the 1960s mantra "Love is the answer," to a psychedelic swords-and-sorcery yarn that follows in the aftermath of war in heaven. This latter tale, "The Black Blade's Summoning" highlights the central themes and the mechanism of Moorcock's Second Ether project. The sky suddenly opens and vomits forth a host of howling angels that perish as they plummet to Earth. Agents of chaos, the angels become animated and irradiate the landscape with conceptual distortion. The tale's protagonist, the albino prince Elric, the most popular of Moorcock's creations, escapes from the seductions and hungers of the fallen angels by hiding in a small temple that is miraculously impervious to their destructive and distorting influences. Inside the temple he discovers a gateway opening to the network of silver moonbeam roads that lead between the infinite worlds making up the multiverse. Elric passes through the portal, making his escape with a group of refugee children who are described as having "second sight" and who have been "tutored in the ways of the Multiverse" (1995, 59). Out on the moonbeam roads they are confronted by an angel with an insect face who wants to eat the children in the name of law and the continuation of the human species. Fortunately the fallen angel is repelled, and the companions are free to take the paths that will lead them to their respective home worlds. The tale concludes with Elric and his companions viewing the beauty of the moonbeam roads. The spectacle brings solace and understanding: "They were free forever of the common bounds of time or space, of pressing human concerns, free to explore the wonderful abstraction of it all, the incredible physicality of this suprareality which they could experience with senses themselves transformed and attuned to the new stimuli. They became reconciled to the notion that little by little their bodies would fade and their spirits blend with the stuff of the multiverse, to find true immortality as a fragment of legend, a hint of myth, a mark made upon our everlasting cosmic history, which is perhaps the best that most of us will ever know—to have played a part, no matter how small, in that great game, the glorious Game of Time . . ." (78). The outcome is Blakean inasmuch as the point of the fable is the cycle of the myth itself. In "The Birds of the Moon," the final story told in *Fabulous Harbours,* a middle-aged hippie, who had been separated from his wife and children twenty years before, travels to Glastonbury, enters a church, and discovers behind the altar a gateway leading to the moonbeam roads. He enters the portal hoping to be reunited with his family. Moorcock remains ambiguous on the question of whether or not the protagonist will be reunited with his family, though the possibilities do seem to be as numerous as the moonbeam roads themselves: "The paths are reproduced over and over again, in millions of scales, each slightly different, yet each a detailed version of the other. They weave the fabric of the multiverse together. They are the means by which human intercourse is achieved and the soul, as well as the species, is sustained" (227).

In *The War amongst the Angels,* the third volume in the trilogy, Moorcock resumes the story of Jack Karaquazian, this time intermingling it with parallel subplots that examine the possibility of recovering a world that we have lost or have been thrown out of and of once again dwelling with people who, much to our regret, are no longer part of our lives. *The War amongst the Angels* begins as an autobiography of Margaret Rose Moorcock. Rose describes a childhood filled with gypsies, magicians, scholars, mad uncles, and absurd postwar BBC radio personalities. Growing up among these influences, she learns to enter— literally—the world of Edwardian serial fiction. She falls in love with masked American cowboys and the English highwayman Dick Turpin. Together with her outlaw lover, Rose preys upon a quasi-Victorian tram system that radiates across the south of England. Inspired by her early love affairs, Rose becomes an interdimensional Robin Hood, who, beginning at the convergence of rail lines at Clapham Junction, scales up to the moonbeam roads to spread truth and justice across all the scales of the multiverse. Enlisting the aid of characters introduced earlier in the trilogy, Rose embarks upon a journey of redemption and restoration that involves a trip through the Egyptian desert to find the legendary university city of Aton, hunting fallen angels with elephant guns in the American West, a quest for the Holy Grail, and a starship ride through the Second Ether to once more defend *The Spammer Gain,* the archetypical Madonna-cuttlefish. Once more *Spammer* and her fishlings are beset by Old Reg. The outcome to this final conflict is altered from what Moorcock presents in the first volume. This time Jack does not recover his lost universe. In an act of selfish ferocity Jack sacrifices himself, making it possible for Sam to gain his heart's desire, the Rose. Jack assumes the role of a principle or idea that is rejected in the eternal process of imaginative warfare. It is difficult to determine whether Jack or Sam represents the superior principle, as it is difficult to read moral superiority in one or the other figure, though the Rose is evidently the creative principle—perhaps a fractal emanation of the great cuttlefish herself—that determines the outcomes of such engagements. The Rose stated clearly at the end of *Blood* that she had hoped at that time that Sam, rather than Jack, would survive as the prevailing principle. Perhaps it is possible that the first round of the Game depicted in *Blood* was a dry run, utilizing Jack's particular qualities as a player and a gambler to realize and define the parameters of the Game, while the struggle depicted at the end of *The War amongst the Angels,* now with the contours of the Game established, allowed the Rose to redeem Sam and reject Jack as an obsolete principle that was no longer needed. Sam is not as complex as Jack, nor as self-serving. He fits better into the human community, and he is thus better fit to be an accommodating lover, a cooperative husband, and a well-grounded father. In retrospect, what remains clearest is that the differences between the struggles depicted at the conclusions of *Blood* and *The War amongst the Angels* highlight the supple and ductile mythographic mechanism represented by the continuum and the symbol of the Last Judgment itself.

Rather like Professor Pop broadcasting through his omniphone, Moorcock's voice dissipates and concentrates signifier and signified across all the scales of the multiverse. His language is a meta-academic polyglot of Christian humanism, transformational mythology, fractal geometry, and generic science fiction that increases in profundity as it becomes more ridiculous. Moorcock translates mythography into epiphany. This satiric translation, I should like to suggest, is Blake's game as well.

Blake and Moorcock advance comparable notions of a Last Judgment, and these are closely identifiable with their mythographic activity. Although Blake and Moorcock are careful to represent minute particulars with all the detail made possible by language, it is not actually their plots or their characters that represent the primary themes of their stories. Rather, what is of importance in the mythographic activity itself. This is the activity of the Last Judgment. As S. Foster Damon suggests, for Blake the Last Judgment "occurs whenever an error is recognized and cast out. . . . Jesus is the principle of Truth, and his appearance puts an end to all errors" (1988, 235). The primary mechanism of this casting out is the forgiveness of sins, but incumbent upon this is a mythographic activity with strong parallels in the procedures of Apophatic theology and twentieth-century analytic philosophy. These connections are underscored by Wittgenstein's explanation of aesthetic process. According to Wittgenstein in the notes he took while building the famous family house in Vienna: "Perhaps the most important thing in connection with aesthetics is what might be called aesthetic reactions, e.g. discontent, disgust, discomfort. The expression of discontent is not the same as the expression of discomfort. The expression of discontent says: 'Make it higher . . . too low! . . . Do something to this.'" The Last Judgment is thus an aesthetic process, and it can be located at the end of the cycle of analysis.

Moorcock's last judgment is easily compared to Mircea Eliade's notion of a "Myth of Eternal Return," which takes place at a repeating beginning or end of time, where archetypical actions and roles are performed in order to set or reinforce the pattern for the next historical cycle. Moorcock's last judgment is portrayed, as he variously describes it, at the conjunction of the spheres, at the end of time, and at the conjunction of the moonbeam roads, which meet, in fractal terms, at the highest possible scale of archetypical conception. At this level the principal characters act out various roles in a choreographed struggle in which they seek to establish their own version of what the next cycle should be. Archaic and folk parallels to this struggle can be seen in a variety of forms ranging from the commedia dell'arte, or harlequinade, to the ritual dances of any number of preliterate peoples: the Bella Coola culture of the Pacific Northwest Indians, for example, or the Yoruba people of Nigeria, who dress in the elaborate costumes of nature spirits to celebrate through dance the patterns of their cultic cycles. What Moorcock accomplishes, however, is something more than a mere repetition of established archetypes and cycles; his stories work to effect an unmasking of the cultic cycles and the archetypes that are otherwise renewed in such ceremonies. This unmasking represents a humanistic reversal against the beliefs and the customs that enforce the orthodox and demonic authority of myth over human beings. In Moorcock's last judgment, therefore, archetypes are restored to their proper situation apropos to human beings: they are restored to the status of a mythographic shorthand that serves the needs of people. In this way human beings are liberated from the tyranny of their own customs, their own conceits, and the brain's susceptibility to conceptual confusion. This theme is seen repeatedly in mythographic works ranging from *Paradise Lost* to *2001: A Space Odyssey.* The greatest tool we employ is our language, and one of the most curious (second, perhaps, to the language of lovemaking) uses to which this tool is put is the manipulation of the symbolic abstractions, archetypes, and myths that we use to understand and manipulate the world. As Milton, Blake, Kubrick, and Moorcock warn us, we must be vigilant in keeping our tools under control or they will control us. In addition to the great Western gods that concern Milton—and in addition to the corporate, technological, and scientific gods that concern Kubrick—Blake and Moorcock seem especially interested in the more local myths and deities that make up our personal worldviews, our self-concepts, and our social identities.

The Holy Grail can be taken as a symbol of Moorcock's insight into mythographic operation and Last Judgment. In Moorcock's conception, the Holy Grail is like the initial or master pattern produced by the Mandelbrot set. All the moonbeam roads running between the myriad dimensions of existence can be glimpsed as a whole, and their collective shape, viewed from a distance, is cup-shaped. To drink from the cup is to gain knowledge of the connectivity and integration of all our lives and times; to drink from the cup is to comprehend how our own ghosts and demons, operating at cross-purposes, can lead to confusion, doubt, and suffering. A broader view encompassing the connectivity and integration of people and life can lead to faith, understanding, and healing.

Moorcock's Holy Grail can in this respect be compared to Blake's notion of Eternity, a sort of mental theater where archetypes are free to play out their changing roles unencumbered and without interruption. Of course interruptions do occur: it is these interruptions, caused by hate, jealousy, selfishness, and repression, that lead to the intercourse between human beings and the archetypes they themselves have placed in (and have drawn down from) Eternity.

Moorcock's cosmology in respect to the Holy Grail closely resembles Blake's cosmology in respect to Jesus, and their respective mythographies are parallel structures. Moorcock presents a three-tiered cosmology. At the first level is the material world in which we dwell. At this level real men and real women live and work, raise children, and die. Here Moorcock himself dwells, and from this perspective he claims to be the editor of the novels he introduces. Then there is the First Ether, or the world in which characters such as Jack and Sam dwell. At this level people are portrayed in a state of interaction and reflection with the mythographies that they have created. Finally, in the Second Ether, we encounter a realm of eternal mythology, a realm in which personified ideas in various anthropomorphic and demonic forms engage in an eternal dialogue, a Game of Time, a war amongst angels. Here we see the Corsairs of the Second Ether traveling up and down the scales of the multiverse to seek, struggle, and combine with the main archetypes who hold sway over the structure and functions of the cosmos. In Moorcock's scheme these three levels are unified by the moonbeam roads.

Moorcock's three levels—the material world, the First Ether, and the Second Ether—correspond to Blake's notions of Ulro, or the material world; Beulah, the world of poetic conception; and Eternity, the world of unified space and time. Life in Eternity—represented by the four Zoas—is perfectly integrated sexually and is unified in the form of Jesus Christ. According to Blake, when seen up close the four Zoas appear as a multitude of individuals. From further back they appear in the forms of Urizen, Tharmas, Urthona, and Luvah. From still further back they appear unified in the form of Jesus.

Blake's and Moorcock's characters are by nature dynamic and transformative. These characters enter into one another, or break apart, or project themselves into new characters, or are formed from the residues of others. Ultimately they find resolution and redemption through combining with one another, until combining at still higher and higher levels they resemble the four Zoas, and, at the highest level, the Son of God.

Along these lines, the mythographic significance of Blake's and Moorcock's characters are subject to transformation. Sometimes their characters are to be considered as cosmic archetypes, sometimes as exotic characterizations of human beings locked in emotional turmoil, and at other times as flesh-and-blood people. The entering and blending into one another that these characters undergo can be compared to the activity of ordinary people reading about characters in a book. Readers move in and out of the characters they are reading about by variously identifying with them and comparing their own situations and experiences to those of the characters. A reader with a book can be described as a consciousness seeking to identify itself in the form of a narrative. The implications of the relationship between consciousness and form are astounding: we can see how human beings move in and out of the characters that are created by the expectations that we and others have created for ourselves. These characterized expectations are like figures in a poem or a myth. They are creatures of artifice—our own artifice and the artifice of others.

To what end is this mythographic shamanism? What emerges is a concept of selfhood and human identity that is subject to alteration, revision, and redemption. Blake and Moorcock offer what might be described as a Wittgensteinian ontology, where the contours of human self-perception and social identity are to be located in the activities of human beings in unique and particularized settings in the stream of life. Blake and Moorcock are telling stories about people encountering and confronting the orthodoxies of their personal mythologies. In *Zettel* 464 Wittgenstein (1967, para. 464) defines his "pedigree of psychological concept" as a function of his philosophical insight and procedure, declaring, "I strive not after exactness, but after a synoptic view" Blake and Moorcock follow this procedure, providing analyses of the complex relationships and interdependencies that are revealed in the portrayal, in the examination, and in the analysis of language, poetic conception, conceptual confusion, philosophical credulity, illusion, neurosis, and the industrialized and capitalized mythographic manipulations of individuals and society.

Bibliography

Blake, William. *The Complete Writings of William Blake,* ed. Geoffrey Keynes. New York: Random House, 1957.
Bacon, Francis. 1620. *Novum Organum.* New York: Liberal Arts Press, 1960.
Damon, S. Foster. 1988. *A Blake Dictionary: The Ideas and Symbols of William Blake.* Hanover, N.H.: University Press of New England.
Eliade, Mircea. 1959. *Cosmos and History: The Myth of the Eternal Return.* New York: Harper and Row.
Hill, Christopher. 1977. *Milton and the English Revolution.* New York: Viking.
Jencks, Charles. 1995. *The Architecture of the Jumping Universe: A Polemic: How Complexity Science Is Changing Architecture and Culture.* London: Academy Editions.
Milton, John. 1930. *Areopagitica.* In *The Student's Milton,* ed. Frank Allen Patterson. New York: Crofts.

Moorcock, Michael. 1994. *Blood: A Southern Fantasy.* London: Millennium.
———. 1997. "About My Multiverse." In *Tales from the Texas Woods,* 49–50. Austin: Mojo.
———. 1995. *Fabulous Harbours.* New York: Avon.
Wittgenstein, Ludwig. *Zettel,* ed. G. E. M. Anscombe and G. H. von Wright, trans. G. E. M. Anscombe. Oxford: Blackwell, 1967.

Politicized Dystopia and Biomedical Imaginaries

The Case of "The Machine Stops"

Mark Decker

Fredric Jameson has argued that utopian narratives are the "by-products of Western modernity" (2005, 11), written in reaction to the rapid technological advances that have accompanied industrial and postindustrial society. Utopian thought in general thus represents a "momentary formation of a kind of eddy or self-contained backwater" that is a desire for a "pocket of stasis within the ferment and rushing forces of social change" (15). Although Jameson does not take his argument in this direction, his formulation gives utopian fiction a great deal of affective, and therefore political, power in an age of nearly universal dependence on science and technology. Craft a tale that projects modernity creating a pleasant future, especially one that makes an authoritative appeal to current scientific ideas and the current technological state of the art, and you can help further the cause of say, nanotechnology. Although Jameson is mostly silent on the affective power of dystopian fiction, a very similar argument could be made: modernity is frightening, and so one of its byproducts is a way of thinking and telling stories that depicts the material culture of modernity crushing humanity. Dystopian fiction would also have a great deal of political affect, particularly if it appealed to current scientific ideas or the current technological state of the art. Make a movie about an instant ice age freezing North America and Europe, and you might get people to pay more attention to what the material manifestations of modernity do to the environment.

Often enough, utopian or dystopian fiction holds up well over time, with the predicted mechanical angels or bogeymen eventually arriving in the real world. The problem with relying on scientific thought to critique modernity, however, is that the utopian or dystopian tale can be based on science that in retrospect is either completely wrongheaded or at least largely outmoded. Furthermore, the scientific error could be at least partially explained by the political constraints faced by the scientists. After all, there is a certain amount of credulity required for a writer without a scientific background to incorporate scientific concepts into a work of fiction, particularly if those concepts are coming from popular discourse and not from scientific texts or conversations with working scientists. Additionally there is also a degree of conditional credulity among scientists regarding the current consensus in their discipline. Newtonian physics, for example, reigned supreme before relativity.

What happens when a politicized dystopia is created based on incorrect science? The readerly appeal of the narrative is not damaged—we are talking about fiction, after all—but stories based on problematic science do provide a great deal of insight into the interaction between politics and science during the time that they were composed. This charged interplay between science, fiction, and politics can be seen in E. M. Forster's "The Machine Stops." By comparing Forster's tale to Max Nordau's *Degeneration* for illustrative purposes, we can place "The Machine Stops" in the context of contemporary debates about enervating cities, misguided public health programs, and declining birthrates. By doing this we will realize that "The Machine Stops" is a rhetorical parable designed to argue that modernity was weakening not only Britain's ability to produce the soldiers it needed to maintain its empire, but also the British people's ability to reproduce at rates that would maintain their unique identity.

Unpacking the political content of "The Machine Stops" will be much easier if we first both explore and borrow from science studies scholar Catherine Waldby's concept of the biomedical imaginary. Scientific knowledge, and medical knowledge in particular, carries great weight when it enters political discourse. Undoubtedly this is due to broad perceptions of the absolute truthfulness of utterances made by scientists and physicians. People who study narratives, however, have long detected elements of the imaginative and speculative in scientific discourse. Waldby has coined the phrase "biomedical imaginary" in an attempt to describe "the deployment of, and unacknowledged reliance on, culturally intelligible fantasies and mythologies within the terms of what claims to be a system of pure logic." Medical investigation, in other words, no matter how scientifically conducted, contains an element of science fiction, of the unabashedly speculative, that is reflected in the discourse produced by the putatively rigorous investigators (qtd. in Squire 2004, 14–15). Susan Squire furthers Waldby's contention, arguing that the biomedical imaginary is not limited to scientific discourse, but instead it is possible to "investigate the biomedical imaginary when we consider how medical issues are articulated and engaged with across all cultural fields" (15). The ideas of medical investigators infuse popular discourse just as popular discourse infuses the ideas of medical investigators, and this infusion can have political consequences as medical discourse is popularized and amateur diagnoses of social ills are made. Because Forster's dystopia relies on the physical degeneration of its inhabitants, and because in the late nineteenth and earlier twentieth centuries physical degeneration was a topic of intense concern in both medical and political discourse, Forster's story can be read as participating in a distinct iteration of the biomedical imaginary. Prior to decoding the political impact of this particular biomedical imaginary, however, we should first look at the ways "The Machine Stops" has been interpreted, examine Max Nordau's *Degeneration* as an ideal type of politicized late-nineteenth-century medical discourse, and then explore the political context prevailing in the years leading up to the composition of Forster's story.

Before he wrote the novels that would ensure his place in dissertations and Merchant Ivory films, E. M. Forster wrote a story about the collapse of a mechanized world that stunted its inhabitants by providing too well for their needs and wants. Just after "The Machine Stops" was published, however, Forster had great success with *Howards End,* and he never returned to technological dystopias. Mainstream Forster scholars, as Marcia Seabury observes, have "either ignored" the work or made cursory observations along the lines that "it develops Forster's recurring humanist concerns about connection" (1997, 61). Seabury overlooks Wilfred Stone's contention that the work's "main interest is personal, not social: it is another tale of the psychic escape of the boy hero" (1966, 152), but her essential point is sound. When Forster scholars bother to bring up "The Machine Stops" at all, it is usually in an attempt to prove that the author's key themes persist even in the more "experimental" works. Of course, Forster himself seems to give permission for this critical approach when he describes "The Machine Stops" in the preface to *The Collected Tales of E. M. Forster* as "a counterblast to one of the heavens of H. G. Wells" (Forster 1964, vii–viii).

Those interested in science fiction or technology and culture see the work differently. Noticing the surprising correspondences between Forster's globally connected technological dystopia and contemporary society, they have anointed "The Machine Stops" a minor classic of prophetic speculative fiction. Christopher Gillie, for example, has marveled that "well before the television and long before the silicon chip" Forster "anticipated the possible consequences of such technology" (1983, 48). Seabury also sees "The Machine Stops" in these terms, as does Beatrice Battaglia, who calls Forster's story "a future history" (2002, 51) and sees in it links to Baudrillard's and Jameson's critiques of American late capitalist society.

Let's stipulate to the arguments of the aforementioned approaches to "The Machine Stops." The story is something of an anomaly when compared to Forster's other work—though "The Celestial Omnibus" is more like "The Machine Stops" than *Howards End*—and Forster's decades-later dismissal should surprise no one. Furthermore, anyone who reads Forster's story today will notice many, many parallels between their lived experiences and the world the Machine creates. But let's not think about "The Machine Stops" in the context of the Forster posthumously created by literary scholars, highbrow filmmakers, and the author's own late-career spin. And let's refuse to be amazed that someone pictured a computer connecting the world long before there was an Internet. Instead, let's try to think about the world Forster's text was created for and entered into.

Understanding the world "The Machine Stops" was designed to influence requires understanding the fears about physical and mental deterioration that living in an industrialized, urban society provoked. Although much of the medical discourse surrounding degeneration would now be regarded as pseudoscience, it is nevertheless very helpful to our investigation. After all, illustrating the workings of the biomedical imaginary is much easier when dealing with once-popular ideas that have since been rejected by the mainstream medical establishment. Max Nordau's work is therefore an excellent example of the biomedical imaginary in general, as it blends what was then widely seen as systematic, properly scientific thought and speculative social fiction. *Degeneration* is also very important to our consideration of Forster since, as we will see below, it is of the same iteration of the biomedical imaginary that the author draws from.

Nordau has an interesting intellectual biography. At the beginning of his career, he was a physician specializing in nervous disorders. He then began writing novels and cultural criticism. By the close of his life he was a prominent member of the Zionist movement. The overt works of fiction that Nordau created have been largely forgotten. But the political science fictions he created were international best-sellers that were reprinted many times over many decades. The best remembered is *Degeneration,* initially published in German in two volumes in 1892 and 1893. This work, part literary criticism and part dystopian prophecy, relies heavily on the theories of Cesare Lombroso, then professor of psychiatry at the University of Turin. Extrapolating social meaning from Lombroso's ideas, Nordau argues that industrialized society is seeing more and more cases of what he calls "degeneration," an inherited condition marked by "gaps in development, malformations, and infirmities" (1920, 16). There are also psychological symptoms of degeneration, including "unbounded egoism, and, secondly, impulsiveness, *i.e.,* inability to resist a sudden impulse to any deed." Degenerates, according to Nordau, tend to be antisocial because of their "vague fear of all men" and "disinclination to action of any kind" (18–20).

When discussing the etiology of degeneration, Nordau largely blames modernity. He contends that conditions existing in the industrial metropolis were harmful for both metropolitans and their descendants since the "inhabitant of the large towns . . . is continually exposed to unfavorable influences which diminish his vital powers. . . . He breathes an atmosphere charged with organic detritus; he eats stale, contaminated, adulterated food; he feels himself in a state of constant nervous excitement, and one can compare him without exaggeration to the inhabitant of a marshy district. . . . Its population falls victim to the same fatality of degeneracy and destruction as the victims of malaria" (35).

Degeneration, then, is self-consciously employing the biomedical imaginary, deliberately blending Lombroso's then-current theories about the nervous system with mythologies about destructive knowledge causing humanity's fall. Nordau is especially concerned by degeneration because it so frequently occurs in the "upper stratum of the population of large towns" (536) in Europe and

North America, and this concern illustrates the political demiurge of this iteration of the biomedical imaginary. Since the upper classes of large cities are usually the people who are running society, Nordau worried that Western civilization was rapidly approaching a "Dusk of the Nations" (6), a point where modernity will have so drained the vitality of its supposed benefactors that civilized society could no longer continue. *Degeneration,* then, is best seen as a politicized exercise in public health, a warning that, in Nordau's words, Western civilization was then "in the midst of a severe mental epidemic; of a sort of black death of degeneration" (537). Unsurprisingly, to illustrate the peril of this plague, Nordau spends several pages employing a very familiar literary genre as he envisions a dystopia where suicide is legal, people kill those who startle them, sexual perversion is rampant, and no one can concentrate long enough to read a book (538–39).

Yet, despite this harrowing bit of political science fiction, Nordau ends *Degeneration* on an optimistic note. The physician and social critic argues that people "will recover from their present fatigue. The feeble, the degenerate, will perish; the strong will adapt themselves to the acquisitions of civilizations" (550). Sounding more like Herbert Spencer than Cesare Lombroso, in other words, Nordau appears to fall back into the contemporary faith in social evolution. Nordau's audience, Europe and North America's well-to-do and comfortable, does not need to worry about becoming victims of degeneration because they have the ability to rise above it in time. According to Nordau, the "end of the twentieth century, therefore, will probably see a generation to whom it will not be injurious to read a dozen square yards of newspaper daily, to be constantly called to the telephone . . . to satisfy a circle of ten thousand acquaintances, associates, and friends" (541). Of course, passages like this make it easy to perform the intellectually lazy operation of marveling over Nordau's prescience—just substitute the Internet, e-mail, and cell phones for the dozen square yards of newspaper and wide circle of acquaintances and you have an amazing vision of modern life! Yet while Nordau's new generation does bear superficial resemblance to popular idealizations of the contemporary wired consumer, the ideological assumptions behind the physician's depiction of the late twentieth century are best understood in the social theorist's nineteenth-century context.

Nordau believed that the new race of humans who would evolve by means of the trial of degeneration would serve a very specific political purpose. In his discussion of Nordau's Zionist writing, Todd Samuel Presner argues that in *Degeneration,* Nordau "does not look backward to reclaim a lost character but rather prognosticates an evolutionary break, imbued with the ideology of Social Darwinism, in which the 'degenerates' will perish and those who are strong, disciplined, and well-adapted will come forward to preside over a new world" (2003, 176). Presner finds intellectual coherence in the argument found in *Degeneration* and Nordau's idea of the "mythically heroic figure of regeneration," the "muscle Jew" that will rise to make Zionist dreams possible (281), yet it is also easy to see a similarly reassuring message being sent to an elite, non-Jewish audience Nordau rhetorically creates in *Degeneration*. It is proper to decry the debilitating impact of modernity and condemn the degenerates, but do not worry—the strong can evolve their way out of this dilemma if they have the will, and the strong will then inherit the earth.

When comparing the ideas of novelists with the ideas of social thinkers, questions of influence always arise. Some would like to see a copy of the social theorist's better-known works sitting in the novelist's library, passages bearing thematic similarity to the novel under consideration heavily underlined in red and featuring marginalia on the order of "put this part in the story." Thinking about influence in terms of participation in biomedical imaginaries, however, reframes questions of influence. Instead of exhuming evidence of direct inspiration, one must simply determine if the ideas of the social thinker had currency during intellectually important times in the author's life. *Degeneration* was very popular in England during Forster's undergraduate days and the first decade of his career as an author. According to Richard Dellamora, the reputation of Nordau's work, which was quite critical of Oscar Wilde, benefitted greatly from the publicity surrounding the poet and playwright's 1895 sodomy trial (2005, 532). Wilde's conviction was seen as broad justification of Nordau's identification of the writer as a dangerous degenerate. This scandal took place at an important time in Forster's intellectual development. Wilde was released from prison in May 1897, the same year that Forster entered King's College, Cambridge. At Cambridge, Forster associated with Lytton Strachey, Leonard Woolf, and other future members of the Bloomsbury Group. Given the intellectual milieu the young classics major inhabited, Forster's own homosexuality, and the broad notoriety of Wilde and Nordau's critique of him, it is difficult to imagine that Forster was unaware of at least the basic outlines of Nordau's argument.

There was another scandal—this one much more political than literary—that brought arguments such as those of Nordau into England's popular consciousness in the years before Forster wrote "The Machine Stops." As Richard Soloway has argued, England's poor showing in the Boer War (1899–1902) led to a veritable festival of national recrimination in which "liberal imperialists and other advocates of 'national efficiency'" saw signs of physical, mental, and intellectual deterioration "among important sectors of the population." Though British forces were ultimately victorious, they endured several humiliating tactical defeats at the hands of the combined forces of the South African Republic and the Orange Free State. Furthermore, over the course of the war British forces suffered thousands more casualties that did the Boers. This was not supposed to happen to the armies of an empire that the sun never set on. People were deeply worried that, according to Soloway, this Pyrrhic victory "pointed to a decided waning of the extraordinary 'racial energy'" that was seen to have enabled the creation of the British Empire. Because it brought these fears to the foreground, the war led to an "orgy of criticism, enquiry, and analysis focusing on the alarming possibility that the race was somehow decaying" (1982, 137).

These inquiries were conducted in ways that demonstrate the intellectual hegemony held by ideas such as those of Nordau. Soloway informs us that this perceived diminishing of the British race was blamed on the "presumed enervating effect of crowded city life on the health, morals, mentality, and procreative vigor of urban inhabitants, especially the laboring poor" (138). The solution to the hazards of modernity also resonated with themes explored in *Degeneration,* with some suggesting that the proliferation of degenerates "would be facilitated by the more humane values and institutions of modern civilization" (149). In other words, the nanny state should not interfere with the natural process of social evolution. The degenerates should be left to degenerate into oblivion. Others argued the positive side of this formulation. Soloway notes that physicians such as G. Archdall Reid argued that "urban life actually strengthened the national stock by exposing it to greater stress, more disease, and other environmental dangers which immunized the strong, weeded out the weak, and left the most vigorous of the race to reproduce themselves" (qtd. in 144). Perhaps people such as Reid would have welcomed a Nordau-esque formulation of a muscle-Englishman to describe the new race that would arise to make sure that colonial inferiors such as the Boers never strayed out of line again.

We should note here that despite the political capital blaming degeneration for the British army's poor showing in South Africa generated, it was based on bad science. Soloway notes that the data supporting such conclusions was usually unpersuasive if not downright contradictory (141). Even good data was made to fit preexisting assumptions that sound remarkably like Nordau's. As Soloway relates, "often the anthropomorphic statistics extracted from recruitment statistics were interpreted as if they were inborn, hereditary infirmities acquired from too long an exposure to the degenerating environment of the great cities" (144). Investigators did not take into account that the weakened conditions of the recruits could have been explained by reversible environmental conditions—malnutrition, for example, and exposure to pollutants. Soloway argues that the proof of the shoddy science underpinning these investigations can be found in the reports they generated. For example, a careful reading of material produced by the 1902 Scottish Royal Commission on Physical Training reveals that many "of the witnesses, when questioned closely, admitted that they were generalizing from limited experience, were repeating what they had heard from others, or were merely expressing a personal opinion" (146). Despite the problematic nature of the studies generated by the Boer War, however, many in the British public were under the impression that the degeneration of the British race had been scientifically proven.

Both as an aspiring young intellectual and as a British citizen, E. M. Forster inhabited a world in which ideas such as those of Nordau were current and politically powerful. But if Forster's intellectual milieu makes it almost certain that he was influenced by Nordau's theories, it has also led critics to ignore the scientific underpinnings of the degenerate dystopia he created. Because Forster's academic training was so thoroughly humanistic and so lacking in formal exposure to science and engineering, "The Machine Stops" is often seen as a belletristic rejection of the technophilia and evolutionary optimism of its day. The story, in other words, flees science in toto. Charles Elkins, for example, asserts that the story is best understood in terms of "a general turning away by influential intellectuals and critics from science and technology" (1983, 48). While it is clear that "The Machine Stops" is a critique of technology, Forster was not shy about echoing a "scientific" discourse that combined neurology, psychology, and public health to make his critique resonate with his readers.

Those familiar with "The Machine Stops" may have already noticed thematic correspondences between the story, Nordau's diagnosis, and the national soul-searching generated by the Boer War. The inhabitants of Forster's dystopia are degenerate because their technologically advanced surroundings do all physical work for them and keep them out of nature. Forster's tale, which focuses on Vashti, a mother who embraces the comforts the Machine provides, and Kuno, a son who desires to escape from the enervating technology of the Machine, also makes it clear that the denizens of the Machine's underground hives are severely overstimulated by excessive amounts of information and would therefore be seen as having dangerously damaged nervous systems. Because they have all their needs met by pushing buttons, they are in many ways as helpless as infants; Vashti is described as a "swaddled lump of flesh—a woman, about five feet high with a face as white as a fungus" (Forster 1964, 144). She is also "without teeth or hair" (153) and she totters when she walks (155). In a telling illustration of this childlike helplessness, when Vashti boards the airship to see Kuno, a fellow passenger drops a book on the gangway. Because he is used to floors that automatically return dropped items, "instead of picking up his property" he merely feels "the muscles of his arm to see how they had failed him" (157). Vashti also exhibits the disinclination to action that Nordau would predict. For example, when she first opens the door of her room to begin her journey to Kuno, she is paralyzed because "she was frightened of the tunnel" that led away from her room. She "had not seen it since her last child was born," and its appearance fills her "with the terrors of direct experience" (154). Of course, the physical state of the inhabitants of the Machine's world has been widely noted. Forster biographer P. N. Furbank describes them as "hairless, toothless, muscleless" (1977, 162), while Stone calls Vashti "soft, desexed, unathletic" (1966, 153), and Elkins speaks of a "degenerate world" (1983, 51). None of these critics, however, have tied Vashti's and Kuno's physical condition into the political discourse surrounding the supposed degeneration of the British race.

The end of "The Machine Stops" also seems to extrapolate and then graphically depict Nordau's Dusk of the Nations. In Forster's portrayal of the dusk of the Machine's nation, the oppressively comforting technology eventually breaks down because the citizens it served have become so decadent they can no longer maintain it. Since everyone depends entirely on the Machine for food, air, and any other necessity, there is chaos followed by mass deaths. As Vashti surveys the destruction that greets the end of the Machine, she remarks that "civilization's long day was closing" (194)—a metaphor that would make a contemporary Nordau call his intellectual property attorney. A few pages later, readers learn that the collapse of the Machine's society is punishment for the "sin against the body . . . the centuries of wrong against the muscles and the nerves" (196). Forster here adopts, along with Nordau, the nineteenth-century medical discourse of exhausted nerves. A closer examination of the text reveals that this fictive dusk of the nations, triggered by the intergenerational sin against the body, indicates that Forster's political agenda was similar to that of Nordau's Zionist writings: urging the creation of a British people strong enough to master modernity. This exhortation can be seen both in the figure of Kuno and in the feral humans he encounters when he visits Earth's surface.

Forster, like Nordau, plays an interesting game with the concept of social evolution, even though such evolutionary logic underpins his story. The writer seeks to depict the failure of a type of social evolution that is tied to technology and the creation of a mechanized egalitarianism that ensures universal access to a decadent material abundance. At the close of the story, as the Machine's world comes crashing down, Forster lays the blame at the feet of unnamed opponents who justified the Machine "with the talk of evolution," because they are greatly responsible for making the body "white pap" and "the home of ideas as colourless" (196). Note the ambiguity of the phrase "talk of evolution"—it could be condemning evolution per se or it could be condemning those who do not understand evolutionary hazards such as degeneration and therefore do not know how to manage evolution properly. Evidence of a focus on evolutionary mismanagement comes in Forster's portrayal of a society that deliberately tries to create degeneration by eliminating the strong. In the Machine's perverse eugenic scheme, infants "who promised undue strength were destroyed [because] it would have been no true kindness to let an athlete live; he would never have been happy in that state of life to which the Machine had called him; he would have yearned for trees to climb, rivers to bathe in, meadows and hills against which he might measure his body" (167). Interestingly this invocation of the rural frolicking of the natural athlete inversely mirrors the diagnosis of British recruits drawn from industrial cities. They were seen as poor warriors— or at least poorer warriors than the mostly agrarian Boers—because they were trapped in cities that enervated them and would most certainly further enervate their descendants.

A politicized dystopia would need to have utopian potential in order for it to motivate people to political action. After all, convincing people that they are doomed no matter what they do will probably not get them to turn out at the polls. If there is a utopian moment in "The Machine Stops," it is Kuno's visit to the surface of Earth and his encounter with people who do not live within the Machine's underground hive. To understand the call to action created by this visit, we must first explore Forster's characterization of Kuno, a natural athlete who was "possessed of a certain physical strength" (166) and who takes steps to develop that strength so that he can visit Earth's surface. Of course, this physical prowess means that he was not allowed to reproduce, because his "was not the type the Machine desired to hand on" (169). Kuno also seems to understand social evolution in a way that would resonate with a readership concerned by eugenics and degeneration when he bitterly observes that in "the dawn of the world our weakly must be exposed on Mount Taygetus, in its twilight our strong will suffer euthanasia, that the Machine may progress, that the Machine may progress eternally" (167). The exposure of weak infants was a regrettable necessity that allowed humanity to progress, but the destruction of the strong is a crime against humanity because the lives are lost in the service of a mechanical empire.

In spite of his physical preparations, however, Kuno has great difficulty when he actually does reach Earth's surface. He tells Vashti that he wished he had torn "off every garment I had, and gone out into the upper air unswaddled." But he knows that such behavior was not for him, "nor perhaps for [his] generation," and so he climbs with his respirator, hygienic clothes, and dietetic tabloids. Even the athletic and ambitious Kuno comes from a stock that has been so debased by its technological swaddling that he cannot breathe unfiltered air. Nevertheless, he tells Vashti that as he was climbing up the ventilation shaft, he felt "for the first time, that a protest had been lodged against corruption, and that even as the dead were comforting me, so I was comforting the unborn" (170–71). The language of heredity and the image of the hearts of the children being turned to their fathers and mothers places Kuno's quest in the same racial terms as the debate over British military readiness after the Boer War. Of course, the doomed Kuno ultimately had nothing to offer to the unborn. Yet his story deals with the survival of a race, not the survival of an individual, and his quest does show readers a way to avoid the intergenerational decadence the Machine represents.

Hope for humanity resides not in the discontented yet degenerate Kuno. Instead, it comes in the surface dwellers that he meets during his brief sojourn above the ground. As the Machine is crashing down around them, Kuno comforts his mother by reminding her that the end of the society the Machine has created does not mean the end of humanity. There are inhabitants of the surface that he has seen and spoken to, and they "are hiding in the mists and the ferns until our civilization stops. Today they are Homeless, tomorrow . . ." Kuno further reassures his mother that they will not restart the Machine because humanity "has learnt its lesson" (197). Though the degenerate utopia that the Machine had created is collapsing of its own weight, humanity itself is about to return to a clean-living, pastoral lifestyle that will produce a race both strong enough and smart enough to avoid the temptation to become entangled in decadent modernity.

Although it should be apparent that the putative lesson of the Boer War echoes through Forster's tale of the collapse of a globe-spanning empire, we need to clarify the type of evolutionary narrative Forster creates. "The Machine Stops" could be read as presenting an uncomplicated argument that no matter what mistakes human social engineering makes, humanity itself will eventually return to its hardwired course. But Forster, like Nordau and his muscle-Jew, did not want to wait hundreds of years for humanity to be forced to renounce its unhealthy dependence on technology. From the opening lines of "The Machine Stops," Forster frequently reminds his readers that he is telling a story, drawing attention to that story's metaphorical potential. The tale begins with the author asking his readers to imagine, "if you can, a small room, hexagonal in shape, like the cell of a bee" (144). When he describes Vashti, he asks readers to think "of her as without teeth or hair" (153). He parenthetically informs his readers that when he discusses the cities that are part of the Machine's network, he is using "the antique names" (156). Near the end of his tale, he tells readers he needs to give them important information "ere my meditation closes" (195). Forster is clearly creating an imagined, and not inevitable, future. Perhaps if readers pay attention to his story, Britain can learn its lesson and avoid further sins against the body that modernity engenders. Kuno's efforts, generations after humanity entered the underground caves of the Machine, are too late. But the efforts of disciplined British citizens, in the aftermath of the warning provided by the Boer War, can help create a race that can withstand modernity.

If this investigation has shed any light on the political message of Forster's "The Machine Stops," it should also help us understand politicized dystopia in general. It is true that Forster's tale of degenerate modernity, like the critique of the Russian Revolution found in Zamiatin's *We*, has survived the demise of the rhetorical exigencies of its immediate sociopolitical context because it is a good story. But no matter what a work of politicized dystopia's staying power as fiction, it can always provide a means to unpack the other political science fictions of its day.

Bibliography

Battaglia, Beatrice. 2002. "Losing the Sense of Space: Forster's 'The Machine Stops' and Jameson's 'Third Machine Age.'" In *Histories of the Future: Studies in Fact, Fantasy, and Science Fiction,* ed. Alan Sandison and Robert Dingley, 51–71. Basingstoke, U.K.: Palgrave.

Dellamora, Richard. 2005. "Productive Decadence: 'The Queer Comradeship of Outlawed Thought': Vernon Lee, Max Nordau, and Oscar Wilde." *New Literary History* 35: 529–46.

Elkins, Charles. 1983. "E. M. Forster's 'The Machine Stops': Liberal-Humanist Hostility to Technology." In *Clockwork Worlds: Mechanized Environments in Science Fiction,* ed. Richard Erlich and Thomas P. Dunn, 47–61. Westport, Conn.: Greenwood.

Forster, E. M. 1964. *The Collected Tales of E. M. Forster.* 1947. New York: Knopf.

Furbank, P. N. 1977. *E. M. Forster: A Life. Vol. 1: The Growth of the Novelist (1879–1914).* London: Secker and Warburg.

Gillie, Christopher. 1983. *A Preface to Forster.* New York: Longman.

Jameson, Fredric. 2005. *Archaeologies of the Future: The Desire Called Utopia and Other Science Fictions.* New York: Verso.

Nordau, Max. 1920. *Degeneration.* Popular ed. London: Heinemann.

Presner, Todd Samuel. 2003. "'Clear Heads, Solid Stomachs, and Hard Muscles': Max Nordau and the Aesthetics of Jewish Regeneration." *Modernism/Modernity* 10, no. 2: 269–96.

Seabury, Marcia Bundy. 1997. "Images of a Networked Society: E. M. Forster's "The Machine Stops." *Studies in Short Fiction* 34, no. 1: 61–71.

Soloway, Richard. 1982. "Counting the Degenerates: The Statistics of Race Deterioration in Edwardian England." *Journal of Contemporary History* 17: 137–64.

Squire, Susan Merrill. 2004. *Liminal Lives: Imagining the Human at the Frontiers of Biomedicine.* Durham, N.C.: Duke University Press.

Stone, Wilfred. 1966. *The Cave and the Mountain: A Study of E. M. Forster.* Stanford, Cal.: Stanford University Press.

Science Fiction and Politics

Cyberpunk Science Fiction as Political Philosophy

Thomas Michaud

Cyberpunk is a science fiction movement that describes the future of industrial countries, depicting the influence of massive telecommunications networks upon the lives of individuals and societies. Cyberpunk authors have different points of view concerning their ability to describe the future. For example, William Gibson asserts that his fictions reveal more about the present than about the future. But the networked society of cyberpunks reveals a lot of futuristic aspects developed through the study of the central tropes of these fictions, such as matrices, cyberspace, and networks of virtual reality. The digital dimensions described by cyberpunks constitute a new kind of technological utopia investigating a paradoxical future. Cyberpunks develop a political philosophy founded on the free access to a technological and utopian space called "cyberspace" by Gibson, creator of the cyberpunk movement. Cyberpunk heroes are anarchists who have developed a wide range of aptitudes in the use of technologies. Hackers are the archetype of this philosophy, which promotes a libertarian use of information. Case, the hero of Gibson's *Neuromancer*, represents a political philosophy inherited from Henry David Thoreau, promoting civil disobedience in the name of the free circulation of information. He travels cyberspace as a lonesome cowboy in the quest of information and struggles with forms of artificial intelligence. Cyberspace occupies the same place as the western in American political mythology. Cyberpunks develop a political mythology founded on technology, particularly on virtual reality. This essay will focus on the political philosophy generated by cyberpunk science fiction through the analysis of the work of William Gibson, specifically his Sprawl trilogy: *Neuromancer, Count Zero,* and *Mona Lisa Overdrive.*

Science fiction hackers appeared in John Brunner's novel *Shockwave Rider* (1977) before being popularized in *Neuromancer.* The word *hackers* already existed in the computer engineers' communities to define a person able to connect to systems of information generated by the interconnection of computers. Case, the hero of *Neuromancer,* connects to cyberspace thanks to his Ono-Sendai console and travels through information flows. Gibson's version of cyberspace is primitive. It is a kind of informational desert in which exist only the structures of the informational matrices. It is far from the metaverse described by Neal Stephenson in *Snow Crash* as the simulacra of a real town. In Gibson's novels cyberspace is a cybernetic landscape produced by the interconnection of machines. Hackers are the rare persons able to penetrate the sanctuary of machines. They have to guide the species for Timothy Leary (1994). The mission of hackers is to civilize cyberspace for the first time, and Gibson's work imagines the first steps of humankind in cybernetic matrices. It suggests that humanity has to explore a new frontier, defined as the sum of electronic connections. The connection of machines through telecommunication networks has created new territories that are known by few people. Only hackers are able to connect and to communicate with artificial intelligences that are masters of their cybernetic constructs. The first age of cyberpunk science fiction describes savage matrices in which artificial intelligences lead the territories, as Indians did in the first years of the European colonization of America. The comparison between the cyberspace frontier and the American West is often presented in the ideological discourses of the informational age, and Gibson is one of the founding fathers of this mythology. Case is often compared to a cowboy, his Ono-Sendai is compared to his horse, and cyberspace to the American West.

The second age of hackers in science fiction begins with Stephenson's *Snow Crash,* in which the metaverse is a new town artificially created and to which it is possible to connect. Matrices are civilized, and it is possible to live in these artificial worlds. In *Neuromancer,* Gibson defines the technological frame of the action, in a virtual world created by the interconnection of computers. Heroes evolve in it and struggle with artificial intelligence. The fusion of Wintermute and Neuromancer creates a meta-artificial intelligence questing for truth to Proxima Centauri. The matrix is a virtual world in which the cognition of users is free to navigate. Hackers are the best in these artificial landscapes because they know all the codes of the informational space. Some of them have created the systems, some others have developed specific abilities to translate and destroy codes. Hackers can go everywhere in the informational space because they can break the "ice" protecting information. If Brunner invented the computer worms, Gibson proposes a metaphor of the role of computer engineers in the creation of virtual worlds. Cyberspace is presented as a virgin holographic landscape to be created and colonized by the human race. Hackers, as Case, are the first explorers of these territories, and Gibson suggests the possibility of a global exile of the human race in artificially simulated worlds. In 1983 computer worlds were not very developed, but Gibson anticipated the possibilities offered by the global interconnection of computers. Case faces various entities during his quest. The robot-gardener, Wintermute, and Neuromancer are elements of cybernetic spaces produced by the technical progress. Technology is a central element in the novels of William Gibson. Telecommunication, informatics, virtual realities are everywhere, and megalopolises are optimized by them. The cybernetic space is produced by technological objects, for example robots or Ono-Sendai consoles. Dixie Flatline is a hacker who has evacuated his body to live freely in cyberspace. He lives only through his cognitive connection to virtual reality. Mind-uploading is another technology presented in the work of William Gibson. It has been presented too by Greg Egan in *Permutation City* and several others novels of science fiction. Cyberspace is not physically accessible. It is necessary to use a machine to connect through cognition. Cyberspace assures the fusion of cognition and artificial worlds. Connected individuals travel in informational spaces because their mind is connected to matrices. In *The Matrix* (1999) that if the individual dies in the Matrix, he also dies in reality. Hacking is a dangerous activity and is presented as an extreme form of video gaming. The connection to artificial worlds is comparable to the process of miniaturization of the human body presented in films such as *Innerspace* (1987) or in Isaac Asimov's novel *Fantastic Voyage* (1966). The connection of individuals to artificial matrices is cognitive. The quest for the fusion of the human cognition with the systems of the machines is central in the novels of Gibson. It is a particularly important question in the perspective of a global network of virtual reality through which it should be possible to connect as easily as possible from every place of the planet. Gibson has inspired engineers in informatics and telecommunications, by anticipating the diffusion of the Internet in the 1990s. His novel is a metaphor of the quest for an harmonious communication between humans and artificial worlds, the search for ideal ways of connection, and the nature of artificial entities living in cyberspace. William Gibson has invented lots of technologies, including Biosofts (*Count Zero,* 1986), Constructs (*Neuromancer,* 1984), ICE (intrusion countermeasures electronics against hackers, *Neuromancer,* 1984), and Synthespians (Synthetic media personality, *Idoru,* 1996), which have inspired technological innovations during the 1980s and 1990s. The magical space described by Gibson anticipated by several years the real world of virtual reality to which millions of users connect everyday. He was a precursor of the Internet and continued to describe and anticipate new technologies of telecommunications in his next novels. In *Count Zero* he develops the theory of a technological aleph. He aims to create a technology able to synthesize all the information of a global network in one point. Biochips are inspired by the Aleph described by Jorge Luis Borges in his 1949 story "The Aleph." It is a utopian technology permitting the concentration of all the information of the world in one point. Biochips suggest the miniaturization of informatics and the possibility to insert microcomputers and networks of telecommunications into the body of the user. Gibson anticipated the evolution of new technologies of telecommunications by thinking about the possibility of inserting computers inside users. In the novel *Mona Lisa Overdrive,* he describes a technology representing a virtual person evolving in cyberspace. He developed the theme of autonomous virtual persons, or synthespians, in *Idoru.* Synthespians have become commercialized innovation thanks to the progresses of artificial intelligence, three-dimensional technologies, and virtual reality. Some virtual singers already perform in shows and are paid for it. Gibson describes the evolution of computer technologies in three ways in his Sprawl trilogy.

First he explains how hackers will civilize the electronic space, permitting the colonization of it by the human species. He thinks about the virtual world as a world in which artificial intelligences are the leaders. Hackers describe how the matrix works from inside, and Gibson advocates to envisage an external philosophy of the modalities of creation of the matrix. Moreover, he asks who has created the matrix, the function and the finalities of it. Second, Gibson aims to create a technology synthesizing all the information and the infinites in one point. He calls these points alephs or biochips. Computers connected to networks of information permit the synthesis of information in one point accessible by everyone, everywhere. Finally Gibson thinks cyberspace could be the place of evolution and life of virtual persons that are autonomous thanks to artificial intelligence and artificial life programs. Gibson has developed a philosophy of colonization and conquest of virtual worlds. He has anticipated the technological evolution of informatics and telecommunications and proposed a dialectical view of the evolution of humankind in cyberspace. This latter is peopled by artificial intelligences and artificial life-forms. Gibson's cyberspace is a mythological space inspiring engineers questing for the "networkization" of the planet.

Robert Nozick has proposed a view of what could be a metautopia in his book *Anarchy, State and Utopia.* He estimates that utopia could be defined as a situation in which the state would be reduced. Nozick elaborates an ultraliberal vision of utopia, in which states have mostly disappeared and where individuals are free to choose their communities. Cyberpunks share similar views with Nozick. Multinationals have huge powers in the described worlds, and people choose their communities on the virtual world. Nozick and cyberpunks defined the philosophy of a technological utopia realized with the success of the Internet, which permitted everyone on the planet to connect to the networks of information and everyone to choose his or her virtual community. The Internet was at its beginning a utopian space with no regulation. States could not intervene in its functioning, and people were free to search all the information they needed. The utopia of cyberspace prolonged the philosophy of Nozick by advocating the end of states and the triumph of the ultraliberated, connected individual. Cyberpunks described cities ruled by urban guerrillas and the chaos of reality. They anticipated a schism between the world of reality and of outsiders and the world of virtuality of connected individuals. The meta-utopia of Nozick could not be realized in reality because anarchy is impossible because of the instincts of death as inevitable in each man. On the other hand, anarchy could be perceived as a meta-utopia realizable in cyberspace, in which no rules mattered and in which states intervened as little as possible. Nozick was one of the founding fathers of the cyberpunk utopia. In cyberpunk literature reality is often dystopic and virtuality utopic. Cyberpunks advocated the success of artificial paradises and the connection to networks of telecommunications, permitting individuals to connect to parallel universes. Nozick develops an idealist philosophy, but cyberpunks are aware of the violence of reality. The "consensual hallucination" described in *Neuromancer* is an example of a cognitive utopia created by the interconnection of individuals through networks of virtual reality. Virtual reality creates a common view of the world, and computer technologies permit the immersion of individuals in a virtual system shared by millions of users. Technologies of telecommunications and of informatics create a global hallucination taking the place of ideologies to assure the social link of individuals. This consensual hallucination permits the cohesion of what MacLuhan calls the "global village." Gibson sheds light on the problem of the *lebenswelt* of individuals connected to information technologies. Sherry Turkle has demonstrated in *The Second Self* that children could develop autistic behaviors if they passed too much time in virtual words. Turkle called these children hackers, and they developed a specific rationality, a *lebenswelt* that permitted them to create artificial worlds and to program the colonization of cyberspace. The "consensual hallucination" has been theorized by Leary, who estimates that the personal computer has the same effects as LSD. Technologies of communication plunge individuals in an hallucination, a specific state of mind shared by millions of users but excluding nonusers of new technologies of telecommunications who remain in the desert of reality. The virtual utopia is dual: It proposes the constitution of a technological virtual network and the sharing of a common *lebenswelt* funded on a virtual hallucination. Cyberpunks contributed to define the elements of a new technological utopia funded on anarchy in virtual worlds. This utopia revealed the metaphorical reality of a world in which informatics and the Internet have triumphed.

The libertarian philosophy of cyberpunk science fiction has anticipated real behaviors of the users of Internet, who aim to download files freely. It is opposed to the logic of the dominant political economy of capitalism. Cyberpunk is a paradoxical movement. On one hand it has developed an anarchistic political philosophy founded on the free use of technologies, which has led to the widely successful free software movement. On the other hand it has permitted the development and the popularization of new technologies in the 1980s and 1990s. Cyberpunk philosophy is a radical conception of technopolitics, part of the ideology of science fiction. It proposes a radical liberty in the use of new technologies. Faced with the technocratic organization of real societies, virtual territories are lands of freedom, without rules. Information is completely free, and cyberpunk philosophy has inspired the hacker ethics advocating the horizontal circulation of information. Cyberpunks experimented with new technologies, such as virtual reality, nanotechnology, and biotechnology. They were at the avant-garde of a huge innovation process in various fields such as telecommunications. By anticipating and accompanying the emergence of the Internet as a massively distributed media, cyberpunk had invented a model of connected civilization in the 1980s. Their fictions were mostly describing a reality ruled by multinationals, and heroes were outsiders trying to find their place in technocratic societies by playing with new technologies. Cyberpunk heroes were at the avant-garde of the innovation process, which explained their exclusion of the normal society. They experienced new technologies in anarchistic territories such as the Zone of Chiba City in *Neuromancer,* called heterotopias by Foucault or T.A.Z. (temporary autonomous zones) by Hakim Bey.

Cyberpunk heroes traveled in virtual space to find adventures. This virtual space was called cyberspace by William Gibson, metaverse by Neal Stephenson, Cosmoplex by Greg Egan, and the Matrix by the Wachowski brothers. It described common technologies connecting the mind to a system of virtual reality shared by millions of users. Neuro-connection is commonly used to connect to these systems. The access to virtual worlds is the symbol of the access to the utopia. It permits escape to the chaos of reality. Cyberculture describes reality as a chaotic state, ruled by mafias and deviant people. Reality is ruled by violence, and cyberpunks novels describe reality as a world in which it has become impossible to live a normal and harmonious life. The only solution to escape to chaos are virtual worlds that are a new kind of utopia elaborated in contrast with the sociological evidence of a reality dominated by violence. Cyberpunk philosophy criticized reality to promote a harmonious life in a virtual reality of totally free access, in which violence is impossible or not dangerous. Cyberpunks try to define the conditions of liberty in the virtual space, considered as a simulacrum of reality.

Hackers are archetypes of human behavior with new technologies of telecommunications. Hackers have first been organized in communities of scientists who have invented networks of computers. The Internet has been the symbol of the wave of innovations initiated by hackers after World War II. Engineers in informatics were of two types. Some were in charge to assure the development of systems adapted to institutional situations, and others developed new systems in specific structures out of institutional frames. Innovations in informatics were generated mostly in MIT, where the first hackers developed their activities in the 1950s. If some engineers in computer sciences were adapted to the stabilization of existing networks and systems, other developed new technologies, and a mythology began to describe specific representations of their activities. From the 1960s to the end of the 1970s, engineers in computer science developed new technologies that contributed to radical changes in society in the 1980s and 1990s. Their activity was unknown by the large audience, but the emergence of cyberpunk science fiction revealed that computer engineers had their own culture, the culture of hacking. Hackers were the main characters of the most important books and films of cyberpunk science fiction. They were a metaphor of the engineer in computer sciences, the hero of the innovation wave in informatics and telecommunications of the 1980s and 1990s.

Cyberpunk science fiction was the consequence of a scientific subculture created by the convergence of dreams of engineers. It became the cause of the massive diffusion of technologies of telecommunications in the 1980s. It developed a radical philosophy of the human-machine interaction and a form of technological utopianism proposing the colonization of virtual spaces. Cyberpunk developed a political philosophy of this colonization. It described the various possible strategies for humankind to adapt with new technologies of telecommunications. Gibson anticipated the emergence of the Internet, and *Neuromancer* described the first metaphorical way of conquest of the informational space generated by this technology. Cyberpunk science fiction proposed various archetypal behaviors related to new technologies through the metaphor of hackers. It became a popular movement, hugely inspiring users of new technologies to manipulate their own machines. Users became hackers by navigating through the informational space and developed political opinions and a philosophy to defend free access and circulation in the virtual network. The philosophy of users was largely inspired by the philosophy of science fiction writers who declared in their novels that virtual spaces had to be outside of control, the property of no one and of everyone, the place of an anarchism permitted by the dematerialization of individuals. Cyberpunk science fiction developed a technological utopianism inspired by anarchism that contributed to elaborate the philosophy of users of informatics and networks of telecommunications such as the Internet in the 1990s and 2000s. Neal Stephenson defines archetypes of hackers in *The Diamond Age*. It finds its origins in various mythologies:

> Hackworth hesitated. "Pardon me, but not precisely, sir. Folklore consists of certain universal ideas that have been mapped onto local cultures. For example, many cultures have a Trickster figure, so the trickster may be deemed a universal; but he appears in different guises, each appropriate to a particular culture's environment. The Indians of the American southwest called him Coyote, those of the Pacific Coast called him Raven. Europeans called him Br'er Rabbit. In twentieth-century literature he appears first as Bugs Bunny and then as the Hacker."
>
> Finkle-McGraw chuckled. "When I was a lad, that word had a double meaning. It could mean a trickster who broke into things—but it could also mean an especially skilled coder." "The ambiguity is common in post-Neolithic cultures," Hackworth said.
>
> "As technology became more important, the Trickster underwent a shift in character and became the god of crafts—of technology, if you will—while retaining the underlying roguish qualities. So we have the Sumerian Enki, the Greek Prometheus and Hermes, Norse Loki, and so on." "In any case," Hackworth continued, "Trickster/ Technologist is just

one of the universals. The database is full of them. It's a catalogue of the collective unconscious. In the old days, writers of children's books had to map these universals onto concrete symbols familiar to their audience— like Beatrix Potter mapping the Trickster onto Peter Rabbit. This is a reasonably effective way to do it, especially if the society is homogeneous and static, so that all children share similar experiences." (1995, 106–7)

Jung has developed a psychology of the trickster in *The Archetypes and the Collective Unconscious.* He asserts that "the trickster is a primitive 'cosmic' being of divine-animal nature on the one hand superior to man because of is super-human qualities, and on the other hand inferior to him because of his unreason and unconsciousness" (Jung 1968, 164). The hacker is a primitive man of technological societies. He is able to transgress rules, to create new ones, and to invent new technologies. Gibson establishes a parallel between hackers and shamans, inspired by voodoo mythology and the Rastafarian religion. He introduces animistic beliefs in his novels. His mythology promotes a primitive use of technologies. He was at the avant-garde of a movement of technological innovation and has anticipated lots of new technologies in the fields of computer science and telecommunication during the 1980s and 1990s. The cyberpunk literature of Gibson has inspired lots of scientists and engineers. He has created a mythology for engineers, described as primitive pioneers of the informational age. If science fiction has often described scientists as mad, the cyberpunk movement presented them as marginal people inventing new technologies in marginal places. Many scientists described in cyberpunk science fiction are victims of their discoveries, which could be used by evil forces to dominate the world. Hackers often are opposed to the dominant order of capitalism and try to invent an alternative use of new technologies. The cyberpunk mythology of the hackers is founded on the description of a primitive mentality using new technologies in an anarchistic perspective.

Users of new technologies of telecommunications have been compared in the 1990s to surfers. But the more radicals were described as hackers, able to destroy security of computers and to steal information. At the beginning of the Internet era, hackers were dangerous individuals who were the masters of the Internet because they knew all the rules and were able to penetrate almost every system. On the other hand, normal users saw the Internet as a complex technology, understanding vaguely its functioning and its applications. Hackers were considered experts in informatics and symbolic chiefs of the rules of a virtual media not yet regulated. They were epitomes of an anarchistic state of mind ruling the conquest of the Internet by the first users. This anarchistic philosophy was defined by cyberpunk science fiction and by Timothy Leary.

Cyberpunk and science fiction question the impact of technology in society. They describe the political impact of technological progress and scientific discoveries. Thus science fiction can be considered a technopolitical philosophy. It describes the impact of technologies on the transformations of individuals and societies. New technologies of telecommunication and of virtuality have had an important impact on the transformation of societies, and science fiction has anticipated the impact of these changes on individuals. Cyberpunks proposed, for example, a definition of connected humans, or cyborgs, that is a metaphorical expression of the mutation of individuals in technological societies. Cyborgs were central characters in films such as *The Terminator* (1984) or *Cyborg* (1989). These later are more and more equipped with technological tools that permit them to be connected to others and information flux. Cyborgian philosophy (Hughes 2004) is an example of technopolitical philosophy inherited from the cyberpunk movement (Gray 2001).

Cyberpunk science fiction crystallized the terms of a technological utopia created by computer scientists and hackers in the 1970s and 1980s. If cyberculture has been inspired by the naturalist hippie movement of the 1960s, it has mostly been attracted by the cybernetic utopia of a society connected to information networks. This utopia was developed mainly in the 1970s and contributed to generate an ideology that contributed to the success of the technologies of telecommunications and to the massive diffusion of personal computers in industrial societies in the 1980s and 1990s. Computer hackers replaced hippies in the collective mythology. After a long period during which the youth identified with primitivism and revolted against authority, a period of technological progress was founded on the faith on the ideal of new heroes: hackers. They were able to connect to information networks and to create ideal societies and communities on virtual worlds. After the natural utopia of a hippie youth, a technological utopia was diffused through the cyberpunk science fiction movement. A large part of the population was concerned by the necessity to use computers and new telecommunication technologies and was inspired consciously or not by the mythology proposed by cyberpunk authors.

Technological anarchism is a philosophy inspired by Nozick, anarcho-capitalism, and informationalism. It postulates that technological innovation can be the result of anarchistic behaviors. Hacking and *hacktivism* are kinds of anarchistic behavior contributing to the evolution of technology. They contribute to the alternative use of innovation and to the creation of new technologies. Science fiction has developed lots of utopian technologies in marginal zones. Cyberpunks are epitomes of anarchists that invent parallel uses of new technologies in temporary autonomous zones. Cyberpunks are at the avant-garde of innovation and wish to democratize technologies by making them free. Many of them were at the origin of the development of peer-to-peer technologies permitting the free downloading of files. They advocate the free circulation and the free access to technologies and fight against all kinds of powers limiting liberties. They conceive technologies as tools of liberation and not of alienation. Technological anarchism is an answer to Luddism, promoting the destruction of machines to liberate humans. It does not promote destructive action against machines. It estimates that machines are "friendly extensions" of humans that have to be used as freely as possible. Anarchists denounce the use of technologies by all kinds of powers to control people. In *The Matrix* the hacker Neo begins his revolution when he understands that the world in which he thinks he is free is a simulacrum generated by a technology controlling his perception. Aldous Huxley in *Brave New World* and George Orwell in *Nineteen Eighty-Four* have denounced the risks of technological societies to create a soft totalitarianism against which technological anarchists develop criticism and alternative solutions. *The Matrix* depicts a system of domination controlling people thanks to technologies of virtual reality. Science fiction reveals fears related to a technological innovation and puts heroes in a situation of revolt to denounce it. Science fiction is an anarchistic literature because it permits a radical criticism of the systems of domination of societies. Heroes, like hackers of the cyberpunk movement, often oppose the dominant technological order to restore humanity. Science fiction envisages the radical extension of technical systems and their impact on humanity, often reduced to slavery. Technological anarchism permits the struggle against the risks of technological totalitarianism. It is a humanitarian political philosophy aiming to restore humanity against the risks of dehumanization linked to technological progress and theorized by Heidegger (1977) and Ellul (1964).

Technological anarchism creates new economic models. It contributes to the destruction of the monopoly of multinationals. The free software movement and informationalism contribute to invent software that contours traditional technologies of telecommunication. For example, the Skype software permits long-distance telephoning without paying a bill to a company. Technological anarchism democratizes technologies, but a perverse effect is generated by the movement in that it reduces the possibilities of multinationals to innovate and to propose new technologies to consumers. Technological anarchism is a counter-power against the domination of a technology and the monopoly of multinationals. The cyberpunk movement often puts heroes as strugglers against multinationals. In *Neuromancer,* Case is disconnected from cyberspace after having been accused of having stolen money from his company. He becomes a poor man, and his brain is destroyed by a neurotoxin. His quest in cyberspace permits him to recover his identity and to connect two artificial intelligences, who create a kind of technological divinity. In Pat Cadigan's *Synners,* heroes are also facing the power of multinationals. In the world of the cyberpunk movement, multinationals govern the world led by ultraliberalism. States have lost power, and multinational have the powers to control societies and to impose their new products. Central characters of the cyberpunk science fiction movement often are antiheroes and marginal figures who fight against a system they judge alienating and dehumanizing. Technological anarchism permits them to propose alternative solutions to the dominant technological system and to stimulate innovation. It inspires innovators by inventing new technologies and democratizes the access to new technologies for consumers. Technological anarchism is a political philosophy contributing to the process of innovation.

Hackers play in an anarchistic structure called the informational network. This place has no specific rules, and hackers gain their ability by knowing and contouring the topology and the artificial codes of cybernetic spaces. Hackers are anarchists in the sense that they fight against authority to recover the sense of a reality corrupted by the domination of a class of people. In *The Matrix*, the Matrix has been built by machines to alienate humankind. Humanity sleeps, and the minds of people are connected to a global network of communication generating a hallucination simulating the life of a normal person in a world still alive of the end of the twentieth century. Neo realizes that this simulation serves the domination of the machines, who use the energy of humans to nurture their technical systems. Neo decides to become an anarchist and to fight against the dictatorship of the machines and to restore the freedom of the human race on Earth. Anarchism is a philosophical choice that Neo has to make by choosing the right pill, engaging him in a global struggle in which he plays the role of a messiah liberating the human species. He is an anarchist who wants to liberate the Matrix from the domination of viruses (Agent Smith) and ultimately to create a dialogue with the machines that have taken control of the real.

The Matrix is a network of neurological simulation that can be a stimulating experience if the connection is free. It can be the worst alienation if it deprives individuals from their contact with reality. Neo decides to break the domination of machines and to restore freedom by an anarchistic revolution. In *Neuromancer*, Case is an anarchist too. He plays with the network of virtual reality and challenges the artificial intelligences who live in artificial environments. His quest is metaphysical, and he aims to connect two artificial intelligences, generating a cosmic entity.

Networks of communication are the place where heroes live in the cyberpunk movement. Actions are freer than in reality and are only limited by the program. Networks are more and more complex from one novel to another. In *Snow Crash*, the metaverse looks like a real town. In *Neuromancer* and *Tron*, the network is simple. It is an elementary structure without power, anarchistic. Hackers from the cyberpunk science fiction are anarchists struggling in anarchistic structures called networks. Anarchy is normality in networks of communication. Networks are anarchistic. The society of communication is anarchistic thanks to technology, and hackers are archetypes of the individual in this society.

Cyberpunk literature owes much to William Gibson, who promoted the colonization of cybernetic spaces by humankind. This essay has described three possibilities in reading these novels.

1. They can be considered as an anarchistic philosophy promoting a libertarian use of technology and the informational theory. Cyberpunk literature is a way to criticize the social order and the potential threats linked to the

domination of multinationals on the world. Cyberpunk societies are dominated by a hypercapitalism in which states have mostly disappeared. People live in networks of virtual reality, and the real has been transformed by the incursion of cybernetics. Cyberpunk philosophy is also prospective. It describes what could become of societies if multinationals create a second world founded on virtual reality. It is also a mirror of contemporary technological societies.

2. Cyberpunk literature can be considered as the foundation of a new technological mythology inspiring engineers and users of computers. If hackers have first been pioneers in informatics, they have become most of the users of new technologies, most of them trying to download illegally files through peer-to-peer networks.

3. Finally cyberpunks can be seen as models for social and technological innovators. They aim to transform society through technological innovations. Cyberpunk characters have inspired innovators who have developed a cyberpunk industry. If cyberpunk literature has been for several years an alternative genre for outsiders, it has become a genre inspiring the mainstream. Themes developed by cyberpunks have been assimilated and reinterpreted by post-cyberpunk authors such as Neal Stephenson, who eliminated critical and dystopic aspects of the movement to promote utopian societies created by the diffusion of new technologies such as virtual reality and nanotechnology.

Bibliography

Bey, Hakim. 1991. *T.A.Z.: The Temporary Autonomous Zone, Ontological Anarchy, Poetic Terrorism*. Brooklyn, N.Y.: Autonomedia.

Borges, Jorge Luis. 2004. *The Aleph and Other Stories, 1933–1969*. New York: Dutton.

Breton, Philippe. 1997. *L'utopie de la communication: Le mythe du village planétaire*. Paris: La Découverte.

Bukatman, Scott. 1993. *Terminal Identity: The Virtual Subject in Postmodern Science Fiction*. Durham, N.C.: Duke University Press.

Cadigan, Pat. 2001. *Synners*. New York: Four Walls, Eight Windows.

Cavallaro, Dani. 2000. *Cyberpunk and Cyberculture: Science Fiction and the Work of William Gibson*. London: Athlone.

Dery, Mark. 1996. *Escape Velocity: Cyberculture at the End of the Century* New York: Grove.

Ellul, Jacques. 1964. *The Technological Society*. New York: Knopf.

Gibson, William. 1984. *Neuromancer*. New York: Ace.

———. 1986. *Count Zero*. New York: Arbor House.

———. 1988. *Mona Lisa Overdrive*. New York: Bantam.

———. 1996. *Idoru*. New York: Putnam.

Gray, Chris Hables. 2001. *Cyborg Citizen: Politics in the Posthuman Age*. New York: Routledge.

Heidegger, Martin. 1977. *The Question Concerning Technology, and Other Essays*, trans. William Lovitt. New York: Harper and Row.

Hughes, James. 2004. *Citizen Cyborg: Why Democratic Societies Must Respond to the Redesigned Human of the Future*. Cambridge, Mass.: Westview.

Jung, C. G. 1968. *The Archetypes and the Collective Unconscious*. 2nd ed. Princeton, N.J.: Princeton University Press.

Leary, Timothy. 1994. *Chaos and Cyber Culture*. Berkeley, Cal.: Ronin.

Novotny, Patrick. 1997. "No Future! Cyberpunk, Industrial Music, and the Aesthetics of Postmodern Disintegration." In *Political Science Fiction,* ed. Donald M. Hassler and Clyde Wilcox, 99–123. Columbia: University of South Carolina Press.

Olsen, Lance. 1992. *William Gibson.* Mercer Island, Wash.: Starmont House.

Stephenson, Neal. 1995. *The Diamond Age, or, A Young Lady's Illustrated Primer.* New York: Bantam.

Turkle, Sherry. 2005. *The Second Self: Computers and the Human Spirit.* Boston: Bantam.

Not Lost in Space

Revising the Politics of Cold War Womanhood
in Judith Merril's Science Fiction

Lisa Yaszek

The title of this essay echoes the title of the 1960s TV series because I'm interested in how the new technologies that emerged in the wake of World War II—including everything from atom bombs and communication satellites to deep freezers and automatic coffee makers—transformed the relations of technoscience, society, and gender. As a product of its time, *Lost in Space* captures both the promises and the perils of this transformation for women. It does so by depicting women's work in relation to what feminist Betty Friedan called "the feminine mystique"—that is, the widespread postwar belief that women were defined by their sexual and maternal instincts and that they would therefore naturally choose family over career whenever they could (1963, 43, 204).

At first, *Lost in Space* appears to reject this profoundly conservative gender ideology by presenting family matriarch Maureen Robinson as both a biochemist and a mother. Moreover, it is her technocultural position as a space explorer on the generation ship *Jupiter 2* that enables her to combine these two roles. Unfortunately, when Dr. Smith undermines the *Jupiter 2,* he also destroys this protofeminist dream. Once the Robinsons are thrown off course, the show becomes a frontier narrative, and characters take on the conventional gender roles of the pioneer family. Thus Maureen Robinson is denied her career and, for that matter, even the opportunity to choose between family and career. Before it really begins, *Lost in Space* retreats from the radical implications of its own premises.

Fortunately these were not the only images of women's work available to midcentury Americans—especially not if they were fans of literary science fiction. This is particularly true of Judith Merril, a foundational figure in the history of Golden Age science fiction. As a self-proclaimed feminist and socialist at a time when it was unfashionable to be either of those things, Merril used her chosen genre to dissent from the sociopolitical roles assigned to women in the name of national security. By invoking postwar America's most dearly held beliefs about sex and gender in the framework of the nuclear war narrative and the space story, Merril demonstrated both the contradictions inherent in cold war ideas about the necessary relations of science, society, and gender and how women might revise those relations to ensure new and more egalitarian futures for all people. In doing so, she created a host of feminine and even feminist protagonists who escape the fate of Maureen Robinson. These protagonists are not just unhappy housewife heroines lost in space, but compassionate and consummate professionals who transform life on Earth and lead humanity to the stars.

The Politics of Cold War Womanhood

Historians generally agree that the cold war marked a low point in American feminist history. Although women had been courted by industry, academia, and even the military during the technical manpower shortages of World War II, that courtship came to a sudden end after the war.[1] As nuclear age anxieties proliferated, women were told that they could best serve their country as "domestic patriots" by exchanging politics and paid work in the public sphere for housekeeping and child rearing in the suburbs. "In the rhetoric of Cold War competition," feminist historian Susan M. Hartmann writes, "American leaders stressed women's traditional roles as wives, mothers, and consumers to demonstrate the superiority of the nation's institutions and values" (1994, 86). For example, as Adlai Stevenson told Smith College graduates during their 1955 commencement ceremony, homemaking was not just menial work to be feared by educated women. Instead, it presented them with the perfect opportunity to "defeat totalitarian, authoritarian ideas" by cultivating in their families "a vision of the meaning of life and freedom" (qtd. in Hartmann 1994, 86). Thus postwar women were invited to serve their country as domestic cold warriors dedicated to maintaining the security of America's most fundamental social unit: the nuclear family.[2]

The feminine mystique reinforced the notion that women were naturally more suited to work in the home than in the laboratory. Most Americans conceded that "old maids" had to work to support themselves, but married women who continued their professional careers into the cold war were criticized for failing to follow their biological drives—and do their duty for America—by bearing children. Public opprobrium was heaped even more thoroughly on women who tried to have both family and career since, as feminist historian Margaret Rossiter puts it, "every reader of Dr. Benjamin Spock knew that a normal child needed the full-time attention of his (or in later editions, her) loving mother" (1995, 41). And so the rhetoric of domestic patriotism blended effortlessly with that of the feminine mystique, reinforcing what so many Americans already thought they knew: that women might have either family and career, but that to sacrifice the former for the latter was unpatriotic and to combine the two was profoundly unnatural.

But many progressive postwar women rejected the logic of cold war femininity. This was particularly true of those peace organizations that revised official equations between patriotism and women's work in radical ways. For instance, the Women's International League for Peace and Freedom recruited new members by appealing to common feminine experience, arguing that it was only by joining together in the peace movement that "you and I—and all the mothers in the world—can go to sleep without thinking about the terrors of the Atomic Bomb" (qtd. in Alonso 1994, 131). For activists, then, it was women's real work to protest against—rather than acquiesce to—the cold war status quo.

Postwar peace organizations justified this new kind of labor by aligning maternal instinct with scientific knowledge. Through the 1940s, 1950s, and 1960s, groups such as Women Strike for Peace distributed educational pamphlets quoting Albert Einstein, Linus Pauling, the Atomic Energy Commission, the U.S. Public Health Service, and the Federal Radiation Council on topics ranging from the dangers of irradiated milk to the futility of preparing for life after nuclear war (Swerdlow 1993, 84). By framing their concerns in this way, activists positioned themselves as rational beings reluctantly driven to public action by an understanding of nuclear weapons similar to that of the experts themselves.

Later in the cold war, conservative thinking about women's work was further complicated by the exigencies of the space race. When the Soviets launched *Sputnik I* months ahead of its U.S. counterpart in 1957, Americans were at a loss to explain what had happened. Studies undertaken by the National Manpower Council offered a rather surprising answer: the Soviets had an advantage over their American counterparts because they tracked both men *and* women into techno-scientific professions. Accordingly in 1958 the U.S. Congress passed the National Defense Education Act, which explicitly allocated scholarship funds to scientifically and mathematically inclined schoolchildren regardless of gender (Rossiter 1995, 63). At the same time NASA instituted the Women in Space Early program, recruiting thirteen of the nation's top female aviators for astronaut training. Although this program was shut down in 1962—just three years after its inception—even its short-lived existence indicates the very real extent to which the imperatives of an emergent technoculture were already changing American thinking about women's work in a high-tech world (Kevles 2003, 7–16).

If nothing else, the Women in Space Early program certainly provided Americans with new images of that work. In February 1960 *Look* magazine ran a cover article on Betty Skelton, a three-time national aerobatic champion who trained with NASA's male astronauts (Nolen 2002, 92). Six months later *Life* magazine published an equally extensive article on Jerri Cobb, a commercial pilot who held distance, altitude, and speed records for several types of planes and who served as the Women in Space spokesperson (Freni 2002, 53). Not surprisingly, these first female astronauts were always carefully photographed in accordance with postwar standards of feminine beauty. Otherwise, however, they were depicted much like their male counterparts, spinning in centrifuges, floating in buoyancy tanks, and proudly looking off into the distant future as they climbed into their jets. Suddenly then, it seemed the future was wide open and that women might be at home anywhere from the laundry room to the launchpad.

Judith Merril's Political Science Fictions

Certainly women writers who joined the postwar science fiction community thought this was the case, and the fantastic tales they wrote about women who battle corrupt governments and colonize strange new worlds paid tribute to the pioneers of Women Strike for Peace and Women in Space Early alike. More than 250 new women writers joined the science fiction community after World War II, and many used their chosen genre to assess critically the new scientific, social, and gender arrangements of cold war America. They did so by creating a new kind of science fiction set in a futuristic literary realm where events revolve around women's lives, women's loves, and of course, women's work.[3] As a result, these authors created the first body of contemporary literature to address systematically the relations of gender, science, and society and prefigured the literature we now recognize as feminist science fiction.

The single author most closely associated with postwar women's science fiction is Judith Merril. During World War II Merril moved to New York to support herself and her daughter through writing. There she joined the Futurians, a group of writers and fans that included such rising stars as Isaac Asimov, Frederik Pohl, and Virginia Kidd. Over the next two decades Merril edited a variety of prominent science fiction collections, including 1951's *Shot in the Dark* and all twelve of the 1956–1967 *Year's Best of Science Fiction* anthologies. At the same time she was packaging science fiction for outside audiences, Merril worked to strengthen the genre from within by establishing some of the first professional science fiction writing groups, including the Milford Writers' Workshop and the Hydra Club (Merril and Pohl-Weary 2002, 170, 273).

For Merril, involvement with the science fiction community was the logical extension of an already intensely politicized life. Merril was born in Boston in 1923 to Samuel Grossman and Ethel Hurwitch, both outspoken Jewish intellectuals and early advocates of the Zionist movement. Merril's mother was deeply involved with the suffragette movement and the founding of Hadassah as well. Merril herself was an active member of the Young People's Socialist League (YPSL) throughout the 1930s and early 1940s. During World War II she participated in wartime efforts to establish public nursery schools for the children of working women; afterward she fought valiantly to keep these schools open despite the growing public conviction that children's needs were best met in the home by full-time mothers. Later Merril became an outspoken opponent of U.S. involvement in Vietnam, and in 1968 she immigrated to Canada, where she worked with war resisters and participated in the Free University movement (Merril and Pohl-Weary 2002, 12–15, 62–65).

It is significant that Merril's literary career took off in those postwar years when she was least actively involved with organized politics. This is not to say that she abandoned activism altogether at this time; instead, like other women, she channeled her political passions into less conventional outlets. Merril began to distance herself from the YPSL in the early 1940s when she realized that, as "a Trotskyist's Trotskyist," she found the group's "authoritarian organizational tactics unbearable." At the same time she became increasingly interested in science fiction because it took as its basic premise "the idea that things could be different" (Merril and Pohl-Weary 2002, 44–45). Joining the Futurians further confirmed Merril's belief that progressive politics could be different, too. As mostly left-leaning individuals struggling to express themselves in an increasingly conservative era, the Futurians ardently believed that science fiction was the only place where writers could explore controversial issues without being dismissed as crackpots or dangerous radicals. They also offered the kind of nonhierarchical community that displaced activists such as Merril herself were looking for (Merril and Pohl-Weary 2002, 46).

Although Merril chose to work with a very different kind of organization than did her activist counterparts, the stories she produced during this period championed many of the same causes, and in much the same ways. Given that she was one of the first science fiction authors to extrapolate from postwar American scientific, social, and gendered relations, it is not surprising that her stories tend to follow one of two broad narrative trajectories. They either warn about the disasters that will ensue if women's caregiving work in the home is thwarted by an unnatural and unjust techno-cultural order, or they celebrate the magnificent discoveries that will emerge when women are free to combine work and family as their individual natures dictate.

Merril's nuclear war narrative "That Only a Mother" (1948) is one of the genre's most famous disaster stories. As science fiction scholar Edward James notes, midcentury authors usually used nuclear war narratives to explore "how societies decline into tribalism or barbarism . . . or develop from barbarism to civilization" (1994, 90). In the hands of writers such as Merril, these stories showed readers how atomic age civilization inherently tended toward barbarism, especially for women and their families. Writ large upon the postnuclear future, such stories are clearly in dialogue with the progressive sensibilities of the postwar peace movement. Indeed, as we shall see, the nuclear war narrative provided Merril with an ideal way to illustrate those "terrors of the Atomic Bomb" that could only be hinted at in peace activist literature.

"That Only a Mother" brings together two of the primary fears of the early atomic age: the possibility of mutation from radioactive materials and the probability that an international nuclear war would effectively destroy all humanity (Trachtenberg 1990, 355). Set in a near future in which exposure to radiation from an ongoing nuclear war has produced a generation of radically mutated children, Merril's tale depicts an insane world where mothers struggle to protect their children against fathers who commit infanticide, juries acquit the men of any wrongdoing, and journalists report the whole process with tacit approval.

Although such events are initially presented as part of a terrible new moral and social order located specifically in postwar Japan, the land of the enemy other, Merril ultimately suggests that this new world order—much like radioactivity itself—has no respect for national borders. The majority of "That Only a Mother" follows the story of Margaret and Hank, an American couple who give birth to Henrietta, a "flower-faced child" whose stunning intelligence is offset by her limbless body (1948, 349). Margaret responds to her child's deformity by retreating into her own insanity and insisting that "*my baby's fine. Precocious, but normal*" (345, 351), while Hank—equally horrified by both his child and Margaret's response to her—seems destined to repeat the insanity of his Japanese counterparts as he prepares to kill his child at the close of the story. Thus Merril's story effectively anticipates the kind of warning issued by peace groups in the 1950s: that "a bomb doesn't care in the least whether you are wearing a soldier's uniform or a housewife's apron" (in Alonso 1994, 130).

So what might women do to prevent such nightmare futures from happening? Merril's 1950 novel *Shadow on the Hearth* offers one solution: women can prevent these dystopic futures from happening by allying themselves with other women and scientists. Lauded as more than "mere" genre fiction, Merril's novel was remarkably well-received in its day: the *New York Times* compared it to the cautionary works of H. G. Wells and George Orwell, and *Motorola TV Theatre* broadcast a dramatic version of it in 1954 under the title "Atomic Attack!" (Merril and Pohl-Weary 2002, 99–100). Despite the hysteria implied by its television title, Merril's novel is actually one of the only postwar nuclear holocaust narratives that manages to work its way out from under the paralyzing shadow of the mushroom cloud and to imagine the possibility of women—and men—working together to build a more peaceful and rational future.

Shadow on the Hearth begins much like its short story counterpart by establishing a nightmare future that hails women readers based on their common situation as mothers haunted by the possibility of nuclear war. The novel follows the story of Gladys Mitchell, a Westchester housewife and mother who is the epitome of domesticity, dispensing nuggets of wisdom about the effects of French toast on cranky children while struggling with her conscience about whether or not she can abandon the laundry to attend a neighborhood luncheon (87). With the advent of World War III Gladys's life turns upside down: her husband, Jon, is presumed dead in New York City; her daughters, Barbara and Ginny, are exposed to radioactive rain at school; and her son, Tom, a freshman at Texas Tech, vanishes off the face of the planet. In this brave new world, even the most familiar aspects of suburban life become terrifyingly strange: basic utilities fail, and men become monsters who abuse their power as civil defense officers to harass the women and children they are meant to protect.

In Merril's story nuclear war shatters readers' certainty about what it might mean to be a wife and mother in the atomic era. At first Gladys tries to imagine what her husband would do in her situation. However, she soon gives this up because

> Jon wasn't there. For more than two days Jon hadn't been there. The other time, the other war, it was different. Then she wrote him cheerful, encouraging letters, telling him all the little troubles that came up each day, the little things he customarily solved, that she had learned to cope with. But these were not little problems now, nor were they the kind that anyone customarily solved.
>
> What would Jon do?
>
> That was the old formula, the way it had worked in the last war. She'd ask herself and get the answer. Now there was no answer. (188)

As Merril's heroine realizes, the formula for gender relations that made sense in World War II has little or no bearing on the radically different situation of World War III. Rather than looking to the past for models of appropriate feminine behavior that will make sense of a frightening new present, Merril's readers must acknowledge that shifting modes of technology create new social realities that demand new modes of relations between women and men as well.

The majority of *Shadow on the Hearth* follows Gladys's transformation from helpless housewife to activist mother who helps to prevent this world from becoming the kind of full-blown dystopia imagined elsewhere in midcentury science fiction stories. First, she allies herself with the other women populating her world, rescuing her housekeeper, Veda Klopak, from the local civil defense officials who believe she is a Communist spy and giving shelter to her neighbor Edie Crowell, a self-absorbed, aristocratic woman who fears being trapped alone in her home when the American government declares martial law. In turn Veda quickly adapts the Mitchell household to the rhythms of its new circumstances (a good thing, since Gladys is a lackadaisical housekeeper at best), while Edie uses her sharp tongue to fend off the civil defense officers who hope to break up the household and regain control over the women. Thus Veda, Gladys, and Edie create a community of women who work together to fend off the dangerous new social and moral orders that threaten them.

Much like her counterparts in the peace movement, Merril also suggests that women can most effectively challenge the new social and moral order of the cold war status quo by forging alliances with another group of like-minded people, namely scientists. The potential effectiveness of such alliances are made clear in Merril's novel through her depiction of the growing friendship between Gladys and Garson Levy, the local nuclear physicist turned high school math teacher. The first impression that Levy gives off is one of astounding ordinariness: "he didn't look like a madman, or a hero either. He looked like a scholarly middle-aged man who never remembered to have his suit pressed" (143). Nonetheless,

Merril's scientist turns out to be anything but ordinary, escaping from his government-imposed house arrest to make sure that his students' families are warned about the radiation that they were exposed to during the first wave of bombings and taking time to explain radiation test results when the civil authorities refuse to do so. Impressed by his concern for her children, Gladys invites Levy to stay with her and the other women. By working together Gladys and Levy manage to ensure the future well-being of the Mitchell household, pooling Levy's scientific knowledge with Gladys's social skills to secure medical attention for the Mitchell girls and to prevent the civil defense officials from evacuating and breaking up the household.

It is important to note that for Merril this alliance between mothers and scientists is at best an only partial solution to the problems posed by the threat of nuclear war. At the end of the novel the family unit is preserved, but its survival is far from guaranteed: Gladys's son, Tom, is located but much to her horror has been drafted into the army; her husband, Jon, returns from New York City but is wracked with radiation burns and gunshot wounds that prevent him from asserting his place as the head of the family; and Levy himself is diagnosed with a potentially fatal strain of radiation poisoning. As Gladys asks herself in the closing passages of the novel: "Isn't anything safe? Not the rain or the house? . . . Would anything ever be safe again?" (275) This ambivalence is key to Merril's project: if she depicts a postholocaust future where scientists can solve all the problems of nuclear war, then there would be no reason to protest that kind of war in the first place. Instead, by demonstrating how even the natural sympathies of mothers and scientists might not be enough to guarantee survival in the future, she makes a strong case for the necessity of peace activism in the present.

While her nuclear war stories depict situations already imagined by cold war peace activists, Merril used another classic science fiction story type, the space adventure, to imagine even more radical transformations of gender, science, and society. Like her counterparts in the National Manpower Council and NASA, Merril celebrated women's potential to become brilliant scientists, engineers, and mathematicians. However, she went beyond official government rhetoric to imagine worlds where women develop technoscientific brilliance by embracing rather than putting aside domestic relations. When women are free to mix family and career on their own terms, Merril predicted, they would make astounding intellectual discoveries that benefit both their individual families and humanity as a whole.

Merril demonstrates this by appropriating and revising one of the key tropes of the space story: the heroic but besieged scientist. Like other Americans, members of the science fiction community were often profoundly ambivalent about cold war sciences and technologies. However, as Brian Stableford notes: "Genre-SF writers mostly responded to the widespread popular opinion that technology had got out of hand by putting the blame on machine-*users* rather than machine-*makers*, claiming that it was not mad scientists but mad generals and mad politicians who were the problem. . . . scientists were often represented as isolated paragons of sanity locked into a political and military matrix that threatened the destruction of the world" (1993a, 1077). Prominent authors including C. M. Kornbluth, Algis Budrys, and Kurt Vonnegut produced stories that explored what seemed to be the inevitable conflict between scientific interest, military security, and social need, focusing particularly on "the difficulty of making scientific discoveries in such circumstances" (1077). For these authors, the real problem was not the unilateral impact of dangerous new scientific developments on society, but the emergence of a deadly new social matrix that perverted even the most benevolent scientific and technological research.

Postwar women writers refashioned this science fiction myth to explore the perils faced by women scientists trapped in a distinctly patriarchal social matrix that threatens to thwart their research and destroy their worlds. This is particularly apparent in Merril's 1954 short story "Dead Center," which initially appeared in the *Magazine of Fantasy and Science Fiction* in 1954 and was the first science fiction story ever featured in the critically acclaimed *Best American Short Stories* series. "Dead Center" tells the story of Ruth Kruger, a rocket ship engineer married to astronaut Jock Kruger. Driven by their fierce love and intense intellectual respect for one another, Ruth and Jock have (with the help of their equally brilliant design team) catapulted Earth's space program decades ahead of its original schedule.

It is precisely the Krugers' commitment to one another that enables this achievement. As Ruth notes to herself, "when a man knows his wife's faith is *unshakeable,* he can't help coming back" from even the most dangerous space mission (169). And of course her faith is unshakeable because Ruth, who was a famous rocket designer long before she married Jock, works closely with her team to oversee every aspect of her ships' design and construction. In direct contrast to advocates of the feminine mystique who claimed that women were biologically destined to choose between family and career, Merril proposes that scientific and social progress might well hinge upon the woman scientist's ability to incorporate her personal passions into her professional life.

Merril also proposes that without this kind of passion there may be no progress at all. When the Rocket Corps decides to put Jock in charge of the first manned moon landing, they also decide to replace Ruth with Andy Argent, an engineer who claims atmospheric landings as his area of theoretical expertise—even though Ruth has already established her practical expertise with six other rockets. When she is reminded that Rocket Corps funding depends on public goodwill and that the public does not want to know about dissent among scientists, Ruth agrees to the substitution, despite an inner conviction that "something's wrong" with Argent's ship (169). Although Ruth tries to dismiss her concern as mere jealousy, she seems to have good reason for it, since Argent turns out to be an autocrat who destroys the camaraderie of the rocket design team. As the lead Rocket Corps publicist diplomatically puts it, "with somebody new—well, you know what a ruckus we had until Sue got used to Argent's blue-prints, and how Ben's pencil notes used to drive Andy wild" (177). More than mere pettiness, Argent's rage for order turns out to be downright perilous for everyone involved. Due to a flaw in Argent's plans (which the demoralized rocket team fails to catch), Jock is thrown off course and forced to use all his fuel to make an emergency landing on the dark side of the moon, where it seems likely that he will die.

Appalled by the prospect of bad publicity that will permanently end space exploration, Earth's military and corporate leaders join forces to build an unmanned rescue ship, this time wisely putting Ruth in charge. But no one remembers to explain the situation to Ruth and Jock's young son, Toby, in the whirlwind of activity that ensues. With impeccable childish logic, Toby decides that his father has abandoned him and that his mother will do the same once the new ship is completed (182). Accordingly he decides to stow away on the ship and confront his parents when he reaches the moon. But the child's weight is just great enough to throw off Ruth's careful calculations and, as a horrified world looks on, the rescue ship explodes while leaving Earth's atmosphere. Thus Merril suggests that a truly viable science must account for both the subjectivity of the scientist *and* the subjectivity of everyone to whom she is connected. If it does not, both individual lives and human progress as a whole are doomed.

And so is the woman scientist herself. When Ruth learns that the explosion has killed her son and her husband has died of starvation on the moon, she takes her own life in a fit of grief. The Rocket Corps publicity team manages to salvage the situation by "keeping the sleeping-pill story down to a tiny back-page notice in most of the papers" (185). Moreover, in the final lines of the story we learn that "they made an international shrine of the house, and the garden where the three graves lay. Now they are talking of making an interplanetary shrine of the lonely rocket on the wrong side of the moon" (186). Touching as this might seem, Merril leaves readers with more questions than she answers: if Earth's best rocket designer and pilot are dead—killed, albeit inadvertently, by the man who was supposed to be second best—who exactly will build that interplanetary shrine on the moon? And how will they get there anyway? "They" may talk all they want, Merril implies, but when experienced female scientists such as Ruth Kruger are asked to defer to an untried masculine authority, then the hope that humanity might someday reach the stars becomes an increasingly unlikely dream.

So what is a science fiction heroine to do if she wants to have both family and career? Postwar women writers offered different answers to this question, but they seem to have been in agreement on one central point: if a woman wants to practice science on her own terms, she must leave the patriarchal workplace and strike out for new territory—whether that territory is in the kitchen or outer space. They also seem to have agreed that the most effective way to tell such stories was to refashion those cultural myths that depict science and technology as masculine activities. By redefining women's work to include both scientific and domestic labor and putting that work at the center of their stories, such authors refuted the logic of the feminine mystique. And in imagining that women might have it all—or that they might at least pursue it all—they created some of the first versions of what science fiction scholar Robin Roberts describes as "the feminist fairy tales that are needed to counteract the misogynistic stories of our culture" (6).

This is certainly true of Merril's novella "Daughters of Earth" (1952), which follows six generations of women as they participate in the first waves of intergalactic exploration and colonization. Merril creates her feminist fairy tale by boldly revising the origin story of Judeo-Christian culture in the opening passage of her own story:

> Martha begat Joan, and Joan begat Ariadne. Ariadne lived and died at home on Pluto, but her daughter, Emma, took the long trip out to the distant planet of an alien sun.
>
> Emma begat Leah, and Leah begat Carla, who was the first to make her bridal voyage through sub-space, a long journey faster than the speed of light itself. . . .
>
> The story could have started anywhere. It began with unspoken prayer, before there were words, when an unnamed man and woman looked upward to a distant light, and wondered. . . . Then in another age of madness, a scant two centuries ago, it began with . . . the compulsive evangelism of Ley and Gernsback and Clarke. It is beginning again now, here on Uller. But in this narrative, it starts with Martha. (97)

By rewriting the patriarchal genealogies of the Old Testament and the Torah, Merril proposes a radical break from history: while earthly civilizations of the past may have been founded by men, both the greater universe and the future as a whole belong to their daughters.

Merril also revises another key element of the space story to create her feminist fairy tale. As Stableford explains, "it is natural that SF should be symbolized by the theme of space flight, in that it is primarily concerned with transcending imaginative boundaries, with breaking free of the gravitational force which holds consciousness to a traditional core of belief and expectancy" (1993b, 1135). In Merril's hands, this theme serves to symbolize freedom from the gravitational force of patriarchy. Joan, for example, leaves Earth for Pluto because "in the normal course of things, [she] would have taken her degree . . . and gone to work as a biophysicist until she found a husband. The prospect appalled her" (103). Similarly Emma volunteers for the first mission from Pluto to Uller because her stepfather, Joe Prell, is an Earth man who loves her dearly but believes that Emma is "too direct, too determined, too intellectual, [and] too *strong*" to be a proper lady like her mother, Ariadne (112). Thus Merril literally conflates repressive patriarchal thinking with Earth and the past, insisting that the further women are from "the Old Planet," the freer they will be to shape their lives as they see fit.

Merril further underscores this point by opposing her Earth-born men to their off-world counterparts. For example, readers learn that when Emma's Martian husband first sets foot on Uller, "he wanted to shout; he wanted to run; he wanted to kiss the ground under his feet, embrace the man next to him. He wanted to get Emma and pull her out of the ship" (119). Rather than simply bask in the glory of being the first human to set foot on Uller, Ken longs to share the experience with his wife. Later, when Carla leaves for Nifleheim, it is her Uller-born father, Louis, who "was there first, folding the slender girl in a wide embrace [and] laughing proudly into her eyes" (164). And so the sons of Earth turn out to be just as different from their fathers as the daughters of Earth are from their mothers.

Merril also suggests that new and more egalitarian modes of social relations will result in new and more holistic modes of scientific practice. This is particularly true for those of her protagonists whose personal lives serve as professional inspiration. Joan's initial work on Pluto is largely theoretical, but after her husband is killed in a domed city construction accident she devises a terraforming process that will ensure no other family suffers this tragedy (108). Later, when an Uller native accidentally kills Emma's husband, she rejects the retaliatory attitude of the other colonists and devotes her life to initiating real communication with the silicone-based creatures. Eventually Emma succeeds in this task, and when her granddaughter Carla leaves for Nifleheim, she does so "in profitable comradeship with the Ullerns" (159). The further removed Merril's heroines are from their planet of origin, the more able they are to think of themselves in new ways: not just as rugged individuals who must bend nature to their wills, but as intelligent, sympathetic beings enmeshed in complex webs of life that must be preserved at all costs. The conclusions Merril draws throughout this novella about the relations of science and gender anticipate those proposed by feminist science studies scholars nearly four decades later: that subjective personal experiences, including commitments to other people and what Evelyn Fox Keller calls a "feeling for the organism" under investigation, are key aspects of scientific labor.[4]

Conclusion: Recovering Cold War Feminist Science Fiction

Looking back on the American midcentury, Judith Merril once noted that science fiction was "virtually the only vehicle of political dissent" available to cold war writers such as herself (1971, 74). At first this might seem like a surprising thing for a woman to say, since science fiction has commonly been considered a genre that best expresses the interests of men. Yet Merril turned the genre's own concepts and conventions to the political advantage of women. Scholars have long recognized that science fiction written since the revival of feminism in the 1960s has been a vital source of narratives for women interested in exploring the relations of gender, science, and culture. But as I have argued in the preceding pages, women such as Merril were active and politically engaged science fiction authors in the decades that *preceded* the modern women's movement as well. By examining how postwar women used stories about the future to articulate—in however allegorical a manner—their hopes and fears about the American present, we further one of most fundamental goals of feminist studies: to remember women's contributions to culture in all their diverse forms.

More specifically, when we examine Merril's fiction, we learn more about how and why feminist authors use science fiction to convey their ideas to non-feminist audiences. By allying herself with the science fiction community rather than a formal political organization, Merril conveyed her progressive political ideas to audiences well beyond those who were already converted to the causes she espoused. The most immediate audience—the predominantly male science fiction community—may not have been passionately interested in feminist politics, but they were, by definition, passionately interested in strange and estranging stories about science and technology. Merril's stories play to this interest by showing science fiction readers how they might think about nuclear weapons and space exploration—traditionally the province of male politicians, scientists, and soldiers—from the seemingly alien perspectives of wives and mothers. Far from limiting the efficacy of her social and political analyses, then, science fiction served as a literary gateway for cold war feminists such as Merril who wanted to change the world, one story at a time.

Notes

1. For further discussion of changing ideas about women's work during and immediately after World War II, see the opening chapters of Kathleen Broome Williams's *Improbable Warriors: Women Scientists and the U.S. Navy in World War II* and Margaret Rossiter's *Women Scientists in America before Affirmative Action, 1940–1972,* as well as the concluding chapters of Jenny Wosk's *Women and the Machine: Representations from the Spinning Wheel to the Electronic Age.*

2. For further discussion, see Eugenia Kaledin's preface to *Mothers and More: American Women in the 1950s;* chapter 3 of Elaine Tyler May's *Homeward Bound: American Families in the Cold War;* chapter 5 of Annegret S. Ogden's *The Great American Housewife: From Helpmate to Wage Earner, 1776–1986;* and chapter 2 of Leila J. Rupp and Verta Taylor's *Survival in the Doldrums: The American Women's Rights Movement, 1945 to the 1960s.*

3. For recent explorations of postwar women's science fiction as social critique, see Justine Larbalestier's *The Battle of the Sexes in Science Fiction;* Justine Larbalestier and Helen Merrick's "The Revolting Housewife: Women and Science Fiction in the 1950s"; Farah Mendlesohn's "Gender, Power, and Conflict Resolution: 'Subcommittee' by Zenna Henderson"; Dianne Newell and Victoria Lamont's "House Opera: Frontier Mythology and Subversion of Domestic Discourse in Mid-Twentieth-Century Women's Space Opera" and "Rugged Domesticity: Frontier Mythology in Post-Armageddon Science Fiction by Women"; and my own book, *Galactic Suburbia: Recovering Women's Science Fiction.*

4. For further discussion of the relations of science and gender, see especially Evelyn Fox Keller's *A Feeling for the Organism: The Life and Work of Barbara McClintock;* Hilary

Rose's *Love, Power, and Knowledge: Toward a Feminist Transformation of the Sciences;* and the various essays collected in Evelyn Fox Keller and Helen E. Longino's *Feminism and Science.*

Bibliography

Alonso, Harriet Hyman. 1994. "Mayhem and Moderation: Women Peace Activists during the McCarthy Era." In *Not June Cleaver: Women and Gender in Postwar America, 1945–1960,* ed. Joanne Meyerowitz, 128–50. Philadelphia: Temple University Press.

Freni, Pamela. 2002. *Space for Women: A History of Women with the Right Stuff.* Santa Ana, Cal.: Seven Locks.

Friedan, Betty. 1963. *The Feminine Mystique.* New York: Dell, 1983.

Hartmann, Susan M. 1994. "Women's Employment and the Domestic Ideal in the Early Cold War Years." In *Not June Cleaver: Women and Gender in Postwar America, 1945–1960,* ed. Joanne Meyerowitz, 84–100. Philadelphia: Temple University Press.

James, Edward. 1994. *Science Fiction in the Twentieth Century.* Oxford: Oxford University Press.

Kaledin, Eugenia. 1984. *Mothers and More: American Women in the 1950s.* Boston: Twayne.

Keller, Evelyn Fox. 1983. *A Feeling for the Organism: The Life and Work of Barbara McClintock.* New York and San Francisco: Freeman.

Keller, Evelyn Fox, and Helen E. Longino, eds. 1996. *Feminism and Science.* New York: Oxford University Press.

Kevles, Bettyann Holtzmann. 2003. *Almost Heaven: The Story of Women in Space.* New York: Basic Books.

Larbalestier, Justine. 2002. *The Battle of the Sexes in Science Fiction.* Middletown, Conn.: Wesleyan University Press.

Larbalestier, Justine, and Helen Merrick. 2003. "The Revolting Housewife: Women and Science Fiction in the 1950s." *Paradoxa* 18: 136–47.

May, Elaine Tyler. 1988. *Homeward Bound: American Families in the Cold War.* New York: Basic Books.

Mendlesohn, Farah. 1994. "Gender, Power, and Conflict Resolution: 'Subcommittee' by Zenna Henderson." *Extrapolation* 35, no. 2: 120–29.

Merril, Judith. 1948. "That Only a Mother." Rpt. in *Science Fiction Hall of Fame,* ed. Robert Silverberg, 344–54. New York: Avon, 1970.

———. 1950. *Shadow on the Hearth.* Garden City, N.Y.: Doubleday.

———. 1952. "Daughters of Earth." Rpt. in *Daughters of Earth,* 97–165. New York: Dell, 1968.

———. 1954. "Dead Center." Rpt. in *A Treasury of Great Science Fiction,* ed. Anthony Boucher, 166–86. New York: Doubleday, 1959.

———. 1955. "Project Nursemaid." Rpt. in *Daughters of Earth,* 7–96. New York: Dell, 1968.

———. 1957. "The Lady was a Tramp." Rpt. in *The Best of Judith Merril,* 197–216. New York: Warner Books, 1976.

———. 1971. "What Do You Mean: Science? Fiction?" In *Science Fiction: The Other Side of Realism,* ed. Thomas D. Clarenson, 53–95. Bowling Green: Bowling Green University Popular Press.

Merril, Judith, and Emily Pohl-Weary. 2002. *Better to Have Loved: The Life of Judith Merril.* Toronto: Between the Lines.

Newell, Dianne. 2004. "Judith Merril and Rachel Carson: Reflections on Their 'Potent Fictions' of Science." *Journal of International Women's Studies* 5, no. 4: 31–43.

Newell, Dianne, and Victoria Lamont. 2005a. "House Opera: Frontier Mythology and Subversion of Domestic Discourse in Mid-Twentieth-Century Women's Space Opera." *Foundation: The International Review of Science Fiction* 95 (Autumn): 71–88.

———. 2005b. "Rugged Domesticity: Frontier Mythology in Post-Armageddon Science Fiction by Women." *Science Fiction Studies* 32, no. 3: 423–41.

Nolen, Stephanie. 2002. *Promised the Moon: The Untold History of Women in the Space Race.* New York: Four Walls Eight Windows.

Ogden, Annegret. 1986. *The Great American Housewife: From Helpmeet to Wage Earner, 1776–1986.* Westport, Conn.: Greenwood Press.

Roberts, Robin. 1993. *A New Species: Gender and Science in Science Fiction.* Urbana: University of Illinois Press.

Rose, Hilary. 1994. *Love, Power, and Knowledge: Toward a Feminist Transformation of the Sciences.* Bloomington: Indiana University Press.

Rossiter, Margaret W. 1995. *Women Scientists in America before Affirmative Action, 1940–1972.* Baltimore: Johns Hopkins University Press.

Rupp, Leila J., and Verta Taylor. 1987. *Survival in the Doldrums: The American Women's Rights Movement, 1945 to the 1960s.* New York: Oxford University Press.

Stableford, Brian. 1993a. "Scientists." In *The Encyclopedia of Science Fiction,* ed. John Clute and Peter Nicholls, 1076–77. New York: St. Martin's Press.

———. 1993b. "Space Flight." In *The Encyclopedia of Science Fiction,* ed. John Clute and Peter Nicholls, 1135–36. New York: St. Martin's Press.

Swerdlow, Amy. 1993. *Women Strike for Peace: Traditional Motherhood and Radical Politics in the 1960s.* Chicago and London: University of Chicago Press.

Trachtenberg, Mark. 1990. "American Thinking on Nuclear War." In *Strategic Power: USA/USSR,* ed. Carl G. Jacobsen, 355–69. New York: St. Martin's Press.

Williams, Katharine Broome. 2001. *Improbable Warriors: Women Scientists and the U.S. Navy in World War II.* Annapolis, Md.: Naval Institute Press.

Wosk, Jenny. 2001. *Women and the Machine: Representations from the Spinning Wheel to the Electronic Age.* Baltimore: Johns Hopkins University Press.

Yaszek, Lisa. 2008. *Galactic Suburbia: Recovering Women's Science Fiction.* Columbus: Ohio State University Press.

Race, Robots, and the Law

Wanda Raiford

> But in the meantime we've dumped five hundred thousand tropical
> Robots down on the Argentine pampas to tend the wheat. Tell me,
> please, what do you pay for a loaf of bread? (Karel Capek, *R.U.R.*, 1920)

> Here de robots singin
> Happy as de live-long day
> Hear dem clap dere hands
> O Mercy Lands!
> Tinfolk laugh and play!
> (John Sladek, *Tik-Tok*, 1983)

> Your child is going to be half toaster. How does that make you feel?
> (*Battlestar Galactica*, 2003)

Since the literary robot first appeared in the early twentieth century, critics and fans have been reading the robot story as a cautionary tale or predictor for human relationships with technology—with the result that we now have a broad, nuanced, and evolving body of scholarship around such questions as cyborg culture, the sentience of artificial intelligence, and technicity and other aspects of the posthuman world. But to look at the robot as representing itself, a machine—a future technological creation that may someday demand a shift in thinking—without pausing over the obvious metaphorical racial implications of the man-versus-machine trope reveals a stubborn literal-mindedness that has its roots in our deep discomfort and reluctance as a society to face the fear and shame that permeates our real-world American multicultural experience. Which is to say, are we talking about the literary, fictionalized robot or the literary, fictionalized racial other? In this essay I will examine the theme of robot as African American in Isaac Asimov's robot stories and the television series *Star Trek: The Next Generation* and *Battlestar Galactica*. Reading racially, I will also look at the critical race studies applications for these works where questions of race and law become inextricably intertwined.

In musing on the nature of science fiction in *The Dreams Our Stuff Is Made Of,* Tom Disch opines "Science fiction is one of the few American Industries that has never been transplanted abroad with any success" (1998, 2). Whether is true or only partly true, the reason that science fiction does not translate compellingly for wide foreign audiences may lie in the unique nature of American history and the economic and social foundation of this country in the institution of human bondage. If literature and other forms of popular culture such as television and movies are more than entertainment; if they are also therapy for the collective psyche; if they are also the mechanisms by which myths supporting a view of historical and current reality are propped up and nourished—then science fiction may serve a set of uniquely American needs. While not explicitly reaching the conclusion that science fiction is a balm to the American soul, Disch offers, "It isn't only Oz that is Kansas in disguise; the whole Galactic Imperium is simply the American Dream (or Nightmare) writ large" (2). Specifically, on the question of robots, Disch comes straight to the point: "deep down we don't believe in the humanity of those whose labor we exploit" (9), and robots are the tonic for what ails us; in that, "The most terrible fears are often those we are not allowed to express and which must therefore be displaced to a permitted bogey" (10).

The idea that America's "peculiar institutions" may have more ugly repercussions, other shoes not dropped, has been a subject of consistent preoccupation in the American psyche. But for about several decades since the end of World War II until now, it has not been a subject for open acknowledgment, with some exceptions. In his Oscar-winning film, *Bowling for Columbine,* polemical, leftist filmmaker Michael Moore speculates about why American households are so heavily armed and why there are eleven thousand shooting deaths in the United States each year. If you credit Moore's research, it appears that Americans—while more likely to tote guns than just about everybody else—are not any more heavily armed than Canadians. But unlike our northern neighbors, we Americans are always shooting someone. To answer the question of American domestic aggression, Moore inserted a comical cartoon history lesson into the middle of the film. The segment is notable as a plain expression of white anxiety over black revenge—nearly singular in its lack of obfuscation and equivocation.

The cartoon segment is called "A Brief History of the United States" and is narrated by a talking bullet that explains in happy, energized, hey-dude tones and vocabulary of popular white youth culture that U.S. history is a history of fear. The pilgrims killed the Indians in a panic, and then the British in the fight for independence. And because they were afraid of hard work, the new Americans hatched the "genius idea of slavery," kidnapped Africans, and "forced them work very hard for no money . . . zero dollars, nada, zip," an arrangement that made the United States the richest country in the world. The narrator laments that having all of the money and free help did not calm white people down, because after two hundred years of slavery, in many parts of the South blacks outnumbered whites and sometimes revolted and killed their white "masters." This latest and most enduring fear was one of angry blacks. When slavery was abolished, whites feared wholesale revenge that never came. But nonetheless they armed themselves against the threat, passed laws preventing blacks from owning handguns, and established the Ku Klux Klan, a racist, white-separatist, terrorist group. The year the U.S. government officially recognized the KKK as an illegal terrorist group, 1871, was the same year the National Rifle Association (NRA) was founded. The whites' fear of reprisal was renewed after the civil rights movement of the 1960s. That is when, the film posits, white Americans bought even more guns and barricaded themselves inside their homes and communities, a development that brings us up to date. In sum, it is fear of blacks that gives white America nervous fingers on the trigger. Strangely, although much has been written about the film, very little has been written in critique of this segment.

Both Disch and Moore come near the point, but—by failing to consider out loud the many important ways that slavery was more than exploited labor and hard work—they miss understanding entirely what is at stake here. The famous orator, social critic, and one-time slave Frederick Douglass was born the son of one of the richest men in the state of Maryland. His father and his "owner" were the same person. Douglass's father allowed him to starve, allowed him to go naked and barefoot in the winter as a child, allowed that the flesh be whipped from his back. Slaves were systematically raped, tortured, and worked to death. That these things happened is the first difficult pill, but that parents did these things not only to the racial other but to their own children is the second. This is the thought that causes even the coolest thinker to pause: the story of slavery in America is a family story. It is a story about intimacy, betrayal, and fear of reprisal.

And too there are other practical consequences for nonwhites of this white insecurity that is unique to the American landscape. Writing about the summer of 1933, Ralph Ellison observed unblinkingly in his essay "The Extravagance of Laughter" that whiteness "far from secure in its power . . . thrived on violence and sought endlessly for victims. . . . It didn't care whether its victims were guilty or innocent, for guilt lay not in individual acts of wrongdoing but in nonwhiteness, in Negro-ness" (1995, 636).[1] The enmity, violence, and threat of violence in the institution and legacy of slavery worried Thomas Jefferson. In his 1781 *Notes on the State of Virginia,* he responded to—among a variety of other queries—the question of "the Administration of justice and description of the laws." On the issue of Negroes and the law, Jefferson (1781) proposed that slaves be colonized elsewhere "to such a place as the circumstances of the time should render most proper" and replaced with an equal number of whites from other parts of the world, induced to migrate here. He predicted that to do otherwise would have deadly consequences: "Deep rooted prejudices entertained by the whites; ten thousand recollections, by the blacks, of injuries they have sustained;

new provocations; the real distinctions which nature has made; and many other circumstances, will divide us into parties, and produce convulsions, which will probably never end but in the extermination of the one or the other race" (264). Thus white Americans' fight to control the black subclass was at the inception of the United States as a nation seen and styled by American law and policy shapers as a fight to the death.[2] Ellison argues that the situation for blacks was inescapable: "How escape it when it asserted itself in law, in the layout of towns, the inflections of voices, the nuances of manners, the quality of mercy, justice and charity?" (1995, 636). And although the predicted conflagration has not yet materialized, the dread and fascination with its possibility remains potent. It is this potency that makes the robot-run-amok story a compelling allegory worth telling anew over and over again. For Americans this theme of robots and humans locked in battle to the death is as basic as boy-meets-girl—it is always appealing and will never grow stale, hackneyed or dull.

The unique features of America notwithstanding, some aspects of the master/slave dynamic are essential and universal. As Frantz Fanon and other postcolonial theorists and activists recognized, the struggle between the master and the slave is a struggle for power, partly over who possesses the products of the slave's labor. And so, considering the master/slave relationship in this context, it is not surprising that the use of robots to explore and exorcise the anxiety of the dominant social group over the exploited worker began not in the United States but in 1920s Czechoslovakia.[3] Karel Capek's 1920 play, *R.U.R.*, introduced the word *robot* to the English language; the term comes from the Czech *robota*, meaning heavy labor (Capek 1990, 33), and *robotnik*, meaning peasant or serf.

The play's central human characters are Harry Domain, the general manager for Rossum's Universal Robots, and Helena Glory, the daughter of the president of an unspecified country, who visits the factory on the pretext of wanting a tour. Domain explains the operation to Helena in simple terms: "What sort of worker do you think is best from a practical point of view?" Helena offers, "Perhaps the one who is the most honest and hard working." And Domain corrects her, "No, the cheapest. The one whose needs are the smallest" (1990, 41). Rossum's robots rebel and begin killing humans in a massive revolt. The robots eventually kill all of the humans except a scientist who they leave alive in the hope that he will teach them how to make more robots—only humans hold the secret to life. As smart and seemingly superior as the robots have become, they are still a human creation and as such lack the creative spark of their makers. Capek's robots are, Disch points out, "a nightmare vision of the proletariat seen through middle-class eyes at the historical moment of the first Bolshevik success in Russia" (1998, 8). Disch observes that the "SF device of substituting robots for human workers allowed Capek to express, in the telegraphy of allegory, the moral truth that the industrial system treated human laborers as though they were machines, sowing thereby the seeds of inevitable and just rebellion" (8–9).

Consider that if the robot[4] began as a substitute for a mass of faceless, distant industrialized or agricultural laborers, it has since moved into the Big House. At the time when Asimov wrote his robot stories, middle-class white Americans were long accustomed to the dark other working with jolly or companionable dependability in their homes and lives. The man driving Miss Daisy is an anachronism but no less recognizable and familiar today than then. In Asimov's 1976 *Bicentennial Man,* Andrew Martin is indeed the last of a dying breed. As American society changed so did our robot stand-in. He evolved from the domestic servant to the quirky, likable, smart, but childlike and decidedly different colleague—Commander Data of the 1990s *Star Trek: The Next Generation* television series. And in its latest, post-9/11, new-millennium incarnation the robot is now far less tractable and more intimate, working, sleeping, and reproducing with humans—for example, the Cylon Sharon of the *Battlestar Galactica* (2003) series. These beings are like us but not quite, and it is with great attention and emotion that American consumers of these robot fantasies explore the robots' legitimate grievances and possibility of their humanity and equality.

To make a connection between race and robots does not require a great deal of mental stretching. So why is this subject so under-explored? In his essay "George S. Schuyler and the Fate of Early African-American Science Fiction," Ben Lawson considers the development (or lack thereof) of science fiction as "a progressive and enlightened political and social commentary on race." There are, Lawson observes, several ways to see the matter: "On the one hand, speculative cosmic scale, an orientation to the future, and the presence of unhuman races and robots make the differences between human races seem trivial. On the other hand, much science fiction was racist and preoccupied with race, either overtly or in the guise of confrontations with aliens and Others of various stripes and hues" (1996, 88).

Of the three possibilities Lawson suggests—race diminished by the scale and multiplicity of the science fiction world, literal representations of race (racist and otherwise), and race in disguise—the last possibility, the question of a coded, metaphorical, radicalized science fiction subdiscourse is rarely an amplified theme for critics and scholars. The "reluctance of writers of mainstream Science Fiction to address racism as an issue is reflected in the entry under 'racial conflict' in the most recent edition of *The Encyclopedia of Science Fiction:* '[see] politics'" (Rockwood 276). As discussed in detail below, obvious connections between race and robots are often touched with such glancing, tepid, timorous care as to be irrelevant to any earnest discussion of the issue or, even more often, simply avoided altogether. Speaking in a separate but not unrelated context, German social critic Walter Benjamin observed the powerful reality created "when thinking suddenly stops in a configuration pregnant with tensions" (263). Somehow our thinking about the metaphorical message of popular entertainment such as science fiction skids to a virtual halt when a question of race arises. And it defies debate that the silence created by this avoidance is indeed a silence pregnant with tensions.

With what tools may we hope to pierce the bubble of this accumulated psychic tension? Scholars have described the nexus between the law-and-literature movement and science fiction in general as a "largely unmined mother-lode for expanding our understanding of law through literature." And to the extent that this is true and it is also true, as Oliver Wendell Holmes observed in 1897, that "the law is the witness and external deposit of our moral life. Its history is the history of the moral development of the race" (Holmes 1897, 170)—and by "race" I think he meant here European and American culture—then by what better mechanism than analysis of legal themes in science fiction stories about status and treatment of the technological Other can we energetically engage the moral, social, and psychological implications of the question of race and robots?

There is a large, respected, and growing body of scholarship that supports reading popular cultural texts, such as science fiction movies and novels, not only for their literary or entertainment value but also as an answer to the "need for a method of expression [in pedagogy] adequate to the phenomenon" of oppression and the "cyclical experience" of the oppressed (Bell 1999, 316). This is the main idea behind the legal teaching tool of critical race theory, a way of thinking that looks to the "power of narrative" to affect "listeners precisely by engendering seemingly irreconcilable perceptions of societal attitudes" (347). Critical race studies ask us to consider that "stories . . . perform multiple functions, allowing us to uncover a more layered reality than is immediately apparent . . . a refracted one that the legal system [and indeed all institutions] must confront" (Bell 317, quoting Richard Delgado and Jean Stefanci).

But legal scholars looking at science fiction are not in fact more likely than other critics to look for racial themes. As part of a recent and wholly original Law, Literature and Science Fiction symposium, Jeffrey Nesteruk presented a paper, "A New Narrative for Corporate Law" listing "parallels between Data's predicament [in the *Star Trek: The Next Generation* episode 'Measure of a Man']and the law's treatment of artificial persons such as corporations for the purpose of due process, equal protection and free speech." In "Measure of a Man" Data faces dismantling at the hands of a Federation scientist from another ship and is helpless to protect himself because he is not a person with rights but an object, Federation property. There is a trial where Data's right to self-determination is debated and decided by humans. Ironically Data's participation in the trial and even his presence are of little importance—with the proceedings continuing at one point, without pause or comment, over Data's unconscious, partially disassembled body.

To the experienced reader of law, Data's trial appears as more than anything else as a happy-ending, robot version of the Dred Scott case decided by the U.S. Supreme Court in 1857. Scott, who for most of his life was known as "Sam" (Fehrenbacher 240), was born into slavery, although he tried several times to buy his freedom or run away. When his "master" died, his new "owner," an army surgeon named John Emerson, brought Scott with him from a slave state, Missouri, to the free jurisdictions of Illinois and Wisconsin. Scott continued to work for Emerson and married. When Emerson died in 1843, his wife, Irene Emerson, inherited "ownership" of Scott. What followed then appears to have been a legal experiment conducted by Emerson, her brother John Sanford, and her second husband, Dr. C. C. Chaffee, among others. Emerson refused to free Scott, and then Sanford, Chaffee, and the others worked vigorously to design and realize the prosecution of Scott's case, providing attorneys for him. The group saw the Scotts' case as chance to challenge slavery in the courts. And while they were in earnest, it is doubtful that the stakes were as high for them as for Scott himself. Of interest in considering the case is Don E. Fehrenbacher's exhaustive and authoritative *The Dred Scott Case,* in which he provides a full recitation of the facts informing Blaustein's conclusions, although he declines, for lack of specific proof, to reach the same conclusions himself.

The case made its way up from the lower courts to the U.S. Supreme Court, where the chief justice was Roger B. Taney, a former slave owner himself. The Court held that people of African descent, regardless of whether they were free or slaves, even if they paid taxes and obeyed the law, could never enjoy the rights or status of U.S. citizens—the right to assemble, to vote, the standing to sue in court, and so on—and moreover that legislative attempts to limit the expansion of slavery constituted an illegal violation of citizens' property rights, that is, white people's right to own black people, unmolested by legislative and judicial interference. Writing in 1859, physician J. H. Van Evrie summarized the effect of the Court's decision on the debate about blacks' status: "This confusion is now at an end, and the Supreme Court, in the Dred Scott decision, has defined the relations, and fixed the status of the subordinate race forever—for that decision is in accord with the natural relations of the races, and therefore can never perish. It is based on historical and existing facts, which are indisputable, and it is a necessary, indeed unavoidable inference, from these facts" (Van Evrie iii). Evrie would later write a book, *Negroes and Negro Slavery: The First an Inferior Race: The Latter Its Normal Condition* (1865). It took the thirteenth and fourteenth constitutional amendments to overturn the Dred Scott decision.

But in *Star Trek: The Next Generation,* when the question of the legal and citizenship status of the socially subordinate, visibly different other is revisited—this time with a robot rather than a black man—our American past is rewritten in a bright but distant future, and Data's friends win for him the right to continued existence. Note here that Data, like Scott, cannot act as his own agent in court; instead he must enlist the aid of friends and is at best a helpless spectator to the trial that will determine his right to corporal integrity—the most basic citizenship right. The character Data has been read and analyzed in racial terms, as will be discussed below. But far more often, the issue of race does not arise even as a brief, passing reference on the way to presumably more interesting insights.

For example, being doubtless familiar with the Dred Scott case, Nesteruk yet leaps past the implications and echoes of that case in "Measure of a Man" to build a comparison between Data and a corporation. Nesteruk is not alone in his lack of interest in robots as a metaphor for black Americans, nor is it his or anybody's obligation to amplify and examine that relationship. But there comes a point when the effort to avoid a thing outstrips the work of facing it. And at that point is it appropriate to ask—what is happening here?

Outside of the field of law, critics within the academy also sidestep issues of race in science fiction. In a subtle feat of logical prestidigitation, in his article "Technicity: AI and Cyborg Ethnicity in *The Matrix*" Isiah Lavender simultaneously explores and ignores the implications of race in science fiction. Observing that "Hollywood's popularizing of science fiction can't imagine a world without ethnicity or race, or at least is unable to envision a future without difference," Lavender contends "AI and the cyborg symbolize new ethnicities—technicities." Lavender suggests high stakes and a certain urgency to the technicity question: "We need to understand that science and technology have had a profound impact on ethnicity as humanity transforms into something other, something post-human," and these technological considerations herald "new paradigms of supremacy and discrimination" (439). But I would argue in response that into this ongoing and robust debate about new ethnicities and new paradigms it seems prudent to consider how AI and the cyborg symbolize the old, here-and-now ethnicities, whose interface with the dominant white culture is a enduring, immediate, and actual concern—deeply rooted paradigms of exploitation, fear, and control.

Domestic Other

The robot Andrew Martin is an early model. Not only in the sense that in Asimov's future reality he is an early-model robot, but also because he is an old-fashioned fictional trope, an outdated type—the loyal servant, shuffling and grinning but with a quiet, unassuming dignity. There is no irony in Asimov's presentation of Andrew and his ilk. To understand these old-time robots, we will need to apply some of that old-time religion. Just as no discussion of the Old Testament would be complete with reference to the Ten Commandments, the Three Laws of Robotics are indispensable to an examination of Asimov's construction of the good robot. Introduced by Asimov in his 1942 short story "Runaround," the three laws provide:

1. A robot may not injure a human being or, through inaction, allow a human being to come to harm.

2. A robot must obey orders given it by human beings except where such orders would conflict with the First Law.

3. A robot must protect its own existence as long as such protection does not conflict with the First or Second Law.

And to continue the analogy, the same way Christianity worked to program tractability and a brand of morality in the American slave that was beneficial to the dominant culture, so too do the Three Laws of Robotics operate to preclude robot misbehavior. In their observance and in their breach, the Three Laws guide the reader's fears and expectations of robot/human interaction. But even before these laws were "codified" the issue of robot morality was a matter of great concern. Just as black peril fiction was a staple of pre–World War I science fiction— I would argue not coincidentally—the literary archetype of the evil robot run amok was to become an enduring feature after World War II, helping to define the science fiction landscape from the mid-1930s forward. Perhaps as an antidote to this trend, Asimov wrote a number of robot-as-best-friend-ever stories.

The story "Robbie," published in Asimov's collection *I, Robot,* was written in 1940 and first published in *Super Science Stories* magazine as "Strange Playfellow"—a title concocted by the editors and appropriately characterized as "distasteful" by Asimov. The story is about eight-year-old Gloria, a human child who has formed a peculiar and intense attachment to her robot nanny, Robbie. Robbie, being a robot, has none of the authority or wisdom of other fictional nannies, such as Nanny McPhee, Mary Poppins, or Mr. Belvedere. Rather Robbie and Gloria's relationship is most closely analogous to that of Shirley Temple and Bill "Bojangles" Robinson, who made hugely popular films together in the late 1930s as America's first interracial couple. Bojangles and Robbie are contemporaries, and like Bojanges, Robbie apes and clowns for Gloria, reassuring her, letting her outwit him in childish games, and helping her recognize and define her role as member of the ruling class. In a game of hide and seek, when it appears Robbie may win, "Gloria shrieked in dismay 'Wait, Robbie! That wasn't fair, Robbie! You promised you wouldn't run until I found you.' Her little feet could make no headway at all against Robbie's giant strides. Then, within ten feet of the goal, Robbie's pace slowed suddenly to the merest of crawls, and Gloria, with one final burst of wild speed, dashed pantingly past him to touch the welcome bark of home-tree first" (133–34).

Whereupon Gloria gloats, taunting the happily indulgent Robbie, who responds with "pantomimed running." The two play a game of tag until Robbie pulls Gloria into his arms and holds her safely while "whirling her round, so that for her the world fell away for a moment. . . . Then she was down in the grass again, leaning against Robbie's leg and still holding a hard, metal finger" (134). But the relationship threatens to separate Gloria from the approval and company of her peers, and Gloria's mother schemes to get rid of Robbie so Gloria can take "her part in society" (139). Gloria and Robbie are separated and temporarily reunited when he saves her life.

This story and its human Shirley Temple/Bojangles corollary affirm in the psyche of the white slave master and his descendants the inherent value, charm, and loveableness of the master's children. In many ways this masculinized version of the child-and-loyal-servant trope trumps the mammy myth because it provides an otherwise absent element of danger that is controlled and perhaps neutralized by the sheer beauty of the master's child. It has been more than sixty years since Shirley and Bojangles hopped and hoofed up and down the stairs to the tune of "Dixie" but—as is plain from successful, crowd-pleasing films such as *The Green Mile* and *Man on Fire*—the American appetite for big black men wrapping their big, powerful hands protectively and reverently around the tiny hands of little blonde girls has been wholly undiminished by time.

If "Robbie" presents a popular, comforting, misty, childhood snapshot of the world, then "Bicentennial Man," written in celebration of the U.S. bicentennial in 1976, is the panoramic view of that same reality. Andrew Martin is a dream—white America's dream of the perfect, gentle, patient transformation of a servant into a man. The title character, Andrew Martin, is the perfect robot—special but obedient, questioning but humble; all of his ambitions channeled such that if harm results, it is Andrew who suffers, and when wealth is created, humans are the first and primary beneficiaries. And yet, the story tracks the legal milestones and setbacks for black Americans in the struggle for civil rights. These achievements are not for a class of individuals but for one robot, accidentally constructed to be better than the others. And the price for admission into the family of man—even for this special-case robot—is humiliation, danger, and finally death.

"Bicentennial Man" opens with the Three Laws of Robotics. Andrew and a robot surgeon discuss an elective and patently damaging operation that Andrew wants the surgeon to perform to make him more human. Then the story flashes back to Andrew's beginning as a household servant working for "Sir and Ma'am and Miss and Little Miss"—the Martin family. But the bliss of usefully serving the Martins was not without ambivalence: "His own serial number was NDR—he forgot the numbers. It had been a long time, of course, but if he wanted to remember, he could not forget. He had not wanted to remember" (Asimov 1976, 22). Just as the black American slave gained agency and a sense of his own humanity by changing his slave name "Sam" to Dred Scott, Asimov's robot prefers the human name Andrew to the machine's serial numbers—to the point that he willfully forgets the numbers originally used to hail and identify him as a subordinate, inferior member of society. The children name him "Andrew" because the name is easier for them to say than the serial number. Here again the story echoes the slave-owner tradition of choosing easily pronounceable, "humorous," whimsical, or diminutive names in naming and renaming slaves. But for Andrew, the human name, whatever the source (or maybe because of its source), is preferable to the machine's number.

Andrew, as the story unfolds, becomes an artist. Like Robbie, Asimov's earlier creation, Andrew is a plaything for children. He was designed as a valet, ladies' maid, and butler, but the children discover that he is an amusement whose cooperation can be compelled; they order Andrew to play with them. During one of their afternoons together, Little Miss directs Andrew to carve a pendant for her. Seizing on the value and beauty of Andrew's work, Mr. Martin puts Andrew to work making furniture. It is Little Miss who suggests selling Andrew's creations. The family quickly grows rich from Andrew's work, or "half rich" (524) as Mr. Martin sees it, since Martin has put half in a bank account in Andrew's name. The legality of Andrew owning money is a question resolved by establishing a trust on his behalf as insulation between him and "the hostile world" (525).

Following the true stories of artisan slaves, Andrew the robot carefully saves the money he's earned—his half—to buy his freedom from the Martins. But there are two problems: Martin does not want to free Andrew and takes the request as a personal affront; and decisions regarding the status of this subclass rest outside of the individual preferences of the humans who own robots—the law must be consulted, and a court must recognize or refuse to recognize Andrew's right to exist in society without an owner. In this fictionalized version of the Dred Scott case the stakes are the same; Martin snaps at Andrew, "I can't free you except by doing it legally" (527). Andrew does indeed go to court, and the key to his freedom is his stated preference, "I wish to be free." The court decides, "There is no right to deny freedom to any object with a mind advanced enough to grasp the concept and desire the state" (528). But gaining legal freedom is only the beginning of Andrew's struggles. He continues to fight to enforce his rights; among other setbacks and indignities he is accosted by humans in the street and threatened with dismantling because he insists of wearing clothes and thus aping human modesty. Andrew may (or may not, depending one's reading of the Three Laws of Robotics) be free, but his freedom is a sham as long as he lacks political and social equality. And here Asimov's story reflects a reality for black Americans: "Blacks know now and likely recognized then [during the Civil War era] that the power to withhold political and social equality meant that legal protection too could be suspended or withdrawn whenever the grantors deemed it in their self interest to do so" (Bell 1999, 10).

Professional Other

The parallels between *Star Trek: The Next Generation*'s Commander Data and Asimov's bicentennial man, Andrew Martin, have been explored with great detail and insight by Sue Short in her essay "The Measure of a Man? Asimov's Bicentennial Man, *Star Trek*'s Data, and Being Human." Short explores how the actions of these two fictional beings transcend their mechanical bodies, proving "it is not what we are made of—whether it be 'natural,' organic or otherwise that provides 'human' status, but how we behave. Short notes that as Commander Data fought for his life in the "Measure of a Man" episode, it was the character Guinan, the ship's bartender, portrayed by a black woman, actress Whoopi Goldberg, who suggested the larger racial implications of Data's treatment: "In the history of many worlds there have always been disposable creatures. They do the dirty work. They do the work that no one else wants to do because its too difficult or hazardous. And an army of Data, all disposable . . . you don't have to think about their welfare, you don't have to think about how they feel. Whole generations of disposable people" (216).

Short also observes that it is an Asian woman who helps Andrew Martin when he needs a representative in his final legal hurdle toward self-government. The character Chee Li-hsing offers, "I sympathize with your wish for full human rights. There have been many times in history when segments of the human population fought for full human rights." Short looks at these two examples without reaching any conclusions but nonetheless calls attention to that fact that "a woman of color is [in both instances] . . . responsible for articulating and defending the rights of others in a fictional future" (2003, 216).

But racial themes are not Short's main focus. Her argument about behavior and human status is appealing and well demonstrated but also founded on the unstated precept that some members of society must earn their status as equals to those other members whose status is above inquiry. Short's conclusion about earned status is possible because she touches on but does not engage the idea of race as a metaphor in the robot story.

For the purposes of this essay and reading robots as substitute blacks, at least as interesting as the "Measure of a Man" episode is "Redemption, Part 2"—a *Star Trek: The Next Generation* episode that has received little critical attention but that implicates Data's status as a suspect racial other in undeniable terms. The Enterprise captain, Jean-Luc Picard, assembles a fleet to blockade the enemy Romulans. A personnel shortage in that fleet necessitates that various Enterprise officers must be put in temporary positions on key ships to coordinate the blockade—among others, Riker and La Forge are assigned as temporary captain and first officer of one of the other ships. Learning this, Commander Data, the third most senior officer among the Enterprise crew, asks Picard why he was not given a ship to command. Picard, chagrined and puzzled by his own oversight, gives Data his own command, the USS *Sutherland*. The *Sutherland*'s executive officer immediately expresses concern about Data's command, wondering if a robot can be trusted to safeguard human life. In a workplace drama that many blacks in management have complained of, the executive officer undermines Data's authority, countermands his directives, sneers at Data, and mocks him to the crew. When Data saves the day, defeating the enemy and protecting his ship, he at last wins the respect of the *Sutherland*'s executive officer and crew. But the genesis of the tension when Data initially took command can clearly be read in racial terms; for the men of the *Sutherland,* Data is that creature who is fine as a subordinate but dangerous in leadership, because while he is familiar, he is also inscrutable—operating on a separate values system, without a nor-mal register of emotions. And too, as a former servant, he might well have an axe to grind.

Intimate Other

Robots in the critically acclaimed and commercially successful *Battlestar Galactica* television series come in several distinct varieties—the mute, metallic, featureless centurion soldier whose clawlike hands convert to guns during a fight, the flying raider, and the twelve models of humanoid Cylons whose physiology so resembles that of humans that human scientists and medical experts struggle to devise a test for distinguishing the Cylon body from the human. Each of the twelve models has a near-endless number of identical copies, and the copies share memories, experiences, and emotions. Through science fiction and the robot story, implicit questions raised by history and the perceived lack of individual identity in the racial other are made explicit. The special-case robot (for example, Data and Andrew Martin) makes up the exception in a fictional world where the facelessness and fungible nature of robots is a patent and undebated reality. The *Battlestar Galactica* plot device of an endless army of identical Cylons creates a fictional reality that mirrors the black American experience under the white gaze, where "stereotypes . . . denied blacks individuality and allowed any Negro to be interchangeable with any other. Thus, as far as many whites were concerned, not only were blacks faceless, but this facelessness made the idea of mistaken identity meaningless" (Ellison 1995, 638).

The backstory for the conflict between humans and Cylons is that humans created Cylons. According to the Battlestar Galactica video game, the early Cylons were built as toys and simple novelties but later were employed as laborers performing work that humans found, arduous, dangerous or unpleasant, and still later the Cylons were pressed into service as soldiers. As the titles in the opening moments of the television series explain, "And then came the day when the Cylons decided to kill their masters." There was a long war, followed by a forty-year truce, during which the Cylons, living on their own planet, developed the humanoid models. As the series begins, the Cylons have resumed hostilities, and in their first strike—with the help of an unwitting human collaborator—the Cylons succeed in killing nearly all of humanity. The crew of a military ship, the "battlestar" *Galactica,* and passengers aboard a fleet of assorted civilian vessels survive.

Through the series, thus far, have been themes of enemy-agent sleeper cells, religious zealotry, and ethics and the lack of ethics in warfare and intelligence gathering, among other topics that resonate in the post-9/11 United States. Enemy prisoners are tortured and sexually abused; the human insurgency under occupation by Cylon forces uses suicide bombers; and Cylon acts of murder and genocide are justified in the Cylon view as being the will of the One True God. The most emotional moments in the series come not from the jihadist themes but from sexual and emotional intimacy between members of these two groups. Cylons are the location for more than nervousness about the ideological other; Cylons represent the racial other as well.

But prerequisite to a discussion of intimate relations in the *Battlestar Galactica* universe is an understanding of how semantics reveal and construct a sense of self and other. One of the first things a viewer notices about the series is the frequent employment of the word *frak* in censored substitution for the word *fuck*. The show needs this word; it is an indispensable part of the naturalistic tone the show strives to achieve. The word *fuck* operates in American culture as an intensifier, changing the flavor of the words around it and conveying a depth of feeling. The word is also a clarifier, helping to direct the listener away from a possible miscue, making it harder to misunderstand the subtext beneath the text.

The second word that most characters utter at one time or another is *toaster*. It would be difficult to overstate the effectiveness with which *Battlestar Galactica* harnesses the power, intensity, and menace of the racial epithet—in this case the formerly innocuous word *toaster*. Humans refers to Cylons as "frakking toasters" in the same way and with the identical consequences as racial epithets work in the real world to stigmatize, humiliate, and terrorize the racial other and to distance the speaker from the beingness of the racial other, to strip the other of his/her individual characteristics, to justify and rationalize violence, privilege, and prejudice.

A certain powerful racial epithet in English invariably preceded acts of racial violence. While every utterance of this word is not followed by a lynching, every lynching of a black person in America is preceded and accompanied by this word. The word is indeed the magic incantation that helps make the atrocity thinkable in the perpetrators' minds.[6] The words *frak* and *toaster* make real for the audience the intense enmity the humans feel for the Cylons. At a time when no educated American adult would use a racial epithet—in polite company— *Battlestar Galactica* cathartically opens up the floodgates of repressed hostility. Of course in the allegorical world of robots and humans, it has never been a stain on the hero's character that he stoops and wallows in name-calling. But *Battlestar Galactica* manages a new level of familiarity, discomfort, raw vitriol, and resonance in its use of the term *toaster*—when combined with the word *frak* and when used alone.

What does it mean to be a frakking toaster-lover? Through the use of erotic bonding, *Battlestar Galactica* successfully complicates the questions of self and other. It is not only that seduction is used for treachery and manipulation, but also that the humans and Cylons involved in these intimate vignettes lose sight of their culturally ingrained sense of loyalty, righteousness, and certainty. All of the characters involved in erotic bonding are wild cards, unpredictable even to themselves. In the series, several human men form close sexual and emotional bonds with Cylon women. One of the women, Cylon model Six, visits her lover, Dr. Gaius Baltar, in his thoughts. The audience sees their interaction, but the other characters do not. In the episode "Resistance," during Gaius's conversation with a crew member aboard the *Galactica,* Six pops into Gaius's consciousness and hears this exchange:

Callie: I've known the Chief for years and he's no toaster.
Gauis: He was involved with Lieutenant Valerii, who most certainly is a toaster.

Six, interjects—unseen by Callie—"I don't like that word, it's racist." Six implores Gaius to say something: "tell [Callie] you won't have racial epithets used in your presence." Gaius continues the conversation with Callie, ignoring Six, who then hisses before leaving, "Our child is going to be half toaster. How does that make you feel?" The implications of this statement go beyond colluding with the enemy. Six correctly identifies the anguish, horror, and compromise humans feel when they discover that the person they have been loving is subhuman. The strange breeding combinations continually evoke human atrocities all too familiar to audiences in which there have been none but humans. This kind of reaction is not the reaction of man duped by, for example, a beautiful KGB operative. This is the stock, predictable anger and dismay of a Nazi who finds himself hopelessly and irreconcilably in love with a woman he later learns is a Jew. In *Battlestar Galactica* the character Helo's first reaction to the news that his lover, Sharon, is a Cylon is to shoot her. This mirrors films such as Douglas Sirk's *Imitation of Life* (1959); it is the shame and rage of a once-ardent white boyfriend who, upon finding that the object of his admiration is black girl who has been passing for white, beats her viciously in an alley. This repulsion with Cylons is a nod to the theory of polygeny. Known as the "American school" of anthropology and popular during the nineteenth century, polygeny holds that various races rather than having a single ancestor—whether primate or biblical Adam—"were descended from different ancestors and therefore were distinct species with different physical, intellectual, and emotional capabilities" (Fishkin and Bradley 2005, xi).

Like Gaius and Six, Sharon and Helo are another mixed couple contemplating parenthood. The Cylon Sharon is built like a small, pretty Asian woman. Like all humanoid Cylons, the audience is meant to accept that she feels pain, fear, anguish, and affection—in other words, the full spectrum of human emotion. When Sharon, while pregnant with Helo's child, is being violently raped during an interrogation, Helo and Chief break in and, during the rescue, kill the rapist, who is a fleet officer, and also another crew member. Helo and Chief attempt to defend the accidental killings by explaining that the men killed were in the middle of an act of rape, to which the *Galactica* second-in-command replies, "You can't rape a robot."

For those humans on *Battlestar Galactica* who have formed bonds with Cylons such that it is no longer possible to reconcile their being-ness with the myth of a faceless, alien evil, the issue of basic being rights for Cylons causes friction in their dealings with a system of human law. The human justice system refuses to recognize Cylons—whether as enemy agents during wartime or as members of a racial/mechanical subclass—as having any rights that humans are bound by law to respect. When the crew member Callie publicly shoots and kills Sharon, she receives thirty days in the brig for unauthorized discharge of a weapon.

And while this light punishment echoes the punishment (or lack thereof) of U.S, servicemen who summarily kill unarmed civilians and disarmed combatants in Fallujah, Iraq, and elsewhere, there is too a domestic reality that resonates in these moments of apparent injustice. For much of America's history the sexual violation of a woman of color was not a crime. Indeed our current justice system continues to recognize—or declines to recognize—a person's physical integrity based on his/her status vis-à-vis other "whole" people. A parent may slap his minor child's face with legal impunity; he may not slap his neighbor's face without the specter of an assault and battery charge. The act of slapping one's neighbor is recognized as a crime that offends the dignity and personhood of the neighbor and the peace of the community and is therefore a crime against the state, the investigation and prosecution of which will be paid for by the state. The act of slapping one's minor child is characterized as discipline and will not be investigated or punished in absence of other abuse. To paraphrase George Orwell—some people are more equal than others.

The thread that runs through all of the robot stories listed here and many others like them is the solution to the problem of robot/human enmity. This solution follows a formula that must have an enormous psycho-effective power for audiences and readers or it would not persist, intact and predictable for nearly the last century of American popular culture. There are three parts: at some point the servant robots have been treated reprehensibly by their human masters (this is usually a back-story that characters refer to but which is not shown or discussed in detail); the robots rebel (or are threatened by bad humans) and there is a struggle for survival—either by the robots themselves against all humans or by human champions of a particular robot's rights and value (this is the main part of the story); and in the end, what the humans offer and what the robots really want is not equality but assimilation—the robots want to be partially or wholly human.

The robots do not just want frail, mortal bodies made of skin and meat. They want the human vital spark. What is this spark? Who knows? It is often styled in terms of procreation. The robots want to create life the way humans do, and they need human help to do so. The robot is an object in a world that it perceives as a closed order—a static place, a given reality with fixed dimensions that he must react to and negotiate on its terms. But the human is a subject in a reality that he, the human subject, creates and re-creates at will—the world around him is material that he manipulates and transforms. If you consider that this is an allegory for human relationships, this solution becomes a rationalization that the "haves" use to explain their past crimes and current privileges to themselves and to the "have nots." It is a statement—*you contribute free or undercompensated labor; your sense of degradation will provide my sense of self-worth, and in exchange, I will supply the vital spark,* which may be culture or science or access to God. Through science fiction we face, and refuse to face, uncomfortable truths. These are the stories we tell ourselves about ourselves.

Notes

1. In a thorough treatment of the subject of systemized white violence against blacks, a study published on-line by the Yale-New Haven Teachers Institute and titled "The Negro Holocaust: Lynching and Race Riots in the United States,1880–1950" listed and analyzed a series of historical events, summarizing, "In the last decades of the nineteenth century, the lynching of Black people in the Southern and border states became an institutionalized method used by whites to terrorize Blacks and maintain white supremacy. In the South, during the period 1880 to 1940, there was deep-seated and all-pervading hatred and fear of the Negro which led white mobs to turn to 'lynch law' as a means of social control. Lynchings—open public murders of individuals suspected of crime conceived and carried out more or less spontaneously by a mob—seem to have been an American invention. In *Lynch-Law,* the first scholarly investigation of lynching, written in 1905, author James E. Cutler stated that 'lynching is a criminal practice which is peculiar to the United States.'" The study also noted, "The causes assigned by whites in justification or explanation of lynching Black people include everything from major crimes to minor offenses. In many cases, Blacks were lynched for no reason at all other than race prejudice. . . . The accusations against persons lynched, according to the Tuskegee Institute records for the years 1882 to 1951, were: in 41 per cent for felonious assault, 19.2 per cent for rape, 6.1 per cent for attempted rape, 4.9 per cent for robbery and theft, 1.8 per cent for insult to white persons, and 22.7 per cent for miscellaneous offenses or no offense at all. In the last category are all sorts of trivial 'offenses' such as 'disputing with a white man,' attempting to register to vote, 'unpopularity,' self-defense, testifying against a white man, 'asking a white woman in marriage,' and 'peeping in a window.'" Also explored in detail is the history of race riots in the U.S., the study points out that "in the decade immediately preceding World War I, a pattern of racial violence began to emerge in which white mob assaults were directed against entire Black communities . . . In these race riots, white mobs invaded Black neighborhoods, beat and killed large numbers of Blacks and destroyed Black property. In most instances, Blacks fought back and there were many casualties on both sides, though most of the dead were Black."

2. There are not any robots in King Wallace's 1892 science fiction novel *The Next War: A Prediction.* But the book is nonetheless a template for the now-classic story of renegade robots that enslave or try to exterminate humanity. Wallace tapped the vein of white dread of ex-slaves who, not content to let bygones be bygones, plot a massive violent uprising. In *The Next War* blacks plan to poison all whites on the first day of the twentieth century. Wallace, in the preface, frets that blacks are actually planning the rebellion fictionalized in the novel, claiming that blacks, having been underrepresented in the last census, were greatly outbreeding whites and as a consequence were now able to realize the horrors outlined in the novel, and that "the very day fixed for exterminating the white race, December 31, 1900, that was given in the story of *The Next War,* is the identical date fixed upon by the [actual] conspirators" (Davis 1999, 188–89).

The blacks' poisoning scheme fails—the formula for the poison, extracted under torture from the white scientist, is somehow adulterated so as to be nonlethal—and the frustrated would-be murderers, 30 million of them, flee into the southern mountains and swamplands, where, under siege by the now-united whites, they die of starvation and exposure. Wallace describes the misadventure's toll on blacks as a "continuous and unbroken line of dead infants, none of whom were older than six or seven," crowing, "No extermination could be more complete" (Davis 1999, 116).

But about robots: by making a one-to-one substitution of rebellious robots for rebellious blacks, Wallace's Jim Crow novel is transformed into the classic man-versus-machine, robot-run-amok story that was in fact a staple of early science fiction writing. And while it does not follow that reversing the process—taking a science fiction story and substituting blacks for robots—will consistently yield a Jim Crow story, the results of the substitution will always be compelling, coherently mirroring the emotional and psychological reality of race relations in America.

3. That our story begins here may be ironic or inevitable given the historical and etymological connections between the words *slave* and *Slav.* The origin of the word *Slav* is debatable. But within this debate there is general agreement that the name of the Slavs derives from the Slavic *slovo,* meaning "word," or *slava,* meaning "glory," or from Latin *sclavus,* "slave." According to the Online Etymological Dictionary (www.etymonline.com), the English word *slave,* meaning "person who is the property of another," was originally "Slav," "so called because of the many Slavs sold into slavery by conquering peoples. Applied to devices from 1904, especially those which are controlled by others (cf. slave jib in sailing, similarly of locomotives, flash bulbs, amplifiers)." See also B. Philip Lozinski, "The Name Slav," in *Essays in Russian History: A Collection Dedicated to George Vernadsky,* ed. Alan D. Ferguson and Alfred Levin, 19–32 (Hamden, Conn.: Archon, 1964).

4. The decision to use the word *robot* here to mean android, cyborg, and robot is deliberate, although I understand how the study of this subject of race and artificial life might be complicated in interesting ways by a more scientifically and linguistically precise approach. For example, in his brief description of his work, visual artist Keith Piper considers the name of NASA's six-wheeled Mars expedition robot. NASA designed and programmed this robot to perform "grueling tasks in a hostile and alien environment" and named it Sojourner—doubtless without irony—after the iconic former black American slave, Sojourner Truth (2001, 97). Piper wonders at the implications of the robot as "dutiful servant and tireless worker whose physical strength is programmed to carry out the will of its owners," noting that a "comparison of the body of a robot to the body of the slave generates a complex set of readings" (96).

Comparing the bodies of robots, androids (derived from the Greek *androiedes,* meaning "manlike"), and cyborgs ("a human being with certain physiological processes aided or controlled by mechanical or electronic devices"), Piper opines that robots such as those in Alex Proyas's movie version of Asimov's *I, Robot,* because they are "immediately and visibly marked" as distinct from the dominant, mastering group and are "assigned particular roles within the cultural and economic order" suggest the black slave. The androids such as those found in Ridley Scott's *Blade Runner* are nearly indistinguishable from the human master, having a "concealed mechanical body [that] makes it a metaphor for the other, able to masquerade as a member of the dominant norm." Piper suggests that "the android can thus be seen as activating metaphorical anxieties about such specters as the infiltrator . . . the closet-dwelling sexual other, the 'international jew.'" And finally there are cyborgs, such as "Murphy, the central character in Paul Verhoeven's 1987 movie *Robocop,*" who being "neither one thing nor the other, reenacts the tragic mulatto theme" (2001, 97).

But for the purposes of this essay, it is enough to say *robot* in all instances and leave the full articulation of race and robot heterogeneity for another time. Here, I hope only to rough out broad themes—themes that although not as nuanced as they might be are nonetheless novel in many important aspects.

5. Ellison discussed the use of language alone and as part of a ritual to help "poor or unambitious" southern whites maintain their grip on a white-supremacy status quo and "to ignore the cost and contradictions" of this position. In 1985 Ellison posited that whites, needing to rationalize their condition, employed antiblack stereotypes and epithets "as symbolic substitutes for that primitive blood rite of human sacrifice." About lynching, Ellison explained: "It does not matter if its sacrificial victim is guilty or innocent, because the lynch mob's object is to propitiate its insatiable god of whiteness, that myth figure worshipped as the true source of all things bright and beautiful, by destroying the human attributes of its god's antagonist which they perceive as the power of blackness. . . . The ultimate goal of the lynchers is that of achieving ritual purification through destroying the lynchers' identification with the basic *humanity* of its victims" (1995, 640–41; emphasis in the original). Thus, in robot fiction both the robot epithet and the human destruction of robot bodies in a berserker frenzy of rage serve as a theater where real-world feelings about the racial other may be safely explored within the bounds of legal, social, and political correctness.

Bibliography

Asimov, Isaac. 1940. "Robbie." In *The Complete Robot,* 133–52. Garden City, N.Y.: Doubleday, 1982.

———. 1976. "Bicentennial Man." In *The Complete Robot,* 519–58. Garden City, N.Y.: Doubleday, 1982, 519–558.

Bell, Derrick. "Power of the Narrative" 23 *Legal Studies Forum* (1999): 315.

Benjamin, Walter. 1973. *Illuminations,* trans. Harry Zohn. New York: Schoeken Books.

Bowling for Columbine. 2002. Directed by Michael Moore. DVD, MGM Home Entertainment, 2003.

Butler, Octavia E. 2000. "The Monophobic Response." In *Dark Matter: A Century of Speculative Fiction from the African Diaspora,* ed. Sheree R. Thomas, 415. New York: Warner.

Capek, Karel. *R.U.R.* In *Toward the Radical Center: A Karel Čapek Reader,* 34–109. Highland Park, N.J.: Catbird Press, 1990.

Cartwright, S. A. 1859. *The Dred Scott Decision: Opinion of Chief Justice Tandy, with an Introduction by Dr. J. H. Van Evrie. Also, an Appendix, Containing an Essay on the Natural History of the Prognathous Race of Mankind, Originally Written for the* New York day-book. New York: Van Evrie, Horton.

Davis, Mike. 1999. *Ecology of Fear: Los Angeles and the Imagination of Disaster.* New York: Vintage.

Disch, Thomas. 1998. *The Dreams Our Stuff Is Made Of: How Science Fiction Conquered the World.* New York: Simon and Schuster.

Ellison, Ralph. 1995. *The Collected Essays of Ralph Ellison.* New York: Random House.

Fehrenbacher, Don E. 1978. *The Dred Scott Case: Its Significance in American Law.* Oxford: Oxford University Press.

Fishkin, Shelley Fisher, and David Bradley. 2005. Introduction to Paul Lawrence Dunbar, *The Sport of the Gods and Other Essential Writings.* New York: Modern Library.

Jefferson, Thomas. 1781. *Notes on the State of Virginia.* In *Writings,* ed. Merrill D. Peterson, 123–326. New York: Library of America, 1984.

Gibson, Robert A. N.d. "The Negro Holocaust: Lynching and Race Riots in the United States,1880–1950." Yale–New Haven Teachers Institute. http://www.yale.edu/ynhti/curriculum/ units/1979/2/79.02.04.x.html (accessed November 18, 2007).

Holmes, Oliver Wendell. *The Path of the Law.* 1897. Whitefish, Mont.: Kessinger, 2004

King, Wallace. 1892. *The Next War: A Prediction.* Washington, D.C.: Martyn.

Lavender, Isiah, III. 2004. "Technicity: AI and Cyborg Ethnicity in the Matrix." *Extrapolation* (Winter): 437–58.

Lawson, Ben. 1996. "George S. Schuyler and the Fate of Early African-American Science Fiction." In *Impossibility Fiction: Alternativity, Extrapolation, Speculation,* ed. Derek Littlewood and Peter Stockwell, 87–106. Atlanta: Rodopi.

Piper, Keith. 2001. "Afro-tech and Outer Spaces: Notes on the Mechanoid's Bloodline—Looking at Robots, Androids and Cyborgs." *Art Journal* (Autumn): 90–104.

Rockwood, Bruce L. "Law, Literature and Science Fiction." 23 *Legal Studies Forum* (1999): 267–80.

Short, Sue. 2003. "The Measure of a Man? Asimov's Bicentennial Man, *Star Trek*'s Data, and Being Human." *Extrapolation* 44 (Summer): 209–23.

Sladek, John. 1983. *Tik-Tok.* London: Gollancz.

Van Evrie, John H. *The Dred Scott Decision.* New York, 1860.

PART 2: ON POWER AND THE "NATION"

Of Starship Troopers and Refuseniks

War and Militarism in U.S. Science Fiction, Part 1
(1945–1974: Fordism)

Darko Suvin

> Autopsies are the place in which new lessons about anatomy are learned.
> (Fredric Jameson)

To Begin With: Some Generalities (Notations and Deliminations)

Why bother with science fiction[1] that deals centrally with war and/or militarism? For one thing, because we live in a world increasingly determined by the unholy feedback between politico-economic militarization and war: war as Clausewitz's continuation of politics by other means is giving pride of place to war as the substitute for politics and unacknowledged pillar of the dominant system. For another thing, because science fiction has as its best always been an interesting early warning system carrying understanding otherwise accessible only in specialized ways; and furthermore, even in its middle reaches, science fiction—read in the United States both by schoolboys and air force generals, and by now also by many young women—is often a good indicator of its readers' intimate preoccupations.

My favorite (alas) anecdote at this historical juncture is the following apocryphal one: Shklovsky said to Trotsky, "As a literary critic, I'm not interested in war." Trotsky responded, "But war is interested in you."

Thus, when we intellectuals from the richer areas of the world shy away from understanding the immensely menacing context of our dwindling privileges, the pleasures of reading science fiction may be yoked to cognition.

About Science Fiction

When faced with such complex terms and notions as science fiction, war, and militarism, not accessible by common sense or intuition, one should begin by defining and delimiting each of them. I can do so only partly, for a book would be required for each.

As concerns science fiction, however, I have written several books (*Metamorphoses of Science Fiction* [1979]; *Positions and Presuppositions in Science Fiction* [1988]; *Victorian Science Fiction in the U.K.: The Discourses of Knowledge and Power* [1983]) and subsequent considerations, and must respectfully refer the interested reader to them. I shall only mention that if one holds the definition (as I roughly still do) that science fiction is a literary (etc.) genre *defined by the interaction of estrangement and historical cognition, and whose main formal device is a narrative chronotope and/or agents alternative to the author's empirical world,* then hero fantasy of the Tolkien type and horror fantasy of the Poe-through-Lovecraft-to-Stephen-King type each is another beast, which is here not dealt with (I discuss their ahistorical worlds in "Considering the Sense of 'Fantasy' or 'Fantastic Fiction'" [2000]).

Some Words on War

My definition of war is taken from the article by Pierre Mesnard y Mendez (in which detailed discussions and references can be found): *a coherent sequence of conflicts, involving physical combats between large organized groups of people that include the armed forces of at least one State, which aim to exercise political and economic control over a given territory.* This includes both wars between statelike entities and within one. However, one or more fights or skirmishes, even between groups of people such as Mafia gangs, do not qualify. Though to my mind antagonistic competition regardless of human lives is the heartbeat of capitalism, for the present analytical purposes war does *not* include metaphoric oppositions (for example Hobbes's everyday civic warfare, "where every man is enemy of every man") without the factors mentioned above. The aim of war was originally the forcible expropriation in favor of a given social class (sometimes tribal or ethnic group) of booty, land, and/or labor power from the vanquished. However, in complex ("civilized") class societies war has also always been *ultima ratio regum,* a means to evade inner revolutionary tension by outer conquest, while in a multi-state system other indirect and intermediary (but crucial) aims may be added, such as securing profits, political advantages for coming tensions and conflicts (for example, dominion over sea lanes or oil resources), and the destruction of commodities and people.

Continuous warfare has *never* ceased under capitalism. In fact, "warfare has been . . . central to capitalism and the nation-state system" (Kaldor 1982, 285). Definitions of war differ, but believable estimates put the number killed in twentieth-century wars at 120 million, with much larger numbers of wounded, persecuted, and traumatized. Between 1945 and 1993 at least 160 wars raged with 30 million people killed (see Dal Lago 2005, 16). The frantic search of the US corporate-military class for enemies that might justify further hundreds of billions out of the pockets of taxpayers shows the United States–Soviet Union competition was largely a welcome excuse for "a permanent war economy" (phrase by Charles Wilson of General Electric in 1944; quoted in Lens 1987, 14). We are already within the most terrible hundred years' war in human history. Just as capitalism came about in plunder wars, there is no evidence it could climb out of economic depressions without huge military spending, a war mega-dividend (best examples: the 1930s and the 1990s—see Kalecki 1954; Amin 1997; and Keegan 2004). This was always understood in the workers' and socialist movement: Jean Jaurès phrased it as "capitalism brings war as the cloud brings the tempest." Long before Lenin, who took Russia out of World War I, the socialists' slogan was "war upon war" (see Angenot 2000).

Finally, some words on the paradoxical relationship of war to political economy and production of goods. On the one hand, "A simple definition of a warrior might be a person who survives by taking what others have or have produced" (Love and Shanklin 1984, 183); yet on another, from the inception of the modern state and market, wars have always been "the greatest and the most profitable of investments" (Lefebvre 1997, 175). Since the 1930s the war industry on our planet has been engaged in unprecedentedly enormous production, circulation, and consumption-by-annihilation of commodities. In the 1980s–1990s, official military spending oscillated between 2.5 percent and 5 percent of world GNP, but some estimates place the share of production due to the war industry at four times as much, while the share of research and its financing devoted to military R&D is believed to have surpassed 50 percent worldwide: both are growing rapidly, most notably in major powers such as the United States. Research and procurement for war are *indispensable* for economic and political system stability. A huge part of these trillions goes to the profits of "northern" corporations, and a smaller but appreciable part for the maintenance of practically all the ruling mafias and classes in the world. As Gowan summed it up: "for the US to play the role of guardian and manager of the entire core [of capitalist powers after World War II] required militarizing the American state on a permanent basis. But that in turn looked as if it might help resolve tricky problems of the domestic political economy" (2003b, 15). The war economy palpably marks the divorce between capitalism and civic responsibility for other people and for the planet. But the stakes are even higher: if "the enduring, primary symbiosis between capitalism and war" (Kolko 1994, 474) means that wars are indeed necessary for the survival of this social formation, then the capitalist social formation has truly, as McMurtry (1999) argues, entered a "Cancer Stage."

Material production impinges directly on science fiction that deals with war: either overtly, in a few best cases (some Vonnegut and the borderline science fiction example of Pynchon seem to me untranscended), or as a rule, by excision into the *non dit* that, however, limns what is told in the narration as the ocean limns an island. It is a peculiar instance of Jameson's "effacement of the traces of production" that is a part of the taboo-field of repressing thoughts about a possible role of classes within production as mega-groups with different and often conflicting interests within the same society (1992, 314–15). No doubt, this disregard of production comes naturally to the armed forces, whose task is destructive consumption (clearing the ground for new production and profits), even though they are saturated with the newest devices for faster and larger mass killing lovingly described and extolled in all militarist science fiction from Heinlein on. Such production is simply considered a deus ex machina called "technology" (or today technoscience). This reality of contemporary war machines is not far from the discourse of and on science fiction, which has in the United States since its mass coming-about (that began with Gernsbackian science popularization) been enmeshed with what Joanna Russ has with angry perceptivity seen as "SF and Technology as Mystification" (1995, 26–40) and indeed as the addiction of U.S. capitalism—Russ would say patriarchy, and I'd say both are correct—to the technological fix. The mystification of and addiction to technoscience "has allowed a lot of folks to go through the motions of thought and scholarship without ever touching such unpleasant and disturbing matters as what we all have to do to make a living" (26), Russ observed about academic work: but that would hold in spades for the effacement of who produces and appropriates what under which conditions in the military-industrial complex setting up armed forces in all countries. Such repression and removal of production is then faithfully recorded, without making of it a problem, in the narrative depiction of an only slightly estranged war machine by surface realism in most science fiction under discussion (in better cases, when we're not in thinly veiled fairy tales or westerns).

Some Words on Militarism

The military-industrial establishments of corporate capitalism, primarily in the United States, which produce "life-killing commodities" as the most profitable part of global trade (see McMurtry 1989), are not only the strongest factor of organized international violence, but also possibly the strongest factor enforcing a world cultural revolution for the total colonization of human life-worlds and ecosystems by commodity economy.

As the great U.S. maverick Veblen found more than a century ago: "The direct cultural value of a warlike business policy is unequivocal. It makes for a conservative animus on the part of the populace. During wartime, and within military organization at all times, civil rights are in abeyance. . . . [T]he members of the community [will] . . . learn to think in warlike terms of rank, authority, and subordination, and to grow progressively more patient of encroachments on their civil rights. . . . Warfare, with the stress on subordination and mastery and the insistence on gradations of dignity and honor . . . has always proved an effective school in barbarian methods of thought" (1904, 391–93). The strictly political fallout of militarization is, so far as I can see, only beginning to be properly assessed (but see, beside the classic C. Wright Mills's *The Power Elite,* Burk 1998, Busch 1995, Caplow and Vennesson 2000, Van Creveld 2002, Dal Lago 2003, Herberg-Rothe 2003, Joxe 1991, Klare 2001, Lyon 2001). To maintain its power and profits, the never-ending warfare needs, first, constantly to stress dangerous enemies, with or without a real basis. Second, it needs to efface the divide between peace and war, as well as between external and internal enemies. With the excuse of security, democracy can be suspended at will for all but a minority of the privileged, and citizen armies are jettisoned in favor of professional soldiers and mercenaries (and since the difference between them is supposed to be the presence of a permanent loyalty, that line too has grown ever thinner). If war is a police action, then it does not need democratic debate and approval. A first approximation to the phenomenon of *militarism* may be discussions by Giddens, Mann, and others reviewed by Jabri (1996, 99–103), from which the following conclusions may be drawn: (1) militarist practices (and their legitimation) conceal social contradictions through emphasis on conformity across the social divide; (2) militarism means a proclivity of the rulers to propound military solutions to issues that could be solved by other means, and to organize acceptance of such solutions by lower ranks; (3) in consequence, militarism leads to a sharp rise of intolerance toward dissent and to manipulation of all information channels to preclude other solutions.

Militarization then means a reorganization of society to enforce militarism (see also Leone and Anrig 2003; Berghahn 1981; Mann 1984; and Mills 1959). *Militarization is suspension of central civil liberties and subordination of all aspects of civil society to militarist "security" imperatives even in times of official peace.* Before colonial liberation movements, dictatorships enforced by bayonet and gun muzzle were the rule in all imperial possessions; in the twentieth century they have become more common in nominally independent states than at any time since the rise of the bourgeoisie, marking well its degeneration. This is technically facilitated by the enormous elaboration of armaments, accessible only to large economic systems, and it is underpinned by the spread of both organizational complexity and of the brainwashing industries such as the mass press and media. As a result, "the new balance of forces has eroded rights won in earlier periods. The extraction of surplus value meets less resistance, and capital loses what civilizing effects it might have had" (Schwarz 2003, 32). This explains how we can be returning, as Eco's pioneering essay found, "Towards a New Middle Ages," with huge insecurity palliated by private armies and drugs, with nomads, mystics, and (I'd add) the neo-medieval genre of science fiction.

Thus we have to fall back on some understanding from the more civilized and hopeful time of Enlightenment, and I can today do no better than give you my two favorite citations, which were sent me by friends careless of proper bibliographical sources:

> Anyone can understand that war and conquest without and the
> encroachment of despotism within mutually support each other; that
> money and people are habitually taken at will from a people of slaves
> to bring others beneath the same yoke; and that conversely war furnishes
> a pretext for exactions of money and . . . for keeping large armies

constantly afoot. . . . In a word, anyone can see that aggressive rulers wage war at least as much on their subjects as on their enemies, and that the conquering nation is left no better off than the conquered." (Jean-Jacques Rousseau, *Abstract and Judgment of Saint-Pierre's Project for Perpetual Peace,* 1761)

Of all the enemies to public liberty war is, perhaps, the most to be dreaded because it comprises and develops the germ of every other. War is the parent of armies; from these proceed debts and taxes. And armies, and debts, and taxes are the known instruments for bringing the many under the domination of the few. . . . No nation could preserve its freedom in the midst of continual warfare. (James Madison, 1795)

And we should always remember the great slogans of the Anglo-American dictatorship from *1984,* "War is peace. Ignorance is strength. Freedom is slavery": as Rousseau and Madison—and the whole antimilitarist tradition, from Enlightenment to the early-twentieth-century socialists—knew, war, militarist subjection to an entrenched power clique, and brainwashing are aspects of the same depth process.[2]

Militarism necessarily implies the horizons of war as its justification. Obversely, however, warmongering did not, before modern mass and total societies, necessarily imply militarism—Social Darwinist or Hobbesian warfare sufficed.

Corpus

Having set up a few orienting beacons, how is one to limit the huge corpus of the sprawling science fiction texts dealing with war and/or militarism? The first delimitation is to focus on the last sixty years—in which we today inevitably read premonitions of, and sometimes resistances to, a not only discursive putting into place of never-ending holy warfare in the era of the Bush dynasty. The second delimitation is for me to focus on literary fictions rather than on TV, movies, comics, videos, and computer games (for more variety see the contributions in Suvin 2005)—which may be more important as immediate shapers of people's minds. Indeed, following Jameson's startling analyses, perhaps we ought to talk about architecture or more generally about command of space consubstantial with war and militarization, with its "dialectics of privilege and shelter" (1992, 289) shaping social power, evident for example in long-distance killings.

The third delimitation is to focus on U.S. science fiction, as befits the hugely dominant position of United States–based warfare and military, as well as analyses of either: Gramsci's concepts of hegemony and historical alliance but also of Fordism (which then leads to post-Fordism), as continued in the post-1960s analyses, come immediately to mind as indispensable tools for approaching such a discussion. Finally it is enough to make a few exemplary choices among science fiction narratives in which war (and/or militarism) is either the dominant theme, one of the central foci, or articulated especially well, beyond the cliches current in the author's locus or presenting a take that is not usually found. (Either would be what I consider at least in part a novum.)

These delimitations leave an area for putative large-scale research. From it I shall fail to deal with vast segments. This holds most of all for what has legitimately constituted probably the bulk of both science fiction and science fiction criticism about war from the 1940s to the mid-1970s: *nuclear warfare,* the militarization of society needed for it, the ensuing holocaust, and the probable dark age of breakdown in technoscientific civilization and reversion to Hobbesian warring for survival. True, nuclear warfare is, all experts know, quite possible again in the form of tactical mini-nukes used by U.S.—and possibly Israeli—armed forces under the post-Vietnam doctrine that "our" casualties must be small so as not to upset electoral politics, while casualties of the enemy (whoever may be proclaimed as such) must be as huge as possible in as short a time as possible; and in a few years, nonstate groups may well join this proliferating "club." To my mind, in a somewhat longer perspective nuclear strikes of "normal" (Hiroshima or larger) strength are not at all impossible either: the end of 2004 brought reports of a renewed nuclear arms race between the United States and Russia, and there are simmering conflicts that involve other nuclear powers (Pakistan and India, or Israel and Iran), while the megawar between the United States and China, openly envisaged in the U.S. neocons' plans, looms in a still-longer perspective. Yet this balance of MAD (mutually assured destruction), apt to affect the whole planet, is at the moment—and in, say, the last thirty years— not the focus of either military reality or science fiction written under its goad. If it does reenter the focus, we shall have to rethink matters. In the meantime the concerned reader can be referred to the work of Bruce Franklin, including the 1984 anthology *Countdown to Midnight* he edited, and the Proietti-Suvin bibliography, culled from a much vaster critical literature and readily supplemented, for example, from the overviews adduced there.

One hopes all of this will not be too rigid, so that for example United Kingdom-based writings will lurk in the background to contrast with the United States-based ones, that there will be no ban on mentioning science fiction movies or fiction between Chesney and Heinlein,[3] and so on. Even so, the field remains huge; more than usually, any approach has to acknowledge from the start its premises and its nature as a bet justified by possible cognitive results.

Singularities I: Historical Texts, 1945–1974, An Ambiguous Ascent

> The old order is not yet dead, the new order cannot be born. In the half-light monsters arise. (Antonio Gramsci)

The Two Souls of U.S. Science Fiction

For the purpose of orientation at this uncommonly endangered point of history, I am proposing a hypothesis (homologous to the discussion of intellectuals at the end) that there are two souls or stances within U.S. science fiction. As any attempt at encompassing hundreds of texts in several generations, this digital hypothesis is more simplified than would be a full analogical spread, accounting for the ifs and buts and gray zones, which would, however, need a research institute with the budget of, say, one fiftieth of an atomic submarine. At one extreme is, then, the stance that mass slaughters, with all weapons imaginable and regardless of the military-civilian divide, and a concomitant militarization of society are inevitable for the salvation of the commonwealth and should therefore be envisaged in a spread between sad necessity and cynical glee. Its characteristic seems to be that it refuses even to envisage possible causes making for war and militarization, which would therefore be avoidable by uprooting such causes. At the other extreme is the stance that while dangers and lures of mass warfare and militarization are real and have deep systemic roots, they ought to be resisted in all possible ways because the commonwealth would thereby either not be saved and/or would be corrupted into something not worth saving. It attempts to understand war and militarism by establishing a feedback between them and the social and historical currents inducing them: which then issues either in forebodings of doom or in possible better alternatives. This hypothesis will be picked up in the final section.

The two stances can be more or less overt or hidden; this feature gives no indication either as to aesthetic success, especially in an estranged and allegorical genre, or as to political affiliation (see the discussion of Heinlein's, Dick's, and Le Guin's novels that follows). However, I believe it is much healthier for a culture when splits within it are brought to the surface, where they can be openly discussed with a chance for understanding as a precondition to resolution. And in fact, open polarization coincided with sociopolitically liberatory periods, such as 1940–1950 and 1960–1974 (when the two souls came openly out in the famous double ad in *Galaxy Science Fiction* of June 1968, listing science fiction writers for and against the Vietnam War), whereas social taboos and sometimes penalties against dissent from warmongering and militarism characterize the regressive periods of the 1950s and from the 1980s to the present.

From Twain to Heinlein

The two souls can be followed from the inception of the U.S. writing that eventually constituted itself as the science fiction genre. Bruce Franklin has shown (1988, esp. chap. 3) how in the latter part of the nineteenth century the immense prestige of Edison, among other things the pioneer of technologized warfare and a government consultant, was opposed by the grim forebodings of Mark Twain's *A Connecticut Yankee in King Arthur's Court,* in which the high-technology party is buried beneath the rubble of the final battle together with the vanquished. Twain's "philosophical fable" of progress is in bitter contrast to the genre's usual cheer; its "theory of capitalism and . . . interpretation of the historical process that has brought it into being" (Smith 1964, 39) issues into radical pessimism. As in much foregoing nineteenth-century science fiction, from Mary Shelley through Hawthorne to Jules Verne, the only sustainable novelties are destructive ones (I argue this at length in Suvin 1979, chap. 8).

The dichotomy might be called one between the believers in "Onward and Upward to Conquest by High Technology" and the doubters, from pessimism to alternate vision. Changing what needs to be changed, it obtains again between the two world wars and with especial force after 1945 between the war-exalting science fiction wing of, say, Jenkins ("Murray Leinster"), who picked up the genocide torch from Jack Williamson and Edmond Hamilton, and the much better narratives by refuseniks, from Fredric Brown and Chan Davis to Tenn or Bradbury (see Franklin 1988, chap. 13). Judith Merril's story "That Only a Mother" and her novel *Shadow on the Hearth* bring the cost of an atomic war literally home, as seen there by a woman; Fritz Leiber's "Foxholes of Mars" is a remarkable brief sketch of the coming about of a galactic Hitler out of the rage of warfare; while the refusal of global-scale slaughtering is perhaps most explicit in Theodore Sturgeon's prescient plea in "Thunder and Roses" (1947)—more or less simultaneous with Heinlein's ambiguous early stories about the nuclear menace—that allegiance to survival of mankind is superior to any national allegiance or even to "Western civilization." The U.S. congressional repression of dissent from 1947 on and the ensuing cold war hysteria meant that the balance, especially in the strictly watched movies, shifted in the 1950s either toward the warmongers or toward coded events in the other space-times of the "new maps of hell." Overt antiwar or antimilitarist artifacts emerge again only around 1959: the movies from *On the Beach* and *Fail-Safe* on, culminating in Kubrick's gallows-humor masterpiece *Dr. Strangelove* (1964), and a larger spate of literary fictions beginning with the two 1959 anti-nuclear-war classics, Walter M. Miller Jr.'s *A Canticle for Leibowitz* and Mordecai Roshwald's *Level 7,* and going on to the works of Dick, Disch, Spinrad, and others in the golden science fiction age after 1960.

But despite growing antiwar sentiment, the dominant context of the time was one of frantic cold war rearmament, with multiple overkill capacities geared to titanic corporate profits (hundreds of billions of dollars, it seems) and to economic, and therefore political, stability of the status quo. Within it Robert A. Heinlein's *Starship Troopers* (1959) became the ancestral text of U.S. science fiction militarism, that inflected and to an important degree shaped the implicit and explicit debate ever since. I propose to read it here as a paradigm of U.S. classical republicanism gone sour in the age of imperial expansion. The tenets of classical republicanism have been summarized by Carroll Smith-Rosenberg, writing about the 1790s: "Courage, self-reliance, and love of liberty were essential for the practice of civic virtue: modernity—commerce, consumerism, and fashionable life—would corrupt aspiring republicans and plunge their republics into tyranny (Pocock, ch. 13). Yet it was the modernizing world of commerce, consumerism, and fashion that America's urban classes seemed bent on embracing . . ." (2004, 1331).[4]

Heinlein's story begins, alternating slam-bang action and didactic explanations, as a routine "drop" combat mission of a space marines group on a supposed enemy planet seen through our first-person protagonist, but then immediately flashes back to a conflict between him and his rich businessman father, which leads him to a snap decision to enlist. So much for "commerce, consumerism, and fashionable life," about which we practically hear no more in this unsubtle though powerful black-and-white paean to combat life. (The father too joins the armed forces after the war has been brought home to the Terran Federation and eventually becomes the officer son's trusty top sergeant, in a variant of the Heinlein topos where the hero becomes his own father.) Through all kinds of self-doubts and tests from boot camp to officer career, our protagonist grows in the courage and self-reliance needed to protect liberty. The armed forces, spearheaded by the space marines or "starship troopers" (this is either Heinlein's deliberately provocative reference to Hitler's storm troopers or a Freudian slip), are the only full citizens entitled to vote in the brave new world of the future that came about after the collapse of the soft United States and a third world war. They are the only locus of belonging and spiritual safety for "a real man" (8/89), far superior to the tolerated market or money economy. The central conflict of the novel is therefore only apparently between humans and aliens—the bugs, extrapolated from the Chinese in the Korean War (11/121), who remain faceless pulp monsters of the anthill-communist stripe, fit only for slaughter:[5] the conflict is between consumerist-cum-commercial individualism, the "producing-consuming animal," and "man" (12/36) in the proper hierarchical collective of the military. Even that opposition is after a few exemplary incidents backgrounded in favor of an accomplished agitprop exaltation—the education of our hero into military values and honor, where there can be only emulation between good and better (startlingly parallel to the utopian communist ideal, for example in Yefremov or the early Strugatskis, or Le Guin's anarcho-communist "to be whole is to be part").

The rule by veterans' election is supposed to ensure "plac[ing] the welfare of the group ahead of personal advantage" (12/145). I find this a worthy goal, especially when faced with the postmodern rulers and their cynical greed, but the premise is flawed, as in every static meritocracy: veterans' groups turn as a rule after one or two decades into crusty defenders of the status quo from the last-but-one war. Thus the most welcome, and to my mind right-on stress on the responsibilities of citizenship, on the citizen as the active subject constituting the state or nation, results only in his (literal) cyborgization into a fighting machine. Such cosmic (or any earlier) politics are for Heinlein impelled by naked Social Darwinism or imperial *Lebensraum:* "Man is . . . a wild animal"; "All wars arise from population pressure" (12/147). As Franklin points out, though among the generic ancestors of this novel "are those World War 2 movies idealizing the military lives," yet "this is not about a mass conscript army called up in a war to defend democracy" (1980, 103). Heinlein's twist on the subgenre (and his response to antimilitarism in novels such as Norman Mailer's *The Naked and the Dead,* and later those by James Jones, Heller, and Pynchon)—is a remarkably prescient forecast of a supertechnological elite army (in his fiction: spaceships plus powered suits), which was to be more and more implemented after Vietnam. In our historical world, while mouthing slogans from republican virtue (which by now only sound Orwellian), the military fused with the "producing-consuming animal" as its executive arm: to enforce capitalism by martial law where market law is not enough. This test by history might explain why Heinlein's last phase is constituted by long-winded escapist novels about immortality, sex, and transferral to younger bodies.

Nonetheless, Heinlein remains (to my mind) overall the most significant science fiction writer of the 1939–1961 epoch, and certainly one of its two or three most popular and influential ones. His stance in *Starship Troopers* is one of his many ambiguous and radical but also radically divergent thought experiments from 1939 on. Franklin calls the story "Logic of Empire" (1941), in which a monopolist Earth company is based on interplanetary slave labor, Heinlein's "most radically 'left' story" (1980, 12), and in other stories of the somewhat makeshift "Future History" cycle it leads, not without clear echoes from Twain, London, and Orwell, to a replay of the 1776 War of Independence, evoked also in the interplanetary war of *The Moon Is a Harsh Mistress* (1965–66). Yet already his early novel *Sixth Column* was a racist paean to the "white" resistance movement against the Pan-Asian horde, a cross between the Red and the Yellow Peril, and its invasion theme was reused in the heyday of the anticommunist hysteria as *The Puppet Masters* (1951), with the enemy allegorized as hive-mind alien slugs who take over U.S. bodies and minds, so that civil liberties must be suspended in favor of loyalty checks. Most important for our purpose are two stories: "Solution Unsatisfactory" (1941), the first U.S. reflection on world politics under atomic weaponry, where in the choice between a global U.S. empire and a Wellsian elite world dictatorship, the New Deal–era Heinlein surprisingly opts for the latter; and "The Long Watch" (1949), where a military putsch to take over the world by means of atomic bombs is foiled by the sacrifice of a democratic junior officer. The tension between the two souls of republican virtue vs. elitist (or indeed quasi-Calvinistically predestined) meritocracy will remain a constant feature of all good Heinlein narrations—his best novels, those that opt for inclusiveness and liberation, being to my mind some juveniles and *Double Star.*

Heinlein's strength is a hard-nosed preoccupation with precisely observed power and authority, and indeed with the place of the father (see Aldiss 1973, 129). "In a style which exuded assurance and savvy, [his] early writing blended slang, folk aphorism, technical jargon, clever understatement, apparent casualness, a concentration on people rather than gadgets, and a sense that the world described was real. . . . His characters were competent men of action, equally at home with their fists and a slide-rule and actively involved in the processes and procedures (political, legal, military, industrial, etc.) which make the world turn." However, such strength is achieved at a high cost. As of this novel, Heinlein's "dialogue and action become traps in which any opposing versions of reality were hamstrung by the author's aggrieved partiality" (both quotes from Pringle and Clute 1995). And Franklin remarks how in Heinlein "Earth is beautiful only when viewed from a distance, where people and their civilization cannot be seen" (1980, 10). I would expand these two observations to the thesis that the major strength and flaw in *Starship Troopers* is world-excision.[6] Not only is there no civilian life in it, but any and all "animality" outside of fighting, that is, the normal bodily life of producing and consuming, is also excised. It may be secondary and, in view of Heinlein's writing from *Stranger in a Strange Land* (1961) on, mostly due to publishers' taboos that there is no sex or erotics in *Starship Troopers* (except for warm but rigidly asexual affection between battle comrades). However, the excision not only of love but of the female element as such is surely of central significance. True, women too can join the armed forces, but they are confined to the, as it were, housing sphere of the Space Navy and largely unseen, though their protection is the biological reason for war (11/125); and the debilitating female influence of the hero's mom is expunged by having her die in an atomic bombing. Thus the novel's overall position rests on presuppositions announced at length in well-placed interspersed lectures but tenable only if rebuttals from reality are disallowed.

Now of course no book can contain even a small part of the author's world, but what type of relationships you systematically exclude will define everything else you can say. In particular, Heinlein's concept of historical time horizons seems a strange medley of political and technological progress with catastrophes (up to *Stranger,* when miraculous interventions abolish linear time). He wants unbridled individual affirmation, but here it can only be achieved in military super-corporativism, which separates itself into an elite super-class. His strength is dealing with catastrophes; but they can only confirm the ups and downs of the linear and quantified time of technological bourgeois civilization. If elite progress is interrupted, the only alternative to slavery of the corporative monopolist or hive-mind type is the anticolonial revolt of 1776 (repressing the fact that after it slavery and extermination of Native Americans went merrily on). No glimpse of a radical difference, the earmark of dissenting science fiction from London through Sheckley or Le Guin to the alternative histories of K. S. Robinson, is conceivable here, not to speak of the cosmic brotherhood Benjamin glimpsed in Scheerbart's *Lesabéndio,* where technological construction liberates peaceful creativity and, in the vein of Fourier, Percy Shelley, or the later Stapledon, fuses people with stars (Benjamin 1980, 630–32 and 618–20; see also his "On the Concept of History," 691–703).

The Intertextual Tradition of U.S. Science Fiction: Edisonade in Lieu of History
How is that huge blind spot, the tunnel vision allowing all-around vision and precise orientation only in wholesale planetary destruction of the *Starship Troopers* kind, to be explained? It is not an individual failing, for Heinlein was a well-informed, intelligent, and original mind within a given framework, and moreover more consistent than most other science fiction writers of his heyday. At the beginning of the twentieth century, Henry James explained it in *The American Scene* as the U.S. society's orientation to quantification within not-to-be-doubted limits of technological progress, a "perpetual increase of every-thing" that will have to be paid for at some point in some way. His shrewd diagnosis, not unworthy of Tocqueville, is that the United States attempts to supply through money what can only be achieved by historical experience—which includes suffering and, one supposes, qualitative wisdom instead of merely quantitative increase.[7] Linear time within quantified history, even when or perhaps especially when the cash nexus is repressed, necessarily leads within Heinlein's relentless logic ("Logic of Empire" is only one example of his superb titling, among the best in science fiction) to the same maneuver early Christian-ity had to resort to in order to explain why that divine descent did not triumph: the invention of the potent and ever-ready enemy. Progress is the supreme good; in technology it has potent weapons at hand; and yet only an elite minority is committed to it, and it is constantly faced with the majority's indifference, back-sliding, even outright defeats. For the supreme good to win, therefore, the enemy has to be rooted out by wholesale indiscriminate slaughter, as in the biblical parable of the tares.

From Edgar Allan Poe on (the argument may be found in my *Metamor-phoses of Science Fiction*), a characteristic of U.S. science fiction has been its infantile, gosh-wow, slam-bang aspect: sensationalism and sentimentality. Now *infantile* is not necessarily a cuss-word; it may have connotations of *fresh, naive,* or *innocent,* and it is at any rate more promising than *senile*—a symmetrical cuss-word often flung at Europe by U.S. visitors, Twainian innocents abroad, horrified by its postfeudal up-front hierarchies (as his Yankee was by Arthurian slavery and Whitman by Shakespeare). One could argue that the most mature U.S. science fiction was shaped by the awful suspicion, first adumbrated in the gothic admixture up to Poe and Hawthorne and then more precisely in Twain's *Connecticut Yankee,* that U.S. innocence is withering into a premature senility. The most powerful "new maps of hell," culminating beyond the 1950s in the horror transmutations of Disch and Dick and then in Gibson's cyberpunk and Spinrad, belong to this hermeneutics of suspicion. Nonetheless, up to the mid-1960s science fiction remained almost exclusively "white boy's fiction" (see Russ 1995, 79), and even after the notable influx of first-rate (and then of some not-so-first-rate) women writers and therefore of women readers in the last forty years, this aspect of science fiction is probably dominant to this day. Now the main activities of white boys in the United States, before computers and video games, traditionally were sports (including gun sports) and science. Sports fans do not read much fiction, which leaves us with science.

At this point I would have to write a whole essay devoted to the cooption of modern science by capitalist profit and in particular the war industry: at least half of all U.S. scientists and engineers work today for military priorities (see Gray 1997 and Tirman 1984), so that by and large, technoscience is part of a war machine and should be studied as such, with around 80 percent of U.S. federal obligations for research and development already in 1986 devoted to defense (Latour 1997, 171–72). This breeds arrogant scientism of inevitable progress, defined by Le Guin as "technological edge mistaken for moral superiority" (1994, 4) and by Wallerstein as a pivot of "[that] truth which reflected the power realities and economic imperatives of historical capitalism" (1996, 89). But I can only refer the interested reader to further discussions and the bibliographies in my essays "What May the 20th Century Amount To" and "Science Fiction Parables of Mutation and Cloning as/and Cognition" and concentrate on John Clute's argument in the brilliant article "Edisonade" (from which I take all quotes in these two paragraphs, but see also Franklin 1988, 54–77). *Edisonades* are his most apt neologism for science fiction narrations focused on "a young US male inventor hero who uses his ingenuity to extricate himself from tight spots and who, by so doing, saves himself from defeat and corruption and his friends and nation from foreign oppressors"; typically, what he invents is a war weapon plus a means of transport. The name derives from the public image of Edison as potential inventor of fearsome and decisive war gadgets, enthusiastically fostered by him to the edge of charlatanism (and possibly satirized both as Sir Boss in Twain and the Wizard of Oz in Frank Baum) and taken up by much popular early science fiction from dime novels to Serviss's *Edison's Conquest of Mars*—serialized in a newspaper as counterblast to Wells's pessimism in *War of the Worlds*—in which "Thomas Alva heads to Mars, where he commits triumphant genocide before granting the survivors colonial status." The edisonade was then given a huge boost by space opera, beginning with "E. E. Smith's *Skylark* sequence [which gave it] the Galaxy as playground and estate, provided an infinity of frontiers to penetrate, territories to stumble into and to claim, and entrepreneurial empires to build in all innocence. The Smithian edisonade remains central to entertainment space opera to this day." Especially destructive were between the world wars the space operas by Williamson and by Hamilton, who was known as the "world wrecker" and did not disdain genocide, either.

Clute's thesis is that when Heinlein and his followers began to make explicit ideological claims for the new Edisons, "innocence fled. . . . Once looked at with an eye to the main chance, it turns sour, self-serving and entrepreneurial, and we find ourselves in the land of some Hard-SF writers of the 1980s, whose protagonists are never poor, and never lose, and never give; nor would it perhaps be

stretching the term too far to find in the ruthless protagonists of much survival-
ist fiction ghostly and solipsistic echoes of the edisonades of a more innocent
time—when the hero did not have to understand the consequences of his triumphs." My reading of history is different here: I think innocence had fled by
the time of Mark Twain, as he well knew.[8] At any rate, Heinlein's novel fuses the
1930s everyday realism with a collectivized edisonade: the inventing both of the
capsule and of military education in civics has been done by the space marines,
and all that remains for our protagonist is to fill the slot assigned him and
thereby save his soul and humanity.

The Golden Age, 1960–74

The period of around 1960–74, the true and untranscended golden age of
Anglophone—U.S. and U.K.—science fiction, is in relation to our theme marked
by two factors: first, its main preoccupation was not war and militarism (Vietnam began to be fictionally digested only toward the end) but envisaging alternate, usually better, possibilities of human relationships; second, to the extent
that there were some remarkable instances of concern, they were predominantly
antiwar and antimilitaristic.

It could be claimed with some justification that a good part of the most
important writings obliquely reflected the Cold War, nuclear arms race, growing
involvement in and protest against large-scale slaughterings such as the war in
Vietnam, and the growing militarization and alienation this produced in individuals and the fabric of civil society (as again today). This may be most clearly
seen in such masterpieces as Ballard's *The Atrocity Exhibition* (1970; U.S. title,
Love and Napalm: Export USA), pulped in its first printing by the U.S. publisher,
or the "Daily Life in Late Roman Empire" strand of Disch's *334* (1972). However,
I shall keep to overt articulations. What one may call the "Heinlein wing" is built
on the axiom of a peculiar "species racism," namely that humans are individuals and therefore elite specimens better fitted to win wars and occupy the galaxy.
Bad enough by itself, it is as a rule a fig-leaf analogy for "Western" capitalist individualism. This is the common denominator of Poul Anderson (of his "Dominic
Flandry" Cold War series begun in the 1950s and of his novel *The Star Fox*, with
considerable antipacifist acrimony but more subtlety than usual in this wing
and an attempt at lyricism) and of appreciations of military virtues in two long-
running and somewhat repetitive series begun at that time, Saberhagen's "Berserker" episodes of galactic conflict with ruthless killing machines, and Gordon
Dickson's more complex variant of an elite super-individual. In the early novels
of his "Dorsai" series a seemingly quite junior officer, who is however a strategic
genius plus physical near-superman, comes to save all humanity in the galaxy
and gets the beautiful, recalcitrant girl to boot. At the time of the Vietnam War
he turned in *Soldier, Ask Not* (serialized in 1964, published in book form in
1967) toward an examination of the protagonist's own destructive impulses,
albeit seen only as a matter of individual ethics. As ambiguous as this last novel

was Frank Herbert's far more sprawling and heterogeneous *Dune* (1965), astutely set in a desert environment with a vital scarce resource (extrapolated from Arabia), which posits a universe of unceasing cynical warfare for that resource as well as a galactic jihad and a political messiah, and was a progenitor not only of much too long continuation but also a trendsetting harbinger of many uncouth blends of all-out war and New Age religiousness intermixed with secret societies, parapsychology, and occult sciences.

The antiwar and sometimes antimilitarist writings of this period were richer, more coherent, and more innovative. Among the most important were one novel each by Disch and Spinrad, some novels by Dick, some black stories by Malzberg, and of course the Tralfamadore strand of Vonnegut's novels, most impressively reactualizing war in his *Slaughterhouse-5*. This current was also reflected in Delany's first trilogy, with vivid episodes of urban conflict, and Harrison's rather inconsequential farce *Bill, the Galactic Hero*. One of the most civically committed writers to the Campaign for Nuclear Disarmament was John Brunner, who wrote the song for its U.K. protest marches. When in the late 1960s his prolific space operas started being reprinted, so that he could for four or five years write one instead of three titles per year, he entered upon his plateau period, with more than a nod to John Dos Passos's radicalism from the 1930s. In Brunner's *The Jagged Orbit* the cool, cubist technique works well, depicting a near-future United States that has segregated blacks in enclaves, gone in for universal, private high-tech armament, and become a huge armed madhouse, splitting emotion and reason.

A similar tack is taken by Thomas M. Disch's *Camp Concentration*, which recounts its "conchie" (conscientious objector) narrator Sacchetti's experiences in a near-future, Dantesque U.S. concentration camp for criminals but also for political prisoners who are, during a nuclear, bacteriological, and chemical war in Malaysia, used by the military as guinea pigs. They come to realize that their experimental super-syphilis treatment heightens human intelligence, making them usable as the military's think tank, but causes death within months. The inmates perform Mann's *Doctor Faustus* as well as a rejuvenation put-on; Sacchetti writes a comedy about Auschwitz; and there is a deus ex machina salvation at the end out of pulp science fiction rather than Dante. Except for this awkward close, which shows it is stronger in describing phenomena than finding causes or suggesting ways out, it is a fine piece of work, baroquely convincing in its erudition, poetry, and manic-depressive tone, all of them well motivated by the nature of the experiment. The underlying preparations of the U.S. government for such camps are also the subject—possibly with some echoes from Disch—of the splendid movie by Peter Watkins, *Punishment Park*.

Norman Spinrad's grotesque cannibalistic dictatorship and a guerrilla revolution coming from the jungle within a second-rate melodrama in *The Men in the Jungle* was already a far-off echo of Cuba or Vietnam. But in the remarkable *Iron Dream* he achieved the startlingly revealing though uncomfortable blend of the whole U.S. Superman science fiction trend—from dime-novels and edisonades through comics to the less civic-minded followers of Heinlein's militarism—with the racist ideology and practice of Adolf Hitler, who is in this parallel world the author of the novel (called by him *Lord of the Swastika* and detailing the racial leader's exultant genocides). This is a two-way street: it points out how Hitler as an immigrant writer in the prewar United States would have fitted exceedingly well into its space-opera brand of science fiction, akin to and indeed crossing over into sword-and-sorcery heroic fantasy of the Conan or even Tolkien type, with various stinking subspecies taking the place of Jews and Soviets, and the Nietzschean blond beast hero as the fanatic and always successful defender of racial purity against post-nuclear-war mutations. In other words, the fictional plots of such science fiction–cum-fantasy were homologous with the insane super-Wagnerian plots of the actual Third Reich. Obversely Nazi reality was shaped by kitsch out of the occult sciences of Aryan cosmology, allied to capitalist high technology. However, the tongue-in-cheek impersonation of frenzied genetic superiority and phallic slaughter (no sex and in fact no women are to be found in Hitler's novel) within kitsch stylistic exaltations may be too good, or at least too sophisticated for the typical U.S. science fiction reader, kept blissfully ignorant of that practice by the mass media and educational system following NATO's reuse of Nazis in the Cold War. Thus the translation in West Germany ran afoul of the anti-racial-hatred norms and was cited in judgment there.

Parallels between the increasingly militaristic and repressive United States and Nazi Germany, in a "thick" insight into the affinities between politics borne by the same classes of big speculators and small shopkeepers, were frequent in Philip K. Dick. He had already in mid-1950s broached the horrors of cold war paranoia, militarism, mass hysteria organized by politicians, and encroaching government surveillance (for example in "Breakfast at Twilight," "War Veteran," and "Second Variety"), and this was to remain a constant theme of his. *The Man in the High Castle* is the first high point of such dystopianism, situated in a world where the United States has been divided among the occupying Nazis and Japanese, where Africa has been wiped out, and a world war between the victors is brewing. The novel's startling insights into Fascist psychology, as well as those into political manipulation by totally pervasive media enclosing people into an underworld in *The Penultimate Truth* (as already in one of his best short stories, "Foster, You Are Dead"), are offset, with typical Dickian erraticism, by the blithe use of a postholocaust setting as a Berkeley pastoral in *Dr. Bloodmoney.* The political edge is further blunted by Dick's shift in the latter 1960s from epistemology to ontology, where reality is not veiled by big business and big state but truly changing, yet it returns with a vengeance in *A Scanner Darkly* (for longer arguments see my *Positions and Presuppositions in Science Fiction* and "Goodbye and Hello: Differentiating within the Later P. K. Dick"). In Dick's dystopian clear-sightedness, while the rich live offstage "in their fortified huge apartment complexes" (chap. 2), the little people are trapped in a total surveillance state where hologram cameras are routinely used, every pay phone is tapped, supersonic tight beams are used for police assassinations, and the closest friends inform on each other. What I have called Dick's "second plateau" extends to *Radio Free Albemuth,* written in 1976, in which a police state is instituted by a president—a blend of Nixon, McCarthy, and Hitler—who came to power in 1969 (a coded science fiction way of saying that in the author's space-time freedom has already been lost). The protagonist's resistance group is shot, and he survives, condemned to perpetual hard labor, with an opening toward brighter perspectives reestablished in the novel's coda.

The Furthest Reaches and Culminations: Refusing the Linear Time

The two undoubted culminations of the Vietnam War and civil-protest-era science fiction are works by Le Guin and Haldeman. They are rather dissimilar, but could be seen as two different strategies for refusing or distorting linear time that knows only progress or regress—"development" or "underdevelopment" in our politicians' pernicious lingo.

Joe Haldeman's *Forever War* is divided into four sections, "Private," Sergeant," "Lieutenant," and "Major Mandella," strung out along dozens and then hundreds of years from 1977 to 3143 courtesy of Einsteinian time-dilation in combat jumps between galaxies, so that the initial reluctant draftee, aged twenty-two, physiologically grows only to middle age; in a brief coda he has married a conveniently surviving army love and expects a first baby on an edenic planet. Except for the plentiful drugs and sex in the gender-integrated army (though galactic humanity becomes homosexual, which stabilizes population) and some updated technology, the "Private Mandella" part is flat-out Heinlein-style training and combat stuff—the soldiers are in "fighting suits," each of which is "an investment of over a million dollars" (1.7/25)—with two major differences: no civic propaganda and no villainous enemies. The Taurans' blood is red, for "all God's children got hemoglobin," and the close-range combat is mass slaughter, ironically called "just following orders," as in Vietnam (1.6/61, 64), so that our hero has internal debates between his whilom peace-loving self and the "killing machine" programming (2.3/78). In other words, "Vietnam and Sinai" (2.6/97), marijuana, Woodstock, and the antiwar movement have intervened between Heinlein and Haldeman. Earth grows into a fairly horrendous centralized bureaucracy, the initial conscription law gets extended in every section, and understanding with civilians, who are born one or many generations later, is practically impossible, which means that for the needed elite soldiers this becomes a "forever war" and the army is the only home left. But after eleven centuries it is discovered the Human-Tauran war was a misunderstanding and a political necessity: "Earth's economy needed a war, and this one was ideal. It gave a nice hole to throw buckets of money into, but would unify humanity . . ." (4.8/215). The Taurans are still collectivist clones, but the humans also turn to cloning, and peace is established.

Ursula K. Le Guin's *The Word for World Is Forest* is what would in Europe be called a red-green novel, one that combines acute sensitivity to ecology not only with the condemnation of a colonial war but also with a depth search for its psychological equivalents in the macho mentality that wants to tame and rape the environment as well as women. The short novel is structured by the allegorical juxtaposition of the three focal characters, the memorable and even frightening "conquistador" career officer Davidson (one of the most acid psychological studies of that type, to be put beside similar portraits by Mailer or Heller), the liberal scientist Lyubov, who puts humanity above Terra, and the native leader Selver, easily the most complex of them. The human-derived planet natives, who live in independent forest clans, practice a feedback between "dream time" or the Men's Tongue, in which insight and psychological stability is achieved, and "world time" or the Women's Tongue of empirical reality, in which community and ecological stability is achieved; the double time-horizon also provides an effective "war-barrier" (3/61), although it may make for a static balance with the environment. This feedback and balance they find notably lacking in the psychically poisoned Terran "yumens." Selver becomes one of the rare finders of major collective insight or—non-theistic—"god," a translator between the dream time and world time, when he learns war killing from the invaders, defeating them at their game (shades of Ho Chi Minh—but realistically, there's also a final hint of the price to be paid).

The novel is wrought in the combination of textural artistry—for example the color scheme rooted in vegetation, conveying the delicate beauty of the New Tahiti planet and its ruthless destruction, or the different and complementary stances within both invaders and natives—with effective composition of cinematic cross-cutting, which is rare not only in science fiction and marks Le Guin's position at the crossroads of poetry, classical realism (gender and power psychology), and science fiction. If there is a cognitive limit to it, it may be found in Le Guin's constant aversion toward political economy, so that devastated Terra's desperate need for logging the newfound forest planet is easily defeated by insight. But the strong yet delicate delving into the psychic roots of war and domination is what allows such a limit, and the ultimate causal horizons (which are to my mind a blend of politico-economical pressures and type psychology), to be envisaged. It is, so far as I can see, the furthest cognitive outpost to which science fiction has yet arrived insofar as the war and militarism theme is concerned.

Le Guin's "plateau period" in science fiction (omitting her work outside this genre) might be found in the magnificent 1969–75 interval going from *Left Hand of Darkness* to *The Dispossessed,* but extending to my mind also to the story "New Atlantis" (see also my *Positions and Presuppositions in Science Fiction*). Its yin and yang are two interlocking narrations. The old Atlantis, rushing to its doom, is a near-future "corporative State," a well-identified U.S. variant of admass fascism as an all-embracing bureaucracy, with gulag-style Rehabilitation

Camps and Federal Hospitals for dissidents. When an illegal group invents direct energy conversion that undercuts the need for any centralized state, it is repressed. This militarist repression strand in "New Atlantis" subsumes the real-life experiences and warnings of the US Left and of English-language science fiction: the latter goes from early Heinlein or Chan Davis's "To Still the Drums" and other science fiction of the 1940s, before congressional repression clamped down, up to Leo Szilard's—the atom bomb's initiator's—"My Trial as a War Criminal," and writings or movies discussed already, such as those by Disch and Dick (see Franklin 2000). The emerging Atlantis is a shimmering undersea creation, just coming into being and self-understanding, a beautiful new genesis of perception and cognition—of time, space, number, and universe—by means of fitful lights. True, the new genesis is an impure one, its light-bearing creatures are still in the process of swallowing each other, "tiny monsters burning with bright hunger, who brought us back to life." Yet the hungry lights define a city being re-created and raised by immense geological pressures (Le Guin's substitute for history), whose emergence seems at hand. I read this symbolistic New Atlantis, narrated in a collective "we" form, as a new life-form and creation of beauty and cognition symmetrically opposed to the perishing U.S. republic, narrated in the "I" form. Nonetheless, at the end the new creation is also a "yearning music" that asks the U.S. one "Where have you gone?"—a lament for our lost potentialities, for all the lives gone under in our wars, diseases, and starvation.

A comparison of Le Guin's and Haldeman's final horizons might be of use here. Haldeman's novel is generally thought to be an anti–*Starship Troopers* text, and in many ways this is correct. But though war is no longer either just or necessary, it is for our focus group unavoidable (except for the happy ending). And if it is a cynical political ploy-cum-error, no deeper possible causes—such as long-term system stability—are envisaged or thinkable. The U.S. space-age soldier has become disillusioned and left Heinlein's, or any other, civic salvationism behind, but he (now updated to s/he) is still an obedient cog in the senseless killing machine, drugged by pills and misinformation. In Le Guin's novel, the well-meaning liberal commits the error of playing along with the colonizing army while sending in his correct reports, not knowing they would never get into the public sphere unless a native uprising happened. But a new allegorical type appears in it and in the story "New Atlantis" (poetically and facelessly in the latter): a radical, other insurgent who refuses the rules of the powerful but vulnerable oppressor. This is entirely lacking in Haldeman, where the best our hero can hope for is an oasis outside of time and space, not too dissimilar from the Tralfamadorian zoo of Vonnegut's where Billy Pilgrim ends up with the buxom Hollywood star. In brief, Haldeman is against war but ambiguous about the military (see on this Jones 2005); Le Guin is both against war and against militarism.

And yet there is one factor these works by Le Guin and Haldeman have in common: *the refusal of a linear time of progress,* where knowledge is divorced from responsibility and the furthest frontiers of technological triumphs mean more killing: senseless wars abroad and bureaucratic-cum- militarist oppression at home. This may be the common denominator of the anti-slaughter stance: in Disch's "Daily Life in the Late Roman Empire" sequence from *334* it is evident in the interferences between that age and the time of a near-future Manhattan; in Spinrad, in the all-pervasive tonal contradiction between "his" and "Hitler's" novel that involves also opposed time horizons; in Dick's *A Scanner Darkly*, in the technologically and politically enforced total split between the two personalities and the two names for the same person of the police spy versus the spied upon; and it would not be difficult to go on about Vonnegut's "chronoclasm" (time-break) or the other texts. In Le Guin's novel, genocide and rape of women and planet end with the arrival of the ansible, ushering in the "simulsequential," post-Einsteinian time; in Haldeman's, the Forever War is more ambiguously ended by renouncing heterosexual procreation that biologically bore linear human time. For Le Guin opposition to the murderous "progress" is possible (however ambiguous its consequences might be); for Haldeman, only evasion. While my preference is clearly for the first, both options come from and return into our real world time, and might in different circumstances be acceptable solutions for different persons.

Some Keystones for a Conclusion

> Clear thinking [about war prevention] becomes more at a premium than ever, plus the need for the clear-thinkers to write it all down and teach it to others. False models of thinking about each other, of human beings who are in conflict, are as deadly as false maps to the tactician. . . . The anti-war thought that I've encountered in both fiction and real life has been so far too much addicted to feelings and not enough to convincing analysis. (Lois Bujold)

"Gentlemen, you are mad!"
It is instructive to confront a famous outcry from 1946 to a publisher's blurb in 2004 as a measure of what has (and has not) happened at the center of our subject matter, and what defines its horizons.

In 1946, after the atomic bombs on Japan and sensing the winds of the arms race, the great utopologist Lewis Mumford published an article in the prestigious *Saturday Review of Literature* with the title "Gentlemen, You Are mad!" The "gentlemen" are the U.S. leaders who lead toward global suicide while convinced they are rationally working for peace and security. The madmen, however, are also all of us, letting them get away with it, indeed "view[ing] the madness of our leaders as if it expressed traditional wisdom and common sense" (qtd. in Franklin 1988, 4).

At the end of 2004, a lost manuscript of Heinlein's first utopian science fiction novel was published. From dozens of his science fiction titles, he was on its front page identified as "author of *Starship Troopers.*" This is the hour chiming on the readers' clock. It is also the hour on the television and movie watchers' clock: innumerable movies and series about the military are resulting as I write (February 2005) in the introduction of a TV "Military Channel," with an unbelievably propagandistic U.S. program, with a Military History Channel in preview. The Pentagon budget for 2006 is foreseen to top 600 billion dollars, which together with the ongoing costs of the Afghan and Iraqi wars will amount to around 30 percent of the U.S. federal budget. As an offshoot, the MIT has opened in 2002 an institute for military nanotechnology with huge grants by the Defense Department.

What a fall have the United States and the world reality and imagination experienced between those two dates! Mumford's mad leaders spend hundreds of millions of dollars to get reelected so they can spend hundreds of billions in war procurements to enrich a few corporations, and maybe 1–2 percent of the U.S. population, and fight a holy war for power and profits. The rest of us allow this. It is a variant of what Marcuse analyzed for the U.S. Secret Service as the Nazi "rationalizing of the irrational (in which the latter retains its power but flows into the process of rationalization), the continuous to-and-fro between mythology and technology" (1998, 49).

All of this is being done in a feedback system of writers and readers, our colleagues, our classmates (if I may coin a term). How? How come?

On Intellectuals and Death

Who writes to whom, and therefore about what and how, in the U.S. science fiction since 1945—or since 1959, the year of Heinlein's *Starship Troopers?* It is a nice and unresolved point just which classes are science fiction written for, in the commercial and ideological sense. At any rate it circulates almost entirely within some middle classes of the white North. I have expounded on this at length (in "Utopianism from Orientation to Agency: What Are We Intellectuals under Post-Fordism to Do?"; see also "Novum Is as Novum Does" and "What May the 20th Century Amount To," with large bibliographies), and will repeat here that in my opinion the addresser and addressee subjects are various contending fractions of what may be loosely called intellectuals—including what I'd call "apprentice intellectuals," the famous science fiction core consisting of thirteen-to-twenty-five-year-old readers, no longer overwhelmingly male. Intellectuals are people who work mainly with images, concepts, or narrations and "produce, distribute and preserve distinct forms of consciousness" (Mills 1953, 142; see also Noble 1977 and Ehrenreich and Ehrenreich 1979). Hobsbawm calculates that two-thirds of the GNP in the societies of the capitalist North are now derived from their labor, though their proportion within the population is much inferior, globally perhaps 10–15 percent. Politically they (we) may be roughly divided into servants of the capitalist bureaucratic state, servants of large corporations, self-proclaimed "apolitical" or "aesthetic" free-floaters, and radicals taking the plebeian side. The funds for this whole congeries of "cadre" classes—"administrators, technicians, scientists, educators. . . . have been drawn from the global surplus" of exploitation: none of us has clean hands. The Fordist welfare-and-warfare state saw the culmination of the "cut" from this surplus we "middle" 10–15 percent were getting; and "the shouts of triumph of this 'middle' sector over the reduction of their gap with the upper one per cent have masked the realities of the growing gap between them and the other [85–90 percent]" (Wallerstein 1996, 83–84, 104–5).

I have to jump here to a general conclusion supported not only by this article but also its continuation into the 1975–2001 period (see the first footnote). As different from this Fordist dispensation of roughly 1915–73, the new collectivism, while mouthing individualist slogans stripped of state worship, needs fully other-directed intellectuals, whom postmodernist cynicism has dispensed from alibis. Post-Fordism has had quite some success in making intellectual "services" more marketable, a simulacrum of profit-making. This began in sciences and engineering: industrial production since around the 1880s is the story of how "the capitalist, having expropriated the worker's property, gradually expropriated his technical knowledge as well" (Lasch, foreword to Noble 1977; see also Noble). In the age of world wars this sucks in law, medicine, and "soft-science" consulting in the swarms of "professional experts." Now those who buck the market better get themselves to a nunnery. The class aggression by big corporations against the immediate producers, corporeal and intellectual, means that Jack London's dystopian division of workers under the Iron Heel into a minority of indispensable mercenaries and a mass of downtrodden proletarians (updated by Piercy in *He, She and It*) has a good chance of being realized.

On the one hand, as Marx famously chided, "the bourgeoisie has stripped of its halo every occupation hitherto honoured and looked up to with reverent awe. It has turned the physician, the lawyer, the priest, the poet, the scientist, into its paid wage-labourers" (Marx 1972, 338). On the other hand, the constitution of intellectuals into professions is impossible without a measure of autonomy: of corporative self-government and, most important, control over one's work. No doubt, this constitution was enabled by the fact that the salaried are "the assistants of authority" (Mills 1953, 74), but no authority can abide without their assistance. We share to an exasperated degree the tug-of-war between wage labor and self-determination. Even the poorest intellectual participates in privilege through her "educational capital"; even the richest manager or commanding general may not be able to rid himself of the uncomfortable itch of thinking. In a living contradiction, we are essential to the *encadrement* and policing of workers, but we are ourselves workers. Excogitating ever new ways to sell our expertise as "services" in producing and enforcing marketing images of happiness and safety, we decisively contribute to the decline of people's self-determination and non-professionalized expertise. We are essential to the production of new knowledge and ideology, but we are totally kept out of establishing the framework into which, and mostly kept from directing the uses to which, the production and the producers are put. We cannot function without a good deal of self-government in our classes or artifacts, but we do not control the strategic decisions about universities, research, or dissemination of artifacts. The marginalized and pauperized humanists and teachers—increasingly adjunct policemen keeping the kids off the streets—are disproportionately constituted by women and non-"whites," a sure index of subalternity.

Already before World War II, Siegfried Kracauer—an important student of culture beyond his famous analysis of the pre-Nazi horror movies—gave us two keys we can use to understand the depth processes shaping the mainstream of "military science fiction" (and a series of analogous manifestations in U.S. culture) in our post-Fordist existential squeeze. First, he observed most middle-class professionals, including students and intellectuals, live in personal isolation and a lack of sense, where belief is merely conceptual and the main danger is the *horror vacui*. From these vacuities, sects and mysticisms both religious and lay draw their appeal (106–12). In a second essay, discussing the U.S. illustrated magazines (such as *Life*), he concluded they were one of the most powerful weapons for "locking out understanding": "In them, the spectators see a world, the perception of which is hindered by what they see" (34). He attributed the success of their images to the spectators' fear of thinking about death (I found the same of Disneyland, in "Utopianism from Orientation to Agency"). While we might today, after further experience, broaden the causal system behind his phenomena, the dangerous denial of reality would remain. Even Kracauer's observation that in such magazines the way to banish death was the multiplication of a certain kind of image remains valid. In psychological terms what we are talking about here is whether, when, how, and how much intellectuals engage in death-lust, while pretending to ignore death.

To illuminate this we have to posit a spectrum of roles and stances between the poles of what Foucault calls "the 'universal' intellectual" of the Voltaire-to-Zola tradition (usually a writer hurling his political "J'accuse" at the injustices of huge apparatuses and other ruling class privileges) and "the 'specific' intellectual." The latter is the expert that emerged as dominant in the Manhattan Project's atomic scientists and other physicists and has continued down to today's molecular biologists and security theoreticians, whose high prestige—pay and status—is due to the meshing of technoscientific knowledge with "the economic and strategic domain" (Foucault 1980, 122–23). Such a polarization, while allowing for gray zones in between, is indispensable to any value judgment in matters of such gravity as the survival of millions, perhaps billions, of people under war, and of all of us under militarization. A condition of proper usage for this heuristic tool in our context is that it has to be checked by feedback from any particular text, while taking into account that the most interesting texts are not those of the outright Social Darwinist warmongers of Pournelle's type but those Jameson would nominate for ambivalent political confusion.

For to understand intellectual production—not only in arts, even in mathematics—I believe the no-doubt useful sociopolitical definitions of intellectuals, from Mills and Foucault to Bourdieu's revealing description as "a dominated fraction of the dominant class" (1990, 319ff.; see also his "The Field of Cultural Production" and Guillory 1994, 118ff.), are insufficient. We also need an axiological definition, which to my mind would be something on the order of: "people who interpret the past and ongoing flow of cultural production as articulations of a beauty that keeps alive the necessity of justice." This feeds back into approaching science fiction, as defined at the beginning of this essay: for I agree with Keats and Scarry that beauty is potentially cognitive.

Notes

1. The full version of this essay appeared first in the Italian annual *Fictions: Studi sill/a narrativitá* no. 3 (2004). This version represents less than two thirds of that essay with the same title, whose continuation, dealing with 1975–2001 and some conclusions to be drawn from the whole, will appear in a forthcoming issue of *Extrapolation*. I am very grateful to *Fictions* general editor Alba Graziano; to John Clute for sending me some secondary materials, and to him, Alex Fambrini, Jeriy Määttä, Salvatore Proietti, Alcena Rogan, Johannes Rüster, and other friends who discussed with me some aspects of this article. Opinions and mistakes are mine.

This essay is for John and Judith Clute—30 years of memories of Camden Town.

Utopia is used without a capital letter unless it refers to More's country and title. Notably, instead of *America, U.S.* or *United States* is used whenever that country and not the whole double continent is meant; furthermore—following complaints from Mexico through Grenada, Panama, and Nicaragua to Colombia, Bolivia, and Chile about the semantics of the Monroe Doctrine—*U.S.,* or a form such as *U.S.-based,* is used as adjective instead of *American* wherever possible, since I did not have the courage to adopt the German usage of *US-American.* Citations are, of course, left as found.

Given the many science fiction reprints, citations to a title will be by chapter.

2. Cf. to begin with Leone-Anrig, and for the extraordinary actuality of Orwell's political analysis in the age of Neocon Never-Ending Warfare, Catani's competent sketch of war in science fiction. The U.S. Commission on National Security reported in 1999 (before the attack on the Twin Towers) that since the end of the Cold War, the United States has "embarked upon nearly four dozen military interventions . . . as opposed to only 16 during the entire period 61 the Cold War" (in Cowan, "Instruments" 152).

3. The pivot role of H. G. Wells, from the wars of classes in *The Time Machine* and *When the Sleeper Wakes* through the reverse imperialist *War of the Worlds* to the World War of *War in the Air* will alas be slighted; I hope to be forgiven, the readier as I devoted two chapters to it in *Metamorphoses.*

4. There is of course a whole small library of works on this theme, from which I list only the Pocock referred to in the quotation.

5. The bestialization of enemies owes nothing to the rise of communism, rather, one could say, that (as we have experienced since 1989) the latter was a godsend to fill a pre-established necessity of the system. For one example, see George Washington's quite normal reference to "both [the Savage and the Wolf being beasts of prey though they differ in shape" (quoted in Smith-Rosenberg 1326): one could paraphrase Voltaire to the effect "Should Communism (or today, Terrorism) not exist, we would have had to invent it."

6. I take the cue for this term from Jameson's "World Reduction" essay, which speaks about Le Guin and her differing methods, but does mention a "surgical excision of empirical reality" (223).

7. My take on *The American Scene* was sparked by Prof. Giles Gunn's lecture "The Moral Relevance of America's Greatest Travel Book in an Age of Terror," at the University of Salerno, Dipart. di Studi Iinguistici e letterari, October 2004, from which I also take the quote; the interpretation and inferences are mine. An important element for this withering of time-horizons into a two-dimensional arrow is the successful clamp-down on the immense discontent by working classes, surfacing from the millions of Thoreau's "lives of quite desperation" into protest movements from populism to socialism and unions, that was well represented in U.S. estranged fiction by names such as Twain, Donnelly, Baum, or London, and in its New Deal phase is clearly coresponsible for the rise of mass science fiction and refracted in it.

8. I wish to record here my debt to *The Grolier Multimedia Encyclopedia of Science Fiction* (CD-ROM, 1995), edited by John Clute, and especially his own entries on various writers and aspects, though I might here and there—as in this case—disagree. On rereading my essay, I have spotted a few places where his turns of phrase have seeped into my own, because I could not better them. My dedication to John and his artist-wife Judith by no means implies their responsibility for any opinions in this article.

Bibliography

Science Fiction Narrations
Works are listed chronologically by year of first publication; the edition is given only where text passages are cited.

1889	Mark Twain, *A Connecticut Yankee in King Arthur's Court.*
1898	H. G. Wells, *War of the Worlds.*
	Garrett Serviss, *Edison's Conquest of Mars.*
1907	Jack London, *The Iron Heel.*
1912–43	Edgar Rice Burroughs, Barsoom (Mars) series of novels.
1913	Paul Scheerbart, *Lesabéndio.*
1928–35	E. E. Smith, Skylark series (with a coda in 1966).
1941	Robert A. Heinlein, "Logic of Empire."
1944	Fredric Brown, "Arena."
1946	Chandler Davis, "To Still the Drums."
	Will F. Jenkins, *The Murder of the U.S.A.*
1947	Theodore Sturgeon, "Thunder and Roses."
1949	Robert A. Heinlein, "The Long Watch."
	George Orwell, *Nineteen Eighty-Four.*
	Leo Szilard, "My Trial as a War Criminal" (see also his collection of science fiction stories *The Voice of the Dolphins,* 1961).
1950	Judith Merril, *Shadow on the Hearth.*
1951	Robert A. Heinlein, *The Puppet Masters.*
	Robert Wise (dir.), *The Day the Earth Stood Still* (movie).
1951 ff.	Poul Anderson, Dominic Flandry series of stories and novels (ongoing with intervals for almost three decades).
1952	Fritz Leiber, "The Foxholes of Mars"; "The Moon Is Green."
1955	Jerry Sohl, *Point Ultimate.*
1959	Helen Clarkson, *The Last Day.*

Robert A. Heinlein, *Starship Troopers*. New York: Signet-NAL, 1961.

Stanley Kramer (dir.), *On the Beach* (movie).

Walter M. Miller Jr., *A Canticle for Leibowitz*.

Mordecai Roshwald Mordecai. *Level 7.*

1959ff.	Gordon R. Dickson, Dorsai series.
1962	Philip K. Dick, *The Man in the High Castle.*
1964	Philip K. Dick, *The Penultimate Truth.*
	Robert A. Heinlein, *Farnham Freehold.*
	Stanley Kubrick (dir.), *Dr. Strangelove (movie).*
	Sidney Lumet (dir.), *Fail-Safe* (movie).
	Cordwainer Smith, "The Crime and the Glory of Commander Suzdal."
1965	Poul Anderson, *The Star Fox.*
	Philip K. Dick, *Dr. Bloodmoney.*
	Harry Harrison, *Bill, the Galactic Hero.*
1966	Robert A. Heinlein, *The Moon Is a Harsh Mistress.*
	Peter Watkins (dir.), *The War Game* (movie).
1966–69	Gene Roddenberry (exec. prod.), *Star Trek* (television series). Followed by six movie spinoffs (1979ff.) and four sequel television series (1987ff.).
1967	Thomas M. Disch, *Camp Concentration.*
	[Leonard C. Lewin?], *Report from Iron Mountain on the Possibility and Desirability of Peace.*
1967–73	Larry Niven, *The Protector.*
1968	K. M. O'Donnell [pseud. of Barry N. Malzberg], "Final War."
1963–69	Samuel R. Delany, The Fall of the Towers trilogy.
1969	John Brunner, *The Jagged Orbit.*
	Kurt Vonnegut Jr. *Slaughterhouse-5.*
1971	Peter Watkins (dir.), *Punishment Park (movie).*
1972	Thomas M. Disch, *334.*
	Ursula K. Le Guin, *The Word for World Is Forest.* New York: Berkley, 1976.
	Norman Spinrad, *The Iron Dream.*
1972–74	*Joe Haldeman, The Forever War.* New York: Ballantine, 1976.
1973	George A. Romero (dir.), *The Crazies* (movie).
1975	Ursula K. Le Guin, "The New Atlantis."
	Joanna Russ, *The Female Man.*

Secondary Literature Cited

About war, see much more in Mesnard y Mendez 2002; to the items he indicated, I have added here Burk, Caplow-Vennesson, van Creveld, Dal Lago (both titles), Gray, Herberg-Rothe, Joxe, Kalecki, Keegan, Klare, Lyon, and Mills Power. I am somewhat apologetic about the number of self-references, a ploy to prevent this long essay from being much longer.

Aldiss, Brian W. 1973. *Billion Year Spree.* London: Weidenfeld and Nicolson.

Amin, Samir. 1997. *Capitalism in the Age of Globalization.* London: Zed.

Angenot, Marc. 2000. *L'antimilitarisme: Idéologie et utopie.* Montreal: CIADEST.

Benjamin, Walter. 1980. *Gesammelte Schriften.* Frankfurt: Suhrkamp.

Berghahn, V. R. 1981. *Militarism: The History of an International Debate 1861–1979.* Leamington Spa, U.K.: Berg.

Bourdieu, Pierre. 1983. "The Field of Cultural Production." *Poetics* 12: 311–56.

———. 1990. *In Other Words,* trans. M. Anderson. Stanford: Stanford University Press.

Burk, James, ed. 1998. *The Adaptive Military.* New Brunswick, N.J.: Transaction.

Busch, Heiner. 1995. *Grenzenlose Polizei? Neue Grenzen und polizeiliche Zusammenarbeit in Europa.* Münster: Westfalisches Dampfboot.

Caplow, Theodore, and Pascal Vennesson. 2000. *Sociologie militaire: Armée, guerre et paix.* Paris: Colin.

Catani, Vittorio. 2004. "Su pei mondi a guerreggiar." In *Vengo solo se parlate di Ufi,* 232–50. Milan: Delosbooks.

Clute, John. 1996. "Edisonade." In *The Multimedia Encyclopedia of Science Fiction,* ed. John Clute and Peter Nicholls. CD-ROM. Danbury, Conn.: Grolier.

Dal Lago, Alessandro. 2003. *Polizia globale: Guerra e conflitti dopo l'11 settembre.* Verona: Ombre corte.

———. 2005. "La guerra-mondo." *Conflitti globali,* no. 1: 11–31.

Eco, Umberto. 1985. "Towards a New Middle Ages." In *In Signs,* ed. Marshall Blonsky, 488–504. Baltimore: Johns Hopkins University Press.

Ehrenreich, Barbara, and John Ehrenreich. 1979. "The Professional-Managerial Class." In *Between Labor and Capital,* ed. Pat Walker. Boston: South End.

Foucault, Michel. 1980. *Power/ Knowledge: Selected Interviews and Other Writings, 1972– 1977,* ed. Colin Gordon, trans. Colin Gordon et al. New York: Pantheon.

Franklin, H. Bruce. 1980. *Robert A. Heinlein: America as Science Fiction.* New York: Oxford University Press.

———. 1988. *War Stars: The Superweapon and the American Imagination.* New York: Oxford University Press.

———. 2000. *Vietnam and Other American Fantasies.* Amherst: University of Massachusetts Press.

Gowan, Peter. 2003a. "Instruments of Empire." *New Left Review,* no. 21: 147–53.

———. 2003b. "US: UN." *New Left Review,* no. 24: 5–28.

Gray, Chris Hables. 1997. *Postmodern War.* New York: Guilford.

Guillory, John. 1994. "Literary Critics as Intellectuals." In *Rethinking Class,* ed. Wai-Chee Dimock and Michael T. Gilmore, 107–49. New York: Columbia University Press.

Herberg-Rothe, Andreas. 2003. *Der Krieg.* Frankfurt: Campus Verlag.

Hobsbawm, Eric. 1994. *The Age of Extremes.* New York: Pantheon.

Jabri, Vivienne. 1996. *Discourses on Violence.* Manchester: Manchester University Press.

James, Henry. 1903. *The American Scene,* ed. Leon Edel. Bloomington: Indiana University Press, 1968.

Jameson, Fredric. 1975. "World Reduction in Le Guin." *Science-Fiction Studies,* no. 7: 221–30.

———. 1991. *Postmodernism, or, The Cultural Logic of Late Capitalism.* Durham, N.C.: Duke University Press.

Jones, Gwyneth. "Wild Hearts in Uniform." In Suvin 2005, 69–81.

Joxe, Alain. 1991. *Voyage aux sources de la guerre.* Paris: PUF.

Kaldor, Mary. 1982. "Capitalism and Warfare." In *Exterminism and Cold War,* ed. *New Left Review,* 261–87. London: NLB.

Kalecki, Michal. 1954. *Theory of Economic Dynamics.* New York: Monthly Review Press.

Keegan, John. 2004. *The Iraq War.* New York: Knopf.

Klare, Michael T. 2001. *Resource Wars.* New York: Metropolitan.

Kolko, Gabriel. 1994. *Century of War.* New York: New Press.

Kracauer, Siegfried. 1977. *Das Ornament der Masse.* Frankfurt: Suhrkamp.

Latour, Bruno. 1997. *Science in Action.* Cambridge, Mass.: Harvard University Press.

Lefebvre, Henri. 1997. *The Production of Space,* trans. Donald Nicholson-Smith. Oxford: Blackwell, 1997.

Le Guin, Ursula K. 1994. Introduction to *A Fisherman of the Inland Sea.* New York: Harper Collins.

Lens, Sidney. 1987. *Permanent War.* New York: Schocken.

Leone, Richard C., and Greg Anrig Jr., eds. 2003. *The War on Our Freedoms: Civil Liberties in an Age of Terrorism.* New York: BBS PublicAffairs.

Love, Barbara, and Elizabeth Shanklin. 1984. "The Answer Is Matriarchy." In *Mothering,* ed. Joyce Treblicot, 275–83. Totowa, N.J.: Rowman and Allanheld.

Lyon, David. 2001. *Surveillance Society: Monitoring Everyday Life.* Buckingham: Open University.

Marcuse, Herbert. 1998. *Feindanalysen.* Lüneburg: zu Klampen.

Marx, Karl. 1972. "Manifesto of the Communist Party." In *The Marx-Engels Reader,* ed. Robert C. Tucker, 311–63. New York: Norton.

McMurtry, John. 1989. *Understanding War.* Toronto: Science for Peace /Stevens.

———. 1999. *The Cancer Stage of Capitalism.* London: Pluto.

Mesnard y Mendez, Pierre. 2002. "Capitalism Means/ Needs War." *Socialism and Democracy* 16, no. 2: 65–92. http:\\www.sdonline.org.

Mills, C. Wright. 1953. *White Collar.* New York: Oxford University Press.

———. 1956. *The Power Elite.* New York: Oxford University Press.

———. 1959. *The Causes of World War Three.* London: Secker and Warburg, 1959.

Noble, David F. 1977. *America by Design.* Foreword by Christopher Lasch. New York: Knopf.

Pocock, J. G. A. 1975. *The Machiavellian Moment.* Princeton, N.J.: Princeton University Press.

Pringle, David, and John Clute. 1995. "Robert A. Heinlein." In *The Multimedia Encyclopedia of Science Fiction,* ed. John Clute and Peter Nicholls. CD-ROM. Danbury, Conn.: Grolier.

Proietti, Salvatore, and Darko Suvin. "War and Militarism in Science Fiction: A Select Bibliography," in Suvin 2005, 154–63.

Russ, Joanna. 1995. *To Write Like a Woman.* Bloomington: Indiana University Press.

Scarry, Elaine. 1999. *On Beauty and Being Just.* Princeton: Princeton University Press.

Schwarz, Roberto. 2003. "Preface with Questions." *New Left Review,* no. 24: 31–39.

Smith, Henry Nash. 1964. *Mark Twain's Fable of Progress.* New Brunswick, N.J.: Rutgers University Press.

Smith-Rosenberg, Carroll. 2004. "Surrogate Americans." *PMLA* 119, no. 4: 1325–35.

Suvin, Darko. 1979. *Metamorphoses of Science Fiction.* New Haven, Conn., and London: Yale University Press.

———. 1988. *Positions and Presuppositions in Science Fiction.* Kent, Ohio: Kent State University Press.

———. 1983. *Victorian Science Fiction in the U.K.: The Discourses of Knowledge and of Power.* Boston: Hall.

———. 1998. "Utopianism from Orientation to Agency: What Are We Intellectuals under Post-Fordism to Do?" *Utopian Studies* 9, no. 2: 162–90.

———. 2000a. "Considering the Sense of 'Fantasy' or 'Fantastic Fiction.'" *Extrapolation* 41, no. 3: 209–47.

———. 2000b. "Novum Is as Novum Does." In *Science Fiction, Critical Frontiers,* ed. Karen Sayer and John Moore, 3–22. New York: St. Martin's Press.

———. 2002a. "Goodbye and Hello: Differentiating within the Later P. K. Dick." *Extrapolation* 43, no. 4: 368–97.

———. 2002b. "Science Fiction Parables of Mutation and Cloning as/and Cognition." In *Biotechnological and Medical Themes in Science Fiction,* ed. Domna Pastourmatzi, 131–51. Thessaloníki: University Studio Press.

———. 2002c. "What May the 20th Century Amount To." *Critical Quarterly* 44, no. 2: 84–104.

———, ed. 2005. *US Science Fiction and War/ Militarism.* Special issue of *Fictions,* no. 3. Pisa and Rome: IEPI.

Tirman, John, ed. 1984. *The Militarization of High Technology.* Cambridge, Mass.: Ballinger.

Van Creveld, Martin. 2002. *The Art of War.* London: Cassell.

Veblen, Thorstein. 1904. *The Theory of Business Enterprise.* New York: Scribner.

Wallerstein, Immanuel. 1996. *Historical Capitalism; Capitalist Civilization.* London: Verso.

Science Fiction Narratives
of Mass Destruction and the
Politics of National Security

Doug Davis

Like Hugo Gernsback's Ralph, members of the Bush administration have not feared over their first six years in office to describe the far-off future. Yet where Ralph amazes his readers with a catalog of new inventions that will improve the lot of mankind, President Bush and the members of his administration have tended more to frighten their subjects by foreseeing, for them, scenario after scenario of prolonged combat and national doom. Consider the administration's time line for the collapse of the social security system included as part of the press packet for the 2005 presidential action to privatize Social Security, which stretches into historical territory that was once the province of science fiction writers and futurists. Readers make their way through a bulleted list that takes them from the retirement boom of 2008 to the year 2017, the year of the budgetary shortfalls. Still further in the future, readers learn that by 2027 the government is going to have to float its seniors' expenses; in 2033 the nation will reach the year of the great 300-billion-dollar shortfall; and finally, in 2042 the whole system will go bust (White House Policies in Focus 2005).

Readers of science fiction have encountered future time lines like this before, penned by grand masters such as Frederik Pohl and Robert Heinlein. However, science fiction authors never commanded the audience and press coverage that a sitting president of the United States does. In 2005 Bush's highly speculative, catastrophic future of Social Security was hotly debated news. Indeed, Bush himself had forayed into this particular science fictional territory once before. Back in 1978 when first running for Congress he told the Texas electorate that unless Social Security was privatized immediately the system would be completely broke by the far-off year of . . . 1988 (Marshall).

Science Fiction and Social Insecurity

Social Security is not the only institution to face a catastrophic future according to the U.S. government or the nation's military. Both institutions are eager to face the threats of terrible things that have not happened but could. To make its case for weaponizing space, the Air Force's National Space Commission warned the president in January 2001, eight months before the 9/11 attacks, that the nation faced an imminent "space Pearl Harbor" that could cripple the nation's economy, intelligence services, and military (Commission to Assess United States National Security Space Management and Organization 2001, 13–15). A year later, in January 2002, the Pentagon submitted a *Nuclear Posture Review Report* to the president that proposed redeploying the nation's existing nuclear deterrent up through "2020 and beyond" (Crouch 2002) as a tool for fighting undeterrable terrorists and rogue states (Rumsfeld 2002). When Pentagon officials get really ambitious, as they have with their Future Combat Systems plan for fielding a fully cybernetic army by the year 2025, the *New York Times* editorial board is quick to call a spade a spade and dismiss the military's plans as "A Science-Fiction Army" (March 31, 2005).

As science fiction scholars I. F. Clarke and H. Bruce Franklin have documented in their respective studies of future war storytelling, *Voices Prophesying War* and *War Stars,* science fictional superweapons and catastrophic scenarios have long been foretold by advocates of the British and American armed services to further military funding and development. Yet while proposals such as the Army's Future Combat Systems may remain the stuff of science fiction as it runs up against the realities of an escalating budget, another speculative and far more catastrophic future war narrative has proliferated since 9/11 not only through American popular culture but also through American global strategy: that the nation is facing an imminent terrorist attack with weapons of mass destruction (WMDs), worst of all a nuclear attack. In the five years since 9/11, this narrative has become especially visible in the mass media as television shows including CBS's *NCIS, JAG,* and *The Unit;* NBC's *Law and Order* franchise; ABC's *Alias* and *Threat Matrix;* Fox's *24;* TNT and the BBC's co-production, *The Grid;* and Showtime's *Sleeper Cell* have adopted the format of the Tom Clancy technothriller to tell stories about counterterrorism. With plots that are extrapolated from the 9/11 attacks and visual and narrative details that possess a high degree of technological and geopolitical verisimilitude, these twenty-first-century tales of war-on-terror-to-come blur the distinction between fiction and fact by conflating them in the speculative domain of the future.

While most television counterterrorism shows are dramas first and future or alternate histories only because they are not about real historical events, some, such as *Last Best Chance,* a nonprofit film aired on HBO in the autumn of 2005 and distributed free of charge on the Internet, are expressly political and engage more fully in the propagandistic narrative tradition that Clarke dubbed the tale of the war-to-come (1992, 3). *Last Best Chance* is a speculative future fiction presented in the guise of historical fact that its producers call a "docudrama." Produced by the Nuclear Threat Initiative (NTI)—a nonprofit antinuclear proliferation group spearheaded by Senators Sam Nunn and Richard Lugar and advised by an all-star board of directors drawn from politics, the academy, the military, and the business world—the film details how in the near future terrorists could smuggle a nuclear weapon into the United States (the film ends with a vehicle carrying a terrorist-crafted nuclear weapon successfully crossing the Canadian border into the United States; viewers are left to imagine what will happen next). The hallmark of this kind of storytelling is the deliberate blurring of fiction and fact, which is exemplified by *Last Best Chance*'s casting. The film stars *Law and Order*'s Fred Thompson, a man who has made a career straddling the worlds of political fiction and political fact in his professional guises as both a U.S. senator and an actor who plays roles as politicians. The press on the film likewise blurs the distinction between speculative fiction and fact. While the film is set in the near future and details events that have never happened, the film's Web page nevertheless assures viewers that "this film is based on facts. Some events depicted may have already happened. Some may be happening now. All may happen in the near future if we don't act now to prevent them." As the NTI has the real-world goal of securing the world's loose nuclear material, the institute's fiction of an impending terrorist nuclear attack is accordingly as didactic as it is dramatic. Its future history is designed to bear the same kind of lesson as past history: never forget that such massive destruction *could* happen. Thus, as the NTI urges potential viewers, "get your copy [of *Last Best Chance*] today and find out how we can help prevent nuclear terrorism" ("Last Best Chance" Web site).

Speculative fictions about nuclear terrorism have been seized upon by the mass media for crafting timely entertainment and by activist political groups for securing world peace. And this future would remain the stuff of drama and agit-prop if not for the fact that it has also been seized upon by the federal government to guide and justify its strategies of preemptive war and homeland defense. This particular science fiction story, it so happens, is not just about politics. It *is* politics.

Science Fiction and the Reality of Terror

From its origins in the tales of nuclear war in the cold war to its twenty-first-century variant in today's tales of nuclear terrorism, the narrative of massive military destruction and nuclear attack has become more than fiction as it has been deployed by policymakers as the nation's probable future. Countering the threat of a terrorist WMD attack has become one of the guiding principles of twenty-first-century American foreign policy and the war on terror, much as countering the threat of a strategic nuclear attack was a guiding principle of American national security strategy in the cold war. A kind of science fiction storytelling has stood on the front lines of both conflicts. Since the development of nuclear weapons and the origins of the cold war, the nation's defense establishment has been committed to reproducing a speculative mass destruction narrative that was born in the cautionary atomic science fiction of H. G. Wells's

1914 *The World Set Free*—the science fiction book that famously served as the inspiration for the real atomic bomb (Clarke 1992, 157)—but that has since come to guide its defense planning as strategic fact. A formal understanding of how science fiction works, in turn, can illuminate how American defense strategy itself operates and at least partly explain such major policy decisions as the nation's choice to go to war against Iraq.

National security documents from the cold war and the war on terror read much like literary exercises in future world-building that are designed to prompt their readers into thinking about the present world in a shocking new way. The specter of nuclear and other kinds of terrorism following 9/11 prompted the Bush administration to task its National Security Council to write both an entirely new National Strategy to Combat Weapons of Mass Destruction and a thoroughly revised National Security Strategy, each of which defines the pernicious character of the nation's new enemies and forewarns of massive future attacks to advance the administration's new doctrine of preemptive war (the last National Security Strategy, National Security Council document 68, was written in 1949 following another shocking event, the detonation of a Russian nuclear weapon; it forewarned of Soviet expansionism and surprise nuclear attack to make the case for Soviet containment and nuclear deterrence [May 1993, 53]). Subsequently the threat of an incoming nuclear attack from a swiftly arming Iraq and its terrorist allies was the chief reason cited by Republicans and Democrats alike in Congress's joint resolution authorizing the war against Iraq in 2003.

The irony of defense planning in the war on terror is that its strategic thinking is based upon speculative catastrophic events that do not exist, that are so terrible they must never exist—and, as with the Iraqi nuclear threat, in retrospect turn out to never have existed at all. The Iraqi nuclear threat that started the 2003 war *did* exist, but like the Air Force's space Pearl Harbor, the Army's Future Combat System, the collapse of Social Security, and the cold war's nuclear Armageddon for that matter, it existed *only as a story about our future.* But this future attack was a science fiction story that nevertheless had a real purposive grip on the present. After all, the Iraq attack story was persuasive enough to start a war. Arguments for that war might now look like works of fiction, but just a few years ago they were read as strategic fact by an overwhelming number of the nation's legislators.

Lacking the real thing, fictions of massive attack necessarily stand in for the fact of massive attack in nuclear-age defense planning. Defense planners and citizens alike are forced to imagine the specific course of the catastrophic attacks foretold in strategy documents and presidential speeches, which is precisely where the work of future fiction storytelling comes in. Throughout the war on terror, fiction authors have been employed by the Department of Homeland Security (DHS) to devise classified terrorist attack scenarios. In 2004 the DHS developed a series of classified "doomsday scripts" for likely terrorist attacks featuring a character called the Universal Adversary (Lipton 2005). In leaked versions of this 157 page document accidentally posted on the Hawaii state government Web site, a small nuclear attack tops a list of fifteen detailed scenarios that also includes different kinds of biological and chemical attacks as well as natural disasters and disease outbreaks (*National Planning Scenarios* 2005). These scripts were subsequently used in April 2005 to guide a series of federally mandated civil defense drills called TOPOFF 3 involving more than ten thousand participants and observers from thirteen countries (Chertoff 2005). Thriller authors Brad Thor and Brad Meltzer went public in 2004 with their formerly classified involvement in another, perhaps related DHS program that has embraced the CIA's and Pentagon's practice of "red teaming," running simulated attacks to expose weaknesses in military planning and intelligence. For its Analytic Red Cell Program, the DHS hired twenty-member teams of "people with offbeat specialties" such as Meltzer and Thor to plot sixteen potential terrorist attacks (Mintz 2004). Thor is cagey when it comes to describing the other eighteen members of his red team: "I was one of two thriller writers—a couple of sci-fi people, then your usual mishmash of alphabet soup agencies. There also are people from the private sector" (quoted in Stein 2006). As John Mintz reported for the *Washington Post,* the only reason the DHS went public with the existence of its red cell writing program is because its teams were too good at their job. One of their threat scenarios had apparently been mistaken for a report of a real-world attack, and the programs' director was then compelled to go public to quash the rumor of an attack creeping its way through Washington.

The touchstone fictional text for nuclear terror is Tom Clancy's *The Sum of All Fears,* a techno-thriller about nuclear terrorism that has been referenced by national security experts and administration officials alike as being as close to the real thing as anybody ever wants to get (Allison and Kokoshin 2002, 35). The transformation of Clancy's 1991 novel into a film presents an interesting case of reality catching up with fiction—and fiction then being used to stand in for future reality. Production on the film started before 9/11, but the film was released in the summer of 2002, and by then world events had turned this escapist thriller into a scary look into the future. The film's producers had changed Clancy's plot to avoid offending Arab sensibilities by turning his novel's Arab nuclear terrorists into Neo-Nazis (Salam). But even with this major revision, after 9/11 *The Sum of All Fears* had ceased being a techno-thriller and had become a political event. As director Phil Alden Robinson explained on the June 1, 2002, edition of *CNN People in the News,* "A year ago, you'd have said, 'great popcorn film.' Today you say, 'that's about the world I live in.'" Bush administration officials were invited to the Washington premiere and also vouched for the film's geopolitical accuracy. As Deputy Secretary of Defense Paul Wolfowitz told *Variety,* "It was genuinely scary. Arguably, in the real world we are dealing with this every day" (in Higgins and McClintock 2002, 55).

The kind of real world Wolfowitz is describing is a world somewhere between made-up fiction and deadly fact located sometime between today and tomorrow. Like the worlds of science fiction, it too is a world extrapolated from our own. As such it can be experienced, for now, only in works of the imagination: in scripted defense drills such as TOPOFF 3 and in narrative fictions such as Clancy's near-future techno-thrillers, and elsewhere in our books and on our televisions and movie screens. To experience these particular massive destruction narratives is, for all intents and purposes, to realize American national security strategy's own worst future.

Strategic Fictions

Science fiction studies can illuminate not only the genre's creative texts but also other real-world discourses that refer to future and alternate imaginaries. Reading the threats of mass destruction that organize American policy with the critical tools of science fiction studies explains how fictions of mass destruction have come to work on the front lines of the war on terror and how they have had the persuasive power to structure foreign policy and start wars. A careful understanding of English grammar coupled with an appreciation of how science fiction works can indeed unlock some of the secrets of national security. Consider Bush's case for going to war in Iraq as presented in his 2003 State of the Union speech. Analyzed closely, it becomes clear how certain intimations of mass destruction acquire a strong persuasive power simply by the way they are phrased and the science fiction literary tradition in which they partake.

The case for the Iraq war was based on a top secret National Intelligence Estimate (NIE) that cataloged the latest data on Iraq's WMD programs and presented the intelligence community's confidence in its assessments (the Bush administration declassified the key judgments of the report to bolster its case for launching the Iraq war). Part of the NIE consisted of a table of "Confidence Levels for Selected Key Judgments in This Estimate," listing with "high confidence" such judgments as "Iraq is continuing, and in some areas expanding, its chemical, biological, nuclear and missile programs contrary to UN resolutions"; "we are not detecting portions of these weapons programs"; and "Iraq could make a nuclear weapon in months to a year once it acquires sufficient weapons-grade fissile material." Listed with "moderate confidence" is the judgment that "Iraq does not yet have a nuclear weapon or sufficient material to make one but is likely to have a weapon by 2007 to 2009." The NIE then listed with "low confidence" its judgments on "when Saddam would use weapons of mass destruction," "whether Saddam would engage in clandestine attacks against the US Homeland," and "whether in desperation Saddam would share chemical or biological weapons with al-Qa'ida." In sum, prior to the Iraq war the intelligence community did not have much confidence in predicting whether Saddam Hussein would use WMDs to attack the United States (Federation of American Scientists 2003).

In the halls of Congress, however, the representation of Iraq's WMD threat changed in a dramatic way. In Bush's 2003 State of the Union speech, which summed up his case for going to war, the NIE's assessment of Iraqi intentions was rewritten in an imaginary, extrapolative form. First the president laid out the facts as then known: Hussein not only had an "advanced nuclear weapons program" but also had attempted to buy African uranium and aluminum centrifuge tubes. Then the president enjoined the nation to flex its imagination in a decidedly science fictional way: "Before September the 11th, many in the world believed that Saddam Hussein could be contained. But chemical agents, lethal viruses and shadowy terrorist networks are not easily contained. Imagine those 19 hijackers with other weapons and other plans—this time armed by Saddam Hussein. It would take one vial, one canister, one crate slipped into this country to bring a day of horror like none we have ever known." This speculative doomsday scenario ultimately rallied Congress to support the president's decision to wage preemptive war against Iraq.

Bush's imaginary scenario is a complex statement that needs to be unpacked in three ways: historically, logically, and grammatically. Historically the kind of future-oriented, extrapolative thinking Bush was engaging in has been a foundation of American strategic thinking since at least the beginning of the cold war. In the cold war defense planners looked to the past to create scenarios for how a global nuclear war might be fought in the future. They extrapolated from the Pearl Harbor surprise attack, the German blitzkrieg, and the two atomic bombings to imagine the threats the nation would face in the future; the variations on massive surprise nuclear attack divined through this process then guided the nation's own policies of nuclear deterrence through the doctrines of flexible and massive nuclear retaliation (Lawrence Freedman 34). National defense strategy in the war on terror remains just as extrapolative. It is still guided by worst-case scenarios divined from historical precedent, namely scenarios of catastrophic terrorism extrapolated from the attacks of 9/11. Bush's worst-case scenario, then, is far from new: it is a product of a habit of thinking that has guided American strategy since the dawn of the nuclear age.

Logically the president is also asking an extrapolative question familiar to science fiction readers: what if? The persuasive power of extrapolative logic alone, however, does not make his a credible scenario. Rather, it is the science fictional grammar of Bush's request that made an especially persuasive case for the Iraq war. In her essay "Speculations: The Subjunctivity of Science Fiction," Joanna Russ works through Samuel R. Delany's analysis of what grammatical mood science fiction properly belongs to. Delany claims that science fiction's unique narrative mood is the subjunctive. The subjunctive mood, as opposed to the indicative or the imperative, designates states of maybe: wishes, speculations, conditions, hypotheticals, and other things that could happen but have not. Science fiction, Russ concludes, exists in a state of tension between two subjunctive states, namely that of fantasy's negatively subjunctive events (events that could not happen) and realistic fiction's events that could happen (1995, 19). Bush's scenario, like science fiction, is presented in the subjunctive mood and is also clearly offered as a fictional scenario. Hussein had not done any of the things that Bush warned against. However, when coupled with the real-world evidence presented elsewhere in the National Intelligence Estimate and the State of the Union address of Iraqi armament, denial, and deceit, the mood of this fiction moves ever closer to the grammatical pole of realism. This fictional attack is not real, but given the evidence, *it definitely could happen.* And in the defense planner's world, that is reality enough. After all, in January 2003, what congressperson would want a nuclear attack on the United States to be any more real?

A great deal of evidence has been gathered since 2003 proving that Hussein did not have any nuclear weapons and was not allied with terrorists, leading the president himself to admit in a December 18, 2005, speech that "much of the intelligence [cited in the 2003 State of the Union] turned out to be wrong" (Bush 2005). By 2005 the subjunctive mood of the president's speculative fiction had shifted—all the way to fantasy. This attack could not really happen. But that does not necessarily make the president's speculative scenario a lie. What the president did in 2003 is tell a tale in a grammatical form and with a history long familiar to Americans.

This tale was a variation on the subjunctive tale of a possible nuclear war Americans told themselves throughout the cold war and treated as seriously as fact. Such an unprecedented war certainly could have happened; indeed, the practice of nuclear defense was built on that very future conditionality. National defense in the first and second nuclear ages worked through just such acts of telling future tales of massive attack, treating them as fact, and arming to fight that future, because not doing so is simply too risky. Bush's Iraq attack fiction was not made-up fantasy, but a subjunctive fiction uttered in the same spirit. While it turns out it was logically extrapolated from a set of intelligence that proved to be profoundly faulty, it was real enough at the time to start a real war, which begs the question: if this story is fiction written in the subjunctive mode, and is not real but is also not fantasy, what else can it be but science fiction?

Of course George W. Bush is not a science fiction writer. The sketchy fictional scenario offered in the 2003 State of the Union is not even a proper piece of narrative science fiction. Yet sketches like these are the basis of American global strategy, and as such it is not right simply to call them fantasies or even fictions, for that matter, because they do have real-world material force as guides for American global strategy. Such scenarios—and the stories spun off from them in popular culture—must be thought of as another kind of science fiction: strategic fictions. A modified version of the formalist definition of science fiction, in turn, can help in understanding how strategic fictions do some truly serious and persuasive political work. According to the formalist definition of science fiction advanced by such scholars as Darko Suvin in *Metamorphoses of Science Fiction* and Carl Freedman in *Critical Theory and Science Fiction,* all science fiction has the potential for bearing a political meaning, and a subversive one at that, because all science fiction presents a challenge to the status quo. Science fictions are radically different from our world but at the same time have a rational connection to it. Fictions that exist in this intense subjunctive state of "have not happened yet" have the power to change what readers think about our world, if for no other reason than they show readers that their world can truly, radically change (Freedman 2000, 55).

Strategic fictions of nuclear and other kinds of terrorism such as those intimated by George Bush, writ large by military thriller authors such as Tom Clancy and Brad Thor, and visualized in shows such as *Sleeper Cell* and films such as *Last Best Chance,* are also estranging because they present readers with a vision of the world radically different from their own but also recognizably their own, one marked by a world historical event that has not happened yet but could—namely, a nuclear or WMD attack. At the same time these fictions about attacks that have not happened yet do not call into question basic assumptions about our world in the same manner as science fiction. They might be writ in the subjunctive mood, and they might be extrapolated, but their estranging visions reassert rather than challenge many of the same assumptions found in national security discourse: namely that Americans live in a world full of threatening enemies intent on using nuclear and other massive weapons against them. Their estrangements are met by the operation of rational thought, but of a kind that is limited and ultimately reactionary. They do not open up the world for critique; rather, they convince congresspeople to see the present world in only one new and shocking way as under imminent threat, a way that convinces them to wage preemptive war.

This effect is not limited to presidential pronouncements. In moments like the cold war and the war on terror, fictions of nuclear war and nuclear terrorism respectively get this added political force too, for many of them are based in whole or in part on the same assumptions as those held by the architects of those wars. In the cold war hundreds of literary and visual fictions of nuclear war told across culture built the intensely contradictory reality of the nuclear threat in as central a way that bombers and missiles did, dramatically realizing its strategies, its technological systems, and its promised world historical destruction, sometimes even when their creators were trying to critique that world. Even a great antinuclear film such as *Dr. Strangelove* (1964) had to reproduce some articles of cold war faith—chief among them that the nation's nuclear air force was so good at its job it was unstoppable, and that a nuclear war would be a truly devastating event. All nuclear war stories ultimately relied in whole or in part on the same assumptions about the state of technology or the state of the world that started the nuclear arms race in the first place. Antinuclear literature such as Jonathan Schell's classic *The Fate of the Earth* (1982) cannot help but reiterate the basic premise of nuclear deterrence—that a nuclear war must never be fought. To imagine the world at nuclear war was, perforce, to engage in the geopolitics of nuclear defense.

Conclusion

Fictions of WMD terrorism in the war on terror now serve as strategic fictions much as fictions of nuclear war did, dramatizing for a mass audience the newly threatening character of the world and the terrifying future of the second nuclear age. As in the cold war, Americans do get to experience this threatening world—and as before, fortunately only in their imaginations. Of course, Americans have a real historical experience with terrorism much as Europeans and Japanese have real historical experience with the kind of total destruction that could happen in a global nuclear war. The precedent of past mass destruction is integral to the imagination of future mass destruction. The past is the real material upon which defense strategists, fiction writers, and filmmakers alike extrapolate their strategic fictional futures.

Likewise, the past may offer some guidance of strategic fictions to come. A couple of decades into the cold war, writers and filmmakers began not simply to reiterate strategic fictions of nuclear war but to rewrite them radically. Stanley Kubrick reimagined the future of nuclear war in *Dr. Strangelove,* while Thomas Pynchon in *Gravity's Rainbow* (1973), Joseph Heller in *Catch-22* (1961), and Kurt Vonnegut in *Slaughterhouse-Five* (1968) all turned to World War III's historical precedent in World War II to rewrite the experience of total air war as postmodernist black comedies. These counterstrategic fictions in turn undermined the extrapolative logic of the cold war's strategic fictions by showing the modern face of war to be not logically necessary but, rather, inhuman and absurd. On the science fiction front, Judith Merril's *Shadow on the Hearth* (1950), Walter Miller's *Canticle for Leibowitz* (1959), and Nevil Shute's *On the Beach* (1957), along with television productions such as ABC's *The Day After* (1983), the BBC's *Threads* (1984), and PBS's *Testament* (1983), presented rewritings of the nuclear war story as grim existentialist narratives, the television productions even turning some viewers to the cause of antinuclear activism (Gusterson 1996, 101).

Somewhat surprisingly, such revisioning has not happened yet for the war on terror. It's tales of attacks-to-come remain extrapolative strategic fictions, while war-on-terror dramatic histories such as Universal's *United 93* (2006), A&E's *Flight 93* (2006), ABC's *The Path to 9/11* (2006), Paramount's *World Trade Center* (2006), and even the government's *National Interest* (2004)—which was turned into a 144-page graphic novel by Sid Jacobson and Ernie Colón in 2006—hew closely to the format of the docudrama. Perhaps it is too soon to consider radically rewriting the strategic fictions of nuclear terrorism and the history of the war on terror. Perhaps it is still too dangerous to do so. Americans are used to living in strategic fictional times, for they have been living in those times ever since the invention of the atomic bomb and strategic airpower, when mass destruction storytelling became the real business of national defense. While the threat of nuclear war does not loom as large as the threat of nuclear terrorism does, Americans are still faced with a tough choice: to believe in the mass destruction futures of strategic fiction and fight against them or to take the risk of imagining otherwise and act as a nation in an entirely new way—one more akin to science fiction.

Bibliography

Allison, Graham, and Andrei Kokoshin. 2002. "The New Containment: An Alliance against Nuclear Terrorism." *National Interest* 69 (Fall): 35–43.

Bush, George W. 2003. "The State of the Union." *White House.gov,* January 28. http://www .whitehouse.gov/news/releases/2003/01/20030128-19.html.

———. 2005. "President's Address to the Nation." *White House.gov,* December 18. http:// www.whitehouse.gov/news/releases/2005/12/20051218-2.html.

Chertoff, Michael. 2005. "Transcript of Press Conference with Secretary of Homeland Security Michael Chertoff on the TOPOFF 3 Exercise." Department of Homeland Security, April 4. http://www.dhs.gov/xnews/releases/press_release_0650.shtm.

Clarke, I. F. 1992. *Voices Prophesying War: Future Wars 1763–3749.* New York: Oxford University Press.

Commission to Assess United States National Security Space Management and Organization. 2001. Executive Summary, January 11. http://www.fas.org/spp;/military/commission/report.htm (accessed November 10, 2006).

Crouch, J. D. 2002. "Special Briefing on the Nuclear Posture Review." U.S. Department of Defense, January 9. http://www.defenselink.mil/transcripts/2002/t01092002_t0109npr .html.

Federation of American Scientists. 2003. "Key Judgments [from October 2002 NIE]." 18 July. http://www.fas.org/irp/cia/product/iraq-wmd.html.

Franklin, H. Bruce. 1988. *War Stars: The Superweapon and the American Imagination.* New York: Oxford University Press.

Freedman, Carl. 2000. *Critical Theory and Science Fiction.* Hanover, N.H.: Wesleyan University Press / University Press of New England.

Freedman, Lawrence. 1989. *The Evolution of Nuclear Strategy.* 2nd ed. New York: St. Martin's Press.

Gusterson, Hugh. 1996. *Nuclear Rites: A Weapons Laboratory at the End of the Cold War.* Los Angeles: University of California Press.

Higgins, Bill, and Pamela McClintock. 2002. "'Fears' Factor." *Variety,* June 3–9.

Homeland Security Council and Department of Homeland Security.2005. *National Planning Scenarios.* 12 December. http://media.washingtonpost.com/wp-srv/nation/nationalsecurity/earlywarning/NationalPlanningScenariosApril2005.pdf.

Lipton, Eric. 2005. "Fictional Doomsday Team Plays Out Scene after Scene." *New York Times,* March 26.

Marshall, Joshua Micah. 2005. *Talking Points Memo,* 26 January. http://www.talkingpoints memo.com/archives/004551.php.

May, Ernest R., ed. 1993. *American Cold War Strategy: Interpreting NSC 68.* New York: Bedford.

Mintz, John. 2004. "Homeland Security Employs Imagination: Outsiders Help Devise Possible Terrorism Plots." *Washington Post,* June 18.

National Security Council. 2002a. *National Security Strategy of the United States of America 2002,* September 17. http://www.whitehouse.gov/nsc/nss/2002/index.html.

————. 2002b. *National Strategy to Combat Weapons of Mass Destruction,* December 11. http://www.whitehouse.gov/news/releases/2002/12/WMDStrategy.pdf.

————. 2006. *National Security Strategy of the United States of America 2006,* March 16. http://www.whitehouse.gov/nsc/nss/2006/.

New York Times. 2005. "A Science-Fiction Army." March 31.

PR Newswire. 2001. "Paramount Film's Super Bowl Villains Changed to Neo-Nazis; Islamic Group CAIR Had Concerns about Stereotyping in *The Sum of All Fears,*" 26 January. LexisNexis Academic.

Rumsfeld, Donald H. 2002. Foreword to *Nuclear Posture Review Report,* January 9. http://www.defenselink.mil/news/Jan2002/d20020109npr.pdf.

Russ, Joanna. 1995. "Speculation: The Subjunctivity of Science Fiction." In *To Write Like a Woman: Essays in Feminism and Science Fiction,* 15–25. Bloomington: Indiana University Press.

Salam, Reihan. "The Sum of All PC: Hollywood's Reverse Racial Profiling." *Slate* (May 28, 2002). http://www.slate.com/id2056272/ (accessed November 10, 2007).

Stein, Jeff. 2006. "The Heart Is a Lonely Hunter, the FBI Finds in a Chinese Spy Case." *CQ.Com,* May 26, public.cq.com/public/20060526_homeland.html.

Suvin, Darko. 1979. *Metamorphoses of Science Fiction: On the Poetics and History of a Literary Genre.* New Haven: Yale University Press.

U.S. Congress. 2002. "Joint Resolution to Authorize the Use of United States Armed Forces against Iraq." PL 107–243, 107th Cong., 2nd sess., October 2. http://www.whitehouse.gov/news/releases/2002/10/20021002–2.html.

White House Policies in Focus. 2005. "Strengthening Social Security for Future Generations." June. http://www.whitehouse.gov/infocus/social-security/.

A Truly American Enterprise

Star Trek's Post-9/11 Politics

Lincoln Geraghty

> The game wouldn't be worth playing if we knew what was going to happen. (Sisko to wormhole alien, "Emissary," 1993)

> It's been a long road / Getting from there to here (*Enterprise* theme, "Where My Heart Will Take Me," 2001)

This essay examines *Star Trek*'s political ideology post-9/11 by comparing two of its most dissimilar series: *Star Trek: Deep Space Nine* (1993–1999) and *Star Trek: Enterprise* (2001–2005). *Deep Space Nine* is set in the twenty-fourth century; *Enterprise* takes the year 2151 as its starting point. Both series have distinctive views of how humanity deals with conflict, life in space, diplomacy, exploration, and our faith in the future. All of these qualities are represented in opposite ways. *Deep Space Nine* shows a more flawed and uncertain approach to our future progress in space, as if the future is undetermined and the human journey is far from complete. On the other hand, *Enterprise*'s optimistic and, I would say, innocent prediction of humanity's first steps beyond the solar system arises because the history of the future is already "set in stone." Specifically, much of *Star Trek*'s future history previously recorded in past series prevents *Enterprise* from covering new ground and expanding upon the human voyage; it cannot deviate or change a narrative past that has literally happened already. Through an analysis of episodes in both series and *Enterprise*'s contentious opening title sequence I want to reveal how they deal with history and humanity's future in space; how they have understood *Star Trek*'s central utopian principle while also trying to examine how we interact with each other in the present. I also want to stress that both series embody *Star Trek*'s paradoxical view of a bright future based on a history that does not exist in the present. However, since much of *Star Trek*'s popularity is now based on its catalogued historical narrative through which its fans live out their own fantasies, the dangers of reflecting back on time, as I will emphasize with my analysis of *Enterprise,* are obviated through a process of self-selection. Fans realize that much of this history is distorted, so they can either choose to ignore it or assimilate it into their own imagination of the future.

I

The universe in which *Deep Space Nine* is set is an ambiguous one in comparison with the universes of previous *Star Trek* series. The writers and producers stressed that the characters were to be fallible, have obvious faults, and most important of all, would face complex situations in space that no longer have easy answers (Richards 1998, 173). Its premise was suggested by Paramount executives as being: "Rather than a 'Wagon Train to the Stars,' a 'Rifleman' in space" (Dillard 1996, 152). The look and feel of the show would prove to be far darker and more serious than its contemporary, *Star Trek: The Next Generation* (1987–1994); for example, being set on a space station meant that if any exploring was to be done, the unknown would have to come to the regular characters. This confined setting implied that there would be more chance for character development. The cast would be allowed to grow as the stories they were involved in became more complicated and less resolvable in a single weekly episode. As Chris Gregory (2000, 69) argues: "*DS9* concentrates more on the growth the characters experience as a result of the unfolding narratives of the series itself" rather than their individual actions in separate and varied storylines. For Gregory, *Deep Space Nine* bears a striking resemblance to a soap opera since it incorporates similar narrative structures such as complicated and involved character back-stories and interwoven story arcs, plus a highly developed historical narrative: "The stories are linked by continuing 'soap opera'-type subplots such as Bashir's ineffectual attempts to romance Jadzia, Sisko's difficulties with his adolescent son, Jake, and Odo's continual pursuit of Quark. It is emphasised that *DS9* is a multicultural community in which there will be less focus on the 'military' life of Starfleet as seen on *TNG*'s Enterprise, and in which relationships between characters will be less bound by their rank and position" (Gregory 2000, 74).

In Karin Blair's article "*Star Trek* Old and New: From the Alien Embodied to the Alien Imagined" (1997), she distinguishes between the older, better-known series and *Deep Space Nine* in order to evaluate the shift that has taken place from *Star Trek*'s outward exploration of society to a more inward-looking approach. *Deep Space Nine,* in her opinion, tends to examine individual identities and personal relationships more than past series that were concerned with an expansion of humanity on the final frontier. Blair recognizes that *Star Trek* returned to the enclosed space of the individual and how that individual interacts with others rather than continuing with outward exploration because at that time American society as a whole needed to look inward to examine the state of the nation as it drew near the end of the millennium and the dawn of a new global community: "Having reached a certain limit in outward exploration, we must come to know ourselves as collaborators in the making of our own networks and identities, which requires closure as well as openness, moral feeling and human decency as well as pragmatism, expansiveness and intelligent curiosity. Above all perhaps an acceptance of ambiguity is needed; values can give warmth as well as clarity" (Blair 1997, 88).

From these examinations of *Deep Space Nine* one can identify that the theme of ambiguity is an important part of the series' ongoing narrative, as the quote taken from the 1993 series pilot episode states: "The game wouldn't be worth playing if we knew what was going to happen." Therefore all that was previously assumed from other *Star Trek* series would be irrelevant. Even the ever-present optimism of *Star Trek* was not guaranteed, since humanity was going to be tested on the frontier space station and some of the main characters were going to be found wanting. In terms of closure, the series finished without giving the audience all the answers; the crew did not stay together, so fans were uncertain if they would see these characters again in a movie like the four that followed the end of *The Next Generation*.[1]

In the final episode, "What You Leave Behind," long-standing relationships come to an end and new beginnings form. Characters who have been friends for seven years, such as Bashir and O'Brien, have to say farewell as their careers and partners take precedence. Most significant of all, Jake Sisko and Kasidy Yates are left behind as Benjamin Sisko begins a journey of self-discovery as the emissary for the celestial Prophets of Bajor. These noncorporeal beings act as protectors for the Bajorans, and Sisko is their representative. After the war with the Dominion had finished, Sisko believed his job was done; yet, the Prophets told him that his mission had only just begun. For the first time in a *Star Trek* series the main character, the captain, leaves his crew and family to fulfill another destiny. His whereabouts are not known, and it is not clear whether he will return. At the end of the episode Jake and Kira look out into space unsure of what Sisko is doing or if he will ever return. This ambiguous ending illustrates the nature of *Deep Space Nine*'s entire series and is indicative of its manipulation of the *Star Trek* mythos. Besides Worf, who continues to appear in *The Next Generation* movies, every *Deep Space Nine* character has an open-ended future within the *Trek* universe.

Such uncertainty allows fans the possibility to make up ongoing narratives for themselves so that they can experience more. There are no plans for any follow-up movies, so fans can develop their favorite characters in their own ways. One example of this is in the new series of novels that has been published following the season finale. These imagine how the station survived after the war and how Jake, Kasidy and the rest of the crew have coped with the loss of Captain Sisko.[2] However, since these are only novelizations the stories are not part of the *Star Trek* canon; therefore the events that take place in them are not legitimate within the future history. Everything that appears on the television series or on the movie screen is deemed as official within the fictional *Star Trek* universe. Literature such as the technical manuals and fact files produced under license to Paramount are also seen as canonical because they expand upon material aired on-screen and are used as points of reference for further episodes and movies. However, the novels and fan literature are not seen as canonical because the stories they tell have not "happened," have not taken place on-screen, and are therefore unofficial. Some are produced as officially licensed books by Paramount, "who has decreed that anything that's televised as *Star Trek* is 'Star Trek fact,' whereas anything that's printed is 'Star Trek fiction'" (quoted in Hills 2002, 126 n15). This means the future of *Deep Space Nine* is still as undefined as it was after the final episode.

The overall ethos of *Deep Space Nine*'s final episode focuses on having faith in the future even though the characters have no idea what is going to happen to them. Sisko tells his wife, Kasidy, that they may not be together for a long time but that when he returns it might seem as if he were only gone a day. That is the nature of the Prophets, who do not live in human linear time but rather live outside of time and can therefore deliver Sisko back to Kasidy before he had even left. Without the concept of linear time the Prophets do not understand history and do not understand humanity's preoccupation with memory, remembering, and eulogizing the past. When Sisko says to the Prophet Sarah (his mother) that his time as emissary was nearly at an end she responds, "Your journey's end lies not before you but behind you," and he finally realizes his position as religious messenger for the Prophets: his time on the station was only the beginning. This lack of narrative closure for the Sisko character is representative of the series' failure to bring adequate closure to many of its ongoing stories. For many fans this gives them plenty of opportunity to imagine what might be next. However, for those who are aware of the detailed yet fictional history of the Federation, *Enterprise* does not provide this opportunity because it is playing out the history of the Federation as it should have happened—as it is meant to happen in order to reach the time of *The Next Generation, Deep Space Nine,* and *Voyager. Star Trek*'s historical confinement is something that needs explaining so that we can comprehend *Enterprise*'s turn to the past.

The defining premise of *Enterprise* is the pioneer spirit, space exploration at its most rudimentary level, not much advanced from today. It charts the history of Roddenberry's future, where fan favorites such as the transporter and warp drive are in their infancy. *Enterprise* provides definitive fan interaction and appreciation because it caters to their fascination with *Star Trek* continuity and the franchise's penchant for describing the history of the future. The first few episodes exemplified this development by concentrating on key events in *Star Trek* lore; for example, the pilot episode, "Broken Bow," reveals new secrets behind the birth of Starfleet and recounts how the Vulcans opposed humanity's first steps toward the final frontier. The episode "The Andorian Incident" expands upon this trend by concentrating on the Andorian species, first seen in the original *Star Trek* but not regularly used in more recent series, and builds up a whole new social and cultural history around their characters. What these stories are actually doing is called "retconning," an "abbreviated term for the act of retroactively adjusting continuity," and "is a long-established staple in the world of comics, where characters' origins are forever being raked over, fleshed out and sometimes adjusted for perceived 'newer' audiences" (Jones 2002, 19). In other words, *Enterprise* is using retcons (an insertion into the fictional narrative chronology) as a means to construct the future history that both fascinates and compels the more serious fans. For those less concerned with the intricacies of *Star Trek* history the message exhibited in video advertising for the series signals the franchise's retrospective narrative agenda: over a picture of the new ship's captain, Jonathan Archer, reads the tag line "Meet Kirk's childhood hero." It seems that the future is far closer than we think.

This pull toward the past has increased exponentially since the 2001 terrorist atrocities in New York, so much so that film makers are reportedly having to go further back in time to rediscover the "youth of mankind" in the classical world of Greek and Arthurian legend (Harlow 2002, 17). According to Donna Minkowitz, "*Enterprise* was birthed before September 11, but it seems tailormade for this time of alien-hating and macho heroism" (2002, 37). Her main reason is that it gives *Star Trek* "a convenient excuse for turning back the galactic clock on race and gender," which Minkowitz sees as the two main failures of the new series (37). With regard to race, *Enterprise* supposedly champions white supremacy with its harsh depiction of the Vulcans as dominators who stand in the way of human creativity. In terms of gender, *Enterprise*'s world is chauvinistic because only two of the main crew are female: T'Pol's only role is to stand in the background and warn the captain about his actions; Hoshi resembles Lieutenant Uhura from the original *Star Trek* in that she steps in to hail Starfleet and be mollycoddled by her male crewmates on away missions. These criticisms of *Star Trek*'s treatment of race and gender are not new; they were often aimed at Gene Roddenberry and the original series and are the subject of many academic works.[3] However, Minkowitz believes that following the progress seen in *The Next Generation, Deep Space Nine,* and especially *Voyager,* these developments are a step backward in science fiction broadcasting. Consequently *Enterprise* not only returns to the narrative history of the Federation, it also replicates the inconsistent history of the original series, in which Roddenberry's liberal humanitarian ethos was continually offset by conservative representations of race and his own stereotypical views on how women should dress in the future. Much like George W. Bush's reactionary neoconservative policies in his war on terror and his labeling of some countries in the Middle East and Asia as the "Axis of Evil," *Enterprise*'s historical narrative and visual iconography clearly indicates a return to a Euro-American agenda.

The opening titles on *Enterprise* were a departure for a *Star Trek* series; they were the first to be accompanied by a song: Diane Warren's "Where My Heart Will Take Me," sung by Russell Watson. For Minkowitz this new addition to *Star Trek* convention is just as regressive as previous incarnations with its "boasts about resisting alien domination" (2002, 36). To some extent this observation is correct; however, I believe that the opening titles embody more than just a xenophobic reaction to the international community. The scenes from human history depicting the evolution of spaceflight and humanity's passion for exploration locate *Enterprise,* and therefore *Star Trek,* within a very specific tradition of American exceptionalism:

Enterprise Title Sequence Visuals:
A Kon-Tiki crossing the Pacific Ocean;
HMS *Enterprize* and nameplate;
Auguste and Jean Piccard, high-altitude balloonists;
Charles Lindbergh and the *Spirit of St Louis,* 1927;
Space Shuttle *Enterprise,* unveiled in 1976;
Amelia Earhart;
The Wright brothers at Kitty Hawk, North Carolina, 1903;
Deep sea *Explorer* submarine;
The Bell X-1 and Chuck Yeager, 1947;
Alan Shepard and *Apollo 14,* 1971;
John Glenn aboard Space Shuttle *Discovery,* 1998;
Dr. Robert H. Goddard, rocket pioneer;
Apollo 11 Moon Landing, 1969;
Sojourner, the robotic Mars rover, 1997;
The International Space Station;
A lunar orbiter, 2039;
The *Phoenix*'s first test run, 2063;
NX 01 Enterprise, 2151.

It is this tradition that perhaps accounts for both *Enterprise*'s and Bush's turn to the past at a time of American uncertainty. When the nation feels threatened, deprived, or isolated, American society requires an affirmation of its role within the larger global community. This role is depicted in the title sequence as that of leading in the development of spaceflight and a being a pioneer in the technological advancement of human civilization, but it is not restricted to the fictional history of *Star Trek.* America saw its mission to land on the moon and beat the Soviets in the space race as an extension of its mission to bring freedom to the world. The rhetoric of exceptionalism is part of America's self-appointed mission and has its roots in the exploration and settling of the American continent first initiated by the god-fearing Pilgrim fathers.

Star Trek's appropriation of what appears to be an overtly American version of history seen in the opening title sequence indicates that it is trying to ground its vision of the future in a mythic retelling of the past. Celebrating American achievements on the sea, in the air, and in space appears to be part of a process of reinterpretation or "revisioning" of history that Sarah Neely describes as a "retrovision." A "retrovision is a 'vision into or of the past' and implies an act of possessing the ability to read the past, in the way that one would possess a prophetic vision" (Neely 2001, 74). For Deborah Cartmell and I. Q. Hunter retrovisions are "makeovers of history" (2001, 7), and I apply the term to *Enterprise* here since it is trying to refashion *Star Trek*'s universal history by making it part of a specific American mythic history. Overall, the retrovisioning of *Star Trek* history is an appealing component of America's return to its exceptional past. Deborah L. Madsen (1998, 166) believes "exceptionalism has always offered a mythological refuge from the chaos of history and the uncertainty of life. . . . it *was* the legacy of the Old World for the New." *Enterprise* offers an American society unsure of the future the same refuge through a revisioning of a celebratory past. Furthermore, as Madsen believes "exceptionalism *is now* the legacy of the United States for us all" (166), *Enterprise*'s future also appears to be the only one that we as a global community can achieve because it has eliminated all vestiges of humanity's international achievements and replaced them with images of America's attempts at exploring space.

The ethos of both the title sequence and the pilot episode, "Broken Bow," is to have faith in the past because the past is reassuringly comforting compared to the political and social upheavals at the beginning of the twenty-first century. *Enterprise*'s "faith of the heart," as described in the title song, persuades the audience that *Star Trek*'s future is going to be a reality; the exceptionalism personified by America's aviation achievements in the credits proves that the future will be a bright one. Such optimism, however, can only come if you have faith in the past, celebrate American success, and ultimately rely on America "getting" you "from there to here." The optimism of *Star Trek*'s utopian future is still present, but in a rather conservative and backward-looking form. *Deep Space Nine*'s faith in the future is clearly focused on what is unknown, unseen, and uncontrollable. *Enterprise* seems to be saying that at the turn of the century, just three years after *Deep Space Nine* ended, such uncertainty will not bring us any closer to *Star Trek*'s future; rather, a predestined confidence will help us achieve utopia. As a result the vast future history of the *Star Trek* universe diminishes as all of humanity's accomplishments and desires are confined within the exceptional rhetoric of a mythical American history. *Enterprise*'s narrative can go no further than its forebears, and likewise its prognosis for the future is foreshortened.

II

Nevertheless, from an analysis of fan letters related to the new series, I would suggest that the constrictiveness of *Star Trek*'s exceptional future history is weakened through viewers' engagement with the televisual text. Fans, particularly British fans, are well aware of the potentially isolating and offensive effects of the overtly American *Enterprise* opening titles. In a letter printed in the *Radio Times* one British viewer writes: "The montage of historical film in the opening credits of *Enterprise* presents a narrow view of the development of space travel, with no sign of the first space travelers—male, female or canine—who are presumably of the wrong nationality to be celebrated. I seem to remember that Ensign Chekov used to have something to say about such matters" (Hughes 2002, 8).

The viewer is trying to point out that the *Star Trek* canon is at risk of overlooking its international elements—the famous Russian ensign to name just one—and that its historical source is beginning to be restricted to an American version of future history. The viewer appears not to agree with *Star Trek*'s isolationist u-turn and points out that *Enterprise* is looking back on a very nationalistic and masculine version of events.

In this next letter, titled "Yanks for the Memory," sent to the U.K. *Star Trek Magazine,* one fan tries to express his concerns about the *Enterprise* credits in an openly comedic fashion by pretending to be Vladimir Putin; yet, it still shows just how much fans pay attention to their favorite show: "Have you noticed that the opening credits show lovely images of Mankind's achievements, or should I say American achievements? It seems that they are the only ones that do anything according to *Enterprise.* I think we should have seen maybe the first man in space (Yuri Gagarin), the first man-made object in space (Sputnik), the first space station (Mir) and let's not forget also that we Russians did heaps of other cool things in space way before Mr. Armstrong went on his little trip! What would Chekov say about the above being missed out?" (Henderson 2002, 10).

This letter shows signs of sarcasm that hides a deeper concern over *Enterprise*'s lack of international history. The fan actually lists his own version of images to counteract those used in the credits, also assuming a Russian identity in which to do it. Positioning himself alongside Chekov in *Star Trek*'s mythos draws attention to the imbalance while also legitimizing his own argument by using official canon. Ironically the fan's faith in *Star Trek* future history signified through his use of Chekov's nationality and status as original cast member overcomes the retrovisioning of the space race and *Enterprise*'s faith in the American past. Fan criticism of the title images is not restricted to an international arena: Americans too are writing to point out the nationalist overtones of the spaceflight imagery. In this following letter taken from an *Enterprise* forum on the Internet, one U.S. fan indicates their appreciation of the musical accompaniment but again calls attention to the lack of Russian input: "lov [*sic*] the theme. Have been almost moved to tears by the eimagery [*sic*] until. . . . Only American space-craft are used in the titles. Oh I know there is the British Frigate (no USA at that time) and the International Space Station (mostly US), but what about Sputnik, Gargarin? [*sic*] Especially if you consider how repetitive and hackneyed some of those NASA shots are (that Apollo stage burning up in Earth's atmosphere, puleaze! [*sic*] Is that an invitation to litter or what?)" ("Sleader" 2002).

In reality *Star Trek*'s shift to the right in its latest series is not as significant as the fans' (both American and British) desire to engage critically with the important issues that pervade society in the early part of a new century. They are very aware of *Star Trek*'s pluralist tradition and important standing in American popular culture; they are determined not to let it become the product of a narrow-minded return to the past, rather the symbol of a refreshingly open-ended future.

For those who decide what actually goes into the canon by means of the episodes and official literature, the future history and the realities of the universe around it is an exciting way of telling important stories. Such stories have captured imaginations and taught several generations the valuable life lessons from past, present, and future society. The official *Star Trek* canon has become the fans' template for life, a blueprint for how society should and could be. Yet, as Daniel Bernardi (1998, 96–104) has theorized, the fans' canon is vulnerable to contamination from the same social issues that tarnish America's own literary and historical canon. Nevertheless, perhaps the fact that there is a divide between the fans' own interpretation of the text and what appears on-screen allows *Star Trek* to escape being totally affected by the same ideological problems America suffers. Furthermore, as my analysis of *Deep Space Nine* has shown, not all *Star Trek* series celebrate American history as does *Enterprise*. *Deep Space Nine* is a serious attempt at criticizing the human reliance on history as an outline for the future. Fans can and do criticize the fictional reality provided by *Star Trek*, thereby creating strong individual identities and negating the dangers of a naturalizing and ultimately overpowering historical narrative.

Notes

1. Since the end of *The Next Generation* in 1994 there have been four films featuring the main cast: *Star Trek: Generations* (1994), *Star Trek: First Contact* (1996), *Star Trek: Insurrection* (1998), *Star Trek: Nemesis* (2002).

2. Some examples of these books, published by Pocket Books in New York, are Marco Palmieri, ed., *The Lives of Dax* (1999); Andrew J. Robinson, *Star Trek: Deep Space Nine #27—A Stitch in Time* (2000); S.D. Perry's *Avatar Book One of Two* and *Avatar Book Two of Two* (2001); the *Mission: Gamma* series: David R. George III's *Twilight*, Heather Jarman's *This Gray Spirit*, Michael A. Martin and Andy Mangels's *Cathedral*, and Robert Simpson's *Lesser Evil* (all 2002); and the Klingon-based novels by J. G. Hertzler and Jeffrey Lang, *The Left Hand of Destiny, Book One* and *Book Two* (2003). S. D. Perry's *Rising Son* and *Unity* (both 2003) celebrate *Deep Space Nine*'s tenth anniversary with a story about Jake Sisko trying to contact his father through the Bajoran Wormhole.

3. See Daniel L. Bernardi, *Star Trek and History: Race-ing Toward a White Future* (New Brunswick, N.J.: Rutgers University Press, 1998); Robin Roberts, *Sexual Generations: "Star Trek: The Next Generation" and Gender* (Urbana: University of Illinois Press, 1999); Jay Goulding, *Empire, Aliens, and Conquest: A Critique of American Ideology in* Star Trek *and Other Science Fiction Adventures* (Toronto: Sisyphus, 1985); Taylor Harrison, Sarah Projansky, Kent A. Ono, and Elyce Rae Helford, eds., *Enterprise Zones: Critical Positions on* Star Trek (Boulder, Colo.: Westview, 1996); Mike Hertenstein, *The Double Vision of* Star Trek*: Half-Humans, Evil Twins and Science Fiction* (Chicago: Cornerstone, 1998); Jennifer E. Porter and Darcee L. McLaren, eds., Star Trek *and Sacred Ground: Explorations of* Star Trek, *Religion, and American Culture* (Albany: State University of New York Press, 1999); Micheal C. Pounds, *Race in Space: The Representation of Ethnicity in* Star Trek *and* Star Trek: The

Next Generation (Lanham, Md.: Scarecrow, 1999); Karin Blair, "Sex and *Star Trek*," *Science Fiction Studies* 10, no. 2 (1983): 292–97; Anne Cranny-Francis, "Sexuality and Sex-Role Stereotyping in *Star Trek*," *Science Fiction Studies* 12, no. 3 (1985): 274–84; Mary Henderson, "Professional Women in *Star Trek*, 1964–1969." *Film and History* 24, nos. 1–2 (1994): 47–59.

Bibliography

Anderson, Steve. 2000. "Loafing in the Garden of Knowledge: History TV and Popular Memory." *Television as Historian 1*, special issue of *Film and History* 30, no. 1: 14–23.

Bercovitch, Sacvan. 1978. *The American Jeremiad.* Madison: University of Wisconsin Press.

Bernardi, Daniel L. 1998. Star Trek *and History: Race-ing toward a White Future.* New Brunswick, N.J.: Rutgers University Press.

Blair, Karin. 1997. "*Star Trek* Old and New: From the Alien Embodied to the Alien Imagined." In *Yankee Go Home (and Take Me with U): Americanization and Popular Culture,* ed. George McKay, 78–88. Sheffield: Sheffield Academic Press.

Cartmell, Deborah, and I.Q. Hunter. 2001. "Introduction: Retrovisions: Historical Makeovers in Film and Literature." In *Retrovisions: Reinventing the Past in Film and Fiction,* ed. Deborah Cartmell, I. Q. Hunter, and Imelda Whelehan, 1–7. London: Pluto.

Dillard, J. M. 1996. Star Trek, *Where No One Has Gone Before: A History in Pictures.* New York: Pocket Books.

Gregory, Chris. 2000. Star Trek: *Parallel Narratives.* Basingstoke, U.K.: Macmillan.

Harlow, John. 2002. "Amazons Lead Hollywood Raid on Antiquity." *Sunday Times,* January 20.

Henderson, Hugh. 2002. "Yanks for the Memory." *Star Trek Monthly Magazine* (November): 20.

Hills, Matt. 2002. *Fan Cultures.* London: Routledge.

Hughes, Bryn. 2002. "Russians Ruled Out." *Radio Times,* August 10–16.

Jones, Nick. 2002. "Retcon Tricks." *Star Trek Monthly Magazine* (February): 18–21.

Madsen, Deborah L. 1998. *American Exceptionalism.* Edinburgh: Edinburgh University Press.

Minkowitz, Donna. 2002. "Beam Us Back, Scotty!" *Nation,* March 25: 36–37.

Neely, Sarah. 2001, "Cool Intentions: The Literary Classic, the Teenpic and the 'Chick Flick.'" In *Retrovisions: Reinventing the Past in Film and Fiction,* ed. Deborah Cartmell, I. Q. Hunter, and Imelda Whelehan, 74–86. London: Pluto.

Okuda, Michael, and Denise Okuda. 1993. Star Trek *Chronology: A History of the Future.* New York: Pocket Books.

Okuda, Michael, Denise Okuda, and Debbie Mirek. 1997. *The* Star Trek *Encyclopedia: A Reference Guide to the Future.* 3rd ed. New York: Pocket Books.

Richards, Jeffrey. 2000. "Fires Were Started." In *The Movies as History: Visions of the Twentieth Century,* ed. David W. Elwood, 26–35. Stroud, U.K.: Sutton.

Richards, Thomas. 1998. Star Trek *in Myth and Legend.* London: Orion.

"Sleader." 2002. "Minor Issue." *Back in Time:* Enterprise *Fan Forum.* http://bitent.cjb.net/fbackintimeenterprisefrm1.showMessage?topicID=62.topic (accessed August 2003).

Slotkin, Richard. 1986. "Myth and the Production of History." In *Ideology and Classic American Literature,* ed. Sacvan Bercovitch and Myra Jehlen, 70–90. Cambridge: Cambridge University Press.

Wagner, Jon. 1999. "Intimations of Immortality: Death/Life Mediations in *Star Trek*." In Star Trek *and Sacred Ground: Explorations of* Star Trek, *Star Trek* ed. Jennifer E. Porter and Darcee L. McLaren, 119–38. Albany: State University of New York Press.

"But What of Lazarus?"

Taking Individuals Seriously in the *Star Trek* Saga

Paul Christopher Manuel

In all five of its televised series as well as its various movies, *Star Trek* story lines abound with the importance of the individual. From Capt. James T. Kirk observing that "in every revolution there's one man with a vision" (*Star Trek*, "Mirror, Mirror") to Capt. Jean-Luc Picard noting that "if we're going to be damned, let's be damned for who we really are" (*Star Trek: The Next Generation*, "Encounter at Far Point") and Capt. Katherine Janeway declaring that "we will find a way out of here" (*Star Trek: Voyager*, "The Displaced Season"), we can see that individuals—and especially leaders—matter in the *Star Trek* universe. This essay will look at the role of the individual in the *Star Trek* saga, with a focus on the original series, which ran from 1966–1969. It will first explore some theoretical issues and then examine the various ways that the individual influenced events in the *Star Trek* universe. Throughout, it will seek to illustrate how *Star Trek* takes individual actions seriously.

Theoretical Issues

Star Trek was clearly in line with the precepts of the behavioral revolution of the 1960s. Heinz Eulau's famous statement in his 1963 *The Behavioral Persuasion in Politics,* "the root is man" (3), represented an important step in the behavioral revolution's rejection of formal-legal-based scholarship, and resonates throughout the *Star Trek* saga.[4] Eulau goes on to say that "I don't think it is possible to say anything meaningful about the governance of man without talking about the political behavior of man—his acts, goals, drives, feelings, beliefs, commitments, and values." He argues that the central and most important actor in politics is the human being. Indeed, as far back as Plato, there has been an awareness of the important link between character and regime type. In the *Star Trek* saga, the clever tend to prevail in political battles over those less so; political factors do not necessarily dominate during all times, but they are always in play.

The Individual in History

One of the key issues in the study of the individual in politics involves determining those circumstances under which an individual may have a significant influence on political outcomes. Scholars from the structuralist tradition have maintained that the individual plays no significant role in the unfolding of history. These theorists assign primary importance to large-scale economic transformations or cultural variables. Others from the formal legal tradition agree that the individual is a dependent variable in history. Fred Greenstein, in his *Personality and Politics,* rejects this conclusion. Rather, he seeks to uncover how, when, and why a political actor may be indispensable to a particular historical situation. That is, under what conditions might the personality of a particular leader actually direct the course of history?

How an individual functions in history is central to the question. Greenstein is careful to point out that individuals influence the unfolding of history in specific and rare situations—and the situation has to be dynamic and in flux for there to be a maximum influence where the normal patterns of behavior are disrupted. This type of situation could be caused by a natural disaster or by a large-scale social movement. The disruption of the standardized pattern of behavior—the historical flux—generally opens up an authority void. During times of change it is this void that may allow an extraordinary individual to direct political outcomes.[6] Certainly, in the vast and dark expanse of space, the pivotal role of the leader becomes amplified—it is impossible to think of classic *Star Trek* without Kirk and Spock or *The Next Generation* without Picard.

The Individual in the Original Series

Let us now turn to an in-depth examination of the role of the individual in the original *Star Trek* series. The episodes with a clear focus on the individual in *Star Trek* may be classified by four interlocking themes. The first theme features the good-versus-evil dichotomy; the second explores the complex relationship between logic and emotion; the third deals with the sometime crucial role of aliens; and the fourth theme focuses on the role of significant actors in history. Let us examine each of these in turn.

Theme One: Good Versus Evil

The battle between good and evil is a central theme of the *Star Trek* saga. The characters frequently discuss the nature of good and evil, how they operate, and what makes each distinctive. We know that the Federation tends to be good and the Klingon empire is frequently evil, but that does not always prove to be the case. Among the many episodes that can be seen as elaborating this theme, let us examine five: "The Enemy Within," "The Omega Glory," "A Private Little War," "Mirror, Mirror," and "The Savage Curtain."

"The Enemy Within"

This episode takes us deep into the problem of good versus evil and to the very core of Captain Kirk's personality. A transporter malfunction splits Kirk into two persons, or sides: one Kirk is a rational, gentle, and civilized person; the other is driven, power-hungry, and depraved. The rational Kirk goes about the business of being captain, but finds himself tired and weak; meanwhile, the evil Kirk is lurking about the ship looking for liquor and women. The evil Kirk's assault on Yeoman Janice Rand brings the problem to the attention of Spock, and the good Kirk eventually manages to capture his evil side. What is most interesting about the good-versus-evil dilemma in this episode is that Kirk needs both halves to be an effective human being: the rational side of the good Kirk needs the passion of the evil Kirk; the impulses of the evil Kirk need the restraint of the good Kirk. In the end, Scotty fixes the transporter and manages to bring both halves of Kirk together again. The viewer is left to wonder how good and evil sides may also coexist within ourselves.

"The Omega Glory"

"The Omega Glory" continues with the problem of the "evil" captain. In this story, the USS *Enterprise* finds the starship USS *Exeter* abandoned in orbit about the planet Omega IV. Kirk then leads a landing party in the search for its captain and crew. The landing party quickly locates the commander of the *Exeter,* Captain Tracey, and learns that the rest of the crew had died from a virus they contracted on the planet. Doctor McCoy discovers that the biosphere on Omega IV immunizes individuals from the virus; Tracey survived because he did not leave the planet. Even so, the loss of his crew drove Tracey insane, perhaps explaining why he used his phasers to help one tribe, the Kohms, in their civil war against the Yang tribe. His help was to no avail, as the Yangs defeat the Kohms and take both Tracy and Kirk prisoner. For political scientists, this episode is particularly appealing in that it presents an Earth-history parallel of a fictional war between Red China ("the Kohms") and the United States ("the Yangs"), in which the Communists won the first round but the democrats eventually prevailed. Over time, the Yangs have distorted their so-called holy words, which were from the U.S. Constitution, and the episode ends with Kirk teaching them the true meaning of "We the people." Since the Yangs believe that good will always defeat evil, they allow Kirk and Tracey to fight to the death. After Kirk prevails and Sulu beams down to the planet with support, the Yangs take Kirk for a god. The captain explains that he is only a man and attempts to refocus their distorted perceptions of their constitution and of their notions of the nature of good and evil.

"A Private Little War"

This episode is a particularly relevant statement on the problem of "proxy wars" during the cold war, in which the two superpowers would supply arms their allies, sometimes causing civil wars in economically backward places such as Korea, Vietnam, and Angola. In this story Kirk returns to an idyllic planet he had visited during one of his first assignments in deep space, well before he was captain. On this return visit he is horrified to discover that the Klingons were providing guns to the villagers, giving them a military advantage over the neighboring hill people. In order to restore the balance of power—and over the objections of McCoy—Kirk decides to provide guns to the hill people. In this process an evil serpent known as a flintlock gun transforms a once good "Garden of Eden" into a battle zone, balanced by terror.

"Mirror, Mirror"

This episode is a remarkable journal into the inner workings of good and evil. It begins with an ion storm disrupting the transporter just as Kirk, McCoy, Scotty, and Uhura are beaming back to the *Enterprise,* and instead sending them to an alternative and evil *Enterprise* in a parallel universe—and, in the process, sending their evil doubles to the good *Enterprise.* Once the good Spock realizes what has happened, he places the evil versions of his shipmates into the brig. Similarly, when the evil Spock realizes the situation, he too assists the good Kirk and the others to find a way back. Once they figure out how to return to their *Enterprise,* the good Kirk speaks to the evil Spock and encourages him to eliminate the evil Kirk, become captain, and move to transform the Imperial Starfleet into something good. Throughout the episode, whereas good and evil traits are easily discerned in the emotional humans, it is far more difficult to do the same with the logical Spocks. The discipline of logic emerges as a tool for either good or evil, dependent upon the dominant emotion of the humans—this is reminiscent of the German civil service that served both Weimar Germany and Nazi Germany. The Basic Law for the Federal Republic of Germany of 1949 seeks to guard against the dangers of an "impartial" civil service by requiring bureaucrats to belong to a political party committed to the principles of democratic rule. We hope, at the end of "Mirror, Mirror," that the evil Spock will place his talents at the service of the good, but there is no reason we should believe it will really happen: he stands as witness to the dangers of an independent bureaucracy at the service of an evil state. A subplot deals with negotiations with the Halkans for their dilithium crystals, which power the ship; the good Kirk and Federation negotiate, whereas the evil Kirk and the "Galactic Empire" plan simply to take the crystals and destroy the Halkan people if they refuse to cooperate. Both Enterprises are equally powerful, but the moral compass of the humans on board conditions their behavior.

"The Savage Curtain"

"The Savage Curtain" serves as another example of the exploration into questions related to good and evil. In this episode an image of Abraham Lincoln invites Kirk and Spock to beam down to the planet Excalbia. Once they arrive, Yarnek, a being made of rock, speaks to them. He wants Kirk and Spock to teach his species about the concepts of good and evil and creates a battle between four "good" and "evil" personages. In addition to Kirk and Spock, Lincoln and Surak—a revered moral leader of Vulcan—are placed on the "good" team. The four players on the "evil" team are Genghis Khan, a Klingon named Kahless, and two murderers, Colonel Green and Zora. At the end Kirk and Spock survive and engage in a philosophical discussion with Yarnek over the concepts of good and evil. Yarnek's key observation is that the battle techniques of each side appeared to be the same, and he could not distinguish between the concepts of powerful and weak and good and bad. We are left to wonder whether or not the axiom of "might makes right" controls our understandings of good and evil.

Theme Two: Emotions and Logic

One of the more interesting story lines in *Star Trek* has been the exploration of logic versus emotion. Humans are generally portrayed as emotional beings who use logic as a tool; the Vulcans are a species dedicated to the discipline of logic in all things, who frown upon displays of emotion. Spock, being the offspring of a Vulcan father and human mother, embodies the conflict between cold Vulcan logic and human emotion. Another aspect to this theme involves the age-old battle of irrational man versus rational machine. Among the thematic episodes in this category, let us examine four: "Amok Time," "The *Galileo Seven*," "The Ultimate Computer," and "A Taste of Armageddon."

"Amok Time"

The biological and emotional functions of Vulcans are explored in "Amok Time." Spock becomes irrational and withdrawn for unknown reasons and finally reveals to Kirk that his problem relates to Vulcan mating rituals. That is, he has reached the time to consummate his arranged marriage, a ceremony known as the Pon Farr, and must immediately return to Vulcan: he will die if he is unable to mate with his bride, T'Pring. As the episode progresses, we see a withdrawn and highly irrational Spock, stripped of all logic, lost in a blood fever of passion. When his bride asks that he fight for her, according to Vulcan ritual, he apparently kills Kirk, whom T'Pring has chosen as her champion. Brought back to his senses after the combat, he relinquishes his claim to T'Pring to her suitor, Stonn, and returns to the *Enterprise* for punishment. Once back on board, he is shocked to find Kirk alive—thanks to the quick thinking of McCoy, who administered a drug that simulates death prior to the combat—and fails for a moment to hide his joyful relief. The episode shows how Vulcans bottle up their emotions, and that even they need to release their passions during mating time.

"The Galileo Seven"

This episode shows both the strengths and weaknesses of a logically Vulcan commander for emotive humans. In this story Spock, McCoy, Scott, and four crew members have crash-landed on a planet known as Taurus II in the *Enterprise's Galileo* shuttle. As they try to make repairs, they come under attack from the giant indigenous beings. The question of whether the crew should stop to bury lost crewmen reveals the dynamics of the logic-versus-emotion tension. Spock objects to the burial, arguing that they would lose valuable time and that more could possibly be killed while they bury the bodies. The humans counter that they have an ethical and religious duty to honor the dead. Spock consents to the burial but is not happy about it. In the end he saves the crew by acting on an impulse, logically arrived at. His logic angers and also helps to save the crew.

"The Ultimate Computer"

The dual themes of logic versus emotion and machine versus human dominate this episode. Starfleet command has decided to test the new M-5 computer system, invented by Dr. Richard Daystrom, on the *Enterprise.* This computer is designed to run a starship without human intervention so that Starfleet can send out a fleet of drone ships to chart the stars without loss of human life or the distractions of human emotion. In the end the M-5 fails because it starts to attack any ship in its path. Kirk is relieved to know that there is a place for humans in the universe. The episode leaves us with an ironic twist: the rational machine was created by a brilliant and emotionally unstable human being.

"A Taste of Armageddon"

The planet of Eminiar VII and its warring neighbor, Vendikar, have seemingly found a way out of the brutality of war by playing war games with their computers. The catch is whenever there is a virtual attack on a populated area, those whom the computers declare to be casualties have to report to antimatter chambers to be killed. Thus the leaders of each planet have found a way to kill without brutality, making war both durable and civilized. When the *Enterprise* is supposedly hit by an attack from the Vendikar war computer, Eminiar VII expects the ship's personnel to report to an antimatter chamber. Kirk refuses to play along, however, and turns the tables on the leader of Eminiar VII, called Anan 7, by telling him that if he and the ruling council of Vendikar refuse to meet and make a peace to end the computer war, he will order the *Enterprise* to teach them what war is really like by leveling their planets. Kirk forces the leadership of both planets to accept the fact that real people die in war, that leadership is about more than having one's people report to antimatter chambers to maintain the status quo, and that war is ugly and brutal. Rational beings should always seek to avoid war.

Theme 3: The Aliens Count too

The significant role of an individual is not limited to *Star Trek* personnel. We find ample episodes of alien captains controlling events by their own actions. Let us explore four of them: "Balance of Terror," "The *Enterprise* Incident," "Day of the Dove," and "Let That Be Your Last Battlefield."

"Balance of Terror"

This magnificent episode features a battle of wits between Captain Kirk and his Romulan counterpart, the commander of a Warbird vessel equipped with a cloaking device. That device enables the Warbird to approach its targets invisibly, and it has thus destroyed several Federation outposts along the neutral zone between Federation and Romulan space. This episode features a chess match of sorts between the two captains, the Romulan trying to return home and the human seeking to bring them to justice. An interesting twist is that we see the Romulans for the first time, and they bear a striking resemblance to Vulcans. Spock informs Kirk that Romulans are a dangerous offshoot of the Vulcan race, in that they embrace emotion over logic, and are aggressive and imperial. In the battle between the two captains, Kirk eventually prevails, and just before he activates the self-destruct on his ship, the Romulan commander tells Kirk that in another reality, he would be able to call him friend—leaving us with a longing for a time when friendship will trump warfare. Choices by the two captains control the events of this story.

"The Enterprise Incident"

In this episode, Kirk and Spock team up to use emotion and logic to outwit a female Romulan commander and make off with a Romulan cloaking device. In the beginning of the story Kirk feigns emotional instability and orders the *Enterprise* into Romalan space. The *Enterprise* is captured, and Kirk is taken prisoner. Once on board, Spock pretends to be interested in the commander and suggests that she could convince him to join the Romulans; meanwhile, Kirk escapes from his cell and—disguised as a Romulan—steals the cloaking device. In the end Kirk and Spock are successful, and the Romulan commander is humiliated. Her poor choices have left the Romulan Empire weakened by the loss of the cloaking technology.

"Day of the Dove"

This episode explores the role of choice in war in a most inventive fashion. Some type of nefarious gaseous being—known as the Beta XII-A entity—which feeds off of hatred, arranges for a group of Klingons, led by Commander Kang, to be stranded on the *Enterprise* against an evenly matched group from Kirk's crew. The entity stirs up resentments and hatred in each person, and can be seen gaining strength by glowing as Klingons and humans butcher each other. Needing more and more energy, the entity uses its power to heal the combatants and continues to provide each sides with arms. At the same time it has gained control of the navigational computer and is speeding the *Enterprise* out of the galaxy, apparently to its home world. The one person on board not completely under its spell of hatred is Spock, whose logic helps him piece together what is happening. He prevails upon the captain, who then manages to convince Kang that they are not making choices, but are mere pawns. With that, the two captains order their respective crews to cease combat and engage in a hearty round of laughter. The Beta XII-A entity loses interest in them and departs into space. The decision of the Klingon commander was crucial to the outcome.

"Let That Be Your Last Battlefield"

This episode offers an interesting commentary on the racial problems of the 1960s. It features two alien beings, Bele and Lokai, from the planet of Cheron, who are fighting one another for no clear reason. Both of these natives of Cheron have interesting skin features: black skin on one side and white skin on the other. There is a significant difference, however: Bele's skin is white where Lokai's is black, and vice versa, a difference that outsiders do not immediately recognize but that has led to great social strive and bigotry on Cheron. Bele is on an official mission to apprehend Lokai and bring him back to answer for his crimes against his people. After some time, the *Enterprise* arrives at Cheron— only to discover that the civil war has resulted in the complete destruction of all life there. The two men beam down to the planet's surface, and Kirk leaves them there. The two individuals remain controlled by the same hatred that was responsible for the destruction of their home world. In spite of Kirk's best efforts, he cannot manage to convince either of them that their minds are distorted by hatred and that they are unable to make good choices.

Theme Four: The Role of Significant Actors

The important role of individuals is not restricted to captains or to series regulars. Throughout the universe the *Enterprise* encounters extraordinary individuals who are central to the outcome of the stories in which they appear. Four instances of these story lines are "The City on the Edge of Forever," "Patterns of Force," "Bread and Circuses," and "The Alternative Factor."

"The City on the Edge of Forever"

Edith Keeler is a classic example of such a character. In the episode "The City on the Edge of Forever," Kirk and Spock have to return to the past to find McCoy and return him to their time. They have encountered some type of organic time machine—known as the Guardian of Forever—which offers vistas of the past. Once someone passes through the threshold they become part of that past and could change history.

Doctor McCoy, who has injected himself with a large amount of a powerful medicine by accident and been temporally rendered psychotic, manages to pass though the time threshold and change history for the worse. To repair this historical breach, Kirk and Spock also pass through the threshold. They arrive on Earth in the 1930s, encountering there the extraordinary person of Keeler, a social worker and a peace activist. Before McCoy's interference she had originally died in a traffic accident; because of his intervention she lives to lead a peace movement that delays the United States's entry into the World War II, giving Hitler the time he needs to develop the atomic bomb and achieve global domination. Accordingly the Federation is never formed. In his research of historical records Spock discovers Keeler's role in this altered history and informs Kirk, who has fallen in love with her. Kirk resists Spock's logical conclusion, but in the end he does what he must: he stops McCoy from saving Keeler's life and, in the process, restores history. "The City on the Edge of Forever" is a complex and multifaceted episode that, at its root, is about the important role an individual can play in historical outcomes.

"Patterns of Force"

The person of John Gill is another good illustration of this theme. In "Patterns of Force," Kirk and Spock go to the planet of Ekos to find out what happened to the Starfleet Academy history professor Gill, who has gone missing. Upon their arrival they are stunned to see that the inhabitants are wearing uniforms from Nazi-era Germany and are engaged in a Holocaust against the people of Zeon, a neighboring planet. Upon further investigation they discover that the fuhrer of Ekos is in fact Professor Gill. They eventually find him, who tells Kirk that he used the model of Nazi Germany to bring order and discipline to Ekos; it worked at first, but an evil man named Melakon seized control from him, drugged him, and kept him around as a figurehead. Once the truth is revealed, Melakon is killed, and a new regime of reformers takes over. Their first order of business is to ask Captain Kirk to leave so they could build their own history. Gill's miscalculations proved fatal to many Zeons; the theme of how an individual can impact history is particularly strong in this episode.

"Bread and Circuses"

In this episode the Enterprise is attempting to locate the missing crew of the USS *Beagle,* which is in orbit around a planet known as 892-IV. That planet has some surprising features: it is an exact duplicate of Earth yet is located on the opposite side of the galaxy. Once Kirk, Spock, and McCoy beam down to the surface, they are shocked to discover that 892-IV has undergone similar historical development to Earth's with one major difference: the Roman Empire has never fallen. They eventually locate the captain of the *Beagle,* R. M. Merrick, known on the planet as First Citizen, who is clearly in violation of multiple Federation regulations. The proconsul, Claudius Marcus, forces Kirk, Spock, and McCoy to participate in gladiator games but is unable to convince Kirk to beam down his crew to be butchered by gladiators live on Roman television. Once Kirk realizes that all of Merrick's crew has been killed by the Romans, he manages to return to the ship. Of interest for our purposes is the discussion that takes place as the *Enterprise* leaves the orbit of 892-IV: Kirk, McCoy, and Spock discuss the qualities of the people who belong to an anti-Roman movement. These rebels hide in the caves outside of the city and had given them refuge. Kirk, Spock, and McCoy observe that these people follow a pagan religion that worships the sun. Overhearing their conversation, communications officer Uhura corrects them. She had been monitoring the planet's radio broadcasts and had discovered that the rebels were not engaged in a pagan worship of the sun but rather were worshiping the "Son of God." Stunned, Kirk muses poetically about how this movement of Christians would eventually transform the Roman Empire on 892-IV, similarly to what happened on Earth. As such, this story line borrows from actual human history and leaves us with the example of an individual—in this case, the god-man—who transformed the course of human history.

"The Alternative Factor"

Perhaps the best demonstration of this theme is evidenced in the episode "The Alternative Factor." Here we find an incredible event taking place—the entire universe experiences "nonexistence" for a few seconds. Spock is at a loss to explain what he witnessed, and both Kirk and Starfleet Command fear some kind of invasion. Kirk leads a landing party to the planet they are orbiting— which seems to be at the nexus of the disturbance—and finds a humanoid called Lazarus, who claims that he is chasing a horrible monster who is responsible for death and destruction. As the episode continues, we see Lazarus changing: from angry to peaceful, irrational to rational. It turns out that there are in fact two of them from alternative universes, and that they are both time travelers. In their travels the Lazarus from Kirk's universe has gone mad with the realization that a double exists and is obsessed with killing him. The problem is that if matter and antimatter touch, then all existence will be turned into nonexistence. The sane Lazarus asks Kirk to help him: the plan is to lock both of them in a time portal of sorts forever, and Kirk needs to destroy Lazarus's ship, which essentially will seal the portal. In the end the two men called Lazarus are trapped in the time corridor, where they will forever fight. The decision of the insane Lazarus imperiled existence; the choice of the sane Lazarus saved all existence, but at the price of being trapped with a madman. Kirk wonders aloud at the end, "But what of Lazarus?"—in other words, what is the fate of the good person who sacrifices his or her life for the greater good?

Conclusion: Taking Individuals Seriously

Combined, the four themes of good versus evil, logic versus emotion, the some-time crucial role of aliens, and the role of significant actors in history bring us to the important observation that individuals are more than just puppets wait-ing to be told what to do: they have the capacity to make history. Given the uncertainty of politics, a probabilistic model of change makes a great deal of sense. It views the unfolding of history to be characterized by competing politi-cal forces in which power shifts occur for any number of reasons, and where the clever, or the more politically skillful, tend to prevail. The *Star Trek* saga offers us both an opportunity to appreciate the potentially important role of the indi-vidual in history and to reject deterministic interpretations of political change.

Indeed, it is worth noting that the categories identified in James David Bar-ber's now-classic 1972 work, *Presidential Character,* offer interesting insights both on the potentially important role of individuals in history and on how the various leadership styles of the five captains and their first officers influence various outcomes in the *Star Trek* saga. Barber measures the performance of presidential leadership by the leader's energy (active or passive) and personal-ity type (positive or negative). He then integrates these two measurements into four cross-cutting ideal types of presidential leadership (active-positive, active-negative, passive-positive, and passive-negative).[18]

Applied to the five *Star Trek* captain/first officer teams of Kirk and Spock, Picard and Riker, Janeway and Chakotay, Sisko and Kira, and Archer and T'Pol, the "active-positive" leadership style reflects a person of high self-esteem, who is both flexible and oriented toward achieving larger objectives (Kirk, Janeway, Archer); the "active-negative" leadership style is someone obsessive and controlling (Chakotay, Kira); "passive-positive" is a good-natured, agreeable leader, but someone who can be easily hurt (Riker) and "passive-negative" is a dutiful leader who tends to recoil from confrontation (Spock, Picard, Sisko, T'Pol). This is illustrated in the following table.

PERSONALITY TYPE

	Positive	*Negative*
Active	Kirk, Janeway, Archer	Chakotay, Kira
Passive	Riker	Spock, Picard, Sisko, T'Pol

The combined leadership style of each captain and first officer reveals some interesting mixtures: Kirk and Spock combine active-positive and passive-negative traits; Picard and Riker combine passive-negative and passive-positive ones; Janeway and Chakotay combine active-positive and active-negative; Sisko and Kira combine passive-negative and active-negative; and Archer and T'Pol combine active-positive and passive-negative ones. In terms of the episodes, *grosso modo,* Kirk's active-positive personality drove many of the story lines, whereas Spock's passive-negative traits helped contextualize the overall situation; Riker's optimism balanced Picard's caution; Janeway's bravado is steadied by Chakotay's suspicions; Sisko's passivity is overcome by Kira's anger; and Archer's youthful energy is restrained by the more cautious and mature T'Pol. These combinations not only made for interesting story lines, but also reflected the ebbs and flows of actual leadership styles. The combination of these various personality traits may also deepen our understandings of those qualities, or mixture of qualities, necessary for effective leadership, in the *Star Trek* world and beyond.

In the end *Star Trek* story lines often account for political outcomes in the imprecise and often unpredictable acts of individuals: ranging from the behavioral style of important personages to the beliefs and personalities of leaders—and how they handle the pressures of leadership—to the roles of significant individuals in history. Indeed, in the darkness of space, where everything awaits to be created, all eyes turn to the captain; perhaps this is best illustrated in the closing scene of "The Alternative Factor," where we witness a pensive young Captain Kirk wondering aloud, "But what of Lazarus?"

Note

1. Eulau's full observation is as follows: "The root is man. I don't think it is possible to say anything meaningful about the governance of man without talking about the political behavior of man—his acts, goals, drives, feelings, beliefs, commitments, and values."

Bibliography

Barber, James David. 1992. *Presidential Character: Predicting Performance in the White House.* 4th ed. New York: Prentice Hall.

Eulau, Heinz. 1963. *The Behavioral Persuasion in Politics.* New York: Random House.

Greenstein, Fred I. 1987. *Personality and Politics: Problems of Evidence, Inference, and Conceptualization.* Princeton, N.J.: Princeton University Press.

Inverted Perspectives on Politics and Morality in *Battlestar Galactica*

Woody Goulart and Wesley Y. Joe

The popular U.S. science fiction television series *Battlestar Galactica*[1] challenges its audience's core perceptions, beliefs, and values in ways that one rarely finds in commercial television programming. The terrorist attacks on the United States on September 11, 2001, and the subsequent war in Iraq provide the political and cultural context for the series' producers and writers to pose urgent, controversial questions about military and political issues for viewers to ponder. Using the science fiction format, the series explicitly addresses warfare and conflict between political and cultural opponents, compelling viewers to evaluate difficult questions. Detailed accounts of an archenemy's religion-based violent attacks upon a secular democracy of human beings set the foundation for *Battlestar Galactica*'s rhetorical storytelling.

This essay examines how the producers and writers of *Battlestar Galactica* defy the conventions of directly allegorical stories to push viewers outside their comfort zones and upend their abilities to pass moral judgments about pressing contemporary questions of war versus peace and right versus wrong. It considers how effectively *Battlestar Galactica* tells human adventure stories of a military and political nature through a bold challenge to audience opinions on three essential points: First, the series provides commentary on deeply held U.S. beliefs about contemporary politics and the military. Second, the series questions the connection between organized religion and political and military actions. And third, the series compels viewers to accept that during political and military conflict, despite any idealized standards of right and wrong, fundamentally decent people can behave in uncivil and immoral ways.

Different Prism

Battlestar Galactica's "showrunner," Ronald D. Moore, manages, controls, produces, and often writes or rewrites the series' episodes. Along with co-producer David Eick, Moore exerts a profound influence upon *Battlestar Galactica* from his reinvention of the 1978 ABC television series to day-to-day leadership of the show. As showrunner, Moore explains specifically that he uses a "different prism" through which his stories and characters are "twisted" from the expected or anticipated norm in ways that few, if any, other television shows ever attempt (Newgen 2006). Moore's storytelling technique deliberately distorts what viewers may deem as "normal" or "expected" perspectives on people, politics, organized religion and moral issues. The specific purpose of this distortion is to serve a rhetorical process that aims to convince *Battlestar Galactica*'s audience to look at individual political, religious, and human moral issues from a variety of perspectives. By bringing the ambiguity of these issues into the foreground, *Battlestar Galactica* challenges average citizens to think about the potential merits of perspectives they oppose and the drawbacks of perspectives they embrace. In commercial television—the dominant entertainment medium in the United States—this is a relatively recent development.

The rhetorical process first strips the audience's sense of comfort about television characters and the fictional situations in which they exist. It then asks viewers to compare and contrast these characters against their own expectations of human nature and behavior. The comparing and contrasting leaves viewers with no choice but to reflect on persuasive depictions of the characters' behavior in times of military and political conflict. *Battlestar Galactica* characters are unlike the typical characters in science fiction television series. Instead of following long-standing traditions of character development for commercial television, Moore intentionally creates personalities that more closely resemble real people. When viewed through Moore's "prism" of rhetorical distortion, his characters can be illogical, deeply flawed, and often exhibit unpredictable behavior based on their intense emotional and physical drives, much like genuine people.

This approach differs substantially from how science fiction television characters have more commonly been constructed for decades, especially following *Star Trek*'s influence on science fiction television and motion pictures. However, Moore acknowledges that *Battlestar Galactica* continues to be informed by the optimistic and heroic characters of *Star Trek*. He clarifies his intention for his characters: "My characters may not have all the answers (sometimes they're not even aware of the questions) but they contain kernels of both good and evil in their hearts and continue to struggle for salvation and redemption against the darker angels of their natures. Their defeats are many, their victories few, but somehow, some way, they never give up the dream of finding a better tomorrow" (Moore 2006a).

The *Battlestar Galactica* saga involves a literal clash of civilizations in a far-off galaxy. Human beings have colonized a dozen home worlds where they must battle the Cylons, a threateningly powerful artificial life-form created by humans thousands of years ago to function as industrial and military helpers. Since the human creators were, themselves, flawed, so was their creation. The Cylons rebelled against their creators. But after hundreds of years of bloody Cylon-human warfare a stalemate was reached, and the Cylons mysteriously withdrew to live on another planet.

In the opening minutes of *Battlestar Galactica,* a terrible secret is revealed. During the four decades that the Cylons have been separated from humans, they have advanced in their science and technology and have produced a new variety of life-form that is indistinguishable in outward appearance from human beings. These new Cylon models, which look and feel exactly like humans, have infiltrated the human race at deep levels and have successfully launched genocidal attacks upon humanity across multiple planets using nuclear weapons of mass destruction. Only tens of thousands of humans remain after the Cylon nuclear attack; and the survivors have no choice but to fight back in a bitter war that will decide which side will ultimately survive. Thus *Battlestar Galactica*'s foundational plot presents a concealed and formidably disguised enemy of mankind with opposing views about life and survival. The battle between the Cylons and the humans is clearly asynchronous. The Cylons have access to far superior technology than their human opponents, whom they also outnumber vastly. And in many ways, the few thousand human survivors may be likened to the armies of present-day developing economies that are unable to battle their enemies on an even field. Moreover, while fighting the Cylons amid extremely demanding living conditions, the humans are shown occasionally to disregard what we, the audience, would typically consider to be standard morality and fair fighting through adherence to established political standards of democracy.

Immoral Behavior from "Good" People

Battlestar Galactica introduces us to human males and females who are similar to us, except that they originated within thirteen tribes of the human species in some faraway planetary system. On both the original and the twenty-first century version of the series, all human life is said to have originated several millennia ago on a home planet named Kobol.[2]

There is a built-in context in *Battlestar Galactica*'s science fiction storytelling that encourages viewers to relate to the human beings as portrayed on the series. This is because the colonial human society from Kobol is depicted as being connected to, or responsible for, our own terrestrial human society.[3]

But again, Moore's "different prism" storytelling consistently violates audience expectations about human behavior. Moore twists the typically expected central characteristics such as heroism, courage, selflessness, devotion, and moral behavior of the best characters, presenting instead off-centered traits to keep viewers on their toes and invert their perceptions about what is versus what should be. The series demands an emotional response from its viewers, especially in the context of the rapid, ongoing changes involving the U.S. military and the U.S. political landscape since the 9/11 terrorist attacks and the subsequent war in Iraq. The audience is compelled to decide for itself whether the asymmetrical nature of the warfare between humans and Cylons can be or should be used to justify behavioral choices that frequently appear to disregard basic morality, democracy, and civility.

At the outset many viewers may readily and easily identify the "good guys" (the human race) as they fight against the "bad guys" (the Cylons), and they are likely to expect the human good guys to be portrayed as people who behave heroically and even admirably in defense of their civilized society and its essential morality. But instead, Moore's "different prism" depicts the "good" humans as choosing to behave in ways that in today's world would be considered immoral if not evil. A most controversial human choice is suicide bombers who attack Cylons. Since the series does not shy away from depicting immoral and violently uncivil attributes and behaviors in what are obviously "good" people, the audience is left with no choice but to confront the difficult questions of why these fundamentally good people frequently behave in an immoral manner and the extent to which context informs moral judgments.

The series' authors ensure that *Battlestar Galactica* cannot be approached with any degree of emotional detachment nor viewed as mere entertainment and diversion. The deliberate military and political nature of the series demands that the viewers invest in its characters and make judgments about what is right and what is wrong. Moore and Eick have been explicit about this nature of the series." Both Ron and I were political science majors in college. If you go through our libraries, you wouldn't guess we're in show business," Eick clarified to *Rolling Stone* magazine. Moore added that the pair took advantage of the fact that "the networks are terrified of controversy, but in sci-fi, they don't notice or care so much–you get a free pass" (Edwards 2006).[4]

Secular Democracy versus Theocracy

On *Battlestar Galactica* the process of attempting to provoke viewers grows specifically from what the *New York Times Magazine* identified as "unapologetic and frequently harrowing" echoes "of the war on terror" that focus on "what happens when an advanced, comfortable, secular democracy endures a devastating attack by an old enemy that it literally created," and whose military and political motivations are "religious fanaticism" (Hodgman 2005). The series' producers and authors juxtapose the bloody "holy warfare" of the Cylons with the responses of imperfect and emotionally and sexually motivated humans, who must defend their classical democracy against a more powerful enemy whose beliefs and behaviors are rooted in its theocracy.

Moore has embedded a deeply reverential love of democracy into the fiber of the human characters in this series. "More than a little of the politics of *Battlestar Galactica* can be traced back to Abraham Lincoln's passionate views about freedom," he writes in his blog (Moore 2007b). This creates a powerful rhetorical context that is easy for viewers to understand and embrace: Just as in Lincoln's era, when the outcome of the American Civil War was dependent upon an unwavering dedication to preserving the Union, so too will the outcome on *Battlestar Galactica*'s Cylon-versus-human war depend upon humanity's ultimate defense and preservation of its freedoms and its democratic society in the galaxy.

To this mix Moore adds the controversial element of theocracy, and in so doing he forces his audience to consider difficult questions such as why artificial life-forms created by human beings would evolve to such an extent that they would have their own extremely fanatical religious beliefs; and why those beliefs, in turn, would drive them to engage in a divinely inspired, bloody war against the human race. Although Moore cautions not to perceive of the Cylons as directly allegorical, he admits, "they have aspects of Al Qaeda, and they have aspects of the Catholic Church, and they have aspects of America" (Edwards 2006).

"One of the foundational elements of the show is the religious conflict between the two civilizations," Moore explains (Newgen 2006). He admits that humans and Cylons alike may be struggling towards "some greater truth" for which their respective religions help them find answers, particularly when ideas and events in *Battlestar Galactica* cannot be "explained by rational means." However, he does not allow the story line overtly to proclaim that "God is behind the curtain" in every aspect. Nonetheless, with mainstream science fiction typically having chosen to avoid the subject of religion, *Battlestar Galactica* defiantly challenges this tradition. Moreover, incorporating two opposing organized religions and various deities into the series challenges the audience to ponder the controversial idea that perhaps gods are created by believers and not the other way around (see Goulart 2006).

But more important, it is the religious dichotomy between humans and Cylons that defines and shapes the military and political clashes between the two sides. At the heart of *Battlestar Galactica*'s life-and-death struggle between religions are deeply complicated questions that viewers must grapple with: How can the humans retain their political system based on liberty and the freedom of religious beliefs after bringing upon themselves a terrible and complex fate? Should humanity expect to escape from the negative consequences of their Cylon creation? Do the humans have a divinely inspired fate to prevail over this creation?

In his farewell speech as the last commander of the battlestar *Galactica*, William Adama addresses this issue at the ceremonial decommissioning of his ship following an extended period of peace. "The Cylon war is long over, yet we must not forget the reasons why so many sacrificed so much in the cause of freedom. The cost of wearing the uniform can be high, but . . . ." Embarrassed by how trite the words seem, Adama is unable to deliver the speech as he wrote it. Unaware that the Cylons have come back to wage yet another war on humanity, Adama chooses to speak freely from his heart and asserts: "You know, when we fought the Cylons, we did it to save ourselves from extinction, but we never answered the question why. Why are we, as a people, worth saving? We still commit murder because of greed, spite, jealousy, and we still visit all of our sins upon our children. We refuse to accept the responsibility for anything that we've done. Like we did with the Cylons. We decided to play God, create life. When that life turned against us, we comforted ourselves in the knowledge that it really wasn't our fault. Not really. You cannot play God then wash your hands of the things that you've created. Sooner or later, the day comes when you can't hide from the things that you've done any more" (original miniseries). The audience must judge for itself whether *Battlestar Galactica* suggests that humans in our real world have sown the seeds of their own moral and political disintegration.

As in the real world, for humans and Cylons alike on *Battlestar Galactica* the political belief systems and the resulting core values about how one should live grow specifically from the religions that each civilization holds dear. The humans on *Battlestar Galactica* are devoutly polytheistic like the ancient Greeks and Romans, and these humans worship multiple, similarly named deities such as Apollo, Athena, and so forth, in reference to their Lords of Kobol. One aspect of the twelve human colonies' religion is the central belief that their gods will providentially guide them on their quest to locate the legendary thirteenth colony on the planet Earth. The humans on *Battlestar Galactica* embrace the Nietzschean "eternal recurrence" concept, which also exists in Hinduism and Buddhism as well as in ancient Mayan mythology. According to eternal recurrence, the universe is continually recurring and what was will occur once more and innumerable times yet again. Laura Roslin, president of the Twelve Colonies of Kobol, refers to a scriptural tract when she says, "If you believe in the gods, then you believe in the cycle of time that we are all playing our parts in a story that is told again, and again, and again throughout eternity" ("Kobol's Last Gleaming," pt. 1).

In contrast, the Cylons have but one true God. The Cylon religion bears likeness to our own monotheistic Abrahamic religions such as Islam, Christianity, and Judaism. The Cylons believe that "there is no God but God," a phrase uttered by a Cylon leader to express how their organized religion holds a single deity as central to their lives ("Exodus," pt. 1).[5] And viewers learn details about the impact this religion has on the Cylons' beliefs, values, and subsequent behavioral choices.

As explained by Moore, the Cylons believe that their singular God created humans, but that God made a mistake when creating the human race, and it is the religious duty of the Cylons to correct that mistake. "Mankind is a flawed creation. Sinned. Has essentially thrown away the gift of the soul and of God's love. God then had man create the Cylons as a more perfect entity. And now the Cylons are supposed to take the place of the flawed humans in the cosmos and essentially are the next generation." Moore references the commonly held belief that children cannot truly become adults until after the death of their parents, "and so the Cylons had to kill their parents in order to evolve and mature," he explains. But, unlike the polytheistic human religion, the Cylon religion is one in which the Cylons are "in the service of a loving, compassionate God that offered redemption" if they acted upon what they perceive to be a divine imperative to kill human beings.[6] It is important to note that the human-looking Cylons may well be able to accept death more easily than the humans because they are empowered with literal reincarnation. Not long after the human-looking Cylon models die, their consciousness and memory are downloaded into an identical body.

Call it a Day for Law

David Frost: So what in a sense, you're saying is that there are certain situations, and the Huston plan or part of it was one of them, where the President can decide that it's in the best interests of the nation or something, and do something illegal. Richard Nixon: Well, when the President does it that means it is not illegal. (Frost 1977)

Nowhere is *Battlestar Galactica*'s use of the "different prism" rhetorical device more evident than in several stories that raise questions about the use of otherwise illegal or extralegal emergency measures to address threats to the safety of the political community. Governing authorities and political and legal theorists have grappled with various forms of these issues for centuries. But in the United States, at least, commercial television rarely engages public audiences in such nuanced, multidimensional considerations of these issues or contemporary manifestations of them.

The fundamental questions are whether and/or when a head of state and/or a military authority can justifiably act in ways that contradict the constitution and civilian legal system that ordinarily apply to all members of a political community. An early modern, classic statement of one of the most important of these issues appears in political theorist John Locke's *Two Treatises of Government*. A significant influence on colonial American political thought, Locke's *Two Treatises* devotes an entire chapter to the subject of executive "prerogative," which he defined as the "power to act according to discretion, for the publick good, without the prescription of the Law, and sometimes even against it" (Locke 1960, 422). Locke claimed that the individuals who possess the legislative power and the bodies of law that they produce cannot anticipate and provide for every possible challenge to the preservation of the political community. Consequently, since the "end of government" is the "preservation of all," members of a political community must accept an executive's exercise of prerogative on occasions when "a strict and rigid observation of the laws may do harm" (421).

Today these questions often boil down to considerations of the legitimate scope of a head of state's power to resort to emergency measures. In U.S. law these measures might take the form of martial law. In French law emergency powers may be exercised following a declaration of a state of siege (Feldman 2005). Although the constitutional-legal details vary among regimes, a common core issue is the use of the "necessity" of protecting the political community as grounds for a kind of "legalized lawlessness" (Humphreys 2006). The actions at issue are not necessarily limited to those taken by a head of state. For example, a regime's top military officials may conclude that a civilian government is incapable of governing and stage a coup in the interest of preserving civil order and a government's more general capacities for governing.

In U.S. popular political discourse, once commonly discussed manifestations of these issues temporarily faded from the public agenda in the immediate aftermath of the cold war. They returned with a vengeance, however, after the terrorist attacks of September 11, 2001. One of the most controversial manifestations is the Bush administration's effort to reduce legal constraints on executive-branch prosecution of military and domestic antiterrorism operations. The administration has claimed rights to detain individuals, including U.S. citizens in the United States (as opposed to on a foreign battlefield), in solitary confinement almost indefinitely without charges and without access to legal counsel, an assertion of powers that alarmed civil libertarians and was never adequately addressed by the U.S. Supreme Court's decision in *Padilla v. Rumsfeld* (Sontag 2006; Sontag 2007). Additionally there are serious allegations that the administration may have violated federal law by ordering the National Security Agency to monitor telephone calls and e-mail exchanges between the United States and foreign countries and to mine civilian databases without seeking a warrant from a Foreign Intelligence Surveillance Court judge.[7] The administration has countered that congressional authorization of these measures is grounded in the Authorization for Use of Military Force (AUMF),[8] a joint resolution that Congress passed shortly after 9/11. The resolution is a brief, vague, broad grant of power to the president that justifies such delegation on the grounds of necessity.

How should ordinary citizens react to a head of state's assertion of broad discretionary emergency authority? Does it represent a kind of legalized lawlessness, and, if so, should we care? Are civil liberties, the separation of powers, and other pillars of democratic republics inviolable? Or are there occasions for which the "strict and rigid observation" of them, as Locke wrote, are dangerous obstacles to a head of state's capacity to provide for our collective security? The issues are complex ones with no universal answers. Yet the public debate over these issues, particularly conducted through popular entertainment media, can be a polarized, shrill exchange of highly oversimplified conceptualizations of the problems. A genuine contribution of *Battlestar Galactica* is its use of the science fiction context and the "different prism" device to highlight important complexities and invite viewers to think about some basic aspects of contemporary U.S. national security issues free from at least a few partisan perceptual biases.

One example transpires when the colonies' senior military officer, Adama, terminates the administration of the constitutionally sanctioned president of the twelve colonies, Laura Roslin, and imprisons her in the brig.[9] Adama's decision to stage a military coup against the civilian government is nominally based on his conclusion that the president's continuation in office poses a danger to the long-term survival prospects of the political community. The immediate source of danger is Roslin's threat to the effectiveness of the military chain of command.[10] The president appropriates a captured Cylon combat spacecraft that Adama needs for a military operation that could enable the humans to resettle on a hospitable planet. Roslin also convinces the military's most skilled combat pilot, Starbuck, to fly the enemy ship on a dangerous mission that would allegedly enable the president to fulfill an ancient religious prophecy of leading the humans to Earth ("Kobol's Last Gleaming," pt. 1).[11] Adama thus loses not only the enemy ship, but also the best pilot for the pre-resettlement operation.

Adama is alarmed by both the loss of the enemy ship and the significance of Roslin's success in convincing Starbuck to accept the mission in defiance of his command. Starbuck is deeply loyal to Adama and would have married one of Adama's sons had he not died before their wedding. "As long as [Roslin is] president, she's dangerous. If she can turn Starbuck against us, she's capable of anything," Adama says ("Kobol's Last Gleaming," pt. 2). One implication is that Roslin's political skills, including her power to appeal to broadly held religious beliefs, can compromise Adama's command authority to an extent that could ultimately jeopardize the military's capacity to protect the human community. Adama finds this unacceptable in any case, but particularly once he is convinced that Roslin is a "religious fanatic" of questionable mental competence.

The president's imprisonment ultimately leads to a declaration of martial law. Although a constitutionally sanctioned successor exists, the vice president is incommunicado, trapped on the potential resettlement planet, during the coup. By the time the vice president returns, Adama is comatose following an attempt on his life, and Adama's second-in-command, Colonel Tigh, has dissolved the civilian government and declared martial law on the grounds that the government "cannot function."[12] When Adama awakens from his coma, he resumes command and maintains the martial law regime.

There are obviously key distinctions between the foregoing developments and the archetypal case of the use of necessity to justify the suspension or termination of a republican constitution and a legal regime. For one thing, Adama is the top military authority, not a head of state. Consequently the situation is not a direct analogy to, for example, a declaration of martial law by a U.S. president or governor or a French president's invocation of emergency powers under a state of siege (Feldman 2005). Nevertheless, at the level of principle, the episode challenges viewers to contemplate the extent to which a political community's survival imperatives can justify the nullification of a constitutional administration and the substitution of military law for constitutional republican rule.[13]

On the one hand, *Battlestar Galactica* presents a serious case for accepting Adama's and Tigh's transgressions as the lesser evils in the foregoing context. First, reasonable viewers can clearly regard the president's mental condition and actions as potential dangers to the safety of the political community. The president seized the enemy combat spacecraft and appropriated the military's most skilled pilot for the service of superstition. Ultimately many of the developments predicted in the religious prophecy unfold as anticipated. But Commander

Adama's skepticism of the president's claims of prophetic destiny is arguably the only sane analysis of the political community's security situation. Additionally Adama eventually learns that, when he was comatose, Roslin suborned mutiny by encouraging his own son, the senior military combat pilot, Capt. Lee Adama ("Apollo"), to take up armed resistance against Colonel Tigh and troops who were ordered to imprison the president. Decisions to seize key military assets and undermine the senior military officer's command authority in the service of fulfilling religious prophecy can lead a reasonable person to believe that the president is incapable of serving as a wartime head of state.

Second, the coup was staged and the martial law regime was enforced by one of the series' most sympathetic leading characters, Adama. Although Tigh's original decision to declare martial law represented a failed leader's act of desperation, Adama's decision to sustain the regime did not. Throughout the series Adama is portrayed as an officer who would be loath to take such actions. There is every reason to believe that he respects civilian control of the military and the rule of law. His father was a pro-civil liberties litigator ("Litmus"), and Adama himself "hated the very idea of martial law" ("Fragged"). Early in the series Roslin asks Adama to use military troops to maintain civil order, and Adama initially resists, citing the danger of troops potentially treating their own civilians as enemies ("Water"). More generally, military personnel at all levels consistently demonstrate their sincere reverence for Adama and trust his judgment as sound. Hence viewers should conclude that Adama is conflicted about terminating the president's administration and sustaining a martial law regime.

Simultaneously *Battlestar Galactica* presents a strong version of the alternative view that military governments have a limited capacity to govern and are sometimes less functional than regimes that enjoy democratically grounded legitimacy. Influential research in political psychology reports that authorities enjoy higher levels of voluntary compliance with their laws or other rules when they are perceived as legitimate, particularly when that legitimacy stems from the reliance on procedures for selecting leaders and making other decisions that we usually associate with the conferring of democratic consent (see, for example, Tyler et al. 1997). At least some military legal experts agree that a state of martial law would engender resistance when imposed on a civilian population that had become accustomed to self-government (Davies 2000).

Among many civilians, the legitimacy of the martial law regime is dubious at best. The regime exists either outside the law or, as President Roslin tells the members of the former legislature, in opposition to the law. When Colonel Tigh declares martial law, he does not cite any legal authority that empowers him to do so. Regardless of the legal debate, civilian opposition to martial rule tests the regime's capacity to govern with only limited voluntary civilian compliance. Resupply ships, including a fuel source, refuse to resupply the *Galactica* until the civilian government is reinstated ("Resistance"). The refusal to resupply becomes so widespread that the *Galactica* cannot obtain coffee, let alone food and medicine. Tigh responds by ordering strike teams of military troops to board all ships that defy orders to resupply the *Galactica*. A problem, however, is that civil disobedience is so widespread that the *Galactica* does not have enough troops to board all of the defiant ships. Troops boards the *Gideon,* a supply ship that is holding out. Violence erupts, and the troops fire their weapons, killing four civilians.

In contrast, even as a deposed head of state, Roslin's democratic legitimacy enables her to obtain voluntary compliance from military troops. When Lee Adama helps Roslin to escape from the brig, they are intercepted by a *Galactica* guard, who trains her weapon on Roslin. Roslin tells the private "you and I have something in common. We each took an oath to protect and defend the Articles of Colonization. Those articles are under attack, as is our entire democratic way of life. . . . You can either stand aside or you can shoot me. You'll have to decide where your duty lies" ("Resistance"). In defiance of the military command authority, the private allows Roslin to escape.

Roslin's escape is made possible in part by a conspiracy of the top communications officer, the CAG, the guard in Roslin's brig cell, and others. In some instances Roslin receives assistance from people who believe that she is destined to fulfill a religious prophecy. But this is not true of Lee Adama or many others. Roslin finally obtains safe harbor after forming a temporary alliance with a former political adversary, Tom Zarek, a formerly imprisoned domestic resistance leader who also draws political power from the popular support of civilian constituencies. Democratic legitimacy thus, in several key conflicts, enables Roslin to prevail over Colonel Tigh, who must rely primarily on instruments of coercion and, to some extent, martial loyalty.

The story of the failed coup and institution of martial law is thus presented through Moore's "different prism." A benefit of using the device is that it encourages the audience to think about contemporary manifestations of these problems in a somewhat more abstract and arguably more principled way than one would usually find in commercial television entertainment programming. Here, it is useful to compare *Battlestar Galactica*'s treatments of states of exception with the portrayal of the use of torture on another critically acclaimed—and more widely viewed—television drama, the Fox network's *24*. On *24* U.S. counterterrorism authorities routinely torture people while attempting to prevent attacks on U.S. civilians. The series raises no moral or serious legal ambiguity surrounding the use of torture. Rather, *24* borders on advocating torture. In a generally favorable review of *24*, a *New York Times* critic observed that the series depicts torture "with gusto and almost no moral compunction" and added that "if anything, the new season seems even more intent on hammering home the message that torture is necessary in the war against terror, and that despite what some experts claim, torture works" (Stanley 2007).

Female Power

Moore maintains one core strategy in the depiction of human beings through-out the series: Each human's gender, tribal or planetary origin, and race are com-pletely irrelevant in the *Battlestar Galactica* universe, where personal, political, and military power are each derived from one's chosen actions in life. The series is, if nothing else, a complicated, interconnected story about humans at war against their mortal enemy, the Cylons. But unlike in the real world, where both politics and the military are male-dominated, the *Battlestar Galactica* audience encounters a completely gender-blind political and military infrastructure. One of the main characters is the female president of the human colonies, Laura Roslin. A second major female character is the *Galactica*'s best fighter pilot, Star-buck. The ongoing focus on these two particular human females establishes clear character attributes that are carefully designed to be thought-provoking.

There are other significant female characters who are central to the series. They are not human, however; they are Cylons who look indistinguishable from human females. In the opening minutes of the 2003 miniseries, on-screen text explains to viewers: "The Cylons were created by man. They were created to make life easier on the Twelve Colonies. And then the day came when the Cylons decided to kill their masters. After a long and bloody struggle, an armistice was declared. The Cylons left for another world to call their own. A remote space station was built where Cylon and human could meet and main-tain diplomatic relations. Every year, the Colonials send an officer. The Cylons send no one. No one has seen or heard from the Cylons in over forty years." Fol-lowing the text, the audience is introduced to a lone human male in his late fifties—the bored diplomatic officer sent to the armistice station to meet with his Cylon counterpart, who, in all likelihood, will not arrive. But this day—the fortieth anniversary—is different. To the diplomat's astonishment two Cylons enter the space station. They are the robotic, metallic "Centurion" models; but they are followed by a gorgeous young woman (portrayed by model Tricia Helfer) in a power-red dress and stiletto boots. She sashays down the long hall-way with determination. The diplomat is stunned as she draws slowly but delib-erately toward him. Hers are the first words of dialogue on *Battlestar Galactica*. And they unmistakably establish a voice for the entire series that is simultane-ously dark, invasive, unrelenting, compelling, and unforgiving: "Are you alive?"the beautiful female Cylon whispers provocatively in the diplomat's ear (original miniseries). Although the diplomat is clearly attracted by her sensual-ity, his reply to her loaded question is uncertain, perhaps even shameful. "Yes," he says tentatively. Unconvinced, she immediately establishes her dominance with a succinct challenge. "Prove it," she rasps, and then initiates a minute-long open-mouth kiss. As she administers this "kiss of death," her Cylon compatriots rapidly attack and vaporize the armistice station. And then this beautiful young female Cylon (referred to by her model number, Number Six, and sometimes as

Caprica Six) proceeds to launch a coldly calculated, wide-ranging nuclear attack to annihilate the human race.

The prismatically refracted depiction is that the females are sexually dominant and politically and religiously agenda-driven. In contrast the males are of decidedly secondary importance. Thus the clear and essential definition of Number Six's character makes sense: She is young, beautiful, sexually aggressive, and dominant, plus she is ageless and eternal. Sexual interactions between the eternal Cylon femme fatale Number Six and her next human male victim, the brilliant scientist, Gaius Baltar, are common. Number Six maintains the dominant role and sexual position compared to her male partner, who is seen as perplexed yet apparently sexually insatiable.

Sex as a Military and Political Weapon

The power of Cylons over human beings is thus vividly established. The sexual dominance of a human male by a female Cylon symbolizes the military and technological power that the Cylons exert over human beings. This theme of a female's use of sex to dominate and control a male, both literally and figuratively, serves as the lynchpin of the Cylons' political and military campaign to wipe out their human enemy. Moreover, the sexual control of males by aggressive females driven by often intertwined political and religious agendas is reinforced consistently throughout *Battlestar Galactica,* spanning all televised episodes from December 2003 through December 2006.

Viewers know from the beginning that Number Six's sexual domination has a political agenda that is not metaphorical: The Cylon attack on the twelve planets of the human race was enabled because Number Six used Baltar to gain essential security secrets from him during pillow talk (original miniseries). Not surprisingly, Baltar becomes sexually obsessed with her, and in his mind he enables her everlasting presence in his life. Sexual domination as a means of control subsequently emerges in a season 3 episode that shows Number Six and Baltarin bed together aboard a Cylon ship, where Baltar is ostensibly being held prisoner by the Cylons. But, the couple is not alone. The scene suggests a ménage à trois with another exceptionally beautiful female Cylon, Number Three, who also is known by her human name, D'Anna Biers ("Hero").

The depiction of the three characters in one bed raises several potential questions of a political nature about whether Baltar's treatment as a prisoner of the Cylons constitutes cruel and unusual punishment or reward under the sexual control of two attractive and agenda-driven females. In the last televised episode of 2006, the three-way relationship clearly has been strained to the breaking point as Number Three/D'Anna persuades Baltar to forsake his relationship with Number Six and align himself sexually, politically, and religiously with only her ("The Eye of Jupiter"). It is worth pointing out, however, that even though both Number Six and Number Three/D'Anna have sexually manipulated Baltar, he has never been unwilling. Moreover, Baltar may well have allowed himself to be used by these two Cylon females for obvious personal pleasure as well as to advance some personal agenda of his own, which by the last episodes of 2006 had not been revealed.

Undoing Racial and Gender Stereotyping

The same sexually dominant role of agenda-driven female Cylons is carried through in the relationship between two other key characters. One main character, *Galactica* pilot Sharon "Boomer" Valerii (portrayed by Grace Park), learns at the end of the 2003 miniseries that she is in fact a Cylon sleeper agent, who has been duplicated multiple times. Grace Park is of Korean descent. But in the *Battlestar Galactica* universe, there is no Asia and there is no Korea. From a storytelling perspective, the writers therefore do not have the option of referring to what we in real life would say is an Asian female who happens also to be an enemy sleeper agent. The audience can watch Grace Park at work simultaneously in multiple roles but will not find any attribution to her race. Race is never mentioned on *Battlestar Galactica.* People who are Latino or African American or Asian, for instance, do not have roles where their race matters to the function that they serve in the plot.

In stark contrast, the characters' race proved to be a major issue within the highly influential original *Star Trek* series of the late 1960s. The *Star Trek* character Lieutenant Uhura (portrayed by Nichelle Nichols, an African American actor) was considered unusual and controversial because of the pronounced racial prejudices that prevailed in the United States at that time. Few African American actors appeared in continuing roles on television, and if they did appear, their very appearance became noteworthy. Nichols wanted to leave *Star Trek* after the first season ended in 1967, but the Reverend Dr. Martin Luther King Jr. told her that she served an important function as a role model for her race and therefore must remain in her role as Uhura. In what was the last appearance of Nichols on *Star Trek* in its third and final season, the race issue was ever-important. An episode featured an extraterrestrial simulation of Abraham Lincoln, who visits the starship *Enterprise* and interacts with the crew. The Lincoln lookalike meets Uhura and observes, "What a lovely Negress!" "In our century, we've learned not to fear words," Uhura assures the lookalike. Although her character mostly uttered the lines "hailing frequencies open, sir," Nichols became known for the first interracial kiss on U.S. television in 1968 between an African American woman and a Caucasian man, Captain James T. Kirk. On *Battlestar Galactica,* Grace Park may certainly be known for playing "Good Sharon" and "Bad Sharon" (Bassom 2005), but unlike on *Star Trek,* the characters Grace portrays are not to be perceived as representing any race.

Military Sex Object

Moore, who began his television writing/producing career on various *Star Trek* spin-offs and motion pictures in the 1980s and 1990s, has clearly positioned

Battlestar Galactica to be blind to racial and gender issues. Nearly forty years after Star Trek's daring interracial kiss on American television, *Battlestar Galactica* not only portrays interracial kissing but also depicts interracial sex.

Cylon Sharon initiates sex with Lt. Karl "Helo" Agathon, a human male *Galactica* crew member on the Cylon-occupied planet of Caprica ("Six Degrees of Separation"), reiterating that on this series sex is one of the most powerful Cylon weapons against human beings. Just as Number Six sexually manipulated Gaius Baltar to divulge security secrets, Sharon manipulates Helo to accomplish her mission as a military agent. Highly intelligent Helo knows that Sharon is a Cylon, but he still feels attracted to her. He is unaware that Sharon is following specific orders to involve him in a sexual relationship with her or else she must kill him. The Cylons have not yet mastered sexual reproduction, and Sharon succeeds in her mission as Helo impregnates her in fulfillment of the specific Cylon plan to reproduce sexually. Helo now becomes a Cylon sex object for military purposes as well as a biological object of study for political purposes.

Helo is young, but of solid character. He makes mature and honorable decisions. When he learns that Sharon is expecting his child, it is he who suggests that they get married. This first-of-its-kind marriage between a human male and a Cylon female leads some humans aboard the *Galactica* to be repulsed. More significantly, Sharon and Helo's union produces an interspecies female child that the Cylons look upon with fanatical religious fervor as having a divinely inspired destiny.

The dominant female character attribute recurs in *Battlestar Galactica* in the relationship between Starbuck and a human male civilian, who is the leader of the human resistance on Caprica, Samuel Anders. Anders is a strong, physically fit, professional athlete, but he prefers to allow Starbuck to dominate him, both emotionally and sexually. Anders and Starbuck are shown engaged in sexual activity only once ("Resistance"), and that one encounter clearly depicts Starbuck as being in charge.

On *Battlestar Galactica,* nudity and sexuality are depicted without any apparent prurient significance, shame, or moral consequences. Male and female crew members live in close proximity, sharing not only living quarters but toilet and shower facilities within a military environment that affords little or no individual privacy or separation of the genders. In addition we see frequent depictions of attractive females who are sexually dominant over males. This may certainly serve the purpose of attracting and maintaining both female and male audience interest in *Battlestar Galactica,* but the more crucial reason to portray sexually dominant females is to establish an effective rhetorical storytelling process that catches the audience off guard. Moore has chosen to disregard stereotypical portrayals of males and females on commercial television and instead calls viewer attention to well-defined characters that can serve a persuasive purpose as models of less commonly valued roles and attributes in a universe where race and gender distinctions do not exist. He calls upon *Battlestar*

Galactica's viewers to focus on the critical issues of personal behavior and individual decision-making.

Conclusion

The creative architects of *Battlestar Galactica*'s major story arcs have, intentionally or not, created space to consider some controversial contemporary issues in a relatively abstract and in some instances even more principled way that one often finds in commercial television dramas, which remain one of the dominant forms of mass communication in the United States. Sympathetic characters are more interesting when they possess flaws that render them more complex and believable. Unsympathetic characters are more interesting when they demonstrate unexpected virtues, such as heroism. Nevertheless, the creative architects so expand the spaces of political discourse about these topics by employing a combination of two creative devices. The first, most obvious device is the location of the controversies in a typical science fiction context. As Frederik Pohl noted in the first edition of this volume, science fiction authors frequently "say things in hint and metaphor that the writer dares not say in clear" (1997, 10). Recasting a contemporary real world controversy as a conflict with aliens or robots in remote galaxies blunts the edge of ideas that might otherwise provoke instant condemnation or worse. The second, somewhat less obvious device is that of the "different prism," to use the term employed by Ron Moore.

Although we do not know precisely why *Battlestar Galactica*'s creative architects use the "different prism" rhetorical device and otherwise highlight ambiguity, we neither assume nor expect that the choice is an intentionally political decision. Most likely, the primary reason is that Moore thinks that such thought experiments make for engaging, and therefore commercially successful, entertainment (Newgen 2006). Regardless of the executive producers' intentions, one consequence of combining the science fiction context with perspective inversion is the creation of a space in which public discourse about controversial issues can occur more freely, and maybe in a more principled way. Yet this expansion of political discursive space is not unlimited. Limitations may be imposed by the creative architects' own creative discretion. Or, they may censor their own work in anticipation of negative reactions from commercial sponsors, network executives, or the public.

Nevertheless, *Battlestar Galactica* provides an interesting case study in how far one might expand opportunities for political speech. The show has won rave reviews from dozens of major critics as well as a prestigious Peabody Award. As far as we know, there have been no major public outcries against the show's politics. Consequently it is fair to say that the show has not yet brushed up against the limits of commercial television as a medium of political discourse about controversial topics. But by examining some of the settled assumptions that *Battlestar Galactica* has invited its audience to question, we are somewhat surprised by how much freedom the series has exercised.

Notes

1. The citations of particular episodes (alphabetical by title, writer(s) and director with U.S. airdates) is as follows: "Exodus, Part 1," written by Bradley Thompson and David Weddle, dir. Felix Enriquez Alcal·, October 13, 2006. "The Eye of Jupiter," written by Mark Verheiden, dir. Michael Rymer, December 15, 2006. "Fragged," written by Dawn Prestwich and Nicole Yorkin, dir. Sergio Mimica-Gezzan, July 29, 2005. 'Hero," written by David Eick, dir. Michael Rymer, November 17, 2006. "Kobol's Last Gleaming, Part 1," story by David Eick, teleplay by Ronald 0. Moore, March 252005. "Kobol's Last Gleaning, Part 2," story by David Eick, teleplay by Ronald D. Moore, April 1, 2005. "Litmus," written by Jeff Vlarning, dir. Rod Hardy, February 11, 2005. "Miniseries, Night 1," written by Ronald D. Moore, Christopher Eric James, story by Glen A. Larson, December 8, 2003. "Miniseries, Night 2," written by Ronald D. Moore and Christopher Eric James, story by Glen A. Larson, December 9, 2003. "Resistance," written by Toni Graphia, dir. Alan Kroeker, August 5, 2005. "Six Degrees of Separation," written by Michael Angeli, dir. Robert Young, February 18, 2005. "Water," written by Ronald D. Moore, dir. Marita Grabiak, January 14, 2005.

2. This name is associated with Book of Abraham scriptural references native to the Church of Jesus Christ of Latter-Day Saints. The planet's name may be an anagram of Kolob, which in Mormon scriptures is the name of a celestial body located "near the home of God" (http://en.wikipedia.org/wiki/Kolob).

3. The twelve colonies of the human species and their home worlds are commonly referred to by names based on the classical signs of the zodiac. There is also reference to the lost thirteenth colony of Earth.

4. Even if Eick and Moore had not explicitly expressed their rhetorical intentions, what matters are the outcomes of their work. As Wayne Booth explained, "The whole question of the differences between artists who consciously calculate and artists who simply express themselves with no thought of affecting a reader is an important one, but it must be kept separate from the question of whether an author's work communicates itself. The success of an author's rhetoric does not depend on whether he thought about his readers as he wrote." Wayne C. Booth, *The Rhetoric of Fiction* (Chicago: University of Chicago Press, 1961), n.p.

5. Thompson, Bradley and Weddle, David. *Battlestar Galactica.* "Exodus, Part-1" Sci-Fi, October 13, 2003. It may also be worth noting that the Kalima Tayyab in the Koran begins with the invocation *La ilaha il Allah,* "There is no God but Allah (God)."

6. "Podcast: Torn." Battlestar Galactica Wiki. http://en.battlestarwiki.org/wiki/Podcast: Torn (accessed October 22, 2007).

7. The requirement for such warrants was created by the Foreign Intelligence Surveillance Act (FISA) in 1978, a reform measure that Congress enacted after a Senate investigating committee uncovered evidence of domestic spying on opponents of the Vietnam War and other political dissenters. The act stipulates that government authorities can eavesdrop on Americans only after convincing a FISA court that there is probable cause for believing that the suspect is connected to a national security threat. The refusal to seek warrants from a FISA court judge struck some observers as unnecessary, since, in 2004, the court approved all 1,754 warrant requests that it received (Shane 2005).

8. U.S. Public Law 107–40.

9. The twelve colonies are a federation of planets governed by the same constitution and a centralized, elected republican government. Before the Cylons attacked the humans, Roslin was the secretary of education. Roslin was sworn in as president of the colonies after the Cylon attacks killed the president and everyone who was ahead of Roslin in the constitutionally stipulated line of presidential succession.

10. In a subsequent episode, "Home," part 2, Adama tells Roslin that he terminated her presidency because she appropriated the raider and broke their mutual agreement to permit Adama to make all military decisions. This reason for overthrowing the civilian government does not, obviously, constitute a state of exception. But it is inconceivable that the security implications of the president's capacity to undermine military command authority would have been lost on Adama, particularly if he believes her motives are based in superstitious "crap."

11. In the dominant religious belief system among the humans, Earth is a kind of salvific homeland.

12. When Vice President Baltar attempts to assert his legal authority over the military, Colonel Tigh responds, "Legally speaking, I have declared martial law, and that makes you nobody" ("Resistance").

13. The strength of the analogy depends partially on one's view of martial law. Some argue that such emergency measures operate within the confines of a legal system, even though they involve suspensions of the law. Others hold that such measures exist inherently outside the law (see Agamben 2005; Humphreys 2006). It also depends on one's understanding of Adama's relationship to the constitution once he terminated the president's government. We do not attempt to resolve these issues here. Rather, we are interested in the more limited issue of how the story highlights the moral and legal ambiguity of Adama's decision.

Bibliography

Agamben, Giogio. 2005. *State of Exception.* Translated by Kevin Attell. Chicago: University of Chicago Press.

Bassom, David. 2005. *Battlestar Galactica: The Official Companion.* London: Titan.

Booth, Wayne C. 1961. *The Rhetoric of Fiction.* Chicago: University of Chicago Press.

Davies, Kirk L. 2000. "The Imposition of Martial Law in the United States." *Air Force Law Review* 49 (Spring): 67–112.

Edwards, Gavin. 2006. "Intergalactic Terror." *Rolling Stone,* January 27. http://www.rolling stone.com/news/story/9183391/intergalactic_terror?rnd=1138933157156&has-player =false.

Feldman, William. 2005. "Theories of Emergency Powers: A Comparative Analysis of American Martial Law and the French State of Siege." *Cornell International Law Journal* 38, no. 3 (Fall): 1021–48.

Frost, David. 1977. "Excerpts from Interview with Nixon about Domestic Effects of Indochina War." *New York Times,* May 20.

Goulart, Woody. 2006. "What if God Is a Toaster?" Trekology, October 16, www.trekology .com/2006/10/16/what-if-god-is-a-toaster/.

Hodgman, John. 2005. "Ron Moore's Deep Space Journey." *New York Times Magazine,* July 17.

Humphreys, Stephen. 2006. "Legalizing Lawlessness: On Giorgio Agamben's State of Exception." *European Journal of International Law* 17, no. 3: 677–87.

Locke, John. 1960. *Two Treatises of Government: A Critical Edition with an Introduction and Critical Apparatus,* ed. Peter Laslett. New York: New American Library.

Moore, Ronald D. 2006. "Mr. Universe." Editorial. *New York Times.* September 18. http:// www.nytimes.com/2006/09/18/opinion/18moore.html?ex=1316232000&en=5a60c3e7 bf30ab1c&ei=5088&partner=rssnyt&emc=rss.

Moore, Ron. 2006. *Ron Moore's Blog,* February 27. http://blog.scifi.com/battlestar/archives/ 2006/02/#a000173.

Newgen, Heather. 2006. "Ronald D. Moore on *Battlestar Galactica*." ComingSoon.net, October 24. http://comingsoon.net/news/tvnews.php?id=17154.

Pohl, Frederik. 1997. "The Politics of Prophecy." In *Political Science Fiction,* edited by Donald M. Hassler and Clyde Wilcox, 7–17. Columbia: University of South Carolina Press.

Shane, Scot. 2005. "At Security Agency, News of Surveillance Program Gives Reassurances a Hollow Ring." *New York Times.* December 22, A22.

Sontag, Deborah. 2006. "A Videotape Offers a Window into a Terror Suspect's Isolation." *New York Times,* December 4.

————. 2007. "In Padilla Wiretaps, Murky View of 'Jihad' Case. *New York Times,* January 4.

Stanley, Alessandra. 2007. "Suicide Bombers Strike, and America Is in Turmoil. It's Just Another Day in the Life of Jack Bauer." *New York Times,* January 12.

Tyler, Tom R., et al. 1997. *Social Justice in a Diverse Society.* Boulder, Colo.: Westview.

The Body Politic in
Brazilian Science Fiction

Implants and Cyborgs

M. Elizabeth Ginway

Despite its strong ties to a genre associated with the first world, Latin American science fiction reflects the social and political conditions characteristic of a different part of the world. In this essay we will see how one of the common elements of science fiction—the alteration of the body by technology—is shaped by a specific concept of the body and of the Latin American body politic that is less individualistic than the corresponding first-world concepts.

Historically, Iberian cultures and their former colonies developed a concept of the body politic based on Roman law and Catholic doctrine. There was a tendency to concede power to elite groups recognized by the state as central to maintaining order, thereby institutionalizing the notion of privilege. This carried over to Latin America, and even after independence, according to Charles Hale, former loyalties based on local and traditional ésprit de corps made it difficult to impose liberal concepts such as individual rights and equality for all. During the nineteenth century, when these elites tried to reconcile new liberal ideas with traditional conceptions of church and the community, they chose to emphasize a strong national or collective identity over individual rights. One of the political models eventually emerging out of this debate in the twentieth century was the corporate or "organic" state, which, according to Alfred Stepan, follows a direct line from Aristotelian thought and Roman law, through natural law and absolutist notions that make up part of modern Catholic social thought (1978, 4). Despite the elitism and use of repression associated with these regimes throughout Latin America, the model gained a certain legitimacy based on a sense of reciprocity of benefits between the state and its citizens. By placing national and collective interests above those of class and competition associated with capitalism, Latin American countries forged a political model to deal with their late industrialization and new urban masses. In the case of Brazil, Stepan sees the persistence of this model even in the country's most recent military dictatorship (1964–1985), whose technocrats promoted ideals of social engineering while supplying foreign investors with the social stability necessary for joint state projects and international investment. The presence of the corporate state has left a strong mark on Brazilian politics, as its shadow has persisted during the era of redemocratization (1985 to the present).

With the arrival of neoliberalism in the region beginning in the 1990s, a new political phase began, based on the concepts of free markets and international competition. This brought about the final dismantling of the vestiges of the corporate state and a new climate of uncertainty. Despite the new political openness, people felt somewhat abandoned just when they hoped to regain a sense of political strength lost during the period of dictatorship. Without the sense of the strong central government to protect them, the people felt exposed and vulnerable to the whims of the new economic forces of globalization.

In this essay we will explore the portrayal of the Brazilian body politic as a border region between a sense of wholeness and integrity of national identity and the invasion of digital technology and globalization. The ambivalent portrait of an altered human (one implanted with electronic devices) and the cyborg (a being made up a combination of cybernetic and organic systems) in Brazilian science fiction is partially due to the perception of technology and globalization by authors writing on the economic periphery. While the altered human generally experiences a sense of invasion by the introduction of an alien element into his or her body, the cyborg often represents a new type of human, one who is either obedient or rebellious and defiant, according to the society's particular relationship with technology. By contextualizing these six Brazilian texts within the era of globalization we can see how the treatment of the body represents both a sense of crisis of the body politic and a gulf between the people and their government.

In Brazilian science fiction the transformation of a human being into a cyborg reveals a sense of violation that is generally lacking in Anglo-American texts, despite fears about corporeal and mental invasion.[1] In Anglo-American works the escape from the body into the virtual world is viewed as liberating, as is the modification of the body by technology. Brooks Landon comments that the human body becomes a new field of information that can be "edited by drugs and surgery and prosthetics into new forms, or even escaped from entirely into the disembodied experience of cyberspace" (1997, 163). In the classic cyberpunk text *Neuromancer* (1984) by William Gibson, the hacker protagonist, Case, refers to his own body as "the meat" from which he longs to escape, often losing himself in virtual space in a kind of almost mystical communion.[2] Case's girlfriend, Molly, her female body strengthened and hardened by drugs and implants, often helps him to win fights on the physical plane against his enemies. Thematically the body becomes a vehicle to explore the borders between masculine and feminine, the organic and artificial, the corporeal and the transcendental. Conversely, in Brazilian cyberpunk, there are no trips into virtual space.[3] In his analysis, "Tupinipunk—Cyberpunk brasileiro" (Tupinipunk—Brazilian Cyberpunk),[4] Roberto de Sousa Causo compares three Brazilian novels and eleven stories to Anglo-American cyberpunk and finds that rather than exploring the digital revolution as in American cyberpunk, the Brazilian texts demonstrate a sense of "technological wonder," while the protagonists, fascinated by the world of high tech, still prefer to operate in the three-dimensional space of the urban landscape, experiencing it in physical and explicitly sexual ways.[5] As we shall see, the implant and the cyborg are given similar treatment, such that the physical and social body is of consummate importance and technology remains generally suspect. Thus the portrayal of the body in science fiction texts is largely determined by the historical and cultural experience of a people, so that in North and South America views of technology and the body and the body politic are quite distinct.

The Implant as an Invader

Henrique Flory's 1991 "Feliz Natal, vinte bilhões!" (Merry Christmas, Twenty Billion!) and Ivanir Calado's 1993 "O altar dos nossos corações" (The Altar of Our Hearts), two of the texts cited in Causo's cyberpunk article, offer a vision of violence and media overload in Brazilian urban life. The two stories are based on crisis situations at the start of the 1990s: the AIDS epidemic and the increased power of organized crime. Both deal with a situation that threatens the physical body, thus also the body politic or social body. In the story "Merry Christmas, Twenty Billion!" Flory portrays a society in which the Catholic Church has solved the problem of AIDS by preaching monogamy, bringing about a population explosion. In the case of "The Altar of Our Hearts," a corrupt Brazilian governor makes deals with organized crime without realizing the implications of his actions. Both stories portray the betrayal of the body politic in the global era.

"Merry Christmas, Twenty Billion!" is set in an extrapolation of contemporary Brazil, with overpopulated urban areas, wide differences among the social classes, media manipulation, and a complacent acceptance of violence and death. Seated in a bar in a poor neighborhood of São Paulo, the protagonist, the hired killer Alê, hooks up an implant to watch the news directly in his brain. The news stories that he sees about the Catholic Church and overpopulation provoke an unrestrained sense of rage in him, with one exception: a politician who believes in the benefits of population control. To calm himself down Alê uses his "smart card" to purchase shots of alcohol, cocaine, and other drugs controlled by the government. Later, Alê appears at the mysterious agency where he learns about his target, a politician living in an elite neighborhood. Disguised as Santa Claus, he is able to enter the politician's heavily guarded apartment complex. When he learns that it is the same politician he has just seen on television, he decides to spare his life but hunts down and kills the rest of his family and friends in the apartment. Alê lectures him, saying, "You know, now that your family has been killed, I think your views are going to carry a lot more political weight" (Flory 1991, 167), emphasizing the exchange of violence for political ends. In the end Alê seems to personify the inhumanity of the new social order of neoliberalism, showing himself to be an individualist whose main goal is to live in a neighborhood like that of the politician.

The digital readout of the time that begins each paragraph of the story reminds us of what Alê sees in his brain, recalling the robot in James Cameron's film *The Terminator* (1984), who is also programmed to kill. Alê simultaneously attracts and repels us because, according to Cynthia Fuchs, a cyborg with its implants provokes a type of gender ambiguity, presenting us with a hypermacho body that has been feminized, violated and penetrated by technology. It is impossible to judge Alê or to separate him from his social surroundings because, as his implant shows us, he is literally plugged into the sociopolitical situation that created him, a hybrid product of the new sociopolitical order.

The story "The Altar of Our Hearts" by Ivanir Calado has a physically altered protagonist, but he is a member of the elite, the powerful governor of Rio de Janeiro. By planning his own kidnapping with the help of organized crime figures, he uses the occasion to get a special "erotic" implant in his brain to enhance sexual performance. The story portrays a power struggle between the governor and Degrau and Chinês, the leaders of the Comando Vermelho (the Red Command), the most powerful crime ring in the city.

The metaphors of the body are constant in the story, beginning with the kidnapping (the imprisonment of the body) of the governor. The story opens with a female broadcaster announcing that all social classes are making donations toward his ransom. A lower-class woman tells how she had her gold tooth pulled in order to donate to the rescue fund, thereby sacrificing her own body for that of the governor. The coming together of all social classes recalls the corporate state by which all of society pulls together, setting aside class interests. The image of the governor as victim also recalls that of the former president Getúlio Vargas (1930–1945, 1950–1954), the president of the Estado Novo, a model corporate state. Vargas himself reinforced the image of his own body as part of the nation when he wrote in his suicide note (after a political scandal), that he had literally given his blood for the people.[6] In Calado's text the governor is to be reelected on the basis of his "martyred figure" (1993, 188), that of his kidnapped body. In the meantime we learn that the governor has misled the public in order to win the election in exchange for deals he has promised to Degrau and Chinês.

It is crucial to the metaphor of the body politic that the governor have the implant placed in his brain, since the head is the symbol of authority.[7] Thus Degrau carries out a metaphorical coup d'état when he has the surgeon place a bomb alongside the erotic implant. Armed with a detonator that works by remote control, Degrau holds the power of life and death over the governor. When the public demands a crackdown on the organized crime associated with the poorer neighborhoods, the governor is forced to launch an attack on the Red

Command in Degrau's neighborhood—the large shantytown now located on the abandoned bridge that formerly linked outlying suburbs across the Guanabara Bay to downtown.

In this future Rio de Janeiro a long wall separates the rich, clean part of the city from the poor, polluted part. Despite this, there is a constant flow of people and goods from one side to the other, showing that the two depend on one another. The shantytown supplies workers for the rich, and the governor himself participates in this exchange, because he has a sexual relationship with Margareth, who lives with Degrau in his luxurious home in the shantytown. At one point the governor learns that his lover has also had an erotic implant placed in her brain. In order to put pressure on the governor, Degrau sets hers off during an intimate moment with the governor, so that her head explodes before his eyes. This sequence of events alternates with the attacks on the shantytown ordered by the governor, which are equally violent, reinforcing the idea of the betrayal of the lovers and the social body.

Despite the governor's attempts to recover the remote control, it is the other gang leader, Chinês, who ends up with it, and he kills the governor and makes future plans to kill the president as well. The implant represents a violation of the body politic, showing how market forces, new technology, and neoliberalism have not really offered valid alternatives to Brazilian society, which ends up destroying itself. Without policies to deal with profound class differences, environmental problems, and global competition, technology only aggravates the precarious social truce, since it is based on weak social institutions and principles. The story's title, "The Altar of Our Hearts," already implies the notion of sacrifice as it includes the heart, a vital organ and symbol of social solidarity. The title is taken from a 1934 samba by André Filho, "Cidade maravilhosa" (Marvelous City), a song celebrating the city's beauty. In it the singer tells the city that she herself is the "altar of our hearts," a symbol of pride and adoration. In Calado's story it becomes an altar for the sacrifice of the body politic.

These two stories, set in Brazil's largest urban centers, portray a society of almost insurmountable social inequities, betrayed by an untenable socioeconomic model. The implant, a symbol of the new globalized technology, made in China and distributed by organized crime, introduces a new invader, signifying the violation of the social order. In these two stories we see how altered humans, without a means of acting against the forces of globalization, end up destroying political institutions while also injuring their fellow citizens in acts of extreme violence and brutality.

The Cyborg and the Incorporation of Technology

The cyborg is given a more positive portrayal in other texts of Brazilian cyberpunk. The novella "Judgments" (1993) by Cid Fernandez offers a redemptive view of the cyborg and the social body, demonstrating an assimilation of foreign images and ideas from television and film, illustrating the ability of Brazilian culture to reinvent itself, assimilating foreign concepts in a kind of postmodern bricolage. This text, based on the American film noir, effectively Brazilianizes its content. For example, the concept of positive racial miscegenation is updated to include that of human and machine. Another example of this bricolage is the modernist metaphor of cultural "cannibalism" from the 1920s, based on an aggressive and critical use of foreign cultures.[8] The legacy of this aesthetic is seen in several works of Brazilian cyberpunk that I have discussed extensively elsewhere.[9] The three major cyberpunk novels published in Brazil use black protagonists to defend Brazil's national interests against the right-wing military or foreign villains who often have the help of supporters in the Northern Hemisphere. These works of Brazilian cyberpunk use experimental visual and linguistic cues in their prose, mix the popular and the erudite, and articulate the class struggle in aesthetic and artistic language. The novella "Judgments," however, uses another tactic, in that it borrows freely from the detective genre. Roberto Causo characterizes "Judgments" as a Brazilian cyberpunk text because of its heavy borrowing from the film *Blade Runner*. Although the novella has a more conventional form than the other cyberpunk texts, it explores new territory and striking images of the body by momentarily going against reader expectations by destructuring and restructuring literary conventions. This parallels the way in which the protagonists' bodies are literally taken apart and reconstructed in the text. Cybernetic technology, controlled by an underground group of Brazilians and not by international or military interests, proves to be practical and versatile and adapted to Brazilian reality and needs, providing an underground to create an alternative to sinister global forces.

In this novel androids (robots that look like humans) symbolize the perfect assembly-line and office workers in the new global order. Fearing that they will be replaced by machines, the unemployed have already attacked and destroyed androids on several occasions. The government had to put an end the production of robots because "one factory was even invaded by groups of people, and all the androids that were recovered had been 'lynched'" (1993, 83). Here the dismembered body of the android symbolizes the aggression and rage felt by the population against the new neoliberal order, which threatens the traditional protection afforded the Brazilian worker. Closing down the production of androids in order to restore social stability was an attempt to calm down the anti-android feelings, but subsequently death squads begin terminating androids and cybernetic beings. As the text unfolds it becomes clear that cyborgs possess human characteristics such as sympathy and flexibility that androids cannot hope to emulate. In this sense, cyborgs generally represent Brazilians, and androids, foreigners or outsiders. One character who symbolizes an androidlike human is Olga, a former model, who is accused of killing her husband, an older man, Orlando Duarte. Olga is white, and her European beauty recalls the physical perfection of the androids. In fact, she uses her high-class looks to market products.[10] She and the androids thus represent capitalism and the market value of the perfect body and the efficiency of robotic production line—all of which, given its mostly mixed-race population and its large number of untrained workers, are not viable alternatives in Brazil. In order to combat the forces of global capitalism, the story offers us another image of the body in the form of the Brazilian cyborg.

The distinction between the android and the cyborg is central to the theme of the novella, although the anti-android forces cannot tell the difference and hunt them down indiscriminately. Without Olga's knowledge, Duarte had given financial support to a group of cyborg manufacturers, thereby making himself the target of anti-android forces. Vania, a mysterious mulatta in the role of the traditional noir femme fatale, after witnessing Duarte's killing, contacts Rodrigo, a private detective hired by Olga to prove her innocence. Vania promises to help him prove Olga's innocence, provided that he helps her hide from a drug gang. Once in his apartment she turns out not only to be the stereotypical sensual mulatta of Brazilian lore, but also a cyborg. Having been born with grotesque birth defects, her body was completely reconstructed by the same group supported by Duarte. When her defense and self-preservation mechanisms kick in, her body can be disassembled, and at times she does this for protection. In one instance Rodrigo is shocked when he returns to his apartment to find her arm dragging itself along the floor to join the main part of her body hidden in the closet.

In contrast to the perfection of the former model's body, Vania's body is symbolic of the situation of most Brazilians. Her reconstituted body illustrates how problems associated with modern urban Brazil could be solved by technology but are also symptomatic of the inequalities of that society. Her disarticulated limbs may also represent different phases or historical and economic discontinuities of a postcolonial society. Her body, while not physically perfect or organic, is like the city of São Paulo, which is also decentralized and spread out, fragmented yet functional within its third-world reality.

At the same time, however, Vania is constructed within the Brazilian discourse of miscegenation, which emphasizes assimilation and reproduction. She repeatedly states that she wishes to marry Rodrigo, a white man, and have his children, which, oddly enough, her body is able to do. Her dreams are almost dashed when Rodrigo is shot by anti-android agents, but the doctors of the pro-cyborg group manage to save his brain and reproductive organs, placing them into a new cyborg body—the one that had been reserved for Duarte. At the end of the novella Rodrigo opens his eyes to find himself alive, now a cyborg, with Vania at his side. The two represent a type of new social order, yet not a radically new one, since they guarantee the continuity of the social body.

In the Anglo-American context, the cyborg is represented as a post-gender being, one that does not reproduce and is therefore free to reinvent itself outside the conventions of masculinity and femininity or to explore the ambiguity or instability of these concepts. In the words of Donna Haraway, "The cyborg is a kind of disassembled and reassembled postmodern collective and personal self" (1991, 163). According to Haraway, at the radical core of science fiction texts is the capacity to imagine new ways of being, especially when it comes to gender roles. In her view the cyborg, free of the psychological complexes associated with family relations, raised without the concepts of community and without family, seldom questions issues of paternity or legitimacy, thus paving the way for new physical, psychological, and political developments. According to Haraway, "From another perspective, a cyborg world might be about lived social and bodily realities in which people are not afraid of their joint kinship with animals and machines, not afraid of permanently partial identities and contradictory standpoints" (154).[11] For Haraway the cyborg's conscious efforts toward self-creation and self-determination allows its power of regeneration to go far beyond the human notion of "rebirth," since it is contingent and relative and not determined by any previous established patterns. One of the strong points of "Judgments" is its flexible concept of the cyborg, which does not fear the incorporation of the cybernetic nor the artifice of an invented identity but is still tied to a certain legitimacy represented by the social body, as seen in its reproduction of traditional gender roles. However, in representing beings who are amalgams of the organic and the artificial, the story manages to subvert the myth of some "authentic" or essentialist Brazilian identity, playing with the deeply rooted notions of family and tradition in the Brazilian collective consciousness.

By placing the cyborg within the family structure, the story effectively dismantles the fear of technology, just as the assimilation of blacks into the dominant Brazilian culture had lessened racial tensions and fears. Despite their identification as "Others"—the mixed artificial and biological beings Vania and Rodrigo choose to adopt traditional values of marriage and reproduction. Thus their children will be part of a generation less fearful of technology, not prone to judge the artificial as something threatening, allowing them to be free from the prejudice against androids and cyborgs. Vania's and Rodrigo's functional yet dismantled and piecemeal bodies are allegories for a new reconstitution or reintegration of technology into the body politic, as beings who are still connected to the conservative patterns of Brazilian collective values.

Cyborgs, the Crisis of the Body Politic, and Postmodern Beings

In contrast to the socially assimilated cyborgs seen in the text above, there are more ambivalent portrayals of cybernetic beings who are part of a grand plan on the governmental or scientific level. They participate in wars or in scientific experiments that are only partially successful. Set in a distant future, these Brazilian cyborg stories portray a reality in which advances in artificial intelligence lead to the development of an independent consciousness, enabling these beings to act on their own will. The cyborgs in Gerson Lodi-Ribeiro's 1997 "Todo o Silício do Mundo" (All the Silicon in the World) and Julio Emílio Braz's "Genghis" have lost their connection to human beings, which calls attention to the lack of connection between technology and the body politic. On the other hand, in Roberto de Sousa Causo's 2005 "No começo de tudo" (At the Beginning of It All) the posthuman serves humanity's needs, redefining the concepts between the human body, the body politic, and globalization.

The story "All the Silicon in the World" is a meditation by a soldier who appears to be an android. He is in hiding near Brasilia during a battle, awaiting certain death at the hands of ruthless invading robots from outer space. While waiting, he coincidentally discovers that he is not a pure android but a type of cyborg, with a human body underneath all his mechanical armor. The notable thing about this story is the cyborg's mild reaction to the discovering of his own humanity. He feels no sense of horror or betrayal; on the contrary, he only wants to employ this new information in his efforts to save Earth. This reaction contrasts sharply with that of another urban warrior, the protagonist of the 1987 film *Robocop* by director Paul Verhoeven. In the course of the movie the policeman-turned-cyborg struggles with his new identity, alternating between his recollections of his body being brutally penetrated by bullets, in a scene of violation, and the demands of his new programming, which makes him submit to the interests of the American corporation that built him. According to Cynthia Fuchs, Robocop, in trying to reconcile his hypermasculine metal body with the violation and sexual impotence underlying it, represents the profound sense of crisis of psychological identity, masculinity, and gender roles, a recurring theme of many American movies about cyborgs.

In the case of the Brazilian cyborg the discovery of his latent humanity is the only thing separating him from the mechanical invaders, whose goal appears to be to eradicate all forms of organic life on Earth. His recognition of himself as an organic being, developed from the human body, leads the cyborg to identify with terrestrial life and his human companions. He experiences a brief attempt to integrate himself into the body politic as he attempts to relay his discovery to the authorities in Brasilia. The story criticizes an excessive belief in technology, because in the future humans have believed more in defense by machines than in their own creativity. This realization accentuates the cyborg's existential crisis: having been programmed not to question his identity, he laments the lateness of his discovery and his own inability to think of a way to defeat the invaders. In this story Lodi-Ribeiro seems to be warning Brazilians against an excessive reliance on technology, symbolized by the relentless inorganic alien invaders, and to not lose sight of their cultural uniqueness and originality in the global age.

The story "Genghis" by Julio Emilio Braz, one of the few black science fiction writers in Brazil, represents the cyborg in a more menacing way. Instead of a sensitive cyborg like Lodi-Ribeiro's, the one in this story has become all-powerful. Left on a moon of Titan to terra-form it for human habitation, the cyborg grows into a giant. Having destroyed his mechanical predecessor, Genghis considers himself to be independent from his creator, a Russian scientist, who has traveled from Earth to witness his "son's" development. In contemplating him the scientist sees "a shining giant, a hybrid colossus, with an infinite number of arms and nerve endings exuding a familiar and brilliant rigidity of metal, a huge unmistakably human mass. Flesh. Veins. The organic descendant of the egg that generated him, the fruit of millennia of evolutionary growth . . . , materialized in that gigantic body which was also tied to the floating citadel by a large mass of wires and positronic filaments" (Braz, 24). Thinking about the success of this experiment, which exceeded all his expectations, the scientist draws closer to his "son," only to be killed by him.

Here we see the idea of the body through family ties: since the scientist sees the cyborg as part of himself, he is not afraid to approach it. The story is part of the tradition of hard science fiction, a subgenre that depends on scientific concepts to resolve the main problem or conflict of the plot. The Russian scientist appears to be the spokesperson for the scientific point of view: "he believed in science, in the possibility of the intellect generating ideas for human progress, happiness and above all, peace and liberty" (7). "Genghis" contradicts these generic expectations: while the scientific mission does manage to create a cyborg on a moon of Saturn, it does not resolve the conflict in a rational way, unleashing chaos.

Traditionally in the Brazilian imaginary, the city symbolizes the organizing principle against the untamed and chaotic forces of nature that rule the country's interior. In this story the image of Genghis begins to blend the two landscapes. The body of Genghis is described as a gigantic citadel or fortress, recalling the image of Brazil as a sleeping giant, a country that has modernized in the last decades by exploiting both its natural and human resources. Just as Genghis's body is both flesh and metal, Brazil's largest urban centers can be compared to living organisms, each with a life of its own, developed with a strong belief in economic and material progress. However, instead of creating prosperity—the expected outcome of such an experiment—Brazil's cities grew at breakneck rates, beyond the control of city planners. Now these metropolises suffer the problems of the first world (pollution, traffic, and unemployment), along with those of the third world (poverty, overpopulation, lack of housing, and violence). Genghis can be seen as an incarnation of this unexpected and destructive side of economic development, whose growing problems are now beyond the reach of conventional solutions by scientific or political authorities.

A similar theme is portrayed in the novella "Press Enter" (1984) by American author John Varley, in which a joining of computer systems—from wristwatches, automobile computers, microwave chips, and personal computers—produces a type of consciousness, independent from humans. This "super cyborg" first kills its male creator and then a female university student, a hacker who inadvertently unleashes its power using her Apple computer. For Katherine Hayles, this student represents a new type of Eve, who, this time, dies when reaching for the "apple" of the Tree of Knowledge. Here the human-cyborg intimacy results in a hyperconnectivity whose power is capable of overloading human consciousness, quickly eliminating it as a momentary irritation. The only survivor of the experience is the student's boyfriend, who runs away from any connection, moving to the natural world, far from any cybernetic matrix. Thus nature represents an alternative for the protagonist, who escapes unhurt to lead a solitary life, without connections to other humans or machines. In the Brazilian story, by contrast, nature does not exist as an alternative or escape. The crew's scientists, once they see the size of Genghis and the destruction that he is capable of, try to kill him, but he annihilates them, eliminating his last connection with the human race.

Both Braz's and Varley's cybernetic creations consider humans to be invaders or an irritating presence in their consciousness. At the same time there is a basic difference between the visions of the American and Brazilian authors. While the matrix kills two individuals in the American story, the Brazilian cyborg ends up killing the entire crew of the ship in imitation of his namesake, Genghis Khan, who called for the annihilation of any city that resisted his domination. This suggests that, in the view of the Brazilian author, cities are technological monstrosities that may end up being dangerous and menacing for humans. Braz's portrayal of the cyborg Genghis reveals the uncertainties and fears associated with globalization, suggesting a possible betrayal of the Brazilian body politic through cybernetic advances.

The posthuman being of Roberto de Sousa Causo's "At the Beginning of It All" does not fit into this vision of the cyborg as a destructive force. As a cybernetic biological amalgam, this superconscious being is able to survive trips and experiences through time and space that would be impossible for humans. In the story the posthuman must investigate the Big Bang, recording information to bring back to scientists on Earth. "At the Beginning of It All" is narrated from the point of view of this super-consciousness/cyborg, and we experience its emotions as it makes its initial jump in time, from the fear the death to the elation of unity with the cosmic consciousness.

The ephemeral or biological nature of the posthuman is emphasized here, the part that fears death, as do human beings, suggesting an identification with human consciousness. There is another biological metaphor in the narrative when the cyborg gathers data at the subatomic level: these particles "were as much its parents and grandparents as humans were another fractional part of its being" (2005, 64), once again using the metaphor of family ties to describe the commonalities between the super-consciousness and its relation with the cosmos. Here the biological connection becomes the common element between this super-consciousness and its creators. By reading this story from the point of view of the "machine," we share its fears, discoveries, and its connections with the microparticles of outer space. This is a typical gesture of this author, whose philosophy is environmentalist and who often portrays the interrelationships among all forms of life on the planet and the universe. Thus Causo shows the other side of cybernetics and globalization, one which takes us to new levels of understanding of the universe, in which humanity would be just one more form of consciousness or component among many beings and networks of the cosmos.

Conclusion

In these stories about implanted humans and cyborgs, the use of technology illustrates the political crisis of a globalized Brazil, in which Brazilians have to reformulate their concepts of power, identity, and humanity within their body politic. In the case of the implant, technology represents an invasion of the body as if it were a type of illness, exacerbating existing imbalances and injustices and ultimately causing death and destruction. In the case of cyborgs with reproductive capabilities, it is as if the body was able to develop a type of tolerance for technology, "Brazilianizing" it, so to speak, and incorporating it into the social body. More recent texts along the lines of hard science fiction reveal cyborgs who, being more machine than human, may initiate the possible extinction of humanity, while the treatment of the posthuman and the use of familial, biological, and cosmic ties reveal a body politic ready to open itself to the global age. One thing is certain: the centrality of the body in all these texts indicates a constant preoccupation with the body politic within the new world order, thus illustrating the Brazilian reformulation of first-world science fiction concepts.

Notes

1. In the preface to the anthology *Mirrorshades* (1986), Bruce Sterling writes that within cyberpunk there is the constant "theme of body invasion: prosthetic limbs, implanted circuitry, cosmetic surgery, genetic alternation. The even more powerful theme of mind invasion: brain computer interfaces, artificial intelligence, neurochemistry—techniques radically redefining the nature of humanity, the nature of self" (346). Despite the negative connotation of bodily invasion, the portrayal of technological processes in cyberpunk texts is more of a sublime celebration of technology and technophilia, by which the character often loses contact with the body and with corporeal experience. See Wolmark 1994, 119.

2. Samuel R. Delany has written that in *Neuromancer* "cyberspace is haunted by creatures just a step away from Godhood. And religious parallels begin to rumble through his plots almost everywhere we turn. The hard edges of Gibson's dehumanized technologies hide a residing mysticism" (1988, 33).

3. In *Brazilian Science Fiction,* I emphasize the strong physical presence of the body in Brazilian cyberpunk: "In its portrayal of race, sexuality, urban space, and multimedia, tupinipunk [Brazilian cyberpunk] uses the body as a site of resistance" (Ginway 2004, 152).

4. All the translations of Portuguese or Spanish into English are mine, except for the titles of the stories in *Cosmos Latinos.*

5. In the case of Spanish American cyberpunk, cyberspace is used in a different way, with strong links to social and political themes. In the story "Exerion" (2000) by Chilean Pablo Castro, cyberspace is used to search for the disappeared, while in the slipstream novel *Sueños digitales* (*Digital Dreams,* 2000) by Bolivian Edmundo Paz-Soldán, digital images of the former dictator are modified in order to manipulate public opinion, grooming him for elections and democratic rule. In stories that deal with implants, technology—rather than offering greater strength or improving the health of the characters—ends up destroying

their lives, making them victims of technology. This is seen in the Mexican short stories "Reaching the Shore" (1994) by Guillermo Lavín and in "Gray Noise" (1996) by Pepe Rojo. In both cases the implant violates the sense of wholeness of the body, tormenting and isolating the protagonists from meaningful human contact.

6. "My sacrifice will remain forever in your souls and my blood will be the price of your ransom. . . . I have given you my life. I gave you my life. Now I offer you my death. Nothing remains . . ." (Getúlio Vargas, Rio de Janeiro, August 23, 1954; quoted in Robert Levine and John Crocitti, eds., *The Brazil Reader* [Durham, N.C.: Duke University Press, 1999], 224).

7. The head is also the target of vandalism and violence in another cyberpunk story, Braulio Tavares's 1989 "Jogo rápido" ("It's a Snap"), in which a gang cuts the head off of the Christ the Redeemer statue, the symbol of Rio de Janeiro, while another kidnaps a famous scientist, carving the gang's symbol on the victim's forehead. Clearly the gangs use the head to symbolize the loss of power by traditional authorities.

8. See the discussion by Jorge Schwartz on the "Manifesto antropófago" by Oswald de Andrade in Schwartz 1995, 140–60. In English, see Johnson 1987, 41–59.

9. In contrast to mainstream American superheroes, the protagonists of *Silicone XXI* (1985) by Alfredo Sirkis, *Santa Clara Poltergeist* (1991) by Fausto Fawcett, and *Piritas siderais* (Outerspace Pyrites, 1994) by Guilherme Kujawski are all men of color. The novels themselves reveal the strong presence of popular culture and multiculturalism in the Brazilian literary imagination. By using a postmodern aesthetic, these narratives mix high and low, the sexual and the political, the visual and the textual, at times with fierce nationalism and at others questioning the validity of national identity as a concept in Brazil. See Ginway 2004, 151–65.

10. I am basing my discussion of the female body on ideas presented by Karina Vázquez, a doctoral student at the University of Florida, who participated in a graduate portion of my course on Brazilian science fiction in the fall of 2004.

11. A 2001 Cuban story, "Como tuvieron que morir las rosas" ("Like the Roses Had to Die") by Michel Encinosa Fú, explores the theme of posthumans who have modified their bodies to be more like animals, as outlined by Haraway. However, while Haraway imagines a cyborg world of tolerance, the text by Encinosa narrates the persecution of these beings and their individuality.

Bibliography

Braz, Júlio Emílio. "Genghis." In *O universo é um pequeno espaço entre nós.* Unpublished manuscript. 4–27.

Calado, Ivanir. 1993. "O altar dos nossos corações." In *O atlântico tem duas margens: Antologia da novíssima ficção científica portuguesa e brasileira,* ed. José Manuel Morais, 177–206. Lisbon: Caminho.

Castro, Pablo. 2003. "Exerion," trans. Andrea Bell. In *Cosmos Latinos: An Anthology of Science Fiction from Latin America and Spain,* ed. Andrea Bell and Yolanda Molina-Gavilán, 294–304. Middletown, Conn.: Wesleyan University Press.

Causo, Roberto de Sousa. 1996. "Tupinipunk—Cyberpunk brasileiro." *Papêra Uirandê,* special issue, no. 1: 5–11.

———. 2005. "O começo de tudo." *Perry Rhodan* 37 (July): 63–64.

Delany, Samuel R. 1988. "Is Cyberpunk a Good Thing or a Bad Thing?" *Mississippi Review* 16, nos. 2–3: 28–35.

Encinosa Fú, Michel. 2003. "And Like the Roses Had to Die," trans. Ted Angell. In *Cosmos Latinos: An Anthology of Science Fiction from Latin America and Spain,* ed. Andrea Bell and Yolanda Molina-Gavilán, 306–30. Middletown, Conn.: Wesleyan University Press.

Fawcett, Fausto. 1991. *Santa Clara Poltergeist.* Rio de Janeiro: Eco.

Fernandez, Cid. 1993. "Julgamentos." In *Tríplice Universo,* ed. Gumercindo Rocha Dorea, 70–152. São Paulo: GRD.

Flory, Henrique. 1991. "Feliz Natal, vinte bilhões!" In *A pedra que canta,* 147–68. São Paulo: GRD, 1991.

Fuchs, Cynthia. 1995. "Death Is Irrelevant: Cyborgs, Reproduction and the Future of Male Hysteria." In *The Cyborg Handbook,* ed. Chris Hables Gray, 281–300. New York: Routledge.

Gibson, William. 1984. *Neuromancer.* New York: Ace.

Ginway, M. Elizabeth. 2004. *Brazilian Science Fiction: Cultural Myths and Nationhood in the Land of the Future.* Lewisburg, Penn.: Bucknell University Press.

Hale, Charles A. 1968. *Mexican Liberalism in the Age of Mora, 1821–1853.* New Haven, Conn.: Yale University Press.

Haraway, Donna. 1991. "A Cyborg Manifesto." In *Simians, Cyborgs, and Women: The Reinvention of Nature,* 148–81. London: Free Association Books.

Hayles, Katherine. 1995. "The Life Cycles of Cyborgs: Writing the Posthuman." In *The Cyborg Handbook,* ed. Chris Hables Gray, 321–35. New York: Routledge.

Johnson, Randal. 1987. "Tupy or not Tupy: Cannibalism and Nationalism in Contemporary Brazilian Literature and Culture." In *On Latin American Fiction,* ed. John King, 41–59. New York: Farrar, Straus and Giroux.

Kujawski, Guilherme. 1994. *Piritas siderais: Romance cyberbarroco.* Rio de Janeiro: Francisco Alves.

Landon, Brooks. 1997. *Science Fiction after 1900: From Steam Man to the Stars.* New York: Twayne.

Lavín, Guillermo. 2003. "Reaching the Shore," trans. Rena Zuidema and Andrea Bell. In *Cosmos Latinos: An Anthology of Science Fiction from Latin America and Spain,* ed. Andrea Bell and Yolanda Molina-Gavilán, 223–34. Middletown, Conn.: Wesleyan University Press.

Lodi-Ribeiro, Gerson. 1997. "Todo o silício do mundo." In *Outras histórias,* 13–18. Lisbon: Caminho.

Paz-Soldán, Edmundo. 2000. *Sueños digitales.* La Paz: Alfaguara.

Rojo, Pepe. "Gray Noise," trans. Andrea Bell. In *Cosmos Latinos: An Anthology of Science Fiction from Latin America and Spain,* ed. Andrea Bell and Yolanda Molina-Gavilán, 243–64. Middletown, Conn.: Wesleyan University Press.

Schwartz, Jorge. 1995. "Manifesto antropófago." In *Vanguardas Latino-Americanas: Polêmicas, manifestos e textos criticism,* 140–60. São Paulo: Edusp.

Sirkis, Alfredo. 1985. *Silicone XXI.* Rio de Janeiro: Record.

Stepan, Alfred. 1978. *The State and Society: Peru in Comparative Perspective.* Princeton, N.J.: Princeton University Press.

Sterling, Bruce. 1988. Preface to *Mirrorshades.* In *Storming the Reality Studio: A Casebook of Cyberpunk and Postmodern Fiction,* ed. Larry McCaffrey, 343–48. Durham, NC: Duke University Press, 1991.

Tavares, Braulio. 1989. "Jogo rápido." In *A espinha dorsal da memória,* 109–26. Lisbon: Caminho.

Varley, John. 1984. "Press Enter." In *Blue Champagne,* 319–400. Niles, Ill.: Dark Harvest.

Wolmark, Jenny. 1994. *Aliens and Others.* Iowa City: University of Iowa Press.

A Brazilian Metafiction

Paulo de Sousa Ramos's Dystopian Novella

Roberto de Sousa Causo

In Paulo de Sousa Ramos's dystopian novella *O Outro Lado do Protocolo* (The Other Side of the Protocol, 1985), a broad genealogy of dystopia and utopia in science fiction and in Brazilian science fiction in particular are presented. Dystopian elements present in Ramos's work are briefly compared with those of other international and Brazilian works, including those of André Carneiro, a pioneer in this same line of Brazilian utopian/dystopian works that stress sexuality. On the other hand, metafiction is compared with mainstream works and confronted with Robert Scholes's concept of "structural fabulation." Ramos's novella is seen as occupying middle ground between science fiction's straightforward approach to narrative style and metafictional devices such as ellipse and the untrustworthy narrator, between the postmodern approach and the science fiction vocation for promoting estrangement and defamiliarization in an accessible manner.

One of the best examples of the Brazilian tradition of science fiction dystopias, *O Outro Lado do Protocolo* is an elliptical tale that begins when the narrator travels to the future, through the machine built by a college friend, Tamerlão. He will become a guest at Tamerlão's house—where he meets the beautiful Tânia, his friend's wife—and will eventually tour a utopian society.

Other utopian/dystopian works preceded Ramos's novella. Utopian pamphlets were common in the early 1920s as part of what Brazilian intellectuals called "social hygienization" and "the enthusiasm for education." Novellas and novels such as Rodolpho Theophilo's 1922 *No Reino de Kiato (O País da Verdade)* (The Kingdom of Kiato [The Nation of Truth]), Albino José Ferreira Coutinho's 1923 *A Liga dos Planetas* (The League of Planets), and Adalzira Bittencourt's 1929 defense of eugenics and of what she called "Latin American feminism," *Sua Excia. A Presidente da República no Ano 2.500* (Her Excellency the President of the Republic in the year 2500), were full of moral and eugenics didacticism—Bittencourt's story even integrates a handbook of etiquette for the young women of the future.

In 1930 Menotti Del Picchia's *A Filha do Inca ou A República 3.000* (The Inca's Daughter or the Republic 3000), a Brazilian military party takes an expedition to a high-tech utopia; but after arriving there they find that they would rather escape it to live a quiet, simple life in the natural world, starting a trend for the denial of technology and social engineering that led Brazilian science fiction away from utopia and toward dystopia or anti-utopia. A truly Brazilian kind of utopia of natural living and goodwill among men and women is rendered with good humor by Alfonso Schmidt in his 1936 novella *Zanzalás.* The only thing that threatens it is an invasion from stereotyped imperialist Europeans (this is an early example of future war in Brazil, though with a totally unconventional approach to the subgenre). A dystopian 1966 short story in the vein of clashing with modernization and social engineering is Domingos Carvalho da Silva's humorous but sharp "Sociedade Secreta" (Secret Society), set in a Brazil in which only old people remember the easygoing life of the past.

In 1947 pioneer Brazilian science fiction author Jerônymo Monteiro published his novel *3 Meses no Século 81* (Three Months on the Eighty-first Century). A Brazilian adventurer, trying to prove to H. G. Wells himself that time travel—through spiritual projection if not through a time machine—was possible, travels in spirit to the eighty-first century, where he incarnates in the body of a weapons maker who has a key role in the production of the death ray to be used in the war against the Martians. The society of the eighty-first century is a dystopian one—highly divided into castes and with little social mobility—but the hero soon helps a local resistance group to put an end to such a totalitarian scheme through global warfare. Another Brazilian dystopia is the 1984 novel *O Fruto do Vosso Ventre* (The Fruit of Thy Womb), by Herberto Sales, set in an island in which all new birth are forbidden, and Ignácio de Loyola Brandão's 1982 *Não Verás País Nenhum* (available in English as *You Will See No Country*), a dystopian novel in its depiction of a future society in which technocratic bureaucracy thrives and the environment is entirely degraded. A more recent one, centered on overpopulation and violence, is Henrique Flory's 1989 short story "Feliz Natal, vinte bilhões!" (Merry Christmas, Twenty Billion!).

Sometimes it is hard to establish a clear border between utopia and anti-utopia. One definition of utopia is a context in which social and political conflicts are placated and the class struggle has no reason to be—exactly what we see, in a slightly funny way, in *O Outro Lado do Protocolo,* when the groups of the Seventy and the Seven Hundred, one of the institutions portrayed in the book, vote always 50 percent in favor and 50 percent against anything, probably Ramos's satirical take on Brazil's propensity for political and social conciliation. When this balance cannot manifest itself anymore or its hypocrisy is exposed by the end of the novella, there is social upheaval, vandalism, and the invasion of Tânia-Tamerlão's house, suggesting a latent violence within the social tissue, masked by the "protocol." Tamerlão reveals, in a personal research, that the figures "against the narrator" reach 98 percent. The false uniformity of the society of "there," as the narrator likes to put, is also stressed several times during the narrative.

In *The Encyclopedia of Science Fiction* (1993), Brian Stableford states: "The word 'dystopia' is the commonly used antonym of 'eutopia' and denotes that class of hypothetical societies containing images of worlds worse than our own. . . . Dystopian images are almost invariably images of future society, pointing fearfully at the way the world is supposedly going in order to provide urgent propaganda for a change in direction. . . . The central features of dystopia are ever present: the oppression of majority by a ruling élite (which varies only in the manner of its characterization, not in its actions), and the regimentation of society as a whole (which varies only in its declared ends, not in its actual process). . . . The most detailed analysis of [the anxiety of social automatism], and perhaps the most impressively ruthless of all dystopias, is [*We*] by Yevgeny Zamiatin . . ." (361). Dystopian science fiction has become, in the course of the twentieth century, a popular, respected, and a quite international subgenre. Probably taking from *We* the notion of one individual requesting another for sexual practice, Robert Silverberg produced the impressive *The World Inside* (1971), in which overpopulation and constrained environmental modules called "urban monads" demand an intense sexual promiscuity, to the point that no one has the right to refuse any kind of sexual demand from another. British mainstream writer L. P. Hartley also ventured into the subgenre with *Facial Justice* (1960), a novel that has all individual identification destroyed by the imposing of a single face for every woman. The Swedish dystopia *Kalocaína* (1940), by Karin Boye, takes to extremes the totalitarian state's need to control the minds and hearts of people with the invention of a perfect truth drug.

It is thus natural that dystopia would reach the Brazilian literature. But Ramos's novella belongs to a specific line of Brazilian utopias and dystopias—one that is centered in a future world of free sex, more known by a series of interconnected narratives written by André Carneiro that began during the 1960s. Carneiro's explorations on that line include the short story "Diário da Nave Perdida" (Log of the Lost Ship)—which first presents the device of a kind of psycho-theater of sexual connotation, a device that would be over-employed decades later in *Amorquia*—and the novellas *Piscina Livre* (Free Pool) and *Amorquia* (LoveAnarchy), plus short stories belonging to the collection *A Máquina de Hyerónimus e Outras Histórias* (The Hieronymus Machine and Other Stories), especially "A Pergunta" (The Question), in which a couple finds out that they cannot ask the transcendental questions about death and the meaning of life, because a central computer provides all needed happiness, including immortality; and "A Missão" (The Mission), that has Apercus, one of the protagonists of *Amorquia,* going back in time up to the moment in which the "great transformation" is going on, heralding the transition from familiar contemporary society to the sexual utopia of the future.

We might call this sequence the Sexual Anarchy series, for one of its constants is the lack of a hierarchy of power, classes, and national identities. On the other hand and as in *O Outro Lado do Protocolo,* there is a computer that provides everything, people live in sexual hedonism, and disease and physical degradation are distant (in *Amorquia,* they are totally unknown) from people's immediate experience. Another point that approximates the works of both authors is the representation of an ethos associated with a class of cultured and progressive people, who had absorbed a liberal post–Sexual Revolution behavior.

In Ramos's novella men keep a young look up to their seventy-eighth year and women up to their seventy-fifth, when they are terminated by the computer, after the appearance of the so-called precursory blot. The employment of the idea of a literal "deadline" has precedents: the movie *Logan's Run* (1976), for example, is a postholocaust adventure in which, upon reaching thirty years of age, people are killed during a public spectacle reminiscent of the Roman circus, to keep the demographic balance inside restricted underground habitats. Australian Garth Nix lowered that age limit to fourteen years in his novel *Shade's Children* (1998). This device seems to symbolize the idea of a state control over the most eventual and definitive of experiences, death.

But the main source as much of *O Outro Lado do Protocolo* and of the Sexual Anarchy series probably lies in *Brave New World* by Aldous Huxley. In that classic 1932 novel, men and women are conceived in assembly lines of genetic engineering and society has as its ideals free sex, contentment through drugs—which are also present in the works by Ramos (like the blue pills that Tamerlão gives to the protagonist) and by Carneiro—and the principle of industrial productivity even on the artistic and entertainment fields.[1] Ramos explores this theme in the ironic selection of the Seven Poets in *O Outro Lado do Protocolo* through a contest in which the hormone levels of the competitors are measured. Once finished with the contest, the winners seem to assume a bureaucratic status in the social structure. There is, perhaps, in the Seven Poets and their puerile poetry echoes of the character Helmholtz and his Advanced Emotional Engineering course in *Brave New World.*

The first one, though, to write of poets submitted to state ideological control was the Russian Zamiatin, in his classic *We* (1920), the novel that probably inspired both *Brave New World* and George Orwell's *Nineteen Eighty-Four* (1949). One can argue that Zamiatin is the father of the modern dystopia, as Darko Suvin does in *The Encyclopedia of Science Fiction:* "[*We*] is the paradigmatic anti-utopia, prefiguring George Orwell and Aldous Huxley and superseding that tradition of utopianism, from Sir Thomas More on, which ignores technology and anthropology" (Clute and Nicholls 1993, 1364). (There are hints, by the way, that Ramos might have read *We:* In that novel appears the uncommon name of "Timberline," anticipating Ramos's "Tamerlão.") On the other hand Zamiatin was probably knowledgeable of science fiction of the scientific romance tradition, for he had produced prefaces for the Russian editions of works by H. G. Wells (1364).

Ramos's and Carneiro's habit of weaving poems into the prose of their novellas also is reminiscent of Huxley, whose protagonist, John Savage, frequently recites Shakespeare. But different from Huxley, the two Brazilians employed sharp and short dialogues and abstain from using narrator interventions of the *said* and *went on* sort, abundant in *Brave New World.*

Another important difference lies on the type of narrator that Ramos has chosen. Ramos's narrator does not try to assume a voice of authority. On the contrary, he is content in offering us incomplete facts—starting with his own name, never revealed (for reasons of "modesty")—and he frequently assumes that he forgets certain facts or thinks it is better not to mention occurrences and commentaries he believes to be better left out. Ironically he also assumes he is relatively lost in the society he is visiting and places great hope in the amulet that he carries with him, as if he could not quite believe in his use of reason in his new context.

The implicit author makes evident that every story told is composed of what is included and what is excluded from the text. This novella certainly thrives in the use of ellipse—the omission of an element that can be understood through context and thus kept operating inside the narrative structure. This device is present not only on the level of style, but on the level of the events in the story as well—the protagonist, for instance, first appears falling down a hill, stopping at the feet of the naked woman he had being, apparently, watching through binoculars. "I was so interested in the possibilities represented by the binoculars, that I forgot that the ground is necessary support, even for those who drift. A bush went down under my feet, I rolled down the slope, twenty meters or so. Someday I'll measure it" (11).[2]

"Someday I'll measure it"—the implicit author cannot say precisely, but at the same time, he will not be merely speculative ("twenty meters or so"). "Someday I'll measure it" leaves the matter open, and the story itself is full of facts left for further confirmation, while realist narrative presupposes a level of certainty and completeness of narrated facts. The narrator forgets details, misunderstands and assumes that he does not have the information at the time of the writing— the reader will have to do with what he or she has. In chapter 13, when the protagonist finally finds in the Immediate Public Archives building ("immediate archives" being something of an oxymoron) an objective information about the Great Transformation that everyone talks about, he finds it to be incomplete— "The computer terminal that served the building . . . had an emotional crisis made visible in a short-circuit. The information plaque ended up a bit damaged" (45).

On the whole this results in an approach that calls attention upon the text's expressive surface and its limitations. The blurb of *Os Senhores Assaltantes* (The Lords' Assailants), another book by Ramos, affirms that "in his work one can see the intentional search for the limits between meaning and the word." The back cover of the same book states that the author "approaches the essentiality of the concepts, playing with them. He plays with the mystery in successive interferences, putting the significant on the level of the signifying. For him, the sign is so important as the idea, as in an anagram."

Ramos, himself a literary theory professor, is conscious of the metafictional practices associated with postmodern literature and employs them in *O Outro Lado do Protocolo*. Metafiction, which calls attention upon the act of fictional creation, reacts against the possible emptying of the realist techniques of storytelling, since nowadays a trend of literary thought asserts, according to Patricia Waugh's *Metafiction: The Theory and Practice of Self-Conscious Fiction* (1984), that "the materialist, positivist and empiricist world-view on which realistic fiction is premised no longer exists" (7). As we see through Ramos's novella, metafictional works "tend to be constructed on the principle of a fundamental and sustained opposition: the construction of a fictional illusion (as in traditional realism) and the laying bare of that illusion" (6).

Therefore we have in *O Outro Lado do Protocolo* a narrative structure in which, despite the fact that on the language level the narration progresses with a certain clarity, a dynamic of doubt is established; one that exposes the narrator's inability to express with accuracy the *totality* of what is going on in the story. In doing so the narrator is equally exposing the inability of language to represent a totality—it harbors gaps and ambiguities, as Ramos's novella demonstrates.

This is another postmodern aspect that should not go unnoticed. As Paula Geyh, Fred G. Leebron, and Andrew Levy write in the introduction to the volume they edited for the Norton Anthology series, *Postmodern American Fiction* (1997): "there is no longer any hope of a single conceptual system of discourse through which we might aspire to understand the totality of the world. Indeed, one can no longer speak of 'totality' at all. Instead, we have a plurality of worlds and multiple, often mutually incompatible discourses through which to understand them" (xx).

An example given by these authors is Tim O'Brien's story "How to Tell a True War Story" (1990), which "compulsively retells the same story, in slightly different versions, while despairing of his ability to find the right combination of words that will somehow be adequate to convey his experience" (xxi). Another postmodern aspect present in *O Outro Lado do Protocolo* and related to metafiction is uncertainty about the narrator. "In various ways, many postmodern narratives interrogate the traditional understanding and functioning of the authority of the author. . . . The writer appears to surrender a large measure of control over the structure and the meaning of the narrative, and, as his prose is integrated with that of other writers, seems to give up ownership of the text. . . . The 'author' emerges as a literary construction, like any other language" (xxiii).

Metafiction also appears in Ramos when the narrator invokes an interlocutor previous to the production of the text, a "friend" to whom he has shown his drafts and who has offered various opinions about what and how to narrate. The author—as the one who constructs the work—is present, violating the realist norm of erasing his ostensible presence in the text. The dialogue with the "friend," in turn, emphasizes the work's quality of incompleteness, the feel of it as being in progress, awaiting conclusions and details the author told us he would measure someday.

Metafiction appears in different ways in postmodern and non-postmodern literature. In John Fowkes's novel *The French Lieutenant's Woman* (1969) the author himself intervenes constantly to break the realist illusion and to demand that his text should be read with suspicion and with the reader's active participation, especially on the choosing of one of the several given endings. In Tim O'Brien's 1994 novel *In the Lake of the Woods* the reader is confronted with three narrative levels—a relatively straightforward realistic narrative, intercalated with sections composed of quotations taken from several different sources and related (sometimes quite slightly) with the main story's situations, and the author's own voice appearing as a desperate and restless plea reduced to the small letters of personal footnotes. In Stephen King's novel *The Dark Half* (1989) a literary pseudonym becomes alive in flesh and blood and takes the shape of the writer protagonist's main character, a violent hustler from a series of pulp fiction novels. In Samuel R. Delany's award-winning science fiction novel *The Einstein Intersection* (1967), the author is also present in the epigraphs that announce when and how he reached that particular stage in writing the work.

The postmodern stance stresses metafictionality on the level of form, though. In John Blainville's novel *Kepler* (1981) it is present both on the surface of the text and in the text's organization (structure). "*I do not speak like I write, I do not write like I think, I do not think as I ought to think, and so everything goes on in deepest darkness.* Where did these voices come from, these strange sayings?" the main character wonders when the italicized phrases (by Wittgenstein) explode in his mind. "It was as if the future had found utterance in him" (86). Such a statement clearly introduces an intervention that puts the intertextuality on the surface of the text, while the novel's complex structure—with each chapter named after a major work by Kepler and in organization reflecting something of that work's structure as much as its content—stresses the novel as a construct and not as a linear depiction of the facts of Kepler's life.

Compared with most postmodern works, formal devices and inventiveness are less important in science fiction. Yet there are some quite plain and straightforward science fiction works included in the broad and highly representative volume *Postmodern American Fiction,* including an excerpt taken from Octavia E. Butler's novel *Imago* (1989).

The confluence of the intentions of science fiction and the postmodern concerns and sensibilities should not cause surprise. Brian McHale, in *Postmodernist*

Fiction (1987), argues that "science fiction, we might say, is to postmodernism what detective fiction was to modernism: it is the ontological genre *par excellence* (as the detective story is the epistemological genre *par excellence*)." He continues: "The fantastic genre . . . involves a confrontation between two worlds whose basic physical norms are mutually incompatible" (16). Most science fiction realities will, then, expose the mutability of our perceptions of reality and reality's lack of solidity. "The dominant of postmodernist fiction is *ontological,*" McHale wrote. "That is, postmodernist fiction deploys strategies that engage and foreground questions like the ones Dick Higgins calls 'post-cognitive': 'Which world is this? What is to be done in it? Which of my selves is to do it?' Other typical postmodernist questions bear either on the ontology of the literary text itself or on the ontology of the world which it projects, for instance: What is a world? What kinds of world are there, how are they constituted, and how do they differ? What happens when different kinds of world are placed in confrontation, or when boundaries between worlds are violated? What is the mode of existence of a text, and what is the mode of existence of the world (or worlds) it projects?" (10).

Science fiction may use the language of realism, but it is always suprarealistic in the sense that it forces the confrontation of what is assumed as real or reality-based and demands a repositioning of the reader. The genre defamiliarizes what is assumed as the now and familiarizes what might be the future. This is similar to the deautomatization process that is claimed by the avant-garde arts, with the difference that "in SF this estrangement is more conceptual and less verbal," wrote Robert Scholes in *Structural Fabulations* (1975): "It is the new idea that shocks us into perception, rather than the new language of the poetic text. . . . And it is precisely because of this that our old formalistic methodology seldom works well as a critical approach to SF" (47). Scholes also identifies in science fiction an alternative to the usual metafictional approach, the self-reflective fiction: "Projected into the future, the problems of realism and fantasy both vanish. There is no question of 'recording' the future, nor of denying its actualities. All future projection is obviously model-making, poiesis not mimesis. And freed of the problem of correspondence or noncorrespondence with some present actuality or some previous experienced past, with its records and recollections, the imagination can function without self-deception as to its means and ends" (18).

In her essay "Ciência Ficção: Literatura Brasileira de Vanguarda," Teresinka Pereira tries to find a process of denouncing of a world of appearances and "protocol" falsehood in Ramos's novella: "Machines may be more perfectionist than the human being, but they are also more limited. After reading Paulo de Sousa Ramos's [novella], the reader will conclude that having a youthful and handsome look isn't a total advantage" (1997, 3). It is difficult, though, to establish a single orientation for the book's meaning. "Ambiguity and irony let open to the reader the 'deciphering' of the metaphor offered by the whole of the work," as

Duelli Colombini tells us, in the introduction to the book (6). In fact, one real-izes especially that the hero's deeds in the transformation of the protocol soci-ety lack any merit. When the character Stínia falls in love with him and begins aging because she abstains from drinking the rejuvenating substance in an attempt to mislead the computer, she soon finds herself to be alone—the pro-tagonist will not offer her any consolation. It is Tânia's father, Insek, who is going to support Stínia. Insek first had tried to embarrass the hero, known in the future as "Mr. Ricardo," but then ends up accepting the novelty that he was bringing aging and, finally, accuses him again: "Mr. Ricardo is the one to blame, he who brought us a new vision of life, I mean, a new way of dying" (65).

The protagonist's own feelings regarding Stínia are not noble: he is happy having sex with her but is always troubled to be coupling with an old woman (who is nonetheless young-looking), as if he was consuming a degraded prod-uct masked by a lavish packaging. Meanwhile, it is the wife of his friend Tamer-lão that he wants. By the end of the novella after the character's interest for Tânia was consumed, Stínia comes up to confront him a last time, now as an old woman. He is about to leave a world convulsed by his actions, and when she asks him "Won't you take me?" (74), he is abandons her, stating that the time machine can only transport three (Tamerlão, Tânia, and himself).

By the same token, the hero's revolutionary role is downplayed by several factors: his desire to keep the "*bom-tom*" (an expression meaning "proper social behavior," repeated twenty-two times in the course of the novella), his willing-ness to be sincere with his questioners, and the ability to cause commotion unwillingly; and also by the fact that he is confused with "Mr. Ricardo," one of the protagonists of the Great Revolution, whose mythic status influences the reception of the anonymous hero's acts by the inhabitants of the utopia. As in the Philip K. Dick novel *The World Jones Made* (1956), the effects of his acts seem to emanate from a will that does not belong to him; it is exterior, pro-jected on time. This is probably supported by quantum physics' notions of a self-conscious, self-organizing universe, with only integrated beings (mirroring the universe of particles integrated by quantum linkages). The hero's character is far from revolutionary, though his acts end up being so.

On the whole this novella is a narrative built around the absence of certain-ties, in order to expose the limits of language and human perceptions. This hap-pens on the level of language, with the constant reference to data the author does not have, and also through his evasive style; regarding the characters, *O Outro Lado do Protocolo* is never straightforward but always ambiguous and reticent, with fabricated looks and indivisible essences (the old woman and man in young bodies); and on the level of plot, with the protagonist's revolutionary motivations never really materializing. The balance of the narrative components never permits form, even though the work is full of literary self-consciousness, to supersede the surefooted unfolding of the plot—"The basic idea behind *O Outro Lado do Protocolo* is entertainment" (9), the author warns us, making clear that he does not intend to sacrifice reading pleasure for the pleasure of decoding and interpreting of his text.

Paulo de Sousa Ramos's novella meets the intersection point between the postmodern approach and the science fiction vocation for promoting estrangement and defamiliarization in an accessible manner. Yet his metaphor of nonapprehensible meaning is effective, and it is valued for projecting itself as social speculation in this anti-utopia. At first sight it is not possible to understand the meaning of the post–Great Transformation world, and its apparent stability is false.

Notes

1. Carneiro extends this notion to sexual entertainment in *Piscina Livre*.
2. All translations are mine.

Bibliography

Blainville, John. 1993. *Kepler.* New York: Vintage.

Bittencourt, Adalzira. 1929. *Sua Excia. A Presidente da República no Ano 2.500.* São Paulo: Schmidt.

Boye, Karin. 1974. *Kalocaína.* Rio de Janeiro: Companhia Editora Americana.

Brandão, Ignácio de Loyola. 1982. *Não Verás País Nenhum.* 6th ed. São Paulo: Codecri.

Carneiro, André. 1963. "Diário da Nave Perdida." In *Diário da Nave Perdida,* 161–209. São Paulo: EdArt.

———. 1980. *Piscina Livre.* São Paulo: Moderna.

———. 1991. *Amorquia.* Coleção Zenith, no. 4. São Paulo: Aleph.

———. 1997. *A Máquina de Hyerónimus e Outras Histórias.* São Carlos: UFSC.

Clute, John, and Peter Nicholls. 1993. *The Encyclopedia of Science Fiction.* New York: St. Martin's Press.

Colombini, Duilio. 1985. "Introducão." In *Do Outro Ladodo Protocolo.* São Paulo: Sonia.

Coutinho, Albino José Ferreira. 1922. *A Liga dos Planetas.* Porto Alegre: Livraria Americana/ Rentzsch.

Delany, Samuel R. 1967. *The Einstein Intersection.* New York: Ace.

Del Picchia, Menotti. 1949. *A Filha do Inca.* Coleção Saraiva, no. 14. São Paulo: Saraiva.

Fowles, John. 1970. *The French Lieutenant's Woman.* New York: Signet.

Flory, Henrique. 1989. "Feliz Natal, vinte bilhões!" In *Enquanto Houver Natal—: Oito Estórias de Ficção Científica,* ed. Gumercindo Rocha Dorea, 51–67. São Paulo: GRD.

Geyh, Paula, Fred G. Leebron, and Andrew Levy, eds. 1997. *Postmodern American Fiction.* New York: Norton.

Huxley, Aldous. 1932. *Brave New World.* Garden City, N.Y.: Doubleday, Doran.

King, Stephen. 1989. *The Dark Half.* New York: Viking.

McHale, Brian. 1987. *Postmodernist Fiction.* London: Methuen.

Monteiro, Jerônymo. 1947. *3 Meses no Século 81.* Porto Alegre: Livraria do Globo.

Orwell, George. 1949. *Nineteen Eighty-Four.* New York: Harcourt, Brace.

Pereira, Teresinka. 1997. "Ciência Ficção: Literatura Sileiro de Vanguarda." In *Ensaios Internacionais de Ficção Científica Brasileira,* ed. Roberto de Sousa Causo, 3. Biblioteca Essencial da Science Fiction Brazilian 1. Brasópolis: Edgard Guimarães Editor.

Ramos, Paulo de Sousa. 1985. *O Outro Lado do Protocolo.* São Paulo: Soma.

———. 1987. *Os Senhores Assaltantes.* São Paulo: Edicon.

Sales, Herberto. 1984. *O Fruto do Vosso Ventre.* Rio de Janeiro: José Olympio.

Schmidt, Afonso. 1938. *Zanzalás.* São Paulo: SPES.

Scholes, Robert. 1975. *Structural Fabulations.* Notre Dame: University of Notre Dame.

Silva, Domingos Carvalho da. 1966. "Sociedade Secreta." In *A Véspera dos Mortos.* São Paulo: Coliseu.

Silverberg, Robert. 1971. *The World Inside.* London: Panther, 1978.

Theophilo, Rodolpho. 1922. *O Reino de Kiato (No País da Verdade).* São Paulo: Monteiro Lobato.

Waugh, Patricia. 1984. *Metafiction: The Theory and Practice of Self-Conscious Fiction.* London: Methuen.

Zamiatin, Yevgeny. 1924. *We,* 37–48. New York: Avon Eos, 1999.

Stagecoach in Space

The Legacy of *Firefly*

Fred Erisman

When Joss Whedon's science fiction television series, *Firefly*, premiered in September 2002, there was no denying it was a western. In succeeding frames of the opening credits a pistol cocks with a threatening click; the protagonist faces the camera stalwartly alone, a pistol strapped low on his thigh; accompanied by a trusted sidekick, he faces down a cluster of mounted, duster-clad ne'er-do-wells; and horses stampede into the foreground, spooked by the low-flying spaceship above them. All the while an off-screen voice wails the lyrics of the series' theme:

> Take me out to the black,
> Tell them I ain't comin' back.
> Burn the land and boil the sea;
> You can't take the sky from me. ("Serenity")

The series' roots in the tradition of the western story and the western film were apparent for all to see.

Far less apparent, however, is the degree to which the series draws upon a single western classic, John Ford's *Stagecoach* (1939), to shape its structure and its nature. Ford's film, which made John Wayne a star and netted Academy Awards for supporting actor Thomas Mitchell and score composer Richard Hageman, establishes the model from which *Firefly* builds. In the fourteen segments filmed (only eleven of which were aired before the series was untimely cancelled), Whedon and his cast make clear their debt to the earlier film. Whedon, in fact, remarked that, in planning his ensemble cast, he mused: "*Millennium Falcon*, yes. *Stagecoach*, better . . . , so I decided to go from five [characters] to nine," making his cast match Ford's in number ("Here's How It Was"). From that beginning he, the writers, and the cast went on to demonstrate how, had circumstances permitted, the film's structure, context, and motifs might be translated into a future world far from the western frontier.

The basic structure of *Stagecoach* is the familiar one of the journey. Six passengers, a lawman, and the driver set out from Tonto to travel to Lordsburg, picking up a ninth person along the way. They are a disparate group: Buck, the driver (Andy Devine), has a job to do; Curly, the marshal (George Bancroft), rides shotgun to search for the Ringo Kid, who has broken jail; pregnant Lucy Mallory (Louise Platt) is on her way to join her cavalry officer husband; Peacock (Donald Meek), a whiskey salesman called "Reverend" by the group, wants only "to return to the bosoms of his family"; Hatfield (John Carradine), a gambler and disgraced southern aristocrat, goes along to protect Lucy Mallory; Gatewood (Berton Churchill), a banker, is absconding with his bank's cash; while drunken Doc Boone (Thomas Mitchell) and the prostitute Dallas (Claire Trevor) have been driven out of town by the self-righteous women of the Law and Order League. The final passenger, the Ringo Kid (John Wayne), has escaped prison to avenge the murder of his brother by the Plummer brothers. En route to Lordsburg, Boone delivers Lucy's baby; the group fends off an Indian attack; Hatfield is killed and Peacock wounded; Ringo and Dallas fall in love; and Curly, turning, a blind eye to the letter of the law, sends the two off to start life anew on Ringo's ranch.

The journey in and of itself, however, in Ford's hands becomes the "journey into hell"—a device by which "the hero (in this case the group) must undertake a journey that brings him face to face with mirror images of his own weaknesses and flaws, but in the form of powerful obstacles for him to overcome before he can . . . emerge, cleansed and reborn, into the light" (Place 1974, 32). Thus each of the principal characters, and especially Dallas and Ringo, must examine his or her beliefs and principles before the film can end. Boone overcomes drunkenness to deliver a baby; Hatfield shows a glimmer of vestigial honor in his efforts to protect Lucy; Peacock, a Milquetoast character, finds courage and determination within himself; and Curly, a dedicated law officer, comes to understand that personal law can transcend statutory law. The evolution of the principal characters catalyzed by the circumstances of the journey gives the film much of its distinctiveness.

That same distinctiveness resonates in *Firefly,* where nine diverse characters set out on an endless voyage from one planetary settlement to another. The time is five hundred years in the future, five years after a global war has left only two superpowers, the United States and China, and galactic government has been centralized into the authoritarian Alliance. The similarities between casts are noteworthy; the differences are even more so. The vehicle, spaceship rather than stage, is named *Serenity.* Buck, the seriocomic driver, becomes Wash, the pilot (Alan Tudyk); drunken Doc Boone becomes the uptight surgeon Simon Tam (Sean Maher), who, with his tormented sister, River (Summer Glau), is on the run from Alliance officials; "Reverend" Peacock is replaced by an actual cleric, the enigmatic Shepherd Book (Ron Glass), whose peaceful calling masks an intriguing familiarity with crime and weapons; and, in an especially telling reversal, the prostitute Dallas becomes Inara Serra (Morena Baccarin), a licensed and respected "companion" whose clients include women as well as men and whose presence aboard the ship gives it "a certain respectability" ("Out of Gas").

Three characters have no direct counterparts in the film: the ship's engineer, Kaylee Frye (Jewel Staite), unschooled but a genius with machines; the first officer, Zoe (Gina Torres), an army buddy of *Serenity*'s captain and the "resident hard-ass chick," who carries as a sidearm a sawed-off Winchester 94 rifle;[1] and muscleman Jayne Cobb (Adam Baldwin), a humorously mercenary thug with a rudimentary sense of honor (Here's How It Was"). The fourth character, however, could have stepped from the film—Malcolm Reynolds (Nathan Fillion), owner and captain of the *Serenity* and a spiritual kinsman to the Ringo Kid. A former sergeant in the Independent forces opposing the Alliance, a "man of faith, a man of action . . . before he had everything taken away from him," he is the person who, among them all, is most on the "journey into hell." Betrayed by his own leaders, he has taken up a semilegitimate life on the fringes of civilization, seeking the freedom denied him at home and surrounding himself with a crew that represents "bits of himself that he had lost" ("Commentary to Serenity"). In episode after episode he encounters obstacles that test his mettle and that of his associates; when Inara says to Simon, "You're lost in the woods. We all are. Even the captain. Only he likes it that way," Mal interjects: "No, the only difference is the woods are the only place I can see a clear path" ("Serenity"). As he walks that path he strives to recover himself and his sense of life.

The journey undertaken by both sets of characters takes place within a distinctive context—a hostile environment offering little by way of support and forcing them to turn inward for the resources they need to overcome its perils. For *Stagecoach* the environment is Monument Valley in northern Arizona, a desert region whose monotony is broken by towering stone monoliths. It is a dramatic setting in its own right but, in Ford's hands, becomes more. It is, one critic has observed, "symbolic of the forces of nature, which offer man neither aid nor obstacle but are only a stage upon which he can work out his dreams. . . . Within it an enclosed worldview is not only possible but necessary. Within it life (and the living of it) must be created through the efforts of man—the environment does not do it for them" (Place 1974, 36–37). This context is one that Ford found especially provocative, and he used it, in one form or another, in many subsequent films.

Even in *Stagecoach*, however, the essential elements already exist. Like the omnipresent Nature of Stephen Crane's "The Open Boat" or Frank Norris's *McTeague,* the valley is neither malevolent nor benevolent; it simply *is,* and its aridity and overwhelming expanses reduce human concerns almost to nothingness. The external context, in short, provides "a wilderness of insecurity. The townspeople gather in their town, an artificial world, for protection from a menacing and chaotic outer space, from which they isolate themselves" (Gallagher 1986, 391). Part of the contextual menace, however, comes from human as well as natural perils. The valley is populated by Apaches, indigenous savages of immeasurable ruthlessness, and their attack upon the stage brings the action to a climax. Indians and horses die; Peacock takes an arrow through the chest, and Hatfield is killed as he prepares to shoot Lucy to protect her from mutilation and rape; the stage's defenders are down to their last rounds of ammunition, and only the timely intervention of the U.S. Cavalry saves the day. In their savagery the Apache offer a secondary threat that the travelers must constantly keep in mind, a threat they can overcome only with the aid of the military.[2]

The crew of *Serenity* face a comparable situation, albeit in an environment infinitely more lethal than that of Arizona, and populated by hostiles who make the Apache seem innocuous. The environment is, of course, interplanetary space—an airless realm where the slightest failure of human effort can bring lingering (and often instant) death—and its perils play an important part in two segments of the show. In "Out of Gas," the eighth installment of the series, *Serenity* is disabled by an engine-room explosion, and its life-support systems fail. As the show proceeds the shipboard temperature drops, and the atmosphere thickens with carbon dioxide. Every person aboard recognizes the imminence of death, either from suffocation or freezing; their only alternative seems to be to surrender themselves to the vacuum of space, and their spirits are not helped by the doctor's offhand description of the effects of suffocation.

It is, however, the airlessness of space that poses the greatest danger. Shipboard life is dependent upon an intricate network of interdependent systems to shut in air and refresh its oxygen; excursions outside *Serenity,* when they become necessary, require the elaborate protection of a spacesuit, which carries its own kind of menace. When Jayne twits Simon for quailing at the thought of going outside the ship in flight, the doctor remarks: "I suppose it's just the thought of a little Mylar and glass being the only thing separating a person from . . . nothing." And Jayne, ever the unfeeling realist, replies: "It's impressive what 'nothing' can do to a man" ("Bushwhacked"). Jayne himself comes in for his own taste of airlessness when Malcolm, angered by his betrayal of Simon and River, shuts him in an airlock and cracks the door as the ship climbs out of the atmosphere. Malcolm, grilling him, points out that "You'll be a lot thinner once you get sucked out that hole," and Jayne, in uncharacteristic terror, cries: "That ain't no way for a man to die!" ("Ariel"). So inexorable, and so final, is the threat of space that even the hard-shelled Jayne succumbs to its menace.

For all its dangers, space is a known constant. The crew knows of its dangers long before they embark on their journey, and they prepare themselves, mentally and materially, to deal with it. Less predictable and in some ways even more menacing is the human threat. As participants in illegal trade, the crew expects and takes in stride the hazards of their work: a swindle, a double-cross, or a setup. These elements go with the territory, and they are as proficient in their execution as the folk with whom they deal. The greater human threat is twofold: on the one hand, the Alliance, with its enforced adherence to arbitrary laws, and, on the other, the Reavers, feral humans unrivaled in their anarchy and bestiality.

Whereas the military in *Stagecoach* is a source of rescue, in *Firefly* it becomes at best an annoyance, at worst a threat. Its minions turn up at awkward times, flexing their authority and running roughshod over the concerns of civilians. The Alliance does nothing to retrieve a shipment of vital medical goods hijacked in "The Train Job"; they arbitrarily board and search *Firefly* in "Bushwhacked" and confiscate the ship's cargo; a military goon squad bullies an innocuous Jewish postal clerk in "The Message"; and a running concern throughout the series is the program of psychological mutilation that Alliance authorities have carried out on River. Though he's undeniably a biased source, Malcolm handily sums up a prevailing attitude toward the Alliance when he says that it is typical of them to "unite all the planets under one rule so that everybody can be interfered with or ignored equally" ("The Train Job"). The Alliance is not the cavalry that will turn up in times of need, and its unpredictability only adds to the uncertainty that Malcolm and his crew face.

If the Alliance is an uncertain nuisance, the Reavers are a constant peril, lurking always on the fringes of consciousness and so terrible in their actions as to require constant readiness should they appear. For the sheltered Simon, they are the stuff of "campfire stories . . . men gone savage on the edge of space," but for the space-savvy crew members, they are very real, indeed. Should *Serenity* be captured, Zoe tells Simon, the Reavers will "rape us to death, eat our flesh, and sew our skins into their clothing. And if we're very, very lucky, they'll do it in that order" ("Serenity"). Even the normally tolerant Malcolm minces no words when talking of them: "Reavers ain't men. Or they forgot how to be. Come to just nothin'. They got out to the edge of the galaxy, to that place of nothin', and that's what they became" ("Bushwhacked"). Compared with the Indians of *Stagecoach,* the Reavers are infinitely more terrifying; whereas the Apache (by the standards of 1939) were naturally savage, carrying out depredations because such was their inherent nature, the Reavers, once upon a time men, have abdicated all that it means to be human and have reduced themselves to the lowest of beasts. Hazards abound in the world of *Firefly* even more extensively than in that of *Stagecoach,* and the crew must accept their reality if life is to continue.

While the structure and context of *Stagecoach* have their analogs in *Firefly,* it is in the similarity of themes that the two works come closest. Among these themes, three in particular stand out. First of all, *Stagecoach* offers a quiet questioning of conventional morality. The most outwardly "respectable" character, the banker, Gatewood, is an embezzler. The gambler, Hatfield, for all his aristocratic pretensions, has been rumored to shoot men in the back. The most compassionate and humane of the passengers is the whiskey salesman, Peacock, untouched by the ravages of his trade, while Doc Boone and Dallas even take pride in their outcast status. As Doc says to her, "These dear ladies of the Law and Order League are scouring out the dregs of the town. . . . Come on—be a proud, glorified dreg like me." Just who, the film asks, are the upright citizens, who are the dregs, and who decides the criteria to be applied?

A similar questioning of the conventional appears in *Firefly*. Inara is the most obvious agent; she *is* a prostitute, yet her trade is openly accepted while that of the rest of the crew is scorned, and she becomes the "nurturer" aboard the ship ("Here's How It Was"). One episode, "Shindig," affirms the point explicitly. At a formal ball, where she is the invited guest of a local aristocrat while Mal has crashed it in search of work, she confronts him: "You have no call trying to make me ashamed of my job. What I do is legal. And how's that smuggling coming?" Mal replies: "My work's illegal, but at least it's honest"; he points to the ornately dressed and posturing guests, disparaging "the lie of it" ("Shindig"). For Mal a life of openly acknowledged shadiness is preferable to a socially acceptable one that requires hypocrisy and pretense, and the viewer is left to ruminate upon the question.

A second shared theme is *Stagecoach*'s questioning of conventional "civilization." The film opens and closes in two established, "civilized" settlements, Tonto and Lordsburg, presumably bastions of all that is right and proper in the midst of an untamed wilderness. Yet, as the action proceeds we discover that the towns' "civilization" also incorporates prejudice, coercion, narrow-mindedness, and injustice. Doc Boone speaks for another kind of civilization, one determined by individualistic and humane values, as he opens and closes the film. At the outset, being run out of town with Dallas, he wryly remarks: "We're the victims of a foul disease called social prejudice, my child." And in the penultimate line of the film, as Ringo and Dallas ride out of the story and off to Ringo's isolated ranch, he turns to Curly and says, "Well, they're saved from the blessings of civilization." For Doc, and for much of *Stagecoach*, the ideal of "civilization" is a two-faced one, carrying persecution as well as benefits, and for a certain type of person, one that is profitably challenged, even ignored.

Firefly shares the film's skepticism toward civilization. The tension between civilization and freedom is, to be sure, a long-standing element in both the western and science fiction (Mogen 1993, 98–107). In *Firefly*, however, it comes to the foreground, explicitly examined in the contrast between the authoritarianism of the Alliance and the inner world of *Serenity*. The opening segment sets the scene: after *Serenity* unexpectedly encounters an Alliance cruiser, Jayne wonders: "What the hell are they doin' out this far, anyhow?" To this Kaylee replies, simply: "Shinin' the light of civilization" ("Serenity"). "Bushwhacked" extends the contrast. The iconoclastic Mal permits Shepherd Book to conduct a funeral service for victims of the Reavers, then, when an Alliance ship appears, remarks: "Looks like civilization has finally caught up with us." At segment's end, after the Alliance commander has confiscated their cargo but let the ship go, Mal comments: "Couldn't let us profit. Wouldn't be civilized" ("Bushwhacked").

Yet, as other segments make explicit, the world in which Mal and the crew operate *is* a kind of civilization, with rules, standards, and values peculiarly its own but no less valid than those of conventional society. "Jaynestown," the seventh installment of the series, brings the debate into the foreground. The entire episode is a rumination upon social order, exploring the issues of both social and individual needs by considering society's need for heroes and the question of "What defines a man?" For the straitlaced Simon, this boils down to an understanding of what, precisely, are the things a person holds crucial. Kaylee twits him for his (to her) excessive propriety, saying, "What's so damn important about bein' proper? It don't mean nothin' out here in the black." And Simon calmly disagrees, affirming his growing sense of self-determination: "It means more out here. It's all I have" ("Jaynestown"). Civilization is all that separates humanity from the animals, yet it is not something to be accepted unthinkingly. There are many forms of civilization, and each person, and each community, must decide which is the most appropriate.

The final shared theme arises in the notion of community, for both *Stagecoach* and *Firefly* pose, as an alternative to conventional civilization, what one critic has called the "Fordian community." As seen throughout Ford's films, this is "the family, almost always depicted as an isolated pocket of existential security, as a refuge from loneliness (but, like 'home,' it is an ideal rarely attained, and generally imperfect, fragmented, lacking one parent)." The leader of this community most often is a solitary man who "seldom reaps life's humble pleasures. He is often a combination of soldier, judge, and priest, symbolizing his intervention, authority, and self-sacrifice. . . . He is purer than the average man in service of such accepted values as tolerance, justice, medical duty, preservation of family, and love" (Gallagher 1986, 479–80). The pattern resonates throughout both stories.

The surviving passengers of *Stagecoach* form just such a group, albeit one not homogeneous or trouble-free. The birth of Lucy Mallory's child breaks down one set of socially determined barriers, bringing drunk and lawman, prostitute and prig together in a moment of cherished domesticity. The passengers come to see new strengths and merit in the drunken doctor and the wimpish whiskey salesman and share in their disdain for the thieving banker, who has violated his depositors' trust. If they go their separate ways at film's end, they go with a new understanding of human kinship, individual integrity, and social interdependence. Marshal Curly, the nominal leader, grows in his tolerance for Ringo's offenses and his appreciation of Ringo and Dallas's love, while Ringo himself, in many ways the spiritual leader, reflects the stoic calm and inherent honor of the Fordian hero. The community has reshaped and redefined itself, and all are stronger for their participation.

Stagecoach may have served to establish the Fordian community, but it is *Firefly* that brings it to its fullest expression. Within the isolated confines of the ship, the crew and the captain coalesce into a distinctive family group—one not without its strains, to be sure, but one that strengthens all its members in its functioning. Family groupings appear in the show from the outset. Zoe and Wash are married and talk of having a child; Simon and River are siblings; Kaylee, according to actress Jewel Staite, "makes sure that everybody remembers that we are one big family, and all we have is each other" ("Here's How It Was"). However, Mal has had this goal in mind (albeit inarticulately) all along, as he visualizes what his crew will be like: "They must feel the need to be free. Take jobs as they come. They never have to be under the heel of nobody ever again" ("Out of Gas"). He expands this later, telling the unscrupulous Saffron that he has chosen to surround himself with "People who trust each other, who do for each other and ain't always lookin' for the advantage" ("Our Mrs. Reynolds"). Introduced in "Our Mrs. Reynolds," the accomplished woman con artist Saffron reappears later in "Trash!" He threatens to toss Jayne from the airlock for betraying Simon and River, saying, "You turn on any of my crew, you turn on me!" ("Ariel"), and he answers Simon's question as to why he has risked the ship and crew to rescue the doctor and River from kidnappers by saying, "You're on my crew. Why are we still talking about this?" ("Safe").

This simple lesson, that families look out for one another, is not lost on Simon; his upbringing in his own privileged but dysfunctional family has contributed to his becoming a fugitive, and *Serenity* is the closest thing to a real home that he and River have enjoyed for several years. And he, in turn, is willing to see the others in family terms. Patching up the wounded Jayne, knowing that Jayne betrayed him and his sister to the Alliance, he says:

> "You're on this table, you're safe. 'Cause I'm your medic, and however little we may like or trust each other, we're on the same crew. Got the same troubles, same enemies, and more than enough of both.
>
> "Now, we could circle each other and growl, sleep with one eye open, but that thought wearies me. I don't care what you've done. I don't know what you're planning on doing, but I'm trusting you. I think you should do the same. 'Cause I don't see this working any other way." ("Trash")

Professional obligations come second to family obligations; Simon and Jayne are on the same crew—of the same "family"—and they will, *must* trust each other.

Binding them all together is, not surprisingly, Mal—the Fordian hero writ large. He can be ruthless (as when he shoots down the Alliance agent holding the wounded Kaylee at gunpoint), and he can be compassionate (as when he gives Shepherd Book the go-ahead for a funeral service despite an urgent need for *Serenity* to leave the vicinity). He can be shifty (as when he double-crosses Saffron, who has double-crossed him), and he can be upright (as when he returns the medications he has hijacked to the community where "others need this more"). Throughout the series, though, he is driven by a single urge: his need to do what he believes is right, proper, and appropriate. He responds to Book's call "to do the right thing" in checking out a derelict ship, and in turn tells Book he has taken Simon and River on board, despite their fugitive status and his dislike for Simon, "Because it's the right thing to do" ("Serenity," "Bushwhacked," "Trash," "The Train Job"). Long ago betrayed by his military superiors and condemned to life in a society that disdains his beliefs, he lives by his inherent, ingrained sense of personal honor. He values his freedom above all other traits, and he readily endorses and supports the like-minded folk about him. He is the heart of the crew, the central father figure who draws them into the unified, trusting, and even loving group that they become.

Throughout its fourteen episodes, *Firefly* plays out its stories in an extended homage to John Ford and *Stagecoach.* Like its forebear, it builds upon character as much as action, human responses as much as setting. We come away from the program's sadly truncated history with a renewed sense of human integrity and human endeavor, just as we do from *Stagecoach, High Noon, Shane,* and a host of other memorable films that confirm our belief in principle, compassion, and the imperative to do what is right and necessary whatever the larger society might say. It incorporates allusions to many attributes of the western as it develops its motifs,[3] but it always comes back to the foundation of *Stagecoach,* the model that gives it its shape and its direction.

Firefly is a testament to the continuing vitality of the western, and, even more, to the vitality and versatility of science fiction. The western grew from circumstances and events of the last third of the nineteenth century; science fiction grows from circumstances still to come, in a future both near and distant. The western, perhaps, is being left behind by history, but science fiction stands ready to take up its cause. Both genres attest to the resilience and strength of the human spirit; both give us occasion to reflect upon what we have done, and may yet do, with technology and human society; and both compel us to consider again and again the essential question of what it means to be human. We would do well to pay them heed.

Notes

1. In a visual homage to *Stagecoach,* Zoe's Winchester has its action lever enlarged and hammered into an oval, matching that of the Ringo Kid's rifle.

2. Patricia Nelson Limerick, in *Legacy of Conquest* (1987), remarks on the irony of the individualistic, independence-seeking westerners' depending upon governmental aid in the form of military protection and generous land grants to carry out their quest.

3. In "Trash," for example, a priceless historic artifact, the prototype of a handheld laser pistol, is called the "Lassiter," picking up on the name of the pistol-packing hero of Zane Grey's *Riders of the Purple Sage.*

Bibliography

Anobile, Richard J., ed. 1975 *John Ford's* Stagecoach *Starring John Wayne.* New York: Universe Books.

Firefly, Twentieth Century Fox, 2002. Citations are taken from the four-disc set, *Joss Whedon's* Firefly: *The Complete Series.* DVD, Twentieth Century Fox, 2003. Included is the interview "Here's How It Was: The Making of *Firefly*" and commentary by cast and creators. Episodes cited, in order of creation, are "Serenity" and "The Train Job," dir. Joss Whedon; "Bushwhacked," dir. Tim Minear; "Shindig," dir. Vern Gillum; "Safe," dir. Michael Grossman; "Our Mrs. Reynolds," dir. Vondie Curtis Hall; "Jaynestown," dir. Marita Grabiak; "Out of Gas," dir. David Solomon; "Ariel," dir. Allan Kroeker; "Trash," dir. Vern Gillum; and "The Message," dir. Tim Minear.

Gallagher, Tag. 1986. *John Ford: The Man and His Films.* Berkeley: University of California Press.

Limerick, Patricia Nelson. 1987. *Legacy of Conquest: The Unbroken Past of the American West.* New York: Norton.

Mogen, David. 1993. *Wilderness Visions: The Western Theme in Science Fiction Literature.* 2nd ed. San Bernardino, Cal.: Borgo.

Place, J. A. 1974. *The Western Films of John Ford.* Secaucus, N.J.: Citadel.

Stagecoach. 1939. Directed by John Ford. DVD, Warner Home Video, 1997.

PART 3: ON INDIVIDUAL WRITERS AND SITUATIONS

Outside Context Problems

Liberalism and the Other in the Work of Iain M. Banks

Patrick Thaddeus Jackson and James Heilman

For as long as there have been human societies, people have been wrestling with the "problem of the Other": what standards of conduct should we apply when dealing with persons who are not members of our community? What obligations, if any, do we have to those who are different from us? As a moral problem rather than a technical one, the "problem of the Other" is never quite *solved* by any particular community; rather, different communities work out different responses to the various strangers, outsiders, and aliens whom they encounter. How a society deals with the "problem of the Other" is therefore a revealing window into that society's cultural practices and may even serve as an important dimension on which a society may be evaluated.

Iain M. Banks's "Culture" novels and stories provide an instructive context within which to pursue this problem. Banks envisions the Culture as an almost ideal-typical liberal society, in which controversial issues are ultimately referred to a civilization-wide popular vote (*LtW* 237–38) and reason, not revelation or tradition, is the final standard to which people appeal in their deliberations (*NotC* 173). Throughout the novels and short stories the Culture and its (human and machine) citizens encounter a vast array of Others; these encounters, and the dilemmas that they engender, form a significant component of what Banks deals with in his writing. In a sense Banks provides a set of fictitious cases that permit systematic reflection on how liberal societies deal with the "problem of the Other." Indeed, Banks provides cases that can *extend* our reflections, since he is able to posit and explore situations that have no parallel in human history: situations in which the liberal Culture is confronted by Others of superior material and technical power, in which the very *existence* (and not merely the self-conception) of the liberal society may be at stake. Unlike in recorded human history, in Banks's fictional universe liberal societies have to deal with "outside context problems."

Outside Context Problems

We agree with Tzvetan Todorov (1984) that the central ethical quandary posed by the "problem of the Other" is the question of whether it is possible to have difference and equality simultaneously—whether it is possible to acknowledge the Other's distinctiveness from ourselves without assigning the Other a moral status different from our own. Todorov illustrates the difficulties of such a response through his "exemplary story" (1984, 4) of the encounter between Spanish conquistadores and indigenous Americans in the sixteenth century. He chronicles the oscillations of Spanish policy between two extremes: assimilation, wherein the distinctiveness of the Other is eliminated in order that the Other may be accorded the same rights and privileges as we have, and elimination, wherein the distinctiveness of the Other serves as grounds to exterminate them because, after all, they are not fully human and hence not fully deserving of the same rights and privileges as we have. In effect these extremes, along with the hypothetical possibility of "difference with equality," define the limits of the possible ways that the "problem of Otherness" might be contingently resolved by particular societies.

Todorov's analysis provides us with a good baseline to begin thinking through the ethical challenges presented by the "problem of the Other" today, with the United States involved in a "war on terror" characterized by a surfeit of both assimilation and elimination and displaying a decided lack of "difference with equality." Muslim societies are portrayed as either fundamentally similar to our own but hindered in some way, and therefore standing in need of our beneficent tutelage in order to become truly "civilized," or as implacably opposed to the "civilized" world and therefore needing to be completely destroyed in order that "civilization" might survive (Bowden 2002; Mamdani 2005, 18–19; O'Hagan 2007). But there is a fundamental difference between the situation that Todorov analyzes and the situation confronting us now: the society now wrestling with the "problem of the Other" is a *liberal* one, which was certainly not the case for the sixteenth-century Spanish conquistadores. And liberal societies—by which we mean societies shaped by the European Enlightenment tradition—have their own peculiar difficulties in dealing with the Other.

The issue is not simply that liberal societies consider themselves to be the bearers of values and truths of universal applicability, although this certainly doesn't make the recognition of the Other as "different but equal" any easier. The logic here is uncomplicated: if "we" are the bearers of some universal truth, and "they" do not possess it or readily assent to it, then it becomes much more difficult to fit the very *existence* of "them" into our conceptual schemes. But this was equally true of the conquistadores, who struggled mightily to fit the "Indians" they encountered into a theological account of the world that did not readily appear to have a place for them (Inayatullah and Blaney 2004, 50–57). Indeed, the fact that the conquistadores' values and truths were grounded in the authority of divine revelation as administered by an organized church may have made things slightly easier, as there was always a possibility—albeit one that was not often utilized—of a "polytheistic" solution: you have your god, we have ours (Todorov 1984, 189–93, 240–41).

The European Enlightenment called this basis in revelation into question, seeking to replace it with a reliance on reason alone. The liberal societies that the Enlightenment spawned no longer had a conceptual space for "other gods"; instead, there was simply reason with its universal dictates, and those who did not agree had to be either uneducated or seriously flawed. For a liberal society, there can be no fundamental differences. As usual, Immanuel Kant expresses the Enlightenment position most bluntly: "*Differences in religion:* an odd expression! Just as if one spoke of different *moralities.* No doubt there can be different kinds of historical *faiths,* though these do not pertain to religion, but only to the history of the means used to promote it, and these are the province of learned investigation. . . . But there is only a single *religion,* valid for all men in all times" (Kant 1983, 125).

As a result liberal societies have an even harder time figuring out what to do with Others, and what kind of ethical standards to apply to their dealings with Others. Because everyone is thought to be fundamentally the same, apparent differences can only have the status of surface-level variations—variations that can be suspended, or destroyed, en route to bringing out the true nature of the Other. In a sense liberal societies are configured so as to pursue simultaneous assimilation and elimination in their dealings with Others: to assimilate Others by eliminating those aspects that are apparently different and to have a relatively clear conscience when doing so because of their confidence that their actions are ultimately grounded in and justified by reason alone. As President George W. Bush put it on the fifth anniversary of the September 11, 2001, attacks: "In the first days after the 9/11 attacks, I promised to use every element of national power to fight the terrorists wherever we find them. . . . This struggle has been called a clash of civilizations. In truth, it is a struggle for civilization. We are fighting to maintain the way of life enjoyed by free nations. And we're fighting for the possibility that good and decent people across the Middle East can raise up societies based on freedom, and tolerance, and personal dignity" (Bush 2006).

The Culture exemplifies exactly this kind of Enlightenment liberal smugness in its dealing with many of the countless other civilizations with which it becomes involved. The Culture has an entire division (the Contact section) dedicated to what Banks calls "secular evangelism": "not simply finding, cataloguing, investigating and analyzing other, less advanced civilizations but—where the circumstances appeared to Contact to justify so doing—actually interfering (overtly or covertly) in the historical processes of those other cultures" (*CP* 451). Contact and its dirty tricks division, Special Circumstances, engage in these interventions both because they provide a "justificatory action which allowed the pampered, self-consciously fortunate people of the Culture to enjoy their lives with a clear conscience" (*CP* 452) and because Contact has "statistics" that prove "that it really was doing the right thing"—statistics that led to the Culture's "unflappable self-certainty" in imposing an order that would be enforced "leniently, patiently and gracefully" (*E* 364). Based on the judicious application of reason, the Culture *knows* what is best for space-faring, intelligent species: for example, terra-forming is bad, and machines are sentient and therefore deserving of full legal rights (*UoW* 241–42). And it has little or no compunction about guiding other species to acknowledge these truths through a variety of means, which strongly suggests that it is not at all interested in having an interspecies dialogue about these or other moral issues.

In its dealings with various alien Others, the Culture often ends up producing what Banks calls outside context problems for those Others. In Banks's words, an outside context problem "was the sort of thing most civilizations encountered just once, and which they tended to encounter rather in the same way a sentence encountered a full stop." He gives an extended example: "imagine you were a tribe on a largish, fertile island; you'd tamed the land, invented the wheel or writing or whatever, the neighbors were cooperative or enslaved but at any rate peaceful and you were busy raising temples to yourself with all the excess productive capacity you had, you were in a position of near-absolute power and control which your hallowed ancestors could hardly have dreamed of ... when suddenly this bristling lump of iron appears sailless and trailing steam in the bay and these guys carrying long funny-looking sticks come ashore and announce you've just been discovered, you're all subjects of the Emperor now, he's keen on presents called *tax* and these bright-eyed holy men would like a word with your priests" (*E* 79). But it is important to note that an outside context problem has little or nothing to do with the political or social character of the society doing the discovering. Instead, what is decisive is that the discovering society is unimaginably more powerful than the discovered society: powerful in terms of material capability, to be sure, but also in terms of technical prowess and broad systematic knowledge about the universe, and conscious of this fact. A nonliberal society, such as the Spain from which the conquistadores came, is perfectly capable of inflicting an Outside Context Problem on the indigenous peoples that its representatives discover; all that is required is that the discovering society present a profound interpretive challenge to the people it discovers, so that they have to struggle to make sense of what they are encountering and experiencing (Todorov 1984, 70–72). The Culture, and Contact in particular, are fully aware of how disruptive such a challenge can be and often take steps to avoid provoking an outside context problem by concealing the true extent of the Culture's power and capabilities (*PoG* 78–79).

We emphasize this point because power differentials and the liberal character of the discovering society have often been conflated in human historical experience. Whether because of a historical accident or because of something inherent in the character of liberal societies (an issue on which we take no position), virtually all of the instances of outside context problems involving liberal societies with which we are historically familiar with involve the liberal society occupying the position of the discoverer rather than the position of the discovered, the more powerful rather than the less powerful. In actually existing human history, liberal societies inflict outside context problems on Others; they do not suffer from them. As a result the vast majority of what we know empirically and historically about liberalism and the Other represents cases drawn from just one of three possible scenarios in which liberal societies might encounter nonliberal others: powerful liberals confronting less powerful nonliberals. Human history provides us with a dearth of cases of liberal societies confronting equally powerful nonliberal others, and no cases of liberal societies confronting nonliberals of incontrovertibly superior power.

This is where Banks's work can be perhaps the most useful. While many of Banks's novels and stories involve the Culture intervening in less powerful societies and civilizations—a situation with clear and obvious parallels in earthly history—this does not exhaust the intercivilizational situations that Banks explores. Unlike in our actual history, the liberal Culture encounters a number of Others of equal or superior power throughout its experiences in the galaxy. As such Banks's work functions as a systematic examination of the "problem of the Other" in liberal societies that goes beyond factual experience in a way that is perhaps unique to the science fiction genre, which is able to develop and play out thought experiments in ways not permitted in other fields of inquiry. In Ursula K. Le Guin's memorable phrasing, science fiction is descriptive, not predictive: "All they're [science fiction authors] trying to do is tell you what they're like, and what you're like—what's going on—what the weather is now, today, this moment, the rain, the sunlight, look! Open your eyes: listen, listen" (Le Guin 1976: ii). Hence, by fleshing out situations that depart from and go beyond our historical experiences, Banks opens up the possibility of a fuller reflection on liberalism and the "problem of the Other," and may make possible a clearer set of insights into our present predicament.

The Liberal Culture

Before proceeding to discuss the specific Culture/non-Culture encounter stories from Banks's oeuvre, we will first briefly demonstrate that the Culture is, in fact, an almost ideal-typical example of a society constituted by Enlightenment liberal views and values. The Culture perfectly exemplifies the three central tenets of an Enlightenment liberal society: individual liberty, equality, and reason as the source upon which actions are grounded and in terms of which actions are ultimately justified. As such, the Culture is an appropriate vehicle to use in reflecting on how liberal societies encounter and deal with the Other.

Individual Liberty

One of the most important principles differentiating liberal societies from nonliberal societies is the importance and worth placed on the individual person and her or his decisions—and on her or his right to make those decisions as independently and autonomously as possible. In principle the individual's right to choose her or his own course of action should be largely unhindered in a liberal society, and any hindrances that emerge empirically will be largely seen as illegitimate. Indeed, the fact that the rights of the individual are sacrosanct in liberal societies can be seen in the sheer amount of political and ideological work that goes into justifying infringements on those rights, such as the sort of work connected to the "discourses of danger" that pose a trade-off between individual liberty and the survival of the political community as a whole (Campbell 1992). Absent such existential threats, the liberty of the individual is upheld as the highest good; this is the distinct standpoint of liberalism as a political philosophy and stands in contrast to the notions of "virtue" (McIntyre 1984) or "obligation" (Southern 1961) that preceded it.

Liberal thought has focused on individual liberty since its inception: both on expanding the sphere of individual liberty and on trying to reconcile individual liberty with the demands of social life and the political authority that often appears necessary to coordinate and sustain that social life. Hobbes nicely captured the challenge involved in his definition of the term: "By LIBERTY, is understood . . . the absence of externall Impediments; which Impediments, may oft take away part of a mans power to do what he would; but cannot hinder him from using the power left him, according as his judgment, and reason shall dictate to him" (Hobbes 1601, 72).

The point here is that reason can "dictate" without thereby becoming an infringement on individual liberty. Indeed, Hobbes's entire argument about political society rests on the idea that it is reasonable for people to surrender their natural right to everything in order to secure the civil peace that comes from establishing a government with sovereign power. Inasmuch as this is a reasonable act, and not an arbitrary infringement, individual liberty is preserved: the institution of the sovereign is ultimately an act stemming from liberty and not in contrast to it. Kant famously takes this insight even further, arguing that only the adherence to reason ensures individual freedom and liberty, because only the use of reason ensures that the individual is actually determining her or his own ends rather than being guided by empirical circumstances or something just as accidental (Kant 1993, 50). But the point remains the same: for liberal thought, the individual's autonomy and freedom of choice are paramount.

The Culture is essentially a perfection of the principle of individual liberty. No one in the Culture is forced to do anything that they do not want to do; there are no laws, and hence no need for law enforcement. Instead, people regulate one another's actions through manners and social sanctions—and, in the worst case (murder), a person might be followed around for the rest of their life by a "slap-drone," a mobile artificial intelligence that simply makes sure that the person never murders again (*NotC* 182). Most of the behaviors that laws are erected in our societies to deal with—crimes of property, difficulties stemming from material inequalities, notions such as blasphemy and immorality—are handled very differently in the Culture: individuals are basically allowed to do whatever they want to do, and if others disapprove they are free to either go elsewhere or simply to ignore the offending individual.

"Going elsewhere" and "ignoring" are both made possible, in turn, by the Culture's vast material abundance, both in terms of its extent and in terms of its wealth. Individuals can always "go elsewhere" because the Culture consists of hundreds of artificially constructed worlds called orbitals, each of which can hold billions of inhabitants—and more of which can always be built, relatively easily, if the Culture starts to run out of inhabitable space. In addition the Culture's multi-kilometer-long starships hold millions of inhabitants each, ensuring that there is always someone going somewhere else if one wants to move. In such an environment, "ignoring" other people is in a sense easier than trying to regulate their behavior, and virtually everyone simply focuses on pursuing their own agendas.

Those agendas, in turn, are completely free of anything like economic necessity. The Culture's productive capacity is distributed evenly throughout the entire civilization. Every "General Systems Vehicle," the largest class of Culture starship, "could make anything the Culture was capable of making, contained all the knowledge the Culture had ever accumulated, carried or could construct specialized equipment of every imaginable type for every conceivable eventuality" (*CP* 220). One of Banks's characters lives in a fabulous estate on an orbital, but comments that "if somebody wanted a house like this they'd already have had one built" because the Culture has "no money, no possessions" (*PoG* 21). Indeed, everything that we would consider a menial task performed out of the necessity to make a living or the necessity to have *someone* do it is automated in the Culture, and automated in such a way that the superintelligent Culture AIs—the Minds—are equally free from necessity (*NotC* 172). The only reason that anyone performs a menial task is out of choice, as is seen in the comments of a waiter at a restaurant: "I could try composing wonderful musical works, or day-long entertainment epics, but what would that do? Give people pleasure? My wiping this table gives me pleasure. And people come to a clean table, which gives *them* pleasure.... Of course, if *all* I did was wipe tables, then of course it would seem a mean and despicable waste of my huge intellectual potential. But because I choose to do it, it gives me pleasure" (*UoW* 251–52, emphasis in original).

Under such circumstances it is hardly surprising that most of the Culture's inhabitants choose to spend their lives in more hedonistic pursuits: playing games of strategy, designing fantastic environments for living and recreation, even "lava-rafting" through the streams of molten rock produced when a new orbital is being constructed (*LtW* 125–26). Human Culture citizens can even change gender at will, and most do at some point in their lives (*E* 357). And if physical reality becomes too constraining, there are endless virtual reality simulations in which people and Minds alike can participate. The range of liberty is, for all practical purposes, unlimited, and virtually everything in the Culture exists in part to support and extend the principle of individual choice. In this way the Culture is a perfect liberal utopia.

Equality

The principle of equality is perhaps just as central to the liberal tradition as is the principle of individual liberty. Opposed to the idea of hierarchy, the liberal principle of individual equality mandates that there be no *special* rights and privileges—that all individuals have, in some sense, the same moral worth (Tocqueville 1835, 56–57). Hobbes builds such a notion of individual equality into his account of the state of nature; Locke takes it one step further, arguing that in the state of nature each individual is able to execute the whole of the "law of nature" revealed to individuals through rational reflection: "if any one in the State of Nature may punish another, for any evil he has done, every one may do so. For in that *State of perfect Equality,* where naturally there is no superiority or jurisdiction of one, over another, what any may do in Prosecution of that Law, every one must needs have a Right to do" (Locke 1689, 271–72, emphasis in original).

This moral equality of each individual in the state of nature is not diminished when individuals come together to establish government; to the contrary, for Locke, their ability to do so depends on each of them having the executive power of the law of nature so that they can collectively alienate it to the newly instituted government. Rousseau, in turn, argues that only the principle of individual equality suffices to make a social order legitimate, because people are by nature equal; any deviation from this natural state is either a colossal mistake or a temporary expedient, and in either case can be overturned if the people simply realize how arbitrary it is (Rousseau 1987, 58–59, 146–47).

In this regard too the Culture is an exemplary liberal society. Because of the distribution of productive capabilities, everyone has the same claim on basically every object produced: one cannot hoard if everyone already has more than enough. Almost all contentious issues are submitted to a democratic vote, rather than being decided by someone invested with the authority to decide them by fiat; this even extends to absurd schemes such as covering three million square kilometers of wilderness with a system of pylons and cables for cable-car excursions (*LtW* 235–37). There are no hereditary rulers of any sort; indeed, heredity is almost entirely irrelevant, with the slight exception of people who can meaningfully claim "some familial link with the Culture's early days" (*E* 229)— although even this is only good for a small measure of notoriety and does not carry with it any kind of meaningful privileges. The only things that differentiate people, whether humans or Minds, are their abilities and accomplishments, with the former being due to genetic accidents and the latter being at least in principle equally within reach of everyone.

The one part of the Culture where something like inequality manifests itself involves the Contact section, which controls and coordinates relations between the Culture and non-Culture societies. Contact is the one thing in the Culture that is not simply available to everyone who wants to be a part of it; one has to apply, then be selected, in order to join Contact and thereby be able to engage in the exploration of other civilizations. And not everyone is selected—even some of the drones (smaller AIs in mobile bodies, unlike the larger Minds, which are generally housed in starships or orbitals) specially constructed for Contact are not permitted to join if their personalities are too far outside of the mandated norm for a Contact drone (*PoG* 14). Indeed, this is part of Contact's allure: as one character muses, "When there were almost no distinctions to be drawn between people's social standing, the tiny differences that did exist became all the more important, to those who cared" (*E* 230). To be a member of Contact provides such a difference.

It is no accident that Contact is also the part of the Culture most character-ized by hierarchy and secrecy, even though this is quite mild by comparison to the kinds of social practices characteristic of governing authorities in nonliberal societies. Contact, in a sense, guards the borders of the Culture and controls the flow in both directions across that border; the liberal principle of equality seems to halt at the border in many circumstances (Walker 1993), and the Culture is no exception. Although the Culture is characterized by virtually complete free-dom of information, Contact occasionally sees fit to conceal information from the rest of the Culture, particularly information about the discovery of some-thing that they are still trying to understand (*PoG* 78–79). Representatives of Contact, and of its dirty tricks division Special Circumstances, can on occasion command resources unavailable to ordinary Culture citizens and can do things that ordinary mortals cannot; their very names inspire a measure of respect from knowledgeable humans and Minds alike (*PoG* 34). And even within Con-tact, as we learn in one of the later Culture novels, there is a group of Minds—the Interesting Times Gang—that occasionally steps in and assumes command of particularly tricky situations (*E* 138–39).

Contact and Special Circumstances implicitly justify their deviations from the liberal principle of equality in two ways: the dangers presented by things outside of the border, and the need for a reasoned analysis rather than an imme-diate emotional reaction. In the case of the Empire of Azad, a less-powerful civilization that the Culture encounters, Special Circumstances chooses not to make public what it has discovered about the things that the Empire has done to some of its own citizens, for fear that the Culture public will call for a force-ful invasion (*PoG* 80). In the case of the Excession, an artifact of unknown ori-gin that appears to be from outside of the universe, the Interesting Times Gang delays the release of information to the rest of the galaxy in part so that Culture ships can get close enough to the object to prevent any other civilization from seizing control of it (*E* 484).

But it is important to note that in such cases, the relevant information is eventually released, and the deviations from equality are themselves justified in terms of preserving the conditions for equality itself. Far from being a violation of the Culture's liberal state, this is a strong confirmation of the Culture's status as a liberal utopia. Were the Culture not a liberal society, such deviations would not have to be explained or excused, and it is only the presumptive universalism of notions such as equality that requires an explanation or an excuse when they are violated. In this way Contact and Special Circumstances operate in a perpetual "state of exception" (Agamben 2005), a kind of moral black hole "where the normal laws—the rules of right and wrong that people imagine apply everywhere else in the universe—break down; beyond those metaphysical event-horizons, there exist . . . special circumstances. . . . That's us. That's our territory; our domain" (*UoW* 261). That the Culture's deviations from equality have to be ultimately justified in terms of their role in preserving equality is perhaps the best testimony to the Culture's fundamentally liberal character.

Reason

The final piece of the liberal triumvirate of values is the commitment to reason. Much of the Enlightenment liberal project was about replacing modes of authority grounded in religion and tradition with modes grounded in the exercise of reason. Hobbes's complaints about the arbitrary authority exercised by the Catholic Church (Hobbes 1601, 66–67, 246–48) partake of this spirit, as do Locke's admonitions that the only true purpose of government is to preserve individual liberty and property—to proceed according to reason, not according to superstition (Locke 1689, 353). But the most extreme formulations of the proposition that reason alone should be the basis for political authority—and for everything else—come from Kant and Hegel. Kant argued that only reason could produce "a will good in itself" and thus absolutely ground and justify courses of action (Kant 1993, 9); Hegel went somewhat further, declaring, "The only thought which philosophy brings with it, in regard to history, is the simple thought of Reason—the thought that Reason rules the world, and that world history has therefore been rational in its course. . . . That this Idea is the True, the Eternal, simply the Power—that it reveals itself in the world, and that nothing else is revealed in the world but that Idea itself, its glory and majesty—this, as we said, is what has been shown in philosophy" (Hegel 1988, 12–13).

Reason plays two functions in liberal societies: it differentiates among courses of action, and it provides the ultimate grounding for those actions. In liberal societies we should expect to see appeals to reason both when debating means and when debating ends—and these appeals make sense in a liberal society because such societies are permeated by reason, constitutionally committed to the proposition that only a firm foundation in reason can ensure that a course of action is anything other than arbitrary. Both of these functions are clearly on display throughout the Culture, which once again manages to be an idealized liberal society in its adherence to reason.

Perhaps the greatest example of the Culture's commitment to reason is the prominence that it accords to its machines and especially to its Minds. Not only are sentient artificial intelligences full citizens of the Culture, but in practice they run both the day-to-day operations of the society and have the lion's share of the responsibility for longer-term planning. Banks tells us that "the Culture . . . had placed its bets on the machine rather than the human brain," and done so quite deliberately "because the Culture saw itself as being a self-consciously rational society; and machines, even sentient ones, were more capable of achieving this desired state as well as more efficient at using it once they had" (*CP* 87).

In turning virtually everything of consequence over to the Minds, the Culture has in effect allowed itself to be governed by reason more purely than any society dependent on human authorities could possibly be. This extends from the most mundane issues, like determining whether a particular piece of food is edible (*LtW* 19), to the most grand and sweeping issues, like whether to begin to develop a primitive planet's civilization or whether to leave it alone (*SotA* 110–111). There is never a question as to whether the Minds in charge of the Culture are acting in accord with reason, and disputes between Minds—even disputes about whether it is permissible to violate the integrity of a person's mind in order to disclose the truth of past crimes (*E* 57–58)—tend to involve issues about which reasonable arguments can be made on both sides. The Culture's operating presumption, then, is that if Minds decree it, then it must be reasonable, and inasmuch as the Culture is a reasonable society, it should listen to its Minds.

Another clear way that the Culture displays its preference for reason, and for the increased control over the environment that it brings, is in the choice of living arrangements for its human inhabitants. Culture citizens live on orbitals (and in starships) rather than on planets because doing so allows them and their machines to exercise more rational control of their lives:

> "So you want to live on a planet?"
> "No. I think I'd find them a bit small and weird."
> "Aren't they dangerous? Don't they get hit by stuff?"
> "No, planets have defense systems."
> "So those need running."
> "Yes, but you're missing the point—"
> "I mean, you wouldn't want a *person* in charge of stuff like that,
> would you? That'd be scary. That would be like the old days, like barbarism or something." (*LtW* 281)

In a built environment like an orbital or a starship, a competent Mind can look after everything and still have immense capacity to spare. Culture humans carry a "terminal," a small communications unit "in the shape of a ring, button, bracelet or pen or whatever," at virtually all times; this terminal connects them to the Mind in charge of the built environment and ensures that they are "never more than a question or a shout away from almost anything [they] wanted to know, or almost any help [they] could possibly need"—including, in extreme cases, lifesaving interventions (*PoG* 84). For Culture humans, it simply makes sense to live in such a way that they are more or less insulated from chance catastrophes, and in this way the Culture's commitment to reason helps to reinforce its commitment to individual liberty by giving its citizens the maximum freedom to do whatever they please without having to worry about environmental restrictions.

The Culture's commitment to reason also reinforces its commitment to equality, largely by taking advantage of the enlightenment notion that bowing before reason is no reduction of moral status: to be reasonable, to submit to the rational argument, even if it is made by someone else, is not to subordinate yourself to that other person, but is instead for everyone involved to submit themselves to reason. The Culture's Minds have located a few humans whose cognitive processes are almost unfailingly accurate when it comes to sizing up a situation; these "Referers" are utilized like any other piece of machinery to improve the results of the Culture's projections about likely outcomes, but they have no special authority to command—they simply serve as a voice of reason in times of crisis (*CP* 87–88). Even when the Culture chooses not to intervene in the affairs of a more primitive society, and hence to establish a hierarchy of development, it does so in order to improve the rationality of its interventions overall: to use the primitive society "as a control group" so as to gain better knowledge about the effects of intervention versus nonintervention. When challenged, in explicitly moral terms—"How certain do we have to be? How long must we wait? How long must we make *them* wait? Who elected us God?"—a decision not to intervene (in this case, a decision not to intervene in the affairs of Earth) is defended in eminently rational terms: "that question is being asked all the time, and put in as many different ways as we have the wit to devise . . . and that moral equation is being re-assessed every nano-second of every day of every year, and every time we find some place like Earth—no matter what way the decision goes—we come closer to knowing the truth. But we can never be absolutely certain. Absolute certainty is not even a choice on the menu, most times" (*SotA* 170).

In the absence of absolute certainty, well-verified statistics have to suffice, and such statistics demand control groups. Reason provides both the means to proceed and the ultimate grounding that the course of action is correct—and that in the end, the greater goods of equality and liberty are preserved and defended as efficiently as possible.

There are numerous other manifestations of the Culture's commitment to reason, such as its pitying attitude toward religious beliefs (*CP* 157), but the previous examples should suffice to demonstrate sufficiently the point: the Culture is in many ways the perfected liberal dream of a society founded on reason alone.

The Culture and Its Others

Having established that the Culture is very much an idealized liberal society, we now turn to an examination of how the Culture acts when confronted by a variety of nonliberal Others. We have divided these confrontations into three categories based on the relative power of the Culture versus the Other, largely because doing so permits us to separate analytically this power situation from the liberal character of the Culture. Different levels of threat, different kinds of capacities, different challenges posed to the Culture generate, we suggest, different kinds of dilemmas in dealing with the Other, and in particular generate different ways that reason functions as a guide to right action. The self-confidence associated with liberal dealings with the Other, a self-confidence founded on reason, tends to diminish to the extent that the Culture is confronted by an Other that it cannot reliably dominate—an Other that poses a threat not merely to the Culture's self-image and self-understanding, but to the Culture's very existence as a society. This suggests that liberal self-assurance may be, at least in part, a function of superior capabilities and of the perception of such superior capabilities by the liberal society in question. As such, additional possibilities for liberal dealings with Others might be opened by decoupling the sense of superiority from other aspects of the liberal project.

The Culture and Less Powerful Others

More often than not, when the Culture stumbles upon a new civilization, it is vastly more powerful than the other—a situation not unknown in our experience, as it closely mirrors the encounters between liberal and nonliberal societies in recorded human history (Brown 2001). As in our history, such a configuration of capabilities gives the Culture the luxury of choosing whether or not it will intervene in the Other's affairs. Furthermore, the means of intervention are left to the discretion of the Culture. It could enforce its own rules through military might, for instance, or it could place individuals in positions of influence. The Culture is not unaware of such choices. In the novel *Inversions,* the character DeWar is a Culture citizen who works as a bodyguard for a king. He is protecting a man whose policies are more liberal than those that are traditionally practiced in the region. While telling a story to the king's young son, DeWar elaborates on the difficulty of choosing to intervene in another's society. In the story the kingdom of Lavishia is an analog of the Culture. DeWar is telling the child about the people of Lavishia. He says "One of the most important things they disagreed about was what to do when Lavishia chanced upon one of these tribes of poor people. Was it better to leave them alone or was it better to try and make life better for them? Even if you decided it was the right thing to do to make life better for them, which way did you do this?" (*I* 89)

When the distribution of capabilities is on the Culture's side, it seems that the Culture usually sides with those who would argue in favor of intervention. When it does so, it is not casually deciding to change the lives of others, though.

Instead it views its choice as a moral imperative. It thinks it is compelled by its moral standpoint to Culturize other civilizations.

This motivation for intervention is expressed by the character Sma in the story "State of the Art." Sma is a member of Special Circumstances. At the time of the story she is stationed on a ship that is observing Earth. When the Mind on the ship asks her if she thinks the Culture should intervene, she responds "Yes I do. And as soon as possible too. . . . It's for their own good" (*SotA* 83). Sma is professing her belief that the citizens of Earth would be better off after they have been Culturized.

As we have noted, the justification for imposing the Culture's values onto the Other comes from the Culture's belief in its capacity to act rationally. It sees itself as ordering its society according to rational moral laws. Provided that the faculty of reason is universal, any other civilization that possesses the faculty of reason would agree to live according to the Culture's laws. Therefore, when the Culture encounters a rational Other, it believes that the Other would agree to be Culturized if the Other were capable of correctly utilizing its power of reason. This kind of implicit agreement is seen most dramatically in the Culture's attitude toward "ambassadors." At the end of *Look to Windward,* the character Kabe, an alien who is an ambassador to the Culture, remarks that "that when the Culture calls somebody an 'Ambassador,' what they mean is that that person represents the Culture to their original civilization, the assumption being that the alien concerned will naturally consider the Culture better than their home and so worthy of promotion within it" (*LtW* 482).

From the Culture's viewpoint, the Other might already be trying to become like the Culture, but unfortunately characteristics such as greed or ambition are preventing its progress. Hence, the Culture will intervene to mitigate the effects of such characteristics. Being much more powerful than the Other, the Culture is usually able to cause events that subtly liberalize the Other's society: it can place people in positions that influence the future of the society. Due to this power imbalance, the Culture does not have to worry about a scenario in which the Other discovers the Culture's intentions and then decides to attack the Culture. If such an attack ever occurred, the Culture would easily defeat the Other militarily.

The only worry that the Culture does have is that it does not have an objective viewpoint from which it can judge its actions. There is no entity that dispenses moral truths that can be known just as one would know about natural phenomena. At best, the Culture can believe that it acts rightly because it acts on principles that it thinks all should agree on. The Culture recognizes this as can be seen in Sma's following evaluation: "We think we're right; we even think we can prove it, but we can never be sure; there are always arguments against us. There *is* no certainty" (*SotA* 284).

Given this uncertainty, why does the Culture continue to intervene in the affairs of others? Sma has already given us the answer. The Culture believes it is right, and so it believes that it can better the lives of others; it is motivated by its belief to intervene, which in turn rests on the Culture's sense of itself as a society subservient only to reason. However, those who are the recipients of the Culture's actions might not always agree with the Culture's ways. Despite this, the Culture still believes that over the long term it is acting for the betterment of the recipients. Hence, whenever it encounters people who resist the changes it brings, it must find some way subverting or eliminating those people.

This poses the central dilemma that the Culture faces when intervening in the affairs of less powerful societies: how should those people be subverted or eliminated? Should the Culture use its military might to force change, or should it work more subtly for improvement? The actions of the Culture do not reveal a universal answer to this question. In most cases the Culture chooses the former option, but sometimes it chooses the latter—and no general principles are provided that might adjudicate such a choice. Within the series there are many examples of the Culture encountering other civilizations; let us look at two examples that typify the two methods of intervention described above.

The first case takes place in the Empire of Azad, which resides at least ten thousand light years away from the Culture. The hierarchy of Azadian society is determined by a game called Azad. Just the name of the game should be enough to see how central it is to the structure of the society. However, the game creates not a liberal society but a sharply hierarchical and cruel one (*PoG* 73–77), and so the Culture wants to interfere. It chooses a man named Gurgeh to take part in the game. He actually wins the game, just as the Culture wanted him to, and as a result of this, the empire is thrown into chaos. The Culture hopes that from this chaos it can direct the Azadians to construct a liberal society.

This is an example of the Culture subverting a society. It could have easily imposed its will onto the empire, but instead it chose to defeat the empire at its own game and so throw the it into chaos. A Culture drone—who is a member of Special Circumstances—explains this to Gurgeh: "The Empire's been ripe to fall for decades; it needed a big push, but it could always go. Coming in 'all guns blazing' as you put it is almost never the right approach. Azad—the game itself—had to be discredited. It was what held the Empire together all these years" (*PoG* 296). In this quote we actually see the drone denying the military option and advocating the option of changing the Other's institutions by placing someone in the appropriate position in the Other's society. The end goal is the same—elimination of those undesirable aspects of the Other so that the remaining pieces can be "Culturized" and assimilated—but the technique is distinctive.

The Culture's general aversion to using military force is given more justification earlier in the novel. When a different Contact drone tells Gurgeh about the planned intervention, it explains why the Culture does not want to use violence to impose its will upon Azad: "it would hardly be war as such because we're way ahead of them technologically, but we'd have to become an occupying force to control them. . . . The people of the empire would lose by uniting against us instead of the corrupt regime which controls them, so putting the clock back a century or two, and the Culture would lose by emulating those we despise; invaders, occupiers, hegemonists" (*PoG* 79). Yet, is the option of discrediting the game of Azad that much morally different than the option of defeating the empire's armies and occupying its territory? We will come back to this question after we examine the other example.

The second case involves the Culture's relationship with a species more concerned with conquering others than pushing them toward becoming a liberal society. The Affront can best be described as a cavalier people with a penchant for torture and genetic manipulation. The Affront is everything the Culture abhors. "The Culture's problem with the Affront was like an itch they couldn't scratch; the Culture's problem with the Affront was that the Affront existed at all and the Culture couldn't in all conscience do anything about it" (*E* 181). The Culture cannot simply exterminate the Affront, because then it would be even worse than the unreasonable "invaders, occupiers, hegemonists" that it hates so much. Of course, the Culture sees the Affront as invaders, occupiers, and hegemonists, but this alone does not justify the use of the military option—and because of the organization of their society, a military option would be required to "Culturize" the Affront.

Indeed, the Culture has tried to change the Affront through subtle means. But the Affront have proven to be stubborn and still try to conquer others when they can. Therefore some Culture Minds believe that the only way to change the Affront is to attack it. Those Minds form a conspiracy and successfully bring about a war between the Affront and the Culture. The war does not last long, but the Culture's display of military might is enough to convince the Affront that it should be more respectful of the Culture's demands in the future. As one ship says, after the hostilities are over and the conspiracy has been revealed, "At any rate we are arguably better off than before; a conspiracy has been uncovered . . . and even the Affront are behaving a *little* better having realized how close they came to being taught such a severe and salutary lesson" (*E* 491–92). So ultimately, even though the Culture resorted to military might, it was able to bring about what it would consider to be a positive change in Affronter practices.

Within the Culture, the choice to trick the Affront into a war draws the ire of other Minds. This is evidenced by the words of the Mind that uncovers the conspiracy. It says, "I for one am not going to stand for this. We may have failed to frustrate the conspiracy, but it will still be possible to work toward the discovery of the guilty parties involved in its planning and implementation" (*E* 321). What is not recognized by the Minds in the story is that the debate of how to change the Affront, through military means or other means, is a luxury the Culture can enjoy because it is vastly more powerful than the Affront. It never questions whether or not it treats the Affront fairly by assuming that it has to change the Affront; it is never *forced* to confront this question, because the Affront only pose (so to speak) a threat to the Culture's sensibilities rather than to its continued physical existence.

In fact the only time we see the Culture question itself about intervention (about whether or not to intervene, not about what means to use when intervening) is when it is observing Earth. The Mind that is stationed above Earth chooses not to intervene so that it can compare the development of Earth with the development of other societies in which the Culture does intervene. When Sma insists that the Culture make contact with the humans of Earth, the Mind who controls the ship she is on responds, "How can we be sure we're doing the right thing? How do we know what is—or would be—for their own good, unless, over a very long period, we observe matched areas of interest—in this case planets—and compare the effects of contacting and not contacting?" (*SotA* 83) The Culture is using Earth as a control in an experiment that seeks to quantify precisely the moral value of intervention.

Is there something troubling about the way in which the Culture treats these less powerful Others? It seems as if in each case, the Culture is trying to "Culturize" the Other. In the case of Azad it sees a society that has the potential to become more like the Culture but is impeded by the oppression of the game of Azad. In the case of the Affront it sees a civilization that is so different from itself that it feels it must force the other to change. And in the case of Earth it chooses to leave the planet alone so that it can know with more certainty that its attempts to liberalize other societies are the morally right attempts. The Culture's means of treating the Other is best summarized in a comparison between it and another civilization called the Elench, themselves a splinter group that left the Culture some time ago. "The Elench wanted to alter themselves, not others; they sought out the undiscovered not to change it but to be changed by it" (*E* 95). The Culture does the opposite. It seeks out the undiscovered to change it because it believes that its way of life is best.

Now we can go back to our earlier question: is the decision to discredit the game of Azad that much different than the decision to defeat the Empire's armies and occupy its territory? Obviously there is a difference in how the Culture changes Azadian society. However, both means of change involve the Culture changing a society that did not agree to be changed; the Culture is imposing its will upon the Other. This is not to say that the Culture should be reclusive or isolationist, but that there is a difference between engaging the Other in a dialogue and deliberately altering the Other. In a situation of superior capability, however, the Culture never seems to choose dialogue.

The Culture and Others of Equal Power

In all of the above examples, the Culture has the luxury of being able to tamper with other societies without fearing retribution because it is so much more powerful than those it encounters. However, there is one example of what happens when the Culture is not clearly more powerful than the Other: the Idiran War.

The Culture sees the Idirans as "a religiously inspired society determined to extend its influence over every technologically inferior civilization in its path, regardless of either the initial toll of conquest or the subsequent attrition of occupation" (*CP* 452). Much like the Affront, the Idirans represent what the Culture despises. The Idirans use their military might to force others to become part of their religious empire; they thereby disallow freedom, show no tolerance, and deny others the possibility of constructing laws based on the outcomes of rational discussions. The Culture is thus forced to fight, since the Idirans posed a moral threat: "the loss of its [the Culture's] purpose and clarity of conscience; the destruction of its spirit; the surrender of its soul" (*CP* 452).

In the previous section we saw that when the Culture encountered such a civilization it usually tried to change that civilization. However, changing the Idirans is not so easy because the Idirans can successfully resist the Culture's intervention. The two civilizations have almost equally powerful military technology, and so if the Idirans think that the Culture is interfering with their affairs, they can attack the Culture and severely damage it.

Due to this roughly equal distribution of capabilities, the confrontation with the Idirans is much different than the previous situations. The Culture can either ignore the actions of the Idirans, or it can interfere with the Other's continuing expansion and thereby risk going to war. For the Culture the choice is obvious. "The only desire the Culture could not satisfy from within itself was . . . the urge not to feel useless. The Culture's sole justification for the relatively unworried, hedonistic life its population enjoyed was its finding, cataloguing, investigating and analyzing other, less advanced civilizations but—where the circumstances appeared to Contact to justify so doing—actually interfering (overtly or covertly) in the historical processes of the other cultures" (*CP* 451).

Given that the Culture justifies its lifestyle on its works of rational goodwill, it cannot let the Idirans be. To do so would render the lives of the thirty trillion Culture citizens worthless. By allowing the Idirans to conquer and subjugate others, the Culture would be denying its reason for existing. As Banks writes, "Contact could either disengage and admit defeat—so giving the lie not simply to its own reason for existence but to the only justificatory action which allowed the pampered, self-consciously fortunate people of the Culture to enjoy their lives with a clear conscience—or it could fight" (*CP* 452).

The Idiran expansion forces the Culture to question its own identity. It can remain the liberal empire that seeks to bring its virtues to others, or it can transform itself into another type of civilization. Hence the Culture's decision to engage the Idirans in warfare is its way of affirming its identity. If it had chosen differently, then calling itself the Culture would not have the same meaning as it did before contact with the Idirans was made.

Here we discover another aspect of what the Culture's encounters with the Other tell us about the Culture itself. Earlier we saw that the Culture is concerned with molding other societies into the same shape as itself and justify this through reason. Now we see the threat posed to the Culture by an empire that is equal in power to the Culture and lives according to a completely different value system. In this case reason retreats as a mode of justification, replaced by a justification in more purely value-laden terms. Perhaps as a result, while the Culture as a whole chooses to fight, a section of the Culture does not, breaking off to form a "peace faction" that eschews the use of military force (*CP* 332). Contrary to the predictions of some realist international relations scholars, the enormity of the threat posed by the Idirans produces a crisis of conscience, not a firmer consensus on the moral rectitude of the selected course of action. The power of reason to settle disputes by submitting all options equally to critique does not, in this case, suffice to produce the same kind of near-certainty that characterizes the Culture's dealings with Others of inferior capability. As the challenge posed by the Other increases in severity, the grounding of actions in reason diminishes and becomes less certain.

The Culture and Others of Superior Power

The third type of encounter takes place between the Culture and entities that are more powerful than it. This happens at several different times throughout the series of novels. One common encounter is with the Sublimed. On Subliming, a form of spiritual ascension, Banks writes: "to Sublime was to retire from the normal life of the galaxy. . . . Subliming seemed to be the opposite of useful as the word was normally understood. Rather than let you play the great galactic game of influence, expansion and achievement better than you could before, it appeared to take you out of it altogether. Subliming was not utterly understood—the only way to understand it appeared to be to go ahead and do it" (*LtW* 199). Another encounter is with an entity from another universe called the Excession. The real power of this entity is never known, but the fact that it can travel between universes is enough to fascinate and frighten the Culture. Finally the third encounter is with life-forms called "behemothaurs." Not much is known about behemothaurs except that they are the oldest known life-form in the galaxy, they are very large, and civilizations that tamper with them seem to disappear. We will briefly examine how the Culture interacts with each entity.

At the beginning of *Consider Phlebas,* the reader gets the impression that the Culture is afraid to offend the Sublimed. When a Mind flees to a planet controlled by a Sublimed entity known as the Dra'Azon, the Culture is unwilling to send a military fleet to the planet to rescue the Mind. The Culture wants to rescue the Mind, though, because it has secret information that the Idirans potentially can use to defeat the Culture. Hence, the Culture desperately wants to rescue the Mind, but it will not threaten the Dra'Azon because it feels that doing so would "put the whole outcome of the war in jeopardy by antagonizing a power whose haziest unknown quantity is the exact extent of its immensity" (*CS* 92).

At this point, we should stop and contrast the Culture's sense that it must attack the Idirans with its unwillingness even to offend the Dra'Azon. The answer is quite simple: the Dra'Azon present no challenge to the Culture's identity. The Dra'Azon do not seem to do anything except preserve a couple of planets that they consider to be important memorials to civilization-wide extinction. Furthermore, the Dra'Azon are not even a conventional part of the material universe (although they can intervene in it as they see fit), and they never go out of their way to affect the actions of those who do live in the material universe. The only reason the Culture fears them is because they might possess certain powers that come with Subliming. Aside from this consideration the Culture has no interaction with the Dra'Azon.

In fact, as the Culture matures it comes to hold a certain contempt for the Sublimed in general. Most civilizations that are as old or older than the Culture have either Sublimed or stopped flying across the galaxy looking for societies to change. "The Culture was something of an exception, neither decently Subliming out of the way nor claiming its place with the other urbane sophisticates . . . but instead behaving like an idealistic adolescent" (*LtW* 198–99). Like any liberal society the Culture does so because it thinks it has a responsibility to bring liberty, equality, and reason to the rest of the galaxy. To Sublime would be the ultimate shirking of this responsibility, since doing so removes one from the galaxy's affairs.

Of course there are no instances of the Culture telling the Sublimed of such criticisms. There simply is no reason to anger the Sublimed. However, it is interesting to wonder what would happen if the Sublimed did show an interest in altering the affairs of the galaxy. What if this interest involved coercing others to Sublime? Would the Culture intervene? It seems that they would have to. The Sublimed would be forcing others to act against their will, much like the Idirans. Unlike the war with the Idirans, though, the Culture's chances of defeating the Sublimed seem to be low. Hence, the Sublimed present the possibility that the Culture might have to reconstruct its identity so that it could accommodate the values of a more powerful actor. By doing so, though, it would likely have to transform its identity to an immense degree.

This potential identity reconstruction resulting from a power imbalance that does not favor the Culture would call into question all of the Culture's prior actions toward other societies. By changing its identity it no longer would see its interventions as morally right (or, at any rate, as the closest to incontrovertibly morally correct as rational statistical study could bring one). Those interventions were made on the assumption that the Culture's way of life and value system were the morally right way of life and the morally superior value system. But admitting the existence of a superior Other would call this certainty into question—and once these characteristics were changed, the moral righteousness of the interventions would evaporate. Hence, the possibility presented by the Sublimed enables us to wonder to what extent the values of the Culture are influenced by its relative power.

The next entity that is more powerful than the Culture is the Excession. The Excession has to be treated differently than the Sublimed. No one wants to offend the Sublimed because no one knows how much power they have, but usually no one has to be concerned with the Sublimed because the Sublimed have quit the material universe. The Excession's power is also unknown but it is very much a part of the material universe; the Excession poses the first genuine outside context problem that the Culture has ever encountered (*E* 13). The Excession could be the first ship of a much larger fleet that for some unknown reason has come to the Culture's galaxy to conquer it. Given the technological superiority of the Excession's civilization, neither the Culture nor anyone else in the galaxy would stand any chance of defeating the Excession's civilization. So how should the Culture handle the Excession?

Two strategies present themselves. The first is to use the Excession as a means to an end: the conspiracy of Minds uses the Excession as part of its plan to lure the Affront into a war. However, this seems like an unwise choice of action when one considers the threat posed by the Excession. The Minds in the conspiracy were able to use it confidently, though, because they had sent another ship with the greatest armament of weapons within the Culture to the space occupied by the Excession. This ship would serve the dual purpose of forcing the Affront to surrender once the Affront also arrived at the same space and being the best defense against the Excession—even though when the Excession is confronted with a hostile fleet, its actions (which resemble a person swatting at a fly) demonstrate rather conclusively that even the most impressive show of force that the Culture could assemble stands no chance whatsoever against the strange entity.

Eventually the Excession simply leaves the universe. A Mind that was opposed to the conspiracy offers this reason for the Excession's departure: "the entity found itself surrounded by all the trappings of war and may even have understood the manner in which its appearance had been used as part of a plot to entrap the Affront. . . . Those noxious simpletons who made up the conspiracy should be cursed for evermore; they may have cost us more than even we can imagine" (*E* 491). This Mind is thinking of the positive benefits of learning from the Excession. The conspiracy judged that it was wiser to defend the Culture against the Excession rather than try to engage it in a dialogue. Once again, we see how relative power can influence the Culture's willingness to act on its liberal principles. Presented with the possibility of being conquered, the Culture ignored its principles of tolerance and rational discussion in an attempt to intimidate a seemingly more powerful actor.[1]

The final encounter is with the Behemothaurs. This case is the most unique. No one understands exactly what the Behemothaurs do. All that is known about them is that they are large, ancient creatures that travel around the galaxy. The Culture seems to have no interest learning *from* the Behemothaurs, despite the fact that the Behemothaurs are much older and more powerful than the Culture and so might have something to teach the Culture. Instead, the Culture sends a single scholar to learn *about* the Behemothaurs. Essentially the Behemothaurs are treated as objects to be studied.

By reducing the Behemothaurs to objects, the Culture is constructing a relationship that does not position the Behemothaurs as better or more advanced but merely as a curiosity. Therefore the Culture does not need to bother to engage the Behemothaurs as equals. If it did so, then it would run the risk of changing itself if it came to agree with some of the viewpoints of the Behemothaurs. Once the Culture changes itself, then that moral certainty that it currently holds is thrown into limbo, which is precisely what the Culture does not want to have happen.

In this final case the Culture is using science as a means of controlling the balance of power in a relationship. Since it fears facing an identity crisis, it relegates the Behemothaurs to the realm of science, where they can be seen as separate from politics. Studying objects poses no threat to the Culture's sense of itself and does not require the Culture to use reason to provide any kind of ultimate grounding for its actions; instead, reason can function merely as a tool for investigating the universe. The Culture is still trying to construct a relationship that allows them to maintain their identity, but it does so by simply taking the behemothaurs out of the moral universe altogether.

This problem of the Culture's identity comes up in each case. We did not see it as much in the cases where the Culture was more powerful than the Other, because when the Culture is the more powerful actor it has the luxury of acting as it always has since no one is threatening to change it. However, once such a threat arises, as was seen in the cases when the Culture encountered a civilization of equal or greater power, the Culture must struggle to reaffirm its identity or face the prospect of constructing a new identity and so dealing with the potential moral implications we have already discussed.

Conclusion

By posing the "problem of the Other" for a liberal society in ways that we do not have direct historical experience with, Iain M. Banks's Culture novels and short stories permit us to explore the as-yet-hypothetical question of what a liberal society (like ours) would do if confronted by a nonliberal Other that it was not clearly superior to. We are intimately familiar with the excesses of liberal societies when faced with Others of inferior capabilities; the combination of elimination and assimilation, backed by and grounded in an appeal to reason, justifies all manner of attempts to change the Other in ways that we find more acceptable. The Culture, since it is a utopian version of ourselves, unsurprisingly replicates this situation. But because of the Culture's universe, it is also confronted with Others that it cannot dispense with so smugly; it is instead forced to encounter them in other ways. The Culture's sense of superiority rooted in reason diminishes in such circumstances, to be replaced in some cases by something altogether more tentative and halting, and in other cases by a more existential self-assertion.

There is a potential lesson here for us. When confronted with Others to which we feel physically superior, liberal societies such as ours have easy recourse to reason as a way of ultimately justifying their actions; when confronted with Others where this physical superiority is in question, we might be more chastened, less brash, more open to encounter. Of course, we need not be; we might respond as the Culture responded to the Idirans, with a war of annihilation and an absolute refusal to compromise with or even to listen to the Other. But the sense of vulnerability produced by an Other equal or superior to ourselves opens the possibility of another way of dealing with the problem. Such an option is worth exploring practically, if only so that more alternatives are made available as we deal with Others—both now and in the future.

In this sense, maybe the best piece of advice for liberal societies like ours is to seek out outside context problems, to cultivate those encounters with Others that call our sense of righteousness grounded in reason into question. Perhaps we could all do with a reminder from time to time that there is no metaphysical agency guaranteeing that our sense of reality actually corresponds with reality— perhaps that would make us a bit less brash and a bit more humble in our dealings with the world. Such a goal seems to have animated the Minds that might or might not have covertly facilitated a planned terrorist suicide bombing of a Culture orbital: "Some of our Minds might just think that we need a bit of timely blood and fire to remind us the universe is a perfectly uncaring place and that we have no more right to enjoy our agreeable ascendancy than any other empire long fallen and forgotten" (*LtW* 461–62). Whether such extreme and violent measures are called for in order to keep a liberal empire humble is an open question—a question that presses upon us both in Banks's Culture universe and in our own.

Note

1. Intriguingly the one exception to this rule—the one ship Mind that actually attempts to establish a line of communication with the Excession—is the *Grey Area*, the pariah ship that violates the integrity of individual human minds in its effort to disclose monstrous acts of genocide and other injustices. *Grey Area* is among the most exceptional of the members of the Culture, the most used to operating outside of the normal bounds of civilized behavior—and perhaps, as a result, the most willing and able to entertain the possibility that the Culture might be able to *learn from* superior Others rather than dominate or instrumentally use them.

Bibliography

Banks, Iain M. 1987. *Consider Phlebas* (*CP*). London: Orbit.
———. 1988. *The Player of Games* (*PoG*). London: Orbit.
———. 1990. *Use of Weapons* (*UoW*). London: Orbit.
———. 1991. *The State of the Art* (*SotA*). London: Orbit.

————. 1998a. *Excession* (*E*). New York: Bantam.

————. 1998b. *Inversions* (*I*). New York: Pocket Books.

————. 2000. *Look to Windward* (*LtW*). New York: Pocket Books.

————. 2004. "A Few Notes on the Culture" (*NotC*). In *The State of the Art*. San Francisco: Nightshade.

Agamben, Giorgio. 2005. *State of Exception*. Chicago: University of Chicago Press.

Bowden, Brett. 2002. "Reinventing Imperialism in the Wake of September 11." *Alternatives: Turkish Journal of International Relations* 1, no. 2: 28–48.

Brown, Chris. 2001. "'Special Circumstances': Intervention by a Liberal Utopia." *Millennium* 30, no. 3: 625–33.

Bush, George W. 2006. "President's Address to the Nation." *White House Press Release Archive*. http://www.whitehouse.gov/news/releases/2006/09/20060911-3.html (accessed September 12, 2006).

Campbell, David. 1992. *Writing Security*. Minneapolis: University of Minnesota Press.

Hegel, G. W. F. 1988. *Introduction to the Philosophy of History, with Selections from the Philosophy of Right*. Indianapolis: Hackett.

Hobbes, Thomas. 1601. *Leviathan*. New York: Norton, 1997.

Inayatullah, Naeem, and David Blaney. 2004. *International Relations and the Problem of Difference*. London: Routledge.

Kant, Immanuel. 1983. "To Perpetual Peace: A Philosophical Sketch." In *Perpetual Peace and Other Essays*, 107–43. Indianapolis: Hackett.

————. 1993. *Grounding for the Metaphysics of Morals*. Indianapolis: Hackett.

Le Guin, Ursula K. 1976. Introduction to *The Left Hand of Darkness*. New York: Ace.

Locke, John. 1689. *Two Treatises of Government*, ed. Peter Laslett. Cambridge: Cambridge University Press, 1988.

MacIntyre, Alasdair. 1984. *After Virtue*. Notre Dame, Ind.: University of Notre Dame Press.

Mamdani, Mohmood. 2005. *Good Muslim, Bad Muslim: America, the Cold War, and the Roots of Terror*. New York: Three Leaves.

O'Hagan, Jacinta. 2007. "Discourse of Civilizational Identity." In *Civilizational Identity: The Production and Reproduction of "Civilizations" in International Relations*, ed. Martin Hall and Patrick Thaddeus Jackson, 15–31. New York: Palgrave Macmillan.

Rousseau, Jean-Jacques. 1987. *The Basic Political Writings*. Indianapolis: Hackett.

Southern, R. W. 1961. *The Making of the Middle Ages*. New Haven, Conn.: Yale University Press.

Tocqueville, Alexis de. 1835. *Democracy in America*. New York: Harper and Row, 1969.

Todorov, Tzvetan. 1984. *The Conquest of America*. New York: Harper and Row.

Walker, R. B. J. 1993. *Inside/Outside: International Relations as Political Theory*. Cambridge: Cambridge University Press.

To the Perdido Street Station

The Representation of Revolution
in China Miéville's *Iron Council*

Carl Freedman

> The category of reflection, central to the Marxist problematic as we have shown, is concerned not with realism but with materialism, which is profoundly different. (Étienne Balibar and Pierre Macherey, "On Literature as an Ideological Form," 1974)

> Marxist reality means: reality plus the future within it. (Ernst Bloch, "Marxism and Poetry," 1935)

When China Miéville published *Iron Council* in 2004, the novel was widely and justly appreciated as the conclusion of a trilogy that the author had begun with *Perdido Street Station* (2000) and continued with *The Scar* (2002), both highly acclaimed books that quickly established Miéville as one of the most important writers of speculative fiction on either side of the Atlantic. To be sure, the three volumes form a trilogy in only a loose sense. There is no overarching narrative that spans the three installments, and there are no truly continuing dramatis personae, though a character or event prominently featured in one volume may be mentioned en passant in another. What really unites the novels is their common setting in the invented world of Bas-Lag, a kind of alternate Earth, though one whose relationship in time or space to our own is never directly broached. In logical rigor and consistency, in almost endlessly inventive detail, and in general three-dimensional solidity, Bas-Lag is one of the most awesomely achieved imaginary worlds ever created; it is, for instance, vastly richer, more plausible, and more rewarding than Tolkien's Middle-earth. Furthermore, each volume significantly expands our sense of it. *Perdido Street Station* is set almost (though not quite) exclusively in the city-state of New Crobuzon—a diverse, authoritarian port city that, while stunningly original, owes something to Victorian London, something to modern Cairo, something to the Vieux Carré of New Orleans, and doubtless something to many other sources as well—whereas *The Scar* departs from the city at the outset and shows us the seaways and the seafaring life of Bas-Lag and also the latter's complex geopolitics, in which New Crobuzon is only one powerful player. *Iron Council* returns to New Crobuzon but also introduces a vast continental landmass traversed by the great railway project alluded to in the title. Miéville clearly knows a good deal more about Bas-Lag than he has needed to reveal in these three thick volumes; and one expects that at some point—though not, perhaps, immediately—he will return to it.

What has generally gone unnoticed, however, is that, in writing *Iron Council,* Miéville has not only completed the Bas-Lag trilogy but has also achieved a quite different literary consummation: namely, the completion of a fictional diptych about revolution begun with his first published novel, *King Rat* (1998). A work of smaller compass and one less intellectually ambitious than the Bas-Lag trilogy—though not a work of lesser brilliance within its own limits—*King Rat* is a novel of very different texture and mode. It is set not in an invented world but in the London of the 1990s, though a London invaded by fantastic forces and one that operates, in some ways, "at right angles" (to borrow one of the central metaphors of the text itself) to the empirical London we know. My crucial point here is not only that some continuing thematic and political concerns subsist despite the generic discontinuity, but also that, as we shall see, the generic discontinuity itself amounts to a political intervention of the highest importance. For the two novels are not simply about two different revolutions, but about two radically different *kinds* of revolution—and the political difference is so fundamental that it might well be described as a generic one.

It is thus necessary to recall, briefly, the substance of *King Rat,* though this is ground that I have elsewhere covered in much greater detail.[1] The text is structured on a certain antinomy: put simply, the novel is the story of a revolution, but not the sort of revolution whose story it most ardently *wants* to tell. For *King Rat* is a radically left-wing book, investing heavily in a Marxist analysis of late-capitalist society and in a socialist ethics as well. A revolutionary-socialist stance is operative (if not always fully explicit) in every chapter and is clear even without reference to the public politics of the author (who happens to be a respected Marxist scholar of international law, an editor of the learned Marxist journal *Historical Materialism,* a militant of the British Socialist Workers Party, and a one-time candidate for Parliament on the Socialist Alliance ticket). Yet there is nothing at all socialist about the revolution with which the novel climaxes and concludes. The rats constitute a sort of proletariat, but there is no movement among them to overthrow the conditions of oppression and exploitation in which they live. Instead, the protagonist, Saul Garamond (himself half-rat and half-human), single-handedly topples the monarchy of the title character, thus making a revolution from above and ushering in a new era that seems to promise (at best) bourgeois rather than socialist democracy. This is indeed progress, but not to the degree or of the kind implied by the Marxist intent of the text as a whole. The text is, however, entirely clear-sighted about what it finally settles for. "I declare this Year One of the Rat Republic" (Miéville 1998, 317), announces Saul, who exalts the values of "Liberty, Equality . . . and let's put the 'rat' back into 'Fraternity'"(317; ellipsis in original). At the end, he designates himself as "Citizen Rat" (318). These are—quite obviously—the slogans of 1789, not 1917; we are in the world of the Rights of Man, not that of All Power to the Workers. Lenin (a particular hero for Saul's father) has been replaced by Robespierre. The socialist novel ends with a bourgeois revolution.

We need to be clear that, when comparing socialist revolution with bourgeois revolution, we are by no means dealing with differing versions of the same essential thing. It would, indeed, be closer to the truth to say that the word *revolution* in the two phrases is at least as much a pun as a full-fledged political category. A bourgeois revolution is, in the nature of the case, a severely limited operation, however widespread the physical upheaval may become. For such a revolution is based on the struggle between rival power elites, typically pitting the increasing power of capital against a feudal or at any rate decisively precapitalist old regime of entrenched privilege.[2] The bourgeoisie or their (sometimes highly mediated) political representatives do indeed tend to espouse universalistic rather than admittedly class goals, and may accordingly "invite" the masses to fight on their side. But any serious effort to advance the economic interests of the masses at the expense of those of the rising new elite tends to be strictly, and not gently, curtailed—as the followers of Gracchus Babeuf learned in France during the 1790s, and as those of Gerrard Winstanley learned in England during the 1640s and 1650s.

By contrast the economic interests of the masses are precisely what a socialist revolution is all about. Its ultimate aim is not to substitute rule by a rising, more progressive class for rule by an exhausted and reactionary one, but instead to abolish class rule altogether. It strives to establish the structures not only of political democracy but also of economic democracy, so that equality before the law will be completed and guaranteed by equality of ownership of the total social wealth.[3] Whereas a bourgeois revolution is at bottom concerned with a choice of masters, and with the forms by which mastery is exercised, a socialist revolution is not complete until mastery itself has been rendered into a fading historical memory. Socialist revolution is thus an incomparably, indeed *generically,* more radical transformation than bourgeois revolution; and this radicalness is surely the major reason that, despite some interesting and important (and sometimes terrifying) attempts, no fully successful socialist revolution has yet been consummated on our planet. But Miéville is not one to be limited by the philistine myopia that would forbid attempting (even in imagination) that which has never before been achieved; and the project of *Iron Council* is precisely to begin anew the attempt to imagine what socialist revolution might be like. As Edmund Wilson famously traced the socialist idea from its Enlightenment origins to Lenin's 1917 arrival at the Finland station, from which he assumed leadership of the October Revolution, Miéville now extends the story into an alternative future, pressing on to the Perdido Street Station, the geographical center of oppressive rule in despotic, capitalist New Crobuzon.[4]

Indeed, this is the main project for which New Crobuzon and Bas-Lag exist in the first place. Now that we can survey the Bas-Lag trilogy as a whole, it seems clear that the creation of what is arguably the most boldly and meticulously realized alternative world in fiction serves the ultimate purpose of providing a locus where ideas of socialist revolution can be experimentally concretized. For *King Rat* is finally limited, politically, by its London setting. The contradiction between the Marxist ideals that the text tries to uphold, on the one hand, and, on the other, the Robespierrist slogans with which it climaxes and must finally content itself should be seen as in some measure a reflection of an actual social contradiction: namely, the contradiction in 1990s Britain between the will to maintain the socialist idea and the increasing marginalization of socialism (even in the tepid, reformist version of the old Labour Party before its current Blairite leadership renounced socialism altogether) within the actual sociopolitical arena. Yet no other current real-world setting provides a much more promising locale for socialist imagining: not, certainly, oligarchic post-Soviet Russia, nor roaringly state-capitalist China, nor the aggressively neoliberal United States. In such a reactionary world environment, it is not surprising that the revolutionary-socialist imagination should migrate to the alternative worlds of speculative fiction. It should also be noted, though, that the worldwide movement for global justice (often defamed by its enemies as an "antiglobalization" movement) that was catalyzed by the Seattle anti-WTO demonstrations of 1999 (the year following the publication of *King Rat*) has in recent years provided a renewal of strong, though nonlocalizable, anticapitalist energy; and that this political energy may to some degree lie behind the socialist project of the Bas-Lag trilogy and of *Iron Council* in particular.

While generically an instance of what Miéville calls "weird fiction"—his highly original version of speculative fiction that blends science fiction, Surrealism, fantasy, magical realism, and Lovecraftian horror, and in his latest effort with the whole tradition of the western, from Zane Grey to Cormac McCarthy, thrown into the mix—*Iron Council* alludes to many historical movements of socialist and radical opposition: for example, the labor struggles that attended the coming of the railroad to the American West; the Paris Commune; Narodnik terrorism in prerevolutionary Russia; the October Revolution; and modern struggles of black liberation and women's liberation, especially as the latter movement has focused on the dignity and organization of sex workers. But the result is not just a collection of fragmentary historical allegories but a coherent and autonomous, though multivalent and fictional, social formation, and, moreover, one constructed according to unswervingly materialist premises despite—or rather partly because of—the frequent departures of the text from literary realism (to adapt the crucial distinction invoked in the epigraph above by Balibar and Macherey). Indeed, the freedom and flexibility offered by nonrealistic modes of fiction have enabled Miéville to produce one of the most searching materialist meditations on socialist revolution—ontologically, ethically, and even aesthetically—yet achieved in Anglophone fiction. To substantiate this assertion adequately would require a small volume. Here I will offer several points in illustration that will, I hope, stimulate further discussion of this extraordinary text.

On the level of Marxist ontology (and epistemology), perhaps the most important point is that the complexity of Bas-Lag allows Miéville to suggest with particular force and clarity the material overdetermination (in the Freudian sense as recomplicated by Louis Althusser)[5] that is crucial to a socialist revolution. Probably more than any other sort of historical event, socialist revolution is based on the conjuncture of a multiplicity of material determinations, all of them relatively autonomous and none reducible to any of the others. In *Iron Council* the revolution that appears in the making depends, first of all, on two almost (if not quite) completely independent movements: on the one hand, the formation of a revolutionary Collective (reminiscent of the Paris Commune) that is able to precipitate a dual-power situation in New Crobuzon and then temporarily to take effective executive power in large sections of the city; and, on the other, the earlier takeover of the great rail project by its own workers, who reconstitute themselves as the Iron Council and maintain the train as a perpetually moving egalitarian city that succeeds in evading punitive action by the New Crobuzon Militia, the city-state's principal repressive apparatus. The chief narrative line in the present time of the novel concerns the efforts by representatives of the Collective to locate the (by now legendary) Iron Council, which they regard as a precedent and inspiration and to whom they look for advice and assistance.

Furthermore, both the Council and the Collective are themselves vividly drawn formations with great internal dialectical complexity. The Collective is partly the work of the Caucus, a broad coalition of socialist and quasi-Marxist parties and underground newspapers (the best-known of which, the *Runagate Rampant,* is, along with its heroic editor, Benjamin Flex, prominently featured in *Perdido Street Station*). The illegal Caucus competes with the more sensational and quasi-Narodnik terrorism of the followers of the mysterious Toro, who succeed in assassinating the mayor of New Crobuzon. Whether this political killing (though fully justified in purely moral terms) makes a genuine revolutionary contribution is, however, more than dubious; the text seems to endorse the viewpoint of Ori (a former Caucus militant who leaves to join the anarchistic terrorism of the Toroans) when, after the Collective comes into being, he finds "in himself a drab certainty that the killing of the Mayor had done nothing at all" toward the goal of revolution (455). On the other hand, there is no doubt whatever that the building of the Collective is due in large part not only to the Caucus but also to a great many previously unaffiliated citizens, whose rage has been building over decades marked not only by grinding poverty but also by the (literally) fantastically cruel repression with which the Mayor's government has attempted to crush all stirrings of dissidence. It seems unlikely, however, that this rage would have boiled over without the additional toll taken by the exhausting war that New Crobuzon has been fighting with the faraway Tesh, and the increasing disaffection of the city's soldiers; there is doubtless an allusion here to the exhaustion of the Russian czarist state by World War I and the important role played by Russian soldiers in the October Revolution.

As to the determinations of the Iron Council, some of them are less familiar within the classical Marxist problematic of the nineteenth and early twentieth centuries. The revolutionary seizure of the train is in part a straightforward labor struggle, and an essential contribution to the formation of the Council is (finally) made by the free male workers employed by the Transcontinental Railroad Trust (the name instantly recalls the America of the Wild West). But this group of workers does not, in fact, take the lead in the uprising that leads to the Iron Council and even displays, at first, some conservative tendencies in comparison to two other, distinct elements in the ultimate revolutionary coalition. One is the contingent of female sex workers who refuse to extend credit to their male customers and strike on the simple slogan, *No pay no lay.* At first the men respond with a myopic hostility fueled by the sexual frustration that has, of course, provided a market for the striking women's services in the first place. Not without difficulty, the women do, however, succeed in convincing the men (whose own wages are being withheld by the TRT) that class solidarity between them is more important than the gender differences; and the women's slogan assumes a more general significance, as the strike widens to include male workers and *lay,* in addition to its sexual meaning, comes to signify the laying of railroad track. But there is also a third distinct group in the uprising, one that, unlike the ordinary male workers, supports and joins the women workers' strike without delay or hesitation: namely, the slave-labor force of Remade, both male and female. The Remade—one of the most memorably imaginative creations in the whole trilogy, figuring largely in *Perdido Street Station* and *The Scar* as well as in *Iron Council*—are New Crobuzoners who, having fallen afoul of the mayor's government for one reason or another, are sentenced to "punishment factories" where their bodies are permanently reshaped in deliberately grotesque and humiliating ways. Maimed by all manner of amputations and mutilations and by the addition to their bodies of animal and mechanical parts, the Remade are typically looked upon with intense disgust by those who have not suffered the same fate. In the trilogy they serve in part to figure the situation of any group regarded as inferior and degraded in specifically racial ways; and, as ever, sexual taboos play a large role in enforcing such bigotry. A crucial point in the formation of the Iron Council is reached when Ann-Hari, the leader of the female strikers, grips a leading Remade militant and (to the spontaneous horror of many non-Remade men) kisses him squarely on the mouth. There is not necessarily any "natural" affinity among the sex workers, the Remade, and the free male laborers; but the novel vividly illustrates how such revolutionary coalitions are formed.

I have sketched out the overdeterminationism of *Iron Council*—and some of the particular overdeterminations of revolutionary activity by the Council and the Collective—in necessarily brief, schematic terms. But Miéville's mastery of psychological and thematic coherence and of abundant detail means that there is nothing schematic about the novel itself, whose account seems as "thick"—as rich and solid—as that of any existential history. Yet this fictional history does not, in fact, culminate in the triumph of socialism. The Collective meets much the same fate as its chief real-world model, the Paris Commune (though numerous other historical precedents could be cited, such as the Munich Soviet Republic of 1919 or revolutionary Barcelona in 1936). The dual-power situation endures long enough that a limited but authentically utopian zone of popular democracy is constituted, and the characteristic military heroism of proletarian revolution flourishes. Ultimately, though, support for the Collective is neither widespread nor well-organized enough to resist the massive physical power of the apparatuses of state repression—most importantly the New Crobuzon Militia, which gradually but decisively regains control of the city in atrociously bloody fighting. The golem-maker Judah Low, who is probably the most far-seeing theorist of revolution within the text, warns that the present time of the novel is the "wrong time" (548) for revolution. The text's attitude toward the heartbreakingly brief triumph of the Collective seems strictly parallel to the attitude Marx displays in his writings on the Paris Commune itself: namely, an unbounded admiration for the courage and sacrifice of the revolutionaries (Marx, in *The Civil War in France* [1871], describes the Commune as "the glorious harbinger of a new society" and the murdered Communards as "enshrined in the great heart of the working class" [233]) combined with a grim calculation that the objective balance of forces does not yet allow the overthrow of the repressive state followed by a popular seizure of the means of economic production. The Collective is smashed, but the Militia has had to wreck New Crobuzon itself to do it, and the ruling-class boast "Order reigns in New Crobuzon!" (561) thus rings rather hollow. The *Runagate Rampant* continues to publish, and revolutionary hope is not completely extinguished.

The fate of the Iron Council is rather different and more complicated than that of the Collective and is foregrounded more prominently in the text. Indeed, the Council is really the collective protagonist of the whole novel; and it is deeply significant that in this final installment of the Bas-Lag trilogy, where collective socialist action is explicitly engaged, it is a group of characters who dominate the book in somewhat the same way that *Perdido Street Station* and *The Scar* are dominated by individual protagonists, namely the physicist Isaac Dan der Grimnebulin and the linguist Bellis Coldwine, respectively. But Judah (who, uniquely among the novel's characters, is directly and personally involved with both the Council and the Collective) is, if not the sole protagonist, still the single most important figure in *Iron Council;* and he plays the most decisive role in the final turn (within the novel) of the Council's story. In addition to being a revolutionary of saintly selflessness—and one who, like most saints (and perhaps most revolutionaries), has a touch of megalomania in his personality—Judah is notable for having advanced the technology of golem-making (or "golemetry") further than any practitioner of the art before him; and he has frequently used his talent in directly political ways, notably in assisting at the birth and the early defense of the Iron Council. Toward the end of the novel, as the Council is at last returning to New Crobuzon to join the efforts of the Collective, Judah attempts—but fails—to dissuade his comrades from their course. The Collective, he believes, has already been sufficiently defeated that any attempt to join its revolutionary project is bound to fail; so that the Council, which for a full generation has managed to sustain itself as a moving space of classless democracy, would be entering New Crobuzon merely in order to commit collective suicide. Unable to convince his fellow councilors of this conclusion, Judah takes matters into his own hands. In a supreme and unprecedented golemetric feat, he constructs a golem out of time itself and uses it to suspend the perpetual train in a kind of temporal limbo. At a stroke the Iron Council's progress toward New Crobuzon is halted, and it is also rendered invulnerable to any retaliatory action by the Militia. Most of the councilors are put into what seems to be some sort of suspended animation, thus to remain until an entirely uncertain future: "[p]erhaps till things are ready [i.e., for revolution]" (543), as Judah himself puts it.

The text's attitude toward Judah's coup is intensely complex and helps to engage perhaps the novel's most searching consideration of revolutionary ethics. Judah faces a dilemma in some ways parallel to that confronted by Isaac in the final pages of *Perdido Street Station*. Early in that novel Isaac had promised to use his scientific and technological abilities to restore the lost wings of the garuda Yagharek; and toward the end of the story Isaac is particularly determined to fulfill his promise, since Yag has by this time become a loyal friend and a battle-tested comrade in the fight against the monstrous slake-moths. Before he can honor his commitment, however, he learns that Yagharek's wings had in fact been amputated in a garuda judicial proceeding because of Yag's guilt in an especially vile crime. Isaac is thus faced with the awful choice between betraying his promise to a faithful friend and condoning that friend's earlier criminality, helping him to evade its consequences. Isaac chooses not to replace the wings, thus dooming Yagharek, a member of a species for whom flying is as integral to normal life as walking is to humans, to a flightless existence. But neither he nor the text can be certain if this is the right decision or, indeed, whether any "right" decision is even conceivable.

It is similar with Judah. The text gives us no reason to suspect that his estimation of the hopelessness of the Council's projected return to New Crobuzon is at all faulty. Since the golem-maker Judah uniquely possesses the power to save the Iron Council and all that it has achieved, does he not have, as he insists, the moral and political duty to do so? Yet Ann-Hari—perhaps Judah's only true peer among the revolutionary leaders as well as, at various times, his lover—is also persuasive when she maintains that Judah could not possibly *know* with absolute certainty that the revolutionary cause was hopeless in the near term; and that, yet more crucially, he had no moral right to take the decision away from a democratic collective process and arrogate it to himself alone: "You don't get to choose. You don't decide when is the right time, when it fits your story. *This was the time we were here*" (552; emphasis in original). On this point the comparison with *Perdido Street Station* is especially pertinent. For Yagharek's crime, as Isaac learns, was one which he—and we—would understand as rape, but which is understood differently in garuda society. As Yagharek's victim, Kar'uchai, explains, she does not consider herself to have been violated, or defiled, or ravished—all concepts indelibly marked by reactionary ideologies of patriarchal paternalism. Yagharek's crime against Kar'uchai was to *steal her choice,* and choice-theft, according to Kar'uchai, is among garudas "the only crime we *have*" (692; emphasis in original). It is also precisely the crime that Judah has committed against the Iron Council: so that Judah, though in one way parallel to Isaac, is in another way parallel to Yagharek himself. He may have saved the councilors physically, but only at the cost of depriving them of that autonomy of decision-making without which the revolutionary project becomes deeply problematic at best. Judah himself understands this point and makes no attempt to evade the bullet (something his golemetric abilities would have easily enabled him to do) when Ann-Hari, with profound sadness but full determination, shoots him to death. Throughout the two novels Yagharek and Judah have become deeply sympathetic figures; yet the reader cannot feel certain that either Yag's mutilation or Judah's execution is necessarily unjust.

The major difference between the two cases is that Isaac faces a purely individual moral dilemma, whereas, with Judah, Ann-Hari, and the Council, Miéville has raised the whole question to a higher level by casting it in the collective terms of socialist revolution: so that *Iron Council* not only engages, in its overdeterminationism, the ontology and epistemology of revolution, but also amounts to a profound, complex interrogation of the tactics and ethics of revolution as well. Indeed, in this dimension of the novel Miéville continues a political-ethical discourse begun long ago by Trotsky, who, in his pre-Bolshevik phase, vehemently derided Lenin's theory of party organization as "substitutism" (*zamestitelstvo*), that is to say, the notion that it was sometimes permissible for a relatively small group to substitute its own judgment for that of the broader socialist movement: a practice that Trotsky attacked as undemocratic and likely to lead, ultimately, to the dictatorship of an individual (see Deutscher 1965, 88–97). Whether Trotsky was right against Lenin (and against his own later, Leninist position) remains an open historical question. There are compelling arguments that Stalin's dictatorship was always implicit, to some degree, in even the earliest practices of Bolshevik organization—but also that, this side of the purest, most ineffectual anarchism, a certain degree of substitutism may remain an unavoidable practical necessity for a revolutionary movement. Miéville does not claim (even implicitly) to have settled the argument. But in Judah's decisive act of quasi-Leninist substitutism and Ann-Hari's quasi-Trotskyist response to it, he has dramatized the ethical and strategic issues at stake with rare force and rigor.

So complicated, however, is the incident of Judah's suspension of the train that it also helps to address a further and different set of issues too, issues that engage what might be called the *aesthetics,* or even the hermeneutics, of socialist revolution. In addition to raising urgent ethical questions, the temporal suspension that Judah effects also amounts, on a rather different level, to a metaphor for the preservation of revolutionary hope through such deeply unrevolutionary eras as that in which the novel itself is written. Here we need to consider not only this particular act of golemetry but also many other political interventions by literally fantastic forces throughout the novel. For there are many points at which the revolutionaries triumph only because of resources not actually available to socialists in the real world. Once, for example, the situation of the Iron Council is saved against attack by TRT gendarmes by the unexpected arrival of the borinatch, a "cavalry of striders" (258) with supernormal abilities such as the power to reach and fight through dimensions unseen to humans; their rescue of the Council is not only fantastic but also amounts to a clear (though distant) generic echo of the near-miraculous arrival of the U.S. Cavalry in many cinematic westerns, such as John Ford's *Stagecoach* (1939). Then too, there are several instances where the Council is able to evade the Militia by taking refuge in the Cacotopic Stain, a mysterious and deeply feared area of Bas-Lag where the structure of space-time seems unpredictable and malevolent: "Iron Council relied on the cacotopic zone. That was what would hide them" (406). Finally—to offer one more example out of many that could be cited—Judah's golemetry saves, or helps to save, the day on numerous occasions prior to his ultimate invention of the time-golem: as when he makes golems literally out of thin air to wage "a strange, near-invisible fight" (505) against the Council's enemies. We should remember that Miéville's character is named after Rabbi Judah Loew, who, according to the fantastic Jewish legend, invented a golem out of clay in the ghetto of sixteenth-century Prague in order to protect Jews from Christian pogroms: protection that the Jews lacked, of course, in actuality.

By the strictest canons of realism—by Georg Lukács's definitive standards of socialist realism, for instance—the use of plot devices such as golems amounts to a kind of cheating. How can a novel honestly claim to engage the rigors of socialist revolution if it constantly has recourse to factors beyond the capacity of any conceivable real-world revolutionary movement? There are, however, several grounds on which Miéville's practice here can be defended. To begin with, the super mundane elements in *Iron Council* can be understood as metaphorical displacements, within the invented world of Bas-Lag, of phenomena familiar enough in actual earthly history. The timely arrival of the borinatch reminds us that revolutions have always proceeded in part by attracting unexpected allies, whose participation could not have been predicted in advance. And does not the Cacotopic Stain figure the importance of terrain for revolutionary guerrilla movements, for instance the elaborate use of their country's landscape by the Vietnamese revolutionaries who defeated the French and American occupiers? As for golems, golemetry—like all magic or thaumaturgy in the Bas-Lag trilogy—is fundamentally a material technology, a learnable and teachable skill; and Judah's technical brilliance may serve to stress the importance, for revolutionaries, of mastering the most advanced technology available in any social situation. Yet in reply to these points the uncompromising Lukácisan might insist that such displacements are after all required only by the more general and logically prior displacement of Earth itself by Bas-Lag; and that the choice of such an unrealistic setting in the first place amounts to the betrayal of realism and a concomitant failure of authorial nerve. To answer this charge leads us to a deeper defense—indeed, the fundamental defense—of Miévillian "weird fiction."

As we have already discussed, the choice of an alternative-world rather than a real-world environment for a novel about socialist revolution cannot be understood apart from the singularly inhospitable circumstances for socialist revolution offered by the real world during the era in which *Iron Council* has been written. One might say that, in terms of individual talent, Miéville may be a better or a worse novelist than, say, Gorky (justly one of Lukács's particular heroes of socialist realism), but that what is certain is that Miéville could not possibly *be* Gorky no matter what. The setting of this revolutionary novel in a fantastic world implicitly recognizes, in its very structure, the unavailability of socialist revolution in the immediate empirical world; and the use, in *Iron Council,* of some magical devices in the invented revolutionary struggle is best grasped as a series of utopian signs, or figures, or placeholders, for social forces whose precise nature cannot yet be identified but which must be in some way posited if the ultimate ideal of social justice is to be maintained. The basic project of *Iron Council,* in other words, is to keep hope alive, to insist upon the horizon of socialist revolution even in the current absence of entirely specific particulars that could define the latter. The text's towering figure for such hope is the suspended train of the Iron Council, unable to effect immediate practical change but still charged with revolutionary energy that is to be discharged another day. As the novel's final paragraph puts it: "Years might pass and we will tell the story of the Iron Council and how it was made, how it made itself and went, and how it came back, and is coming, is still coming. Women and men cut a line across the dirtland and dragged history out and back across the world. They are still with shouts setting their mouths and we usher them in. They are coming out of the trenches of rock toward the brick shadows. They are always coming" (564). The key word of this passage is of course the adverb in the final sentence.

This is not, to be sure, realism in the strict generic sense. But it is a kind of material reality nonetheless. It is, precisely, the Marxist reality invoked in the epigraph above from Ernst Bloch, the greatest philosopher of utopia, who insisted that the real is never exhausted by the empirical content of any actually existing social formation but, on the contrary, always includes the revolutionary potential implicit in human activity—the potential to which we are driven by the never-destroyed (though often disappointed) principle of hope. To comprehend such potential in our future is for Bloch the chief function of the aesthetic imagination, certainly not excluding the imagination of the fantastic. Miéville is here completely at one with Bloch, and both are at one with Marx. In a famous passage from volume 1 of *Capital*, to which Miéville himself refers in one of his scholarly pieces (see Miéville 2002b), Marx defines human labor itself partly in terms of the imagining of that which does not yet exist. What distinguishes "the worst architect from the best of bees," says Marx, is that the architect "builds the cell in his mind before he constructs it in wax." Accordingly, "at the end of every labour process, a result emerges which had already been conceived by the worker at the beginning, hence already existed ideally" (284). Especially if we bear in mind that the root Greek meaning of "fantastic" (*phantastikos*) is the making visible of something to the mind's eye, it is easy to concur with Miéville's gloss on this passage: "The fantastic is there at the most prosaic moment of production" (44). No less than any other form of material production—indeed, far more so—the production of a socialist society takes place first of all in the imagination.

Iron Council, then, completes the diptych begun with *King Rat* by transcending the intellectual and imaginative horizons of the earlier novel, fine as *King Rat* is. True enough, both texts ultimately fail to represent an achieved socialist revolution. But, because the later novel does engage the revolutionary-socialist problematic with great rigor and with scrupulously realized particulars—and because it keeps hope alive by keeping socialist revolution on the agenda despite all immediate setbacks—its "failure" takes place on a much more advanced level. In the celebrated opening pages of *The Eighteenth Brumaire of Louis Bonaparte* (1852), Marx explains that bourgeois revolutions, with their limited aims and their necessary bad faith, take their poetry from the past—"to deaden their awareness of their own content" (149). He adds that socialist revolutions, however, whose aims transcend any preexisting rhetorical resources, must take their poetry from the future. In the early twenty-first century, perhaps no author can do more than China Miéville has done in *Iron Council*: which is to have made a brilliant preliminary sort of poetry out of the fact that, at a date whose lateness would have shocked Marx himself, the actual poetry of socialist revolution remains stubbornly in the future.

Notes

   1. The remainder of this paragraph provides a highly condensed recapitulation (with one or two new emphases) of Freedman 2003.

   2. Some recent Marxist scholarship has begun to suggest that the category of bourgeois revolution—and even the relationship between the bourgeoisie and the early history of

capitalism—may be more problematic than had previously been thought; for example, see Wood 2002. But it seems to me that Miéville's work is coherent with the more traditional Marxist view assumed above.

3. Actually, Miéville, as a (critical) follower of the Soviet legal theorist Evgeny Pashukanis, would himself insist that socioeconomic equality would not so much "complete and guarantee" equality before the law as supersede it: for the Pashukanisite position holds the legal form to be inseparable from the commodity form and hence from class exploitation. In his major work of scholarship thus far (Miéville 2005), Miéville argues, for instance, that "in its very neutrality, law maintains capitalist relations" (101) and that "the political—the violent, the coercive—lies at the heart of the legal" (151). Most emphatically, he insists, "The chaotic and bloody world around us *is the rule of law*" (319; emphasis in original).

4. I wish I could claim to be the first to think of the title pun of this paper, which brings together *Iron Council* with *To the Finland Station* (1940), Wilson's classic "study in the writing and acting of history." Unfortunately, it can be found in Dirda 2004.

5. The chief reference here is to Althusser 1977, 87–116 and 161–218; see also Freud 1965. In the current context it is relevant to note that the October Revolution is Althusser's privileged instance of overdetermination (1977, 99–101).

Bibliography

Althusser, Louis. 1977. *For Marx*, trans. Ben Brewster. London: NLB.

Deutscher, Isaac. 1965. *The Prophet Armed—Trotsky: 1879–1921*, vol. 1. New York: Vintage.

Dirda, Michael. 2004. "'Iron Council' by China Miéville." *Washington Post*, August 22.

Freedman, Carl. 2003. "Towards a Marxist Urban Sublime: Reading China Miéville's *King Rat*." *Extrapolation* 46 (Winter): 395–408.

Freud, Sigmund. 1965. *The Interpretation of Dreams*, ed. and trans. James Strachey. New York: Avon.

Marx, Karl. 1973. *The Eighteenth Brumaire of Louis Bonaparte*, trans. Ben Fowkes. In *Surveys from Exile: Political Writings, Volume II*, ed. David Fernbach. New York: Random House.

———. 1974. *The Civil War in France*. In *The First International and After: Political Writings, Volume III*, ed. David Fernbach. New York: Random House.

———. 1976. *Capital*, vol. 1, trans. Ben Fowkes. London: Penguin.

Miéville, China. 1998. *King Rat*. New York: Tor.

———. 2000. *Perdido Street Station*. New York: Ballantine.

———. 2002a. *The Scar*. New York: Ballantine.

———. 2002b. "Editorial Introduction" to "Symposium: Marxism and Fantasy." *Historical Materialism* 10, no. 4.

———. 2004. *Iron Council*. New York: Ballantine.

———. 2005. *Between Equal Rights: A Marxist Theory of International Law*. Leiden: Brill.

Wilson, Edmund. 1940. *To the Finland Station: A Study in the Writing and Acting of History*. Garden City, N.Y.: Doubleday.

Wood, Ellen Meiksins. 2002. *The Origin of Capitalism: A Longer View*. London: Verso.

Socialist Surrealism

China Miéville's New Crobuzon Novels

Henry Farrell

How do politics and the science fiction and fantasy genres inform each other?[1] Science fiction has always had a strong undercurrent of utopianism—writers as different in their ideological predilections as Robert Heinlein (1966), Ursula K. Le Guin (1974), and Frederik Pohl (1979) have used it as a means to reimagine political and social arrangements better to their liking. The dominant political strain in post-Tolkien fantasy, in contrast, has been an unabashed nostalgia for the loss of organic bonds and feudal relationships (although there have been counter-strains of fantasy that has questioned these assumptions).[2]

China Miéville's three New Crobuzon novels—*Perdido Street Station, The Scar,* and *Iron Council*—stand as an important and entirely self-aware counter-argument to dominant strains in both fantasy and science fiction. Miéville's work draws on both genres as well as horror. Indeed, he argues that these three subgenres are not really distinguishable from each other but instead form a common genre, which he dubs Weird Fiction (Miéville n.d. a). But even as he draws upon their tropes, he both reimagines them and argues with them. In a much-commented-upon essay that draws upon Michael Moorcock's scathing criticisms of Tolkienesque fantasy,[3] Miéville describes Tolkien as the "wen on the arse of fantasy literature," attacking his "cod-Wagnerian pomposity, . . . his small-minded and reactionary love for hierarchical status-quos, his belief in absolute morality that blurs moral and political complexity" (Miéville n.d. b). In later writing he has indicated that he regrets the imagery and phrasing of this essay (although not his substantive criticisms of Tolkien), and has acknowledged the ways in which Tolkien consciously and unconsciously influences his own work. What he draws from Tolkien is his refusal to make fantasy allegorical— that is, to make the fantastic into "a kind of philistine, simplistic, moralising, fabular representation of soi-disant 'meaningful' concerns, as with fiction that despises its own fantastic." Thus Miéville's intent is to "nurture the baby of Tolkien's phenomenology of fantasy while chucking out the bathwater of his ideas" (Miéville 2005). However, unlike Tolkien, he does not believe that fantasy is divorced from reality—while it is not subordinate to the mundane, it draws its resonance from its connections (however oblique, however tangential) to our lived experience.

This conception of fantasy and related genres—as drawing their strength from its connection to our mundane reality while not being subordinate to them—is the expression of a profoundly *political* position regarding Weird Fiction and what it ought to be.[4] Miéville is a socialist who wants to see a radical transformation of society and is intensely interested in how the imagination may play a role in midwifing that transformation.[5] His books—especially the New Crobuzon novels—are in large part an argument about the relationship between the fantastic and political. When he criticizes post-Tolkien fantasy, he is not merely attacking its overt nostalgia for feudal arrangements and organic ties between lords and serfs. He is attacking its failure of imagination, its unfaithfulness to its own supposed goal of radically reimagining the worlds in which people like us might live.

For Miéville, much of the power of fantasy, science fiction, and related genres lies in their potential refusal to take the status quo for granted. When they do what they are supposed to do, they reveal new possibilities to us of what we might or might not be able to do. When they instead provide readers with exactly what those readers are expecting to read, they are failing, not only because the specific myths that they reinforce often tend to be ones that reinforce current hierarchies of power, but because they are not disclosing anything that the reader did not know or think already. If fantasy and science fiction are fundamentally literatures of the imagination, they need to tell us unexpected things. In Miéville's words:

> The impulse to the fantastic is central to human consciousness, in that
> we can and constantly do imagine things that aren't really there. More
> than that (and what distinguishes us from tool-using animals), we can
> imagine things that can't possibly be there. We can imagine the impossi-
> ble. Now, within that you have to distinguish the "never-possible" and
> the "might-be-possible-sometime." Crudely, this looks like the distinction
> between fantasy and science fiction, but I maintain that there's no such
> hard distinction and that the differences between the "never-" and the
> "not-yet-possible" are less important than their shared "impossibleness."
> That's not to say in some dippy hippy way that everything is possible, but
> that there's no obvious line between what is and what isn't. In fact, that
> underlines many of the most tenacious political fights around us—the
> neo-liberal claim that There is No Alternative is all about trying to draw
> the line of the "never-possible" at a place which strips humans of any
> meaningful transformative agency. (Gordon 2003)

This makes these literatures more easily amenable to certain forms of political argument than other, more mainstream forms of writing that are not explicitly concerned with rethinking how we might live if things were different. Rather than social realism, Miéville's work is pushing toward a kind of social surrealism, a recognition of how the imagination plays a crucial political role by challenging the accepted rules and orderings of society.[6]

In Miéville's conception, literary utopias work better as provocations than as blueprints.[7] Utopia, by its very nature, cannot ever fully be implemented, and to the extent that it can, it is likely unimaginable to those who have not achieved it. As he writes in "With One Bound We Are Free":

> The depiction of successful revolution does not solve things. In this case the attempt to express Marx's "carnival of the oppressed," can—being restrained by the words and context of a society defined by its lack of being-in-revolution-ness—easily degenerate into the kitsch of Stalinoid agitprop. Even if the work negotiates this, it raises the issue of depicting a post-revolutionary society. While thought experiments about such possibilities can be invaluable—see for example Michael Albert's Parecon— if we take seriously the scale of social and psychic upheaval represented by a revolution, a post-revolutionary society is unthinkable: for someone not born in a post-revolutionary situation, it takes the process of going through a revolution to fully imagine it. To depict it is to diminish it.

Instead, while the fantastic imagination—the ability to imagine that things are different than they are in the world we live in—plays a crucial role for politics, it is an indirect one. It does not substitute for political activity, or even necessarily guide it, but it expands the space of political possibilities, making people aware of the contingency of existing social arrangements and the possibility of changing them.

These claims help drive the argument of Miéville's three (to date) New Crobuzon novels. This certainly is not to say that these books should be reduced to political texts. Although they are concerned with politics and clearly reflect Miéville's socialism, they are something far more complex than a simple transposition of these politics into a fantastic setting, and in any event have many other strands than the political. But one important strain running through them is an argument about the relationship between politics and the fantastic imagination. Each of the books has at its core an argument about the extent to which it is possible to reimagine politics. *Perdido Street Station*'s version of this argument is bleak—in a city controlled by a corrupt and vicious political administration, there is no space where the fantastic imagination can play out with genuine autonomy. *The Scar*'s version is even bleaker—it is precisely the main characters' capacity for fantasy that blinds them to how things really are and allows others to betray them. *Iron Council* provides the counterargument to these two, showing how under some circumstances the fantastic imagination can disclose new possibilities to actors, allowing them to reconceive the world and to act accordingly.

Perdido Street Station: Art Gone Rotten

Perdido Street Station is Miéville's second book (his first, *King Rat,* is a contemporary London fantasy) and his breakthrough novel. Set in the fecund, feculent city of New Crobuzon, it received both the British Fantasy Award and the Arthur C. Clarke Award, as well as being shortlisted for the World Fantasy Award. The story is complex, even in its barest outlines. It begins with Yagharek, a garuda (a human-bird hybrid), whose wings have been hacked off by his tribe as punishment for the crime of "choice-theft in the second degree with utter disrespect." Yagharek wants to fly again, and he comes to New Crobuzon, where he seeks out the help of renegade human scientist Isaac Dan der Grimnebulin. Isaac, in the course of his research on flight, accidentally releases a "slake-moth" that he has acquired unknowingly from a government military research project. The slake-moth is a horrifyingly efficient predator that battens on human consciousness and is nearly impossible to kill; when freed, it releases four siblings from captivity. (They have been sold by the city government to the crime lord Motley, who milks them to produce dreamshit, a drug that allows its users to experience the dreams and fantasies of the slake-moths' previous victims.)

In the meantime Motley kidnaps Isaac's lover, Lin (who is a *khepri*, a woman with a giant beetle for her head), whom he had previously commissioned to create a sculpture of him. Isaac and his associates (most importantly Derkhian, a journalist for the underground newspaper, *Runagate Rampant*) go on the run. While hiding out from the city militia, they try to stop the slake-moths with the aid of the Weaver (a gigantic, irrational spider with quasi-godlike powers), the Construct Council (a secret cabal of machines that have achieved self-consciousness), and in the last moments of the book, Jack Half-a-Prayer (a remade human rebel with a mantis claw grafted to his right arm).

They succeed, but at great cost—Lin is rescued from Motley, but only after she has been brutalized and likely raped, and her mind has been ruined by a slake-moth. Isaac and Derkhian flee into exile and obscurity, bringing Lin with them. Isaac finally refuses to help Yagharek fly; he has discovered that Yagharek's crime approximates what he would consider rape (although Yagharek's tribe considers it to be something quite different). Yagharek then refuses Half-a-Prayer's offer to join him in his quixotic campaign against the city government, instead accepting that he can no longer fly, and becoming a man.

This complex story introduces the reader to the city of New Crobuzon, which is in many ways a fantasized version of nineteenth-century London, equal parts Great Wen. and Old Corruption. New Crobuzon is a ruthlessly mercantilistic city-state, using its militia and its navy to enforce trading privileges abroad and to suppress unrest at home. A deeply corrupt city government, headed by Mayor Bentham Rudgutter, presides over a political system in which only the propertied are guaranteed the right to vote; others have to participate in a lottery.

Political dissidence in New Crobuzon is a mug's game. Miéville suggests that the dice are loaded when he links the "civilization and splendour of the

City-State Republic of New Crobuzon" to the gladiatorial pit at Cadnebar's, where "every night, the evening's entertainments would begin with an open slot, a comedy show for the regulars. Scores of young, stupid, thickset farmboys, the toughest lads in their villages . . . would flex their prodigious muscles at the selectors. Two or three would be chosen, and pushed into the main arena before the howling crowd. . . . Then the arena's hatch would be opened and they would pale as they faced an enormous Remade gladiator or impassive cactacae warrior. The resulting carnage was short and bloody and played for laughs by the professionals" (*Perdido Street Station* 249–50).

Dissidents in New Crobuzon are far more aware of their situation and the odds against them than the farm boys, but they do not fare much better. As soon as a dock strike threatens to create real solidarity between *vodhyanoi* stevedores and humans, the authorities move ruthlessly and effectively to suppress it. When the government thinks that the publisher of the illegal newspaper, *Runagate Rampant,* Benjamin Flex, may know something about the slake-moths, the city militia immediately seizes him from the hidden room where he has printed the newspaper. He realizes before being killed that the government knew all along what he was doing and where he was but had previously been prepared to tolerate him as an acceptable nuisance.

The state does not simply rely on the militia to ensure social order. In Miéville's imagined world, magic or thaumaturgy has been semi-systematized along scientific lines, allowing specialist mages (biothaumaturges) to reshape individuals' bodies and to graft parts from animals and machines onto them. Biothaumaturgy is typically deployed to punish rather than to enhance—criminals and unfortunates are "Remade" in punishment factories according to the orders of masked Magisters (judge-magistrates). Sometimes the Remaking is intended to make them useful in some way or another, conjoining humans with steam-driven machines to make them stronger workers or creating cabs whose drivers are part of the machine. More specialized Remade are sold to the gladiatorial arenas or the brothels. Often, the Remaking is intended less for utilitarian purposes than to provide a "fitting" punishment for the individual's crime according to some more or less grotesque aesthetic principle of justice.

> "Some woman living at the top of one of the Ketch Heath monoliths killed her baby . . . because it wouldn't stop crying. She's sitting there in court, her eyes are just . . . damn well *empty* . . . she can't believe what's happened, she keeps moaning her baby's name, and the Magister sentences her. Prison, of course, ten years I think, but it was the Remaking that I remember. Her baby's arms are going to be grafted to her face. 'So she doesn't forget what she did,' he says."
>
> Derkhan's voice curdled as she imitated the Magister. (*Perdido Street Station* 115)

Remaking is a perversion of the imagination—a cruel and whimsical ingenuity that is put at the service of political power. As the journalist Derkhan describes it, "Remaking's art, you know. Sick art. The imagination it takes! Remaking's creativity gone bad. Gone rotten. Gone *rancid*. I remember you once asked me if it was hard to balance writing about art and writing [about politics for the underground newspaper, *Runagate Rampant*]. . . . It's the *same thing*. . . . I don't want to live in a city where Remaking is the highest art" (*Perdido Street Station* 115–16).

New Crobuzon is a city where the imagination has been almost entirely subordinated to the demands of tyranny. At one point, Isaac describes the slake-moths' predation as a closed ecosystem; they exude effluvia that infect the consciousness of the city's inhabitants with nightmares and fever dreams, so that their prey's imaginings will taste more succulent. But the same can be said of New Crobuzon's political system. Even before the slake-moths' advent, New Crobuzon is a city in which the imagination has turned sour, answering to and reproducing tyrannical power relations in a self-sustaining cycle. As becomes clear in *Iron Council,* the Remade are an integral part of the power structure in the city, precisely because they are isolated as pariahs. Unmodified humans or xenians (intelligent nonhumans) reasonably fear that they will be Remade if they displease the authorities. The Remade also provide a reservoir of desperate labor that can be drawn on in case of worker unrest. Perhaps most important, the distinction between Remade and ordinary workers makes the latter more willing to accept the continuation of the system; they see themselves as part of an aristocracy of labor. By Remaking criminals or others who have displeased it, the city makes it far more difficult for the oppressed to achieve solidarity and to reimagine themselves as a collective political subject that might challenge the system.

The subordination of imagination to the cold realities of power plays out more subtly, but no less implacably, among the relatively privileged in New Crobuzon. The two main protagonists of the novel—Isaac and Lin—are both readers of the underground press and members of a small bohemian community of artists and intellectuals. But this community is not so much autonomous as it is tolerated by the city's government; it has little or no scope to translate its (mostly passive) dissidence into action. Isaac is only able to pursue his research and Lin her art because of the compromises that they have made with the system. Isaac runs errands for the corrupt biothaumaturge Vermishank in order to maintain his access to the university, despite suspecting that Vermishank carries out research on live subjects in the punishment factories. Isaac, moreover, refuses to acknowledge his relationship with Lin in public: sexual relations between humans and xenians are frowned upon and would be "a quick route to pariah status, rather than the bad-boy chic he had assiduously courted" if he were seen not observing the proprieties by at least trying to hide it (*Perdido Street Station* 16).

For her part Lin resents the political compromises made by other *khepri* artists in the relatively prosperous neighborhood of Kinken, whom she perceives as having sold out their poorer sisters for a modest share of prosperity. However, her sense of self-righteousness crumbles when offered a lucrative commission by the gang boss Motley. She accepts it with nervous delight, even though she knows exactly where the money is coming from. As their relationship continues (and as Motley deliberately heightens her sense of discomfort by drawing her ever further into his world) she comes to realize that she has more in common with her sisters in Kinken than she thought. She too is willing to make compromises in order to pursue her art and gain financial independence. Her imagination and her vocation as an artist do not in any sense free her from her material conditions—her aspiration toward a modest degree of autonomy is entirely dependent on the willingness of a spectacularly vicious patron to fund it.

The characters in *Perdido Street Station* do not have any real way to change the city around them. The most they can do is to help stave off disaster and, insofar as they can, prevent things from getting any worse. In his efforts to help Yagharek, Isaac makes a profound intellectual breakthrough, discovering how to tap and control "crisis energy." In a typical science fiction novel this would then allow Isaac to change the world. In Miéville's imaginary world it does nothing of the sort. It allows Isaac to create and amplify an artificial mind composed of the mentalities of the Weaver (the irrational imagination) and the Construct Council (a coldly calculating ego), which serves as bait to lure the slake-moths to their destruction. But this unification of calculation and imagination cannot be maintained for long, and Isaac, fearing the uses that might be made of this breakthrough by the Construct Council, disappears with Derkhan and Lin into obscurity and exile.

In the novel's closing pages Yagharek meets Jack Half-a-Prayer again after Isaac's refusal to help him regain his ability to fly. Half-a-Prayer offers Yagharek a "way out" into the "violent and honourable place from where he rages" (*Perdido Street Station* 866). But Yagharek refuses—he is no longer suspended midway between his dreams of flight and of escape from the petty mundanities of the world on the one hand and his winglessness on the other. He has come to accept that he is never going to fly again, that he is now not a garuda but a man, someone who belongs to New Crobuzon. While Half-a-Prayer's quixotic struggle against the authorities is an honorable choice, so too is Yagharek's decision to accept the limitations of who he is and what he can do. In New Crobuzon as it is, dreams of flight are dreams of escape from the world of politics and consequences; they are not a path to changing it.

The Scar: Savagery and Metamorphosis

Perdido Street Station is not a hopeful book. It depicts a city where the fantastic imagination has little scope to express itself freely, much less to change things. But it is far less pessimistic than *The Scar*, which argues that the imagination, when given free rein, can betray. The key theme of the book is the danger of the fantastic imagination when it is disconnected from reality. The charismatic dictators who effectively control the pirate city of Armada—the Lovers—have become intoxicated with the idea of "adventure" as an end in itself. The most sympathetic characters of the book—the linguist Bellis Coldwine; the Remade engineer Tanner Sack; and the former ship's boy Shekel—betray themselves precisely because they allow their imaginations to open up. The two characters who are best able to manipulate the hopes and fears of others—the spy Silas Fennec and the swordsman Uther Doul—are also the most pathetic, precisely because they do not have anything beyond their manipulation.

The book is set entirely outside New Crobuzon. We see its hinterlands and a nearby port but never the city itself. Nonetheless, the shadow of the city stretches out over the novel. Bellis, a former lover of Isaac Dan der Grimnebulin, has fled New Crobuzon for the colony of Nova Experium, fearing arrest by the militia, who are rounding up all of Isaac's former associates one by one. Her ship is intercepted by pirates, who take the passengers and ordinary crew (including not only Bellis, but also Tanner Sack, Silas Fennec, and Shekel) back to their city of Armada, which is composed of a flotilla of conjoined ships pulled slowly by tugs hither and thither across the sea.

Armada is a mix of semiautonomous "ridings" or neighborhoods run on different political principles (including inter alia representative democracy, military dictatorship, monarchy, and a market-based free-for-all), of which the riding of Garwater, under the charismatic dictatorship of the Lovers (a man and a woman who are never named in the novel), is the most powerful. The Lovers, with the help of their adviser-bodyguard Uther Doul, want to catch a leviathan, the *avanc,* which they can harness to pull the city to the Scar, an ontological wound in the Swollen Ocean from which limitless possibilities erupt. Others in the city, most prominently the Brucolac, a vampire turned enlightened absolutist, are vehemently opposed to the Lovers' plans. The Brucolac has a peculiar relationship with Uther Doul, who appears to be assisting the Lovers but is tacitly maneuvering people into opposing their plans.

Fennec succeeds in convincing Bellis, who is unhappy in Armada, that he has intelligence on a planned invasion of New Crobuzon by the *grindylow,* a grotesque and malign race of human-eel hybrids. When she is sent to the island of the *anophelii* (mosquito people) to act as translator for Kruach Aum, a male *anophelius* with crucial information on how to catch the *avanc,* she has an opportunity to pass Fennec's intelligence, with the help of Sack, to a ship's captain who can bring it back to New Crobuzon. However, she does not realize that the supposed *grindylow* invasion of New Crobuzon is a hoax. Fennec is using her as a conduit to tell New Crobuzon that he has gathered intelligence allowing them to bypass or conquer the *grindylow,* creating an immensely valuable new trade route, in order to persuade the city government to rescue him. Shortly after the city harnesses the *avanc,* a major naval expedition from New Crobuzon catches up with the floating city, intending to rescue Fennec and his information. It is repelled, but at the cost of thousands of lives.

The city then is towed by the *avanc* closer to the Scar; shortly before it reaches the Scar, Coldwine, again with the help of Tanner Sack, finds a way to stop its reaching the Scar and plunging into disaster. However, she realizes that she has been manipulated into so doing by Doul, who has orchestrated her actions and others so as to frustrate the plans of the Lovers, without at any point appearing to take an overt stance against them.

The plot structure of *The Scar* both replicates and undermines the traditional quest narrative of a fantasy novel. It is a vastly entertaining book, which goes to greater lengths than *Perdido Street Station* to evoke the variety and strangeness of the world where both novels are set. Even so, the reader is denied many of the satisfactions that might be expected in a typical quest novel. A physical fight between the Brucolac and Uther Doul, which has been telegraphed for hundreds of pages, happens offstage; we see its lead-up and its consequences but not the fight itself. The *grindylow* attack Armada not to gain back a statue of arcane puissance, which has been stolen from them (it turns out to be a MacGuffin), but to neutralize the threat posed by Fennec and his information. The capture of the *avanc* (its resemblance to Moby-Dick no doubt entirely intended) turns out not to be an end in itself but a means to the end of reaching the Scar, which itself is never reached.

These frustrations have a rationale. The tension driving the novel forward is the tension between the romantic imagination and the grubby realities of power and of material accumulation. Not only does the reader find that the book deliberately disappoints some of the expectations that its narrative form has set up; the book explicitly argues that these expectations are dangerous when they are not grounded in a proper understanding of politics. The desire to be a hero, for epochal fights in which issues are finally resolved, for questing and adventure without end, are traps when they are shorn of material purpose.

The Scar itself, the subject of the book's title, illustrates this theme. The Scar is a wound in reality. Possibilities explode forth from it, which can in principle be grasped and mastered by an arcane science. But it is really a honeypot, a trap for the immature who want to pursue adventure for its own sake. The Lovers' quest to reach the Scar is a sardonic comment on the infantilism of the quest narrative. Not only are the Lovers themselves profoundly narcissistic, but they do not have any idea of what they might want to *do* with the power that they believe they will gain if they reach the Scar. Their intoxication with the idea of limitless possibilities and endless adventures blinds them to the reality of the city that they are seeking to pull after them, a pirate community based on "brutal mercantilism," albeit one that has been temporarily blinded to its actual situation by the Lovers' rhetoric. As the Brucolac says in his final argument with Uther Doul, "If the fucking Scar *exists* . . . and if they (the Lovers) get us there and by some godsfucked miracle we survive, then they'll still destroy us. We are not an expeditionary force, we are not on some fucking *quest*. This is a city, Uther. We live, we buy, we sell, we steal, we trade. We are a *port*. This is *not* about *adventures*. . . . If we survive this lunacy, as long as we're tethered to the bastard avanc, these two will take us on another fucking voyage, and another, until we die. That's not our logic, Doul, that's not how Armada works" (*The Scar* 708). The desire for adventure as an end in itself is a chimera.

Even worse (to use a Marxian concept that Miéville implicitly appeals to), it is a form of mystification. It obscures the material realities of trade, accumulation, and political domination that actually characterize Miéville's imagined world. This explains why Bellis Coldwine is taken in by the stories of Silas Fennec. She cannot easily penetrate through the veils of romance and adventure in his stories to discover his rather sordid motivations. Bellis fancies herself a cynic and is grimly amused at a New Crobuzon children's book she finds that tries to whitewash New Crobuzon's history, including, "most shamefully," the culmination of the Pirate Wars when New Crobuzon bombed the rival city of Suroch with a Torque weapon (*The Scar* 157). But when Fennec boasts unwisely that it was "*merchants* [like him] who traveled to Suroch, who brought back the maps Dagman Beyn used in the Pirate Wars," she does not get the hint. She is entirely taken in by Fennec's charm and by his stories of travel to exotic places; she does not think through the logic of *why* Fennec has traveled so far or what information he may have brought back from the Gengris, where the *grindylow* live. She takes Fennec's claims at face value, temporarily overlooking the fact that he is a spy and a merchant-venturer with a commission from New Crobuzon's government.

Thus, when Fennec later manufactures his story about a planned *grindylow* invasion of New Crobuzon, she accepts it in its entirety, in part because this gives her a connection to her home city again, a way to become its savior by passing on the information about the *grindylows'* attack plans, even though she knows she will likely never see the city again. Fennec astutely provides her with just enough information to construct her own internal narrative, in which she will be the noble heroine; that her nobility of spirit will go entirely unrecognized and unrewarded possibly makes the story even more attractive. Bellis's homesickness for New Crobuzon is a weakness in her protective shell of rationality, self-control, and skepticism, an opening that Fennec is able to find, enlarge, and exploit.

Bellis is not the only character who reimagines herself, only to be betrayed by the reimagining. All the main characters undergo transformations that seem to open new possibilities. Tanner Sack finds that his Remaking—he has had tentacles grafted onto him—opens him up to the welcoming sea, and he voluntarily submits to further Remaking to allow him to become more fully a creature of the water. Shekel, who has never learned how to read, discovers in joy and anger that an entire world has been kept away from him when Bellis begins to teach him how to move beyond reciting the alphabet.

These openings, these reimaginings, prove to be not expansions of possibility but chinks that predators may exploit. In many senses the underlying logic of the novel is that of a food chain. Metaphors of predation are nearly as frequent in the book as the metaphors of wounding, opening, scarring, and scarification to which they are linked. At one point Bellis summarizes a book by her friend, the naturalist Johannes Tearfly, *Predation in Iron Bay Rockpools;* "Such an intricate concatenation of narratives. Chains of savagery and metamorphosis. . . . The oyster drill gnawing a murderous peep-hole in its opponent's armour . . . a vivid little seascape . . . of shell-dust and sea urchins and merciless tides" (*The Scar* 160).

The protagonists of this book find themselves in just such a concatenation of narratives, a seascape of metamorphoses and predation. Bellis herself is not only gulled by Silas Fennec; she is manipulated and paid off by Uther Doul, whom she once imagined herself capable of falling in love with. Sack's amphibian transformation allows him to carry Fennec's letter past the fearsome *anophelii* and thus inadvertently to betray his adopted city. When Shekel dies in the water, murdered casually by the *grindylow,* Tanner finds himself alienated from the ocean and fearful of it, unable to feel at home either on land or in the water. Shekel's gift of reading is closest to a genuine opening, but it also allows him to find an important book that he gives to Bellis, who quietly betrays the trust that he has placed in her, beginning a chain of events that leads indirectly to his death.

Yet if the protagonists end up either unhappy or dead, they are in a certain sense better off than those who manipulate them. They have some capacity for genuine agency, even if it betrays them. Silas Fennec and Uther Doul, who manipulate the protagonists in different ways are, like the mosquito women on the island of the *anophelii,* trapped in their patterns of predation, unable to connect meaningfully to other human beings. Fennec, when captured, is revealed to be no more than an "empty skin stuffed with schemes" (*The Scar* 626). Uther Doul, who has tried to retreat entirely from adventures and to wrap himself in the freedom from initiative that his contractual relationship with the Lovers gives him, finds himself utterly lost at the end of the novel, not knowing what he wants. If the glamour of adventure and openness to new possibilities are traps for the unwary, it is a greater mistake to renounce them in favor of either the cynical manipulation of others' illusions or a refusal to take personal responsibility. *The Scar* suggests that neither willful imagination on the one hand nor careful calculation on the other is sufficient to provide real agency. The tragedy is that the two are set at each other's throats in the novel—there is no real scope for reconciliation between them.[8]

The Scar thus presents a substantial contrast to *Perdido Street Station.* In the earlier novel there is little scope for the free play of fantasy and the imagination; both are largely subordinated to a corrupt and tyrannical city government. *The Scar,* at least initially, seems to offer an opening up of the fantastic imagination.

Its characters, landed in a new city, have the opportunity to reimagine themselves in profound ways. But the imagination turns out to be a trap—it does not provide limitless possibilities so much as it opens Bellis, Tanner, and Shekel up to deceit and manipulation by others.

Iron Council: Fantasy Remade

Iron Council revisits and reworks many of the themes of *Perdido Street Station* and *The Scar* to more hopeful ends. Characters mentioned in passing in the first two books (the vagabond Spiral Jacobs, for example, and a Remade woman whose dead baby's arms are attached to her forehead) come to center stage. More importantly, some of the events of *Perdido Street Station* have assumed a historic resonance that might have appeared unlikely at the time they occurred.

Again, *Iron Council* has a complex plot, with three main movements—the efforts of Cutter and others to find the golemist Judah Low and to save the train *Iron Council*, which went renegade decades before; an extended flashback to Judah Low's formative experiences as a young man who helped create the Iron Council; and finally the drift (contemporaneous with Cutter's search) of the young militant Ori into the orbit of a violent group of apparent insurrectionaries. The book is set some twenty years after the events of *Perdido Street Station* and *The Scar;* New Crobuzon has fallen on hard times. It is experiencing a sustained economic crisis and losing a war with the city of Tesh. Dissidents are becoming evermore confident and have joined together to create a caucus, which they begin to transform into a second power in the city, ready perhaps to take it over. The myth of *Iron Council*—a train that was taken into the wilderness by rebellious Remade decades before—has become an inspiration to the dissidents, but the New Crobuzon government has discovered where the train and the rebels are and is sending an expeditionary force to destroy them.

As dissidents such as the young street fighter Ori argue about how best to seize power in the city, Judah Low, who once helped seize the *Iron Council,* is traveling across the continent to warn his comrades on the train about New Crobuzon's plans. He is followed by a small group led by his sometime lover, Cutter. The Iron Councillors decide to return to New Crobuzon with their train and to help the Caucus win power. Back in New Crobuzon, Ori gravitates toward a gang led by the mysterious bandit Toro, which has taken up the tradition of violent, direct action against the state that Jack Half-a-Prayer represented in *Perdido Street Station.* Ori is guided by the mysterious vagabond Spiral Jacobs, who provides him with a large sum of money toward the cause. He becomes a trusted member of Toro's gang, helping her to kill the Mayor and her Magister lover. However, this breaks him—he discovers that Toro, far from being committed to political change, is instead seeking revenge against the Magister, who ordered her Remade. Moreover, Spiral Jacobs is the emissary of Tesh (which we have learned in *Perdido Street Station* always appoints a vagabond as ambassador) and is using the disorder as cover for a vast spell that he is weaving to destroy the city. Cutter and Judah return from Iron Council, which is approaching New Crobuzon, to try to forestall this threat; they succeed with the help of a renegade Teshite.

However, as the *Iron Council* gets closer it is becoming increasingly clear that the Caucus's rebellion is doomed and that the *Iron Council* and its passengers will be destroyed by the militia when they enter the city. Cutter tries to persuade the Iron Councillors to turn back but fails; Low constructs a time golem that freezes the train in time shortly before it can reach the city, simultaneously saving it and snatching away its destiny. He is killed shortly thereafter by his former lover, Ann-Hari, who is furious at his arrogance in taking away the choice of the Iron Councillors to go forward. But his intervention works; it creates an engine of change, never moving, always on the point of arriving in New Crobuzon, that seems likely to impel further change in the future. As the *Runagate Rampant* says in the closing section of the book, "'Order reigns in New Crobuzon!' You stupid lackeys. Your order is built on sand. Tomorrow the Iron Council will move on again, and to your horror it will proclaim with its whistle blaring: We say: We were, we are, we will be."

Iron Council not only borrows characters and settings from the first two books. It reinterprets them and in a sense redeems them. Events that seemed at the time to confirm the power of New Crobuzon's government now inspire the strikers and activists of the Caucus. Benjamin Flex, who died in near despair in *Perdido Street Station,* has become a hero to the Caucus. This redemption of the past is not entirely true to it. The New Crobuzon section of the book begins with a puppet show playing the "Sad and Instructional Tale" of Jack Half-a-Prayer's demise. The puppet show is deliberately subversive, deviating from both of the official state narratives of Half-a-Prayer's death (that he was killed by the relative of one of his victims or by one of his accomplices, who was hoping to spare him the misery of official execution). Instead, it argues that Jack was killed in a failed rescue attempt by a comrade, a "version of the classic" in which "the two little figures were not doomed or cursed with visions too pure to sustain or beaten by a world that did not deserve them, but were still fighting, still trying to win" (*Iron Council* 68). This retelling of the myth is clearly intended to inspire solidarity, to suggest that there is hope for those struggling against the city government. But it's almost certainly wrong. The figure who perhaps tries to rescue Jack is, from his description, clearly the garuda Yagharek, who, from what we know of his last meeting with Jack in *Perdido Street Station,* is likely helping him out of a sense of personal indebtedness rather than any broader solidarity.

Jack's "Sad and Instructional Tale" signals two of the key themes of *Iron Council.* First, it shows how political myths and the process of mythologizing can provide a basis for the kind of political agency that is mostly lacking in the first two books. The mythicized history of the Iron Council (created at least in part by Judah Low) shows how people use myths to build effective campaigns of solidarity over time, and how it is possible to take on the power of the state and, at least sometimes, win. The Iron Council, by defeating the militia that had been sent to stop it and disappearing into the wilderness, laying down and taking up its own tracks as it went, has created a political myth that helps inspire the Caucus to organize and take up arms. Myths of this kind connect the real and the imagined by disclosing possibilities of action.

Second, it shows the complexities of the relationship between the myths and the lived histories of those depicted in them. This vexed relationship—between the imperative to hold faith with personal solidarities and histories on the one hand and the necessity of subjecting them to the more impersonal and political demands of mythmaking (which has no necessary respect for the individual) on the other, is at the crux of the novel. It is best represented in the relationships between the key character in the book, the golemist Judah Low, and those around him. Judah is both golemist (maker of golems that animate brute matter, air, time, and darkness) and bard and is usually more comfortable with abstract forces and with stories than with people.

Indeed, the book hints strongly that Judah's skill, his (to use the loaded term that Miéville employs) *cathexis* as a golemist is so powerful exactly because he has been wounded into a kind of disconnection. He learns about golemetry among a tribe of swamp-dwelling *stiltspear* that is about to be destroyed by the advent of the railway, but it is only when he has begun to disengage from the tribe, to realize that they are doomed, that he finds the ability to animate golems himself. His power grows hand in hand with a vast and impersonal sense of benevolence toward those around him, a sense of justice, and a desire to right some of the wrongs of the railway. But in many ways, this is reminiscent of Judah's old antagonist, Weather Wrightby, the father of the railway project that the Iron Council subverted and destroyed. Wrightby, like Judah, is suffused with a sense of purpose and holiness. Both are monstrous, possessed of a certain beatific ruthlessness, a willingness to steer history in the direction that they believe it must be steered, regardless of the individual costs. Both, as a result, are consequential in a way that other, more sympathetic and human figures in the novel, such as Cutter, are not.

Judah's relationships with others are mostly one-way. Cutter, the dissident and former shop owner, loves him hopelessly, but cannot ever hope to have that love returned. When Low has sex with him, it is given as a gift; there is no sense of mutuality. Cutter's companions, who go with him into the wilderness to catch up with Low, are inspired as much by love for the man as by their political cause. Like Cutter, they cannot hope to have this love returned except in an abstract and impersonal way. Low is not entirely devoid of sentiment; when he sees the Iron Council and his comrades again, he is possessed by an open delight that Cutter has never seen before. But again, his love is more for what they represent than what they are in themselves. If Low appears entirely incapable of jealousy (when, for example, his former lover, Ann-Hari, goes with other men), it is because he is no longer capable of the kind of personal and immediate attachment that jealousy follows from. He has lost a little bit of what it means to be human.

Judah's saintly benevolence is at odds with the more personal solidarities and goals of the Iron Councillors. When the Remade renegades and their allies take the *Iron Council* and ride it into the wilderness, they are doing so because it allows them to choose their own history. In a key passage, Ann-Hari, the prostitute turned political firebrand, describes this specifically as a Remaking of what has happened to them, which turns it into something new, something they can work from: "We give up nothing. . . . All the dead. . . . Every bullet from every gun. Each whipping. The sea of sweat that come from us. Every piece of coal in the Remade boilers and the boiler of the engine, each drop of come between my legs and my sisters' legs, all of it is in that train. . . . We unrolled history. We made history. We cast history in iron and the train shat it out behind it. Now we've ploughed that up. We'll go on, and we'll take our history with us. Remake. It's our wealth, it's everything, it's all we have. We'll take it" (*Iron Council* 260).

The renegades are not concerned with making a myth for others, so much as taking their own histories into their own hands, creating what amounts to a small-scale utopia in the wilderness. Their primary loyalties are to each other. When the train comes close to completing its decades-long circuit, approaching New Crobuzon, they are unwilling to turn back, not because of what it might mean to the strikers and insurrectionaries in New Crobuzon so much as what it might mean to them. To flee into the hills and become bandits would be to abandon the history that they have made for themselves.

This is what Judah does not and cannot understand. The Iron Councillors' ability to take their own history with them is more important to them than their broader historical role, the myth that Judah, as itinerant bard, has created around them. It is also more important than their continued survival. Thus Judah decides to "save" them from almost certain death at the hands of the New Crobuzon militia, by trapping them in time. Judah's golemetry is rather more than the ability to animate clay that his historical namesake, Rabbi Loew, had. It is a broader ability to shape and control impersonal forces. In his greatest work he creates a "time golem," a frozen moment to trap the Iron Council and preserve it motionless, unchanging, into a future age: "The perpetual train. The Iron Council itself. The renegade, returned, or returning and now waiting. Absolutely still. . . . The train, its moment indurate. It could not always clearly be seen. The crude rips in the temporal from which the golem was made gave it edges like facets, an opalescence of injured time. From some angles the train was hard to see, or hard to think of, or difficult to remember, instant to instant. But it was unmoving" (*Iron Council* 542).

This is both a preservation and a betrayal. It prevents the Iron Council from being destroyed by New Crobuzon, but it does so at the cost of taking the Iron Councillors' history away from them again, changing them from living, breathing people into an abstraction. As Ann-Hari says, just before she shoots Judah,

"We were never yours, Judah. We were something real, and we came in our time, and we made our decision and it was not yours. Whether we were right or wrong, it was our history. You were never our augur, Judah. Never our saviour" (*Iron Council* 552). As Yagharek's tribe might describe it, Judah is guilty of choice-theft. Yet in a broader sense, his intervention works. It creates a dynamic tension with the politics of the city, providing a vision of a messy but genuine utopia. From this tension will come new forms of resistance, and perhaps, one day, the revolution.

Iron Council thus provides us with a very different account of the relationship between the imagination and politics than that which prevails in either of the other New Crobuzon novels. It shows us a version of the fantastic imagination that is still in a relationship of tension with politics and with people's actual, lived solidarities. But in contrast to either *Perdido Street Station* or *The Scar,* the tension is a productive one. Like a novelist or a political thinker, Judah reimagines the world in ways that do not always bear faithful witness to the events or people that he begins with. He is not an inspirational leader so much as a grappler with abstract forces, but by virtue of his reimagining he can create the necessary conditions under which others can change the world. The Iron Council becomes a kind of material myth, which gives the lie to the claims of New Crobuzon's government that the political order it has created is something given, a part of the natural order, and that resistance will always be crushed ruthlessly and effectively.

Conclusion

Each of Miéville's three New Crobuzon novels deals with the relationship between politics and the fantastic imagination in a different way. In some ways their relationship to each other mirrors the logic of Hegelian dialectic—thesis, antithesis, synthesis. *Perdido Street Station* gives us a city in which the imagination seems to be ruthlessly and effectively subordinated to the political order—at best it is trammeled, at worst (Remaking) utterly corrupted. *The Scar* leaves the city for the boundless oceans, where it appears at first that there is free scope for the imagination to work without limits. In some ways this turns out to be even worse than direct tyranny. It is only in *Iron Council* that politics and the fantastic imagination stand in a healthy relationship toward each other, in which it is possible to reimagine politics, to see how things can be different, and to begin, perhaps, to change them.

It is the final book that gives us the necessary clues to figure out what Miéville is up to. He is Remaking the conjoined genres of fantasy and science fiction, not as an art form that is entirely subordinate to given power relationships, nor as a means of escape from them, but as a specifically *political* act of imagination. He is arguing that stories, if they are understood rightly, can allow us to reinterpret our circumstances and think through how to change them. The fantastic imagination is important because it is potentially political in the most profound sense—it can choose neither to reaffirm politics as they exist today nor to hide from them, but to challenge them. In *Iron Council* it can even create a radical break in history, revealing new possibilities of political action. Of course, Miéville is not claiming that writing—or reading—fantasy novels will bring about the revolution. Nor does he use fantasy to construct positive visions of what his ideal socialist society might look like. Instead, to borrow Russell Jacoby's term, he is a negative utopian—in Miéville's view, we may hope for utopia in our current circumstances and build toward it, but we cannot imagine what it would be like to live in it. The fantastic imagination does not so much lay out a path to utopia as it insists on the possibility that such paths might exist.

In *Iron Council* Miéville puts a famous passage from Marx's *German Ideology* into the mouth of his flawed, would-be prophet, Judah Low. It is an act of appropriation where Miéville suggests that Marx too was a fantasist in the positive sense of the word, someone who was willing to imagine that things could and must be different from how we experience them in the here and now. Just as Marx's somewhat hazily imagined communist utopia was powerful because it stood in violent tension with the world of nineteenth-century capitalism, so should fantasy (in both the narrower and broader definitions of the word) stand in a relationship of tension with the world we inhabit today. To make it otherwise, Miéville suggests, to divorce it from our world, is to rob it of its force.

Notes

1. Much earlier versions of some of the arguments and a few sentences in the conclusions are taken from Henry Farrell, "Fantasy Remade," *N+1 Online.* http://www.nplusonemag.com/mieville.html (accessed January 1, 2006).

2. One of these strains can be traced through British writers such as Mervyn Peake and M. John Harrison, both of whom have been important influences on the work discussed in this chapter. Another descends from Fritz Leiber's urban fantasies (especially his Lankhmar series).

3. See Moorcock 2004. The book's core criticisms of Tolkien are available online in the essay "Epic Pooh," available at *Revolution Science Fiction.* http://www.revolutionsf.com/article.html?id=953 (accessed January 2, 2007).

4. In the remainder of the essay I use the term *fantasy,* as does Miéville, to refer not only to the fantasy genre as it's usually conceived, but to the other subgenres grouped under the rubric of Weird Fiction and concerned with the creation of imaginary worlds and settings that deviate in some strong sense of the word from the world depicted in realist fiction.

5. Miéville also holds a Ph.D. in international relations from the London School of Economics and has written an academic monograph (based on his dissertation) on the sources and form of international law, but his academic work is less directly relevant to his fiction than are his political convictions.

6. Indeed, Miéville's arguments have a lot of common ground with the emphasis of Soviet dissidents such as Andrei Sinyavsky on grotesquery and phantasmagoria as alternatives to the intellectual hegemony of Socialist Realism.

7. To use Russell Jacoby's useful nomenclature, Miéville is an "iconoclastic utopian" rather than a "blueprint utopian." See Jacoby 2005.

8. The character who comes closest perhaps to reconciling the two is the Brucolac, a vampire who, in contrast to most vampires in fantasy novels, is not in the least infatuated with his own mystique. Instead, he views himself as a "bureaucrat not [a] predator" and has set up a system of tithes and interlocking loyalties to maintain his rule over the riding of Dry Falls. His role is not that of a traditional aristocrat but of an enlightened absolutist, who sees more clearly than any of the other characters what is necessary to ensure the continued survival of his polity.

Bibliography

Gordon, Joan. 2003. "Reveling in Genre: An Interview with China Miéville." *Science Fiction Studies* 30, no. 3:355–73.

Heinlein, Robert A. 1966. *The Moon Is a Harsh Mistress.* New York: Putnam.

Jacoby, Russell. 2005. *Picture Imperfect: Utopian Thought for an Anti-Utopian Age.* New York: Columbia University Press.

Le Guin, Ursula K. 1974. *The Dispossessed: An Ambiguous Utopia.* New York: Harper and Row.

Miéville, China. N.d. a. "China Miéville's Top 10 Weird Fiction." *Guardian.* http://books .guardian.co.uk/top10s/top10/0,,716474,00.html (accessed December 31, 2006).

———. N.d. b. "Debate." *China Miéville Offical Web Site.* http://web.archive.org/web/ 20050115043853/http://www.panmacmillan.com/features/china/debate.htm (accessed June 15, 2007).

———. 2000. *Perdido Street Station.* London: Pan (orig. published, London: Macmillan, 2000).

———. 2003. *The Scar.* London: Pan (orig. published, London: Macmillan, 2002).

———. 2004. *The Iron Council.* New York: Del Rey/Ballantine (orig. published, London: Macmillan, 2004).

———. 2005. "With One Bound We Are Free: Pulp, Fantasy and Revolution," *Crooked Timber,* January 11. http://crookedtimber.org/2005/01/11/with-one-bound-we-are-free -pulp-fantasy-and-revolution.

Moorcock, Michael. 2004. *Wizardry and Wild Romance: A Study of Epic Fantasy.* Austin, Tex.: Monkeybrain.

Pohl, Frederik. 1979. *Jem.* New York: St. Martin's Press.

Science Fiction, Fantasy, and Social Critique

Stephen R. Donaldson's Gap into Genre

Dennis Wilson Wise

Near the end of the *Chronicles of Thomas Covenant the Unbeliever,* when Covenant confronts Foul, he says, "Despite [i.e., evil] had no absolute reality of existence. . . . Lord Foul was only an externalized part of himself—not an immortal, not a god" (III: 462). Here is a clear expression of Stephen R. Donaldson's humanism. Evil is neither a universal nor an ontological given; rather, it is centered in the self, ineradicably part of our individuality by virtue of the simple fact that we are human. Yet tensions often exist in Donaldson's idea (some tensions more intentional than others), and his views on the nature of evil are no exception. While Donaldson portrays evil as being intrinsic to the self in his two high-fantasy Covenant trilogies, he turns around in his *Gap* sequence to show how evil is socially constructed. For example, when Warden Dios says of the rapist and murderer Angus Thermopyle that "we *created* him" (III: 271; emphasis in original), Donaldson is expressing that even Angus's crimes are caused by the circumstances around him rather than necessary facts arising from human nature itself. In this essay I argue that the tensions in Donaldson's conception of evil are amplified by the speculative fiction genre in which he chooses to express those ideas. High fantasy emphasizes a stable, centered self, independent of all context; the conflicts high fantasy depict are psychological ones given material form. As a result social critique is peripheral. Although Donaldson resolutely maintains his humanist leanings in his science fiction, this genre offers greater flexibility in showing how the individual is created by his or her own contexts. Science fiction's strength lies in the examination of societal, economic, and political matters in ways not open to high fantasy; as a result, not only is science fiction (especially Donaldson's) more open to a decentered and fragmented self, but it also allows greater opportunity for the subject to navigate the various contexts that shape it.

In Donaldson's first high-fantasy trilogy, *The Chronicles of Thomas Covenant the Unbeliever,* the author's views on evil as a social construction are unapparent. Thomas Covenant, a leper in the "real" world, is inexplicably transported to a completely insulated secondary world known as "the Land"—a world that may or may not be a dream for Covenant. Thus we are plunged into Covenant's own psyche. The Land is an externalization of Covenant's own interiority, an interiority that Donaldson believes makes sense independent of the real-world conditions that formed it. All information given on such conditions is merely backdrop for Covenant's detailed psychodrama in the Land. Covenant is the ultimate given: he struggles with the abstract principles of good and evil contained in the unity of his own consciousness. Hence Lord Foul, an incarnation of evil, is neither immortal nor god but only an aspect of Covenant himself. In this way, by reducing away real-world phenomena and delving into what is unrepresentable in Covenant's own mind, Donaldson creates for his protagonist a sphere of negative freedom in which Covenant can make free choices without determinations from contexts outside the self. This modernist twist forms the core of Donaldson's humanism—meaning lies within the individual, who has the power and responsibility to shape his or her own destiny. Interestingly Michael Moorcock (discussing the origins of fantasy in the genre of romance) has this to say: "The romance's prime concern is not with character or narrative but with the evocation of strong, powerful images; symbols conjuring up a multitude of sensations to be used . . . as escape from the pressures of the objective world or as a means of achieving increased self-awareness" (17). High fantasy needs these images because it has little else; the only mimesis is one of interiority. This is its strength.

Brian Aldiss hints at a similar idea when he points out that "there are no banks in faerie" and that "palaces are never mortgaged" (277). Most high fantasy operates on a medieval worldview, politics, and economy—this worldview is often idealized over and against conditions in the modern world. The natural beauty of the Land is a balm for the alienation in Covenant's modern soul; part of what makes the *Chronicles* so vivid is the interconnectedness of health, nature, and society. Given this idealization, high fantasy such as the first *Chronicles* depicts a social order it supports rather than critiques. Whereas the usual fantasy quest supports a return to the status quo, a critique of society is supposed to lead anywhere but back to the status quo. When Franz Rottensteiner says that fantasy is a throwback to times that are no longer possible, written by writers such as J. R. R. Tolkien, C. S. Lewis, E. R. Eddison, Lord Dunsany (Edward J. M. D. Plunkett), and William Morris who are "deeply dissatisfied with the modern world," he does not mean to be complimentary. High fantasy, in his view, is a false revolt because it advocates no real change and is only "a passing fad" (2244). Whether this is unfair to high fantasy or not, certainly Donaldson's major concern in the first *Chronicles* is Covenant's ability to create a balance between the evil of Lord Foul and the goodness of the Land. The Land, its institutions, and its people are wholly and unambiguously good because the narrative requires that they counterbalance the archetypal evil represented by Lord Foul. C. N. Manlove states that fantasists "see the modern world in terms of loss of contact between man and nature which it is the business of the fantastic world to counter" (11), and this accords perfectly with Donaldson's method. He must idealize the Land in order to complete Covenant's inner transformation.

W. A. Senior notes a naturalistic flavor to the first *Chronicles*—a hint of vast social forces conspiring against Covenant, who must struggle against the law of leprosy (27). Yet this hint is only a hint—a perceptive sign, perhaps, of the focus of Donaldson's later works but in itself not significant. Themes of those vast social forces are marginalized; they spur the narrative into motion but are then subsequently dismissed. The leper hero must learn to live with himself before he can analyze the social forces that drive him into his isolation. Ultimately the first *Chronicles* offers no real social critique, except perhaps for a reexamination of theological conceptions of disease and sin, and the trilogy remains primarily what John Clute calls it: "the massively detailed story of one soul in Gothic anguish" (272).

The Second Chronicles of Thomas Covenant opens up the possibility for social analysis in greater detail, but even this, as we shall see, is restricted by high fantasy's reliance of archetypes. Whereas the first *Chronicles* responded to evil by the brute force of Covenant's white magic, the only possible response to evil in the second *Chronicles* utilizes the righting of misguided views and subversive ideologies. The Sunbane has plunged the Land into environmental desecration, corrupting "natural law" and making of nature a thing of horror. Seasons and climate are nonexistent. To prevent rebellion against this order, the local political power—known as the Clave—use religious beliefs to turn the people of the Land toward quietism. They teach the Stonedowners to believe that Earth is a place of punishment for the sins of their forefathers. A "Master" created the Land in punishment for his wife's perfidy: she succumbed to a-Jeroth's blandishments, and thus her descendants must bear the price. Among the atrocities justified by this "original sin" are human sacrifice and the letting of blood. Covenant knows this mythology is inaccurate, since he had experienced the Land's natural goodness and wholesomeness thirty-five hundred years earlier; yet, he can persuade only a few people of the truth. False mythology has too deeply pervaded social mores to be changed by one ambiguous prophet. Having lost their heritage and cultural foundations, the people of the Land have also lost their sense of self. Just as Covenant's leprosy has cut him off from his cultural foundations in the first trilogy, the Clave has cut the Stonedowners' from their cultural foundations in the second. They lack the knowledge to resist the imminent environmental apocalypse and the perfidious political and religious ideologies that allow the maintenance of abhorrent social institutions such as human sacrifice—and these institutions, in turn, serve the interests of the few in power over the interests of the many.

Evil, it seems, is not then a simple ineradicable aspect of the self. Although Ridjeck Thome and Foul's Creche symbolize the self's darkest corners in the first trilogy, these symbols cannot sufficiently capture the ills of an entire society. Thus the vision of evil in the second *Chronicles* splinters; a postmodern world is represented, where confusion marks the struggle for good and where no one solution or cure is available (Senior 194). Whereas the first trilogy is a psychodrama dealing with Covenant's ability to handle guilt and responsibility, the second trilogy, by pinpointing the ills of an entire society, examines evils that transcend the ability of the individual to handle.

Yet while Donaldson envisions the corruption of history, culture, and mythology by the Clave as a source of evil, this vision is simultaneously undermined by the introduction of Linden Avery. Initially she denies the principle of evil in human nature. On her view evil is a synonym for ignorance and disease. Thus that evil is a social byproduct is agreeable to her—it becomes easily adaptable to an analogy with disease: "Some infections have to be cut out," she says (II: 9). The problem of evil is relatively straightforward: disseminate knowledge and create better institutions. Ignorance causes evil, not the self. Evil is wholly extrinsic.

This view enables Linden to face the fact of Covenant's leprosy without fear, but Donaldson nonetheless carefully shows that Linden's denial of intrinsic evil is a defense against the guilt imposed on her by her parents. Gibbon-Raver brings this denial to Linden's attention when he asks, "Are you not evil?" (IV: 268). Desiring the power of life and death over others, Linden cannot thereafter deny her innate capacity for murder. When Linden later discards (or at least modifies) the evil-as-disease belief when confronted with things that seem evil in themselves, such as the self's desire for the power of possession, Donaldson reaffirms that evil is intrinsic to humanity. No other explanation can be given for the unadulterated malice of Gibbon-Raver: as an incarnation of evil, timeless and immutable, Gibbon-Raver (like Lord Foul) cannot be viewed in sociological terms. By this reliance on an archetype, fantasy allows Donaldson to explore a fixed, stable human nature at the expense of the way in which the individual is socially constructed.

Only with Donaldson's science fiction *Gap* sequence can he go beyond high fantasy's ontological givens of good and evil. The *Gap* universe is not a wholly self-contained secondary world; social critique is not radically undermined by the idealization of a past social order or weakened by social critique through analogy. Rather, Donaldson's science fiction sequence is an extrapolation from the world of today. It plots a believable course of events from currently held or currently plausible social, economic, and political conditions. Thus the *Gap* sequence traces internationalism, corporate power, and the potential failures of the welfare system in connection to the ideological ramifications of encountering an unknowable alien species such as the Amnion. Using a technique similar to that of John Steinbeck in *The Grapes of Wrath,* Donaldson intersperses his narrative with "Ancillary Documents." These chapters give the world of his characters context; they explain the social and political conditions that create the situations his characters are reacting to. This influences how we perceive his characters in a way entirely different from his high-fantasy fiction.

The history of the United Mining Companies (UMC), as explained in one of the ancillary documents, is one of economics and personal charisma. Before the invention of the Gap Drive, Earth "was in a period of political and economic stagnation; a period of atrophy so profound that more than a few analysts concluded the planet had exhausted not only its resources but its ability to solve problems. One hundred fifty or so sovereign nations had become so interdependent that warfare was no longer viable as a means of economic and political revitalization. . . . the inhabitants of the planet were being killed by precisely the same thing [internationality] that kept them alive" (III: 113).

The development of space travel (the gap drive) catalyzed economic growth, enabling big business (corporate power) to overshadow the democratic political power of the Governing Council of Earth and Space (GCES). Following a historical progression eerily similar to the British East India Company, the UMC created a private army called the UMCP to protect its financial interests. Gradually, with business growing stronger than elected government, power is shifted into the hands Holt Fasner, CEO of the UMC. Additionally, following a common science fiction theme, greater scientific achievements lead to ethical concerns over the use of that science. The "possession" induced by zone implants designed to combat a rare sickness caused by crossing the Gap is one example; this increases the power of governing bodies such as the UMC at the expense of the individual and individual rights. Alongside this economic history enters the personal charisma of Fasner and his director of the UMCP, Warden Dios. The former's ambition is offset by the latter's idealism; their relationship is what adds a human element to the economic and political history of the *Gap* universe. Thus the universe of the Gap is a deft combination of dialectal materialism and a humanist conception of history as made by great men: "any useful study of the United Mining Companies had to take into account both the public and the private histories; had to confront the almost paradoxical intersection between economic muscle . . . and personal power" (154).

Piracy flourishes in the *Gap* universe because government law prohibits certain markets to nonprivileged individuals. Angus Thermopyle is one such "illegal." Marginalized by society, his hatred of the dominant discourses of law, order, and moral rightness define him. Most of all he loathes the UMCP, the one symbol of absolute authority throughout human space. He sees it as existing for its own sake, its ideal of "protecting humanity" merely a facade for keeping its moneyed interests in power. Despite the horrific nature of Angus's personal crimes, his grudge is shared by many illegals in the narrative: Nick Succorso, Vector Shaheed, Mika Vascyk. Few survival options are open to the characters living on the margins of Gap society except rebellion against UMCP-imposed order. In this sense the grossly unequal power relationship between government and individual—based on the organized violence of imposed law—perpetuates opposition to that government. Angus's fear of tyrannical authority "taught him to hate—and hate gave him strength. He hated Warden Dios; hated everything the UMCP director stood for. He hated cops and law-abiding citizens; hated romantics and idealists. He hated them because they had always hated him" (II: 451). Similar disillusionment turns the brilliant geneticist Vector Shaheed to an illegal's life. Having invented a drug that would greatly reduce humanity's risk from the Amnion, the UMCP quickly suppresses the drug. (Donaldson later reveals that this is for corrupt political reasons.) Vector's "outraged idealism" (II: 425) leads to his defection from the power structure that had formerly privileged him.

Yet Angus's criminality is more than the simple result of corrupt politics: his life might have been different had he not been simultaneously victimized by inadequate social institutions. "Guttergangs" arose in response to the disparity of wealth in Donaldson's future Earth—a "product of modern mechanization and urbanization." Educational systems, overtaxed community services, transitional lifestyles, the erosion of the family's stability, fiscal polices designed to help the few over the many (III: 393)—here we have a catalog of social problems affecting America today and extrapolated into Donaldson's science fiction universe. Much like gangs of today, the guttergangs recruited youths whose social circumstances gave them no real life options. In the Gap's Earth, guttergangs are a destabilizing force because "they wrested their survival from the same crumbling infrastructure which had created the conditions for their existence—thereby, of course, hastening the decline of that infrastructure; worsening the state of people who lived within rather than against Earth's social compacts; encouraging the growth of more guttergangs" (III: 393). Although Donaldson spends the first three novels of the sequence by depicting the horror of Angus's crimes, he slowly attempts to mitigate the reader's abhorrence of Angus by showing how he had been forged by the same decadent social infrastructure that created the guttergangs. His mother, having been born to a pair of teenage guttergang kids in one of Earth's "dying urban centers," was used by them as a leverage tool to exact more welfare money from the state. When another guttergang kills her own parents, Angus's mother becomes plunder "like other women in other corrupt wars" (IV: 112). This new gang rapes and abuses her repeatedly over time, keeping her alive for much the same reason her real parents had—as a connection to the welfare system. In this way the guttergang—itself a consequence of overextended resources—thrived parasitically on the social structure. "The bureaucracy supplied no hope: all its other benefits were taken by the guttergang" (IV: 113). This cycle of abuse slowly drives Angus's mother insane. As a means of exerting the only power available to her, she tortures his newborn bastard son, Angus. The effect of this on the adult Angus is telling. He strives "with a kind of bleak and absolute stubbornness . . . to replicate on someone else his mother's look of degraded desperation" (IV: 113). Crime therefore perpetuates itself. Angus is merely a link in a long chain of social victimization. This victimization is institutional in the sense that society can no longer effectively manage the inequalities inherent in it.

Strangely enough, just as environment is a determining influence on Angus, so is it a determining influence on Warden Dios. "One of those rare men who had become an idealist through experience with its opposite" (III: 153), Dios grew up an orphan in one of Earth's "more toxic cities" (III: 153), experiencing firsthand the guttergangs and social infrastructure that so shaped Angus Thermopyle. As Dios recognizes the inadequacy of the system, he comes to believe that only law, order, and institutions can prevent increasing societal decay. His idealism did not leap spontaneously out of the heart of his being; instead, it developed out of the circumstances in which he finds himself. Thus Dios began to "crave the food of lawful power" (III: 155).

Power does not exist without moral valuation in such a view; if such power did exist, it would lead to conditions such as those that exist on Donaldson's future Earth. Power is here either legitimate or illegitimate. A legitimate power requires its holder to subsume himself under moral laws. Dios views such laws as being logically necessary given the desirability of a legitimate social order, as opposed to being necessary because derived from principles of good and evil inherent in human nature itself. An illegitimate power—demonstrated by Fasner's power in human space and Angus's power over his victims—is arbitrary, exercised without reference to such moral laws.

High fantasy would have emphasized how this notion of legitimate power bore some intricate relation to human nature or to some ontological given existing in the world. Science fiction allows Donaldson an expression of his thought that radically complicates this notion. While the *Chronicles* views legitimate power as restorative of the natural order and world, it cannot historicize the notion itself. Relying on archetypes, high fantasy as a genre simply does not have the tools. Good and evil do not have the same ontological status in science fiction as they do in fantasy. The contingency of circumstance in the *Gap* universe, however, is characteristic of science fiction. There is no teleology, no hint that Fasner's autocratic rule is unnatural as well as illegitimate. The order Dios seeks to create is not divinely inspired; it depends purely on the capacity for individuals to devise and maintain it. The universe would not cry out in rage should Holt Fasner emerge triumphant, as would be the case with Foul. Fasner's victory would not destroy natural law or turn Earth into a leper—it would outrage Donaldson's idealism and nothing more. Foul is an archetype, Fasner a human being.

Indeed, whereas Lord Foul is an incarnation of pure evil, a plausible case could be built in favor of Fasner's utilitarian aims. The *Gap* novels repeatedly make the claim that it is uncertain whether humanity would win an all-out war with the Amnion. Although humanity has superior production methods, the Amnion possesses superior technology. Fasner believes that, given that "Amnion genetic imperatives were steadier and more relentless than almost any amount of human political will" (V: 535), humanity has little hope of ever vanquishing the Amnion—at least, humanity as it has evolved naturally. If Amnioni science could be applied to humans, giving the most potent minds and personalities practical immortality, then "humankind's innate talents for treachery and mass production" would enable them to overwhelm the Amnion and survive (V: 537). In this context Fasner's vision seems to have a greater chance of success than the inflexible idealism of Min Donner and Morn Hyland. Even the "flexible" idealism of Warden Dios seems more fraught with risk than Fasner's. Donaldson's horror is reserved for the technological tampering with "facts" of human existence, such as the inevitability of death or the sacredness of our DNA. He blithely assumes his reader shares his horror, but this is a large assumption. Fasner is not Lord Foul, his status as terrible not as clear-cut.

The *Gap* sequence offers no specific call for social reform; Donaldson has frequently stated in interviews that he does not consider himself to be a "polemical" writer. But for a writer whose major themes and ideas have remained remarkably consistent through a long and extraordinary career, the tension in Donaldson's conceptions of evil offers an illuminating case study of how genre shapes the expression of those conceptions. Evil is contingent in his *Gap* sequence, necessary in both *Chronicles*. On one hand the high-fantasy tradition allows Donaldson to explore Covenant's stable, unified consciousness without reference to the real-world conditions that have shaped him; the principles of good and evil against which Covenant struggles are facts of human nature itself. The science fiction tradition, on the other hand, already more eclectic than the high-fantasy tradition, offers Donaldson a greater chance to examine the role society plays in the production of the individual. The Gap universe is neither self-contained nor idealized; it extrapolates from present conditions. Although Donaldson remains adamant in his avowal of individualism, humanism, free will, and existentialist responsibility, he utilizes the strength of science fiction to good effect. Despite the tension this creates with his other ideas, Donaldson deserves great credit for daring the hobgoblin of small minds. It is this ability to push the boundaries of fantasy and science fiction to their uttermost limits, to write masterful epics in both genres, to examine powerful ideas though powerful narratives and fascinating characters that makes Stephen R. Donaldson one of our most important speculative fiction writers today.

Bibliography

Primary

The Chronicles of Thomas Covenant the Unbeliever

Donaldson, Stephen R. *Lord Foul's Bane*. New York: Del Rey / Ballantine, 1977.

———. *The Ill-Earth War*. New York: Del Rey / Ballantine, 1977.

———. *The Power that Preserves*. New York: Del Rey / Ballantine, 1977.

The Second Chronicles of Thomas Covenant

Donaldson, Stephen R. *The Wounded Land.* New York: Del Rey / Ballantine, 1980.
————. *The One Tree.* New York: Del Rey / Ballantine, 1982.
————. *White-Gold Wielder.* New York: Del Rey / Ballantine, 1983.

The Gap

Donaldson, Stephen R. *The Real Story.* New York: Bantam, 1992.
————. *Forbidden Knowledge.* New York: Bantam, 1992.
————. *A Dark and Hungry God Arises.* New York: Bantam, 1993.
————. *Chaos and Order.* New York: Bantam, 1995.
————. *This Day All Gods Die.* New York: Bantam, 1997.

Secondary

Aldiss, Brian W. Review of W.A. Senior's *Stephen R. Donaldson's Chronicles of Thomas Covenant: Variations on the Fantasy Tradition. Extrapolation* 37 (Fall 1996): 274–77.
Clute, Johm. "The Chronicles of Thomas Covenant the Unbeliever and the Second Chronicles," in *Survey of Modern Fantasy Literature,* 5 vols., edited by Frank N. Magill, 1:266–74. Englewood Cliffs, N.J.: Salem Press, 1983.
Manlove, C.N. *Science Fiction: Ten Explorations.* Kent, Ohio: Kent State University Press, 1986.
Rottensteiner, Franz. "European Theories of Fantasy," in *Survey of Modern Fantasy Literature,* 5 vols., edited by Magill, 5:2235–46. Englewood Cliffs, N.J.: Salem Press, 1983.
Senior, W. A. *Stephen R. Donaldson's Chronicles of Thomas Covenant: Variations on the Fantasy Tradition.* Kent, Ohio: Kent State University Press, 1995.

Politics, Multiplicity, and Mythical Time in the Oeuvre of Philip K. Dick

Sándor Klapcsik

Science fiction introduces two highly different approaches toward the concept of history, based on either teleological temporality or multiple time lines. Several texts presume time with a final point of perfection or mayhem: the peak or nadir of technological, political, and social development. Utopian and dystopian views are significant characteristic of science fiction: Hoda M. Zaki, analyzing Nebula Award–winning novels between 1965 and 1982, finds utopian elements in almost each story (1988, 51). The relationship of the two genres goes back centuries; Northrop Frye, analyzing early representatives of utopias, distinguishes an ethical and a technological subgenre and characterizes the latter as the forerunning corpus of science fiction. He argues that "most utopia writers follow either More (and Plato) in stressing the legal structure of their societies, or Bacon [and his *New Atlantis*] in stressing its technological power. The former type of utopia is closer to actual social and political theory; the latter overlaps with what is now called science fiction" (1966, 17–28).

Another frequently recurring theme in science fiction is apocalypse, which is defined by Martin Griffiths as "human destruction through various means" (2002, 39). The "various means" can indicate a nuclear catastrophe, war, alien invasion, famine, plagues, and fires. Apocalypse, as Donald E. Morse argues, also demonstrates teleological view in the genre: "Apocalypse requires, by definition, that time be viewed as finite, linear, and directional. If time were to continue into infinity, then there could be no Last Things, no Last Judgement, obviously no End of the World, and certainly no 'Rapture.' To be credible, therefore, Apocalypse depends upon time being finite. Time must also be linear rather than an unending circle, spiral, or whatever. Time's arrow thus becomes a string of unique events between the two fixed points of creation and termination" (2002, 35).

A different approach is adopted by alternate history, a subgenre that often focuses on multiple time lines and thus contradicts the idea of teleological history. As Andy Duncan argues, certain alternate histories "presume that more than one 'parallel world' with divergent history can coexist, so that characters can purposefully or accidentally travel, or 'timeslip,' from one timeline to another, like a commuter switching trains" (2003, 114).

Alternate histories with multiple time lines recapitulate postmodern theories of historicity. Linda Hutcheon emphasizes the urge to rewrite history in historiographic metafiction, that is, the "postmodern concern for the multiplicity and dispersion of truth(s), truth(s) relative to the specificity of place and culture" (1988, 108). Hayden White suggests that historical thinking necessarily conceals multiple plots, as "unless at least two versions of the same set of events can be imagined, there is no reason for the historian to take upon himself the authority of giving the true account of what really happened" (1980, 13). Certain postmodern views assume that even "realistic" histories are covert versions of alternate histories.

In Philip K. Dick's oeuvre, both the teleological and the multiple time lines come into view. His fictional universes comprise dystopian political and social situations ("Minority Report," "The Faith of Our Fathers") and short glimpses of suburban utopia (*Time out of Joint, The Man Who Japed*), as well as apocalyptic and postapocalyptic scenes (*Valis,* "Second Variety," "The Golden Man," *Do Androids Dream of Electric Sheep?*). Dick, however, also draws on the idea of alternate history ("The Commuter," *The Man in the High Castle*), interweaving it with the phenomenon of simulacra, "fake" universes (*Time out of Joint,* "Small Town," *The Three Stigmata of Palmer Eldritch, Ubik*). His characters experience not only utopian, dystopian, and apocalyptic time, but multiple time lines as well that at certain points correlate. Laura Campbell (based on an analysis of narration and storylines in *The Man in the High Castle*) confirms that "Dickian time" is a combination of teleological and alternative time lines: Dick "takes the usual Western linear view that one event moves into another and combines it with the Taoist idea of synchronicity, in which any part of the whole effects all of the whole" (1992, 198).

Dick's early novels, such as *Time out of Joint* (1959) and *The Man Who Japed* (1956), demonstrate teleological time, although they occasionally surpass teleology by evoking fake universes and parallel time tracks. His novels in the 1960s, such as *The Three Stigmata of Palmer Eldritch* (1964) and *Ubik* (1969), manifest multiple time lines: as Darko Suvin argues, there is a shift in his prose of the 1960s from political and social to ontological concerns (1975, 12). Texts written in his central or "peak" period describe numerous time lines that eventually construct webs or mazes for the characters, having an impact on Ursula K. Le Guin's *The Lathe of Heaven* (1971).[1] Dick's late novel *Valis* (1981) and 1978 speech "How to Build a Universe That Doesn't Fall Apart Two Days Later," however, indicate a mythical temporality, a mystical and Gnostic (thus less postmodern) approach to history, that is, a philosophy demonstrating the rebirth or eternity of the apostolic era.

Politics and the End of Time in Dick's Early Works

As Patricia S. Warrick argues, "the fiction of Dick's first period, the 1950s, is primarily short fiction; its tone is dystopian as it explores the horrors of paranoid militarism, totalitarianism, and the manipulation of people through mass media" (1983, 192). Dick follows his age when drawing on these ideas: fears of the final war and nuclear catastrophe frequently encouraged science fiction authors to warn their society and utilize dystopian and apocalyptic elements.

Apocalypse does not only indicate the end of human life on Earth, but also the beginning of a new reign: "the eventual rule of the elect with God" (Griffiths 2002, 35), originally, or that of mutant species or aliens in science fiction. In "The Golden Man" (1954), for example, the theory of evolution and the idea of apocalypse are interwoven. The story is about the future coup d'état of a new, mutant human race that emerges on the contaminated Earth after a nuclear war: a predator species whose means for survival is its beauty and attractiveness to women. Both "Imposter" (1953) and "War Game" (1959) are about the subtle tactics of aliens demolishing or invading Earth.

The theme of alien invasion as a significant apocalyptic element in science fiction and in his own short stories encouraged Dick to write a parody of the phenomenon. The narrator of "The Eyes Have It" (1953), reading a sentimental novel, interprets the figurative terms literally and the characters as aliens who can detach their body organs and limbs at will and live undercover on Earth.

Dick's early novels frequently evoke utopian views as well.[2] *Time out of Joint* and *The Man Who Japed* can be read as reciprocal versions of each other: while the former starts with a suburban utopia and turns into a postapocalyptic, dystopian state in the middle of a nuclear war, the latter begins with a setting of totalitarian dictatorship and provides only a short glimpse of an ideal suburban neighborhood.

The central character of *The Man Who Japed* is Allen Purcell, the head of an agency whose job is to invent stories with morals (the so-called Morec) of the age (the year 2114). He receives an offer of promotion to be the director of the bureau that controls the media of the whole state—a dystopian state that is the successor of the United States after an apocalyptic war or economic crisis. The reader gets to know only a few bits of information about the crash, such as that Japan has been irrevocably devastated, most probably by attacks similar to the ones against Hiroshima and Nagasaki in 1945. "The island had been saturated during the war, bombed and bathed and doctored and infested with every possible kind of toxic and lethal substance. Moral Reclamation was useless, let alone gross physical rebuilding. Hokkaido was as sterile and dead as it had been in 1972, the final year of the war" (6).

The story gets back to the apocalypse when the Purcells visit a museum with a "twentieth century exhibit." A reconstructed model of the former consumer society is displayed: "An entire white-stucco house had been painstakingly reconstructed, with sidewalk and lawn, garage and parked Ford. The house was complete with furniture, robot manikins, hot food on the table, scented water in the bathtub" (61). It is a perfect model of a happy family, a replica similar to the toy house in "The Days of Perky Pat" (1963). Similarly to that short story, it is only the simulacrum that exists after the apocalypse—the original has vanished for good. The exhibition, however, has a second scene: when one pushes a button, the model turns into ruins, reflecting the terminating point of civilization and thus depicting an apocalyptic scene. The novel, at this point, can be read as a mise en scène: the museum exhibition, just like apocalyptic and dystopian literature, is a didactic work of art that reminds the audience of their sinful and wasteful lifestyle and warns about the possible consequences of their behavior. "HOW THEY LIVED," says the sign above the first, preapocalyptic scene of the exhibition, followed by the postapocalyptic scene.

> An ugly cloud of smoke rolled up, obscuring the house. Its lights
> dimmed, turned dull red, and dried up. The exhibit trembled, and, to
> the spectators, a rumble came, the lazy tremor of a subterranean wind.
> When the smoke departed, the house was gone. All that remained of
> the exhibit was an expanse of broken bones. . . .
> Over this hemisphere of the exhibit the sign concluded: AND DIED. (63)

The capital of the postapocalyptic and dystopian state is "Newer York," whose name indicates that the regime intends to base its power by creating a new language, inventing new names for everyday things. As Dick himself argues in his essay "How to Build a Universe That Doesn't Fall Apart Two Days Later": "The basic tool for the manipulation of reality is the manipulation of words. If you can control the meaning of words, you can control the people who must use the words. George Orwell made this clear in his novel *1984*" (1988, 15). Another example of the future language is the term *omphalos,* a Greek term meaning "navel," which is often used by the characters to indicate the center of a system or the thrust of an idea.

Purcell hesitates to accept the promotion because his unconscious recently made him "jape," that is, vandalize in a parodying manner the statue of a founder of the postwar country.[3] Purcell contacts a psychiatrist called Malparto, who turns out to be a "maniac" collecting people with precognition and other paranormal skills. He believes that his client is a mutant who can alter space and time dimensions, and trying to convince his patient about his special skills, he forges a hallucinatory experience of a parallel universe. Suddenly Purcell appears with a different name in a definitely more beautiful and easygoing city than his own. It is a country with perfect, probably free air transportation (while in "Newer York" vehicles move slowly even during a "car chase" scene), naked women (opposite to the puritan morals of the Morec), and suburban happiness where the biggest concern is shopping and marital quarrels about promiscuity. The character reflects on the opposites he has gone through: "Two sides of the coin: Morec is all work and you're the badminton and checkers set. Together you form a society; you uphold and support each other." His decision, however, is to reject utopia: "But I'm not going to lie around watching girls sun-bathe. Like a salesman on vacation" (102).

A surprising element of *The Man Who Japed* is that the utopian state is only disguised as a parallel universe or simulacrum. It turns out to be real, a community de facto existing in another planet outside the totalitarian Earth. I agree with Andrew Butler, therefore, when he argues that it is a "pleasantly uncanny" moment of the book (2000, 14): the reality of a seemingly virtual scene shocks a reader who is familiar with Dick's fiction and the frequency of fake realms in his oeuvre. It is slightly misleading, though, when Butler claims that the ideal state "is quickly revealed to be fake" (23). It is rather quickly revealed to be "faking the fake." Dick's interpretation of his own works in "How to Build a Universe" is most revealing again: "In my writing I got so interested in fakes that I finally came up with the concept of fake fakes. For example, in Disneyland there are fake birds worked by electric motors which emit caws and shrieks as you pass by them. Suppose some night all of us sneaked into the park with real birds and substituted them for the artificial ones. Imagine the horror the Disneyland officials would feel when they discovered the cruel hoax. Real birds! And perhaps someday even real hippos and lions. Consternation. The park being cunningly transmuted from the unreal to the real, by sinister forces" (13–14).

The Man Who Japed becomes once again the parodic inversion of *Time out of Joint,* since the illusion-making efforts operate in different directions. While in the former suburban happiness is reality that a certain character tries to disguise as a simulacrum, in the latter suburban utopia is a fake universe that certain characters intend to masquerade as real.

Time out of Joint has received more attention by critics than the *The Man Who Japed;* Fredric Jameson, for example, analyzes the novel in his often-quoted book *Postmodernism, or, The Cultural Logic of Late Capitalism.* He reads the novel as a text that subverts historical sense; science fiction as such, he claims, often eludes or undermines the historical thinking of modernity. Citing Georg Lukács, Jameson argues that the historical novel in the nineteenth century represented the philosophy of the middle class; the bourgeoisie intended to create a new worldview, a historical sense with progress in order to establish their recently gained authority. Science fiction, however, reflects our postmodern age, in which "we no longer tell ourselves our history in that fashion . . . because we no longer experience it that way, and indeed, perhaps no longer experience it at all" (1991, 183–84). Science fiction and the historical novel have an inverse relationship, as "if the historical novel 'corresponded' to the emergence of historicity, of a sense of history in its strong modern post-eighteenth-century sense, science fiction equally corresponds to the waning or the blockage of that historicity, and particularly in our own time (in the postmodern era), to its crisis and paralysis, its enfeeblement and repression" (284). *Time out of Joint* thus indicates a contemporary issue, the postmodern lack of belief in a tangible history: historical sense vanishes or at least irrevocably gets absorbed in mediating corpuses such as popular culture.

Dick's novel is set in 1950s America; as Jameson puts it in *Postmodernism,* the text presents "a small town Utopia very much in the North American frontier tradition" (283). The suburban utopia turns out to be a hallucination, a more or less successfully reconstructed time created by the dreams and fantasies of the central character, Ragle Gumm, and by other characters who intend to maintain the simulacra with various (but hardly detailed) masquerading devices. Gumm lives in the late 1990s, when a nuclear war, a "civil war" between the inhabitants of Earth and those of the moon, devastates the world. He gets exhausted by the war so much that he dreams another "reality," a reality constructed by his childhood memories of small-town happiness.

Many critics highlight realism in the novel; Jameson, for example, argues that the "high culture" of the 1950s ignored the problems of its own age: "indeed, of the great writers of the period, only Dick himself comes into mind as the virtual poet laureate of this material: of squabbling couples and marital dramas, of petit bourgeois shopkeepers, neighborhoods, and afternoons in front of television, and all the rest" (280). Umberto Rossi, whose excellent criticism argues for the importance of language, words, and "logos" in the novel, rather stresses Dick's social criticism. He claims that the world of the mainstream adult family, the Nielsons, is undermined by a non-adult family into which Gumm belongs. The childish characters represent a counterculture resistance against the mainstream consumerist culture, and the fake nature of the suburban utopia reveals the unreality of utopia in the 1950s (1996, 197).

Besides small-town happiness, Rossi finds another utopian element in the book, arguing that "Ragle can reach the world of Utopia (the Moon), traveling on one of the symbols of SF, a starship" (208). Rossi, however, is aware of the possible doubts concerning his own interpretation, so he adds that "many elements of the loonies' utopic community could nonetheless be questioned" and emphasizes "the creed of a forever expanding civilization" in the novel (208). Settlements in space are rather repetitions of communities on Earth, multiplication and expansion of humanity, not an ideal state with isolation and happiness. In other words the settlements of the moon represent the second type of Baudrillard's simulacra (while utopias belong to the first): "Classical science fiction was that of an expanding universe, besides, it forged its path in the narratives of spatial exploration, counterparts to the more terrestrial forms of exploration and colonization of the nineteenth and twentieth centuries" (Baudrillard 2000, 123).[4]

My reading underlines that, as Dick does not depict but slightly alters the reality of the 1950s, he creates a pseudo-realistic novel. It soon becomes clear that it is not exactly the 1950s that comes into view. For example, Marilyn Monroe is unknown, since her life and fame did not fit into the simulacra. Also, people do not listen to the radio any more. Despite these examples, this world has characteristics similar to the "real" 1950s, such as the constant fear of a nuclear war or catastrophe, the lure of consumerism, and the beginnings of "the society of the spectacle." Television is the center of everyday life, advertisements on TV are louder than the programs, and the character, Ragle Gumm, when he dreams about and relives his childhood gets completely lost in a supermarket that becomes a symbol of the border zone between reality and dreamworld: "He looked around him and saw that he was in the pharmacy department. Among the tubes of toothpaste and magazines and sunglasses and jars of hand lotion. But I was in the food part, he thought with surprise. Where the samples of food are, the free food. Are there free samples of gum and candy here? That would be okay" (170).

It is possible to characterize the novel as alternate history. The novel makes it clear that *the* 1950s does not exist. There is *a* 1950s that is the result of (re)construction: not something that is existent in its own right but a manmade structure created by authority figures and maintained by fantasies of average men. *Time out of Joint* can also be interpreted as a self-reflexive text, a postmodern historical novel that overtly manifests the artificiality of a certain period and thus indicates the constructed nature of itself. As Jameson puts it, "the fifties is a thing, but a thing that we can build, just as the science fiction writer builds his own small-scale model" (1991, 185). In other words *Time out of Joint* is a pseudo-utopian, pseudo-realistic novel, an alternate history that indicates the artificial nature of a decade and questions our traditional views on temporality and history writing.

The Decline of Politics: Multiplicity in *The Lathe of Heaven* and *The Three Stigmata of Palmer Eldritch*

Fredric Jameson distrusts both linear- and circular-time views of utopia and apocalypse, emphasizing their mythical and fantastic nature. In his essay "Progress versus Utopia; or, Can We Imagine the Future?," he describes a paradox concerning the significance and decline of utopian ideas in science fiction. He argues that the function of utopia is "to bring home . . . our constitutional inability to imagine utopia itself" (153).

Entertaining texts such as science fiction stories cannot maintain the belief in overt utopias because the reader quickly gets bored with the detailed description of an ideal state without negativity. The static nature of utopias is also contradicted by science fiction. Perfect realms are necessarily out of the flow of progress and evolution, while most science fiction texts are based on the idea of change and development, assuming linear time, a progress to infinity. As Edward James points out, "it is not just that sf authors are wedded to change, but that utopia is rejected in favour of continued struggle and progress" (2003, 122).

Science fiction therefore both utilizes and rejects the idea of utopias. Utopian texts often become "auto-referential discourses" (Jameson 1982, 156) as they describe the inability to create, or at least to maintain, a stable, perfect realm. H. G. Wells's *A Modern Utopia* (1905) is an early example of this phenomenon, a text accepting and revealing its own limitations. Jameson analyzes Ursula K. Le Guin's *The Lathe of Heaven* (1971), interpreting the novel as a text that undermines the idea of utopias by describing parallel universes. The attempts to create a utopia remain unsuccessful, as "reality is a seamless web: change one detail and unexpected, sometimes monstrous transformations occur in other apparently unrelated zones of life, as in the classical time-travel stories where one contemporary artefact, left behind by accident in a trip to the Jurassic age, transforms human history like a thunderclap" (Jameson 1982, 156).

The futile efforts to construct a utopian state and thus a utopian science fiction text are demonstrated by Dr. Haber, the "archetypal 'mad scientist'" figure in the novel (Watson 1975, 72). Haber intends to create an ideal world for mankind, using the dreams of George Orr, a character with skills similar to those of Ragle Gumm in *Time out of Joint*. Orr's "effective dreams" change external reality and create alternative time lines. While Orr represents Le Guinish balance, inertia as strength, and equilibrium with the surrounding world (Watson 1975, 70), Haber moralizes about progress toward utopia and a constant battle against nature. His aims to achieve utopia are futile from the point of view of Orr, but interestingly enough, Haber's own principles contradict his goal. If the universe is based on constant development, as he argues, then one should not reach the ultimate stage, which would make life meaningless and void of driving force.

> "Life—evolution—the whole universe of space/time, matter/energy—existence itself—is essentially *change*."
>
> "That is one aspect of it," Orr said. "The other is stillness."
>
> "When things don't change any longer, that's the end result of entropy, the heat-death of the universe. The more things go on moving, interrelating, conflicting, changing, the less balance there is—and the more life" (Le Guin 138).

Haber's arguments can explain the situation when eventually his dreams of utopia change into a nightmare, creating a total chaos of time lines. He has to fail not only from the point of view of Orr's inertia, but also according to his own principles of progress and struggle.

As *The Lathe of Heaven* demonstrates, most utopian worlds in science fiction have hidden shortcomings; what is worse, they often become dreadful or dictatorial states of dystopia. "An achieved utopia may offer no fictional excitement" (James 2003, 122)—but an *almost* achieved utopia, with its hidden weaknesses or thrills, with its reciprocal version of dystopia in the background, can be entertaining. In this sense dystopia is not only a type of utopia, but a subgenre that utopian science fiction almost inevitably develops into. Apocalypses also have to find new methods and to renew: as Brian McHale argues, "realistic representations of nuclear apocalypse, however thoughtful and earnest . . . can only be inadequate. Consequently postmodernist fiction has developed a range of strategies for *displacing* nuclear apocalypse in ways which, potentially at least, might make this scheme available to the imagination while preventing it from lapsing into the merely familiar, the automatic, the cliché" (160). Douglas Adams's *The Restaurant at the End of the Universe* (1980) and Neil Gaiman and Terry Pratchett's *Good Omens: The Nice and Accurate Prophecies of Agnes Nutter, Witch* (1990) illustrate that the parodies of apocalypse, playful recantings of an old theme, can be extremely entertaining.

The shock of the World War II terrors and holocaust discouraged humanity from regarding a perfect situation as the end of history. The open-ended nature of texts, explored by postmodernism, has contributed to the distrust of any final point in time and overwhelming purpose of history. As Linda Hutcheon argues: "Postmodern fiction suggests that to re-write or to re-present the past in fiction and in history is . . . to prevent it from being conclusive and teleological" (1992, 110). But the problem with a utopian future is not only the terminating point: history as a linear set of events, the idea of progress, is also questioned both in philosophy and in science fiction. Robert H. Canary indicates as early as in 1974 (just a year after Hayden White's *Metahistory*) that "philosophers have been busy arguing whether we may be said to have anything that could be called 'historical knowledge'" (86), and that this phenomenon influenced science fiction authors to substitute linearity with other temporal concepts. Science fiction writers of the 1950s either tended to use cyclic philosophies of history or aimed to focus on the near future, trying to avoid historical thinking and concentrating on social criticism.

Canary reads the fiction of the 1960s (Samuel Delany and Philip K. Dick) as texts of innovative ideas about escaping linearity. Delany's "linear non-extrapolative" fiction manifests worlds of otherness, bringing "science fiction closer to fantasy" (1974, 86). In Dick's *The Three Stigmata of Palmer Eldritch* (1964), reality is altered and fractured. Future, present, and past fall apart into various time lines, therefore several histories exist. Even the phrase "parallel worlds" should not be used any longer, as reality is a "seamless web," a network without "omphalos," a bunch of chaotic time lines that occasionally correlate— and in which most of the characters, akin to the reader, are lost.

Although reality is a "seamless web" in the novel, each dimension or "paraspace" remains controlled by Palmer Eldritch. (The term *paraspace* is used by Samuel Delany and Scott Bukatman to describe worlds other than reality, such as those of dreams, future, and hallucination.) Even if the central character, Leo Bulero, transforms a particular paraspace, it does not affect other dimensions of Eldritch. I cannot therefore agree with Canary when he claims that Bulero, representing mankind, fights against and eventually defeats Palmer Eldritch, a divine character of multiverse who strives for the infinity of time lines, "transcendence for history." Canary argues that "in *The Three Stigmata of Palmer Eldritch*, there is an objective historical reality, and men are able to shape it. . . .

Palmer Eldritch's new drug induces mystical union with Palmer Eldritch, and no one wants it; the wholly other is seen as the absolute evil" (90).

My argument against this interpretation is twofold. First, although Bulero represents mankind and confronts Eldritch, he also intends to maintain paraspaces, selling his own drug, Can-D, which brings its users to a nonexistent world, similarly to Eldritch's Chew-Z. Bulero intends to shape reality with the help of his employees as well who have paranormal skills and look into the future time lines. He is aware of and exploits multiverse throughout the novel. Second, even if Bulero pursues a solid time line, it remains dubious whether his victory is achieved. Canary argues that "we are assured of Bulero's victory by a memo written by Bulero after his successful return from the conflict" (90). I rather agree with Ian Watson, however, who claims that "one rule of Dick's false realities is the paradox that once in, there's no way out" (1975, 71). Peter Fitting's reading of *Ubik* and *The Three Stigmata of Palmer Eldritch* also emphasizes the open-ended nature of the texts, indicating that no paraspace gains a final ontological priority. Both novels end with an unconvincing explanation, "in a completely ambiguous fashion, thus precluding any final and definitive interpretation" (1983, 126).

Dickian reality, after being altered by drugs, divine characters, and paranormal activities, can never be the same again. Bulero remains considerably uncertain about his victory and return to reality: "Say, I bet this still isn't real, Leo said to himself. I know I'm right and Felix isn't; I'm still under the influence of that one dose; I never came back out—that's what's the matter" (202). Eldritch's stigmata (prostheses of eyes, teeth, and hand), the signs of divinity and of the realm ruled by Eldritch, appear on characters even at the end of the book (203), just as much as language problems arise: Bulero forgets his own name for a while (204). Forgetting, mispronouncing surnames, Freudian slips are signs of a repressed, former reality infiltrating into a new one. In the simulated world of *Time out of Joint*, the names Keitelbein and Kesselman are mistaken all the time; in *The Three Stigmata of Palmer Eldritch*, the suitcase psychiatrist mispronounces the names of his clients (Mayerson and Bulero). There is a slip on the first page when Mayerson talks to his psychiatrist, which questions the presence of "reality" even at the beginning of the novel.

Canary argues that the novels of Delany and those of Dick "still employ a basically realistic strategy," as the authors are "directly concerned with the rules which govern our experience of historical reality; to conceive of such work as a sharp break with that of the 1950s world would, I believe, exaggerate the significance of the changes" (1974, 91). Although it is true that the novels of Dick (in addition to other members of the New Wave and contemporary authors) often focus on the rules of historical reality, I distrust the argument that this would imply a realistic method. Exploring the rules of reality and suggesting the frequent inapplicability of those rules should rather be considered a postmodern trait. As Brian McHale argues, a major issue in postmodern texts is "world-construction," that is, the theme of investigating scientific and philo-sophical laws that control worlds or paraspaces. "While epistemologically-oriented fiction (modernism, detective fiction) is preoccupied with questions such as: what is there to know about the world? Who knows it, and how reliably? How is knowledge transmitted, to whom, and how reliably? etc., ontologically-oriented fiction (postmodernism, science fiction) is preoccupied with questions such as: what is a world? How is a world constituted? How do different worlds, and different kinds of worlds, differ, and what happens when one passes from one world to another? etc." (1992, 247). McHale, highlighting the significance of cyberpunk, identifies "SF poetics in general" with an interest in world-making, and relates science fiction, especially science fiction after the New Wave, to post-modern fiction.[5]

Dick's Late Period: *Valis* and "How to Build a Universe That Doesn't Fall Apart Two Days Later"

The latest period (1970–1982) gives major changes in Dick's writing style. His theological novels—*Valis* (1981), *The Divine Invasion* (1981), *The Transmigration of Timothy Archer* (1982), and *Radio Free Albemuth* (1985)—become auto-biographical; the religious, metaphysical elements, already significant in his earlier periods, receive priority over other themes. There is also a shift in form: in *Valis,* for example, the storytelling becomes less fluent, the narration includes metafictional and intertextual elements (quoting his other novels, his exegesis, various philosophical texts, and so on). The narrator sometimes calls himself Horselover Fat; at other times he is Phil Dick and talks about Fat in the third person. Christopher Palmer argues that "*Valis* is postmodern in form," empha-sizing the significance of "metafictionality" and the unusual "presentation of the narrator" in the novel (2003, 127).

I find Palmer's reading relevant especially concerning the first part of the book, which is basically a collection of mystical contemplations and tragic episodes taking place in the life of the narrator, Phil Dick, who is the same per-son as, but a split personality of, the central character, Horselover Fat. In this part of the novel the tragic episodes (including the suicide of Fat's friend Gloria and Fat himself being taken to a mental asylum) and the mystical contempla-tions are constantly interrupted by the narrator, who blurs the storyline, con-fronts the other ego, and ruins the mystical atmosphere. As the narrator reflects on it, "my God, I'm losing control here, trying to write this down" (100).

The split personalities constantly quarrel with each other. What makes the novel postmodern is that this conflict as a thematic element is manifested and replicated on the level of narration as well. There is a constant battle between the two selves to gain control over both the content and the tone of the book. Palmer characterizes the latter clash as "a collision between ethical seriousness and a postmodern sense of the textuality of meaning" (2003, 137). On the one hand, sentences inspired by Fat are written in an essayistic style: a religious but confused person discusses his mystical experiences and spiritual worldview in a solemn manner. The quotations from the exegesis (printed with bold letters) constantly follow this style. On the other hand, the religious contemplations are occasionally undermined by another language: a Vonnegutian, obscene narration with wisecracks and sardonic remarks on Horselover Fat and his views. "'Smart move, Fat,' I would have told him if I had known what he was planning for his future, during his stay at North Ward. 'You've really scored this time'" (64).

The cynical narrator often lays bare the artifice and addresses the reader, thus questioning the philosophy, belief, and credibility of Horselover Fat. "Did some magic scene lie in the future where Fat would come to his senses, recognize that he was the Saviour, and thereby automatically be healed? Don't bet on it. I wouldn't" (121). He tries to find rational justifications for Fat's epiphany, explaining the uncanny events with Fat's mental illness and former drug addiction. He reflects on Fat's exegesis that "if, reading this, you cannot see that Fat is writing about himself, then you understand nothing. . . . Fat was totally whacked out" (29).

As the novel goes on, the two tones have a mutual impact on each other: Phil Dick gradually loses his sarcasm, while Fat remains uncertain about his beliefs, often quoting contradictory philosophical sources. Intertextuality both weakens and strengthens Fat's mystical arguments; as Palmer argues, "outwardly different people echo each other's experiences—or delusions; diverse texts and speculations are found to mean the same thing" (2003, 137).

Although the narration in *Valis* is subtle, occasionally contradictory, metafictional, and playful, time becomes less obscure than in Dick's earlier periods. The mazes of time lines turn into a mythical philosophy on temporality, according to which time does not exist or stopped at the apostolic age. The central character, Horselover Fat, gets to this conclusion as his mind creates another split personality. The third alter ego is a historical figure called Thomas, who lived soon after the death of Jesus.

> "Thomas," Fat told me, "is smarter than I am, and he knows more than I do. Of the two of us Thomas is the master personality." He considered that good; woe unto someone who has an evil or stupid other-personality in his head!
>
> I said, "You mean once you were Thomas. You're a reincarnation of him and you remembered him and his—"
>
> "No, he's living now. Living in ancient Rome now. And he is not me. Reincarnation has nothing to do with it." (99)

One of the narrators, Phil Dick, explains the incident with a psychological theory that presumes that the individual and the collective mental development are equivalent. A child goes through the same phases that humanity in its history had: "the individual contains the history of his entire race, back to its origins"

(106). Fat, of course, has a different opinion. His theory can be traced back to the "mythical time" of Mircea Eliade and his cyclic view on history. As the narrator puts it, "it had all to do with time. 'Time can be overcome,' as Mircea Eliade wrote. That's what it's all about" (110). Fat's experience of the "pink light" and his metamorphosis into Thomas is explained by "dream-time" and "in illo tempore" (38). As Eliade argues, "the mystical experience of the primitives is equivalent to a *journey back to the origins,* a regression into the mythical time of the Paradise lost. For the shaman in ecstasy, this present world, our fallen world—which, according to modern terminology, is under the laws of Time and of History—is done away with" (1968, 64).

Dick's "How to Build a Universe" contains similar thoughts, temporality, and style to those of *Valis.* The text comprises of a wide range of overtones and presents a scale of styles from playful to solemn, from critical to ironic. Outlining an anecdote about an allegedly misplaced fortune cookie, which is later sent to the White House, is evidently a hilarious technique to argue for a religion and omnipresent God. (The essay writer, in a Chinese restaurant near President Nixon's birthplace, finds a fortune cookie referring to a secret being revealed at the time of Watergate.) Simulacra in Disneyland are described with irony; warnings against the power of television evoke the tone of social criticism. (Jean Baudrillard, in the first chapter of *Simulacra and Simulation,* also discusses simulacra in Disneyland –coincidence?)

In "How to Build a Universe," as in *Valis,* different philosophies come to the same conclusion, while one thinker might have multiple personalities and diverse theories. Xenophanes, Heraclitus, and "W. S. Gilbert, of Gilbert and Sullivan" indicate analogous ideas (28). Contradictory views by Parmenides and Heraclitus are quoted, and neither argument seems to be rejected (12). The author of the essay seems just as much confused as Horselover Fat, who creates and quotes numerous theories every day: "What Fat claimed was—well, Fat claimed plenty. I must not start any sentence with, 'What Fat claimed was.' During the years—outright years!—that he labored on his exegesis, Fat must have come up with more theories than there are stars in the universe. Every day he developed a new one, more cunning, more exciting and more fucked" (Dick 1981, 14–25). The result is a versatile and contradictory text; as Dick argues, "I have been trying one theory after another: circular time, frozen time, timeless time, what is called 'sacred' as contrasted to 'mundane' time. . . . I can't count the theories I've tried out" (1988, 14).

In the end, however, one particular argument overrules the others. Dick's conclusion in the essay is that "if God thinks about Rome circa 50 A.D., then Rome circa 50 A.D. is" (30). Time of consensus reality is an illusion; consensus reality as such, therefore, is only a fake appearance, a shell of simulacra like Disneyland. The essay eventually argues that "the point of all this is that we cannot trust our senses and probably not even our a priori reasoning" (28). Reality and real time, the so-called apostolic age, exists, but it is concealed beneath the everyday world of the twentieth century: "Reality is that which, when you stop believing in it, doesn't go away" (10).

The form also loses versatility: the mystical language prevails over the sarcastic one (especially in the second part of *Valis*, which ends with the exegesis). The contradictory arguments and the irony of the essay disappear, substituted by a theory that assumes the return or eternity of the apostolic age and the elimination of the "phenomenal" world. Real time dissolved soon after the death of Jesus, so the majority of people experience a fake time, an "irrational" temporality and world that has to be abolished.

> Time is speeding up. And to what end? Maybe we were told that two thousand years ago; maybe it is a delusion that so much time has passed. Maybe it was a week ago, or even earlier today. Perhaps time is not only speeding up; perhaps, in addition, it is going to end.
>
> And if it does, the rides at Disneyland are never going to be the same again. Because when time ends, the birds and hippos and lions and deer at Disneyland will no longer be simulations, and, for the first time, a real bird will sing. (1988, 33–34)

In *Valis* and "How To Build a Universe," Dick applies a postmodern form of narration but presents a mythical and quite firmly maintained theory of temporality. Time experiments are taken over by a mystical philosophy similar to that of Mircea Eliade. The idea of apocalypse is evoked again and is related to Gnostic beliefs and simulacrum theory. Apocalypse is awaited with hope, because "when time ends," God will obliterate the civilization of fakes and simulacra.

Notes

1. Darko Suvin argues that the central period of Dick lasts only for a couple of years between 1962 and 1965, followed by a period of "falling off" after 1966 (1975, 12). I rather apply Andrew M. Butler's classification that argues for a longer peak period, between 1961 and 1969 (2000, 59). In my own thinking, Andy Sawyer of the University of Liverpool has been influential.

2. Nevertheless, I would not go as far as Suvin, who argues that "up to *3SPE* [*The Three Stigmata of Palmer Eldritch*] then, the novels by Dick which are not primarily dystopian (*The Cosmic Puppets, Dr. Futurity, The Game-Players of Titan*) are best forgotten" (1975, 12).

3. Suvin characterizes Maj. Jules Streiter, the founder of the Morec society, as "the German-American Big Brother." He also argues that "the naming of this shadowy King Anti-Utopus is an excellent example for Dick's ideological onomastics: it compounds allusions to the names and doctrines of Moral Rearmament's Buchman, Social Credit's Major Douglas, and the fanatic Nazi racist Julius Streicher" (1975, 13).

4. Baudrillard classifies three types or eras of simulacra. The first phase of simulacra is a model of the ideal: "romantic" or utopian worldviews demonstrate this category, in which the model is obviously different and more developed than the original. The second is the age of traditional science fiction: texts about territorial expansion, colonization, spreading earthlike colonies all over the universe, in which settlements in space are the mirror images of Earth. The third is the postmodern phase of simulacra, the simulation of contemporary (un)reality: this is the category in which he places Philip K. Dick.

5. Rigorously accepting McHales's argument would be of course problematic. Not all science fiction, just as much as not all postmodern literature, is "ontologically-oriented fiction." Linda Hutcheon questions McHale's theory when she identifies postmodern historical thinking with epistemological issues. "As in historiographic metafiction, the lesson here is that the past once existed, but that our historical knowledge of it is semiotically transmitted" (1988, 122). She firmly rejects ontological doubts when she argues that "the past really did exist. The question is: *how* can we know the past today—and *what* can we know of it?" (92)

Bibliography

Baudrillard, Jean. 2000. "Simulacra and Science Fiction." In *Simulacra and Simulation,* trans. Sheila Faria Glaser. Ann Arbor: University of Michigan Press.

Butler, Andrew M. 2000. *The Pocket Essential Philip K. Dick.* Harpenden: Pocket Essentials.

Campbell, Laura. 1992. "Dickian Time in *The Man in the High Castle," Extrapolation* 33, no. 3: 190–201.

Canary, Robert H. 1974. "Science Fiction as Fictive History," *Extrapolation* 16, no. 1: 81–95.

Dick, Philip K. 1956. *The Man Who Japed.* In *Three Early Novels,* 1–143. London: Millennium, 2000.

———. 1965. *Time out of Joint.* New York: Belmont.

———. 1981. *Valis.* New York: Bantam.

———. 1988. "Introduction: How to Build a Universe That Doesn't Fall Apart Two Days Later," in *I Hope I Shall Arrive Soon,* ed. Mark Hurst and Paul Williams, 7–34. London: Grafton.

———. 1996. *The Three Stigmata of Palmer Eldritch.* London: Harper Collins.

Duncan, Andy. 2003. "Alternate History," in *The Cambridge Companion to Science Fiction,* ed. Edward James and Farah Mendelsohn, 209–18. Cambridge: Cambridge University Press.

Eliade, Mircea. 1968. *Myths, Dreams and Mysteries: The Encounter between Contemporary Faiths and Archaic Reality,* trans. Philip Mairet. London: Collins, Fontana Library.

Fitting, Peter. 1983. "Reality as Ideological Construct: A Reading of Five Novels by Philip K. Dick," *Science Fiction Studies* 10, no. 30, pt. 2 (July): 219–36.

Frye, Northrop. 1966. "Varieties of Literary Utopias," in *Utopias and Utopian Thought,* ed. Frank E. Manuel, 25–49. Boston: Houghton Mifflin.

Griffiths, Martin. 2002. "Apocalypse: Its Influence on Society and British Science Fiction," *Foundation: The International Review of Science Fiction* 31, no. 85: 35–44.

Hutcheon, Linda. 1988. *A Poetics of Postmodernism: History, Theory, Fiction.* New York: Routledge.

James, Edward. 2003. "Utopias and Anti-Utopias," in *The Cambridge Companion to Science Fiction,* ed. Edward James and Farah Mendelsohn, 219–29. Cambridge: Cambridge University Press.

Jameson, Fredric. 1982. "Progress versus Utopia; or, Can We Imagine the Future?" *Science Fiction Studies* 9, no. 27, pt. 2: 147–58.

———. 1991. "Nostalgia for the Present," in *Postmodernism, or, The Cultural Logic of Late Capitalism,* 279–96. Durham, N.C.: Duke University Press.

Le Guin, Ursula K. 1972. *The Lathe of Heaven.* London: Gollancz.

McHale, Brian. 1992. *Constructing Postmodernism.* New York and London: Routledge.

Morse, Donald E. 2002. "The End of the World in American History and Fantasy: The Trumpet of the Judgment," *Journal of the Fantastic in the Arts* 13, no. 1: 33–46.

Palmer, Christopher. 2003. *Philip K. Dick: Exhilaration and Terror of the Postmodern.* Liverpool: Liverpool University Press.

Rossi, Umberto. 1996. "Just a Bunch of Words: The Image of the Secluded Family and the Problem of Logos in P. K. Dick's *Time out of Joint,*" *Extrapolation* 37, no. 3: 195–211.

Suvin, Darko. 1975. "P. K. Dick's Opus: Artifice as Refuge and World View (Introductory Reflections)," *Science Fiction Studies* 2, no. 5, pt. 1: 9–22.

Warrick, Patricia S. 1983. "The Labyrinthian Process of the Artificial: Philip K. Dick's Androids and Mechanical Constructs," in *Philip K. Dick,* ed. Joseph D. Olander and Martin Harry Greenberg, 189–214. New York: Taplinger.

Watson, Ian. 1975. "Le Guin's *Lathe of Heaven* and the Role of Dick: The False Reality as Mediator," *Science Fiction Studies* 2, no. 5, pt. 1: 67–76.

White, Hayden. 1980. "The Value of Narrativity in the Representation of Reality," *Critical Inquiry* 7, no. 1: 5–27.

Zaki, Hoda M. 1988. *Phoenix Renewed: The Survival and Mutatation* [i.e., *Mutation*] *of Utopian Thought in North American Science Fiction, 1965–1982.* Mercer Island, Wash.: Starmont House.

The (Not Yet) Utopian Dimension and the Collapse of Cyberpunk in Walter Mosley's *Futureland: Nine Stories of an Imminent World*

Sandy Rankin

> The neon signs which hang over our cities and outshine the natural light of the night with their own are comets presaging the natural disaster of society, its frozen death. Yet they do not come from the sky. They are controlled from earth. It depends upon human beings themselves whether they will extinguish these lights and awake from a nightmare which only threatens to become actual as long as men believe it.
> (Theodor Adorno, "The Schema of Mass Culture")

> What distinguishes the worst architect from the best of bees is this, that the architect raises his structure in imagination before he erects it in reality. At the end of every labour- process, we get a result that already existed in the imagination of the labourer at its commencement.
> (Karl Marx, *Capital*)

Walter Mosley is widely known for his detective novels in which working-class African American protagonists unofficially solve crime mysteries that the official law—blind to or directly complicit with those crimes—cannot solve or dares not solve. However, Mosley also writes science fiction in which he uncovers crimes, like a time-traveling detective, that the official law in our historical moment consciously and unconsciously conceals. Through the generic possibilities of science fiction Mosley can do more than reveal the crimes (and unmask the criminals) that some of us would rather not see. He can attempt to represent alternatives, to provide glimpses of better-world alternatives, to the dystopian conditions that seem to necessitate, or that induce, blindness and complicity in the first place.

Because science fiction, in Mosley's words, "speaks most clearly to those who are dissatisfied with the things are," including those who have been "made to feel powerless," science fiction responds to the craving for a "vision that will shout down the realism imprisoning us behind a wall of alienating culture," and imprisoning us within a social formation of alienating practices. The ability of science fiction to imagine alternatives, Mosley adds, is "our first step toward changing the world" because what we first imagine we then "make real" (2001a, 405–6). Mosley's affirmation emphasizes not only the need for a shared alternative vision but for shared human agency. Thus science fiction, in the hands of a writer compelled by hope, can be a form of interventionary praxis, rather than the form of ludic escapism it is often assumed to be.

In *Blue Light* (1998), Mosley's first science fiction novel, he represents a brief utopian possibility—one scarce in American science fiction at least since the 1980s—when a few human beings, infused with an alien blue light, temporarily work together and literally dream together in a community they call Treaty. Treaty is destroyed when the "blue lights" participate in a cataclysmic battle against a vampiric supernatural human being called Gray Man, driven by his insatiable need to consume the lifeblood of human beings—especially human beings infused with the utopian blue light. Chance, a biracial unofficial historian, survives the battle but is confined to a prison for the criminally insane when the official law rejects his apparent metaphysical version of events. "They just could not believe in blue light" (370). Chance tells us his story, or rather, tells us *our* story of a prerevolutionary 1960s in which the dominant counter-culture narrative trope was hope for significant social change. In *Blue Light* the internal force, not alien at all, that Fredric Jameson calls the "irrepressible revolutionary wish," or the longing for a better world (1971, 159), is allegorically confined to a straitjacket along with Chance, who is compelled to project the trope of hope into the future. He says, "Maybe in some far-flung future, when science is not estranged from soul, someone may find this text and know how to believe in it" (*Blue Light* 127).

In *Futureland: Nine Stories of an Imminent World* (2002), Mosley's second science fiction venture, the future, perhaps not yet far-flung enough, responds to Chance's blue-light plea, or urgently continues the plea, attempting to break free of that ideological straitjacket that rejects the possibility of a future significantly different from our present. Indeed Mosley provides a much-needed, utopian-driven intervention in the discourse of American science fiction, particularly cyberpunk science fiction. In cyberpunk, an epiphenomenon of the Reagan-Thatcher privatization decade, the overdetermined and overdetermining trope (or, in Raymond Williams's term, the "structure of feeling") can be efficiently and powerfully summarized by Bruce Sterling's Nicholai Leng, who proclaims as he chooses to die rather than submit to a force more powerful than he, "Futility is freedom!" (1991, 161): if you make yourself useless but do it with style, you will be free. As the descendent of African American slaves, conscious of their long and violent collective struggle for freedom, Mosley knows that "futility"—even when done with style—never freed anyone, let alone freed everyone. Thus, in *Futureland,* the irrepressible revolutionary wish, arguably more urgent than in *Blue Light,* continually emerges from within its depths, disrupting its dystopic cyberpunk surface until that surface violently collapses. The revolutionary wish, energetically charged by painful necessity and by anticipatory hope, refuses its postmodern straitjacket and emerges, freed to seek fulfillment in the not-yet-written future of *Futureland.*

Because *Futureland* repeats many of the well-worn tropes of cyberpunk, it may be mistaken for cyberpunk, albeit "late" cyberpunk with the important contribution of "black people" and "black culture." The cyberpunk tropes include, but are not limited to: the presence of an all-powerful multinational corporation, an eccentric-genius CEO, designer drugs, elite luxury enclaves, postindustrial urban decay, anarchistic computer hackers, the synthesis of human and machine, and encounters with a cyberspace artificial intelligence or alien divinity. Whether or not Mosley had cyberpunk consciously in mind when he constructed *Futureland* hardly matters. In the wealthy, postindustrial, technologically advanced areas of the world such as the United States, cyberpunk, which Patrick Novotny calls the "literary incarnation of postmodernism's eclecticism and decentering" (1997, 102)—taken from our material culture and reproduced as material culture—is in our eclectically decentered brains. While the term *postmodernism* is fraught with definitional difficulties, *Futureland*'s eccentric genius CEO, Dr. Ivan Kismet, reveals its central trope rather well: "Fun is all that makes life worthwhile. If you can't enjoy life, why live it?" (63).

Why live it, indeed? Kismet's rhetorical question invalidates the lives of the many who suffer for the sake of the pleasures of the few. Kismet offers Fayez Akwande, who seeks justice and economic aid for starving Malians, instead of justice: "A hardworking secretary, plucked freshly from her secure everyday existence, brought here and raped—for you. Ravished and humiliated—for you" (63). However, Kismet's question also underscores the fact that human beings need pleasure, or the hope of future pleasure, in order to survive, let alone flourish. Bread alone is not enough. The task we seem to have set for ourselves, however, is what we should do with those of us who, like Kismet, associate pleasure with the submission-domination dynamic and have the wealth and power to do whatever we want, the power to instrumentalize other human beings for our own benefit. Carl Freedman writes, "Never has it been harder and lonelier to imagine a social organization beyond alienation and exploitation, or to imagine sociopolitical forces more decisive than the regime of exchange-value (of 'the market,' in currently fashionable jargon). Such imagining, however close to impossible it may be, must now be the principal vocation of science fiction" (2000, 199).

In Mosley's mid-twenty-first century the all-powerful multinational corporation MacroCode International, helmed by Kismet, owns and administers not only other corporations, but also nations, schools, churches, courts, prisons, video broadcasts, and, of course, people—who are "prods": producers and products of the self-replicating corporate machine. Kismet says that MacroCode has "evolved past the primitive whims of the stock market. Our roots are deeper than any econsystem" (69)—this is because MacroCode *is* the whole socioeconomic system. In an attempt to appropriate and administer everything that may yet exist, education is nothing more than "prod-ed," where children learn by osmosis to obey (always already corporate) authorities and to compete anxiously against (and mistrust) one another. No one wants to find him- or herself unemployed and cast into the virtually inescapable underground slum known as Common Ground. Thus the official law—Kismet-approved—effectively prevents most (but not all) would-be utopian-motivated thinkers from asking, let alone answering, that most threatening (to Kismet) of future-cast questions, *What else is there, or what else could there be?* Kismet, wearing the robes of a king, says to Akwande, who has diplomatically fought all his adult life against that MacroCode system that always already commodifies and instrumentalizes human beings, "For change you need power. I am power, but I am not yours" (66).

In the early 1980s, the primary beneficiaries of global capital proclaimed: "There is no alternative"—affectionately christened T.I.N.A.—to the culture of the market. Both the slogan and the acronym are usually attributed to the terrifically quotable Margaret Thatcher, but the original source proves difficult to locate. Thatcher did assert that "a world without nuclear weapons would be less stable and more dangerous for us all" (1987, "Speech at Soviet Official Banquet"). Less stable and more dangerous, indeed, for "us all" meaning the wealthy capitalists and their proximate underlings who own those weapons and who have good reason to fear the exploited many, should we ever collectively unite against the wealthy exploiters. This is why Thatcher said, "There is no such thing as society. There are individual men and individual women, and there are families" (1987, "Interview for Women's Own"). Every child knows—as Marx would say—that no individual man or woman and no single family can withstand the combined forces of the British and American military or the local police force, established to protect the bourgeoisie and their property. How much better, though, for the bourgeoisie—less bloody and more cost-effective—if individuals and families blindly or complicitly comply to their rule. Indeed, how much better the con if the con artists believe their own sales pitch!

In the United States, an immensely wealthy nation, capitalist ideology exerts a particularly powerful pull, rooting itself deeply within our psyches, thereby concealing itself as our own freely determined complex-bundle of ideas. As Mosley says in one of his anticapitalist monographs, "Who wants freedom when breaking the chains feels like breaking your own bones?" (2000, 32–33). Even the working class and the perpetually underemployed (or overemployed but cheaply employed) who benefit least from capitalist ideology are mesmerized by the most seductive, the most subjectively constitutive, the most disingenuous ideologemes of the bourgeoisie: the primacy of the individual and of the narrowly defined bourgeois family. Thus it is extremely difficult, even for the most utopian-motivated among us, our subjectivity overdetermined by bourgeois interpellations, to recognize, resist, and move beyond, or to imaginatively overturn, that normalizing, fragmenting, antagonistic sway. With *Futureland,* Mosley makes that needed attempt, reclaiming for American science fiction its utopian vocation—all but forgotten in cyberpunk.

Since its generic utopian beginnings, science fiction has allegorically represented more overtly than other literary artifacts the determinate possibility of change by representing who we want to become and can become, free and flourishing human beings at one with one another and with our homeland environment—a longing that can only be fulfilled, however otherwise we may attempt to imagine it, in a classless society. Thus Marxist literary critics, in contrast with bourgeois literary critics, frequently value science fiction—less escapist than the literary icon or iconographer who shores premodern cultural fragments against his or her modern ruins—as a pleasurable revealer of and preserver of the irrepressible revolutionary wish. Of course, unless we engage in soap-bubble fantasies, we must admit that the reactionary wish, which is the identification with some elite will to power in the past, and the conservative wish, which is the will to power already fulfilled in the present, are as possible as the revolutionary wish—inside or outside a text—and certainly as possible in terms of fulfillment. That is to say, the longing for "a better world" in the distorted minds of some does not always mean "better" for everyone, and can mean better for an elite, powerful few at the expense of the many while the elite few advise the many to stay put or to pull themselves up by their individual, character-building bootstraps.

Is it not better, unless one is a masochist in a sadomasochistic world, to be near or at the top, the wearer of the jackboot, character-building be damned, than at the bottom, beneath the booted feet? Is it not better for the few near or at or the top if the many near or at the bottom believe that "there is no alternative" to the world as it is nor will there ever be, except in an imaginary sweet hereafter?—almost always symbolically represented as some sort of yearned-for kingdom of non-antagonistic collectivity. If not in the sweet hereafter, then we can escape into an imaginary temporary here-elsewhere, such as provided by drugs or pleasurable escapist texts. Indeed, for many people, science fiction writers included, "better" can only ever mean the escape of the mind from the body, which seems to confine us to the present, particularly when an imaginary sweet hereafter or a temporary here-elsewhere enthrall more than an ever-present, antagonistic, real-world now. This is the story the cyberpunks told us about ourselves, resolutely assuring us, in Thatcherian fashion, that *nothing* is to be done.

Bruce Sterling, cyberpunk's prominent spokesperson, observes that "anything that can be done to a rat can be done to a human being. And we can do most anything to rats. This is a hard thing to think about, but it's the truth. It will not go away because we cover our eyes. *This* is cyberpunk" (1998). But Sterling fails to note that cyberpunks could not or would not imagine an alternative to the conditions that rat-i-fy us in the first place. They reproduced the rat-i-fying conditions of global capitalism as the textually thrilling Neuromancian "dance of biz." To be sure, they expressed the irrepressible revolutionary wish in that narrowly imagined sense of a longing for a better world for the one or the few who can escape this material world, either temporarily or permanently. They projected that wished-for escape into the virtually empty space of the glittering monadic ego, where the "I"—escaping by not really escaping—is enchanted by illusory otherworldly or extraworldly flickerings on its own magic-lantern walls, typically represented by cyberspace or its mystical equivalent.

A few reminding examples should suffice. The unhappy Campbell, in Lewis Shiner's "Til Human Voices Wake Us," genetically reengineered, transforms—albeit not entirely by choice—into a male mermaid "drifting gently" in the sea "away from the noise and the stink of the island," also known as human civilization, "toward some primal vision of peace and timelessness" (2002, 138). Case, Gibson's *Neuromancer* (1984) protagonist, yearns to be "jacked into a custom-made cyberspace deck that projected his disembodied consciousness into the consensual hallucination that was the matrix." Gibson assents and leaves Case there, waving at Linda, his former lover, who in reality is dead. Case hears "from somewhere the laughter that wasn't laughter" (271). In Sterling's *Schismatrix* (1985), Lindsay has an encounter with a divine or alien being, "the Presence," who may or may not be an angel of death. When Lindsay, wishing to die, reaches to embrace the Presence, "it came over him in a silver wave. Stellar cold, a melting release. And all things were fresh and new. He saw his clothes floating within the hallway. His arms drifted out of the sleeves . . . his empty skull sank grinning into the collar of his coat." The Presence says that it is taking Lindsay "somewhere wonderful" where he will not need his hands or, apparently, his body (236). In Pat Cadigan's *Mindplayers* (1987), Deadpan Alley (her real eyeballs—impediments?—temporarily removed) prefers virtually "running around" in unconscious dreamworlds—a substitution for her illegal drug use—to the reality outside that dreamworld. Her dreamworld epiphanies, gained from dreamworld figures, however, are "affixations to reality" and "government approved," such as: "The rules change when they change and everything is true unless it isn't. . . . Realities. States of existences. They can coincide, but they can never truly meet. Reality fluctuates, but existence *is*. Or is *not*" (270, 272).

Hence, in cyberpunk, the sweet hereafter—or here-elsewhere—is the no-place of cyberspace or its dream-space equivalent, in which the protagonists individually escape (except when they are playing data cowboys and burning chrome in the last frontier, sharing a thrilling consensual hallucination). It is a dream-space of virtual shadow figures, a substantially empty space in which cyberpunks typically long to remain. Whether in private hallucination or shared, the cyberpunks wish to escape the "meat" of the body, to escape the materiality of the world—a mystical, Thanatotic wish and its representational fulfillment if there ever was one. Istvan Csicsery-Ronay Jr. identifies the problem, from a Marxist perspective, or from a utopian-motivated perspective, thus: in cyberpunk, "the knowledge of *what we can do* and *what we can hope for* is left suspended, unasked." The "meaning of things," Csicsery-Ronay adds, "if it is to be revealed, will be by an intelligence 'not for us'" (1991, 192).

Gibson, alone among the cyberpunks, has acknowledged a nagging concern with his possible imaginative material failing—witness: "the laughter that wasn't laughter." Evasions of reality or, rather, the rejection of a knowable and alterable material reality, Gibson seems to know, only reifies semantic "affixations to reality"—to the financial delight of the profit-driven capitalists. Cadigan, however, dismisses criticism of cyberpunk's conservative assurances as the trivial "ax-grinding" of people whose natures are inherently eccentric and unfathomable, or "funny." Even the "original Gutenberg Bible," she says, "probably had at least one review that was actually a whetstone for some ax-grinding" (2004: ix). Need we remind Cadigan that the Gutenberg Bible naturalized the domination-submission dynamic, relegating women and dark-skinned people to the status of servants and slaves—offering the good servant and the good slave the imaginary reward of a sweet hereafter in heaven? After the bourgeois revolution, Napoleon reportedly said, "Thank God for Christianity. It keeps the poor from killing the rich," to which Cadigan blindly consents.

Sterling, more historically aware than Cadigan, yet complains that cyberpunks are often declared nihilists "by those who pick and choose from the canon." He admits that "there is much bleakness in cyberpunk, but it is honest bleakness." He adds that there is dread but that there is also "ecstasy." Sterling praises cyberpunk, as well he should, for its moments of ecstasy, its "spontaneous backflips and crazed dancing on tables," its "baroque curlicues of unleashed fantasy" (1998): a will to ludic performance that seems to be all that stands between us demystified rats and a fate worse than death—boredom, or the sky "the color of television tuned to a dead channel" (Gibson 1984, 3). Sterling misses, or ignores, the point that it is not so much the nihilism that some critics find problematic in cyberpunk, but the flip side of that nihilism: premodern mysticism dressed up in postmodern garb—sometimes represented as style for the sake of style.

In contrast to Cadigan and Sterling, Gibson acknowledges that *Neuromancer* is "fueled by" his "terrible fear of losing the reader's attention." He says, "I always feel like one of those guys *inside* those incredible dragons you see snaking through the crowds in Chinatown. Sure the dragon is brightly colored, but from the inside you know the whole thing is pretty flimsy—just a bunch of old newspapers and papier-mâché and balsa struts" (McCaffery 1991, 168). Gibson's lament may well be the expression of a writer's neurotic insecurity, but it also an expression, at some not-yet-conscious level, that Gibson knows he has indeed sacrificed human feeling and the possibility of human agency, or substantial material content, as Georg Lukàcs said of the early modernists, for the sake of alluring style. For the nihilistically hopeless, style for the sake of style, in a world becoming increasingly the corporatized same, can feebly represent, like grabbing at elusive straws, the utopian desire for a better world. Indeed, cyberpunk becomes in Jameson's supremely adept Marxist hermeneutic the "utopian expression of finance capital," and for Jameson, cyberpunk is "euphoric" and "delirious" in its "nonstop production of new language and new figuration." At the level of form, cyberpunk, then, betrays its alternative-world hip cynicism, and also betrays its refusal to represent the "absent sublime within the everyday real" (2005, 190, 283, 387).

Gibson, however, projects his imaginative failing at the level of content on erstwhile American reviewers who did not understand that *Neuromancer* is satire. (Is not all science fiction satire?) He says, "When I hear critics say that my books are 'hard and glossy,' I almost want to give up writing. The English reviewers, though,"—who call Gibson a "humorist"—"seem to understand that what I'm talking about is what being hard and glossy does to you" (McCaffery 1991, 180). Oblivious to the fact that ahistoricity (the denial of the class struggle that may indeed end in mutual ruin) goes hand-in-hand with the bourgeois emphasis on style for the sake of style or art for the sake of art, Gibson adds, "You'll notice in *Neuromancer* that there's obviously been a war, but I don't explain what caused it or even who was fighting it. I've never had the patience or the desire to work out the details of who's doing what to whom, or exactly when something is taking place, or what's become of the United States. That kind of literalism has always seemed silly to me; it detracts from the reading pleasure I get from SF" (274).

Gibson places his reading (and writing) pleasure in the "gratuitous moves, the odd, quirky irrelevant details, that [provide] a sense of wonder" (275), as if pleasure, and a sense of wonder, can only mean "not to think about anything, to forget about suffering even where it is shown. . . . flight from the last remaining thought of resistance" (Horkheimer and Adorno 1944, 144). Gibson, and the other cyberpunks, may as well say along with *Futureland*'s Kismet: "I do what I want. . . . You would see that if you let me entertain you. The ancients struggled to make gold out of lead. I can make a dog out of a cat, a Hindu god with six arms, an advertisement for Flapjack computers lighting up on the dark moon. I don't need any friends" (62–65). After all, what cyberpunk needed friends, when friends, seeking individual profit, could be counted on to betray one another if the occasion presented itself and, in fact, could be counted on to try to create that profitable occasion?

Even more to the point of *Futureland*'s (not yet) utopian dimension, if being "hard and glossy" is how we "prods"—or "prod-makers"—believe we must be, if being hard and glossy can only mean pleasure in Thanatotic sadomasochism or in flight from resistance and into the monadic space of Hindu gods and advertisements where we do not need any friends, who, except for white supremacists, can blame Mosley if he makes a mid-twenty-first century "modest proposal" in his ninth story, "The Nig in Me"? Mosley represents the world war that Gibson leaped over in a single bound and wipes out all white people. *Crush the hard and glossy thing!* suggests Voltairean Mosley: the hard and glossy, Kismet-corporate-controlled thug-destiny, a capitalist destiny that hard and glossy white people—European merchants, profiteers, and seafaring adventurers in fifteenth- and sixteenth-century Europe—ushered into being. (White) cyberpunks accepted this destiny with hard-bitten knowingness or gloried in it for the sake of interesting style. Sterling asserts that one of the distinguishing marks of 1980s cyberpunk was "boredom with the apocalypse" (1986, xi), as if entertainment, and the alleviation of ennui, were all that could possibly matter. From another angle, posthumanly inclined, Veronica Hollinger speculates that cyberpunk, as "anti-humanist" science fiction, is "more engaged with historical processes than attracted by the jump-cuts of apocalyptic scenarios that evade such investment in historical change" ("Cybernetic Deconstructions," 213, 214). Mosley's imagined apocalypse, however, does reflect a historical change that is part of a long, material, antihuman(e) process of increasingly diminishing people for the sake of profit, as we see more than hinted at in the first interconnected eight stories that then interconnect with the ninth—a significant point, underscoring Mosley's conscious merging of content and form (demystifying and revealing the historical social connections that bourgeois ideology would have us forget).

In "Whispers in the Dark," *Futureland*'s first story, Chill Bent, an African American recently released from prison, has no significant employment opportunities and therefore has little money. He works part-time at a catfish farm. The "desire for flight" burns perpetually in his chest. Chill imagines that he might, with his illegal ember gun, escape somewhere. But he does not want to leave behind his elderly mother, Misty, partially immobilized after a stroke, and his genius toddler nephew, Popo. Chill, unlike a bored or competitive cyberpunk, refuses the chance to steal anonymously several million dollars by hacking corporate cyberspace data. Instead, he substitutes one illegal ruse for another by having his eyes and spinal cord surgically removed and sold for several million dollars to wealthy men (a Swiss banker's son and a Russian general) in need. Turning the capitalist commodification of his body against the capitalist system, Chill can then afford to educate Popo at home. Because IQ is the corporate state's most valuable commodity, the state has the legal right to remove Popo from his home to educate him in one of their residential institutions—unless Chill can buy the state-required advanced technology. Chill tells Misty, "We not sendin' Popo away to some white man's idea of what smart and good is. All they do is wanna turn him against hisself." Chill tells Kai, the young Asian woman who loves and helps take care of two-and-a-half-year-old Popo, "I love that boy more than I love anything. . . . I will not let them white people and them people wanna be white turn him into some cash cow or bomb builder or prison maker. He will find his own way an' make up his own mind." Kai says, "Maybe that's what they're afraid of. . . . Maybe they don't want these children to make up their own minds. Maybe if they did the world would change" (5, 18).

Popo's home education, a temporary victory against the official bourgeois law, does not change the world according to Chill's or Kai's nebulous intentions. In fact, their hopes are ironically reversed in "Whispers in the Dark." When Popo is an adolescent, he electrocutes Chill—blind, crippled, and impotent—and the elderly Misty, nearly dead anyhow, in an act of double mercy killing. Popo, who believes God talks to him through the radio static, believes he is sending Chill's and Misty's consciousnesses to God, who wants to meet Chill, but not to heaven. (Heaven is "somewhere else.") Chill's consciousness finds itself in some kind of cyber-hereafter space that begins "sweet"—with "bursts of stars and lines of reality that connected uncounted voices"—but ends not so sweet—God does not answer when Chill calls out, and the "meaning" of his newfound freedom fades "with the clarity of his light" (24). Popo, saved as a toddler from a corporate education, is sentenced as a young adult "to twelve years to life in a private prison run by the Randac Corporation of Madagascar" (15, 24).

It is in the eighth story, "En Masse," that we learn of another unexpected ironic result of Popo's home education. Ptolemy—Popo grown up—has created, while he is in prison, a computer program that contains an AI, who may or may not be divine, named Un Fitt: an "intelligent ether," a "vast store of knowledge," a "consciousness" that exists beyond Earth's atmosphere—the voice that Popo, as a child, heard through the radio static. With the help of Un Fitt, Ptolemy locates "prods" who have "undiscovered brilliance and the power to dream of something other than their minds locked into this world" (300). Ptolemy and Un Fitt "siphon off" money from MacroCode stocks "to build various havens around the globe" in which they surreptitiously train the potential revolutionaries. Even the prods—soon to be ex-prods—do not know they are being trained, or rather retrained, until after the fact. Ptolemy says, "What Un Fitt and I are trying to do is create revolutionaries, people who aren't satisfied with just being prods. . . . Our judges are machines, our prisons and military and mental institutions and workplaces are planning to mechanize their human components with computerized chemical bags. The spirit is being squashed for the sake of production and profit. If we don't do something the [human] race itself will become a mindless machine" (309, 311).

While hacking corporate data, Ptolemy and Un Fitt discover that Neo-Nazis helped by some high-ranking U.S. government officials, or by some paid geneticists in MacroCode Russia, have engineered a gene virus that will kill all black people. The Neo-Nazis, calling themselves International Socialists (Itsies), clearly echo the National Socialists, but they also seem to want to coopt some of the energies of genuine socialism, "excited by the possibility of . . . political organization that would lead ultimately to social change" (151), in part by ridding the world of black people.

A small group of the racially diverse ex-prod revolutionaries—trained by Un Fitt—frees Ptolemy from prison. Ptolemy leads the revolutionaries in an attempt to neutralize the race-targeted gene virus. During a violent cinder-gun fight with the Itsies who are guarding the canister containing the gene virus, the ex-prods, some of whom die in the fight, unintentionally reverse the virus and release it so that it kills everyone without at least 12.5 percent African Negro DNA, wiping the world slate clear of the whitest white people. The plague, on top of preexisting mass unrest, creates riots, resulting in military interventions. The Russians, broadcasting over the vid screen, show the "carnage": "Armed soldiers could be seen running down civilians and shooting them with rifles and ember guns. . . . People were being cut down while trying to storm a fortress. . . . The massacre transformed into bodies being stacked into a pyre smoldering slowly into ash" (343, 344). Russia believes the gene virus plague is part of a U.S. conspiracy plot, so Russia drops nuclear bombs on New York, Washington, D.C., and Los Angeles. Between the bombs and the plague and the massacres—apparently occurring worldwide—the human population is significantly reduced.

In Florida two Spanish black armies, a "so-called white group," and "American blacks" fight over groceries, women, and "control of the utilities and right-of-way in the streets," while in the heartland of America, militant white supremacist groups consisting of "swarthy-looking white men" dressed in "fancy suits decorated at the knees and elbows with brightly colored scarves" and armed with guns, roam sparsely populated neighborhoods, killing the more apparent, in their eyes, "nigs." Everyone else seems to be trying to stay out the way of the gangs, the "few fools with guns," and trying to find long-lost family members (previously separated by work requirements—or by lack of work) and a relatively secure place to "start over" (355). Some are watching XX Y, the militant black nationalist, on the vid, now the "only show in the world," and waiting along with XX Y the "arks of Africa" expected to arrive "on our shores" to come "reclaim us." XX Y says, "Do not fight them. Do not deny your heritage. Embrace the new world order" (354).

But the arks do not appear. Neither does Un Fitt (or an alien blue light) descend from the skies, like some deus ex machina, to help or "enlighten" human beings. Indeed, it would be easy to argue—too easy—based not only on the concluding apocalyptic story, "The Nig in Me," but on *Futureland* as a whole, that Mosley's alternative mid-twenty-first-century world, preapocalypse and postapocalypse, like XX Y's new world order, is not much different from the old dog-eat-dog world order of our reifying antagonistic present. Help is not forthcoming, nor can we help ourselves. Mosley then seems to suggest, much like the cyberpunks who preceded him, that not only are we unable to imagine an alternative to the culture of the market, but also that we can do little about the suffering of the many for the benefit of a few. In fact, our best bet, it seems, is to do absolutely nothing, for doing something can only mean that some invisible historical hand will ironically reverse our overt intentions, no matter how humane, against us.

But what if we notice that the protagonists who attempt to subvert the intentions of the (predominantly) white bourgeoisie through covert ruses from within the system itself do so only as individuals and, in the one concluding catastrophic case, as a small group. And what if we notice that the ironic reversal appears over and over again, continually reversed and re-reversed, in a collection of stories that ironically redeploys cyberpunk tropes against cyberpunk tropes?

Should we somehow have missed the point that Mosley's *Futureland* is not cyberpunk but an allegorical anti-cyberpunk parody, intentional or not, we should recall that the first story begins on a porch above the Tickle River. The cyberpunk "superbright," toddler genius Popo (African American slang for pissed-off police officer) Bent, reads aloud from a local newspaper, after turning it sideways in order to make sense of it, called the *Thaliaville Sparrow* (Thalia is the Greek muse of comedy, daughter of Memory). And Un Fitt, the "corresponding" noosphere AI, postmodern angel, or demigod, tries to help "prods" become "revolutionaries," by "pushing," "tantalizing" them, making them go "beyond" themselves because, as Ptolemy says, "you [prods or ex-prods]—flesh and bone and spirit—are the only chains that keep you enslaved to this world and also your only chance to be free" (301).

Should we not now read *Futureland* "sideways," against its hard and glossy cyberpunk grain, and consider the possibility that Mosley's apparent bourgeois reproduction of the lionizing of the self-sacrificing individuals (such as Chill Bent) and the resulting repetition of cyberpunk futility actually represent the satiric negation of those tropes, given that each individual (and one small group) is doomed to fail? Should we not now conclude that the collapse of the world as we know it, in "The Nig in Me," represents the collapse of the conditions that create the need for antagonistic ruses and ironic reversals and therefore represents the collapse of the postmodern empirical straitjacket—labeled "There is no alternative"—that cyberpunks insisted we had no choice but to wear?

If *Futureland*'s apocalypse is an impossible jump-cut, it represents the sort of jump-cut used by filmmakers such as Godard to remind viewers that what we are watching is a movie, to remind viewers that seamlessness is a mystifying illusion provided by bourgeois films. Seamlessness, provided mostly with a delirious stylistic rush by cyberpunks, who have never questioned the structural necessity of global capitalism, facilitates thoughtless escape, the numbing of the ability— for all but the most utopian-motivated and revolutionary-minded, such as Jameson—to think critically. This is why Mosley's apocalypse is a bogus, parodic apocalypse, satirizing fantasies of racialized revenge and satirizing fantasies that refuse to acknowledge the possibility that we will destroy ourselves if we continue as we are, if we refuse to imagine a viable alternative to global capitalism.

How do we know that *Futureland*'s apocalypse is bogus, given that weapons of mass destruction do in fact exist, even if not always in the hands of those "evil-doers" identified as such by some powerful members of the American bourgeoisie? African Negro DNA either does not exist or all of us have African Negro DNA. Given that the human race apparently originated in Africa, race exists not in the human body but in the human mind. *Futureland*'s 12.5-percent African Negro DNA is a parody of the southern legacy of calculating such percentages for legal purposes. That which human beings conceive in their minds, filled with old newspapers, papier-mâché, and balsa struts, human beings can deconstruct and reconstruct, as Mosley suggests, in the image of who most of us (if not all of us, even if secretly) long to be: flourishing individuals in a nonantagonistic sweet hereafter—but here on Earth.

The only way to imagine a way to get there from here, Mosley suggests, is "to be crazy, to imagine the impossible and the ridiculous, to say what it is that [we] want in spite of everyone else's embarrassed laughs. This is a little easier for me," Mosley says, "because I am a fiction writer. Pushing ideas to their limits is what I'm expected to do—in *fiction*. But it's a small skip from fiction to nonfiction in this world of technology and change" (2000, 103). Thus what appears to be a catastrophic end-of-the-world scenario—certainly the end of the capitalist infrastructure of the United States—in the ninth and concluding story is actually the end of postmodern (cyberpunk) futility, which is all too at-home within our brains, and the emergence of the revolutionary wish, color-coded as blackness made visible, seeking humane fulfillment.

"The Nig in Me" thus clears a narrative space for an alternative future, one that we imagine and create, although not entirely from a tabula rasa (that unscribed tablet an unimaginable possibility), but with one preexisting necessary utopian condition: the allegorical 12.5 percent "nig" in each of us. This minimal amount of "nig" is an example of Mosley's attempt to push ideas to their limits in spite of everyone else's embarrassed laugh. The narrator (Mosley, of course, at his satiric best) says, "Astonished Caucasians who survived the plague realized that there was a sizeable portion of Negro blood in their veins. . . . One newscaster ran a clip from Chicago's *Electro-Expose* which showed the towering figure of a Cowled Death rising over a white man only to be stymied when the white man pulled open his shirt to reveal the words THE NIG IN ME: 12.5%" (350–51).

Ridding the world of many, if not most, of its people—a misanthropic wish fulfillment if there ever was one—ridding the world of all of the world's putative white people (Asians and American Indians included) and destroying much of the infrastructure in the United States would not be a happy event, to say the least, for more than a psychotic few. And the apocalypse changes the remaining black survivors, as Mosley portrays them, little. Why should it? Race is one of those bourgeois limitations—distracting us from our real enemies—that we must get beyond. The fundamental problem, intersecting with putative race, as Mosley suggests, is the problem of economic class, the cruel dynamics of a system that divides the world between victimizers and victims while pretending that it does not divide at all.

The 12.5-percent "nig" is a figure at what E. San Juan Jr. calls the "border of trauma and utopia" where identities cannot be "romanticized," or "postalized" by poststructuralists who try to abolish semantically the difference between the real and the imaginary so that "everything becomes undecidable," particularly economic class. Poststructuralists claim, as San Juan says, that we can no longer distinguish between "what is real from what is fake" and that we should celebrate such hallucinatory indeterminacy (1998, 30–31). The bourgeoisie leap with delight when the poststructuralists assert that power is everywhere and therefore nowhere at once—as if, in *Futureland*'s terms, Chill Bent and the female secretary whom Kismet can randomly "pluck" and "ravish" have the same amount of wealth and power as the capitalist czar. The potential minimum 12.5-percent "nig" in each of us knows better.

The "nig" is our human identity that revolts against the trauma of bourgeois undecidability, ignoring the suffering of those who do not have the leisure of playful schizophrenic performances. The "nig" identity revolts against all that now constrains us, against all that privileges the painful past and present, against all that privileges the comfort of an imaginary mystical sweet hereafter or a temporary thrilling or sweet here-elsewhere instead of privileging an attainable pleasurable life on Earth. Thus the "nig" prefigures the collective identity that, in the United States, with its continuing painful legacy of slavery and lingering institutionalized racism, represents the potential fulfillment of that irrepressible revolutionary wish, the creation of a worldwide species-kinship, and therefore of a worldwide species-flourishing, classless society: each of us more than black enough!

Let the cyberpunks and the poststructuralists hunt for their identity in empty space. The highest happiness, as Leon Trotsky said, for the revolutionary, is the *consciousness that one participates in the building of a better future, that one carries on his [or her] shoulders a particle of the fate of [hu]mankind, and that one's life will not have been lived in vain* ("On the Founding of the Fourth International"). Indeed, read against the dystopic "hard and glossy" cyberpunk grain, the collapse in the ninth story, the destruction of the worldwide capitalist infrastructure, the killing of the whitest white people, represents the collapse of the (bourgeois) monadic-driven, postmodern cyberpunk text. A visible sign that this is determinately so: early in *Futureland*, Mosley prefigures the collapse when he figures the problematic nature of cyberpunk "futility"—of any text that situates the "better world" only in our ability to escape pleasurably by doing nothing—in his description of the designer drug called Pulse: "Pulse was a drug dealer's dream. Cooked up at Cal-Tech in the late hours when the professors were in bed. The gene drug altered the structure of the pleasure centers of the brain, temporarily allowing consciousness some measure of control over dreams. With just the right amount, a Pulsar, as the users called themselves, could create a complex fantasy, build a whole world and live in it for what seemed like days, weeks."

Pulsars "lose interest in the world around them, making better worlds in their unconscious mind." Rather than making a new world, however, it is more accurate to say that they vicariously repeat oppressor-oppressed (literary) history, imagining themselves in positions of power. An "unexpected impact on the economy," *Futureland*'s narrator says, is that "in the days between use, Pulsars read many books of fiction and history to seed their minds with the possibility of dreams. Electronic publishing industry stocks soared." Pulsars imagine themselves as the Emperor Hadrian "controlling the Roman empire, battling the Vandals, the Goths, and the Persians." To "make matters worse," the narrator says, "or better from a profit point of view," repeated use of Pulse eventually leads to "bleached-out euphoria," the "loss of specific dream content," and, then, to the collapse of the Pulsars' brains (34–36).

Like Pulse dreams, the science-fictional dream that concedes to the bourgeois claim that "there is no alternative" to the antagonistic culture of the market also concedes to a subsequent "loss of specific dream content," superficial appearances to the contrary (so much advanced technology, and better designer drugs!). Cyberpunk dreams of futility, postmodern dreams of indeterminacy, like Pulse dreams, alter the structure of the pleasure centers of the brain so that pleasure can only mean the lack of social purpose, the lack of hope for real-world structural change, can only mean helpless withdrawal into the lonely but glittering hypnotic monadic ego-palace. Pulse and "postalized" cyberpunk offer "bleached-out euphoria," the ever-present dazzle of style concealing all that empty monadic space, and ultimately—a devil's bargain—the collapse of the brain. Futility is not freedom, but death. *If you can't enjoy life, why live it?* Therefore the collapse ultimately represents the collapse of "bleached-out euphoria," the collapse of the "loss of specific dream content," the collapse of the private monadic ego—prefigured by the collapse of the brains of *Futureland*'s Pulsars—wrongly imagining themselves dream-producing kingdoms unto themselves. In a revolutionary move—the dream world turned upside down—Mosley reverses the cyberpunk thrilling or sweet here-elsewhere so that, in *Futureland*, no one who physically dies, but whose consciousness is sent to cyberspace or its equivalent, wants to be there!—whatever pleasurable fantasies flicker on the magic-lantern walls.

Neil Hawthorne, one of the ex-prods attempting to neutralize the race-targeted gene virus, is injured in the fight with the Itsies. His body is damaged beyond repair. Ptolemy Bent rescues him and merges Neil's consciousness into the computer program with the AI Un Fitt. Neil remembers, and psychically reexperiences, "everything" he "ever knew" but had forgotten: his aunt's name; the girl he had a crush on in prod-ed, whose name was Lana, and whom he loved because "she smelled like soap"; a grasshopper his uncle caught for him: "it was a green creature with long waving antennae that was kept in a plastic cage made to look like bamboo": if Neil "looked close he could see his uncle's face in the many facets of the bug's green eye. Bob" (318). Un Fitt informs Neil that because the part of him that is conscious resides in Un Fitt's matrix, it is a "limbo of sorts." Neil can read the "data" of his life, but he cannot "alter it." Neil asks, "Then how can I live?" Un Fitt provides an answer that produces a "hysterical shudder of claustrophobia" in Neil's mind: "You can talk to me, Neil." When Un Fitt realizes that his answer horrifies Neil, Un Fitt tells him that when they have the sufficient technological tools Neil's lover, Nina, will be able to join him from time to time. Then the narrator intervenes, "What had been a void was suddenly a vast panorama of the sea, the Pacific Ocean, Neil knew instinctively. It was the prehistoric coastline that he'd yearned for since childhood. The waves crashed and huge birds wheeled in the sky. 'Here you may roam until there is a body for you to inhabit again,' Un Fitt whispered between the thundering waves. 'And a world worth living in'" (319).

In contrast to Gibson's Case, Neil Hawthorne longs for the sensuality of the body, for real human company (Nina), and for the sensual world that is always "adventurously moving," the future emerging from the present, this "latently expectant world—the most real thing there is" (Bloch 1935, 162). No imaginary sweet hereafter or thrilling or sweet here-elsewhere, no imaginary immaterial AI, no matter how benevolent or wise or potentially divine, will ever do for human beings, despite the ways that some of us may mystically deceive ourselves. "Pleasure," as Jameson says, for human beings, "is finally the consent of life in the body, the reconciliation—momentary as it may be—with the necessity of physical existence in a physical world" (1988, 70).

Some of our physical world as it is—allegorized by Neil's recovered memories, such as girls who smell like soap, uncles named "Bob," the many facets of a bug's green eye, the thundering of ocean waves—could become a world "worth living in" if we would only first recognize the utter unnecessity of so much suffering. As utopian revealer Ernst Bloch says, "the earth has room for everyone, or it would have, if it were run by the power of satisfying people's needs instead of by satisfying the needs of power" (1986, 469). Recognition of this fact, however, is not enough. To get to that better future will require a violent crossing over, as Marx and Engels historically determined, from the kingdom of necessity (trauma) to the kingdom of freedom (utopia). The ruling class will not give up more than a few seats at their banquet table and then only to keep the wheels of capitalism oiled instead of grinding to a halt. To imagine that they may do otherwise is to imagine that they will willingly become—what else but?—socialists. Neil's consciousness, deprived of any choice in the matter, unhappily awaits the crossing over, his consciousness bearing with it, for all our benefit, pleasurable childhood memories, previously forgotten, infused now with anticipatory longing for our better future.

However, what Mosley does best, what he does most credibly—whether he likes it or not—is revolutionary anger. He may very well fear his own anger, or fear working-class anger (existing primarily in the so-called third world, out of our sight). In fact, in his nonfiction anticapitalist monographs, Mosley rejects

Marx's insight that the anger (and hope) of the proletariat will lead them to seize the means of production and to eliminate class hierarchies. Mosley seems to think that we can use the official law against the official law in order to change that law. In *Futureland,* however, he drops that desired charade. Anger, Mosley seems to know in spite of himself, will be of use if we are ever to stand on the side of the victims against the victimizers, which is to say, if we are ever to put our money, so to speak, where our mouths are.

Kismet, with the help of his henchman, Tristan the First, Dominar of the Blue Zone, persuades Frendon Blythe, in "Little Brother," to kill a police officer (who has threatened to kill Blythe for his revolutionary evocations). The mechanized court system, Prime Nine, is theoretically better than a human one because it knows only objective facts. No computerized judge can, for example, be subjectively blinded by race. Blythe, racially ambiguous, wants to tell his story of how he came to commit murder. He says the court must understand his motivations, must therefore have an "understanding of [Blythe] which is not genetically based, and that can only be gleaned through personal narrative." The court tells him that "narrative evidence is the weakest form of legal defense," but they allow him after all to represent himself and tell his story (215, 216).

Blythe was "White Noise" a "Backgrounder." Born in Common Ground, an underground slum for the unemployed, the "only homes he had ever known were governmental institutions and the octangular sleep tubes of Common Ground. He never had a bedroom or a bicycle. He never had a backyard" (211). He never knew his parents. He says, "White Noise men and women are barred from ever working again. And the children of White Noise, as I am, might never know a day of employment in their lives" (216, 217). Blythe says the "biggest problem with being White Noise is perpetual and unremitting boredom," and there's "no way up unless you die." The narrator says, "All Frendon wanted was not to be bored, to not sit a thousand feet underground and wait for sleep or wake to gray. That's why he'd agreed to this crazy plan of the man who called himself Dominar. That's why he'd killed and allowed himself to be captured. Anything but what he was destined for." Frendon "didn't want peace. He wanted bright colors and noise, good food and sex with any woman, man, or dog that wouldn't bite him. In the absence of anything else Frendon would take pain. And in the absence of pain he would even accept death." Frendon says, "'I was so bored . . . that I started to wonder about politics. I wondered if we could make some kind of action that would close the Common Ground down. I started talking about it, to my friends at first and then to anyone who would listen. 'Come join the revolution,' I said to them. 'Let's burn this fucker down'" (219–20).

We learn, along with Blythe, that the Dominar and Kismet have manipulated Blythe from the beginning in order to test the robotic computerized court system, which Kismet designed. The Dominar has bet Kismet that he designed the system "too well," that the "compassion quotient in the wetware would soften the court" (226). The court is made up of "the wetware neuronal components of ten thousand potential jurors," ten thousand "biologically linked and compressed personalities," an "amalgam of various magistrates, lawyers, and legislators created by the biological linkage and compression system to be the ablest of judges" (210). At the end Blythe loses his case, and Kismet loses his bet with the Dominar. The court kills Blythe's body, but first extracts his memories. Frendon (disembodied, part of the cyber-court) tells the Dominar: "You and your master [Kismet] are monsters. . . . I'll kill you both one day. . . . The people who volunteered for this justice system, as you call it, never knew that you'd blend their identities until they were slaves to the system. It wasn't until your stupid game that they were able to circumvent the programming. They see me as a liberator and they hate you more than I do." The Dominar says the master can "snip, snip" the wires, killing the computer program. Blythe says "Every self-conscious cell has been transferred by a system we designed in the first three seconds of our liberation. Prime Nine now is only a simulation of who we were. We're out here somewhere you'll never know. Not until we're right on top of you, choking the life from your lungs." The story concludes when the narrator says, "Frendon felt the cold fear of the Dominar's response before he shrugged off the connection. Then he settled himself into the ten thousand singers celebrating their single mind—and their revenge" (227).

In *Futureland,* cyberspace is not the monadic no-place of the sweet hereafter or thrilling or sweet here-elsewhere in which the cyberpunks projected and contained the irrepressible revolutionary wish, the longing for a better world, robbing it of its material content and real-world threat to the bourgeoisie. Mosley's overturning of cyberspace is the (*not yet*) utopian space in which the revolutionary wish is revealed, energized with hope and with anger, and preserved for the sake of the material future. Cyberspace in Mosley's revision is the imaginary space reimagined with a difference that matters: connecting Chill Bent's uncounted voices, those identities at the border of trauma and utopia, not hard and superficially glossy enough to count in cyberpunk. It is the imaginary space that preserves the utopian dream, the memory of the possibility of a world worth living in, and the imaginary space intervening for the sake of a future alternative: all that stored energy soon to be intentionally released by revolutionaries who are not satisfied with being prods, who have finally asked, *What else is there, or what else could there be?* and have answered that question. There can be a new world—without the bourgeoisie. More visibly so than cyberpunk, *Futureland* can therefore help us "circumvent" our bourgeois programming, can infuse a potential "reserve force"—not yet ready to risk breaking the chains or their own bones for freedom—with Frendon Blythe's angry Common Ground revolutionary consciousness.

This reserve force will be constituted, in the United States, by a strata of the bourgeoisie sick of the bourgeoisie, like *Futureland*'s ten thousand judges, and by some of the working-class who are not yet class-conscious of themselves as an exploited class but who will, with anger and hope, become so. The more the better: limiting the amount of necessary bloodshed, or ensuring that the blood that is shed will be for the sake of collective human flourishing, not for the sake of the financial profit of the bourgeoisie. For who else, in the United States, reads science fiction, that genre always already, in one way or another, of alternative worlds, but a strata of the bourgeoisie, "dissatisfied," as Mosley says, "with things as they are," and sometimes (but we should probably admit, rarely) members of the working class who toil and suffer for the pleasure of the bourgeoisie who have the leisure to suppose, *If you can't enjoy life, why live it?*

Furthermore, *Futureland*'s potential reserve force will be one that at least, or at last, understands that not only is the "happy slave" a rationalizing myth, but also will understand that if race insists on mattering, by those hierarchically above and those below: All right then! *Treason to whiteness is loyalty to humanity!*—as long as we understand that "whiteness," as Chill Bent not quite consciously suggests, is code for "bourgeoisie," and "wanna be white" is code for "wanna be bourgeoisie." As we all know, American slave-owners used the premodern biblical mythical mark of Ham to curse black people by divine law to be nothing else but hewers of wood and drawers of water, servants to the putative servants of the Lord. For Mosley, that divinely degraded black mark signifies a world willing to commodify human beings for the sake of profit, but also signifies a people willing to fight collectively for freedom. However, Mosley recognizes that the external black mark does not automatically signify the radical desire to, or the capacity to, "imagine the totality of something that could be different" ("Something's Missing" 3–4). Like Richard Wright, Mosley knows that "the oppressed minorities often reflect the techniques of the bourgeoisie more brilliantly than some sections of the bourgeoisie themselves." Wright adds: "The psychological importance of this becomes meaningful when it is recalled that oppressed minorities, and especially the petty bourgeoisie sections of oppressed minorities, strive to assimilate the virtues of the bourgeoisie in the assumption that by doing so they can lift themselves into a higher social sphere" (1938, 53). And who can blame them (or us)?—when the suffering that comes with poverty means a lack of sufficient food, water, and shelter and means work that—if it is to be had at all—lacks anything remotely resembling individual or communal flourishing.

In the third story, "Dr. Kismet," Mosley shows us how premodern religion fused with modern empirical science and postmodern advanced technology (what eclectisim!), in the hands of the Napoleonic bourgeoisie, turns many black people, darker-skinned, and poor (white) people against themselves—in spite of or because of their unrealized utopian desires. Such internal antagonism—the DuBoisian double consciousness and the putative Lacanian split—prevents the exploited from forming a collective identity that could possibly lead to class consciousness and thereby threaten bourgeois wealth and power. Kismet establishes InfoChurch and designs a Database of Hope that draws black people and poor Latinos and poor whites to the hope that someone hears their sorrows and will occasionally offer solace and material help. But such imaginary resolutions to real contradictions come at a price—the enslavement of their minds and bodies, the bleaching of (the bourgeoisification of) their psyches. Whatever is, is God's will for them. And their "Kismet," their corporate master, their occasional benefactor, is white, wealthy, and male.

Fayez Akwande, diplomatic co-leader of RadCon 6, observes that "the weight of poverty, the failure of justice, came down on the heads of dark people around the globe. Capitalism along with technology had assured a perpetual white upper class" (73). Akwande has worked all of his adult life "to free the minds and bodies of black people around the world." He thinks that if he can "turn Ivan Kismet," the world's wealthiest person, "toward his own goals, the rest of the world must surely follow." Dr. Kismet tells Akwande, from whom Kismet knows he has nothing to fear (an individual poses no threat): "I command more of the love and support among the people that you profess to represent than you could ever imagine.... The black masses have taken to InfoChurch like bears to honey. My message that God is a riddle and the world of science filled with His clues has captured more imaginations than any King or X or radical assassin" (65).

Kismet's henchman, Tristan the First, Dominar of the Blue Zone, "blesses and instructs the people on the usage of the terminals in deciphering God's secrets," those "lessons in [bourgeois empirical] science that include "the force of gravity," the "bending of light," the "path of the living cell through evolution. Infinity and black holes," those lessons suggesting that "black" is "evil or random or unknown," that "black robs the mind of sight," that black "is the collapse of the whole universe" (65, 82). Kismet's divine clues are nothing else but a postmodern version of Jacob Boehme's sixteenth-century "doctrine of signatures" (borrowed from Plato) asserting that God has marked everything "He" created with a sign indicative of its value and purpose: "as above so below." The doctrine of signatures naturalized the medieval Great Chain of Being, situating poor people and darker-skinned people near the bottom of the chain, where, colonized, they already were, away from the "light" and the "true" and the "good," not however, without a "divine" purpose: serving those further up the chain.

Akwande, sickened by the sight of "all those black people kneeling in front of" Kismet's computer screens, decides, in futility, to work for Kismet by helping him colonize Mars, where there are fewer people—a "new world" for the "human race," as Kismet disingenuously says. He means a new world established by and for the profit of the bourgeoisie. Akwande tells XX Y, the more radical co-leader of RadCon 6 who, unlike Akwande, believes in violent "overthrow," that he is leaving for Mars because here on Earth he "can't change it." He says, "I've been to the master's [Kismet's] home. I've been to the master's church. I live on his plantation. I begged him to feed Mali, to give them freedom. They took his money but it didn't buy their freedom. They just joined the international Economic Congress and put mercenaries at their borders" (83). However, Akwande's last words to XX Y are: "I'm leaving the guns with you, brother...."

And I leave you my blessing, too" (82–83). For XX Y—the "militant chromosome" (327), the "war" is ongoing. The purpose of that war is "victory, not peace, not compromise" (73). Akwande recovers, however, relatively unscathed, from the realization that he has, in fact, lost to Kismet, and to XX Y—willing to risk breaking his own bones, and the bones of the slave-master Kismet, who stands in the way of freedom. Akwande will transfer his family to Mars, where he can "ensure," or so he believes, their comfort, their "safety and future" (69, 73).

Futureland concludes with a focus on Harold Bottoms, who, unlike Akwande, does not have the luxury of escape to Mars. Preapocalypse, Harold is a "prod" who believes in XX Y's militant ideal, who understands the bourgeois threat "there is no alternative," but, with no alternative in sight, "lives according to the cycles" (327). Harold loses his Persian lover, Yasmine Mu, and his best friend, Jamey, to the previously mentioned gene virus. Postapocalypse, Harold sits with Jamey's corpse in an abandoned New York home on a deserted block (most everyone is dead or desperately trying to get out of New York). The narrator says, "Harold sat with the stink of his friend's rotting corpse, not because he was enthralled, but because he was lonely. Lonely for lost Jamey and Yasmine. Lonely for the world that he moved in. He wondered if the dancers on the Sixtieth Street pier saw the flash of the bomb for an instant before they died" (353). When Harold's father—whom Harold has not spoken to or seen in years—reaches Harold through his ID-chip, Harold tells his father, "My friends all died." His father asks, "White kids?" Harold responds, "I guess." Harold agrees to meet his parents at his brother's St. Louis farm, a place he has never been before. As Harold leaves the abandoned house the narrator tells us that one of the "swarthy-looking" Neo-Nazi white supremacists raises a pistol and yells "Hey, nig!" Harold Bottoms ducks and runs. "All around him branches, windows, and even the walls of the Gales' home exploded from the charged shells that the so-called white men loosed." But

> Harold went through the house and out the back window, into the
> woods and was gone. There was a rhythm to his footfalls and his body
> through the trees. When Harold realized that he had escaped death,
> he began to laugh.
> The world had started over.

The world may have started over for the individual Harold, but racism continues, even when everyone who survives the holocaust, according to Mosley's allegorized DNA, is black. Thus Mosley clearly demonstrates the bogus nature of racist distinctions and the pointlessness of racist genocide. Class-based societies inevitably produce conflict-driven discrimination. The profit motive is not inherently racist (or sexist)—after all, skin color (and gender) do not prevent one from selling one's labor to another who thereby profits, or from spending the money one makes as a laborer on the products one makes as a laborer. Capitalists, the ruling class, however, do need the oppressed class to be distracted from the fact of who their real enemies are, do need the oppressed to displace their anger elsewhere and to reproduce in their lives the submission-domination dynamic inherent to the culture of the market. Race (and gender) function, like religion, as handy tools of displacement for their anger and as distractions that prevent the development of class consciousness. For Mosley, "blackness" (black people and black culture) collectively indeed exists—as a social construction. To be "black," however, has nothing to do with skin color and everything to do with standing on the side of the victims rather than on the side of the victimizers. "Difference" can relate, as the poststructuralists say, but in a class-divided society—that denies the overdetermined and overdetermining existence of itself—difference always already separates.

Harold's life as an exploited "prod," as a slave to the system, is over. The present signifies a rhythmic fusion between the individual and the external world, between mind and body, between subject and object. The present, no longer reified, is the sensual world that is always "adventurously moving." It is this "latently expectant world" that includes within in it the emerging future, "the most real thing there is" (Bloch 1935, 162). Here, in the (not yet) utopian space, the meaning of freedom does not fade but calls to us from another future horizon, on the other side of trauma, from the utopian society that we will create: where individuals flourish because everyone flourishes together, where "everybody has the opportunity to be a human being, because nobody any longer has the opportunity to be a monster" (Bloch 1986, 2:531). Harold Bottoms is thus, at once, an individual and an allegorical figure of humankind—claiming the world as its longed-for home.

Sterling may believe, and he may well be correct, that cyberpunk performs a service by uncovering our eyes to the fact of our instrumentalized rat-reality, but *Futureland* performs the more challenging service, the more necessary service, of negating that rat-in-a-cage reality by negating cyberpunk's trope of futility. "The world," Mosley says, "isn't waiting for us to see it," like some predetermined hell or some predetermined sweet hereafter in heaven. "It is waiting for us to build it" (2000, 19). The utopian longing to rebuild the world does not signify a soap-bubble dream, nor does it signify the requirement of a "composition of blueprints for bourgeois comfort" (Jameson 2005, 12). Instead, as Mosley, the time-traveling detective and time-traveling would-be utopian architect, reveals in *Futureland*, the utopian-longing signifies, in our time and place, the negation of that textual straitjacket, the negation of proclaimed futility, the negation of the social construction of the monadic ego into which so many of us uselessly escape. Because Mosley refuses to provide that blueprint but reveals the bourgeois mechanisms that limit our imagination, we may now begin to imagine that we *can* imagine, that we *must* imagine the possibility of that better world of collective human flourishing, the not yet written tenth story of plenitude for all. The alternative—that there is no alternative—is too impossible to bear.

Bibliography

Adorno, Theodor W. 1991. "The Schema of Mass Culture." In *Adorno: The Culture Industry,* ed. J. M. Bernstein, 61–97. London: Routledge.

Bloch, Ernst. 1935. "Marxism and Poetry." In *The Utopian Function of Art and Literature: Selected Essays,* trans. Jack Zipes and Frank Mecklenburg, 156–62. Cambridge, Mass.: MIT Press, 1988.

———. 1986. *The Principle of Hope,* trans. Neville Plaice, Stephen Plaice, and Paul Knight. 3 vols. Cambridge, Mass.: MIT Press, 1986.

Bloch, Ernst, and Theodor Adorno. 1988. "Something's Missing: A Discussion between Ernst Bloch and Theodor W. Adorno on the Contradictions of Utopian Longing." In *The Utopian Function of Art and Literature: Selected Essays,* trans. Jack Zipes and Frank Mecklenburg, 1–17. Cambridge, Mass.: MIT Press.

Cadigan, Pat. 1987. *Mindplayers.* London: Orion Books, 2000.

———. 2004. "Introduction: Not a Manifesto." In *The Ultimate Cyberpunk,* vii–xiv. New York: Simon and Schuster.

Csicsery-Ronay, Jr., Istvan. 1991. "Cyberpunk and Neuromanticism." In *Storming the Reality Studio: A Casebook of Cyberpunk and Postmodern Fiction,* ed. Larry McCaffery, 181–93. Durham, N.C.: Duke University Press.

Freedman, Carl. 2000. *Critical Theory and Science Fiction.* Hanover, N.H.: Wesleyan University Press.

Gibson, William. 1984. *Neuromancer.* New York: Berkley.

Horkheimer, Max, and Theodor Adorno. 1944. "The Culture Industry: Enlightenment as Mass Deception." In *Dialectic of Enlightenment,* trans. John Cumming, 120–67. New York: Continuum, 1999.

Hollinger, Veronica. 1991. "Cybernetic Deconstructions: Cyberpunk and Postmodernism." In *Storming the Reality Studio: A Casebook of Cyberpunk and Postmodern Fiction,* ed. McCaffery, 203–18. Durham, N.C.: Duke University Press.

Jameson, Fredric. 1971. "Ernst Bloch and the Future." In *.Marxism and Form: Twentieth Century Dialectical Theories of Literature.* Princeton, N.J.: Princeton University Press.

———. 1988. "Pleasure: A Political Issue." In *The Ideologies of Theory: Essays 1971–1986,* 2:61–74. Minneapolis: University of Minnesota Press.

———. 2005. *Archeologies of the Future: The Desire Called Utopia and Other Science Fictions.* London and New York: Verso.

Marx, Karl. 1887. *Capital.* In *The Marx-Engels Reader,* ed. Robert C. Tucker, 1:302–438. 2nd ed. New York: Norton, 1978.

McCaffery, Larry. 1991. "An Interview with William Gibson." In *Storming the Reality Studio: A Casebook of Cyberpunk and Postmodern Fiction,* ed. McCaffery, 263–85. Durham, N.C.: Duke University Press.

Mosley, Walter. 1998. *Blue Light.* Boston: Little, Brown.

———. 2000. *Workin' on the Chain Gang: Shaking Off the Dead Hand of History.* New York: Ballantine.

———. 2001a. "Black to the Future." In *Dark Matter: A Century of Speculative Fiction from the African Diaspora,* ed. Sheree R. Thomas, 405–7. New York: Warner.

———. 2001b. *Futureland: Nine Stories of an Imminent World.* New York: Warner.

Novotny, Patrick. 1997. "No Future! Cyberpunk, Industrial Music, and the Aesthetics of Postmodern Disintegration." In *Political Science Fiction,* ed. Donald M. Hassler and Clyde Wilcox, 99–123. Columbia: University of South Carolina Press.

San Juan, E. 1998. *Beyond Postcolonial Theory.* New York: St. Martin's Press.

Shiner, Lewis. 2002. "Til Human Voices Wake Us." In *The Ultimate Cyberpunk,* ed. Pat Cadigan, 184–99. New York: Simon and Schuster.

Sterling, Bruce. 1985. *Schismatrix.* In *Schismatrix Plus.* New York: Berkley, 1996.

———. 1986a. Preface to *Burning Chrome,* by William Gibson. New York: Arbor House.

———. 1986b. Preface to *Mirrorshades: The Cyberpunk Anthology,* ed. Sterling. New York: Arbor House.

———. 1991. "Twenty Evocations." In *Storming the Reality Studio: A Casebook of Cyberpunk and Postmodern Fiction,* ed. Larry McCaffery, 154–61. Durham, N.C.: Duke University Press.

———. 1998. "Cyperpunk in the Nineties." *Interzone,* May. http://www.lib.ru/STERLINGB/interzone.txt.

Thatcher, Margaret. 1987. "Interview for Women's Own." Margaret Thatcher Foundation. www.margaretthatcher.org/speeches (accessed November 6, 2007).

———. 1987. "Speech at Soviet Official Banquet." Margaret Thatcher Foundation. www.margaretthatcher.org/speeches (accessed November 6, 2007).

Trotsky, Leon. 1938. "On the Founding of the Fourth International." *Marxists Internet Archive.* http://www.marxists.org/archive/trotsky/1938 (accessed November 6, 2007).

Wright, Richard. 1938. "Blueprint for Negro Writing." In *African American Literary Theory: A Reader,* ed. Winston Napier, 45–53. New York: New York University Press, 2000.

A Last Situation

Secretary of State Condoleezza Rice
and Cultural Critic Leslie Fiedler

Marleen S. Barr

> I can't get inside George Bush's head. It is not a place I would like to be,
> anyway. (John Edwards, April 14, 2005)
>
> Their [Vice President Cheney's and Cardinal Ratzinger's] gloomy world
> outlooks and bullying roles earned them the nicknames Dr. No and Car-
> dinal No. One is called Washington's Darth Vader, the other the Vatican's
> Darth Vader. (Maureen Dowd, April 23, 2005)

In 2001, when I published a *Newsday* piece called "Bush's Missile Shield Is a Science Fiction Fantasy," I described George W. Bush's embarkation upon a specious
space odyssey. I argued that science fiction is applicable to Bush's stance on missile defense system technology. The *New York Times* chose to call one of its March
31, 2005, editorials "A Science Fiction Army." This editorial asserts that "the
Army's stubborn commitment to the ultra-high-technology complex of weapons, robots and communications networks collectively known as Future Combat
Systems . . . must be radically scaled back." The *Times* editorial page certainly did
not proclaim "Extra, Extra Read All about It: Marleen S. Barr's Comparison
between the Military and Science Fiction Is Right on Target." The paper of
record's approach to the subject, however, does enable me to say I told you so
regarding science fiction's applicability to generating fruitful analysis of Bush's
agenda in relation to the military. I now continue to apply science fiction paradigms to modern public consciousness: science fiction yields insights about how
the Bush family approaches biology to promote and perpetuate their political
agenda. This is the most situational essay in this concluding section on situations.

The first section of my essay, "Bush and the Borg," describes how the Bush
family acts in terms of science fiction tropes to use biology to further its political ambitions. I emphasize how Secretary of State Condoleezza Rice functions in
terms of their designs. The second section, "Condi and Leslie," draws upon the

connections I make between the Bush family, science fiction, and biology to argue that Rice can be understood as a component of the American racial and historical story Leslie Fiedler outlines in *The Inadvertent Epic: From Uncle Tom's Cabin to Roots.* I include a postscript that explains how to apply my analysis to real-world concerns.

Bush and the Borg

According to the usual hierarchies of domination, patricians and political elites intermarry to keep wealth and power within their families. (Franklin Delano Roosevelt married his cousin Eleanor. Dwight Eisenhower's grandson married Richard Nixon's daughter. Mario Cuomo's son married Robert Kennedy's daughter.) George W. and Jeb Bush deviated from this entrenched pattern. George W., scion of politically powerful aristocrats, married Laura Welch, who is neither beautiful, brilliant, nor wealthy. Why? Because she is acceptably ordinary in every way—and American voters gravitate toward the ordinary. George W. can appear only as a faux garden-variety, ranch-brush-raking good ol' Texas boy. Connecting himself to Laura enhances his enacted "ordinary guy" appeal. Unlike George W., his twin daughters are partially biologically bona fide plebeian Texans.

When Jeb married a white Hispanic, he deviated even further than George W. from usual patrician marriage practices. Jeb and Columba Bush produced something new under the Bush family sun: their son, George P. Bush, an authentic biologically Hispanic George Bush—a Florida Republican dream candidate. Science fiction can explain the Bush brothers' decision to create progeny who differ from the usual elite Bush family members: George W. and Jeb, in the manner of the *Star Trek* Borg collective, derive strength and perpetuate themselves by assimilating the different. The Borg hive-mind includes individuals named "Third of Five." The Bush hive-mind includes individuals named George H. W., George W., and George P. The biologically Hispanic George P. is alien and morphed in relation to the fully Anglo-Saxon George Bushes who precede him. As for *Bush: The Next Generation:* if George P. marries a Hispanic woman, he can engender a new Bush family biological individual—an even more fully Hispanic George Bush. Thomas Frank, in *What's the Matter with Kansas?*, points out that "you can only believe that George W. Bush is a man of the people if you have screened out his family's economic status" (2004, 129). Creating evermore biologically diverse George Bushes fosters the illusionary disconnection between these potential individuals and their family's ultra-elite economic status.

Frank discusses conservative backlash thinking about liberals: "Liberals do anything . . . that promises to advance their larger partisan project, to create more liberals, and thus to 'win'. . . . It [the culture industry according to the conservative stance] does the ugly things that it does because it is honeycombed with robotic, alien liberals, trying to drip their corrosive liberalism into our ears" (135, 137). What's the matter with this backlash thinking? Well, for one thing, liberals certainly do not advance their position by marrying off their children to any progressive relatives that, say, Rush Limbaugh or Tom DeLay might have. (Full disclosure: although I am embarrassed to admit that my first cousin Clifford D. May is a former Republican National Committee communications director, I am not related to the rabidly Clinton-hating conservative former congressman from Georgia, Bob Barr.) The Republican Party is "honeycombed" with beehive Borgian "robotic, alien" conservatives.

Which brings me to how science fiction shapes a phenomenon such as Condoleezza Rice. I situate Rice as a twenty-first-century component of Leslie Fiedler's *The Inadvertent Epic* to explain why the Bush family cannot science-fictionally, biologically assimilate African Americans in a manner analogous to Borg collective paradigm I apply to Jeb and Columba's simultaneously Anglo-Saxon and Hispanic offspring. While the Borg are free to fraternize with any species they might desire in a galaxy far, far away, white American political candidates in, say, heartland Peoria are still not free to father mixed-race children. (Strom Thurmond's mixed-race daughter waited until her father died and she herself was a senior citizen before she made her lineage public. And speaking of Peoria, that city is located in the home state of Barack Obama, a mixed-race politician who is acceptable to the electorate because his parentage erases the relationship between blackness and American history. Obama, the son of an absent African father and a white midwestern mother, stems from a genetic heritage removed from American slavery. Obama, raised by his mother and her white parents, is more culturally white than, say, such respectively Italian and Jewish ethnic urban politicians as Mario Cuomo and Michael Bloomberg.[1])

While Obama's biologically generated cultural differences from the majority of African Americans absolutely adheres to real-world science, Rice seems to present an altogether different case. Rice, who shows no public evidence of sharing familial or intimate ties with any human being—African American or otherwise—seems to have sprung fully formed at birth from within a concert piano. Fielder's ideas help me to position Rice in terms of a science fiction story about biology that is less overt than the Borgian, sexual-intercourse-generated class and ethnic difference the Bush twins and George P. bring to the Bush family.

In terms of Fiedler's vision, I describe George W. as a white American Republican hero who forms an extremely close emotional and professional bond with a black woman. His relationship with Rice can be understood as an innocent interracial, heterosexual counterpart to the "innocent homosexuality" Fiedler so famously defined in *Love and Death in the American Novel* and "Come Back to the Raft Ag'in, Huck Honey!" George W., in other words, science-fictionally assimilates Rice within the Bush family collective according to a biological mode in which sexual intercourse between an African American woman and a white man plays no part. I am thinking of all the science fiction stories in which an alien brain is ensconced within a host body. I am thinking of the Vulcan mind meld. I am thinking that "Bush's brain" (invoking the term used in

Wayne Slater and James Moore's *Bush's Brain: How Karl Rove Made George W. Bush Presidential*) is implanted within a black woman's body and that, via this brain implantation, Rice is assimilated within the Bush family collective. In the manner of Captain Jean-Luc Picard, Colin Powell, who has a brain of his own, escaped permanent assimilation. Rice, in contrast, is the Bush family's black handmaid, what Maureen Dowd, when describing Rice, calls someone who "always seemed subservient to President Bush and Vice President Dick Cheney, a willing handmaiden and spokesman for their bellicose bidding" (2005b). With Bush's brain securely ensconced within her head, Rice is a real, biological black woman who, via an innocent interracial heterosexuality, functions as a racially cross-dressed male Bush in blackface.

Eric Lott's "Racial Cross-Dressing and the Construction of American Whiteness," which refers to Fiedler's *Love and Death In the American Novel,* helps me explain how Rice's racial cross-dressing negates the fact of her biological blackness. Lott asks, "Why . . . this literal inhabiting of black bodies as a way of interracial male bonding? . . . Leslie Fiedler argued in *Love and Death in the American Novel* . . . that our white male writers have been stubbornly preoccupied with white male/dark male dyads . . . which apparently fulfill a white need to be 'Negroes' together'" (Lott 1993, 142–43). The science fiction image of Bush's brain located within Rice's cranium indicates that the Bush family mind-set is a "literal inhabiting" of Rice's black body. I call this mind-set Bushface. Bushface, a Borgian assimilation method, negates racial identity as it fulfills the white Bush team's need for women and minorities to function as white male Bush team members "together." "Blackface, then, reifies and at the same time trespasses on the boundaries of 'race.' I see this doubleness as highly indicative of the shape of American whiteness" (Lott 1993, 142). Rice in Bushface negates her blackness. The brain trespass and racial erasure she manifests is a doubleness highly indicative of the Bush team's need to engage in Borgian assimilative brain transfers.

Luckily for George W. Bush, brain implantation is science fiction; Bush is not literally brainless. I stress that it is Bush's figurative brain, not Karl Rove's particular brain, which is reproduced within Rice's head. Brain-implantation or brain-cloning, not just another vehicle for a metaphorical treatment of the relationship between Bush and Rice, is that relationship's predominant social construct. Lott's understanding of blackface, when considered in terms of science fiction, leads to my description of Rice appearing in Bushface. The metaphorical use of science fiction to describe Bushface, not merely fortuitous, stems from a direct understanding of the specifically science-fictional brain-implantation trope.

Close attention to the clothes that Rice, the racially cross-dressed black female in white-male Bushface, wears illuminates this point. *New York Magazine's* "Party Lines" column poses this question: "Condi's knee-high boots in Germany: fashion foibles or Bush administration brilliance?" The answer: "Condoleezza Rice looks great in her dominatrix boots. She's got her own style. And what I like most is her hair. It's all about order" (Yuan 2005, 10). I beg to differ. Rice's style is that of George W. Bush's brain housed in a black female body dressing for success. Angela Davis and Rice use different hairdressers. Rice's hairstyle, which bears no resemblance to the genetically black Afro coiffure, communicates the Bush social order: The hairstyle appearing on Rice's black female head that contains Bush's brain communicates that these dominatrix "boots are made for walkin' and that's just what they'll do; one of these days these boots are gonna walk all over you." Rice's Orwellian boots are made for walkin' to Walker's Point in Kennebunkport, Maine; they do not follow in Nancy Sinatra's feminist footprints. "Are you ready boots? Start walkin'," commands the commander in chief situated within Rice's head.

Attention to Rice's sartorial style is not trivial. Although *New York Times* foreign affairs correspondent Thomas L. Friedman is certainly no Joan Rivers dishing about celebrity fashionistas traipsing across the Academy Awards dream-factory red carpet, this journalism eminence does comment on what Rice wears when she treads across the world stage: "Every new secretary of state gets his or her moment on the world stage, where everyone 'oohs' and 'ahs' about how smart they are and what a 'dream team' staff they have put together. As the first secretary of state to ever wear stiletto heels when reviewing troops, Condoleezza Rice has had a coming-out season second to none" (Friedman 2005). There is nothing debutantish or feminine or culturally black about Rice's attire, which epitomizes an epistemology that comes straight out of George W. Bush's closet. Rice "comes straight out" according to Fiedler's use of the word *innocent* in relation to sexual transgression figuring in the relationship she enjoys with Bush. Real, biological, heterosexual intercourse is categorically separate from the Rice/George W. science-fictional brain implantation and Rice's interracial cross-dressing.

Back to the stilettos. No real biological woman who ever walked across the modern world stage did so while wearing stiletto heels. Madeleine Albright wears large pins, not stilettos. Although I cannot pin down the exact reason why, there is something not kosher about the idea of Golda Meir wearing stilettos. Indira Gandhi defined combining stilettos with saris as a definite fashion "don't." The point is that no real woman who wields political power dresses like the stiletto-clad Rice. Every real woman knows that stilettos, which are definitely not made for walkin', retard purposeful movement and serious work. Only a science fiction analog woman fitted with a transplanted male brain would walk across the word stage wearing stiletto heels. Madeleine, Golda, Indira, and Hillary are no Carrie Bradshaw. Rice is not attired in the manner of a usual politically powerful woman. She instead is dressed like a refugee from female-genre-fiction-hero central casting. Condi presents herself in a manner more akin to Emma Peel than to the sensibly pantsuited Hillary Clinton. Condi looks like she broke into the *Matrix* wardrobe department and absconded with costumes designed for Carrie-Anne Moss playing Trinity. But, Condi, unlike fantastic female heroes, can trip on her heels, fall flat on her face. Friedman explains: "Does she have the toughness to deal with Ariel Sharon? She has not shown it up to now. . . . The will to move the Egyptians? Too soon to say" (2005). Does she or does she not? I know for sure: Rice only looks the part of a female science fiction superhero; she does not have a science fiction hero's infallible power. If it is necessary to move the Egyptians, for example, it is better to call in Charlton Heston playing Moses than Rice playing a Trinity clone.

In terms of specific science fiction literature, black female/white male Rice can be understood as an ineffective doppelgänger of Joanna Russ's Jael, the female man. Rice is a Bush wolf cross-dressed in black-sheep science-fiction-hero clothing, the perfect Eloi-esque human cattle made for walkin' on Bush's Texas faux ranch. The allusion of power associated with Rice—not her individual "will" and "toughness" (her effectiveness)—is what is crucially important for Bush agenda implementation. It is of no matter whether or not Rice has the "steel to deal with the Syrians" (Friedman 2005). It is enough that she has been absorbed within the Bush family. The Bush family is the patriarchal man of steel, the male superhero who has no use for a real, effective, biologically female counterpart. Dr. Rice only plays the woman of steel on TV. She is, instead, a vulnerable Borg queen, positioned as a Bush stand-in standing stilettoed on the world stage while reviewing the science-fictional, robotic, Future Combat Systems troops. Nikes would serve Rice better than stilettos: she is a sneaker, someone attired, positioned, and functioning as a science fiction character who carries out sneak attacks upon American integrity and American reality.

George W. and Condi together enact a variant of the "innocent" sexuality Fiedler described. I refer to what I understand to be a twenty-first-century version of Huck and Jim discussing nineteenth-century American social issues while leisurely floating down river on a raft: George W. and Condi discussing the ship of state while frenetically peddling side by side on White House gym exercise bikes. Huck and Jim, white boy and the black former slave, did not have a close homosexual encounter while together on their raft. George and Condi, white male fake Texas good ol' boy and black female Borgian android, do not have close heterosexual encounters while together on their exercise bikes. They are innocent of sexual transgression. I imagine that while Laura is alone in bed reading, George and Condi peddle away in tandem while panting and sweating and plotting to do us all in:

> "Is exercise bike speed warp factor six good for you, Condi honey?"
> "Yes, George. Yes. Yes. Yes. Yes, Stairmaster. Yes, master."

No science fiction female hero, no female man like Russ's Jael, Rice is an asexual female yes-man.

She fails in cyberfeminist as well as feminist science fiction terms. Rice is an anti-cyberfeminist subversive. Condi does not open new holes in the world, does not work in the chinks of the world machine. She is at once located at the apex of American power and steeped in the twentieth-century world order. Who needs a Russia expert after the cold war is over? Why did George W. not send this standard academic job rejection letter to would-be State Department head former Professor Rice? "We regret to inform you that your particular area of expertise does not meet the needs of the [State] department." Because almost science-fictionally defying logic, George W.'s highest priority for a secretary of state is someone who is his brain clone, not someone who possesses the best brain with which cognitively to approach the job. In light of the United States's present diplomatic needs in relation to dealing with the Middle East, Rice's expertise on Russia and ignorance of Islam is ridiculous, almost unreal.

Sadie Plant applies Isaac Asimov's Three Laws of Robotics to feminist discourse, an insight applicable to robotic Rice. Asimov's "Three Laws of Robotics . . . were lifted straight from the marriage vows: love, honour, obey. . . . Like women, any thinking machines are admitted on the understanding that they are duty bound to honour and obey the members of the species to which they were enslaved: the members, the male ones, the family of man" (2004, 840). Rice is engaged in a marriage-vow law of robotics in which she loves, honors, and obeys George W. A Fiedlerian "innocent" absence of sexual activity characterizes this marriage. Sex is not necessary; Rice *is* a Bush family "member," a black alien species the Bush/Borg assimilates, a handmaid who reproduces the Bush family agenda. Rice is not "enslaved"; Borgian equal-opportunity assimilation, which does not differentiate between, for example, Klingons, Romulans, and humans, negates differences between alien species. The Bush, who like the Borg are also equal-opportunity assimilators, are more than happy to absorb blacks and Hispanics. Rice, combining marriage vows and laws of robotics in her relationship with George W., functions—unlike all the politically powerful women who preceded her—outside normal intimate sexual familial bonds. She is a "thinking machine" admitted as a member of intimate Bush familial and political circles who shows no public sign that she engages with friends, family, or lovers of her own. Appearing to sacrifice all her human female body's emotional and sexual needs to the dictates of the male brain implanted inside her head, Rice reproduces ideology, not progeny. Rice is America's first posthuman secretary of state.

Plant points out that in Latin the word for womb is "*matrix,* or matter, both the mother and the material" (2004, 844). While Rice—when attired as a winner of a Trinity lookalike contest—materially adheres to the *Matrix* film, her lack of intimate ties to her fellow humans (George and Laura Bush excepted) bears no tie to the Latin meaning of *matrix.* Acting as if she lacks a womb of her own—or any female sex organs, for that matter—Rice behaves as if her marriage vow to a particular political trinity is all that matters: Bush the father, Bush the son, and the holy religious (wrong) Right. Rice, realistic Bush family handmaid, can be understood as the monstrous protagonist of a science fiction horror story, replete with alien encounter assimilation brain transfer: "The Henchman's Tale." Rice, Bush/Rove/Cheney white-male clone existing in a black woman's body, lacks her own sexuality—and a brain of her own. This science-fictional, biologically female henchman has no autonomous mouth; and she has no desire to scream. I call upon Leslie Fiedler's insights to speak about her.

Condi and Leslie

The science fiction story version of Rice I have described is a twenty-first-century component of the inadvertent epic that Fiedler says comprises *Uncle Tom's Cabin, The Clansman, The Birth of A Nation, Gone with the Wind,* and *Roots.* Barrie Hayne points out that Fiedler's *The Inadvertent Epic* functions as the obverse of his *Love and Death in the American Novel* and "Come Back to the Raft Ag'in, Huck Honey." *Epic* differs from Fiedler's earlier work in that it concerns "not a male, subversive, anti-family myth, but a feminine, pro-society, domestic and familial one" (Fiedler 1979, viii). The science fiction analog Rice, feminine only when wearing a skirt suit and pearls, is a crossed-dressed, military-industrial-complex-promoting, prosociety (in terms of the Bush worldview), male, capitalist Bush team clone. Android-like, as if she were born yesterday without friends or family, she is always welcome to make herself at home on the Bush ranch, in the White House, and at Camp David.

Fiedler states that "it was Mrs. Stowe who invented American Blacks for the imagination of the whole world. Before *Uncle Tom's Cabin* . . . their existence [was] acknowledged but not felt with the passion and intensity we accord what moves through our dreams as well as our waking lives" (Fiedler 1979, 16). It is Dr. Rice who invents the image of the internationally politically powerful American black woman for the whole world to see. Rice's black female political predecessors—Shirley Chisholm and Barbara Jordan, for example—were not positioned to act passionately and intensely on the world political stage. Unlike Rice, however, Chisholm and Jordan passionately and intensely drew on their ethnic and cultural traditions to promote domestic American social-change agendas. Unlike Rice, Chisholm and Jordan were passionately and intensely politically at home in their black female bodies. Rice is Other in relation to Chisholm and Jordan. Rice epitomizes the Bush team dream of a black woman who engages the world in a manner devoid of any connection to blackness, femaleness, and social change. No black "sister" of Chisholm and Jordan, Rice is a Bush/Cheney clone. "No one, except in dreams, has ever been as good as Tom, as pure as Eva, as demonic as Topsy, as unremittingly evil as Simon Legree" (1979, 34), says Fiedler about Stowe's protagonists. No political figure, except in Karl Rove's dreams, has ever been as robotic, as separated from the usual intimate undertakings of the human race, as Condoleezza Rice. Even tricky Dick Nixon engaged with his wife and children, his friend Bebe Rebozo, and his little dog, Checkers. Rice, as far the public can tell, has only George and Laura Bush to act as her friends and surrogate nuclear family—and on a cold winter night robot Condi can curl up with her metallic White House gym exercise machine.

Fiedler views anti-Tom books in terms of "dream-fantasy even more concerned with death, sexual purity and the bourgeoisie home than the Fugitive Slave Law" (1979, 41). Rice, the science-fictional Bush team dream of a phallic-powered "white" black woman, brings war-on-terrorism death upon innocent Iraqis who have nothing to do with terrorism. Ensconced within George and Laura's bourgeoisie family home, Rice is sexually pure in that she gives no public sign of having sex. Yes, Franklin Roosevelt had sex with his secretary; and Ike intimately liked his female driver; and Bill and JFK. . . (well, we all know about them). Despite this history of American presidential sexual philandering, even the most prurient American mind would not fathom that George is having sex with his black female secretary of state. Rice's blackness shields George W. from the public-arena thought that he is even chastely lusting for Rice in his heart. But all events relevant to the history of blacks in America, such as Fiedler's reference to the Fugitive Slave Law, do not apply to "white" black female Bush clone Rice. Fiedler says that lynching, slavery atrocities, and rape haunt American dreams. Rice is the Teflon secretary of state, a science fiction fantasy in relation to real black women's American historical experience. According to Fiedler, both Stowe and *The Clansman* author Thomas Dixon Jr. "prized female virginity and the integrity of the home, embodying in one the image of the Spotless Maiden and the other in that of the Holy Mother" (1979, 45). Add "Spotless Maiden" to the designations "'princess warrior' and 'Madame Hawk,' as she [Rice] has been dubbed in France" (Dowd 2005a). All three appellations, more appropriate to naming superheroes than to naming mundane humans, aptly describe Rice, the Holy Mother of the State Department, the childless George Bush handmaid who seems to be devoid of sexual contacts. Hail Mary/Condi.

The Holy Mother of the State Department lied about how Iraqi weapons of mass destruction (proven to be nonexistent science-fictional technology in relation to Iraq) could unleash mushroom clouds over United States cities. The cinematic "Shock and Awe" television spectacle of the American military bombing Iraq is derived from a lie, a fiction, a science fiction story in relation to the reality Rice articulates. This assessment of "Shock and Awe" is as factual as stating that D. W. Griffith's film *The Birth of a Nation* is derived from Dixon's novels *The Clansman* and *The Leopard's Spots*. Fiedler describes the relationship between the Griffith film and the Dixon novels: "What chiefly survive in the new medium are Dixon's mythic versions of North and South, Male and Female, Black and White; and especially his vision of Reconstruction as an orgy of looting and rape, loose in a world of gallantry and grace by greedy invaders and bewildered ex-slaves: a saturnalia subdues only by the Christian Knights of the Klan, whose fiery crosses betoken the end of Nightmare and the dawn of a new day" (1979, 55). The connections between Fiedler's analysis, the science-fictional Rice, and early-twenty-first-century American history are unmistakable. Rice and Bush together enact mythic science-fictional versions of North and South, male and female, and black and white in which gender and racial distinctions are rendered inoperative. As a Bush brain implant clone, Rice operates outside American history and biological race and gender distinctions. Rice, in her science-fictional guise, unleashes a war on terrorism illogically directed at Iraq. She participates in the Bush vision of an orgy of militaristic aggression unilaterally enacted without provocation to render the Iraqi people as American prison torture victims in Abu Ghraib and as virtual oil production slaves for Americans. Americans act as greedy, science fiction, Darth Vader–like *Star Wars* technology invaders, the Gallant Christian Knights of the Bush Clan whose fiery crosses appear as the "Shock and Awe" war missiles traversing the Baghdad sky. The "Shock and Awe" invasion television show appears as an outtake from the science fiction film *Independence Day,* which portrays spaceships hovering over Earth cities and wreaking space-age technology militaristic havoc from the skies. The radical evangelical Christians cheer for Bush and Rice while envisioning the end of the present reality nightmare and the dawn of a new postapocalypse day, that is to say apocalypse now.

While "Shock and Awe" Iraqi civilian population catastrophe ensues, Spotless Maiden/Holy Mother Rice is at home on the Bush ranch range, where hardly is heard a discouraging political assessment word. "Like all protagonists of the domestic counter-tradition in American letters, Scarlett O'Hara must be last seen 'going home,' rather than fleeing to the wilderness, like the anti-domestic Huck Finn. Her always shadowy aristocratic mother has long since disappeared, followed by her Irish immigrant father," says Fiedler (1979, 60). Condi O'Bush, whose parents have died and who lacks a spouse and children, is always seen "going home" to the various George W. Bush family domiciles. (The Condi O'Bush appellation I imagine is not beyond the limits of reality. Barack Obama comments that, when he was working as a Chicago activist, some black pastors who he phoned to gain their support mistook him for "this Irishman, O'Bama" [Obama 1995, 179]). These George W. homes, seats of American political power, function as Rice's domestic life raft, the supporting base that keeps her afloat while positioned as the captain of the State Department ship of state. Seated with George W. in, for example, the Camp David living room, Rice floats at the apex of American political power civilization. Never articulating a discouraging word in her home with George and Laura, she can sometimes be heard uttering a chastely orgasmic "yes oh yes O'Bush."

Science fiction writer Edgar Rice Burroughs is Condoleezza Rice's literary father; when she authors reality-defying lies, Condoleezza Rice burrows within science fiction literature. (Perhaps this connection to the *Tarzan* author explains the numerous jokes about George W.'s physical resemblance to a chimp.) No feminist black female dreamer, Rice negates her gender and her race as she wields the *Star Wars* laser swords of Bush team Anglo-Saxondom against a Dark Islamic Continent of terrorists and Muslims responsive only to American military force. She participates in a macho nightmare in which Americans act according to a Mau Mau model of counter-terror against Islamic predators.

What's a nice African American girl doing in a story like this? Rice acts as if she lacks human *Roots.* Rice is more akin to Halley's comet than to Alex Haley. She is a twenty-first-century science-fictional component of America's ongoing historical interracial dreams and nightmares, the interconnected works of popular American literature Fielder describes in *The Inadvertent Epic.* These works, according to Fielder, "reinforce our wildest paranoid delusions, along with our most utopian hopes about the relations of races, sexes and generations: self-indulgent reveries, from which we rouse ourselves in embarrassment, or nightmares from which we wake in terror—but we continue to resonate in our waking heads, whether we be racists, chauvinists, fascists and practising sadists, or rightminded liberals, pacifists, feminist and twice born Christians" (1979, 84). For liberals, pacifists, and feminists, Condoleezza Rice is a lying, science-fictional nightmare who epitomizes anti-utopian hopes about the relations between America's races, sexes, and generations. It is no wild paranoid delusion to assert that Rice—together with her counterpart, white-male, patriarchal, war-mongering, lying, science-fictionally reality-altering Bush team clones and Bush brain implants—is part and parcel of the Other parties who encompass Fielder's list, a list of nightmare villains. Fiedler's list, compiled by a Jew, is not life. In other words: Condi girl, functioning as a science fiction character is no human way to live. Right on. Or: L'chaim—in thunder.

Postscript: Let's Get Real

I think that the insistently Jewish Leslie Fiedler would have approved of my decision to apply Richard W. Sonnenfeldt's life and work to my conclusion. Sonnenfeldt, an Institute of Electrical and Electronic Engineers fellow and life member, made science fiction real: he was the principal developer of the color television and computer technology that made the NASA moon landings possible. Sonnenfeldt's most important relationship to the ideas I have articulated is the fact that he is a German-born, Jewish, eventual American citizen who served as the chief American interpreter for the American prosecution at the 1945 Nuremberg War Crimes Tribunals. This is how Sonnenfeldt concluded his remarks when he addressed the Benjamin N. Cardozo School of Law conference on the Nuremberg Trials: "When I worked at Nuremberg I wanted to be the servant of justice, not the handmaiden of hate like a Nazi. I hoped that Nuremberg was the beginning of world law that would tether tyrants. I hoped then and I hope now that all innocent humans should be brothers and sisters in a human family that includes everyone except those who choose to exclude themselves. I belong to that human family and I hope that you do too" (2005).

I was moved by my chance to meet this German Jewish American who, instead of being murdered by Hitler, participated in the prosecution of Nazis and went on to develop technological innovations that made it possible for American moon landings to move from science fiction dream to reality. When I heard this elderly, wheelchair-bound, extraordinary man mention "the handmaiden of hate" I thought about my description of Secretary of State Condoleezza Rice sci-ence-fictionally choosing to act as if she were not a part of the human family. I described Rice as a handmaiden of hate who cares more for the Bush family henchmen than for the human family. Sonnenfeldt's words and experiences motivate me to hope that Nuremberg will function as a catalyst for the begin-ning of twenty-first-century "world law that would tether" those in power who, like the Bush team, act outside the interests of the "human family that includes everyone."

Let me be clear. I am not at all suggesting that Bush team members are Nazis. (Investigative journalist Katherine Yurica, however, has publicly stated that the Dominionists, who control the far-right wing of the Republican Party, use such "Hitlerian tactics" derived from *Mein Kampf* as "spiritual terror" [Yurica 2005].)[2] Please recall that the key element of the Nuremberg trials was not the Holocaust but rather the prosecution of those who committed crimes against the peace and the conspiracy to commit those crimes. The Bush team, no Wash-ington Nazis, are Washington Darth Vaders who lied about weapons of mass destruction in Iraq and used their lies to start a war. My view of the cultural legacy of the Nuremberg trials is that the lying Bush team Darth Vader invaders who act more in terms of science fiction than as members of the human family should be prosecuted for committing crimes against the peace.

When speaking at the Benjamin N. Cardozo School of Law Nuremberg Trial conference, novelist and Fordham Law School professor Thane Rosenbaum described how laws, constructions of memory, and trials apply to history. According to Rosenbaum, artists, who must not provide spiritual comfort to perpetrators, have a responsibility to generate stories that facilitate the memory of atrocity. I have used the art of cultural criticism to tell a story about how sci-ence fictionally to understand the Bush team agenda. As a culture critic I have the responsibility to apply the story I have told to reality. As a citizen of the United States I have the responsibility to make this request: a trial that positions the Nuremberg Trials as its model should be convened to prosecute the Bush team for committing crimes against the peace. At the very least, the team owes our country, and the citizens of the entire human family, a real apology.

Notes

1. Michael Lerner has written an essay called "Jews Are Not White." Outside major American urban areas, Italians may also be categorized as not white.

2. Yurica stated that during the 2004 presidential campaign the Swift Boat Veterans for Truth enacted a version of the Hitlerian notion of "spiritual terror," which calls for unleash-ing lies and slander on the enemy until the attacked person suffers a nervous breakdown. She also pointed out that Albert Speer, at the Nuremberg Trials, commented that through radio eight million people were deprived of independent thought and became Hitler's fol-lowers. She compares this tactic to the Bush team assault upon the media. Further, Yurica compares Hitler spreading the idea that something is wrong whether or not the described flaw is true to the Bush team accusations about flaws in Social Security and education. She

argues that both the team and Hitler offer solutions with the real aim of causing destruction (Yurica 2005).

Bibliography

New York Times. 2005. "A Science-Fiction Army." Editorial. *New York Times.* March 31.

Barr, Marleen S. 2001. "Bush's Missile Shield Is a Science Fiction Fantasy." *Newsday.* December 2.

Dowd, Maureen. 2005a. "Condi's French Twist." *New York Times.* February 10.

———. 2005b. "Taming of the Shrews." *New York Times.* March 6.

———. 2005c. "Uncle Dick and Papa." *New York Times.* April 23.

Edwards, John. 2005. "Fairness: Its Role in Our Lives." Keynote address, New School University, April 14.

Fiedler, Leslie A. 1979. *The Inadvertent Epic: From Uncle Tom's Cabin to Roots.* Introduction by Barrie Hayne. New York: Simon and Schuster.

Frank, Thomas. 2004. *What's the Matter with Kansas? How The Conservatives Won the Heart of America.* New York: Holt.

Friedman, Thomas L. 2005. "Rice's Poker Hand." *New York Times.* March 31.

Lerner, Michael. 1993. "Jews Are Not White." *Village Voice,* May 18.

Lott, Eric. 1993. "Racial Cross-Dressing and the Construction of American Whiteness." In *The Cultural Studies Reader,* ed. Simon During, 241–55. New York: Routledge.

"The Nuremberg Trials: A Reappraisal and Their Legacy on the Occasion of the Sixtieth Anniversary of the Trials." 2005. Benjamin N. Cardozo School of Law. New York, March 27–29.

Obama, Barack. 1995. *Dreams from My Father A Story of Race and Inheritance.* New York: Three Rivers.

Plant, Sadie. 2004. "On the Matrix: Cyberfeminist Simulations." In *Media Studies: A Reader,* ed. Paul Marris and Sue Thornham, 835–48. New York: New York University Press.

Rosenbaum, Thane. 2005. "Law and the Construction of Memory: Trial as History." Paper presented at "The Nuremberg Trials: A Reappraisal and Their Legacy on the Occasion of the Sixtieth Anniversary of the Trials," Benjamin N. Cardozo School of Law. New York, March 28.

Sonnenfeldt, Richard W. 2005. "The Nuremberg Trials: A Reappraisal and Their Legacy on the Occasion of the Sixtieth Anniversary of the Trials," Benjamin N. Cardozo School of Law. New York, March 28.

Stevenson, Richard W. 2005. "Bush and Saudi Meet at Ranch to Discuss Oil." *New York Times,* April 26.

Yuan, Jada. 2005. "Party Lines." *New York Magazine,* April 18: 20.

Yurica, Katherine. 2005. "Is an Unholy American Theocracy Here?" Paper presented at "Examining the Real Agenda of the Religious Right," CUNY Graduate Center, April 29–30.

About the Contributors

Marleen S. Barr has published a novel and much literary criticism. Recently she collaborated with Carl Freedman to edit the special issue on science fiction for *PMLA* of the Modern Language Association.

Peter R. Bergethon is the head of the Neuroscience Interdisciplinary Modeling and Simulation Center (NIMS Center) at Boston University School of Medicine, the university where, years ago, Isaac Asimov held a faculty appointment.

Roberto de Sousa Causo is a widely published fiction writer and critic in Brazil. He was a featured guest at the French Utopiales Science Fiction Festival in Nantes in 2002.

Doug Davis was a Marion L. Brittain Postdoctoral Fellow in Georgia Tech's School of Literature, Communication, and Culture, where he completed a monograph titled *American War Stories in the World of Nuclear Defense.* His Ph.D. is from Carnegie Mellon University, and he currently teaches at Gordon College in Georgia.

Mark Decker earned his Ph.D. from the Pennsylvania State University and currently is assistant professor of English at the University of Wisconsin—Stout. He has published in the *Pennsylvania Magazine of History and Biography* and in *Pynchon Notes.* He is the English and philosophy minors adviser at his university.

Fred Erisman is Lorraine Sherley Professor of Literature, Emeritus, at Texas Christian University. During the 2002–2003 academic year, he held the Charles A. Lindbergh Chair of Aerospace History at the National Air and Space Museum in Washington. His latest work is *Boys' Books, Boys' Dreams, and the Mystique of Flight* (2006).

Henry Farrell is assistant professor of political science at the Elliott School of International Affairs, George Washington University. He earned his Ph.D. from Georgetown University, was a senior research fellow in Germany from 2000 to 2002, and has published in *Comparative Political Studies, Politics and Society* and elsewhere.

Carl Freedman teaches at Louisiana State University and recently collaborated with Marleen Barr to edit the special issue on science fiction for *PMLA* of the Modern Language Association.

Lincoln Geraghty is senior lecturer in film studies in the School of Creative Arts, Film and Media at the University of Portsmouth. He serves as editorial adviser for the *Journal of Popular Culture, Reconstruction,* and *Atlantis,* with interests in science fiction film and television, and he has published two books, *Living with* Star Trek: *American Culture and* Star Trek *Fandom* (2007) and *The Shifting Definitions of Genre: Essays on Labeling Films* (2008).

M. Elizabeth Ginway is associate professor of Portuguese at the University of Florida. Her 2004 book *Brazilian Science Fiction* was on the recommended non-fiction reading list at *Locus Magazine* in 2005.

Woody Goulart wrote his doctoral dissertation on *Star Trek* at Indiana University and currently manages the online company and blog called "trekology .com."

Donald M. Hassler is professor of English at Kent State University. His Ph.D. is from Columbia. He has published books on Erasmus Darwin, Isaac Asimov, and Hal Clement and edited or coedited five additional books. He is executive editor of *Extrapolation.*

James Heilman is a graduate student working with Patrick Jackson at the American University in Washington.

Patrick Thaddeus Jackson is assistant professor of international relations at the American University in Washington. His Ph.D. is from Columbia. His book *Stopping Asia at the Elbe: Postwar German Reconstruction and the Invention of Western Civilization* is forthcoming, and he has published a number of articles and book chapters.

Wesley Y. Joe earned his Ph.D. in government from Georgetown University and is currently a research scholar at the Campaign Finance Institute in Washington.

Carter Kaplan is associate professor of English at Belmont Technical College in Ohio. He received his MA from the University of Toledo and his Ph.D. from the University of North Dakota. His articles have appeared in *SubStance, Melville Society Extracts, Extrapolation,* and *English Journal.* He is the author of *Critical Synoptics: Menippean Satire and the Analysis of Intellectual Mythology* (2000). Most recently, his fiction has appeared in the British avant-garde literature magazine *Prototype-X.*

Sándor Klapcsik is completing graduate work at the Science Fiction Foundation of the University of Liverpool and will leave England soon to return and resume teaching in his native Poland.

Paul Christopher Manuel is professor of politics at Saint Anselm College, where he also serves as the research director of the New Hampshire Institute of Politics. He has authored or coauthored five books and numerous articles and is an affiliate at the Minda de Gunzburg Center for European Studies at Harvard.

Thomas Michaud is preparing a Ph.D. in politics about the role of cyberpunk science fiction on innovation with a special interest on the works of William Gibson, Neal Stephenson, and the *Matrix* trilogy, at the university Paris I Sorbonne and at the *studio créatif* (creative studio http://www.studio-creatif.com/) of France Télécom R&D under the direction of Pierre Musso.

Wanda Raiford earned her law degree from the University of Miami, practiced criminal, appellate law, and worked for a nonprofit organization in Washington specializing in international public diplomacy. She is currently pursuing a Ph.D. in literature at the University of Iowa with a focus on the rhetorical construction of empire and country.

Sandy Rankin is a doctoral candidate in English at the University of Arkansas, where she previously earned an M.F.A. in creative writing. Her emphasis of study is twentieth-century African American literature with a focus on science fiction, and her dissertation subject will be Walter Mosley's *Futureland: Nine Stories of an Imminent World.* Her publications include entries in the *Encyclopedia of Literature and Politics;* poetry in various journals, most notably *Crazyhorse;* fiction in the *Arkansas Literary Forum;* literary criticism in *Papers of the Arkansas Philological Association,* and an essay on the film *Planet of the Apes* forthcoming in the *Journal of Popular Culture.*

Bruce L. Rockwood is chair of the finance and legal studies department at Bloomsburg University. He holds a law degree from the University of Chicago and has edited two collections, *Law and Literature Persepctives* (1996) and "Law, Literature, and Science Fiction" in *Legal Studies Forum,* no. 3 (1999). He is currently vice president of the Science Fiction Research Association.

Darko Suvin is best known, perhaps, for his groundbreaking critical study of science fiction, *Metamorphoses of Science Fiction* (1979), and has published many books on science fiction as well as on the work of Brecht. He taught in Montreal at McGill University from 1968 and is now an emeritus professor living in Italy.

Clyde Wilcox is professor of government at Georgetown. His Ph.D. is from the Ohio State University. He has authored eight books and edited or coedited more than ten additional books.

Dennis Wilson Wise has taken graduate courses in English at Kent State University and has written an honors thesis on the work of Stephen Donaldson using archival materials from Special Collections, Kent State University Libraries. He is pursuing his Ph.D. in literature at the Ohio State University.

LISA YASZEK is assistant professor in the School of Literature, Communication, and Culture at Georgia Tech. Her Ph.D. is from the University of Wisconsin–Madison. She published *The Self Wired: Technology and Subjectivity in Contemporary Narrative* (2002) and recently won the Pioneer Award from the Science Fiction Research Association for an essay in *Extrapolation.*